"Prose that unfolds at warp speed and rarely fails to sing."

—*The Observer* (London)

"A page-turning thrill ride that you won't want to put down."

—*Sacramento Book Review*

THE LOVERS

"Unfailingly compelling."

—*The New Orleans Times-Picayune*

"Expertly melds a hard-boiled plot with the supernatural."

—*Publishers Weekly* (starred review)

"Provides all the pleasures fans expect."

—*Kirkus Reviews*

THE UNQUIET

"The haunting creepiness . . . will guarantee late-night goose bumps."

—*Richmond Times-Dispatch*

"Charlie Parker stands unique and consistently complex."

—*Rocky Mountain News* (Denver)

"The tangible and the metaphysical often collide, emitting sparks of blood, phantom whispers, and the secrets that entomb the living."

—*The Clarion-Ledger* (Jackson, MS)

THE REAPERS

"Veteran crime fans will want to savor every note-perfect word."

—*Booklist* (starred review)

"Powerful, disturbing prose."

—*Omaha World-Herald* (NE)

"A definite nail-biter."

—*Pittsburgh Post-Gazette*

"A lightning strike of a novel."

—*Rocky Mountain News* (Denver)

"Sets the standard in noir."

—*The Myrtle Beach Sun News* (SC)

THE WRATH OF ANGELS

"Connolly writes seamlessly about an array of forces both criminal and supernatural, killings, and torture alongside the plethora of more prosaic human failings that he delineates so compassionately."

—*Library Journal* (starred review)

"Few thriller writers can create a sense of menace and evil as deftly as Connolly does. Compelling."

—*The Irish Independent*

"An exciting fusion of the occult and the hard-boiled . . . a gruesomely entertaining ride."

—*Publishers Weekly*

"The best kind of book for long winter nights."

—*New York Newsday*

"It's Evil versus Good versus an entity indifferent to both."

—*Booklist*

THE WOLF IN WINTER

"Connolly is at his very best here. . . . A brilliant performance from one of our finest writers."

—*The Irish Times*

Praise for #1 Internationally Bestselling Author
JOHN CONNOLLY

"A genre of one."

—*Bookreporter.com*

"Compulsively readable."

—*The New Orleans Times-Picayune*

"Truly masterful."

—*The Herald* (Ireland)

"Dark . . . and haunting."

—*Fantasy Book Critic*

"Strongly recommended for plot, characterization, authenticity . . . horror . . . and humanity."

—*Library Journal* (starred review)

"Powerful . . . Both harrowing and memorable."

—*Kirkus Reviews* (starred review)

"One of the best thriller writers we have."

—#1 *New York Times* bestselling author Harlan Coben

"A unique voice."

—*New York Times* bestselling author Michael Connelly

"The intensity of a madman and the subtlety of a poet."

—#1 *New York Times* bestselling author Vince Flynn

"Think Thomas Harris by way of Stephen King."

—*Publishers Weekly*

"Leaves unshakable images lurking on the edge of the reader's consciousness."

—*Booklist*

"He writes like a poet about terrible horrors . . . His words sing."

—*Houston Chronicle*

"For Connolly, the 'unknown' remains unknown, lending an air of mystery and tension that's as unrelenting as it is unsettling. Connolly truly understands both horror and crime fiction, and his deft blend of the two makes for a powerful and heady brew, resulting in one of the most potent and emotionally wrenching P.I. series in recent memory. And his characterizations are so sharp they could draw blood."

—*The Thrilling Detective*

Acclaim for the Charlie Parker Thrillers

EVERY DEAD THING

"Terrific . . . a complex tale as riveting and chilling as *The Silence of the Lambs*."

—*San Francisco Examiner*

"A spellbinding book . . . that holds the reader fast in a comfortless stranglehold."

—*Los Angeles Times*

"Extravagantly gifted . . . Ambitious, grisly."

—*Kirkus Reviews*

"Darkly ingenious."

—*Publishers Weekly* (starred review)

"An ambitious, moral, disturbing tale with a stunning climax."

—*The Times* (London)

"Speeds us through a harrowing plot to a riveting climax."

—*New York Times* bestselling author Jeffery Deaver

THE BURNING SOUL

"The latest Charlie Parker thriller offers a powerful story line that weaves together suspense, mystery, and a small touch of the supernatural."

—*Kirkus Reviews*

"The portrayal of the perpetually troubled Charlie as ever rings true."

—*Publishers Weekly*

"Another strong entry in this always exciting series."

—*Booklist*

THE WHISPERERS

"Macabre narrative couched in prose that is often allusive and poetic."

—*The Independent* (London)

"Visionary brand of neo-noir . . . written in an uncommonly fine, supple, sensuous prose."

—*The Irish Times*

"[Connolly] provides a rational chain of evidence and deduction for the plot while simultaneously creating a real atmosphere of numinous dread."

—*Publishers Weekly*

THE CHARLIE PARKER STORIES

DARK HOLLOW

THE KILLING KIND

THE WHITE ROAD

THE REFLECTING EYE
(A NOVELLA IN THE NOCTURNES COLLECTION)

THE BLACK ANGEL

THE UNQUIET

THE REAPERS

THE LOVERS

THE WHISPERERS

THE BURNING SOUL

THE WRATH OF ANGELS

THE WOLF IN WINTER

OTHER WORKS

BAD MEN

THE BOOK OF LOST THINGS

NOCTURNES

THE CHRONICLES OF THE INVADERS
(WITH JENNIFER RIDYARD)

CONQUEST

EMPIRE

THE SAMUEL JOHNSON STORIES (FOR YOUNG ADULTS)

THE GATES

THE INFERNALS

THE CREEPS

NONFICTION

BOOKS TO DIE FOR (EDITED BY
JOHN CONNOLLY AND DECLAN BURKE)

EVERY DEAD THING

A CHARLIE PARKER THRILLER

JOHN CONNOLLY

EMILY BESTLER BOOKS

ATRIA

NEW YORK LONDON TORONTO SYDNEY NEW DELHI

An Imprint of Simon & Schuster, Inc.
1230 Avenue of the Americas
New York, NY 10020

This Emily Bestler Books/Atria Paperback edition June 2015

EMILY BESTLER BOOKS / ATRIA PAPERBACK and colophons are trademarks of Simon & Schuster, Inc.

For information about special discounts for bulk purchases, please contact Simon & Schuster Special Sales at 1-866-506-1949 or business@simonandschuster.com.

The Simon & Schuster Speakers Bureau can bring authors to your live event. For more information or to book an event contact the Simon & Schuster Speakers Bureau at 1-866-248-3049 or visit our website at www.simonspeakers.com.

Interior design by Paul J. Dippolito

Manufactured in the United States of America

10 9 8 7 6 5 4 3

Library of Congress Cataloging-in-Publication Data is available.

ISBN 978-1-5011-2262-0
ISBN 978-1-4165-1725-2 (ebook)

AUTHOR INTRODUCTION

Every Dead Thing was not only my first published novel but also the first piece of fiction that I had written since leaving school. I thought that I was going to become a journalist, and even went so far as to study journalism at the postgraduate level, and then convince a reputable newspaper, the *Irish Times*, to pay me to produce work. Only gradually did I come to realize that my heart wasn't really in journalism, and my love of the supposedly incompatible genres of mystery and the supernatural eventually caused me to sit down and begin writing what became the prologue to *Every Dead Thing*.

And, in the beginning, the prologue was all that I wrote, over and over again. I think I spent six months just rewriting those first pages. I somehow convinced myself that I couldn't continue with the rest of the book until the prologue was perfect, which is the stuff of madness. But the prologue was crucial to what would follow, and I instinctively understood this, even as a neophyte writer. In the years since, I've often thought about changing it (that madness never really goes away) because it's difficult, and brutal, and too explicit for some, but I wanted readers to understand how a man could be broken by shock and grief. I wanted them to see through Parker's eyes, to feel as he felt, because only then would the journey that he takes in *Every Dead Thing* make any kind of sense.

In many ways, *Every Dead Thing* is a novel about grief and regret, but it's also, ultimately, about hope and forgiveness. I think there are two basic human responses to great trauma and loss. Some will turn inward, and grow bitter and isolated. Their pain will feed on them, and they, in turn, will feed on it. At their worst, they will want others to hurt as they do, because the only thing worse than suffering is suffering alone.

Then there are those for whom personal tragedy results in an incredible compassion and empathy—having suffered, they will do all in their power to ensure that no one else should suffer in the same way—and out of this comes a form of release. In *Every Dead Thing*, Charlie Parker starts out as the first kind of man and ends up as the second, but to transform himself he must wade through blood.

When I first began writing *Every Dead Thing* I thought that it might take two books to complete Parker's transformation, but ultimately the novel took on the structure of an hourglass, with two connected plots, one feeding into the other. Parker wants to find and punish the individual responsible for killing his wife and child. He cannot do that if he is mired in his own rage because the Traveling Man, the killer he seeks, will use that rage against him. Instead Parker takes on a case that appears to be entirely distinct from his own mission, and unleashes within himself a capacity for empathy so powerful as to be almost overwhelming. In doing so he comes to an understanding of his own responsibilities and of the nature of the Traveling Man, thus denying the killer the satisfaction of turning Parker into his creature.

The supernatural elements that would become so important later in the series are only glimpsed here, and they are ambiguous, for Parker may simply be unhinged by grief. I always believed that they were real from the start, although I wouldn't communicate a firm position on it until later in the series. The hybrid nature of the Parker books, their fusion of the mystery and supernatural genres, was the result of a conscious decision on my part, although I didn't realize at the time how strongly the more conservative elements of the mystery genre would react to the intermingling of the two traditions.

The roots of the detective novel lie in rationalism, in the belief that the basis of truth is intellectual and deductive. Edgar Allan Poe described his Dupin stories, regarded as the foundation stones of the detective genre in English, as "tales of ratiocination," even if the solutions to the mysteries themselves, which include a crazed orangutan as a killer, suggest otherwise, a view given further substance by Poe's own status as something less than a pillar of rationality. Regardless, this emphasis on intellect and reason as the best path to understanding human behavior was later embodied in Sir Arthur Conan Doyle's descriptions of the deductive powers of Sherlock Holmes (even if, in reality, Conan Doyle himself was fascinated by spiritualism) and in Agatha Christie's Hercule Poirot and his reliance on his "little gray cells." Once this worldview began to concretize, it was always unlikely that the supernatural—which is based not on irrationality, as some might like to believe, but anti-rationalism—would find any kind of welcome in the genre, although early practitioners were happy to flirt with its conventions, including Wilkie Collins in *The Moonstone* and Conan Doyle in *The Hound of the Baskervilles.*

Perhaps it's because I come from a Catholic tradition, allied to a love of supernatural fiction that goes back to childhood, but I've never really believed that rationalism is the sole—or even the most appropriate—means of gauging human behavior, or of understanding the world we inhabit. At the very least, people are a lot odder than rationalism allows, and make decisions based on a great many criteria, of which what might be the most rational or sensible thing to do in any given situation is often pretty far down the list.

But from the very start I also viewed Parker's story as one of redemption, and the word "redemption"—if one comes from a Christian tradition—arrives freighted with a certain amount of spiritual baggage. We redeem ourselves through sacrifice, and that is the path Parker chooses, even if he has not yet quite realized this when we meet him in *Every Dead Thing.*

The other issue that frequently arises in the context of this novel is its setting. As a young Irish writer born in Dublin, living in the city, and working for an Irish newspaper, I might not have been expected to produce a novel that wholeheartedly rejected Ireland as a location for its action. In part, this was a consequence of my reading: my models were American mystery writers (I had no real fondness for, or connection with, the British tradition), and Ross Macdonald and James Lee Burke in particular. I don't think I ever even considered trying to import the American tradition into an Irish setting, although I now understand that I brought something of a European sensibility to that American model, of which the mythological and supernatural aspects of my work are the clearest manifestations.

I was also very consciously reacting to the expectation, even obligation, that to be an Irish writer was to engage with the nature of Irishness. My being a product of the insular, repressed, and depressed Ireland of the seventies and eighties, there were few things with which I less wanted to engage than the nature of Irishness. Just as America had provided a means of actual escape and reinvention for generations of Irish immigrants, so too it provided for me a means of imaginative escape, and the possibility of being a writer who just happened to be Irish instead of an "Irish writer," with all of the connotations both positive, and, for me, largely negative of that term.

The most crucial research volume for *Every Dead Thing* was *The Body Emblazoned: Dissection and the Human Body in Renaissance Culture* by Jonathan Sawday. I can't quite recall how I first came upon Sawday's work. *The Body Emblazoned* might even have turned up in one of the *Irish Times*'s frequent book sales, but I have a feeling that I read about it somewhere, and set out to hunt it down. Its subject matter, and explicit illustrations, formed a connection in my mind with the ossuary at Sedlec in the Czech Republic, which would subsequently feature in the fifth Parker novel, *The Black Angel*. It wasn't a great leap from the beautiful medical art of Vesalius and Albinus, which celebrate the human form while reminding us of its fragility, to the concept of the memento mori, those pieces of art and architecture, often funereal in nature, that remind us of the passing of earthly concerns and our own inevitable mortality. Together they informed the strange, bleak worldview of the Traveling Man.

Every Dead Thing took about five years to complete its journey from conception to eventual publication, although for most of that time publication of any kind seemed hugely unlikely. About midway through that period, with half of the book written, I sent out the first three chapters, a synopsis, and a covering letter to every likely publisher and agent in the *Writers' and Artists' Yearbook*, in the hope that someone might stump up enough of an advance to enable me to make a research trip to the United States, and give me the spur of even mild support that I felt I needed in order to finish the book. Instead I received a steady trickle of rejections, some of them quite emphatic. One editor even scribbled a note at the end of her publishing house's standard rejection letter to tell me how much she hated the book.

But one or two publishers expressed an interest in reading the finished novel (no money, though), and one agent in particular, Darley Anderson, took the time to call and offer me a place on his list. He couldn't promise anything, but his support and enthusiasm were enough. I maxed out my credit card, drained my bank account of funds, sweated through a couple of summer weeks in Louisiana, returned to Maine (where I'd worked when I was younger) to refamiliarize myself with Portland, and completed the novel, all while keeping the fact of its existence secret from my colleagues at the newspaper on the grounds that failure is one of those problems that is doubled, not halved, by sharing it with other people. (It would be fair to say, therefore, that news of the book's purchase by Hodder & Stoughton in 1998 came as something of a surprise to most of the staff of the *Irish Times*. One leading light of the paper's literary section pretty much had to be helped to a chair, wailing as she went: "But he wasn't even a good journalist!")

In a strange way, that early rejection of the book by multiple publishers was the best thing that could have happened to me. With no expectations, no financial hold over my work, and no obligations to editors, I was free to write a novel that was structurally odd, crossed genres with no concern for entrenched opinion or possible commercial appeal, had a pair of gay criminals as its models for success in love and life, and revolved around a central character who was violent, haunted, and perhaps even maddened by grief and loss.

The money would still have been nice, though.

1

For I am every dead thing . . . I am re-begot
Of absence, darknesse, death; things which are not.

John Donne, "A Nocturnall Upon S. Lucies Day"

PROLOGUE

It is cold in the car, cold as the grave. I prefer to leave the a/c on full, to let the falling temperature keep me alert. The volume on the radio is low but I can still hear a tune, vaguely insistent over the sound of the engine. It's early R.E.M., something about shoulders and rain. I've left Cornwall Bridge about eight miles behind and soon I'll be entering South Canaan, then Canaan itself, before crossing the state line into Massachusetts. Ahead of me, the bright sun is fading as day bleeds slowly into night.

THE PATROL CAR ARRIVED *first on the night they died, shedding red light into the darkness. Two patrolmen entered the house, quickly yet cautiously, aware that they were responding to a call from one of their own, a policeman who had become a victim instead of the resort of victims.*

I sat in the hallway with my head in my hands as they entered the kitchen of our Brooklyn home and glimpsed the remains of my wife and child. I watched as one conducted a brief search of the upstairs rooms while the other checked the living room, the dining room, all the time the kitchen calling them back, demanding that they bear witness.

I listened as they radioed for the Major Crime Scene Unit, informing them of a probable double homicide. I could hear the shock in their voices, yet they tried to communicate what they had seen as dispassionately as they could, like good cops should. Maybe, even then, they suspected me. They were policemen and they, more than anyone else, knew what people were capable of doing, even one of their own.

And so they remained silent, one by the car and the other in the hallway beside me, until the detectives pulled up outside, the ambulance following, and they entered our home, the neighbors already gathering on their stoops, at their gates, some moving closer to find out what had happened, what could have been visited on the young couple beyond, the couple with the little blond girl.

"Bird?" I ran my hands over my eyes as I recognized the voice. A sob shuddered through my system. Walter Cole stood over me, McGee farther back, his face bathed by the flashes of the patrol car lights but still pale, shaken by what he had seen. Outside there was the sound of more cars pulling up. An EMT arrived at the door, distracting Cole's attention from me. "The medical technician's here," said one of the patrolmen as the thin, whey-faced young man stood by. Cole nodded and gestured toward the kitchen.

"Birdman," Cole repeated, this time with greater urgency and a harder tone to his voice. "Do you want to tell me what happened here?"

I PULL INTO THE parking lot in front of the flower shop. There is a light breeze blowing and my coattails play at my legs like the hands of children. Inside, the store is cool, cooler than it should be, and redolent with the scent of roses. Roses never go out of style, or season.

A man is bending down, carefully checking the thick waxy leaves of a small green plant. He rises up slowly and painfully as I enter.

"Evening," he says. "Help you?"

"I'd like some of those roses. Give me a dozen. No, better make it two dozen."

"Two dozen roses, yessir." He is heavy-set and bald, maybe in his early sixties. He walks stiffly, hardly bending his knees. The joints of his fingers are swollen with arthritis.

"Air-conditioning is playing up," he says. As he passes by the ancient control unit on the wall, he adjusts a switch. Nothing happens.

The store is old, with a long glass-fronted hothouse along the far wall. He opens the door and begins lifting roses carefully from a bucket inside. When he has counted twenty-four, he closes the door again and lays them on a sheet of plastic on the counter.

"Gift wrap 'em for ya?"

"No. Plastic is fine."

He looks at me for a moment and I can almost hear the tumblers fall as the process of recognition begins.

"Do I know you from someplace?"

In the city, they have short memories. Farther out, the memories last longer.

Supplemental Crime Report

NYPD **Case Number:** 96-12-1806

Offense: Homicide

Victim: Susan Parker, W/F
Jennifer Parker, W/F

Location: 1219 Hobart Street, kitchen

Date: Dec. 12, 1996

Time: Around 2130 hrs

Means: Stabbing

Weapon: Edged weapon, possibly knife (not found)

Reporting Officer: Walter Cole, Detective Sergeant

Details: On December 13, 1996, I went to 1219 Hobart Street in response to a request by Officer Gerald Kersh for detectives to work a reported homicide.

Complainant Detective Second Grade Charles Parker stated he left house at 1900 hrs following argument with wife, Susan Parker. Went to Tom's Oak Tavern and remained there until around 0130 hrs on December 13. Entered house through front door and found furniture in hallway disturbed. Entered kitchen and found wife and daughter. Stated that wife was tied to kitchen chair but daughter's body appeared to have been moved from adjacent chair and arranged over mother's body. Called police at 0155 hrs and waited at scene.

Victims, identified to me by Charles Parker as Susan Parker (wife, 33 years old) and Jennifer Parker (daughter, 3 years old), were in kitchen. Susan Parker was tied to a kitchen chair in center of floor, facing door. A second chair was placed beside it, with some ropes still attached to rear struts. Jennifer Parker was lying across her mother, faceup.

Susan Parker was barefoot and wearing blue jeans and white blouse. Blouse was ripped and had been pulled down to her waist, exposing breasts. Jeans and underwear had been pulled down to her calves. Jennifer Parker was barefoot, wearing a white nightdress with blue flower pattern.

I directed Crime Scene Technician Annie Minghella to make a full investigation. After victims were confirmed dead by Medical Examiner Clarence Hall and released, I accompanied bodies to hospital. I observed Dr. Anthony Loeb as he used rape kit and turned it over to me. I collected following items of evidence:

96-12-1806-M1: white blouse from body of Susan Parker (Victim No. 1)

96-12-1806-M2: blue denim jeans from body of Victim 1

96-12-1806-M3: blue cotton underwear from body of Victim 1

96-12-1806-M4: combings from pubic hair of Victim 1

96-12-1806-M5: washings from vagina of Victim 1

96-12-1806-M6: scrapings from under Victim 1's fingernails, right hand

96-12-1806-M7: scrapings from under Victim 1's fingernails, left hand

96-12-1806-M8: combings from Victim 1's hair, right front

96-12-1806-M9: combings from Victim 1's hair, left front

96-12-1806-M10: combings from Victim 1's hair, right rear

96-12-1806-M11: combings from Victim 1's hair, left rear

96-12-1806-M12: white/blue cotton nightdress from body of Jennifer Parker (Victim No. 2)

96-12-1806-M13: washings from vagina of Victim 2

96-12-1806-M14: scrapings from under Victim 2's fingernails, right hand

96-12-1806-M15: scrapings from under Victim 2's fingernails, left hand

96-12-1806-M16: combings from Victim 2's hair, right front

96-12-1806-M17: combings from Victim 2's hair, left front

96-12-1806-M18: combings from Victim 2's hair, right rear

96-12-1806-M19: combings from Victim 2's hair, left rear

It had been another bitter argument, made worse by the fact that it followed our lovemaking. The embers of previous fights were stoked back into glowing life: my drinking, my neglect of Jenny, my bouts of

bitterness and self-pity. When I stormed from the house, Susan's cries followed me into the cold night air.

It was a twenty-minute walk to the bar. When the first shot of Wild Turkey hit my stomach, the tension dissipated from my body and I relaxed into the familiar routine of the drunk: angry, then maudlin, sorrowful, remorseful, resentful. By the time I left the bar only the hard core remained, a chorus of drunks and sots battling with Van Halen on the jukebox. I stumbled at the door and fell down the steps outside, barking my knees painfully on the gravel at their base.

And then I stumbled home, sick and nauseous, cars swerving wildly to avoid me as I swayed onto the road, the faces of the drivers wide with alarm and anger.

I fumbled for my keys as I arrived at the door, and scraped the white paint beneath the lock as I struggled to insert the key. There were a lot of scrapes beneath the lock.

I knew something was wrong as soon as I opened the front door and stepped into the hall. When I had left, the house had been warm, the heating on full blast because Jennifer especially felt the winter cold. She was a beautiful but fragile child, as delicate as a china vase. Now the house was as cold as the night outside. A mahogany flower stand lay fallen on the carpet, the flowerpot broken in two pieces amid its own soil. The roots of the poinsettia it had contained were exposed and ugly.

I called Susan's name once, then again, louder this time. Already the drunken haze was clearing and I had my foot on the first step of the stairs to the bedrooms when I heard the back door bang against the sink unit in the kitchen. Instinctively I reached for my Colt DE but it lay upstairs on my desk, upstairs where I had discarded it before facing Susan and another chapter in the story of our dying marriage. I cursed myself then. Later, it would come to symbolize all of my failures, all of my regrets.

I moved cautiously toward the kitchen, the tips of my fingers glancing against the cold wall on my left. The kitchen door was almost closed and I edged it open slowly with my hand. "Susie?" I called as I stepped into the kitchen. My foot slid gently on something sticky and wet. I looked down and I was in Hell.

IN THE FLORIST'S, THE old man's eyes are narrowed in puzzlement. He shakes his finger good-naturedly in front of me.

"I'm sure I know you from someplace."

"I don't think so."

"You from around here? Canaan, maybe? Monterey? Otis?"

"No. Someplace else." I give him a look that tells him this is a line of inquiry he doesn't want to pursue, and I can see him backing off. I am about to use my credit card but decide not to. Instead, I count out the cash from my wallet and lay it on the counter.

"Someplace else," he says, nodding as if it has some deep, inner meaning for him. "Must be a big place. I meet a lot of fellers from there."

But I am already leaving the store. As I pull away, I can see him at the window, staring after me. Behind me, water drips gently from the rose stems and pools on the floor of the car.

Supplemental Crime Report (Contd.)

Case Number: 96-12-1806

Susan Parker was seated in a pine kitchen chair, facing north toward the kitchen door. Top of the head was ten feet, seven inches from north wall and six feet, three inches from east wall. Her arms were pulled behind her back and . . .

tied to the bars at the back of the chair with thin cord. Each foot was in turn tied to a leg of the chair, and I thought her face, mostly concealed by her hair, seemed so awash with blood that no skin could be seen. Her head hung back so that her throat gaped open like a second mouth, caught in a silent, dark red scream. Our daughter lay splayed across Susan, one arm hanging between her mother's legs.

The room was red around them, like the stage of some terrible revenger's tragedy where blood was echoed with blood. It stained the ceiling and the walls as if the house itself had been mortally wounded. It lay thick and heavy on the floor and seemed to swallow my reflection in a scarlet darkness.

Susan Parker's nose had been broken. Injury was consistent with impact against wall or floor. Bloodstain on wall near kitchen door contained fragments of bone, nasal hair, and mucus . . .

Susan had tried to run, to get help for our daughter and herself, but she had made it no farther than the door. Then he had caught her, had grabbed her by the hair and smashed her against the wall before dragging her, bleeding and in pain, back to the chair and to her death.

Jennifer Parker was stretched, facing upward, across her mother's thighs, and a second pine kitchen chair was positioned beside that of her mother. Cord wrapped around the back of the chair matched marks on Jennifer Parker's wrists and ankles.

There was not so much blood around Jenny, but her nightdress was stained by the flow from the deep cut in her throat. She faced the door, her hair hanging forward, obscuring her face, some strands sticking to the blood on her chest, the toes of her naked feet dangling above the tiled floor. I could only look at her for a moment because Susan drew my eyes toward her in death as she had in life, even amid the wreckage of our time together.

And as I looked upon her I felt myself slide down the wall and a wail, half-animal, half-child, erupted from deep inside me. I gazed at the beautiful woman who had been my wife, and her bloody, empty sockets seemed to draw me in and envelop me in darkness.

The eyes of both victims had been mutilated, probably with a sharp, scalpel-like blade. There was partial flensing of the chest of Susan

Parker. The skin from the clavicle to the navel had been partially removed, pulled back over the right breast and stretched over the right arm.

The moonlight shone through the window behind them, casting a cold glow over the gleaming countertops, the tiled walls, the steel faucets on the sink. It caught Susan's hair, coated her bare shoulders in silver, and shone through parts of the thin membrane of her skin pulled back over her arm like a cloak, a cloak too frail to ward off the cold.

There was considerable mutilation . . .

And then he had cut off their faces.

It is darkening rapidly now and the headlights catch the bare branches of trees, the ends of trimmed lawns, clean white mailboxes, a child's bicycle lying in front of a garage. The wind is stronger now, and when I leave the shelter of the trees I can feel it buffeting the car. Now I am heading toward Becket, Washington, the Berkshire Hills. Almost there.

There was no sign of forcible entry. Complete measurements and a sketch of the entire room were noted. Bodies were then released.

Dusting for fingerprints gave the following results:

Kitchen / hall / living room—usable prints later identified as those of Susan Parker (96-12-1806-7), Jennifer Parker (96-12-1806-8), and Charles Parker (96-12-1806-9).

Rear door of house from kitchen—no usable prints; water marks on surface indicate that door was wiped down. No indication of robbery.

No prints were developed from tests on victims' skin.

```
Charles Parker was taken to Homicide and gave
statement (attached).
```

I knew what they were doing as I sat in the interrogation room: I had done it so many times myself. They questioned me as I had questioned others before, using the strange formal locutions of the police interrogation. "What is your recollection as to your next move?" "Do you recall in relation to the bar the disposition of the other drinkers?" "Did you notice the condition as to the lock on the rear door?" It is an obscure, convoluted jargon, an anticipation of the legalese that clouds any criminal proceedings like smoke in a bar.

When I gave my statement Cole checked with the bartender from Tom's and confirmed that I was there when I said I was, that I could not have killed my own wife and child.

Even then, there were whispers. I was questioned again and again about my marriage, about my relations with Susan, about my movements in the weeks coming up to the killings. I stood to gain a considerable sum in insurance from Susan, and I was questioned about that as well.

According to the ME, Susan and Jennifer had been dead for about four hours when I found them. Rigor mortis had already taken hold at their necks and lower jaws, indicating that they had died at around 21.30, maybe a little earlier.

Susan had died from severing of the carotid artery, but Jenny . . . Jenny had died from what was described as a massive release of epinephrine into her system, causing ventricular fibrillation of the heart and death. Jenny, always a gentle, sensitive child, a child with a traitor-weak heart, had literally died of fright before her killer had a chance to cut her throat. She was dead when her face was taken, said the ME. He could not say the same for Susan. Neither could he say why Jennifer's body had been moved after death.

```
Further reports to follow.
Walter Cole, Detective Sergeant
```

I had a drunk's alibi: while someone stole away my wife and my child, I downed bourbon in a bar. But they still come to me in my dreams, sometimes smiling and beautiful as they were in life and sometimes faceless and bloodied as death left them, beckoning me further into a darkness where love has no place and evil hides, adorned with thousands of unseeing eyes and the flayed faces of the dead.

It is dark when I arrive and the gate is closed and locked. The wall is low and I climb it easily. I walk carefully, so as not to tread on memorial stones or flowers, until I stand before them. Even in the darkness, I know where to find them, and they in their turn can find me.

They come to me sometimes, in the margin between sleeping and waking, when the streets are silent in the dark or as dawn seeps through the gap in the curtains, bathing the room in a dim, slow-growing light. They come to me and I see their shapes in the darkness, my wife and child together, watching me silently, ensanguined in unquiet death. They come to me, their breath in the night breezes that brush my cheek and their fingers in the tree branches tapping at my window. They come to me and I am no longer alone.

CHAPTER I

The waitress was in her fifties, dressed in a tight black miniskirt, white blouse, and black high heels. Parts of her spilled out of every item of clothing she wore, making her look like she had swollen mysteriously sometime between dressing and arriving for work. She called me "darlin'" each time she filled my coffee cup. She didn't say anything else, which was fine by me.

I had been sitting at the window for over ninety minutes now, watching the brownstone across the street, and the waitress must have been wondering exactly how long I was planning to stay and if I was ever going to pay the check. Outside, the streets of Astoria buzzed with bargain hunters. I had even read the *New York Times* from start to finish without nodding off in between as I passed the time waiting for Fat Ollie Watts to emerge from hiding. My patience was wearing thin.

In moments of weakness, I sometimes considered ditching the *New York Times* on weekdays and limiting my purchase to the Sunday edition, when I could at least justify buying it on the grounds of bulk. The other option was to begin reading the *Post,* although then I'd have to start clipping coupons and walking to the store in my bedroom slippers.

Maybe in reacting so badly to the *Times* that morning I was simply killing the messenger. It had been announced that Hansel

McGee, a state Supreme Court judge and, according to some, one of the worst judges in New York, was retiring in December and might be nominated to the board of the city's Health and Hospitals Corporation.

Even seeing McGee's name in print made me ill. In the 1980s, he had presided over the case of a woman who had been raped when she was nine years old by a fifty-four-year-old man named James Johnson, an attendant in Pelham Bay Park who had convictions for robbery, assault, and rape.

McGee overturned a jury award to the woman of $3.5 million with the following words: "An innocent child was heinously raped for no reason at all; yet that is one of the risks of living in a modern society." At the time, his judgment had seemed callous and an absurd justification for overturning the ruling. Now, seeing his name before me again after what had happened to my family, his views seemed so much more abhorrent, a symptom of the collapse of goodness in the face of evil.

Erasing McGee from my mind, I folded the newspaper neatly, tapped a number on my cell phone, and turned my eyes to an upper window of the slightly run-down apartment building opposite. The phone was picked up after three rings and a woman's voice whispered a cautious hello. It had the sound of cigarettes and booze to it, like a bar door scraping across a dusty floor.

"Tell your fat asshole boyfriend that I'm on my way to pick him up and he'd better not make me chase him," I told her. "I'm real tired and I don't plan on running around in this heat." Succinct, that was me. I hung up, left five dollars on the table, and stepped out onto the street to wait for Fat Ollie Watts to panic.

The city was in the middle of a hot, humid summer spell, which was due to end the following day with the arrival of thunderstorms and rain. Currently, it was hot enough to allow for T-shirts, chinos, and overpriced sunglasses, or, if you were unlucky enough to be holding down a responsible job, hot enough to make you sweat like a pig under your suit as soon as you left the a/c behind. There wasn't even a gust of wind to rearrange the heat.

Two days earlier, a solitary desk fan had struggled to make an impact on the sluggish warmth in the Brooklyn Heights office of Benny Low. Through an open window I could hear Arabic being spoken on Atlantic Avenue and I could smell the cooking scents coming from the Moroccan Star, half a block away. Benny was a minor-league bail bondsman who had banked on Fat Ollie staying put until his trial. The fact that he had misjudged Fat Ollie's faith in the justice system was one reason why Benny continued to remain a minor-league bondsman.

The money being offered on Fat Ollie Watts was reasonable, and there were things living on the bottom of ponds that were smarter than most bail jumpers. There was a fifty-thousand-dollar bond on Fat Ollie, the result of a misunderstanding between Ollie and the forces of law and order over the precise ownership of a 1993 Chevy Beretta, a 1990 Mercedes 300 SE, and a number of well-appointed sport utility vehicles, all of which had come into Ollie's possession by illegal means.

Fat Ollie's day started to go downhill when an eagle-eyed patrolman familiar with Ollie's reputation as something less than a shining light in the darkness of a lawless world spotted the Chevy under a tarpaulin and called for a check on the plates. They were false and Ollie was raided, arrested, and questioned. He kept his mouth shut but packed a bag and headed for the hills as soon as he made bail, in an effort to avoid further questions about who had placed the cars in his care. That source was reputed to be Salvatore "Sonny" Ferrera, the son of a prominent capo. There had been rumors lately that relations between father and son had deteriorated in recent weeks, but nobody was saying why.

"Fuckin' goomba stuff," as Benny Low had put it that day in his office.

"Anything to do with Fat Ollie?"

"Fuck do I know? You want to call Ferrera and ask?"

I looked at Benny Low. He was completely bald and had been since his early twenties, as far as I knew. His glabrous skull glistened with tiny beads of perspiration. His cheeks were ruddy and flesh hung from his chin and jowls like melted wax. His tiny office, located above a halal store, smelled of sweat and mold. I wasn't even sure why I had said I would take the job. I had money—insurance money, money from the sale of the house, money from what had once been a shared account, even some cash from my retirement fund—and Benny Low's money wasn't going to make me any happier. Maybe Fat Ollie was just something to do.

Benny Low swallowed once, loudly. "What? Why are you lookin' at me like that?"

"You know me, Benny, don't you?"

"Fuck does that mean? Course I know you. You want a reference? What?" He laughed halfheartedly, spreading his pudgy hands wide as if in supplication. "What?" he said again. His voice faltered, and for the first time, he actually looked scared. I knew that people had been talking about me in the months since the deaths, talking about things I had done, things I might have done. The look in Benny Low's eyes told me that he had heard about them too and believed that they could be true.

Something about Fat Ollie's flight just didn't sit right. It wouldn't be the first time that Ollie had faced a judge on a stolen vehicles rap, although the suspected connection to the Ferreras had forced the bond up on this occasion. Ollie had a good lawyer to rely on; otherwise his only connection to the automobile industry would have come from making license plates on Rikers Island. There was no particular reason for Ollie to run, and no reason why he would risk his life by fingering Sonny over something like this.

"Nothing, Benny. It's nothing. You hear anything else, you tell me."

"Sure, sure," said Benny, relaxing again. "You'll be the first to know."

As I left his office, I heard him mutter under his breath. I couldn't be sure what he said but I knew what it sounded like. It sounded like Benny Low had just called me a killer like my father.

It had taken me most of the next day to locate Ollie's current squeeze through some judicious questioning, and another fifty minutes that morning to determine if Ollie was with her through the simple expedient of calling the local Thai food joints and asking them if they had made any deliveries to the address in the last week.

Ollie was a Thai food freak and, like most skips, stuck to his habits even while on the run. People don't change very much, which usually makes the dumb ones easy to find. They take out subscriptions to the same magazines, eat in the same places, drink the same beers, call the same women, sleep with the same men. After I threatened to call the health inspectors, an Oriental roach motel called the Bangkok Sun House confirmed deliveries to one Monica Mulrane at an address in Astoria, leading to coffee, the *New York Times*, and a phone call to wake Ollie up.

True to form and dim as a ten-watt bulb, Ollie opened the door of 2317 about four minutes after my call, stuck his head out, and then commenced an awkward, shambling run down the steps toward the sidewalk. He was an absurd figure, strands of hair slicked across his bald pate, the elasticated waistband of his tan pants stretched across a stomach of awesome size. Monica Mulrane must have loved him a whole lot to stay with him, because he didn't have money and he sure as hell didn't have looks. It was strange, but I kind of liked Fat Ollie Watts.

He had just set foot on the sidewalk when a jogger wearing a gray sweat suit with the hood pulled up appeared at the corner, ran up to Ollie, and pumped three shots into him from a silenced pistol. Ollie's white shirt was suddenly polka-dotted with red and he folded to the ground. The jogger, left-handed, stood over him and shot him once more in the head.

Someone screamed and I saw a brunette, presumably the by now recently bereaved Monica Mulrane, pause at the door of her apartment block before she ran to the sidewalk to kneel beside Ollie, passing her hands over his bald, bloodied head and crying. The jogger was already backing off, bouncing on the balls of his feet like a fighter waiting for the bell. Then he stopped, returned, and fired a single shot into the top of the woman's head. She folded over the body of Ollie Watts, her back shielding his head. Bystanders were already running for cover behind cars, into stores, and the cars on the street ground to a halt.

I was almost across the street, my Smith & Wesson in my hand, when the jogger ran. He kept his head down and moved fast, the gun still held in his left hand. Even though he wore black gloves, he hadn't dropped the gun at the scene. Either the gun was distinctive or the shooter was dumb. I was banking on the second option.

I was gaining on him when a black Chevy Caprice with tinted windows screeched out from a side street and stood waiting for him. If I didn't shoot, he was going to get away. If I did shoot, there would be hell to pay with the cops. I made my choice. He had almost reached the Chevy when I squeezed off two shots, one hitting the door of the car and the second tearing a bloody hole in the right arm of the jogger's top. He spun, firing two wild shots in my direction as he did so, and I could see his eyes were wide and ultrabright. The killer was wired.

As he turned toward the Chevy it sped away, the driver spooked by my shots, leaving Fat Ollie's killer stranded. He fired off another shot, which shattered the window of the car to my left. I could hear people screaming and, in the distance, the wail of approaching sirens.

The jogger sprinted toward an alley, glancing over his shoulder at the sound of my shoes hammering on the road behind him. As I made the corner a bullet whined off the wall above me, peppering me with pieces of concrete. I looked up to see the jogger moving beyond the midpoint of the alley, staying close to the wall. If he got around the corner at the end, I would lose him in the crowds.

The gap at the end of the alley was, briefly, clear of people. I decided to risk the shot. The sun was behind me as I straightened, firing twice in quick succession. I was vaguely aware of people at either side of me scattering like pigeons from a stone as the jogger's right shoulder arched back with the impact of one of my shots. I shouted at him to drop the piece but he turned awkwardly, his left hand bringing the gun up. Slightly off balance, I fired two more shots from around twenty feet. His left knee exploded as one of the hollow points connected, and he collapsed against the wall of the alley, his pistol skidding harmlessly away toward some trash cans and black bags.

As I closed on him I could see he was ashen faced, his mouth twisted in pain and his left hand gripping the air around his shattered knee without actually touching the wound. Yet his eyes were still bright and I thought I heard him giggle as he pushed himself from the wall and tried to hop away on his good leg. I was maybe fifteen feet from him when his giggles were drowned by the sound of brakes squealing in front of him. I looked up to see the black Chevy blocking the end of the alley, the window on its passenger side down, and then the darkness within was broken by a single muzzle flash.

Fat Ollie's killer bucked and fell forward on the ground. He spasmed once and I could see a red stain spreading across the back of his top. There was a second shot, the back of his head blew a geyser of blood in the air and his face banged once on the filthy concrete of the alley. I was already making for the cover of the trash cans when a bullet whacked into the brickwork above my head, showering me with dust and literally boring a hole through the wall. Then the window of the Chevy rolled up and the car shot off to the east.

I ran to where the jogger lay. Blood flowed from the wounds in his body, creating a dark red shadow on the ground. The sirens were close now and I could see onlookers gathered in the sunlight, watching me as I stood over the body.

The patrol car pulled up minutes later. I already had my hands in the air and my gun on the ground before me, my permit beside it. Fat Ollie's killer was lying at my feet, blood now pooled around his head and linked to the red tide that was congealing slowly in the alley's central gutter. One patrolman kept me covered while his partner patted me down, with more force than was strictly necessary, against the wall. The cop patting me down was young, perhaps no more than twenty-three or twenty-four, and cocky as hell.

"Shit, we got Wyatt Earp here, Sam," he said. "Shootin' it out like it was *High Noon*."

"Wyatt Earp wasn't in *High Noon*," I corrected him, as his partner checked my ID. The cop punched me hard in the kidneys in response and I fell to my knees. I heard more sirens nearby, including the telltale whine of an ambulance.

"You're a funny guy, hotshot," said the young cop. "Why'd you shoot him?"

"You weren't around," I replied, my teeth gritted in pain. "If you'd been here I'd have shot you instead."

He was just about to cuff me when a voice I recognized said: "Put it away, Harley." I looked over my shoulder at his partner, Sam Rees. I recognized him from my days on the force and he recognized me. I don't think he liked what he saw.

"He used to be a cop. Leave him be."

And then the three of us waited in silence until the others joined us.

Two more blue-and-whites arrived before a mud brown Nova dumped a figure in plain clothes on the curb. I looked up to see Walter Cole walking toward me. I hadn't seen him in almost six months, not since his promotion to lieutenant. He was wearing a long brown leather coat, incongruous in the heat. "Ollie Watts?" he said, indicating the shooter with an inclination of his head. I nodded.

He left me alone for a time as he spoke with uniformed cops and detectives from the local precinct. I noticed that he was sweating heavily in his coat.

"You can come in my car," he said when he eventually returned, eyeing the cop called Harley with ill-concealed distaste. He motioned some more detectives toward him and made some final comments in quiet, measured tones before waving me toward the Nova.

"Nice coat," I said appreciatively as we walked to his car. "How many girls you got in your stable?"

Walter's eyes glinted briefly. "Lee gave me this coat for my birthday. Why do you think I'm wearing it in this goddamned heat? You fire any shots?"

"A couple."

"You do know that there are laws against discharging firearms in public places, don't you?"

"I know that but I'm not sure about the guy dead on the ground back there. I'm not sure that the guy who shot him knows either. Maybe you could try a poster campaign."

"Very funny. Now get in the car."

I did as he said and we pulled away from the curb, the onlookers gaping curiously at us as we headed off through the crowded streets.

CHAPTER II

Five hours had elapsed since the death of Fat Ollie Watts, his girlfriend, Monica Mulrane, and the shooter, as yet unidentified. I had been interviewed by a pair of detectives from Homicide, neither of whom I knew. Walter Cole did not participate. I was brought coffee twice but otherwise I was left alone after the questionings. Once, when one of the detectives left the room to consult with someone, I caught a glimpse of a tall, thin man in a dark linen suit, the ends of his shirt collar sharp as razors, his red silk tie unwrinkled. He looked like a fed, a vain fed.

The wooden table in the interrogation room was pitted and worn, caffeine-stamped by the edges of hundreds, maybe thousands, of coffee cups. At the left-hand side of the table, near the corner, someone had carved a broken heart into the wood, probably with a nail. And I remembered that heart from another time, from the last time I sat in this room.

"SHIT, WALTER . . ."

"Walt, it ain't a good idea for him to be here."

Walter looked at the detectives ranged around the walls, slouched on chairs around the table.

"He's not here," he said. "As far as everyone in this room is concerned, you never saw him."

The interrogation room was crowded with chairs and an additional table had been brought in. I was still on compassionate leave and, as it happened, two weeks away from quitting the force. My family had been dead for two weeks and the investigation had so far yielded nothing. With the agreement of Lieutenant Cafferty, soon to retire, Walter had called a meeting of detectives involved in the case and one or two others who were regarded as some of the best homicide detectives in the city. It was to be a combination of brainstorm and lecture, the lecture coming from Rachel Wolfe.

Wolfe had a reputation as a fine criminal psychologist, yet the Department steadfastly refused to consult her. It had its own deep thinker, Dr. Russell Windgate, but as Walter once put it: "Windgate couldn't profile a fart." He was a sanctimonious, patronizing bastard but he was also the commissioner's brother, which made him a sanctimonious, patronizing, influential bastard.

Windgate was attending a conference of committed Freudians in Tulsa, and Walter had taken the opportunity to consult Wolfe. She sat at the head of the table, a stern but not unattractive woman in her early thirties, with long, dark red hair that rested on the shoulders of her dark blue business suit. Her legs were crossed and a blue pump hung from the end of her right foot.

"You all know why Bird wants to be here," continued Walter. "You'd all want the same thing, if you were in his place." I had bullied and cajoled him to let me sit in on the briefing. I had called in favors I didn't even have the right to call in, and Walter had relented. I didn't regret doing what I had done.

The others in the room remained unconvinced. I could see it in their faces, in the way they shifted their gaze from us, in the shrug of a shoulder and the unhappy twist of a mouth. I didn't care. I wanted to hear what Wolfe had to say. Walter and I took seats and waited for her to begin.

Wolfe took a pair of glasses from the tabletop and put them on. Beside her left hand, the carved broken heart shone wood-bright.

She glanced through some notes, pulled out two sheets from the sheaf, and began.

"Right, I don't know how familiar you are with all this, so I'll take it slowly." She paused for a moment. "Detective Parker, you may find some of this difficult." There was no apology in her voice; it was a simple statement of fact. I nodded and she continued. "What we're dealing with here appears to be sexual homicide, sadistic sexual homicide."

I TRACED THE CARVED heart with the tip of my finger, the texture of the grain briefly returning me to the present. The door of the interrogation room opened, and through the gap, I saw the fed pass by. A clerk entered with a white *I Love NY* cup. The coffee smelled as if it had been brewing since that morning. When I put in the creamer it created only the slightest difference in the color of the liquid. I sipped it and grimaced.

"A SEXUAL HOMICIDE GENERALLY involves some element of sexual activity as the basis for the sequence of events leading to death," continued Wolfe, sipping at her coffee. "The stripping of the victims and the mutilation of the breasts and genitals indicate a sexual element to the crime, yet we have no evidence of penetration in either victim by either penis, fingers, or foreign objects. The child's hymen was undamaged and there was no evidence of vaginal trauma in the adult victim.

"We also have evidence of a sadistic element to the homicides. The adult victim was tortured prior to death. Flensing took place, specifically on the front of the torso and the face. Combined with the sexual elements, you're dealing with a sexual sadist who obtains gratification from excessive physical and, I would think, mental torture.

"I think he—and I'm assuming it's a white male, for reasons I'll go into later—wanted the mother to watch the torture and killing of her child before she herself was tortured and killed. A sexual sadist gets his kicks from the victim's response to torture; in this case, he had two victims, a mother and child, to play off against each other. He's translating sexual fantasies into violent acts, torture, and, eventually, death."

OUTSIDE THE DOOR OF the interrogation room I heard voices suddenly raised. One of them was Walter Cole's. I didn't recognize the other. The voices subsided again, but I knew that they were talking about me. I would find out what they wanted soon enough.

"OKAY. THE LARGEST FOCUS group for sexual sadists consists of white, female adults who are strangers to the killer, although they may also target males and, as in this case, children. There is also sometimes a correspondence between the victim and someone in the offender's own life.

"Victims are chosen through systematic stalking and surveillance. The killer had probably been watching the family for some time. He knew the husband's habits, knew that if he went to the bar then he would be missing for long enough to allow him to complete what he wanted to do. In this case, I don't think the killer managed that completion.

"The crime scene is unusual in this case. Firstly, the nature of the crime means that it requires somewhere solitary to give the offender time with his victim. In some cases, the offender's residence may have been modified to accommodate his victim, or he may use a converted car or van for the killing. In this case, the killer chose not to do this. I think he may like the element of risk involved. I also think he wanted to make, for want of a better term, an 'impression.'"

An impression, like wearing a bright tie to a funeral.

"The crime was carefully staged to impact in the most traumatic way on the husband when he returned home."

Maybe Walter had been right. Maybe I shouldn't have come to

the briefing. Wolfe's matter-of-factness reduced my wife and child to the level of another gruesome statistic in a violent city, but I hoped that she would say something that would resonate inside me and provide some clue to drive the investigation forward. Two weeks is a long time in a murder case. After two weeks with no progress, unless you get very, very lucky, the investigation starts to grind to a halt.

"This seems to indicate a killer of above-average intelligence, one who likes playing games and gambling," said Wolfe. "The fact that he appeared to want the element of shock to play a part could lead us to conclude that there was a personal element to what he did, directed against the husband, but that's just speculation, and the general pattern of this type of crime is impersonal.

"Generally, crime scenes can be classified as organized, disorganized, or some mix of the two. An organized killer plans the murder and targets the victim carefully, and the crime scene will reflect this element of control. The victims will meet certain criteria which the killer has set: age, hair color maybe, occupation, lifestyle. The use of restraints, as we have in this case, is typical. It reflects the elements of control and planning, since the killer will usually have to bring them to the scene.

"In cases of sexual sadism, the act of killing is generally eroticized. There's a ritual involved; it's usually slow, and every effort is made to ensure that the victim remains conscious and aware up to the point of death. In other words, the killer doesn't want to end the lives of his victims prematurely.

"Now, in this case he didn't succeed, because Jennifer Parker, the child, had a weak heart and it failed following the release of epinephrine into her system. Combined with her mother's attempted escape and the damage caused to her face by striking it against the wall, which may have resulted in temporary loss of consciousness, I believe the killer felt he was losing control of the situation. The crime scene moved from organized to disorganized, and shortly after he commenced flensing, his anger and frustration got the better of him and he mutilated the bodies."

I wanted to leave then. I had made a mistake. Nothing could come of this, nothing good.

"As I said earlier, mutilation of the genitals and breasts is a feature of this type of crime, but this case doesn't conform to the general pattern in a number of crucial ways. I think the mutilation in this case was either a result of anger and loss of control, or it was an attempt to disguise something else, some other element of the ritual which had already commenced and from which the killer was trying to divert attention. In all likelihood, the partial flensing is the key. There's a strong element of display—it's incomplete, but it's there."

"Why are you so sure it's a white male?" asked Joiner, a black Homicide detective with whom I'd worked once or twice.

"The most frequent perpetrators of sexual sadism are white males. Not women, not black males. White males."

"You're off the hook, Joiner," someone said. There was a burst of laughter, an easing of the tension that had built up in the room. One or two of the others glanced at me but for the most part they acted as if I wasn't there. They were professionals, concentrating on amassing any information that might lead to a greater understanding of the killer.

Wolfe let the laughter fade. "Research indicates that as many as forty-three percent of sexual murderers are married. Fifty percent have children. Don't make the mistake of thinking that you're looking for some crazy loner. This guy may be the hero of his local PTA meetings, the coach of the Little League team.

"He could be engaged in a profession that brings him into contact with the public, so he's probably socially adept and he may use that to target his victims. He may have engaged in antisocial behavior in the past, although not necessarily something serious enough to have gotten him a police record.

"Sexual sadists are often police buffs or weapons freaks. He may try to stay in touch with the progress of the investigation, so keep an eye on individuals who ring in with leads or who try to trade off information. He also owns a clean, well-maintained car: clean so it doesn't attract attention, well maintained because he has to be sure he doesn't get stranded at or near the crime scene. The car could have been modified to allow him to transport victims; the door and window handles in the rear will have been removed, the trunk may have been soundproofed. If you think you have a possible suspect, check the trunk for extra fuel, water, ropes, cuffs, ligatures.

"If you go for a search warrant, you'll be looking for any items relating to sexual or violent behavior: pornographic magazines, videos, low-end true-crime stuff, vibrators, clamps, women's clothing, particularly undergarments. Some of these may have belonged to victims or he may have taken other personal items from them. Look out also for diaries and manuscripts; they may contain details of victims, fantasies, even the crimes themselves. This guy may also have a collection of police equipment and almost certainly has a knowledge of police procedures." Wolfe took a deep breath and sat back in her chair.

"Is he going to do it again?" asked Walter. There was silence in the room for a moment.

"Yes, but you're making one assumption," said Wolfe. Walter looked puzzled.

"You're assuming this is the first. I take it a VICAP has been done?"

VICAP, operational since 1985, is the FBI's Violent Criminal Apprehension Program. Under VICAP, a report is completed on solved or unsolved homicides or attempted homicides, particularly those involving abductions or that are apparently random or motiveless or sexually oriented; on missing persons cases, when foul play is suspected; and on unidentified dead bodies, when the manner of death is known or suspected to be homicide. The report is then submitted to the National Center for the Analysis of Violent Crime at the FBI's academy in Quantico, in an effort to determine if similar pattern characteristics exist elsewhere in the VICAP system.

"It was submitted."

"Have you requested a profile?"

"Yes, but no profile as yet. Unofficially, the MO doesn't match. The removal of the faces marks it out."

"Yeah, what about the faces?" It was Joiner again.

"I'm still trying to find out more," said Wolfe. "Some killers take souvenirs from their victims. There may be some kind of pseudo-religious or sacrificial element to this case. I'm sorry, I'm really not sure yet."

"You think he could have done something like this before?" said Walter.

Wolfe nodded. "He may have. If he has killed before, then he may have hidden the bodies, and these killings could represent an alteration in a previous pattern of behavior. Maybe, after killing quietly and unobtrusively, he wanted to bring himself to a more public arena. He may have wanted to draw attention to his work. The unsatisfactory nature of these killings, from his point of view, may now cause him to revert to his old pattern. Alternatively, he could recede into a period of dormancy; that's another possibility.

"But if I was to gamble, I'd say that he's been planning his next move carefully. He made mistakes this time and I don't think he achieved the effect he was looking for. The next time, he won't make any mistakes. The next time, unless you catch him first, he's really going to make an impact."

THE DOOR OF THE interrogation room opened and Walter entered with two other men.

"This is Special Agent Ross, FBI, and Detective Barth from Robbery," said Walter. "Barth was working the Watts case. Agent Ross here deals with organized crime."

Close up, Ross's linen suit looked expensive and tailored. Barth, in his JCPenney jacket, looked like a slob by comparison. The two men stood against opposite walls and nodded. When Walter sat, Barth sat as well. Ross remained standing against the wall.

"Anything you're not telling us here?" Walter asked.

"No," I said. "You know as much as I do."

"Agent Ross believes that Sonny Ferrera was behind the killing of Watts and his girlfriend and that you know more than you're saying." Ross picked at something on the sleeve of his shirt and dropped it to the floor with a look of distaste. I think it was meant to represent me.

"There was no reason for Sonny to kill Ollie Watts," I replied. "We're talking stolen cars and fake license plates here. Ollie wasn't in a position to scam anything worthwhile from Sonny and he didn't know enough about Sonny's activities to take up ten minutes of a jury's time."

Ross stirred and moved forward to sit on the edge of the table. "Strange that you should turn up after all this time—what is it? six, seven months?—and suddenly we're knee deep in corpses," he said, as if he hadn't heard a word I'd said. He was forty, maybe forty-five, but he looked to be in good condition. His face was heavily lined with wrinkles that didn't seem like they came from a life of laughter. I'd heard a little about him from Woolrich, after Woolrich left New York to become the feds' assistant special agent in charge in the New Orleans field office.

There was silence then. Ross tried to stare me out, then looked away in boredom.

"Agent Ross here thinks that you're holding out on us," said Walter. "He'd like to sweat you for a while, just in case." His expression was neutral, his eyes bland. Ross had returned to staring at me.

"Agent Ross is a scary guy. He tries to sweat me, there's no telling what I'll confess to."

"This is not getting us anywhere," said Ross. "Mr. Parker is obviously not cooperating in any way and I—"

Walter held up a hand, interrupting him. "Maybe you'd both leave us alone for a while, get some coffee or something," he suggested. Barth shrugged and left. Ross remained seated on the table and looked like he was going to say more, then he stood up abruptly and quickly walked out, closing the door firmly behind him. Walter exhaled deeply, loosened his tie, and opened the top button of his shirt.

"Don't dump on Ross. He'll bring a ton of shit down on your head. And on mine."

"I've told you all I know on this," I said. "Benny Low may know more, but I doubt it."

"We talked to Benny Low. The way Benny tells it, he didn't know who the president was until we told him." He twisted a pen in his hand. "'Hey, it's just bidness,' that's what he said." It was a pretty fair imitation of one of Benny Low's verbal quirks. I smiled thinly and the tension in the air dissipated slightly.

"How long you been back?"

"Couple of weeks."

"What have you been doing?"

What could I tell him? That I wandered the streets, that I visited places where Jennifer, Susan, and I used to go together, that I stared out of the window of my apartment and thought about the man who had killed them and where he might be, that I had taken on the job for Benny Low because I was afraid that, if I did not find some outlet, I would eat the barrel of my gun?

"Not a lot. I plan to look up some old stoolies, see if there's anything new."

"There isn't, not at this end. You got anything?"

"No."

"I can't ask you to let it go, but—"

"No, you can't. Get to it, Walter."

"This isn't a good place for you to be right now. You know why."

"Do I?"

Walter tossed the pen hard on the table. It bounced to the edge and then hung there briefly before dropping to the floor. For a moment I thought he was going to take a swing at me but then the anger went from his eyes.

"We'll talk about this again."

"Okay. You going to give me anything?" Among the papers on the table, I could see reports from Ballistics and Firearms. Five hours was a pretty short time in which to get a report. Agent Ross was obviously a man who got what he wanted.

I nodded at the report. "What did Ballistics say about the bullet that took out the shooter?"

"That's not your concern."

"Walter, I watched the kid die. The shooter took a pop at me and the bullet went clean through the wall. Someone's got distinctive taste in weaponry."

Walter stayed silent.

"No one picks up hardware like that without someone knowing," I said. "You give me something to go on, maybe I might find out more than you can."

Walter thought for a minute and then flicked through the papers for the Ballistics report. "We got submachine bullets, five-point-seven millimeters, weighing less than fifty grains."

I whistled. "That's a scaled-down rifle round, but fired from a handgun?"

"The bullet is mainly plastic but has a full-metal jacket, so it doesn't deform on impact. When it hits something—like your shooter—it transfers most of its force. There's almost no energy when it exits."

"And the one that hit the wall?"

"Ballistics reckons a muzzle velocity of over two thousand feet per second."

That was an incredibly fast bullet. A Browning 9 millimeter fires bullets of one hundred ten grains at only eleven hundred feet per second.

"They also reckon that this thing could blow through Kevlar body armor like it was rice paper. At two hundred yards, the thing could penetrate almost fifty layers." Even a .44 Magnum will only penetrate body armor at very close range.

"But once it hits a soft target . . ."

"It stops."

"Is it domestic?"

"No, Ballistics say European. Belgian. They're talking about something called a Five-seveN—that's big *F*, big *N*, after the manufacturers. It's a prototype made by FN Herstal for antiterrorist and hostage rescue operations, but this is the first time one has turned up outside national security forces."

"You contacting the maker?"

"We'll try, but my guess is we'll lose it in the middlemen."

I stood up. "I'll ask around."

Walter retrieved his pen and waved it at me like an unhappy schoolteacher lecturing the class wise guy. "Ross still wants your ass."

I took out a pen and scribbled my cell phone number on the back of Walter's legal pad.

"It's always on. Can I go now?"

"One condition."

"Go on."

"I want you to come over to the house tonight."

"I'm sorry, Walter, I don't make social calls anymore."

He looked hurt. "Don't be an asshole. This isn't social. Be there, or Ross can lock you in a cell till doomsday for all I care."

I stood up to leave.

"You sure you've told us everything?" he asked to my back.

I didn't turn around. "I've told you all I can, Walter."

Which was true, technically at least.

TWENTY-FOUR HOURS EARLIER, I had found Emo Ellison. Emo lived in a dump of a hotel on the edge of East Harlem, the kind where the only guests allowed in the rooms are whores, cops, or criminals. A Plexiglas screen covered the front of the super's office, but there was no one inside. I walked up the stairs and knocked on Emo's door. There was no reply but I thought I heard the sound of a hammer cocking on a pistol.

"Emo, it's Bird. I need to talk."

I heard footsteps approach the door.

"I don't know nothin' about it," said Emo, through the wood. "I got nothin' to say."

"I haven't asked you anything yet. C'mon, Emo, open up. Fat Ollie's in trouble. Maybe I can do something. Let me in."

There was silence for a moment and then the rattle of a chain. The door opened and I stepped inside. Emo had retreated to the window but he still had the gun in his hand. I closed the door behind me.

"You don't need that," I said. Emo hefted the gun once in his hand and then put it on a bedside cabinet. He looked more comfortable without it. Guns weren't Emo's style. I noticed that the fingers of his left hand were bandaged. I could see yellow stains on the tips of the bandages.

Emo Ellison was a thin, pale-faced, middle-aged man who had worked on and off for Fat Ollie for five years or so. He was an average mechanic but he was loyal and knew when to keep his mouth shut.

"Do you know where he is?"

"He ain't been in touch."

He sat down heavily on the edge of the neatly made bed. The room was clean and smelled of air freshener. There were one or two prints on the walls, and books, magazines, and some personal items were neatly arrayed on a set of Home Depot shelves.

"I hear you're workin' for Benny Low. Why you doin' that?"

"It's work," I replied.

"You hand Ollie over and he's dead, that's your work," said Emo.

I leaned against the door.

"I may not hand him over. Benny Low can take the loss. But I'd need a good reason not to."

The conflict inside him played itself out on Emo's face. His hands twisted and writhed over each other and he looked once or twice at the gun. Emo Ellison was scared.

"Why did he run, Emo?" I asked softly.

"He used to say you were a good guy, a stand-up guy," said Emo. "That true?"

"I don't know. I don't want to see Ollie hurt, though."

Emo looked at me for a time and then seemed to make a decision.

"It was Pili. Pili Pilar. You know him?"

"I know him." Pili Pilar was Sonny Ferrera's right-hand man.

"He used to come once, twice a month, never more than that, and take a car. He'd keep it for a couple of hours, then bring it back. Different car each time. It was a deal Ollie made, so he wouldn't have to pay off Sonny. He'd fit the car with false plates and have it ready for Pili when he arrived.

"Last week, Pili comes, collects a car, and drives off. I came in late that night, 'cause I was sick. I got ulcers. Pili was gone before I got there.

"Anyway, after midnight I'm sittin' up with Ollie, talkin' and stuff, waitin' for Pili to bring back the car, when there's this bang outside. When we get out there, Pili's wrapped the car around the gate and he's lying on the wheel. There's a dent in the front, too, so we figure maybe Pili was in a smash and didn't want to wait around after.

"Pili's head is cut up bad where he smacked the windshield and there's a lot of blood in the car. Ollie and me push it into the yard and then Ollie calls this doc he knows, and the guy tells him to bring Pili around. Pili ain't movin' and he's real pale, so Ollie drops him off at the doc's in his own car, and the doc insists on packing him off to the hospital 'cause he thinks Pili's skull is busted."

It was all flowing out of Emo now. Once he began the tale he wanted to finish it, as if he could diminish the burden of knowing by telling it out loud. "Anyway, they argue for a while but the doc knows this private clinic where they won't ask too many questions, and Ollie agrees. The doc calls the clinic and Ollie comes back to the lot to sort out the car.

"He has a number for Sonny but there's no answer. He's got the car in back but he doesn't want to leave it there in case, y'know, it's a cop thing. So he calls the old man and lets him know what happened. So the old man tells him to sit tight, he'll send a guy around to take care of it.

"Ollie goes out to move the car out of sight but when he comes back in, he looks worse than Pili. He looks sick and his hands are shakin'. I say to him, 'What's wrong?' but he just tells me to get out and not to tell no one I was there. He won't say nothin' else, just tells me to get goin'.

"Next thing I hear, the cops have raided the place and then Ollie makes bail and disappears. I swear, that's the last I heard."

"Then why the gun?"

"One of the old man's guys came by here a day or two back." He gulped. "Bobby Sciorra. He wanted to know about Ollie, wanted to know if I'd been there the day of Pili's accident. I said to him, 'No,' but it wasn't enough for him."

Emo Ellison started to cry. He lifted up his bandaged fingers and slowly, carefully, began to unwrap one of them.

"He took me for a ride." He held up the finger and I could see a ring-shaped mark crowned with a huge blister that seemed to throb even as I looked at it. "The cigarette lighter. He burned me with the car cigarette lighter."

Twenty-four hours later, Fat Ollie Watts was dead.

CHAPTER III

Walter Cole lived in Richmond Hill, the oldest of the Seven Sisters neighborhoods in Queens. Begun in the 1880s, it had a village center and town common and must have seemed like Middle America recreated on Manhattan's doorstep when Walter's parents first moved there from Jefferson City shortly before World War II. Walter had kept the house, north of Myrtle Avenue on 113th Street, after his parents retired to Florida. He and Lee ate almost every Friday in Triangle Hofbräu, an old German restaurant on Jamaica Avenue, and walked in the dense woods of Forest Park during the summer.

I arrived at Walter's home shortly after nine. He answered the door himself and showed me into what, for a less educated man, would have been called his den, although "den" didn't do justice to the miniature library he had assembled over half a century of avid reading: biographies of Keats and Saint-Exupéry shared shelf space with works on forensics, sex crimes, and criminal psychology. Fenimore Cooper stood back to back with Borges; Barthelme looked uneasy surrounded by various Hemingways.

A Macintosh PowerBook sat on a leather-topped desk beside three filing cabinets. Paintings by local artists adorned the walls, and a small glass-fronted case in the corner displayed shooting trophies, haphazardly thrown together as if Walter was simultaneously proud of his ability yet embarrassed by his pride. The top half of the window was open and I could smell freshly mown grass and hear the sound of kids playing street hockey in the warm evening air.

The door to the den opened and Lee entered. She and Walter had been together for twenty-four years and they shared each other's lives with an ease and grace that Susan and I had never approached, even at the best of times. Lee's black jeans and white blouse hugged a figure that had survived the rigors of two children and Walter's love of Oriental cuisine. Her ink black hair, through which strands of gray wove like moonlight on dark water, was pulled back in a ponytail. When she reached up to kiss me lightly on the cheek, her arms around my shoulders, the scent of lavender enfolded me like a veil and I realized, not for the first time, that I had always been a little in love with Lee Cole.

"It's good to see you, Bird," she said, her right hand resting lightly on my cheek, lines of anxiety on her brow giving the lie to the smile on her lips. She glanced at Walter and something passed between them. "I'll be back later with some coffee." She closed the door softly behind her on the way out.

"How are the kids doing?" I asked as Walter poured himself a glass of Redbreast Irish whiskey—the old stuff with the screw top.

"Good," he replied. "Lauren still hates high school. Ellen's going to study law in Georgetown in the fall, so at least one member of the family will understand the way it works." He inhaled deeply as he raised the glass to his mouth and sipped. I gulped involuntarily and a sudden thirst gripped me. Walter noticed my discomfiture and reddened.

"Shit, I'm sorry," he said.

"It's all right," I responded. "It's good therapy. I notice you're still swearing in the house." Lee hated swearing, routinely telling her husband that only oafs resorted to profanity in speech. Walter usually countered by pointing out that Wittgenstein once brandished a poker in the course of a philosophical argument, proof positive in his eyes that erudite discourse sometimes wasn't sufficiently expressive for even the greatest of men.

He moved to a leather armchair at one side of the empty fireplace and motioned to its opposite number. Lee entered with a silver coffeepot, a creamer, and two cups on a tray and then left, glancing anxiously at Walter as she did. I knew they had been talking before I arrived; they kept no secrets from each other and their unease seemed to indicate that they had discussed more than their concerns about my well-being.

"Do you want me to sit under a light?" I asked. A small smile moved across Walter's face with the swiftness of a breeze and then was gone.

"I heard things over the last few months," he began, looking into his glass like a mystic examining a crystal ball. I stayed silent.

"I know you talked to the feds, pulled in some favors so you could take a look at files. I know you were trying to find the man who killed Susan and Jenny." He looked at me for the first time since he had begun talking.

I had nothing to say, so I poured some coffee for both of us, then picked up my own cup and sipped. It was Javan, strong and dark. I breathed deeply. "Why are you asking me this?"

"Because I want to know why you're here, why you're back. I don't know what you've become if some of the things I've heard are true." He swallowed and I felt sorry for him, for what he had to say and the questions he had to ask. If I had answers to some of them, I wasn't sure that I wanted to give them, or that Walter really wanted to hear them. Outside, the kids had finished their game as darkness drew in, and there was a stillness in the air that made Walter's words sound like a portent.

"They say you found the guy who did it," he said, and this time there was no hesitation, as if he had steeled himself to say what he had to say. "That you found him and killed him. Is that true?"

The past was like a snare. It allowed me to move a little, to circle, to turn, but in the end, it always dragged me back. More and more, I found things in the city—favorite restaurants, bookshops, tree-shaded parks, even hearts carved bone white into the wood of an old table—that reminded me of what I had lost, as if even a moment of forgetfulness was a crime against their memories. I slipped from present to past, sliding down the snake heads of memory into what was and what would never be again.

And so, with Walter's question, I fell back to late April, back to New Orleans. They had been dead for almost four months.

WOOLRICH SAT AT A table at the rear of the Café du Monde, beside a bubble gum machine, with his back against the wall of the main building. On the table before him stood a steaming cup of café au lait and a plate of hot beignets covered in powdered sugar. Outside, people bustled down Decatur, past the green-and-white pavilion of the café, heading for the cathedral or Jackson Square.

He wore a tan suit, cheaply made, and his silk tie was stretched and faded so that he didn't even bother to button his shirt at the collar, preferring instead to let the tie hang mournfully at half mast. The floor around him was white with sugar, as was the only visible part of the green vinyl chair upon which he sat.

Woolrich was an assistant SAC of the local FBI field office over at 1250 Poydras. He was also one of the few people from my police past with whom I'd stayed in touch in some small way, and one of the only feds I had ever met who didn't make me curse the day Hoover was born. More than that, he was my friend. He had stood by me in the days following the killings, never questioning, never doubting. I remember him standing, rain-soaked, by the grave, water dripping from the rim of his outsized fedora. He had been transferred to New Orleans soon after, a promotion that reflected a successful apprenticeship in at least three other field offices and his ability to keep his head in the turbulent environment of the New York field office in downtown Manhattan.

He was messily divorced, the marriage over for maybe twelve years. His wife had reverted to her maiden name, Karen Stott, and lived in Miami with an interior decorator whom she had recently married. Woolrich's only daughter, Lisa—now, thanks to her mother's efforts, Lisa Stott—had joined some religious group in Mexico, he said. She was just eighteen. Her mother and her new husband didn't seem to care about her, unlike Woolrich, who cared but couldn't get his act together enough to do anything about it. The disintegration of his family pained him in a very particular way, I knew. He came from a broken family himself, a white-trash mother and a father who was well meaning but inconsequential, too inconsequential to hold on to his hellcat wife. Woolrich had always wanted to do better, I think. More than the rest, I believed, he shared my sense of loss when Susan and Jennifer were taken.

He had put on more weight since I last saw him, and the hair on his chest was visible through his sweat-soaked shirt. Rivulets rolled down from a dense thatch of rapidly graying hair and into the folds of flesh at his neck. For such a big man, the Louisiana summers would be a form of torture. Woolrich may have looked like a clown, may even have acted that way when it suited him, but no one in New Orleans who knew him ever underestimated him. Those who had in the past were already rotting in Angola penitentiary.

"I like the tie," I said. It was bright red and decorated with lambs and angels.

"I call it my metaphysical tie," Woolrich replied. "My George Herbert tie."

We shook hands, Woolrich wiping beignet crumbs from his shirtfront as he stood. "Damn things get everywhere," he said. "When I die, they'll find beignet crumbs up the crack of my ass."

"Thanks, I'll hold that thought."

An Asian waiter in a white paper cap bustled up and I ordered coffee. "Bring you beignets, suh?" he asked. Woolrich grinned. I told the waiter I'd skip the beignets.

"How you doin'?" asked Woolrich, taking a gulp of coffee hot enough to scarify the throat of a lesser man.

"I'm okay. How's life?"

"Same as it ever was: gift wrapped, tied with a red bow, and handed to someone else."

"You still with . . . what was her name? Judy? Judy the nurse?"

Woolrich's face creased unhappily, as if he'd just encountered a cockroach in his beignet. "Judy the nut, you mean. We split up. She's gone to work in La Jolla for a year, maybe more. I tell you, I decide to take her away for a romantic vacation a couple of months back, rent us a room in a two-hundred-dollar-a-night inn near Stowe, take in the country air if we left the window of the bedroom open, you know the deal. Anyway, we arrive at this place and it's older than Moses's dick, all dark wood and antique furniture and a bed you could lose a team of cheerleaders in. But Judy, she turns whiter than a polar bear's ass and backs away from me. You know what she says?"

I waited for him to continue.

"She says that I murdered her in the very same room in a previous life. She's backed up against the door, reaching for the handle and looking at me like she's expecting me to turn into the Son of Sam. Takes me two hours to calm her down and even then she refuses to sleep with me. I end up sleeping on a couch in the corner, and let me tell you, those goddamned antique couches may look like a million bucks and cost more, but they're about as comfortable to sleep on as a concrete slab."

He finished off the last bite of beignet and dabbed at himself with a napkin.

"Then I get up in the middle of the night to take a leak and she's sitting up in bed, wide awake, with the bedside lamp upside down in her hand, waiting to knock my head off if I come near her. Needless to say, this put an end to our five days of passion. We checked out the next morning, with me over a thousand dollars in the hole.

"But you know what the really funny thing is? Her regression therapist has told her to sue me for injuries in a past life. I'm about to become a test case for all those donut heads who watch a documentary on PBS and think they were once Cleopatra or William the Conqueror."

His eyes misted over at the thought of his lost thousand and the games Fate plays on those who go to Vermont looking for uncomplicated sex.

"You heard from Lisa lately?"

His face clouded over and he waved a hand at me. "Still with the Jesus huggers. Last time she called me, it was to say that her leg was fine and to ask for more money. If Jesus saves, he must have had all his cash tied up with the savings and loan." Lisa had broken her leg in a roller-skating accident the previous year, shortly before she found God. Woolrich was convinced that she was still concussed.

He stared at me for a time, his eyes narrowed. "You're not okay, are you?"

"I'm alive and I'm here. Just tell me what you've got."

He puffed his cheeks and then blew out slowly, marshaling his thoughts as he did so.

"There's a woman, down in St. Martin Parish, an old Creole. She's got the gift, the locals say. She keeps away the gris-gris. You know, bad spirits, all that shit. Offers cures for sick kids, brings lovers together. Has visions." He stopped and rolled his tongue around his mouth, and squinted at me.

"She's a psychic?"

"She's a witch, you believe the locals."

"And do you?"

"She's been . . . helpful, once or twice in the past, according to the local cops. I've had nothing to do with her before."

"And now?"

My coffee arrived and Woolrich asked for a refill. We didn't speak again until the waiter had departed and Woolrich had drained half of his coffee in a steaming mouthful.

"She's got about ten children and thousands of goddamn grandchildren and great-grandchildren. Some of them live with her or near her, so she's never alone. She's got a bigger extended family than Abraham." He smiled but it was a fleeting thing, a brief release before what was to come.

"She says a young girl was killed in the bayou a while back, in the marshlands where the Barataria pirates used to roam. She told the sheriff's office but they didn't pay much attention. She didn't have a location, just said a young girl had been murdered in the bayou. Said she had seen it in a dream.

"Sheriff didn't do nothing about it. Well, that's not entirely true. He told the local boys to keep an eye out and then pretty much forgot all about it."

"What brings it up again now?"

"The old woman says she hears the girl crying at night."

I couldn't tell whether Woolrich was spooked or just embarrassed by what he was saying, but he looked toward the window and wiped his face with a giant grubby handkerchief.

"There's something else, though." He folded the handkerchief and stuffed it back in his trouser pocket.

"She says the girl's face was cut off." He breathed in deeply. "And that she was blinded before she died."

WE DROVE NORTH ON I-10 for a time, past an outlet mall and on toward West Baton Rouge with its truck stops and gambling joints, its bars full of oil workers and, elsewhere, blacks, all drinking the same rotgut whiskey and watery Dixie beer. A hot wind, heavy with the dense, decayed smell of the bayou, pulled at the trees along the highway, whipping their branches back and forth. Then we crossed onto the raised Atchafalaya highway, its supports embedded beneath the waters, as we entered the Atchafalaya swamp and Cajun country.

I had been here only once before, when Susan and I were younger and happier. Along the Henderson Levee Road we passed the sign for McGee's Landing, where I'd eaten tasteless chicken and Susan had picked at lumps of deep-fried alligator so tough even other alligators would have had trouble digesting it. Then a Cajun fisherman had taken us on a boat trip into the swamps, through a semisubmerged cypress forest. The sun sank low and bloody over the water, turning the tree stumps into dark silhouettes like the fingers of dead men pointing accusingly at the heavens. It was another world, as far removed from the city as the moon was from the earth, and it seemed to create an erotic charge between us as the heat made our shirts cling to our bodies and the sweat drip from our brows. When we returned to our hotel in Lafayette we made love urgently and with a passion that superseded love, our drenched bodies moving together, the heat in the room as thick as water.

Woolrich and I did not go as far as Lafayette. We abandoned the highway for a two-lane road that wove through the bayou country for a time before turning into little more than a rutted track, pitted by holes filled with dank, foul-smelling swamp water around which insects buzzed in thick swarms. Cypress and willow lined the road and, through them, the stumps of trees were visible in the waters of the swamp, relics of the harvestings of the last century. Lily pads clustered at the banks, and when the car slowed and the light was right, I could see bass moving languidly in their shadows, breaking the water occasionally.

I had heard once that Jean Lafitte's brigands had made their home here. Now others had taken their place, killers and smugglers who used the canals and marshes as hiding places for heroin and marijuana, and as dark, green graves for the butchered, their bodies adding to the riotous growth of nature, their decay masked by the rich stench of vegetation.

We took one further turn, and here the cypress overhung the road. We rattled over a wooden bridge, the wood gradually returning to its original color as the paint flaked and disintegrated. In the shadows at its far end I thought I saw a giant figure watching us as we passed, his eyes white as eggs in the darkness beneath the trees.

"You see him?" said Woolrich.

"Who is he?"

"The old woman's youngest son. Tee Jean, she calls him. Petit Jean. He's kinda slow, but he looks out for her. They all do."

"All?"

"Six of 'em live in the house. The old woman, her son, three kids from her second-eldest's marriage—he's dead; died with his wife in a car crash three years back—and a daughter. She has five more sons and three daughters all living within a few miles of here. Then the local folks, they look after her too. She's kind of the matriarch around these parts, I guess. Big magic."

I looked to see if he was being ironic. He wasn't.

We left the trees and arrived in a clearing before a long, single-story house raised above the ground on stripped stumps of trees. It looked old but lovingly built, the wood on the front unwarped and carefully overlapped, the shingles on the roof undamaged but, here and there, darker where they had been replaced. The door stood open, blocked only by a wire screen, and chairs and children's toys littered the porch, which ran the length of the front of the house and disappeared around the side. From behind, I could hear the sound of children and the splashing of water.

The screen door was opened and a small, slim woman appeared at the top of the steps. She was about thirty, with delicate features and lush dark hair drawn back in a ponytail from her light coffee-colored skin. Yet as we stepped from the car and drew nearer, I could see her skin was pitted with scars, probably from childhood acne. She seemed to recognize Woolrich for, before we said anything, she held the door open so I could step inside. Woolrich didn't follow. I turned back toward him.

"You coming in?"

"I didn't bring you here, if anyone asks, and I don't even want to see her," he said. He took a seat on the porch and rested his feet on the rail, watching the water gleam in the sunlight.

Inside, the wood was dark and the air cool. Doors at either side opened into bedrooms and a formal-looking living room with old, obviously hand-carved furniture, simple but carefully and skillfully crafted. An ancient radio with an illuminated dial and a band dotted with the names of far-flung places played a Chopin nocturne. The music followed me through the house and into the last bedroom, where the old woman waited.

She was blind. Her pupils were white, set in a huge moon face from which rolls of fat hung to her breastbone. Her arms, visible through the gauze sleeves of her multicolored dress, were bigger than mine and her swollen legs were like the trunks of small trees ending in surprisingly small, almost dainty, feet. She sat, supported by a mountain of pillows, on a giant bed in a room lit only by a hurricane lamp, the drapes closed against the sunlight. She was at least three hundred and fifty pounds, I guessed, probably more.

"Sit down, chile," she said, taking one of my hands in her own and running her fingers lightly over mine. Her eyes stared straight ahead, not looking at me, as her fingers traced the lines on my palm.

"I know why you here," she said. Her voice was high, girlish, as if she were a huge speaking doll whose tapes had been mixed up with a smaller model. "You hurtin'. You burnin' inside. Little girl, you woman, they gone." In the dim light, the old woman seemed to crackle with hidden energy.

"*Tante,* tell me about the girl in the swamp, the girl with no eyes."

"Poor chile," said the old woman, her brow furrowing in sorrow. "She the fust here. She was runnin' from sumpin' and she los' her way. Took a ride wi' him and she never came back. Hurt her so, so bad. Didn't touch her, though, 'cept with the knife."

She turned her eyes toward me for the first time and I realized she was not blind, not in any way that mattered. As her hands traced the lines of my palm, my eyes closed and I felt that she had been there with the girl in her final moments, that she might even have brought her some comfort as the blade went about its business. "Hush, chile, you come with *Tante* now. Hush, chile, take my hand, you. He done hurtin' you now."

As she touched me, I heard and felt, deep within myself, the blade cutting, grating, separating muscle from joint, flesh from bone, soul from body, the artist working on his canvas; and I felt pain dancing through me, arcing through a fading life like a lightning flash, welling like the notes of a hellish song through the unknown girl in the Louisiana swamp. And in her agony I felt the agony of my own child, my own wife, and I was certain that this was the same man. Even as the pain faded to its last for the girl in the swamp, she was in darkness and I knew he had blinded her before he killed her.

"Who is he?" I said.

She spoke, and in her voice there were four voices: the voices of a wife and a daughter, the voice of an old obese woman on a bed in a wine-dark room, and the voice of a nameless girl who died a brutal, lonely death in the mud and water of a Louisiana swamp.

"He the Travelin' Man."

WALTER SHIFTED IN HIS chair and the sound of his spoon against the china cup was like the ringing of chimes.

"No," I said. "I didn't find him."

CHAPTER IV

Walter had been silent for a while, the whiskey now almost drained from his glass. "I need a favor. Not for me but for someone else."

I waited.

"It has to do with the Barton Trust."

The Barton Trust had been founded in his will by old Jack Barton, an industrialist who made his fortune by supplying parts for the aeronautical industry after the war. The trust provided money for research into child-related issues, supported pediatric clinics, and generally provided child-care money that the state would not. Its nominal head was Isobel Barton, old Jack's widow, although the day-to-day running of the business was the responsibility of an attorney named Andrew Bruce and the trust's chairman, Philip Kooper.

I knew all this because Walter did some fund-raising for the trust on occasion—raffles, bowling tournaments—and also because, some weeks before, the trust had entered the news for all the wrong reasons. During a charity fete held on the grounds of the Barton house on Staten Island, a young boy, Evan Baines, had disappeared. In the end, no trace of the boy had been found and the cops had pretty much given up hope. They believed he had somehow strayed from the grounds and been abducted. It merited some mention in the newspapers for a time and then was gone.

"Evan Baines?"

"No, at least I don't think so, but it may be a missing person. A friend of Isobel Barton, a young woman, seems to have gone missing. It's been a few days and Mrs. Barton's worried. Her name's Catherine Demeter. Nothing to link her with the Baines disappearance; she hadn't even met the Bartons at that point."

"Bartons plural?"

"Seems she was dating Stephen Barton. You know anything about him?"

"He's an asshole. Apart from that, he's a minor drug pusher for Sonny Ferrera. Grew up near the Ferreras on Staten Island and fell in with Sonny as a teenager. He's into steroids, also coke, I think, but it's minor stuff."

Walter's brow furrowed. "How long have you known about this?" he asked.

"Can't remember," I replied. "Gym gossip."

"Jesus, don't tell us anything we might find useful. I've only known since Tuesday."

"You're not supposed to know," I said. "You're the police. Nobody tells you things you're supposed to know."

"You used to be a cop too," Walter muttered. "You've picked up some bad habits."

"Gimme a break, Walter. How do I know who you're checking up on? What am I supposed to do, go to confession to you once a week?" I poured some hot coffee into my cup. "Anyway, you think there might be a connection between this disappearance and Sonny Ferrera?" I continued.

"It's possible," said Walter. "The feds were tracking Stephen Barton for a while, maybe a year ago, before he was supposed to have started seeing Catherine Demeter. They were chasing their tails with that kid, so they let it go. According to the Narcotics file she doesn't seem to have been involved, at least not openly, but what do they know? Some of them still think a crack pipe is something a plumber fixes. Maybe she could have seen something she wasn't supposed to see."

His face betrayed how lame he thought the link was, but he left me to voice it. "C'mon, Walter, steroids and minor coke? There's money in it but it's strictly Little League compared to the rest of Ferrera's business. If he knocked off someone over musclehead drugs, then he's even more stupid than we know he is. Even his old man thinks he's the result of a defective gene."

Ferrera senior, sick and decrepit but still a respected figure, had been known to refer to his only son as "that little prick" on occasion. "Is that all you've got?"

"As you say, we're the police. No one tells us anything useful," he replied dryly.

"Did you know Sonny is impotent?" I offered.

Walter stood up, waving his empty glass in front of his face and smiling for the first time that evening. "No. No, I didn't. I'm not sure I wanted to know, either. What the hell are you, his urologist?" He glanced over at me as he reached for the Redbreast. I waved my fingers in a gesture of disregard that went no farther than my wrist.

"Pili Pilar still with him?" I asked, testing the waters.

"Far as I know. I hear he pushed Nicky Glasses out of a window a few weeks back because he fell behind on the vig."

The World Bank had loans out that attracted lower interest than Sonny Ferrera's financial operations. Then again, the World Bank probably didn't throw people out of the tenth floor because they couldn't keep up with the interest, at least not yet.

"Tough on Nicky. Another hundred years and he'd have had the loan paid off. Pili'd better ease up on his temper or he's gonna run out of people to push through windows."

Walter didn't smile.

"Will you talk to her?" he asked as he resumed his seat.

"MPs, Walter . . ." I sighed. Fourteen thousand people disappear in New York every year. It wasn't even clear if this woman was missing—in which case she didn't want to be found or someone else didn't want her found—or simply misplaced, which meant that she had merely upped sticks and moved off to another town without breaking the news to her good friend Isobel Barton or to her lovely boyfriend, Stephen Barton.

Those are the kinds of issues PIs have to consider when faced with missing persons cases. Tracing missing persons is bread and butter for PIs, but I wasn't a PI. I had taken on Fat Ollie's skip because it was easy work, or seemed to be at the time. I didn't want to file for a PI license with the state licensing services in Albany. I didn't want to get involved in missing persons work. Maybe I was afraid it would distract me too much. Maybe I just didn't care enough, not then.

"She won't go to the cops," said Walter. "The woman isn't even officially missing yet, since no one has reported her."

"So how come you know about it?"

"You know Tony Loo-Loo?" I nodded. Tony Loomax was a small-time PI with a stammer who had never graduated beyond skips and white trash divorces.

"Loomax is an unusual candidate for Isobel Barton's patronage," I said.

"It seems he did some work for one of the household staff a year or two back. Traced her husband, who'd run off with their savings. Mrs. Barton told him she wanted something similar done, but wanted it done quietly."

"Still doesn't explain your involvement."

"I have some stuff on Tony, mild overstepping of legal boundaries, which he would prefer I didn't act on. Tony figured I might like to know that Isobel Barton had been making low-key approaches. I spoke to Kooper. He believes the trust doesn't need any more bad publicity. I figured maybe I could do him a favor."

"If Tony has the call, then why are you approaching me?"

"We've encouraged Tony to pass it on. He's told Isobel Barton that he's passing her on to someone she can trust because he can't take the case. Seems his mother just died and he has to go to the funeral."

"Tony Loo-Loo doesn't have a mother. He was brought up in an orphanage."

"Well, *someone's* mother must have died," said Walter testily. "He can go to *that* funeral."

He stopped and I could see the doubt in his eyes as the rumors he had heard flicked a fin in the depths of his mind. "And that's why I'm approaching you. Even if I tried to do this quietly through the usual channels, someone would know. Christ, you take a drink of water at headquarters and ten guys piss it out."

"What about the girl's family?"

He shrugged. "I don't know much more but I don't think there is one. Look, Bird, I'm asking you because you're good. You were a smart cop. If you'd stayed on the force the rest of us would have been cleaning your shoes and polishing your shield. Your instincts were good. I reckon they still are. Plus you owe me one: people who go shooting up the boroughs don't usually walk away quite so easily."

I was silent for a while. I could hear Lee banging around in the kitchen while a TV show played in the background. Perhaps it was a remnant of what had taken place earlier, the apparently senseless killing of Fat Ollie Watts and his girlfriend, the death of the shooter, but it felt as if the world had shifted out of joint and that nothing was fitting as it should. Even this felt wrong. I believed Walter was holding back on me.

I heard the doorbell ring and then there was a muffled exchange of voices, one of them Lee's and the other a deep male voice. Seconds later there was a knock on the door and Lee showed in a tall, gray-haired man in his fifties. He wore a dark blue double-breasted suit—it looked like Boss—and a red Christian Dior tie with an interlocking gold *CD* pattern. His shoes sparkled like they'd been shined with spit, although, since this was Philip Kooper, it was probably someone else's spit.

Kooper was an unlikely figure to act as chairman and spokesman of a children's charity. He was thin and pale faced, and his mouth managed the unique trick of being simultaneously slim and pursed. His fingers were long and tapering, almost like claws. Kooper looked like he had been disinterred for the express purpose of making people uneasy. If he had turned up at one of the trust's kids' parties, all of the children would have cried.

"This him?" he asked Walter, after declining a drink. He flicked his head at me like a frog swallowing a fly. I played with the sugar bowl and tried to look offended.

"This is Parker," nodded Walter. I waited to see if Kooper would offer to shake hands. He didn't. His hands remained clasped in front of him like a professional mourner at a particularly uninvolving funeral.

"Have you explained the situation to him?"

Walter nodded again but looked embarrassed. Kooper's manners were worse than a bad child's. I stayed seated and didn't say anything. Kooper sniffed and then stood in silence while he looked down on me. He gave the impression that it was a position with which he was entirely familiar.

"This is a delicate situation, Mr. Parker, as I'm sure you'll appreciate. Any communication in this matter will be made to me in the first instance before you impart any information to Mrs. Barton. Is that clear?"

I wondered if Kooper was worth the effort of annoying and decided, after looking at Walter's look of discomfort, that he probably wasn't, at least not yet. But I was starting to feel sorry for Isobel Barton and I hadn't even met her.

"My understanding was that Mrs. Barton was hiring me," I said eventually.

"That's correct, but you will be answerable to me."

"I don't think so. There's a small matter of confidentiality. I'll look into it, but if it's unconnected with the Baines kid or the Ferreras, I reserve the right to keep what I learn between Isobel Barton and myself."

"That is not satisfactory, Mr. Parker," said Kooper. A faint blush of color rose in his cheeks and hung there for a moment, looking lost in the tundra of his complexion. "Perhaps I am not making myself clear: in this matter, you will report to me first. I have powerful friends, Mr. Parker. If you do not cooperate, I can ensure that your license is revoked."

"They must be very powerful friends because I don't have a license," I said. I stood up and Kooper's fists tightened slightly. "You should consider yoga," I said. "You're too tense."

I thanked Walter for the coffee and moved to the door.

"Wait," he said. I turned back to see him staring at Kooper. After a few moments, Kooper gave a barely perceptible shrug of his shoulders and moved to the window. He didn't look at me again. Kooper's attitude and Walter's expression conspired against my better judgment, and I decided to talk to Isobel Barton.

"I take it she's expecting me?" I asked Walter.

"I told Tony to tell her you were good, that if the girl was alive you'd find her."

There was another brief moment of silence.

"And if she's dead?"

"Mr. Kooper asked that question as well," said Walter.

"What did you say?"

He swallowed the last of his whiskey, the ice cubes rattling against the glass like old bones. Behind him, Kooper was a dark silhouette against the window, like a promise of bad news.

"I told him you'd bring back the body."

IN THE END, THAT'S what it all came down to: bodies—bodies found and yet to be found. And I recalled how Woolrich and I stood outside the old woman's house on that April day and looked out over the bayou. I could hear the water lapping gently at the shore, and farther out, I watched a small fishing boat bobbing on the water, two figures casting out from either side. But both Woolrich and I were looking deeper than the surface, as if, by staring hard enough, we could penetrate to the depths and find the body of a nameless girl in the dark waters.

"Do you believe her?" he said at last.

"I don't know. I really don't know."

"There's no way we're gonna find that body, if it exists, without more than we've got. We start trawling for bodies in bayous and pretty soon we're gonna be knee deep in bones. People been dumping bodies in these swamps for centuries. Be a miracle if we didn't find something."

I walked away from him. He was right, of course. Assuming there was a body, we needed more from the old woman than she had given us. I felt like I was trying to grip smoke, but what the old woman had said was the closest thing yet to a lead on the man who had killed Jennifer and Susan.

I wondered if I was crazy, taking the word of a blind woman who heard voices in her sleep. I probably was.

"Do you know what he looks like, *Tante*?" I had asked her, watching as her head moved ponderously from side to side in response.

"Only see him when he comes for you," she replied. "Then you know him."

I reached the car and looked back to see a figure on the porch with Woolrich. It was the girl with the scarred face, standing gracefully on the tips of her toes as she leaned toward the taller man. I saw Woolrich run his finger tenderly across her cheek and then softly speak her name: "Florence." He kissed her lightly on the lips, then turned and walked toward me without looking back at her. Neither of us said anything about it on the journey back to New Orleans.

CHAPTER V

It rained throughout that night, breaking the shell of heat that had surrounded the city, and the streets of Manhattan seemed to breathe easier the next morning. It was almost cool as I ran. The pavement was hard on my knees but large areas of grass were sparse in this part of the city. I bought a newspaper on the way back to my apartment, then showered, changed, and read over breakfast. Shortly after 11 A.M. I headed out to the Barton house.

Isobel Barton lived in the secluded house her late husband had built in the seventies on Todt Hill, an admirable if unsuccessful attempt to replicate the antebellum houses of his native Georgia in an East Coast setting and on a smaller scale. Old Jack Barton, an amiable soul by all accounts, had apparently made up with money and determination for what he lacked in good taste.

The gate to the drive was open as I arrived, and the exhaust fumes of another car hung in the air. The cab turned in just as the electronic gates were about to rumble closed, and we followed the lead car, a white BMW 320i with tinted windows, to the small courtyard in front of the house. The cab looked out of place in that setting, although how the Barton household might have felt about my own battered Mustang, currently undergoing repairs, I wasn't so sure.

As I pulled up, a slim woman dressed conservatively in a gray suit emerged from the BMW and watched me curiously as I paid the cabdriver. Her gray hair was tied back in a bun that did nothing to soften her severe features. A large black man wearing a chauffeur's uniform appeared at the door of the house and moved quickly to intercept me as I walked from the departing cab.

"Parker. I believe I'm expected."

The chauffeur gave me a look that told me, if I was lying, he'd make me wish I'd stayed in bed. He told me to wait, before turning back to the woman in gray. She glanced at me briefly but nastily before exchanging a few words with the chauffeur, who moved off to the back of the house as she approached me.

"Mr. Parker, I'm Ms. Christie, Mrs. Barton's personal assistant. You should have stayed at the gate until we were sure who you were." In a window above the door, a curtain twitched slightly and then was still.

"If you have a staff entrance I'll use that in future." I got the impression from Ms. Christie that she hoped that eventuality wouldn't arise. She eyed me coldly for a moment, then turned on her heel.

"If you'll come with me, please," she said over her shoulder as she moved toward the door. The gray suit was threadbare at the edges. I wondered if Mrs. Barton would haggle over my rates.

If Isobel Barton was short of cash she could simply have sold off some of the antiques that furnished the house, because the interior was an auctioneer's wet dream. Two large rooms opened out at either side of a hallway, filled with furniture that looked like it was used only when presidents died. A wide staircase curved up to the right; a closed door lay straight ahead while another nestled under the stairs. I followed Ms. Christie through the latter and into a small but surprisingly bright and modern office with a computer in a corner and a TV and video unit built into the bookshelves. Maybe Mrs. Barton wouldn't haggle about the rates after all.

Ms. Christie sat down behind a pine desk, removed some papers from her valise, and shuffled through them in obvious irritation before finding what she wanted.

"This is a standard confidentiality agreement drawn up by the trust's legal advisers," she began, pushing it toward me with one hand while clicking a pen simultaneously with the other. "It is an undertaking on your behalf to keep all communication relating to the matter in hand between Mrs. Barton, myself, and yourself." She used the pen to point to the relevant sections on the agreement, like an insurance salesman trying to slip a bum contract past a sucker. "I'd like you to sign it before we proceed any further," she concluded.

It seemed like nobody involved with the Barton Trust had a particularly trusting nature. "I don't think so," I said. "If you're concerned about possible breaches of confidentiality, then hire a priest to do your work. Otherwise you'll have to take my word that what passes between us will go no further." Perhaps I should have felt guilty about lying to her. I didn't. I was a good liar. It's one of the gifts God gives alcoholics.

"That's not acceptable. I am already unconvinced about the necessity of hiring you and I certainly feel it is inappropriate to do so without—"

She was interrupted by the sound of the office door opening. I turned to see a tall, attractive woman enter, her age indeterminable through a combination of the gentleness of nature and the magic of cosmetics. At a glance I would have guessed she was in her late forties, but if this was Isobel Barton, then I knew she was closer to fifty-five, maybe older. She wore a pale blue dress that was too subtly simple to be anything but expensive and displayed a figure that was either surgically enhanced or extremely well preserved.

As she drew closer and the tiny wrinkles in her face became clearer, I guessed it was the latter: Isobel Barton did not look like the sort of woman who resorted to plastic surgery. Around her neck gold and diamonds glittered, and a pair of matching earrings sparkled as she walked. Her hair too was gray, but she let it hang long and loose on her shoulders. She was still an attractive woman and she walked like she knew it.

Philip Kooper had borne the brunt of the media attention following the disappearance of the Baines boy, but that attention had not been significant. The Baines boy was from a family of dopers and no-hopers. His disappearance merited a mention only because of the trust, and even then the trust's lawyers and patrons had called in enough favors to ensure that speculation was kept to a minimum. The boy's mother was separated from his father and they hadn't been getting along any better since he left.

The police were still trying to trace the father in case of a possible snatch, even though every indication was that the father, a petty criminal, hated his child. In some cases, that might be enough to justify taking the child and killing him to get at his estranged wife. When I was a rookie patrolman, I once arrived at a tenement to find a man had abducted his baby daughter and drowned her in the bath because his ex-wife wouldn't let him have the TV after they separated.

Only one piece of coverage of the Baines disappearance stuck in my mind: a picture of Mrs. Barton, snapped head-bowed as she visited the mother of Evan Baines in a run-down project. It was supposed to have been a private visit. The photographer, returning from the scene of a drug killing, just happened to be passing. One or two papers took the picture, but they ran it small.

"Thank you, Caroline. I'll talk to Mr. Parker alone for a while." She smiled as she said it but her tone brooked no argument. Her assistant affected a lack of concern at the dismissal but her eyes flashed fire. When she had left the room, Mrs. Barton seated herself on a stiff-backed chair away from the desk and motioned me toward a black leather couch, then turned her smile on me.

"I'm sorry about that. I didn't authorize any such agreement but Caroline can be overprotective of me at times. Can we offer you coffee, or would you prefer a drink?"

"Neither, thank you. Before you go any further, Mrs. Barton, I should tell you that I don't really do missing persons work." In my experience, searching for missing persons was best left to specialist agencies with the manpower to chase up leads and possible sightings. Some solo investigators who took on that kind of work were at best ill equipped and at worst little better than parasites who preyed on the hopes of those who remained to keep funding minimal efforts for even smaller returns.

"Mr. Loomax said you might say that, but only out of modesty. He told me to say he would regard it as a personal favor."

I smiled, despite myself. The only favor I would give Tony Loo-Loo would be not to piss on his grave when he died.

According to Mrs. Barton, she had met Catherine Demeter through her son, who had seen the girl working at DeVries's department store and had pestered her for a date. Mrs. Barton and her son—her stepson, to be accurate, since Jack Barton had been married once before, to a Southern woman who had divorced him after eight years and moved to Hawaii with a singer—were not close. She was aware that her son was engaged in activities that were, as she put it, "unsavory," and had tried to get him to change his ways, "both for his own sake and the sake of the trust." I nodded sympathetically. Sympathy was the only possible emotion to feel for anyone involved with Stephen Barton.

When she heard he was seeing a new girlfriend she asked if they could all meet together, she said, and a date had been arranged. In the end her son had failed to appear but Catherine had turned up, and after an initial awkwardness, the two quickly struck up a friendship far more amicable than the relationship that existed between the girl and Stephen Barton. The two had continued to meet occasionally for coffee and lunch. Despite invitations, the girl had politely refused offers from Mrs. Barton to come out to the house, and Stephen Barton had never brought her.

Then Catherine Demeter had simply dropped out of sight. She had left work early on Saturday and had failed to keep an early dinner appointment on Sunday with Mrs. Barton. That was the last anyone had heard of Catherine Demeter, said Mrs. Barton. Two days had now passed and she had heard nothing from her.

"Because of, well, the publicity that the trust has received recently over the disappearance of that poor child, I was reluctant to cause a fuss or draw any further adverse attention down on us," she said. "I called Mr. Loomax and he seemed to think that Catherine may simply have drifted on somewhere else. It happens a lot, I believe."

"Do you think there's something more to it than that?"

"I really don't know, but she was so happy with her job and she appeared to be getting on well with Stephen." She stopped for a moment at this mention of her son's name, as if considering whether or not to proceed. Then: "Stephen has been running wild for some time—since before his father's death, in fact. Do you know the Ferrera family, Mr. Parker?"

"I'm aware of them."

"Stephen fell in with their youngest son, despite all of our efforts. I know he keeps bad company and I know he's involved with drugs. I'm afraid he may have dragged Catherine into something. And . . ." She paused again, briefly. "I enjoyed her company. There was something gentle about her and she seemed so sad sometimes. She said that she was anxious to settle down here, after moving around for so long."

"Did she say where she had been?"

"All over. I gather that she had worked in a number of states."

"Did she say anything about her past, give any indication that something might be troubling her?"

"I think something may have happened to her family when she was young. She told me that she had a sister who died. She didn't say any more. She said she couldn't talk about it and I didn't press her on it."

"Mr. Loomax may be right. She may simply have moved on again."

Mrs. Barton shook her head insistently. "No, she would have told me, I'm sure of it. Stephen hasn't heard from her and neither have I. I'm afraid for her and I want to know that she is safe. That's all. She doesn't even have to know that I hired you, or that I was concerned for her. Will you take the case?"

I was still reluctant to do Walter Cole's dirty work and to take advantage of Isobel Barton, but I had little else on my plate except an appearance in court the following day on behalf of an insurance firm, another case I had taken for the money and to pass the time.

If there was a connection between the disappearance of Catherine Demeter and Sonny Ferrera, then she was almost certainly in trouble. If Sonny had been involved in the killing of Fat Ollie Watts, it was clear that he was going off the rails.

"I'll give it a few days," I said. "As a favor," I added. "Do you want to know my rates?"

She was already writing a check, drawn on her private account and not that of the trust. "Here's three thousand dollars in advance and this is my card. My private number is on the back."

She moved her chair forward. "Now, what else do you need to know?"

THAT EVENING, I HAD dinner at River on Amsterdam Avenue, close to Seventieth Street, where the classic beef made it the best Vietnamese in town and where the staff moved by so softly that it was like being waited on by shadows or passing breezes. I watched a young couple at a nearby table intertwining their hands, running their fingers over each other's knuckles and fingertips, tracing delicate circles in their palms, then gripping their hands together and pressing the heel of each hand forcefully against the other. And as they simulated their lovemaking, a waitress drifted by and smiled knowingly at me as I watched.

CHAPTER VI

The day after I visited Isobel Barton, I made a brief visit to court in connection with the insurance case. A claim had been made against a phone company by a contracted electrician, who said he had fallen down a hole in the road while examining underground cables and was no longer able to work as a result.

He may not have been able to work, but he had still been able to power lift five hundred pounds in a cash contest in a Boston gymnasium. I had used a palm-size Panasonic video camera to capture his moment of glory. The insurance company presented the evidence to a judge, who suspended any further decision on the matter for one week. I didn't even have to give evidence. Afterward I had coffee in a diner and read the paper before heading over to Pete Hayes's old gym in Tribeca.

I knew Stephen Barton worked out there sometimes. If his girlfriend had disappeared, then there was a strong possibility that Barton might know where she had gone or, equally important, why. I remembered him vaguely as a strong, Nordic-looking type, his body obscenely pumped from steroid use. He was in his late twenties but the combination of training and tanning salons had worn his face to the consistency of old leather, adding at least ten years to his age.

As artists and Wall Street lawyers had started moving into the

Tribeca area, attracted by loft space in the cast iron and masonry buildings, Pete's gym had moved upmarket, filling what used to be a spit and sawdust place with mirrors and potted palms and, sacrilege upon sacrilege, a juice bar. Now heavyweight boneheads and serious power lifters worked out alongside accountants with paunches and female executives with power-dress business suits and cell phones. The bulletin board at the door advertised something called "spinning," which involved sitting on a bike for an hour and sweating yourself into a red agony. Ten years ago, even the suggestion that the gym might be used for such a purpose would have caused Pete's regular clientele to bust the place up.

A wholesome-looking blonde in a gray leotard buzzed me into Pete's office, the last bastion of what the gym had once been. Old posters advertising power lifting competitions and Mr. Universe shows shared wall space with pictures of Pete alongside Steve Reeves, Joe Weider, and, oddly, the wrestler Hulk Hogan. Bodybuilding trophies sat in a glass-fronted cabinet while behind a battered pine desk sat Pete himself, his muscles slackening in old age but still a powerful, impressive figure, his salt-and-pepper hair cut in a short military style. I had trained in the gym for almost six years, until I was promoted to detective and started to destroy myself.

Pete stood and nodded, his hands in his pockets and his loose-fitting top doing nothing to conceal the size of his shoulders and arms.

"Long time," he said. "Sorry about what happened to . . ." He trailed off and moved his chin and shoulders in a kind of combination shrug, a gesture to the past and what it contained.

I nodded back and leaned against an old gunmetal gray filing cabinet adorned with decals advertising health supplements and lifting magazines.

"*Spinning*, Pete?"

He grimaced. "Yeah, I know. Still, spinning makes me two hundred dollars an hour. I got forty exercise bikes on the floor above us and I couldn't make more money with a printing press and green ink."

"Stephen Barton around?"

Pete kicked at some imaginary obstacle on the worn wooden floor. "Not for a week or so. He in trouble?"

"I don't know," I replied. "Is he?"

Pete sat down slowly and, wincing, stretched his legs out in front of him. Years of squatting had taken their toll on his knees, leaving them weak and arthritic. "You're not the first person to come here asking about him this week. Couple of guys in cheap suits were in here yesterday trying to find him. Recognized one of them as Sal Inzerillo. Used to be a good light-middleweight until he started taking falls."

"I remember him." I paused. "Works for old man Ferrera now, I hear."

"Might do," nodded Pete. "Might do. Might have worked for the old man in the ring too, if you believe the stories. This about drugs?"

"I don't know," I replied. Pete glanced at me quickly to see if I was lying, decided I wasn't, and went back to examining the tops of his sneakers. "You hear of any trouble between Sonny and the old man, anything that might have involved Stephen Barton?"

"There's trouble between them, sure, otherwise what's Inzerillo doing damaging my floor with his black rubber soles? Don't know that it involves Barton, though."

I moved on to the subject of Catherine Demeter.

"Do you remember a girl with Barton recently? She may have been around here sometimes. Short, dark hair, slight overbite, maybe in her early thirties."

"Barton has lots of girls but I don't remember that one. Don't notice, mostly, unless they're smarter than Barton, which makes me wonder."

"Not difficult," I said. "This one probably was smarter. Is Barton a hitter?"

"He's mean, sure. Popping pills frazzled his brain, gave him bad 'roid rage. It's fight or fuck with him. Fuck, mainly. My old lady could take him in a fight." He looked at me intently. "I know what he was into, but he didn't sell here. I'd have force-fed his shit to him till he burst if he tried it." I didn't believe Pete but I let it go. Steroids were part of the game now and there was nothing Pete could do except bluster.

He pursed his lips and pulled his legs slowly in. "A lot of women were attracted to him by his size. Barton was a big guy and he sure talked big. Some women just want the protection someone like him seems to offer. They believe if they give the guy what he wants he'll look out for them.

"Pity she chose Stephen Barton, then," I said.

"Yeah," agreed Pete. "Maybe she wasn't so smart after all."

I had brought my training gear with me and did ninety minutes in the gym, the mirrored walls reflecting my efforts back at me from every angle. It had been some time since I trained properly. To avoid embarrassment I skipped the bench and stuck to shoulders, back, and light arm work, enjoying the sensation of strength and movement in the bent-over rows and the pressure on my biceps during the curls.

I still looked pretty good, I thought, although the assessment was a result of insecurity instead of vanity. At just under six feet, I still retained some of my lifter's build—the wide shoulders, definition in the biceps and triceps, and a chest that was at least bigger than two eggs frying on the sidewalk—and I hadn't regained much of the fat I had lost during the year. I still had my hair, although there was gray creeping back from the temples and sprinkling the fringe. My eyes were clear enough to be recognizably gray-blue, set in a slightly long face now deeply etched at the eyes and mouth with the marks of remembered grief. Clean shaven, with a decent haircut, a good suit, and some flattering light, I could look almost respectable. In the right light, I could even have claimed to be thirty-two without making people snigger too loudly. It was only two years less than my age on my driver's license, but these little things become more important as you get older.

When I was finished, I packed my gear, declined Pete's offer of a protein shake—it smelled like rotten bananas—and stopped off for a coffee instead. I felt relaxed for the first time in weeks, the endorphins pumping through my system and a pleasant tightness developing across my shoulders and back.

THE NEXT CALL I made was to DeVries's department store on Fifth Avenue. The personnel manager called himself a human resources manager and, like personnel managers the world over, was one of the least personable people one could meet. Sitting opposite him, it was difficult not to feel that anyone who could happily reduce individuals to resources, to the same level as oil, bricks, and canaries in coal mines, probably shouldn't be allowed to have any human relations that didn't involve locks and prison bars. In other words, Timothy Cary was a first-degree prick from the tip of his close-cropped dyed hair to the toes of his patent leather shoes.

I had contacted his secretary earlier that afternoon to make the appointment, telling her that I was acting for an attorney in the matter of an inheritance coming to Ms. Demeter. Cary and his secretary deserved each other. A wild dog on a chain would have been more helpful than Cary's secretary, and easier to get past.

"My client is anxious that Ms. Demeter be contacted as soon as possible," I told him as we sat in his small, prissy office. "The will is extremely detailed and there are a lot of forms to be filled out."

"And your client would be . . . ?"

"I'm afraid I can't tell you that. I'm sure you understand."

Cary looked like he understood but didn't want to. He leaned back in his chair and gently rubbed his expensive silk tie between his fingers. It had to be expensive. It was too tasteless to be anything else. Crisp lines showed along his shirt as if it had just been removed from its packaging, assuming Timothy Cary would have anything to do with something so plebeian as a plastic wrapper. If he ever visited the shop floor it must have been like an angel descending, albeit an angel who looked like he'd just encountered a bad smell.

"Miss Demeter was due in work yesterday." Cary glanced down

at a file on his desk. "She had Monday off, so we haven't seen her since Saturday."

"Is that usual, to have Monday off?" I wasn't anxious to know, but the question distracted Cary from the file. Isobel Barton didn't have Catherine Demeter's new address. Catherine would usually contact her, or Mrs. Barton would have her assistant leave a message at DeVries's. As Cary brightened slightly at the opportunity to discuss a subject close to his heart and started mouthing off about work schedules, I memorized her address and SSN. I eventually managed to interrupt him for long enough to ask if Catherine Demeter had been ill on her last day at work or had complained of being disturbed in any way.

"I'm not aware of any such communication. Miss Demeter's position with DeVries is currently under review as a result of her absence," he concluded smugly. "I hope, for her sake, that her inheritance is considerable." I don't think he meant it.

After some routine delaying tactics, Cary gave me permission to speak with the woman who had worked with Catherine on her last shift in the store. I met her in a supervisor's office off the shop floor. Martha Friedman was in her early sixties. She was plump, with dyed red hair and a face so caked with cosmetics that the floor of the Amazon jungle probably saw more natural light, but she tried to be helpful. She had been working with Catherine Demeter in the china department on Saturday. It was her first time to work with her, since Mrs. Friedman's usual assistant had been taken ill and someone was needed to cover for her.

"Did you notice anything unusual about her behavior?" I asked, as Mrs. Friedman took the opportunity afforded by some time in the supervisor's office to discreetly examine the papers on his desk. "Did she seem distressed or anxious in any way?"

Mrs. Friedman furrowed her brow slightly. "She broke a piece of china, an Aynsley vase. She had just arrived and was showing it to a customer when she dropped it. Then, when I looked around, she was running across the shop floor, heading for the escalators. Most unprofessional, I thought, even if she was sick."

"And was she sick?"

"She *said* she felt sick, but why run for the escalators? We have a staff washroom on each floor."

I got the feeling that Mrs. Friedman knew more than she was saying. She was enjoying the attention and wanted to draw it out. I leaned toward her confidentially.

"But what do *you* think, Mrs. Friedman?"

She preened a little and leaned forward in turn, touching my hand lightly to emphasize her point.

"She saw someone, someone she was trying to reach before they left the store. Tom, the security guard on the east door, told me she ran out by him and stood looking around the street. We're supposed to get permission to leave the store when on duty. He should have reported her, but he just told me instead. Tom's a *schvartze*, but he's okay."

"Do you have any idea who she might have seen?"

"No. She just refused to discuss it. She doesn't have any friends among the staff, far as I can tell, and now I can see why."

I spoke to the security guard and the supervisor, but they couldn't add anything to what Mrs. Friedman had told me. I stopped at a diner for coffee and a sandwich, returned to my apartment to pick up a small black bag my friend Angel had given me, and then took another cab, to Catherine Demeter's apartment.

CHAPTER VII

The apartment was in a converted four-story redbrick in Greenpoint, a part of Brooklyn that was populated mainly by Italians, Irish, and Poles, the latter counting a large number of former Solidarity activists among them. It was from Greenpoint's Continental Iron Works that the ironclad *Monitor* had emerged to fight the Confederate ship *Merrimac,* when Greenpoint was Brooklyn's industrial center.

The cast iron manufacturers, the potters, and printers were all gone now, but many of the descendants of the original workers still remained. Small clothing boutiques and Polish bakeries shared frontage with established kosher delis and stores selling used electrical goods.

Catherine Demeter's block was still a little down at heel, and kids wearing sneakers and low-slung jeans sat on the steps of most of the buildings, smoking and whistling and calling at passing women. She lived in apartment 14, probably near the top of the building. I tried the bell but wasn't surprised when there was no answer from the intercom. Instead I tried 20, and when an elderly woman's voice responded, I told her I was from the gas company and had a report of a leak but the super's apartment was empty. She was silent for a moment, then buzzed me in.

I guessed she'd probably check with the super, so time was limited, although if the apartment didn't reveal anything about where Catherine Demeter might have gone, I'd have to talk to the super anyway, or approach the neighbors, or maybe even talk to the mailman. As I passed into the lobby I used a pick to open the mailbox for apartment 14, finding only a copy of the most recent *New York* magazine and what looked like two junk mail drops. I closed the box and took the stairs up to the third floor.

The third floor was silent, with six newly varnished apartment doors along the hall, three on each side. I walked quietly to number 14 and took the black bag from under my coat. I knocked once more on the door, just to be sure, and removed the power rake from the bag. Angel was the best B&E man I knew, and even as a cop I'd had reasons to use him. In return, I'd never hassled Angel and he'd stayed out of my way professionally. When he did go down, I'd done my best to make things a little easier for him inside. The rake had been a thank-you of sorts. An illegal thank-you.

It looked like an electric drill but was smaller and slimmer, with a prong at its tip that acted as a pick and tension tool. I stuck the prong in the lock and squeezed the trigger. The rake clattered noisily for a couple of seconds and then the lock turned. I slipped in quietly and closed the door behind me, seconds before another door in the corridor opened. I stayed still and waited until it closed again, then put the rake back in the bag, reopened the door, and took a toothpick from my pocket. I snapped it into four pieces and jammed them into the lock. It would give me time to get to the fire escape if someone tried to enter the apartment while I was there. Then I closed the door and turned on the lights.

A short hallway with a threadbare rug led to a clean living room, cheaply furnished with a battered TV and a mismatched sofa and chairs. To one side was a small kitchen and to the other a bedroom.

I checked the bedroom first. Some paperback novels stood on a small shelf beside the bed. The only other furniture consisted of a wardrobe and dressing table, both of which appeared to have been made up from IKEA kits. I checked under the bed and found an empty suitcase. There were no cosmetics on the dressing table, which meant that she had probably packed a small overnight bag when she left and taken them with her. She probably hadn't intended to stay away for long and she certainly didn't appear to have left for good.

I checked the closet but there were only clothes and a few pairs of shoes inside. The first two drawers in the dresser also contained only clothes, but the last one was filled with papers, the accumulated documents, tax forms, and employment records of a life spent moving from city to city, from job to job.

Catherine Demeter had spent a long time in the waitressing game, moving from New Hampshire to Florida and back again with the social season. She had also spent some time in Chicago, Las Vegas, and Phoenix, as well as numerous small towns, judging by the collection of wage slips and tax documents in her drawer. There were also various bank statements. She had about nineteen thousand dollars in a savings account in a Citibank, as well as some stocks and bonds, bound carefully with a thick blue ribbon. Finally, there was a passport, updated recently, and within it three extra passport-size photos of herself.

Catherine Demeter, true to Isobel Barton's description, was a small attractive woman in her mid-thirties, five-two, with dark hair cut short in a bob, pale blue eyes, and a fair complexion. I took the extra photos and put them in my wallet, then turned to examine the only item of a very personal nature in the drawer.

It was a photo album, thick and worn at the corners. Within it was what I assumed to be a history of the Demeter family, from sepia-tinted photos of grandparents through the wedding of what I guessed were her parents and on through the photos of two girls growing up, sometimes with parents and friends, sometimes together, sometimes alone. Pictures from the beach, from family holidays, from birthdays and Christmas and Thanksgiving, the memories of two sisters starting off in life. The resemblance between the two was clear. Catherine was the younger, the overbite visible even then. The girl I took to be her sister was perhaps two or three years older, with sandy-colored hair, a beautiful girl even at eleven or twelve.

There were no more pictures of the older girl after that age. The rest consisted of Catherine alone or with her parents, and the record of her growth was more periodic, the sense of celebration and joyfulness gone. Eventually, the photos dwindled away to nothing, with a final picture of Catherine on the day of her high school graduation, a solemn-looking young woman with dark rings beneath eyes that seemed close to tears. The testimonial attached came from the principal of Haven High School, in Virginia.

Something had been removed from the final pages of the album. Small pieces of what appeared to be newspaper rested at the base of the album pages, most merely tiny fragments as thin as threads, but one about an inch square. The paper was yellowing with age, with a fragment of a weather report on one side and part of a picture on the other, the tip of some sand-blond hair visible in one corner. Tucked into the last page were two birth certificates, one for Catherine Louise Demeter, dated March 5, 1962, and the other for Amy Ellen Demeter, dated December 3, 1959.

I returned the album to the drawer and went into the bathroom next door. It was clean and neat like the rest of the apartment, with soap, shower gels, and foam bath arranged neatly on the white tiles by the bath and towels stored in a small cabinet under the sink. I opened one side of the mirrored cabinet on the wall. It contained toothpaste, floss, and mouthwash, as well as some nonprescription medicines for cold relief and water retention, evening primrose capsules, and assorted vitamin pills. There were no birth control pills or other contraceptives. Maybe Stephen Barton took care of that, although I doubted it. Stephen didn't seem like the sensitive type.

The other side of the cabinet contained a miniature pharmacy with enough uppers and downers to keep Catherine moving like a roller coaster. There were Librium, for mood swings; Ativan, to combat agitation; and Valium, Thorazine and Lorazepam for anxiety. Some were empty, others half empty. The most recent came from a prescription from Dr. Frank Forbes, a psychiatrist. I knew the name. "Fucking Frank" Forbes had screwed or attempted to screw so many of his patients that it was sometimes suggested that they should charge him. He had been on the verge of losing his license on a number of occasions, but the complaints were either withdrawn, never got to court, or were suppressed through the judicious application of some of Fucking Frank's funds. I heard he had been unusually quiet lately after one of his patients had contracted a dose of the clap after an encounter with Frank and then had promptly slapped a lawsuit on him. This one, I gathered, was proving difficult for Fucking Frank to bury.

Catherine Demeter was clearly a very unhappy woman and was unlikely to get any happier if she was seeing Frank Forbes. I wasn't too keen on visiting him. He had once tried to come on to Elizabeth Gordon, the daughter of one of Susan's divorced friends, and I'd paid him a visit to remind him of his duties as a doctor and to threaten to throw him from his office window if it ever happened again. After that, I tried to take a semiprofessional interest in Frank Forbes's activities.

There was nothing else of note in Catherine's bathroom, or in the rest of her apartment. As I was leaving I stopped at her telephone, picked it up, and pressed the redial button. After the beeps subsided a voice answered.

"Haven County Sheriff's Office, hello?"

I hung up and called a guy I knew in the telephone company. Five minutes later he came back with a list of local numbers called from Friday to Sunday. There were only three and they were all mundane—a Chinese take-out, a local laundry, and a movie information line.

The local company couldn't give me any details of any long distance calls made, so I tried a second number. This one connected me with one of the many agencies that offer PIs and those with a deep and abiding interest in other people's business the opportunity to purchase confidential information illegally. The agency was able to tell me within twenty minutes that fifteen calls had been made to Haven, Virginia, numbers on Saturday evening through Sprint, seven to the sheriff's office and eight to a private residence in the town. I was given both numbers and I went with the second. The message on the answering machine was terse: "This is Earl Lee Granger. I'm not here right now. Leave a message after the beep or, if it relates to police business, contact the sheriff's office at . . ."

I punched in the number, got the Haven County Sheriff's Office again, and asked to speak to the sheriff.

I was told that Sheriff Granger wasn't available, so I asked to speak to whoever was in charge in his absence. The ranking deputy was Alvin Martin, I learned, but he was out on a case. The deputy on the phone didn't know when the sheriff would be back. From his tone, I guessed the sheriff hadn't simply gone out to buy cigarettes. He asked me my name and I thanked him and hung up.

It seemed that something had caused Catherine Demeter to get in touch with the sheriff in her hometown, but not with the NYPD. If there was nothing else, I'd have to pay a visit to Haven. First, though, I decided to pay a visit to Fucking Frank Forbes.

CHAPTER VIII

I stopped off at Azure on Third Avenue and bought myself some expensive fresh strawberries and pineapple from the deli, then took them around to the Citicorp Center to eat in the public space. I liked the building's simple lines and its strange, angled top. It was also one of the few new developments where a similar imagination had been applied to its interior: its seven-story atrium was still green with trees and shrubs, its shops and restaurants were packed with people, and a handful of worshipers sat silently in its simple, sunken church.

Two blocks away, Fucking Frank Forbes had a swank office in a seventies smoked-glass development, at least for the present. I took the elevator up and entered the reception area, where a young and pretty brunette was typing something on the computer. She looked up as I entered and smiled brightly. I tried not to let my jaw hang as I smiled back.

"Is Dr. Forbes available?" I asked.

"Do you have an appointment?"

"I'm not a patient, thankfully, but Frank and I go way back. Tell him Charlie Parker wants to see him."

Her smile faltered a little but she buzzed Frank's office and gave him the message. Her face paled slightly as she listened to his response but she held herself together remarkably well, all things considered.

"I'm afraid Dr. Forbes can't see you," she said, the smile now fading rapidly.

"Is that really what he said?"

She blushed slightly. "No, not quite."

"Are you new here?"

"This is my first week."

"Frank select you personally?"

She looked puzzled. "Ye-es."

"Get another job. He's a deviant and he's on his way out of business."

I walked past her and entered Frank's office while she took all this in. There was no patient in Frank's consulting room, just the good doctor himself leafing through some notes on his desk. He didn't look pleased to see me. His thin mustache curled in distaste like a black worm, and a red bloom spread from his neck to his high-domed forehead before disappearing into his brush of wiry black hair. He was tall, over six feet, and he worked out. He looked real good, but looks were as far as it went. There was nothing good about Fucking Frank Forbes. If he handed you a dollar, the ink would be running before it got to your wallet.

"Get the fuck out, Parker. In case you've forgotten, you can't come barging in here anymore. You're not a cop now and the force is probably all the richer for your absence." He leaned toward the intercom button but his receptionist had already entered behind me.

"Call the police, Marcie. Better still, call my lawyer. Tell him I'm about to file for harassment."

"Hear you're giving him a lot of business at the moment, Frank," I said, taking a seat in a leather upright opposite his desk. "I also hear Maibaum and Locke are handling the lawsuit for that unfortunate woman with the social disease. I've done some business with them in the past and they're real hot. Maybe I could put them onto Elizabeth Gordon. You remember Elizabeth, don't you, Frank?"

Frank cast an instinctive glance over his shoulder at the window and twisted his chair away from it.

"It's okay, Marcie," he said, nodding uneasily to the receptionist. I heard the door close softly behind me. "What do you want?"

"You have a patient called Catherine Demeter."

"Come on, Parker, you know I can't discuss my patients. Even if I could, I wouldn't share shit with you."

"Frank, you're the worst shrink I know. I wouldn't let a dog be treated by you because you'd probably try to fuck it, so save the ethics for the judge. I think she may be in trouble and I want to find her. If you don't help me I'll be in touch with Maibaum and Locke so fast you'll think I'm telepathic."

Frank tried to look like he was wrestling with his conscience, although he couldn't have found his conscience without a shovel and an exhumation order.

"She missed an appointment yesterday. She didn't give any notice."

"Why was she seeing you?"

"Involutional melancholia, mainly. That's depression to you, characteristic of middle to later stages of life. At least that's what it seemed like, initially."

"But . . . ?"

"Parker, this is confidential. Even I have standards."

"You're joking. Go on."

Frank sighed and fiddled with a pencil on his blotter, then moved to a cabinet, removed a file, and sat back down. He opened it, leafed through it, and began to talk.

"Her sister died when Catherine was eight, or rather her sister was killed. She was one of a number of children murdered in a town called Haven, in Virginia, in the late sixties, early seventies. The children, males and females, were abducted, tortured, and their remains dumped in the cellar of an empty house outside the town." Frank was detached now, a doctor running through a case history that might have been as distant as a fairy tale to him for all the emotion he put into the telling.

"Her sister was the fourth child to die, but the first white child. After she disappeared the police began to take a real interest. A local woman, a wealthy local woman, was suspected. Her car had been seen near the house after one of the children disappeared, and then she tried an unsuccessful snatch on a kid from another town about twenty miles away. The kid, a boy, scratched up her face, then gave a description to the cops.

"They went after her but the locals heard and got to the house first. Her brother was there. He was a homosexual, according to locals, and the cops believed she had an accomplice, a male who might have driven the car while she made the snatches. The locals figured the brother was a likely suspect. He was found hanged in the basement."

"And the woman?"

"Burned to death in another of the old houses. The case simply . . . faded away."

"But not for Catherine?"

"No, not for her. She left the town after graduating from high school, but her parents stayed. The mother died about ten years ago, father shortly after. And Catherine Demeter just kept moving."

"Did she ever go back to Haven?"

"No, not after the funerals. She said everything was dead to her there. And that's it, pretty much. It all comes back to Haven."

"Any boyfriends, or casuals?"

"None that she mentioned to me, and question time is over. Now get out. If you ever bring this up again, in public or in private, I'll sue your ass for assault, harassment, and anything else my lawyer can come up with."

I got up to leave.

"One more thing," I said. "For Elizabeth Gordon and her continued nonacquaintance with Maibaum and Locke."

"What?"

"The name of the woman who burned to death."

"Modine. Adelaide Modine and her brother William. Now please, get the fuck out of my life."

CHAPTER IX

Willie Brew's auto shop looked run down and unreliable, if not blatantly dishonest, from the outside. Inside it wasn't a whole lot better, but Willie, a Pole whose name was unpronounceable and had been shortened to Brew by generations of customers, was just about the best mechanic I knew.

I had never liked this area of Queens, only a short distance north from the roars of the cars on the Long Island Expressway. Ever since I was a boy, I seemed to associate it with used car lots, old warehouses, and cemeteries. Willie's garage, close by Kissena Park, had been a good source of information over the years, since every deadbeat friend of Willie's with nothing better to do than listen in on other people's business tended to congregate there at some time or another, but the whole area still made me uneasy. Even as an adult, I hated the drive from JFK to Manhattan as it skirted these neighborhoods, hated the sight of the run-down houses and liquor stores.

Manhattan, by comparison, was exotic, its skyline capable of seemingly endless change, depending upon one's approach. My father had moved out to Westchester County as soon as he could afford to, buying a small house near Grant Park. Manhattan was somewhere we went on weekends, my friends and I. Sometimes we would traverse the entire length of the island to stand on the walkway over the Brooklyn Bridge and stare back at the evolving skyline. Beneath us, the boards would vibrate with the passage of the traffic, but to me, it seemed like more than that: it was the vibration and hum of life itself. The cables linking the towers of the bridge would cut and dissect the cityscape before us, as if it had been clipped by a child's scissors and reassembled against the blue sky.

After my father's death, my mother had moved us back to Maine, to her hometown of Scarborough, where tree lines replaced cityscapes and only the racing enthusiasts, traveling from Boston and New York to the races at Scarborough Downs, brought with them the sights and smells of the big cities. Maybe that was why I always felt like a visitor when I looked at Manhattan: I always seemed to be seeing the city through new eyes.

Willie's place was situated in a neighborhood that was fighting gentrification tooth and nail. Willie's block had been bought by the owner of the Japanese noodle house next door—he had other interests in downtown Flushing's Little Asia and seemed to want to extend his reach farther south—and Willie was involved in a partially legal battle to ensure that he wasn't shut down. The Japanese responded by sending fish smells through the vents into Willie's garage. Willie sometimes got his own back by getting Arno, his chief mechanic, to drink some beers and eat a Chinese meal, then stumble outside, stick his fingers down his throat, and vomit outside the noodle house. "Chinese, Vietnamese, Japanese—all that shit looks the same when it comes out," Willie used to say.

Inside, Arno—small, wiry, and dark—was working on the engine of a beat-up Dodge. The air was thick with the smell of fish and noodles. My '69 Mustang was raised up on a platform, unrecognizable bits and pieces of its internal workings strewn around on the floor. It looked no more likely to be on the road again in the near future than James Dean. I'd called earlier to tell Willie I'd be dropping by. The least he could have done was pretend to be doing something with it when I arrived.

The sound of loud swearing came from inside Willie's office, which was up a set of wooden stairs to the right of the garage floor.

The door flew open and Willie rumbled down the steps, grease on his bald head and his blue mechanic's overalls open to the waist to show a dirty white T-shirt straining over his huge belly. He climbed arduously up a set of boxes placed beneath the vent in a step pattern and put his mouth to the grille.

"You slant-eyed sons of bitches," he shrieked. "Quit stinkin' my garage out with fish or I'm gonna get nuclear on your ass." There was the sound of something shouted in Japanese from the other end of the vent, and then a burst of Oriental laughter. Willie thumped the grille with the heel of his hand and climbed down. He squinted at me in the semidarkness before recognizing me.

"Bird, how you doin'? You want a coffee?"

"I want a car. My car. The car you've had for over a week now."

Willie looked crestfallen. "You're angry with me," he said in mock-soothing tones. "I understand your anger. Anger is good. Your car, on the other hand, is not good. Your car is bad. The engine's shot to shit. What have you been running it on, nuts and old nails?"

"Willie, I need my car. The taxi drivers are treating me like an old friend. Some of them have even stopped trying to rip me off. I've considered hiring a rental car to save myself embarrassment. In fact, the only reason I haven't hit you for a car is that you said the repairs would take a day or two at most."

Willie slouched over to the car and nudged a cylindrical piece of metal with the toe of his boot.

"Arno, what's the deal on Bird's Mustang?"

"It's shit," said Arno. "Tell him we'll give him five hundred dollars to scrap it."

"Arno says to give you five hundred to scrap it."

"I heard him. Tell Arno I'll burn his house down if he doesn't fix my car."

"Day after tomorrow," came a voice from under the hood. "Sorry for the delay."

Willie clapped me on the shoulder with a greasy hand.

"Come up for a coffee, listen to the local gossip." Then, quietly: "Angel wants to see you. I told him you'd be around."

I nodded and followed him up the stairs. Inside the office, which was surprisingly neat, four men sat around a desk drinking coffee and whiskey from tin mugs. I nodded to Tommy Q, who I'd busted once for handling pirated videocassettes, and a thickly mustached hot-wire guy known, unsurprisingly, as Groucho. Beside him sat Willie's other assistant, Jay, who, at sixty-five, was ten years older than Willie but looked at least ten years older than that again. Beside him sat Coffin Ed Harris.

"You know Coffin Ed?" said Willie.

I nodded. "Still boosting dead guys, Ed?"

"Naw, man," said Coffin Ed. "I gave all that up a long time ago. I got a bad back."

Coffin Ed Harris had been the kidnapper to beat all kidnappers. Coffin Ed figured that live hostages were too much like real work, since there was no telling what they might do or who might come looking for them. The dead were easier to handle, so Coffin Ed took to robbing mortuaries.

He would watch the death notices, pick a decedent who came from a reasonably wealthy family, and then steal the corpse from the mortuary or the funeral home. Until Coffin Ed came along and bucked the system, funeral homes weren't usually well guarded. Coffin Ed would store the corpses in an industrial freezer he kept in his basement and then ask for a ransom, usually nothing too heavy. Most of the relatives were quite happy to pay in order to get their loved ones back before they started to rot.

He did well until some old Polish aristocrat took offense at his wife's remains being held for ransom and hired a private army to go looking for Coffin Ed. They found him, although Coffin Ed just about got away through a bolt-hole in his cellar that led to his neighbor's yard. He got the last laugh, too. The power company had cut off Ed's electricity three days before because he hadn't been paying his bills. The old Pole's wife stank like a dead possum by the time they found her. Since then, things had gone downhill for Coffin Ed, and he now presented a down-at-the-heel figure in the back of Willie Brew's garage.

There was an uneasy silence for a moment, which was broken by Willie.

"You remember Vinnie No Nose?" said Willie, handing me a steaming cup of black coffee, which was already turning the tin mug red hot but still couldn't hide the smell of gasoline from its interior. "Wait'll you hear Tommy Q's story. You ain't missed nothing yet."

Vinnie No Nose was a B&E guy out of Newark who had taken one fall too many and had decided to reform, or at least to reform as far as any guy can who has made a living for forty years by ripping off other people's apartments. He got his nickname from a long, unsuccessful involvement with amateur boxing. Vinnie, small and a potential victim for any New Jersey lowlife with a penchant for inflicting violence, saw an ability to use his fists as his potential salvation, like lots of other short guys from rough neighborhoods. Sadly, Vinnie's defense was about as good as the Son of Sam's, and his nose was eventually reduced to a mush of cartilage with two semiclosed nostrils like raisins in a pudding.

Tommy Q proceeded to tell a story involving Vinnie, a decorating company, and a dead gay client that could have put him in court if he'd told it in a respectable place of employment. "So the fruit ends up dead, in a bathroom, with this chair up his ass, and Vinnie ends up back in jail for peddling the pics and stealing the dead guy's video," he concluded, shaking his head at the strange ways of nonheterosexual males. He was still laughing his ass off at the story when the smile died on his face and the laugh turned into a kind of choking sound in his throat. I looked behind me to see Angel in the shadows, curly black hair spilling out from under his blue watch cap and with a sparse growth of beard that would have made a thirteen-year-old laugh. A dark blue longshoreman's jacket hung open over a black T-shirt, and his blue jeans ended in dirty, well-worn Timberlands.

Angel was no more than five-six, and to the casual onlooker, it was difficult to see why he should have struck fear into Tommy Q. There were two reasons. The first was that Angel was a far better boxer than Vinnie No Nose and could have pummeled Tommy Q to horse meat if he wanted to, which might well have been the case since Angel was gay and might have found the source of Tommy's humor less than amusing.

The second and probably more compelling reason for Tommy Q's fear was that Angel's boyfriend was a man known only as Louis. Like Angel, Louis had no visible means of support, although it was widely known that Angel, now semiretired at the age of forty, was one of the best thieves in the business, capable of stealing the fluff from the president's navel if the money was good enough.

Less widely known was the fact that Louis, tall, black, and sophisticated in his dress sense, was a hit man almost without equal, a killer who had been reformed somewhat by his relationship with Angel and who now chose his rare targets with what might be termed a social conscience.

Rumor had it that the killing of a German computer expert named Gunther Bloch in Chicago the previous year had been the work of Louis. Bloch was a serial rapist and torturer who preyed on young, sometimes very young, women in the sex resorts of Southeast Asia, where much of his business was transacted. Money usually covered all ills, money paid to pimps, to parents, to police, to politicians.

Unfortunately for Bloch, someone in the upper reaches of the government in one of his nations of choice couldn't be bought, especially after Bloch strangled an eleven-year-old girl and dumped her body in a trash bin. Bloch fled the country, money was redirected to a "special project," and Louis drowned Gunther Bloch in the bathroom of a thousand-dollar-a-night hotel suite in Chicago.

Or, like I said, so rumor had it. Whatever the truth of the matter, Louis was regarded as very bad news and Tommy Q wanted in future to be able to take a bath, however rarely, without fear of drowning.

"Nice story, Tommy," said Angel.

"It's just a story, Angel. I didn't mean nothing by it. No offense meant."

"None taken," said Angel. "At least, not by me."

Behind him there was a movement in the darkness, and Louis appeared. His bald head gleamed in the dim light, his muscular neck emerging from a black silk shirt within an immaculately cut gray suit. He towered over Angel by more than a foot, and as he did so, he eyed Tommy Q intently for a moment.

"Fruit," he said. "That's a . . . *quaint* term, Mr. Q. To what does it refer, exactly?"

The blood had drained from Tommy Q's face and it seemed to take him a very long time to find enough saliva to enable him to gulp. When he did eventually manage, it sounded like he was swallowing a golf ball. He opened his mouth but nothing came out, so he closed it again and looked at the floor in the vain hope that it would open up and swallow him.

"It's okay, Mr. Q, it was a good story," said Louis in a voice as silky as his shirt. "Just be careful how you tell it." Then he smiled a bright smile at Tommy Q, the sort of smile a cat might give a mouse to take to the grave with it. A drop of sweat ran down Tommy Q's nose, hung from the tip for a moment, and then exploded on the floor. By then, Louis had gone.

"Don't forget my car, Willie," I said, then followed Angel from the garage.

CHAPTER

We walked a block or two to a late-night bar and diner Angel knew. Louis strolled a few yards ahead of us, the late evening crowds parting before him like the Red Sea before Moses. Once or twice women glanced at him with interest. The men mostly kept their eyes on the ground, or found something suddenly interesting in the boarded-up storefronts or the night sky.

From inside the bar came the sound of a vaguely folky singer performing open-guitar surgery on Neil Young's "Only Love Can Break Your Heart." It didn't sound like the song was going to pull through.

"He plays like he hates Neil Young," said Angel as we entered.

Ahead of us, Louis shrugged. "Neil Young heard that shit, he'd probably hate himself."

We took a booth. The owner, a fat, dyspeptic man named Ernest, shambled over to take our order. Usually the waitresses in Ernest's took the orders, but Angel and Louis commanded a degree of respect, even here.

"Hey, Ernest," said Angel, "how's business?"

"If I was an undertaker, people'd stop dying," replied Ernest. "And before you ask, my old lady's still ugly." It was a long-established exchange.

"Shit, you been married forty years," said Angel. "She ain't gonna get no better lookin' now."

Angel and Louis ordered club sandwiches and Ernest wandered away. "I was a kid and looked like him, I'd cut my dick off and make money singin' castrato, 'cause it ain't gonna be no use no other way," remarked Angel.

"Bein' ugly ain't done you no harm," said Louis.

"I don't know." Angel grinned. "I was better looking, I coulda screwed a white guy."

They stopped bickering and we waited for the singer to put Neil Young out of his misery. It was strange meeting these two, now that I was no longer a cop. When we had encountered one another before—in Willie's garage, or over coffee, or in Central Park if Angel had some useful information to impart, or if he simply wanted to meet to talk, to ask after Susan and Jennifer—there had been an awkwardness, a tension between us, especially if Louis was nearby. I knew what they had done, what Louis, I believed, still did, silent partnerships in assorted restaurants, dealerships, and Willie Brew's garage notwithstanding.

On this occasion, that tension was no longer present. Instead, I felt for the first time the strength of the bond of friendship that had somehow grown between Angel and me. More than that, from both of them I felt a sense of concern, of regret, of humanity, of trust. They would not be here, I knew, if they felt otherwise.

But maybe there was something more, something I had only begun to perceive. I was a cop's nightmare. Cops, their families, their wives and children, are untouchables. You have to be crazy to go after a cop, crazier still to take out his loved ones. These are the assumptions we live by, the belief that after a day spent looking at the dead, questioning thieves and rapists, pushers and pimps, we can return to our own lives, knowing that our families are somehow apart from all this, and that through them we can remain apart from it too.

But that belief system had been shaken by the deaths of Jennifer and Susan. Someone wasn't respecting the rules, and when no easy answer was forthcoming, when no perp with a grudge could conveniently be apprehended, enabling all that had taken place to be explained away, another reason had to be found: I had somehow drawn it on myself, and on those closest to me. I was a good cop who was well on the way to becoming a drunk. I was falling apart and that made me weak, and someone had exploited that weakness. Other cops looked at me and they saw not a fellow officer in need, but a source of infection, of corruption. No one was sorry to see me go, maybe not even Walter.

And yet what had taken place had somehow brought me closer to both Angel and Louis. They had no illusions about the world in which they lived, no philosophical constructions that allowed them to be at once a part of, and apart from, that world. Louis was a killer: he couldn't afford delusions of that kind. Because of the closeness of the bond that existed between them, Angel couldn't afford those delusions either. Now they had also been taken away from me, like scales falling from my eyes, leaving me to reestablish myself, to find a new place in the world.

Angel picked up an abandoned paper from the booth next door and glanced at the headline. "You see this?" I looked and nodded. A guy had tried to pull some heroic stunt during a bank raid in Flushing earlier in the day and ended up with both barrels of a sawed-off emptied into him. The papers and news bulletins were full of it.

"Here's some guys out doin' a job," began Angel. "They don't want to hurt nobody, they just want to go in, take the money—which is insured anyway, so what does the bank care?—and get out again. They only got the guns 'cause no one's gonna take them seriously otherwise. What else they gonna use? Harsh words?

"But there's always gotta be some asshole who thinks he's immortal 'cause he's not dead yet. This guy, he's young, keeps himself in good condition, thinks he's gonna get more pussy than Long Dong Silver if he busts up the bank raid and saves the day. Look at him: realtor, twenty-nine, single, pulling down one-fifty a year, and he gets a hole blown in him bigger'n the Holland Tunnel. Lance

Petersen." He shook his head in wonderment. "I never met anyone called Lance in my whole life."

"That's 'cause they all dead," said Louis, glancing seemingly idly around the room. "Fuckers keep standing up in banks and getting shot. Guy was probably the last Lance left alive."

The clubs arrived and Angel started eating. He was the only one who did. "So how you doin'?"

"Okay," I said. "Why the ambush?"

"You don't write, you don't call." He smiled wryly. Louis glanced at me with mild interest and then returned his attention to the door, the other tables, the doors to the restrooms.

"You been doin' some work for Benny Low, I hear. What you doin' working for that fat piece of shit?"

"Passing time."

"You want to pass time, stick pins in your eyes. Benny's just using up good air."

"Come on, Angel, get to it. You're rattling away and Louis here is acting like he expects the Dillinger gang to walk in and spray the counter."

Angel put down his half-eaten section of club and dabbed almost daintily at his mouth with a napkin. "I hear you've been asking after some girlfriend of Stephen Barton's. Some people are very curious to know why that might be."

"Such as?"

"Such as Bobby Sciorra, I hear."

I didn't know if Bobby Sciorra was psychotic or not, but he was a man who liked killing and had found a willing employer in old man Ferrera. Emo Ellison could testify to the likely result of Bobby Sciorra taking an interest in one's activities. I had a suspicion that Ollie Watts, in his final moments, had found that out as well.

"Benny Low was talking about some kind of trouble between the old man and Sonny," I said. " 'Fuckin' goombas fighting among themselves' was how he put it."

"Benny always was a diplomat," said Angel. "Only surprise is the UN didn't pick up on him before now. There's something weird going on there. Sonny's gone to ground and taken Pili with him. No one's seen them, no one knows where they are, but Bobby Sciorra's looking real hard for all of them." He took another huge bite of his sandwich. "What about Barton?"

"I figure he's gone underground too, but I don't know. He's minor league and wouldn't have much to do professionally with Sonny or the old man beyond some muling, though he may once have been close to Sonny. May be nothing to it. Barton may not be connected."

"Maybe not, but you've got bigger problems than finding Barton or his girl."

I waited.

"There's a hit out on you."

"Who?"

"It's not local. It's out of town. Louis don't know who."

"Is it over the Fat Ollie thing?"

"I don't know. Even Sonny isn't such a moron that he'd put a contract out over some hired gun who got himself wasted 'cause you stepped in. The kid didn't mean anything to anyone and Fat Ollie's dead. All I know is you're irritating two generations of the Ferrera family and that can't be good."

Walter Cole's favor was turning into something more complicated than a missing persons case, if it was ever that simple.

"I've got one for you," I said. "Know anyone with a gun that can punch holes through masonry with a five-point-seven-millimeter bullet weighing less than fifty grains? Submachine rounds."

"You gotta be fuckin' kidding. Last time I saw something like that it was hangin' on top of a tank turret."

"Well, that's what killed the shooter. I saw him blown away and there was a hole knocked through the wall behind me. The gun's Belgian made, designed for antiterrorist police. Someone local picked up a piece of hardware like that and took it to the range, it's gotta get around."

"I'll ask," said Angel. "Any guesses?"

"My guess would be Bobby Sciorra."

"Mine too. So why would he be cleaning up after Sonny's mess?"

"The old man told him to."

Angel nodded. "Watch your back, Bird."

He finished his sandwich and then stood to go. "C'mon. We can give you a ride."

"No, I want to walk for a while."

Angel shrugged. "You packing?"

I nodded. He said he'd be in touch. I left them at the door. As I walked, I was conscious of the weight of the gun beneath my arm, of every face I passed in the crowd, and of the dark pulse of the city throbbing beneath my feet.

CHAPTER XI

Bobby Sciorra: a malevolent demon, a vision of ferocity and sadism that had appeared before the old man, Stefano Ferrera, when he was on the verge of insanity and death. Sciorra seemed to have been conjured up from some bleak corner of Hell by the old man's anger and grief, a physical manifestation of the torture and destruction he wished to inflict on the world around him. In Bobby Sciorra he found the perfect instrument of pain and ugly death.

STEFANO HAD WATCHED HIS own father build a small empire from the family's modest house in Bensonhurst. In those days Bensonhurst, bordered by Gravesend Bay and the Atlantic Ocean, still had a small-town feel. The scent of deli food mingled with that of wood-burning ovens from the local pizza parlors. People lived in two-family houses with wrought iron gates, and when the sun shone, they would sit out on their porches and watch their kids play in their tiny gardens.

Stefano's ambition would take him beyond his roots. When his time came to take over the operation, he built a big house on Staten Island; when he stood at his rear-facing windows, he could see the edge of Paul Castellano's mansion on Todt Hill, the $3.5

million White House, and probably, from his topmost window, the grounds of the Barton estate. If Staten Island was good enough for the head of the Gambino family and a benevolent millionaire, then it was good enough for Stefano. When Castellano died after being shot six times at Sparks Steak House in Manhattan, Stefano was, briefly, the biggest boss on Staten Island.

Stefano married a woman from Bensonhurst named Louisa. She hadn't married him out of any kind of love familiar from romantic novels: she loved him for his power, his violence, and mainly, his money. Those who marry for money usually end up earning it. Louisa did. She was emotionally brutalized and died shortly after giving birth to her third son. Stefano didn't remarry. There was no grief there; he just didn't need the bother of another wife, especially after the first had produced his heirs.

The first child, Vincent, was intelligent and represented the best hope for the family's future. When he died in a swimming pool from a massive brain hemorrhage at twenty-three, his father didn't speak for a week. Instead, he shot Vincent's pair of Labradors and retired to his bedroom. Louisa had been dead for seventeen years.

Niccolo, or Nicky, two years younger than his brother, took his place at his father's right hand. As a rookie, I watched him roam the city in his huge bullet-proofed Cadillac, surrounded by soldiers, carving himself a reputation as a thug to match his father. By the early 1980s, the family had overcome an initial distaste for the drug trade and was flooding the city with every kind of poison it could lay its hands on. Most people stayed out of the way, and any potential rivals were warned off or ended up as fish chum.

The Yardies were another matter. The Jamaican gangs had no respect for established institutions, for the old ways of doing business. They looked at the Italians and saw dead meat; a shipment of cocaine worth two million dollars was boosted from the Ferreras and two soldiers were left dead. Nicky responded by ordering a cull of the Yardies: their clubs were hit, their apartments, even their women. In a three-day period, twelve of them died, including most of those responsible for the cocaine theft.

Maybe Nicky imagined that would be the end of it and things would return to normal again. He still cruised the streets in his car, still ate in the same restaurants, still acted as if the threat of violence from the Jamaicans had dissipated in the face of this show of force.

His favorite haunt was Da Vincenzo, an upscale mom-and-pop operation in his father's old Bensonhurst neighborhood that was smart enough not to forget its roots. Maybe Nicky also liked the echoes of his brother in the name, but his paranoia led him to have the glass in the windows and doors replaced with some military-strength panes, the sort used by the president. Nicky could enjoy his fusilli in peace, undisturbed by the imminent threat of assassination.

He had only just ordered one Thursday evening in November when the black van pulled into the side street opposite, its back facing toward the window. Nicky may have glanced at it as it stopped, may have noticed that its windshield had been removed and replaced with a black wire grille, may even have frowned as the rear doors sprang open and something white flared briefly in the darkness of its interior, the back blast rattling the grille.

He may even have had time to register the RPG-7 warhead as it powered toward the window at six hundred feet per second, smoke trailing it from behind, its roar penetrating the thick panes before they exploded inward, glass and hot metal fragments and the slug from the missile's copper liner tearing Nicky Ferrera into so many pieces that his coffin weighed less than sixty pounds when it was carried up the aisle of the church three days later.

The three Jamaicans responsible disappeared into the underworld and the old man vented his fury on his enemies and his friends in an orgy of abuse, of violence, and of death. His business fell apart around him and his rivals closed in, recognizing in his madness the opportunity to rid themselves of him once and for all.

Just as his world seemed about to implode on itself, a figure appeared at the gates of his mansion and asked to speak with the old man. He told the guard he had some news about the Yardies, the guard passed on the message, and after a search, Bobby Sciorra was admitted. The search was not a complete one: Sciorra held a black plastic bag, which he refused to open. Guns were trained on him as he approached the house, and he was told to halt on the lawn, about fifty feet from the steps of the house, where the old man stood in wait.

"If you're wasting my time, I'll have you killed," said the old man. Bobby Sciorra just smiled and tipped the contents of the bag on the illuminated lawn. The three heads rolled and bumped against one another, the dreadlocks coiled like dead snakes, with Bobby Sciorra smiling above them like some obscene Perseus. Thick, fresh blood hung languorously from the edges of the bag before dripping slowly onto the grass.

Bobby Sciorra "made his bones" that night. Within one year he was a made guy, an ascent up the family ladder made doubly unique by its speed and the relative obscurity of Sciorra's background. The feds had no file on him, and Ferrera appeared able to add little more. I heard rumors that he had crossed the Colombos once, that he had operated out of Florida for a while on a freelance basis, but nothing more than that. Yet the killing of the linchpins of the Jamaican posse was enough to earn him the trust of Stefano Ferrera and a ceremony in the basement of the Staten Island house that resulted in the pricking of Sciorra's trigger finger over a holy picture and his tie-in to Ferrera and his associates.

From that day on, Bobby Sciorra was the power behind the Ferrera throne. He guided the old man and his family through the trials and tribulations of post-RICO New York, when the FBI's Racketeer Influenced Corruption Organization statutes allowed the feds to prosecute organizations and conspirators that benefited from crime, instead of just the individuals who committed those crimes. The major New York families—Gambino, Lucchese, Colombo, Genovese, and Bonanno—numbering maybe four thousand made guys and associates, all took big hits, losing the heads of their families to jail or the Reaper. But not the Ferreras. Bobby Sciorra took care of that, sacrificing some minor players along the way to ensure the survival of the family.

The old man might have preferred to take even more of a backseat in the family operation if it hadn't been for Sonny. Poor dumb, vicious Sonny, a man without the intelligence of either of his brothers but with at least their combined capacity for violence. Any operations he controlled degenerated into bloodshed, but none of it bothered Sonny. Corpulent and bloated even in his twenties, he enjoyed the mayhem and the killing. The death of the innocent in particular seemed to give him an almost sexual thrill.

Gradually, his father sidelined him and left him to his own devices—steroids, small-time drug deals, prostitution, and occasional violence. Bobby Sciorra tried to keep him under some sort of control, but Sonny was beyond control or reason. Sonny was vicious and evil, and when his father died, a line of men would form to ensure Sonny joined him as soon as possible.

CHAPTER XII

I never expected to end up living in the East Village. Susan, Jennifer, and I had lived out in Park Slope, in Brooklyn. On Sundays we could stroll up to Prospect Park and watch the kids playing ball, Jennifer kicking at the grass with her sneakers, before heading to Raintree's for a soda, the sound of the band in the band shell drifting in through the stained-glass windows.

On such days, life seemed as long and welcoming as the green vista of Long Meadow. We would walk Jenny between us, Susan and I, and exchange glances over her head as she burst forth with an endless stream of questions, observations, strange jokes that only a child could understand. I would hold her hand in mine, and through her, I could reach out to Susan and believe that things would work out for us, that we could somehow bridge the gap that was growing between us. If Jenny ran ahead, I would move close to Susan and take her hand and she would smile at me as I told her that I loved her. Then she would look away, or look at her feet, or call Jenny, because we both knew that telling her I loved her was not enough.

When I decided to return to New York at the start of the summer, after months of searching for some sign of their killer, I informed my lawyer and asked him to recommend a realtor. In New York, there are about three hundred million square feet of office space and not enough places to put the people who work in them. I couldn't say why I wanted to live in Manhattan. Maybe it was just because it wasn't Brooklyn.

Instead of a realtor, my lawyer produced a network of friends and business acquaintances that eventually led to me renting an apartment in a redbrick house in the East Village with white shutters on the windows and a stoop that led up to a fanlighted front door. It was a little closer to St. Mark's Place than I would have preferred, but it was still a good deal. Since the days when W. H. Auden and Leon Trotsky had roomed there, St. Mark's had become the East Village with a vengeance, full of bars, cafés, and overpriced boutiques.

The apartment was unfurnished and I pretty much left it that way, adding only a bed, a desk, some easy chairs, and a stereo and small TV. I removed books, tapes, CDs, and vinyl from storage, along with one or two personal belongings, and set up a living space to which I had only the minimum attachment.

It was dark outside as I lined the guns before me on the desk, stripped them down, and cleaned each one carefully. If the Ferreras were coming after me, I wanted to be prepared.

In all my time on the force, I had been forced to draw my weapon to protect myself on only a handful of occasions. I had never killed a man while on duty and had only once fired at another human being, when I shot a pimp in the stomach as he came at me with a long-bladed knife.

As a detective, I had spent most of my time in Robbery and Homicide. Unlike Vice, which was a world in which the threat of violence and death to a cop was a real possibility, Homicide involved a different type of police work. As Tommy Morrison, my first partner, used to say, anybody who's going to die in a Homicide investigation is already dead by the time the cops arrive.

I had abandoned my Colt Delta Elite after the deaths of Susan and Jennifer. Now I had three guns in my possession. The .38 Colt Detective Special had belonged to my father, the only thing of his that I had retained. The prancing-pony badge on the left side of the rounded butt was worn and the frame was scratched and pitted, but it remained a useful weapon, light at about a pound in weight and easily concealed in an ankle holster or a belt. It was a simple, powerful revolver, and I kept it in a holster taped beneath the frame of my bed.

I had never used the Heckler & Koch VP70M outside a range. The 9 millimeter semiautomatic had belonged to a pusher who had died after becoming hooked on his own product. I had found him dead in his apartment after a neighbor had complained about the smell. The VP70M, a semiplastic military pistol holding eighteen rounds, lay, still unused, in its case, but I had taken the precaution of filing away the serial number.

Like the .38, it had no safety. The attraction of the gun lay in the accessory shoulder stock that the pusher had also acquired. When fitted, it made an internal adjustment to the firing mechanism that turned the weapon into a full-automatic submachine gun that could fire twenty-two hundred rounds per minute. If the Chinese ever decided to invade, I could hold them off for at least ten seconds with all the ammunition I had for it. After that, I'd have to start throwing furniture at them. I had removed the H&K from the compartment in the Mustang's trunk where I usually stored it. I didn't want anyone stumbling across it while the car was being serviced.

The third-generation Smith & Wesson was the only gun I carried, a 10 millimeter model specially developed for the FBI and acquired through the efforts of Woolrich. After cleaning it, I loaded it carefully and placed it in my shoulder holster. Outside, I could see the crowds making for the bars and restaurants of the East Village. I was just about to join them when the cell phone buzzed beside me, and thirty minutes later I was preparing to view the body of Stephen Barton.

RED LIGHTS FLASHED, BATHING everything in the parking lot with the warm glow of law and order. A patch of darkness marked the nearby McCarren Park, and to the southwest, traffic passed over the Williamsburg Bridge heading for the Brooklyn-Queens Expressway. Patrolmen lounged by cars, keeping the curious and the ghoulish behind barriers. One reached out to block my way—"Hey, gotta keep back"—when we recognized each other. Tyler, who remembered my father and would never make it beyond sergeant, withdrew his hand.

"It's official, Jimmy. I'm with Cole." He looked over his shoulder and Walter, who was talking with a patrolman, glanced over and nodded. The arm went up like a traffic barrier and I passed through.

Even yards from the sewer I could smell the stench. A frame had been erected around the area and a lab technician in boots was climbing out of the manhole.

"Can I go down?" I asked. Two men in neatly cut suits and London Fog raincoats had joined Cole, who barely nodded. The FBI letters weren't visible on the backs of their coats so I assumed they were keeping a low profile. "Uncanny," I said as I passed. "They could almost be regular people." Walter scowled. They joined in.

I slipped on a pair of gloves and climbed down the ladder into the sewer. I gagged with my first breath, the river of filth that ran beneath the tree-lined avenues of the city forcing a taste of bile into the back of my throat. "It's easier if you take shallow breaths," said a sewer worker who stood at the base of the ladder. He was lying.

I didn't step from the ladder. Instead, I pulled my Maglite from my pocket and pointed it to where a small group of maintenance workers and cops stood around an arc-lit area, their feet sloshing through stuff about which I didn't even want to think. The cops gave me a brief glance, then returned with bored looks to watching the med guys go about their business. Stephen Barton lay about five yards from the base of the ladder in a tide of shit and waste, his blond hair moving wildly with the current. It was obvious that he had simply been dumped through the manhole at street level, his body rolling slightly when it hit the bottom.

The ME stood up and pulled the rubber gloves from his hands. A plainclothes Homicide detective, one I didn't recognize, directed a quizzical look at him. He returned one of frustration and annoyance. "We'll need to look at him in the lab. I can't tell shit from shit down here."

"Come on, give us a fucking break," the detective whined lamely.

The ME hissed through his teeth in irritation. "Strangled," he said as he elbowed his way through the small group. "Knocked unconscious first with a blow to the back of the head, then strangled. Don't even ask for a time of death. He could have been down here for a day or so, probably no longer. The body's pretty flaccid." Then the sound of his feet echoed through the sewer as he began to clack up the ladder.

The detective shrugged. "Ashes to ashes, shit to shit," he said, then turned back toward the body.

I climbed up to street level, the ME behind me. I didn't need to look at Barton's body. The blow to the head was unusual, but not extraordinary. It can take as long as ten minutes to kill a man by strangulation, assuming he doesn't manage to break free in the process. I had heard of would-be assassins losing handfuls of hair, patches of skin, and in one case, an ear to a struggling victim. Far better, where possible, to tap him on the head first. Tap him hard *enough and strangling him might not be necessary at all.*

Walter was still talking to the feds, so I moved as far away from the sewer as I could get while still remaining within the police cordon and drew deep breaths of night air. The smell of human waste underpinned everything, clinging to my clothes with the grim resolution of death itself. Eventually the feds returned to their car and Walter walked slowly toward me, hands stuck in his trouser pockets.

"They're going to bring Sonny Ferrera in," he said.

I snorted. "For what? His lawyer will have him out before he even has time to take a leak. That's assuming he was even involved, or that they can find him. This bunch couldn't find the ground if they fell over."

Walter wasn't in the mood. "What do you know? The kid was running shit for Ferrera; he fucks him over and ends up dead, strangled what's more." Strangulation had become the mob's preferred method of dispatch in recent years: quiet and no mess. "That's the feds' line, and anyway, they'd bring Sonny Ferrera in on suspicion of ignoring a no-smoking sign if they thought it would stick."

"C'mon, Walter, this isn't a Ferrera job. Dumping a guy in a sewer isn't . . ." But he was already walking away, a raised right hand indicating that he didn't want to hear any more. I followed him. "What about the girl, Walter? Maybe she fits in somewhere?"

He turned back to me and put a hand on my shoulder. "When I called you, I didn't think you were going to come running in like Dick Tracy." He glanced back at the feds. "Any sign of her?"

"I think she blew town. That's all I'm saying for the present."

"The ME thinks Barton could have been killed early Tuesday. If the girl left town after that, it could tie her in."

"Are you going to mention her to the feds?"

Walter shook his head. "Let them go chasing after Sonny Ferrera. You stay on the girl."

"Yassuh," I said. "I'ma keep lookin'." I hailed a cab, conscious that the feds were looking at me even as I got in and we drove away into the night.

CHAPTER XIII

It was common knowledge that the old man was having trouble keeping his only surviving son under control. Ferrera had watched the Cosa Nostra tear itself apart back in Italy as it tried, with increasing brutality, to intimidate and destroy the state's investigators. Instead, its methods had served to reinforce the determination of the braver ones to continue the fight; the families were now like one of their own victims bound in the *incaprettamento,* the method of execution known as the goat strangling. Like a victim bound with ropes to his arms, legs, and neck, the more the families struggled, the more the rope around them grew tighter. The old man was determined that this should not happen to his own organization.

By contrast, Sonny saw in the violence of the Sicilians a method of tyranny that suited his own aspirations for power. Maybe that was the difference between father and son. Wherever possible old Ferrera had used the "white *lupara*" when an assassination was necessary, the complete disappearance of the victim without even a trace of blood to give away the truth of what had taken place. The strangling of Barton was certainly a Mafia hallmark, but the dumping was not. If the old man had been responsible for his death, then his final resting place would probably have been the sewers, but not before he had been dissolved in acid and poured down a drain.

So I didn't believe the old man had ordered the killing of Isobel Barton's stepson. His death and the sudden disappearance of Catherine Demeter had come too close together to be mere coincidence. It was possible, of course, that Sonny had ordered them both to be killed for some reason, for if he was as crazy as he seemed to be, then another corpse would be unlikely to trouble him. On the other hand, it was also possible that Demeter had killed her own boyfriend and then fled. Perhaps he hit her once too often, in which case Mrs. Barton was now paying me to find someone who was not only a friend but, potentially, her son's killer.

THE FERRERA HOUSE WAS set in tree-shrouded grounds. Entry was by a single iron gate, electronically operated. An intercom was set into the pillar on the left-hand side. I buzzed, gave my name, and told the voice I wanted to see the old man. From the top of the pillar a remote camera was focused on the cab, and although no one was visible in the grounds, I guessed three to five guns were in my immediate vicinity.

Some one hundred yards from the house sat a dark Dodge sedan with two males sitting in the front seat. I could expect a visit from the feds as soon as I got back to my apartment, possibly sooner.

"Walk through. Wait inside the gate," said the voice from the intercom. "You'll be escorted to the house." I did as I was told and the cab pulled away. A gray-haired man in a dark suit and standard-issue shades appeared from behind the trees, a Heckler & Koch MP5 held at port arms. Behind him was another younger man, similarly dressed. To my right I could see two more guards, also armed.

"Lean against the wall," said the gray-haired man. He frisked me professionally while the others watched, removing the clip from my own Smith & Wesson along with the spare clip on my belt. He pulled back the slide to eject the round in the chamber and handed the gun back to me. Then he motioned me toward the house, walking to my right and slightly behind me so that he could keep an eye on my hands. One man shadowed us at either side of the road. It was hardly surprising that old man Ferrera had lived so long.

The house was surprisingly modest from the outside, a long two-story dwelling with narrow windows at the front and a gallery running along the upper level. More men patrolled the meticulously kept garden and the graveled driveway. A black Mercedes stood at the right of the house, its driver waiting nearby if needed. The door was already open as we approached, and Bobby Sciorra stood in the hallway, his right hand clasping his left wrist like a priest waiting for the offerings.

Sciorra was six feet five inches tall and probably weighed less than one-sixty, his long thin limbs like blades beneath his gray single-breasted suit, his striated neck almost feminine in its length, its pallor enhanced by the pristine whiteness of the collarless shirt buttoned beneath it. Short dark hair surrounded a bald pate, which ended in a cone so sharp as to appear pointed. Sciorra was a knife made flesh, a human instrument of pain, both surgeon and scalpel. The FBI believed that he had personally committed more than thirty killings. Most of those who knew Bobby Sciorra believed the FBI was conservative in its estimate.

He smiled as I approached, revealing perfectly white teeth glistening behind narrow, slash lips, but the smile never reached his blue eyes. Instead it disappeared in the jagged scar that ran from his left ear across the bridge of his nose and ended just below the right earlobe. The scar devoured his smile like a second mouth.

"You got some balls coming here," he said, still smiling, his head shaking gently from side to side as he said it.

"That an admission of guilt, Bobby?" I asked.

The smile never faltered. "Why do you want to see the boss? He's got no time for shit like you." The smile broadened perceptibly. "By the way, how are your wife and kid? Kid must be—what?—four by now."

A dull red throbbing began to pulse in my head but I held it back, my hands tightening at my sides. I knew I'd be dead before my hands closed on Sciorra's white skin.

"Stephen Barton turned up dead in a sewer this evening. The feds are looking for Sonny and probably for you as well. I'm concerned for your welfare. I wouldn't want anything bad to happen to either of you that I wasn't a part of."

Sciorra's smile remained the same. He seemed about to answer when a voice, low but authoritative, sounded over the house intercom system. Age gave it a gravelly resonance from which the rattle of death was not absent, lurking in the background like the traces of Don Ferrera's Sicilian roots.

"Let him in, Bobby," it said. Sciorra stepped back and opened a set of draft-excluding double doors halfway down the hall. The gray-haired guard walked behind me as I followed Sciorra, who waited until he had closed the draft doors before opening a second door at the end of the hall.

Don Ferrera sat in an old leather armchair behind a big office desk, not entirely dissimilar from Walter Cole's desk, although its gilt inlay raised it into a different league from Walter's comparatively Spartan possession. The curtains were drawn and wall lights and table lamps gave a dim yellow glow to the pictures and bookshelves that lined the walls. I guessed from their age that the books were probably worth a lot and had never been read. Red leather chairs stood against the walls, complementing Don Ferrera's own chair and some sofas that surrounded a long low table at the far end of the room.

Even sitting down and stooped by age, the old man was an impressive figure. His hair was silver and greased back from his temples, but an unhealthy pallor seemed to underlie his tanned complexion and his eyes appeared rheumy. Sciorra closed the door and once more assumed his priestlike stance, my escort remaining outside.

"Please, sit," said the old man, motioning toward an armchair. He opened an inlaid box of Turkish cigarettes, each ringed with small gold bands. I thanked him but refused. He sighed: "Pity. I like the scent but they are forbidden me. No cigarettes, no women, no alcohol." He closed the box and looked longingly at it for a moment, then clasped his hands and rested them on the desk before him.

"You have no title now," he said. Among "men of honor," to be called Mister when you had a title was a calculated insult. Federal investigators sometimes used it to belittle mob suspects, dispensing with the more formal Don or Tio.

"I understand no insult is intended, Don Ferrera," I said. He nodded and was silent.

As a detective I had some dealings with the men of honor and always approached them cautiously and without arrogance or presumption. Respect had to be met with respect and silences had to be read like signs. Among them, everything had meaning and they were as economical and efficient in their modes of communication as they were with their methods of violence.

Men of honor spoke only of what concerned them directly, answered only specific questions and would stay silent rather than tell a lie. A man of honor had an absolute obligation to tell the truth and only when the behavior of others altered so far as to make it necessary to break these rules of behavior would he do so. All of which assumed that you believed pimps and killers and drug dealers were honorable in the first place, or that the code was anything more than the incongruous trapping of another age, pressed into service to provide a sheen of aristocracy for thugs and murderers.

I waited for him to break the silence.

He stood and moved slowly, almost painfully, around the room and stopped at a small side table on which a gold plate gleamed dully.

"You know, Al Capone used to eat off gold plates. Did you know that?" he asked. I told him that I hadn't known.

"His men used to carry them in a violin case to the restaurant and lay them on the table for Capone and his guests, and then they'd all eat off them. Why do you think a man would feel the need to eat from a gold plate?" He waited for an answer, trying to catch my reflection in the plate.

"When you have a lot of money, your tastes can become peculiar, eccentric," I said. "After a while, even your food doesn't taste right unless it's served on bone china, or gold. It's not fitting for someone with so much money and power to eat from the same plates as the little people."

"It goes too far, I think," he replied, but he no longer seemed to be talking to me and it was his own reflection he was examining in the plate. "There's something wrong with it. There are some tastes that should not be indulged, because they are vulgar. They are obscene. They offend nature."

"I take it that isn't one of Capone's plates."

"No, my son gave it to me as a gift on my last birthday. I told him the story and he had the plate made."

"Maybe he missed the point of the story," I said. The old man's face looked weary. It was the face of a man who had not enjoyed his sleep for some time.

"The boy who was killed, you think my son was involved? You think this was a piece of work?" he asked eventually, moving back into my direct line of vision and staring away from me at something in the distance. I didn't look to see what it was.

"I don't know. The FBI appears to think so."

He smiled an empty, cruel smile that reminded me briefly of Bobby Sciorra. "And your interest in this is the girl, no?"

I was surprised, although I should not have been. Barton's past would have been common knowledge to Sciorra at least and would have been passed on quickly when his body was discovered. I thought my visit to Pete Hayes might have played a part too. I wondered how much he knew, and his next question gave me the answer: not much.

"Who are you working for?"

"I can't say."

"We can find out. We found out enough from the old man at the gym."

So that was it. I shrugged gently. He was silent again for a while.

"Do you think my son had the girl killed?"

"Did he?" I responded. Don Ferrera turned back toward me, the rheumy eyes narrowing.

"There is a story told about a man who believes he is being cuckolded by his wife. He approaches a friend, an old, trusted friend, and says: 'I believe my wife is cheating on me but I don't know with whom. I have watched her closely but I cannot find out the identity of this man. What do I do?'

"Now his friend is the man who is cheating with his wife, but to divert the other's attention he says that he saw the wife with another man, a man with a reputation for dishonorable conduct with other men's wives. And so the cuckold turns his gaze on this man and his wife continues to cheat on him with his best friend." He finished and gazed intently at me.

Everything has to be interpreted, everything is codified. To live with signs is to understand the necessity of finding meanings in seemingly irrelevant pieces of information. The old man had spent most of his life looking for the meanings in things and expected others to do likewise. In his cynical little anecdote lay his belief that his son was not responsible for Barton's death but that whoever was responsible stood to benefit from the concentration of the police and FBI on Sonny's assumed guilt. I glanced at Bobby Sciorra and wondered how much Don Ferrera really knew about what went on behind those eyes. Sciorra was capable of anything, even of undermining his boss for his own gains.

"I hear maybe Sonny has taken a sudden interest in my good health," I said.

The old man smiled. "What kind of interest in your health, Mr. Parker?"

"The kind of interest that could result in my health suddenly ceasing to be good."

"I don't know anything about that. Sonny is his own man."

"That may be, but if anyone pulls anything on me, I'll see Sonny in Hell."

"I'll have Bobby look into it," he said.

That didn't make me feel a whole lot better. I stood up to leave.

"A clever man would be looking for the girl," said the old man, also standing up and moving toward a door in a corner of the room behind the desk. "Alive or dead, the girl is the key."

Maybe he was right, but the old man must have had his own reasons for pointing me toward her. And as Bobby Sciorra escorted me to the front door, I wondered if I was the only person looking for Catherine Demeter.

THERE WAS A CAB waiting at the gates of the Ferrera house to take me back to the East Village. As it turned out, I had enough time to shower and make a pot of coffee at my apartment before the FBI came knocking on my door. I had changed into tracksuit bottoms and a sweatshirt so I felt a little casual next to Special Agents Ross and Hernandez. The Blue Nile was playing in the background, "A Walk Across the Rooftops," causing Hernandez to wrinkle his nose in distaste. I didn't feel the need to apologize.

Ross did most of the talking, while Hernandez ostentatiously examined the contents of my bookshelf, looking at covers and reading the dust jackets. He hadn't asked if he could and I didn't like it.

"There are some picture ones on the lower shelf," I said. "No Crayolas, though. I hope you brought your own."

Hernandez scowled at me. He was in his late twenties and probably still believed everything he had been taught about the agency in Quantico. He reminded me of the tour guides in the Hoover Building, the ones who herd the Minnesota housewives around while dreaming of gunning down drug dealers and international terrorists. Hernandez probably still refused to believe that Hoover had worn a dress.

Ross was a different matter. He had been involved with the feds' Truck Hijack Squad in New York in the seventies and his name had been linked to a number of high-profile RICO cases since then. I believed he was probably a good agent, but a lousy human being. I had already decided what I was going to tell him: nothing.

"Why were you at the Ferrera house this evening?" he began, after declining an offer of coffee like a monkey refusing a nut.

"I've got a paper route." Ross didn't even grin. Hernandez's scowl deepened. If I'd had a nervous disposition, the strain might have proved too much for me.

"Don't be an asshole," said Ross. "I could arrest you on suspicion of involvement with organized crime, hold you for a while, let you go, but what good would that do either of us? I'll ask you again: why were you at the Ferrera house this evening?"

"I'm conducting an investigation. Ferrera might have been connected to it."

"What are you investigating?"

"That's confidential."

"Who hired you?"

"Confidential." I was tempted to put on a singsong voice, but I didn't think Ross was in the right frame of mind. Maybe he was right, maybe I was an asshole; but I was no nearer to finding Catherine Demeter than I had been twenty-four hours ago, and her boyfriend's death had opened up a range of possibilities, none of which was particularly appealing. If Ross was out to nail Sonny Ferrera or his father, then that was his problem. I had enough of my own.

"What did you tell Ferrera about Barton's death?"

"Nothing he didn't know already, seeing as how Hansen was at the scene before you were," I replied. Hansen was a reporter with the *Post*, a good one. There were flies that envied Hansen's ability to sniff out a corpse, but if someone had time to tip Hansen off it was pretty certain that someone had informed Ferrera even earlier. Walter was right: parts of the Police Department leaked like a poor man's shoes.

"Look," I said, "I don't know any more than you do. I don't think Sonny was involved, or the old man. As for anyone else . . ."

Ross's eyes flicked upward in frustration. After a pause, he asked if I'd met Bobby Sciorra. I told him I'd had that pleasure. Ross stood and picked at some microscopic speck on his tie. It looked like the sort you picked up in Filene's Basement after the good stuff has gone.

"Sciorra's been mouthing off about teaching you a lesson, I hear. He thinks you're an interfering prick. He's probably right."

"I hope you'll do everything in your power to protect me."

Ross smiled, a minute hitching of the lips that revealed small, pointed canines. He looked like a rat reacting to a stick poked in its face.

"Rest assured, we'll do everything in our power to find the culprit when something happens to you." Hernandez smiled too as they headed for the door. Like father, like son.

I smiled back. "You can let yourselves out. And Hernandez . . ." He stopped and turned.

"I'm gonna count those books."

Ross was right to be concentrating his energies on Sonny. He may have been strictly minor league in many ways—a few porn parlors near Port Authority, a social club on Mott with a handwritten notice taped above the phone reminding members that it was bugged, assorted petty drug deals, shylocking, and running whores hardly made him Public Enemy Number One—but Sonny was also the weak link in the Ferrera chain. If he could be broken, then it might lead to Sciorra and to the old man himself.

I watched the two FBI men from my window as they climbed into their car. Ross paused at the passenger side and stared up at the window for a time. It didn't crack under the pressure. Neither did I, but I had a feeling that Agent Ross wasn't really trying, not yet.

CHAPTER XIV

It was after ten the next morning when I arrived at the Barton house. An unidentified flunky answered the door and showed me into the same office in which I had met Isobel Barton the day before, with the same desk and the same Ms. Christie wearing what looked like the same gray suit and the same unwelcoming look on her face.

She didn't offer me a seat so I stood with my hands in my pockets to stop my fingers getting numb in the chilly atmosphere. She busied herself with some papers on the desk, not sparing me a second look. I stood by the fireplace and admired a blue china dog that stood at the far end of the mantelpiece. It was part of what had probably once been a pair, since there was an empty space on the opposite side. He looked lonely without a friend.

"I thought these things usually came in pairs?"

Ms. Christie glanced up, her face crumpled in annoyance like an image on old newspaper.

"The dog," I repeated. "I thought china dogs like that came in matching pairs." I wasn't particularly concerned about the dog but I was tired of Ms. Christie ignoring me and I derived some petty pleasure from irritating her.

"It was once part of a pair," she replied after a moment. "The other was . . . damaged some time ago."

"That must have been upsetting," I said, trying to look like I meant it while simultaneously failing to do so.

"It was. It had sentimental value."

"For you, or Mrs. Barton?"

"For both of us." Ms. Christie realized she had been forced to acknowledge my presence despite her best efforts, so she carefully put the cap on her pen, clasped her hands together, and assumed a businesslike expression.

"How is Mrs. Barton?" I asked. What might have been concern moved swiftly across Ms. Christie's features and then disappeared, like a gull gliding over a cliff face.

"She has been under sedation since last night. As you can imagine, she took the news badly."

"I didn't think she and her stepson were that close."

Ms. Christie tossed me a look of contempt. I probably deserved it.

"Mrs. Barton loved Stephen as if he were her own son. Don't forget that you are merely an employee, Mr. Parker. You do not have the right to impugn the reputation of the living or the dead." She shook her head at my insensitivity. "Why are you here? There's a great deal to be done before . . ."

She stopped and, for a moment, looked lost. I waited for her to resume. "Before Stephen's funeral," she finished, and I realized that there might be more to her apparent distress at the events of last night than simple concern for her employer. For a guy who had all the higher moral qualities of a hammerhead shark, Stephen Barton had certainly attracted his share of admirers.

"I have to go to Virginia," I said. "It may take more than the advance I was given. I wanted to let Mrs. Barton know before I left."

"Is this to do with the killing?"

"I don't know." It was becoming a familiar refrain. "There may be a connection between Catherine Demeter's disappearance and Mr. Barton's death but we won't know unless the police find something or the girl turns up."

"Well, I can't authorize that kind of spending at the present time," began Ms. Christie. "You'll have to wait until after—"

I interrupted her. Frankly, I was getting tired of Ms. Christie. I was used to people not liking me, but most at least had the decency to get to know me first, however briefly.

"I'm not asking you to authorize it, and after my meeting with Mrs. Barton, I don't think you have anything to do with it. But as a common courtesy I thought I'd offer my sympathies and tell her how far I've got."

"And how far have you got, *Mr.* Parker?" she hissed. She was standing now, her knuckles white against the desk. In her eyes something vicious and poisonous raised its head and flashed its fangs.

"I think the girl may have left the city. I think she went home, or back to what used to be home, but I don't know why. If she's there I'll find her, make sure she's okay, and contact Mrs. Barton."

"And if she isn't?" I let the question hang without a reply. There was no answer, for if Catherine Demeter wasn't in Haven, then she might as well have dropped off the face of the earth until she did something that made her traceable, like using a credit card or making a telephone call to her worried friend.

I felt tired and frayed at the edges. The case seemed to be fragmenting, the pieces spinning away from me and glittering in the distance. There were too many elements involved to be merely coincidental, and yet I was too experienced to try to force them all together into a picture that might be untrue to reality, an imposition of order upon the chaos of murder and killing. Still, it seemed to me that Catherine Demeter was one of those pieces and that she had to be found so that her place in the order of things could be determined.

"I'm leaving this afternoon. I'll call if I find anything." Ms. Christie's eyes had lost their shine and the bitter thing that lived within her had curled back on itself to sleep for a while. I was not even sure that she heard me. I left her like that, her knuckles still resting on the desk, her eyes vacant, seemingly staring somewhere within herself, her face slick and pale as if troubled by what she saw.

AS IT TURNED OUT, I was delayed by further problems with my car and it was 4 P.M. before I drove the Mustang back to my apartment to pack my bag.

A welcome breeze blew as I walked up the steps, fumbling for my keys. It sent candy wrappers cartwheeling across the street and set soft drink cans tolling like bells. A discarded newspaper skimmed the sidewalk with a sound like the whisperings of a dead lover.

I walked the four flights of stairs to my door, entered the apartment, and turned on a lamp. I prepared a pot of coffee and packed as it percolated. About thirty minutes later I was finishing my coffee, my overnight bag at my feet, when the cell phone rang.

"Hello, Mr. Parker," said a man's voice. The voice was neutral, almost artificial, and I could hear small clicks between the words as if they had been reassembled from a completely different conversation.

"Who is this?"

"Oh, we've never met, but we had some mutual acquaintances. Your wife and daughter. You might say I was with them in their final moments." The voice alternated between sets of words: now high, then low, first male, then female. At one point, there seemed to be three voices speaking simultaneously, then they became a single male voice once again.

The apartment seemed to drop in temperature and then fall away from me. There was only the phone, the tiny perforations of the mouthpiece, and the silence at the other end of the line.

"I've had freak calls before," I said, with more confidence than I felt. "You're just another lonely man looking for a house to haunt."

"I cut their faces off. I broke your wife's nose by slamming her against the wall by the kitchen door. Don't doubt me. I am the one you've been looking for." The last words were all spoken by a child's voice, high-pitched and joyous.

I felt a stabbing pain behind my eyes and my blood sounded loudly in my ears like waves crashing against a headland bleak and gray. There was no saliva in my mouth, just a dry dusty sensation. When I swallowed the feeling was that of dirt traveling down my throat. It was painful and I struggled to find my voice.

"Mr. Parker, are you okay?" The words were calm, solicitous, almost tender, but spoken by what sounded like four different voices.

"I'll find you."

He laughed. The synthesized nature of the sound was more obvious now. It seemed to break up into tiny units, just as a TV screen does when you get too close and the picture becomes merely a series of small dots.

"But I've found *you,*" he said. "You wanted me to find you, just as you wanted me to find them and to do what I did. You brought me into your life. For you, I flamed into being.

"I had been waiting so long for your call. You wanted them to die. Didn't you hate your wife in the hours before I took her? And don't you sometimes, in the deep dark of the night, have to fight back your sense of guilt at the feeling of freedom it gave you knowing she was dead? I freed you. The least you could do is show some gratitude."

"You're a sick man, but that isn't going to save you." I checked caller ID on the phone and froze. It was a number I recognized. It was the number of the public phone at the corner of the street. I moved toward the door and began making my way down the stairs.

"No, not 'man.' In her final moments your wife knew that, your Susan, mouth to mouth's kiss as I drew the life from her. Oh, I lusted for her in those last, bright red minutes, but then, that has always been a weakness of our kind. Our sin was not pride, but lust for humanity. And I chose her, Mr. Parker, and I loved her in my way." The voice was now deep and male. It boomed in my ear like the voice of a god, or a devil.

"Fuck you," I said, the bile rising in my throat as I felt sweat bead my brow and run in rivulets down my face, a sick, fearful sweat that defied the fury in my voice. I had come down three flights of stairs. There was one flight left to go.

"Don't go yet." The voice became that of a female child, like my child, my Jennifer, and in that moment I had some inkling of the nature of this Traveling Man. "We'll talk again soon. By then, maybe my purpose will be clearer to you. Take what I give you as a gift. I hope it will ease your suffering. It should be coming to you right . . . about . . . *now.*"

I heard the buzzer sound in my apartment upstairs. I dropped the phone to the floor and drew the Smith & Wesson from my holster. I took the remaining steps two at a time, racing down the stairs with adrenaline pumping through my system. My neighbor Mrs. D'Amato, startled by the noise, stood at her apartment door, the one nearest the front entrance, a housecoat held tight at her neck. I rushed past her, wrenched open the door, and came out low, my thumb already clicking down the safety.

On the step stood a black child of no more than ten years, a cylindrical, gift-wrapped parcel in his hand and his eyes wide in fear and shock. I grabbed him by the collar and flung him inside, shouting for Mrs. D'Amato to hold him, to get both of them away from the package, and ran down the steps of the redbrick and on to the street.

It was deserted except for the papers and the rolling cans. It was a strange desertion, as if the East Village and its inhabitants had conspired with the Traveling Man against me. At the far end of the street, beneath the streetlight, a telephone booth stood. There was no one there and the handset was hanging in its place. I ran toward it, moving away from the corner wall as I approached in case anyone was waiting at the other side. Here, the street was alive with passersby, gay couples hand in hand, tourists, lovers. In the distance I saw the lights of traffic and I heard around me the sounds of a safer, more mundane world I seemed to have left behind.

I spun at the sound of footsteps behind me. A young woman was approaching the telephone, fumbling in her purse for change. She looked up as she saw me approach and backed off at the sight of the gun.

"Find another," I said. I took one last look around, clicked the safety, and stuck the gun in the waistband of my pants. I braced my foot against the pillar of the phone booth and with both hands I wrenched the connecting cable from the phone with a strength that was not natural to me. Then I returned to my apartment house, carrying the receiver before me like a fish on the end of a line.

Inside her apartment Mrs. D'Amato was holding the kid by his arms while he struggled and fought, with tears rolling down his cheeks. I held his shoulders and squatted down to his level.

"Hey, it's okay. Take it easy. You're not in any trouble, I just want to ask you some questions. What's your name?"

The boy quieted down a little, although he still shook with sobs. He glanced around nervously at Mrs. D'Amato and then made an attempt to break for the door. He nearly made it, too, his jacket slipping from his body as he pulled out his arms, but the force of his efforts made him slip and fall and I was on him. I hauled him to a chair, sat him down, and gave Mrs. D'Amato Walter Cole's number. I told her to tell him it was urgent and to get over here fast.

"What's your name, kid?"

"Jake."

"Okay, Jake. Who gave you this?" I nodded toward the parcel that stood on the table beside us, wrapped in blue paper decorated with teddy bears and candy canes, and topped with a bright blue ribbon.

Jake shook his head, the force sending tears flying off in both directions.

"It's all right, Jake. There's no need to be scared. Was it a man, Jake?" Jake, Jake. Keep using his name, calm him, get him to concentrate.

His face swiveled toward me, the eyes huge. He nodded.

"Did you see what he looked like, Jake?"

His chin crumpled and he started to cry in loud sobs that brought Mrs. D'Amato back to the kitchen door.

"He said he'd hurt me," said Jake. "He said he'd *cu-cut my face off.*"

Mrs. D'Amato moved beside him and he buried his face in the folds of her housecoat, wrapping his small arms around her thick waist.

"Did you see him, Jake? Did you see what he looked like?"

He turned from the housecoat.

"He had a knife, like doctors use on TV." The boy's mouth hung wide with terror. "He showed it to me, touched me with it here." He lifted a finger to his left cheek.

"Jake, did you see his face?"

"He was all dark," said Jake, his voice rising in hysteria. "There was nuh-nuhthin' there." His voice rose to a scream: "*He didn't have no face.*"

I TOLD MRS. D'AMATO to take Jake into the kitchen until Walter Cole arrived, then sat down to examine the gift from the Traveling Man. It was about ten inches high and eight inches in diameter and it felt like glass. I took out my pocket knife and gently pulled back an edge of the wrapping, examining it for wires or pressure pads. There was nothing. I cut the two strips of tape holding the paper in place and gently removed the grinning bears, the dancing candy canes.

The surface of the jar was clean and I smelled the disinfectant he had used to erase any traces of himself. In the yellowing liquid it contained I saw my own face doubly reflected, first on the surface of the glass and then, inside, on the face of my once-beautiful daughter. It rested gently against the side of the jar, now bleached and puffy like the face of a drowning victim, scraps of flesh like tendrils rising from the edges and the eyelids closed as if in repose. And I moaned in a rising tide of agony and fear, hatred and remorse. In the kitchen, I could hear the boy named Jake sobbing, and mingled with his cries, I suddenly heard my own.

I DON'T KNOW HOW much time elapsed before Cole arrived. He stared ashen faced at the thing in the jar and then called Forensics.

"Did you touch it?"

"No. There's a phone as well. The number matches the caller ID but there won't be any traces. I'm not even sure he was at that phone: that number shouldn't have come up on the cell phone ID. His voice was synthesized in some way. I think he was running his words through some form of sophisticated software, something with voice recognition and tone manipulation, and maybe bouncing it off that number. I don't know. I'm guessing, that's all." I was babbling, words tripping over one another. I was afraid of what might happen if I stopped talking.

"What did he say?"

"I think he's getting ready to start again."

He sat down heavily and ran his hand over his face and through his hair. Then he picked up the paper by one edge with a gloved hand and almost gently used it to cover the front of the jar, like a veil.

"You know what we have to do," he said. "We'll need to know everything he said, anything at all that might help us to get a lead on him. We'll do the same with the kid."

I kept my eyes on Cole, on the floor, anywhere but on the table and the remains of all that I had lost.

"He thinks he's a demon, Walter."

Cole looked once again at the shape of the jar.

"Maybe he is."

As we left for the station, cops milled around the front of the building, preparing to take statements from neighbors, passersby, anyone who might possibly have witnessed the actions of the Traveling Man. The boy, Jake, came with us, his parents arriving shortly after with that frightened, sick look that poor, decent people get in the city when they hear that one of their children is with the police.

The Traveling Man must have been following me throughout

the day, watching my movements so he could put into action what he had planned. I traced back my movements, trying to remember faces, strangers, anyone whose gaze might have lingered for just a moment too long. There was nothing.

At the station, Walter and I went through the conversation again and again, pulling out anything that might be useful, that might stamp some distinguishing feature on this killer.

"You say the voices changed?" he asked.

"Repeatedly. At one point, I even thought I heard Jennifer."

"There may be something in that. Voice synthesis of that kind would have to be done using some sort of computer. Shit, he could simply have routed the call through that number, like you said. The kid says he was given the jar at four P.M. and told to deliver it at four-thirty-five P.M. exactly. He waited in an alley, counting the seconds on his Power Rangers digital watch. That could have given this guy enough time to get to his home base and bounce the call. I don't know enough about these things. Maybe he needed access to an exchange to do what he did. I'll have to get someone who knows to check it out."

The mechanics of the voice synthesis were one thing, but the reasons for the synthesis were another. It might have been that the Traveling Man wanted to leave as few traces of himself as possible: a voice pattern could be recognized, stored, compared, and even used against him at some point in the future.

"What about the kid's comment, that this guy with the scalpel had no face?" asked Walter.

"A mask of some kind, maybe, to avoid any possibility of identification. He could be marked in some way, that's another option. The third choice is that he is what he seems to be."

"A demon?"

I didn't reply. I didn't know what a demon was, if an individual's inhumanity could cause him to cross over in some way, to become something less than human; or if there were some things that seemed to defy any conventional notion of what it meant to be human, of what it meant to exist in the world.

When I returned to the apartment that night, Mrs. D'Amato brought me up a plate of cold cuts and some Italian bread and sat with me for a time, fearful for me after what had taken place that afternoon.

When she left, I stood beneath the shower for a long time, the water as hot as I could take it, and I washed my hands again and again. I lay awake then for a long time, sick with anger and fear, watching the cell phone on my desk. My senses were so heightened that I could hear them hum.

CHAPTER XV

Read me a story, Daddy."

"What story do you want to hear?"

"A funny story. The three bears. The baby bear is funny."

"Okay, but then you have to go to sleep."

"Okay."

"One story."

"One story. Then I go to sleep."

In an autopsy, the body is first photographed, clothed and naked. Certain parts of the body may be X-rayed to determine the presence of bone fragments or foreign objects embedded in the flesh. Every external feature is noted: the hair color, the height, the weight, the condition of the body, the color of the eyes.

"Baby Bear opened his eyes wide. 'Somebody's been eating my porridge, and it's all gone!' "

"All gone!"

All gone.

The internal examination is conducted from top to bottom, but the head is examined last. The chest is examined for any sign of rib fractures. A Y-shaped incision is made by cutting from shoulder to shoulder, crossing over the breasts, then moving down from the lower tip of the sternum to the pubic region. The heart and lungs are exposed. The pericardial sac is opened and a sample of blood is taken to determine the blood type of the victim. The heart, lungs, esophagus, and trachea are removed. Each organ is weighed, examined, and sliced into sections. Fluid in the thoracic pleural cavity is removed for analysis. Slides of organ tissue are prepared for analysis under a microscope.

"And then Goldilocks ran away and the three bears never saw her again."

"Read it again."

"No, we agreed. One story. That's all we have time for."

"We have more time."

"Not tonight. Another night."

"No, tonight."

"No, another night. There'll be other nights, and other stories."

The abdomen is examined and any injuries are noted before the removal of the organs. Fluids in the abdomen are analyzed and each separate organ is weighed, examined, and sectioned. The contents of the stomach are measured. Samples are taken for toxicological analysis. The order of removal is usually as follows: the liver, the spleen, the adrenals and kidneys, the stomach, pancreas, and intestines.

"What did you read?"

" 'Goldilocks and the Three Bears.' "

"Again."

"Again."

"Are you going to tell me a story?"

"What story would you like to hear?"

"Something dirty."

"Oh, I know lots of stories like that."

"I know you do."

The genitalia are examined for injuries or foreign material. Vaginal and anal swabs are obtained and any foreign matter collected is sent to a DNA lab for analysis. The bladder is removed and a urine sample is sent to toxicology.

"Kiss me."

"Kiss you where?"

"Everywhere. On my lips, my eyes, my neck, my nose, my ears, my cheeks. Kiss me everywhere. I love your kisses on me."

"Suppose I start with your eyes and move down from there."

"Okay. I can live with that."

The skull is examined in an effort to find evidence of injury. The intermastoid incision is made from one ear to the other, across the top of the head. The scalp is peeled away and the skull exposed. A saw is used to cut through the skull. The brain is examined and removed.

"Why can't we be like this more often?"

"I don't know. I want us to be, but I can't."

"I love you like this."

"Please, Susan . . ."

"No . . ."

"I could taste the booze on your breath."

"Susan, I can't talk about this now. Not now."

"When? When are we going to talk about it?"

"Some other time. I'm going out."

"Stay, please."

"No. I'll be back later."

"Please . . ."

REHOBOTH BEACH IN DELAWARE has a long boardwalk bordered on one side by the beach and on the other by the sort of amusement arcades you remember from your childhood: twenty-five-cent games played with wooden balls that you roll into holes to score points; horse races with metal horses loping down a sloped track, with a glass-eyed teddy bear for the winner; a frog pond game played with magnets on the end of a child's fishing line.

They've been joined now by noisy computer games and space flight simulators, but Rehoboth still retains more charm than, say, Dewey Beach, farther up the coast, or even Bethany. A ferry runs from Cape May in New Jersey to Lewes on the Delaware coast, and from there, it's maybe five or six miles south to Rehoboth. It's not really the best way to approach Rehoboth, since you run the gamut of burger joints, outlet stores, and shopping malls on U.S.1. The approach north through Dewey is better, running along the shore with its miles of dunes.

From that direction, Rehoboth benefits from the contrast with Dewey. You cross into the town proper over a kind of ornamental lake, go past the church, and then you're on Rehoboth's main street, with its bookstores, its T-shirt shops, its bars and restaurants set in big old wooden houses, where you can drink on the porch and watch people walk their dogs in the quiet evening air.

Four of us had decided on Rehoboth as the place to go for a weekend break to celebrate Tommy Morrison's promotion to lieutenant, despite its reputation as something of a gay hot spot. We ended up staying in the Lord Baltimore, with its comfortable, antiquated rooms harking back to another era, less than a block away from the Blue Moon bar, where crowds of well-tanned, expensively dressed men partied loudly into the night.

I had just become Walter Cole's partner. I suspected Walter had pulled strings to have me assigned as his partner, although nothing was ever said. With Lee's agreement, he traveled with me to Delaware, along with Tommy Morrison and a friend of mine from the academy named Joseph Bonfiglioli, who was shot dead a year later while chasing a guy who had stolen eighty dollars from a liquor store. Each evening at 9 P.M., without fail, Walter would call Lee to check on her and the kids. He was a man acutely aware of the vulnerability of a parent.

Walter and I had known each other for some time—four years

by then, I think. I met him first in one of the bars in which cops used to hold court. I was young, just out of uniform, and still admiring my reflection in my new tin. Great things were expected of me. It was widely believed that I would get my name in the papers. I did that, although not in the way that anyone would have imagined.

Walter was a stocky figure wearing slightly worn suits, a dark shadow of a beard on his cheeks and chin even when he had shaved only an hour before. He had a reputation as a dogged, concerned investigator, one who had occasional flashes of brilliance that could turn an investigation around when legwork had failed to produce a result and the necessary quota of luck upon which almost every investigation depends was not forthcoming.

Walter Cole was also an avid reader, a man who devoured knowledge in the same way that certain tribes devour their enemies' hearts in the hope that they will become braver as a result. We shared a love of Runyon and Wodehouse, of Tobias Wolff, Raymond Carver, Donald Barthelme, the poetry of e. e. cummings, and, strangely, of the earl of Rochester, the Restoration dandy tortured by his failings: his love of alcohol and women and his inability to be the husband that he believed his wife deserved.

I recall Walter wandering along the boardwalk at Rehoboth with a Popsicle in his hand, a garish shirt hanging over a pair of khaki shorts, his sandals slapping lightly on the sand-scattered wood, and a straw hat protecting his already balding head. Even as he joked with us, examining menus and losing money on the slots, stealing fries from Tommy Morrison's big Thrasher's paper tub, paddling in the cool Atlantic surf, I knew that he was missing Lee.

And I knew, too, that to live a life like Walter Cole's—a life almost mundane in the pleasure it derived from small happinesses and the beauty of the familiar, but uncommon in the value it attached to them—was something to be envied.

I met Susan Lewis, as she then was, for the first time in Lingo's Market, an old-style general store that sold produce and cereals alongside expensive cheeses and boasted its own in-store bakery.

It was still a family-run operation—a sister, a brother, and their mother, a tiny, white-haired woman with the energy of a terrier.

On our first morning in the resort, I stumbled out to buy coffee and a newspaper in Lingo's, my mouth dry, my legs still unsteady from the night before. She stood at the deli counter, ordering coffee beans and pecans, her hair tied loosely in a ponytail. She wore a yellow summer dress, her eyes were a deep, dark blue, and she was very, very beautiful.

I, on the other hand, was very much the worse for wear, but she smiled at me as I stood beside her at the counter, oozing alcohol from my pores. And then she was gone, trailing a hint of expensive scent behind her.

I saw her a second time that day, at the YMCA as she stepped from the pool and entered the dressing rooms, while I tried to sweat out the alcohol on a rowing machine. It seemed to me that, for the next day or two, I caught glimpses of her everywhere: in a bookshop, examining the covers of glossy legal thrillers; passing the launderette, clutching a bag of donuts; peering in the window of the Irish Eyes bar with a girlfriend; and finally I came upon her one night as she stood on the boardwalk, the sound of the arcades behind her and the waves breaking before her.

She was alone, caught up in the sight of the surf gleaming white in the darkness. Few people strolled on the beach to obscure her view, and at the periphery, away from the arcades and the fast food stalls, it was startlingly empty.

She looked over at me as I stood beside her. She smiled.

"Feeling better now?"

"A little. You caught me at a bad time."

"I could *smell* your bad time," she said, her nose wrinkling.

"I'm sorry. If I'd known you were going to be there, I'd have dressed up." And I wasn't kidding.

"It's okay. I've had those times."

And from there it began. She lived in New Jersey, commuted to Manhattan each day to work in a publisher's office, and every second weekend she visited her parents in Massachusetts. We were married a year later and we had Jennifer one year after that. We had maybe three very good years together before things started to deteriorate. It was my fault, I think. When my parents married they both knew the toll a policeman's life could take on a marriage, he because he lived that life and saw its results reflected in the lives around him, she because her father had been a deputy in Maine and had resigned before the cost became too high. Susan had no such experience.

She was the youngest of four children, both of her parents were still alive, and they all doted on her. When she died, they ceased to speak to me. Even at the graveside, no words passed between us. With Susan and Jennifer gone, it was as if I had been cut adrift from the tide of life and left to float in still, dark waters.

CHAPTER XVI

The deaths of Susan and Jennifer attracted a great deal of attention, although it soon faded. The more intimate details of the killing—the skinning, the removal of the faces, the blindings—were kept from the public, but it didn't stop the freaks from coming out of the woodwork. For a time, murder tourists would drive up to the house and videotape one another standing in the yard. A local patrolman even caught one couple trying to break in through the back door in order to pose in the chairs where Susan and Jennifer had died. In the days after they had been found, the phone rang regularly with calls from people who claimed to be married to the killer, or who felt certain that they had met him in a past life or, on one or two occasions, called only to say they were glad my wife and child were dead. Eventually I left the house, remaining in touch by phone and fax with the lawyer who had been entrusted with the business of selling it.

I had found the community in southern Maine, when I was returning to Manhattan from Chicago after chasing up one more obscure non-lead, a suspected child killer named Myron Able, who was dead by the time I arrived, killed in the parking lot of a bar after he tangled with some local thugs. Maybe I was also looking for some peace in a place I knew, but I never got as far as the house in Scarborough, the house that my grandfather had left me in his will.

I was sick by that time. When the girl found me retching and crying in the doorway of a boarded-up electronics store and offered me a bed for the night, I could only nod. When her comrades, huge men with muddied boots and shirts that smelled of sweat and pine needles, dragged me to their pickup and dumped me in the back, I half hoped that they were going to kill me. They nearly did. By the time I left their community, out by Sebago Lake, six weeks later, I had lost more than twelve pounds and my stomach muscles stood out like the plates on an alligator's back. During the day, I worked on their small farm and attended group sessions where others like me tried to purge themselves of their demons. I still craved alcohol but fought back the desire as I had been taught. There were prayers in the evenings and every Sunday a pastor would give a sermon on abstinence, tolerance, the need for each man and woman to find a peace within himself or herself. The community funded itself through the produce it sold, some furniture it made, and donations from those who had availed themselves of its services, some of them now wealthy men and women.

But I was still sick, consumed by a desire to revenge myself upon those around me. I felt trapped in a limbo: the investigation had ground to a halt and would not resume again until a similar crime was committed and a pattern could be established.

Someone had taken my wife and child from me and escaped unpunished. Inside me, the hurt and anger and guilt ebbed and flowed like a red tide waiting to spill its banks. I felt it as a physical pain that tore at my head and gnawed at my stomach. It led me back to the city, where I tortured and killed the pimp Johnny Friday in the toilet of the bus station where he had been waiting to feast on the waifs and strays drifting into New York.

I think now that I had always set out to kill him but that I had hidden the knowledge of what I intended to do in some corner of my mind. I draped it with self-serving justifications and excuses, the sort I had used for so long each time I watched a shot of whiskey poured in front of me, or heard the gassy snap of a bottle cap. Frozen by my own inability and the inability of others to find the killer of Susan and Jennifer, I saw a chance to strike out and I took it. From the moment I packed my gun and gloves and set out for the bus station, Johnny Friday was a dead man.

Friday was a tall, thin black man who looked like a preacher in his trademark dark three-buttoned suits and his collarless shirts fastened at the neck. He would hand out small Bibles and religious pamphlets to the new arrivals and offer them soup from a flask, and as the barbiturates it contained began to take effect, he would lead them from the station and into the back of a waiting van. Then they would disappear, as surely as if they had never arrived, until they turned up on the streets as beaten junkies, whoring for the fix that Johnny supplied at inflated prices while they pulled in the tricks that kept him rich.

His was a hands-on operation, and even in a business not noted for its humanity, Johnny Friday was beyond any kind of redemption. He supplied children to pedophiles, delivering them to the doors of selected safe houses, where they were raped and sodomized before being returned to their owner. If they were rich and depraved enough, Johnny would give them access to "the basement," in an abandoned warehouse in the garment district. There, for a cash payment of ten thousand dollars, they could take one of Johnny's stable, boy or girl, child or teen, they could torture, rape, and if they wished, kill, and Johnny would take care of the body. He was noted, in certain circles, for his discretion.

In my search for the killer of my wife and child, I had learned of Johnny Friday. From a former snitch I learned that Johnny sometimes dealt in pictures and videos of sexual torture, that he was a leading source of this material, and that anyone whose tastes ran in that direction would, at some point, come into contact with Johnny Friday or one of his agents.

And so I watched him for five hours from an Au Bon Pain in the station, and when he went to the washroom, I followed him. It was divided into sections, the first mirrored, with sinks, the second lined with urinals along the end wall and two sets of stalls opposite, divided by a central aisle. An old man in a stained uniform sat in a small, glass-lined cubicle beside the sinks but he was engrossed in a magazine when I entered behind Johnny Friday. Two men were washing their hands at the sinks, two were standing at the urinals, and three of the stalls were occupied, two in the section to the left, one in the section to the right. Piped music was playing, some unrecognizable tune.

Johnny Friday walked, hips swinging, to the urinal at the far right of the wall. I stood two urinals away from him as I waited for the other men to finish. As soon as they had finished I moved behind Johnny Friday, clasping my hand on his mouth and pressing the Smith & Wesson into the soft skin beneath his chin as I pushed him into the end stall, the farthest away from the other occupied stall on that side.

"Hey, don't, man, don't," he whispered, his eyes wide. I brought my knee up hard into his groin and he fell down heavily on his knees as I locked the door behind us. He tried weakly to rise and I hit him hard in the face. I brought the gun close to his head again.

"Don't say a word. Turn your back to me."

"Please, man, don't."

"Shut up. Turn."

He inched slowly round on his knees. I pulled his jacket down over his arms and then cuffed him. From my other pocket I took a rag and a roll of duct tape. I stuffed the rag in his mouth and wrapped the tape around his head two or three times. Then I pulled him to his feet and pushed him down on to the toilet. His right foot came up and caught me hard on the shin and he tried to push himself up, but he was off balance and I hit him again. This time he stayed down. I held the gun on him and listened for a moment in case anyone came to see what the noise was. There was only the sound of a toilet flushing. No one came.

I told Johnny Friday what I wanted. His eyes narrowed as he realized who I was. Sweat poured from his forehead and he tried to blink it from his eyes. His nose was bleeding slightly and a thin trickle of red ran from beneath the duct tape and rolled down his chin. His nostrils flared as he breathed heavily through them.

"I want names, Johnny. Names of customers. You're going to give them to me."

He snorted in disdain and blood bubbled from a nostril. His eyes were cold now. He looked like a long, black snake with his slicked-back hair and slitted, reptilian eyes. When I broke his nose they widened in shock and pain.

I hit him again, once, twice, hard blows to the stomach and head. Then I pulled the tape down hard and dragged the bloodied rag from his mouth.

"Give me names."

He spat a tooth from his mouth.

"Fuck you," he said. "Fuck you and your dead bitches."

What happened after is still not clear to me. I remember hitting him again and again, feeling bone crunch and ribs break and watching my gloves darken with his blood. There was a black cloud in my mind and streaks of red ran through it like strange lightning.

When I stopped, Johnny Friday's features seemed to have melted into a bloody blur. I held his jaw in my hands as blood bubbled from his lips.

"Tell me," I hissed. His eyes rolled toward me, and like a vision of some craggy entrance to Hell, his broken teeth showed behind his lips as he managed one last smile. His body arched and spasmed once, twice. Thick black blood rolled from his nose and mouth and ears, and then he died.

I stood back, breathing heavily. I wiped my blood-spattered face as best I could and cleaned some of the blood from the front of my jacket, although it hardly showed against the black leather and my black jeans. I took the gloves from my hands, stuffed them in my pocket, and then flushed the toilet before peering carefully out and pulling the door closed behind me as I left. Blood was already seeping out of the stall and pooling in the cracks between the tiles.

I realized that the noise of Johnny Friday's dying must have echoed around the washroom but I didn't care. As I left I passed only an elderly black man at the urinals and he, like a good citizen who knows when to mind his own business, didn't even glance at me. There were other men at the sinks, who gave me a cursory look in the mirror. But I noticed that the old man was gone from his glass cubicle and I ducked into an empty departure gate as two cops came running toward the washroom from the upper level. I made my way to the street through the ranks of buses beneath the station.

Perhaps Johnny Friday deserved to die. Certainly no one mourned his passing and the police made little more than a cursory effort to find his killer. But there were rumors, for Walter, I think, had heard them.

But I live with the death of Johnny Friday as I live with the deaths of Susan and Jennifer. If he did deserve to die, if what he got was no more than he merited, yet it was not for me to act as his judge and executioner. "In the next life we get justice," someone once wrote. "In this one we have the law." In Johnny Friday's last minutes there was no law and only a kind of vicious justice that was not for me to give.

I DID NOT BELIEVE that my wife and child were the first to die at the hands of the Traveling Man, if that was who he was. I still believed that somewhere in a Louisiana swamp lay another and in her identity was the clue that would open up the world of this man who believed he was not a man. She was part of a grim tradition in human history, a parade of victims stretching back to ancient times, back to the time of Christ and before that, back to a time when men sacrificed those around them to placate gods who knew no mercy and whose natures they both created and imitated in their actions.

The girl in Louisiana was part of a bloody succession, a modern-day Windeby Girl, a descendant of that anonymous woman found in the fifties in a shallow grave in a peat bog in Denmark, where she had been led nearly two thousand years before, naked and blindfolded, to be drowned in twenty inches of water. A path could be traced through history leading from her death to the death of another girl at the hands of a man who believed he could appease the demons within himself by taking her life but who, once blood had been spilled and flesh torn, wanted more and took my wife and child.

We do not believe in evil anymore, only evil acts that can be explained away by the science of the mind. There is no evil and to believe in it is to fall prey to superstition, like checking beneath the bed at night or being afraid of the dark. But there are those for whom we have no easy answers, who do evil because that is their nature, because they are evil.

Johnny Friday and others like him prey on those who live on the periphery of society, on those who have lost their way. It is easy to get lost in the darkness on the edge of modern life, and once we are lost and alone, there are things waiting for us there. Our ancestors were not wrong in their superstitions: there is reason to fear the dark.

And just as a trail could be followed from a bog in Denmark to a swamp in the South, so I came to believe that evil, too, could be traced throughout the life of our race. There was a tradition of evil that ran beneath all human existence like the sewers beneath a city, that continued on even after one of its constituent parts was destroyed, because it was simply one small part of a greater, darker whole.

Perhaps that was part of what made me want to find out the truth about Catherine Demeter, for as I look back, I realize that evil had found its way to touch her life too and taint it beyond retrieval. If I could not fight evil as it came in the form of the Traveling Man, then I would find it in other forms. I believe what I say. I believe in evil because I have touched it, and it has touched me.

CHAPTER XVII

When I telephoned Rachel Wolfe's private practice the following morning, the secretary told me that she was giving a seminar at a conference at Columbia University. I took the subway from the Village and arrived early at the main entrance to the campus. I wandered for a while around the Barnard Book Forum, students jostling me as I stood browsing in the literature section, before making my way to the main college entrance.

I passed through the university's large quadrangle, with the Butler Library at one end, the administration building at the other, and like a mediator between learning and bureaucracy, the statue of Alma Mater in the grass center. Like most city residents, I rarely came to Columbia, and the sense of tranquillity and study only feet away from the busy streets outside was always surprising to me.

Rachel Wolfe was just finishing her lecture as I arrived, so I waited for her outside the theater until the session ended. She emerged talking to a young, earnest-looking man with curly hair and round spectacles, who hung on her every word. When she saw me she stopped and smiled a good-bye at him. He looked unhappy and seemed set to linger, but then turned and walked away, his head low.

"How can I help you, Mr. Parker?" she asked, with a puzzled but not uninterested look.

"He's back."

WE WALKED OVER TO the Hungarian Pastry Shop on Amsterdam Avenue, where intense-looking young men and women sat reading textbooks and sipping coffee. Rachel Wolfe was wearing jeans and a chunky sweater with a heart-shaped design on the front.

Despite all that had happened the previous night, I was curious about her. I had not been attracted to a woman since Susan's death, and my wife was the last woman with whom I had slept. Rachel Wolfe, her long red hair brushed back over her ears, aroused a sense of longing in me that was more than sexual. I felt a deep loneliness within myself and an ache in my stomach. She looked at me curiously.

"I'm sorry," I said. "I was thinking of something."

She nodded and picked at a poppy-seed roll before pulling off a huge chunk and stuffing it in her mouth, sighing with satisfaction. I must have looked slightly shocked, because she covered her mouth with her hand and giggled softly.

"Sorry, but I'm a sucker for these things. Daintiness and good table manners tend to go out the window when someone puts one in front of me."

"I know the feeling. I used to be like that with Ben & Jerry's until I realized that I was starting to look like one of the cartons."

She smiled again and pushed at a piece of roll that was trying to make a break for freedom from the side of her mouth. The conversation sagged for a time.

"I take it your parents were jazz fans," she said eventually.

I must have looked puzzled for a moment, because she smiled in amusement as I tried to take in the question. I had been asked it many times before but I was grateful for the diversion, and I think she knew that.

"No, my father and mother didn't know the first thing about

jazz," I replied. "My father just liked the name. The first time he heard about Bird Parker was at the baptismal font, when the priest mentioned it to him. The priest was a big jazz fan, I was told. He couldn't have been happier if my father had announced that he was naming all of his children after the members of the Count Basie Orchestra. My father, by contrast, wasn't too happy at the idea of naming his firstborn after a black jazz musician, but by then it was too late to think of another name."

"What did he call the rest of his children?"

I shrugged. "He didn't get the chance. My mother couldn't have any more children after me."

"Maybe she thought she couldn't do any better?" She smiled.

"I don't think so. I was nothing but trouble for her as a child. It used to drive my father crazy."

I could see in her eyes that she was about to ask me about my father but something in my face stopped her. She pursed her lips, pushed away her empty plate, and settled herself back in her chair.

"Can you tell me what happened?"

I went through the events of last night, leaving nothing out. The words of the Traveling Man were burned into my mind.

"Why do you call him that?"

"A friend of mine led me to a woman who said that she was receiving, uh, messages from a dead girl. The girl had died in the same way as Susan and Jennifer."

"Was the girl found?"

"No one looked. An old woman's psychic messages aren't enough to launch an investigation."

"Even if she exists, are you sure it's the same guy?"

"I believe it is, yes."

Wolfe looked like she wanted to ask more, but she let it go. "Go back over what this caller, this Traveling Man, said, again, slowly this time."

I did until she lifted her hand to stop me. "That's a quote from Joyce: 'mouth to mouth's kiss.' It's the description of the 'pale vampire' in *Ulysses.* This is an educated man we're dealing with. The stuff about 'our kind' sounds biblical; I'm not sure of it. I'll have to check it. Give it to me again." I spoke the words slowly as she took them down in a wire-bound notebook. "I have a friend who teaches theology and biblical studies. He might be able to identify a source for these."

She closed the notebook. "You know that I'm not supposed to get involved in this case?"

I told her that I hadn't known.

"Following our earlier discussions, someone got in touch with the commissioner. He wasn't pleased at the snub to his relative."

"I need help with this. I need to know all I can." Suddenly I felt nauseous, and when I swallowed, my throat hurt.

"I'm not sure that's wise. You should probably leave this to the police. I know that's not what you want to hear, but after all that's happened, you risk damaging yourself. Do you understand what I mean?"

I nodded slowly. She was right. Part of me wanted to draw back, to immerse myself once again in the ebb and flow of ordinary life. I wanted to unburden myself of what I felt, to restore myself to some semblance of a normal existence. I wanted to rebuild but I felt frozen, suspended, by what had happened. And now the Traveling Man had returned, snatching any possibility of that normality from me and, simultaneously, leaving me as powerless to act as I had been before.

I think Rachel Wolfe understood that. Perhaps that was why I had come to her, in the hope that she might understand.

"Are you okay?" She reached over and touched my hand and I almost cried. I nodded again.

"You're in a terribly difficult situation. If he has decided to contact you, then he wants you to be involved and there may be a link that can be exploited. From an investigative point of view, you probably shouldn't deviate from your routine in case he contacts you again, but from the point of view of your own well-being . . ." She let the unstated hang in the air. "You might even want to consider some professional help. I'm sorry for being so blunt about it, but it has to be said."

"I know, and I appreciate the advice." It was strange to find myself attracted to someone after all this time and then have her advise me to see a psychiatrist. It didn't hold out the promise of any relationship that wasn't conducted on an hourly basis. "I think the investigators want me to stay."

"I get the feeling you're not going to do it."

"I'm trying to find someone. It's a different case, but I think this person may be in trouble. If I stay here, there's no one to help her."

"It may be a good idea to get away from this for a time, but from what you're saying, well . . ."

"Go on."

"It sounds like you're trying to save this person but you're not even sure if she needs saving."

"Maybe I need to save her."

"Maybe you do."

I TOLD WALTER COLE later that morning that I would continue looking for Catherine Demeter and that I would be leaving the city to do so. We were sitting in the quietness of Chumley's, the Village's old speakeasy on Bedford. When Walter called, I had surprised myself by nominating it for our meeting, but as I sat sipping a coffee I realized why I had chosen it.

I enjoyed its sense of history, its place in the city's past, which could be traced back like an old scar or the wrinkle at the corner of an eye. Chumley's had survived the Prohibition era, when customers had escaped raids by leaving hastily through the back door, which led onto Barrow Street. It had survived world wars, stock market crashes, civil disobedience, and the gradual erosion of time, which was so much more insidious than all the rest. Right now, I needed its stability.

"You have to stay," said Walter. He still had the leather coat, now hanging loosely over the back of his chair. Someone had whistled at him when he entered wearing it.

"No."

"What do you mean, no?" he said angrily. "He's opened an avenue of communication. You stay, we wire up the phone, and we try to trace him when he calls again."

"I don't think he will call again, at least not for a while, and I don't believe we could trace him anyway. He doesn't want to be stopped, Walter."

"All the more reason to stop him, then. My God, look at what he's done, what he's going to do again. Look at what you've done for his—"

I leaned forward and broke in on him, my voice low. "What have I done? Say it, Walter. Say it!"

He stayed silent and I saw him swallow the words back. We had come close to the edge, but he had pulled back.

The Traveling Man wanted me to remain. He wanted me to wait in my apartment for a call that might never come. I could not let him do that to me. Yet both Walter and I knew that the contact he had established could well be the first link in a chain that would eventually lead us to him.

A friend of mine, Ross Oakes, had worked in the police department of Columbia, South Carolina, during the Bell killings. Larry Gene Bell abducted and smothered two girls, one aged seventeen and abducted close to a mailbox, the other aged nine and taken from her play area. When investigators eventually found the bodies of the children they were too decomposed to determine if they had been sexually assaulted, although Bell later admitted to assaulting both.

Bell had been tracked through a series of phone calls he made to the family of the seventeen-year-old, conversing primarily with the victim's older sister. He also mailed them her last will and testament. In the phone calls he led the family to believe that the victim was still alive, until her body was eventually found one week later. After the abduction of the younger girl he contacted the first victim's sister and described the abduction and killing of the girl. He told the first victim's sister that she would be next.

Bell was found through indented writing on the victim's letter, a semiobliterated telephone number that was eventually tracked to an address through a process of elimination. Larry Gene Bell was a thirty-six-year-old white male, formerly married and now living with his mother and father. He told Investigative Support Unit agents from the FBI that "the bad Larry Gene Bell did it."

I knew of dozens of similar cases where contact with the killer by the victim's family sometimes led to his capture, but I had also seen what this form of psychological torture had done to those who were left behind. The family of Bell's first victim were lucky because they had to suffer Bell's sick wanderings for only two weeks.

Amid the anger and pain and grief that I had felt the night before, there was another feeling that caused me to fear any further contact with the Traveling Man, at least for the present.

I felt relief.

For over seven months there had been nothing. The police investigation had ground to a halt, my own efforts had brought me no nearer to identifying the killer of my wife and child, and I feared that he might have disappeared.

Now he had come back. He had reached out to me and, by doing so, opened the possibility that he might be found. He would kill again, and in the killing, a pattern would emerge that would bring us closer to him. All these thoughts had raced through my head in the darkness of the night, but in the first light of dawn, I had realized the implications of what I felt.

The Traveling Man was drawing me into a cycle of dependency. He had tossed me a crumb in the form of a telephone call and the remains of my daughter, and in doing so had caused me to wish, however briefly, for the deaths of others in the hope that their deaths might bring me closer to him. With that realization came the decision that I would not form such a relationship with this man. It was a difficult decision to make but I knew that if he decided to contact me again, then he would find me. Meanwhile, I would leave New York and continue to hunt for Catherine Demeter.

Yet deep down, perhaps only half recognized by me and suspected by Rachel Wolfe, there was another reason for continuing the search for Catherine Demeter.

I did not believe in remorse without reparation. I had failed to protect my wife and child, and they had died as a result. Perhaps I was deluded, but I believed that if Catherine Demeter died because I stopped looking for her, then I would have failed twice, and I was not sure that I could live with that knowledge. In her, maybe wrongly, I saw a chance to atone.

Some of this I tried to explain to Walter—my need to avoid a dependent relationship with this man, the necessity of continuing the search for Catherine Demeter, for her sake and my own—but most of it I kept to myself. We parted uneasily and on bad terms.

TIREDNESS HAD GRADUALLY TAKEN hold of me throughout the morning and I slept fitfully for an hour before setting off for Virginia. I was bathed in sweat and almost delirious when I awoke, disturbed by dreams of endless conversations with a faceless killer and images of my daughter before her death.

Just as I awoke, I dreamed of Catherine Demeter surrounded by darkness and flames and the bones of dead children. And I knew then that some terrible blackness had descended on her and that I had to try to save her, to save us both, from the darkness.

2

Eadem mutata resurgo.

(Though changed, I shall arise the same.)

Epitaph of Jakob Bernoulli, Swiss pioneer of fluid dynamics and spiral mathematics

CHAPTER XVIII

I drove down to Virginia that afternoon. It was a long ride but I told myself that I wanted time to open up the car's engine, to let it cut loose after its time off the road. As I drove, I tried to sort through what had happened in the last two days, but my thoughts kept coming back to the remains of my daughter's face resting in a jar of formaldehyde.

I spotted the tail after about an hour, a red Nissan four wheel drive with two occupants. They kept four or five vehicles behind but when I accelerated, so did they. When I fell back they kept me in view for as long as they could, then they began to fall back too. The plates were deliberately obscured with mud. A woman drove, her blond hair pulled back behind her and sunglasses masking her eyes. A dark-haired male sat beside her. I put them both in their thirties but I didn't recognize them.

If they were feds, which was unlikely, then they were lame. If they were Sonny's hired killers, then it was just like Sonny to hire cheap. Only a clown would use a 4WD for a tail, or to try to take out another vehicle. A 4WD has a high center of gravity and rolls easier than a drunk on a slope. Maybe I was just being paranoid, but I didn't think so.

They didn't make a move and I lost them in the backroads between Warrenton and Culpeper as I headed toward the Blue Ridge.

If they came after me again, I'd know: they stood out like blood in snow.

As I drove, sunlight speared the trees, causing the weblike cocoons of caterpillars to glisten. I knew that, beneath the strands, the white bodies of the larvae were twisting and writhing like victims of Tourette's syndrome as they reduced the leaves to brown lifelessness. The weather was beautiful and there was a kind of poetry to the names of the towns that skirted Shenandoah: Wolftown, Quinque, Lydia, Roseland, Sweet Briar, Lovingston, Brightwood. To that list could be added the town of Haven, but only if you decided not to spoil the effect by actually visiting it.

It was raining heavily by the time I reached Haven. The town lay in a valley southeast of the Blue Ridge, almost at the apex of a triangle formed with Washington and Richmond. A sign at the limits read, *A Welcome in the Valley,* but there was little that was welcoming about Haven. It was a small town over which a pall of dust appeared to have settled that even the driving rain seemed unable to dislodge. Rusting pickups sat outside some of the houses, and apart from a single fast food joint and a convenience store attached to a gas station, only the weak neon of the Welcome Inn bar and the lights of the late-night diner opposite beckoned the casual visitor. It was the sort of place where, once a year, the local Veterans of Foreign Wars got together, hired a bus, and went somewhere else to commemorate their dead.

I checked into the Haven View Motel at the outskirts of the town. I was the only guest and a smell of paint hung around the halls of what might once have been a considerable house but had now been converted into a functional, anonymous three-story inn.

"Second floor's being redecorated," said the clerk, who told me his name was Rudy Fry. "Have to put you upstairs, top floor. Technically, we shouldn't be accepting guests at all but . . ." He smiled to indicate the big favor he was doing me by letting me stay. Rudy Fry was a small overweight man in his forties. There were long-dried yellow sweat stains under his arms and he smelled vaguely of rubbing alcohol.

I looked around. The Haven View Motel didn't look like the sort of place that would attract visitors in the best of times.

"I know what you're thinkin'," said the clerk, his smile revealing sparkling dentures. "You're thinkin', 'Why throw good money away by decoratin' a motel in a shit hole like this?' " He winked at me before leaning over the desk conspiratorially. "Well, I'm tellin' you, sir, it ain't gonna be a shit hole much longer. Them Japanese is comin' and when they do, this place is gonna be a gold mine. Where else they gonna stay round here?" He shook his head and laughed. "Shit, we gonna be wipin' our asses with dollar bills." He handed me a key with a heavy wooden block chained to it. "Room twenty-three, up the stairs. Elevator's busted."

The room was dusty but clean. A connecting door led into the room next door. It took me less than five seconds to break the lock with my pocketknife, then I showered, changed, and drove back into town.

The recession of the seventies had hit Haven hard, putting an end to what little industry there was. The town might have recovered, might have found some other way to prosper, had its history been other than it was, but the killings had tainted it and the town had fallen into decay. And so, even after the rain had sluiced its way over the stores and streets, over the people and the houses, over trees and pickups and cars and Tarmac, there was no freshness about Haven. It was as if the rain itself had been sullied by the contact.

I stopped in at the Sheriff's Office but neither the sheriff nor Alvin Martin was available. Instead, a deputy named Wallace sat scowling behind the desk and shoveling Doritos into his mouth. I decided to wait until the morning in the hope of finding someone more accommodating.

The diner was closing as I walked through the town, which left only the bar or the burger joint. The interior of the bar was ill lit, as if it was expending too much power on the pink neon sign outside. *The Welcome Inn:* the sign glowed brightly, but the interior seemed to give the lie to the sign.

Some kind of bluegrass music was playing over a speaker, and a TV above the bar was showing a basketball game with the volume turned down, but no one seemed to be listening or watching anyway. Maybe twenty people were scattered around the tables and the long, dark wood bar, including a mountainous couple who looked like they'd left the third bear with a baby-sitter. There was a low tide of conversation, which ebbed slightly when I entered, although it refused to cease entirely, and then resumed at its previous level.

Near the bar, a small knot of men lounged around a battered pool table, watching a huge, heavy-set man with a thick dark beard playing an older man who shot pool like a hustler. They eyed me as I walked by but continued playing. No conversation passed between them. Pool was obviously a serious business in the Welcome Inn. Drinking wasn't. The hard men around the pool table were all clutching bottles of Bud Light, the real drinker's equivalent of a club soda and lime.

I took an empty stool at the bar and asked for a coffee from a bartender whose white shirt seemed dazzlingly clean for such a place. He studiously ignored me, his eyes seemingly intent on the basketball game, so I asked again. His glance moved lazily to me, as if I were a bug crawling on the bar and he had just had his fill of squashing bugs but was wondering whether he couldn't squash one more for the road.

"We don't do coffee," he said.

I glanced along the bar. Two stools down an elderly man in a lumber jacket and a battered Cat cap sipped at a mug of what smelled like strong black coffee.

"He bring his own?" I inquired, gesturing with a nod down the bar.

"Yep," said the bartender, still looking at the TV.

"A Coke'll do. Right behind your knees, second shelf down. Don't hurt yourself leaning over."

For a long time it seemed he wasn't going to move, then he shifted slowly, leaned down without taking his eyes from the screen, and found the opener on the edge of the counter by instinct. Then he placed the bottle in front of me and set an iceless glass beside it. In the mirror behind the bar, I saw the amused smiles of some of the other patrons and heard a woman's laugh, low and boozy with a promise of sex in it. In the mirror over the bar, I traced the laugh to a coarse-featured woman in the corner, her hair huge and dark. Beside her, a stout man whispered sour somethings in her ear like the cooings of a sick dove.

I poured the drink and took a long swig. It was warm and sticky and I felt it cleave to my palate, my tongue, and my teeth. The bartender spent a while idly polishing glasses with a bar towel that looked like it had last been cleaned for Reagan's inauguration. When he got bored with redistributing the dirt on the glasses he wandered back toward me and put the bar towel down in front of me.

"Passin' through?" he asked, although there was no curiosity in his voice. It sounded more like advice than a question.

"Nope," I said.

He took it in and then waited for me to say more. I didn't. He gave in first.

"Whatcha doin' here, then?" He looked over my shoulder at the pool players behind and I noticed that the sound of balls colliding had suddenly ceased. He smiled a big shit-eating grin. "Maybe I can"—he stopped and the grin got wider, his tone changing to one of mock formality—"be of some *a*-ssistance."

"You know anyone named Demeter?"

The shit-eating grin froze and there was a pause.

"No."

"Then I don't believe you can be of any *a*-ssistance."

I stood up to leave, placing two dollar bills on the counter.

"For the welcome," I said. "Put it toward a new sign."

I turned to find a small, rat-featured guy in a worn blue denim jacket standing in front of me. His nose was dotted with blackheads and his teeth were prominent and yellow-stained like walrus tusks. His black baseball cap was marked with the words

Boyz N the Hood, but this wasn't any logo John Singleton would have liked. Instead of homies, the words were surrounded by the hooded heads of Klan figures.

Beneath his denim jacket, I could see the word *Pulaski* under a seal of some sort. Pulaski was the birthplace of the Ku Klux Klan and the site of an annual rally for Aryan crackers everywhere, although I bet the face of old Thom Robb, grand high ass-wipe of the Klan, must have just lit up at the sight of Rat Features and his pinched, subintelligent face arriving to take in the Pulaski air. After all, Robb was trying to make the Klan appeal to the educated elite, the lawyers and the schoolteachers. Most lawyers would have been reluctant to have Rat Features as a client, still less a brother in arms.

But there was probably still a place for Rat Features in the new Klan. Every organization needs its foot soldiers, and this one had cannon fodder written all over him. When the time came for the Boyz to storm the steps of the Capitol and reclaim the Jewnited States for their own, Rat Features would be in the front line, where he could be certain to lay down his life for the cause.

Behind him, the bearded pool player loomed, his eyes small, piggy, and dumb looking. His arms were enormous but without definition, and his gut bulged beneath a camouflage T-shirt. The T-shirt bore the legend *Kill 'em all—Let God sort 'em out,* but the big guy was no marine. He looked as close to retarded as you can get without someone coming by twice a day to feed you and clean up your mess.

"How you doin'?" said the Rat. The bar was quiet now and the group of men at the pool table were no longer lounging but stood rigid in anticipation of what was to come. One of them smiled and poked his neighbor with an elbow. Obviously, the Rat and his buddy were the local double act.

"Great till now."

He nodded as if I'd just said something deeply profound with which he had a natural empathy.

"You know," I said, "I once took a leak in Thom Robb's garden."

Which was true.

"It'd be better if you just got back on the road and kept driving, I reckon," said the Rat, after a pause to figure out who Thom Robb was. "So why don't you just do that?"

"Thanks for the advice." I moved to go past him but his pal put a hand like a shovel against my chest and pushed me back against the bar by flexing his wrist slightly.

"It wasn't advice," said the Rat. He gestured back at the big guy with his thumb.

"This here's Six. You don't get back in your fuckin' car now and start raisin' dust on the highway, Six is gonna fuck you up bad."

Six smiled dimly. The evolutionary curve obviously sloped pretty gently where Six came from.

"You know why he's called Six?"

"Let me guess," I replied. "There are another five assholes like him at home?"

It didn't look like I was going to find out how Six got his name, because he stopped smiling and lunged past the Rat, his hand clutching for my neck. He moved fast for a man his size, but not that fast. I brought my right foot up and released it heel first onto Six's left knee. There was a satisfying crunching sound, and Six faltered, his mouth wide with pain, and stumbled sideways and down.

His friends were already coming to his aid when there was a commotion from behind them and a small, tubby deputy in his late thirties pushed his way through, one hand on the butt of his pistol. It was Wallace, Deputy Dorito. He looked scared and edgy, the kind of guy who became a cop to give him some sort of advantage over the people who used to laugh at him in school, steal his lunch money, and beat him up, except he found that now those people still laughed at him and didn't look like they'd let the uniform stand in the way of another beating. Still, on this occasion he had a gun and maybe they figured he was scared enough to pull it on them.

"What's goin' on here, Clete?"

There was silence for a moment and then the Rat spoke up. "Just some high spirits got out of hand, Wallace. Ain't nothin' to concern the law."

"I wasn't talking to you, Gabe."

Someone helped Six to his feet and brought him to a chair.

"Looks like more than high spirits to me. I reckon you boys better come on down to the cells, cool off for a time."

"Let it go, Wallace," said a low voice. It came from a thin, wiry man with cold, dark eyes and a beard flecked with gray. He had an air of authority about him and an intelligence that went beyond the low cunning of his associates. He watched me carefully as he spoke, the way an undertaker might eye up a prospective client for his casket.

"Okay, Clete, but . . ." Deputy Dorito's words trailed off as he realized there was nothing he could say that would matter to any of the men before him. He nodded to the crowd, as if the decision not to pursue things any further had been his to make.

"You'd better leave, mister," he said, looking at me.

I stood up and walked slowly to the door. No one said anything as I left. Back at the motel, I rang Walter Cole to find out if anything had developed in the Stephen Barton killing, but he was out of the office and his machine was on at home. I left the number of the motel and tried to get some sleep.

CHAPTER XIX

The sky was gray and dark the next morning, heavy with impending rain. My suit was wrinkled from the previous day's travel, so I abandoned it for chinos, a white shirt, and a black jacket. I even dug out a black silk-knit tie, so I wouldn't look like a bum. I drove once through the town. There was no sign of a red jeep or the couple I had seen driving it.

I parked outside the Haven Diner, bought a copy of the *Washington Post* in the gas station across the road, and then went into the diner for breakfast. It was after nine but people still lounged around at the counter or at the tables, mumbling about the weather and, I guessed, about me, since some of them glanced knowingly in my direction, directing the attention of their neighbors toward me.

I sat at a table in the corner and scanned the paper. A mature woman in a white apron and blue uniform with *Dorothy* embossed at her left breast walked over to me carrying a pad and took my order of white toast, bacon, and coffee. She hovered over me after I finished ordering. "You the fella who whupped that Six boy in the bar last night?"

"That's me."

She nodded in satisfaction.

"I'll give you your breakfast for free, then." She smiled a hard smile, then added: "But don't you go confusin' my generosity with an invitation to stay. You ain't that good lookin'." She strolled back behind the counter and pinned my order to a wire.

There wasn't much traffic on Haven's main street, or much human activity in sight. Most of the cars and trucks seemed to be passing through on their way to someplace else. The town seemed to be permanently stuck in a grim Sunday morning.

I finished my food and left a tip on the table. Dorothy slouched forward over the counter, her breasts resting on its polished surface. "Bye now," she said as I left. The other diners briefly looked over their shoulders at me before returning to their breakfast and coffee.

I drove to the Haven Public Library, a new single-story building at the far side of the town. A pretty black woman in her early thirties stood behind the counter with an older white woman whose hair was like steel wool and who eyed me with obvious distaste as I entered.

"Morning," I said. The younger woman smiled slightly anxiously while the older one tried to tidy the already immaculate area behind the counter. "What's the local paper around here?"

"Used to be the *Haven Leader*," answered the younger woman after a slight pause. "It's gone now."

"I was looking for something older, back issues."

She glanced at the other woman as if for guidance, but she continued to shift pieces of paper behind the counter.

"They're on microfiche, in the cabinets beside the viewer. How far back do you want to go?"

"Not far," I said, and strolled over to the cabinets. The *Leader* files were arranged in date order in small square boxes in ten drawers, but the boxes of files for the years of the Haven killings were not in their place. I ran through them all, in case they had been misfiled, although I had a feeling that those files weren't available to the casual visitor.

I returned to the counter. The elderly woman was no longer in sight.

"The files I'm looking for don't appear to be there," I said. The younger girl looked confused but I didn't get the impression that she was.

"What year were you looking for?"

"Years. Nineteen sixty-nine, nineteen seventy, maybe nineteen seventy-one."

"I'm sorry, those files aren't"—she seemed to search for an excuse that might be plausible—"available. They've been borrowed for research."

"Oh," I said. I smiled my best smile. "Never mind, I'll manage with what's there."

She seemed relieved and I returned to the viewer, idly flicking through the files for anything useful with no return other than boredom. It took thirty minutes before the opportunity presented itself. A party of schoolchildren entered the junior section of the library, separated from the adult section by a half-wood, half-glass screen. The younger woman followed them and stood with her back to me, talking to the children and their teacher, a young blonde who didn't look long out of school herself.

There was no sign of the older woman, although a brown door was half open in the small lobby beyond the adult section. I slipped behind the counter and began rifling through drawers and cupboards as quietly as I could. At one point I passed, crouching, by the entry door to the junior section, but the librarian was still dealing with her young clients.

I found the missing files in a bottom drawer, beside a small coin box. I slipped them into my jacket pockets and was just leaving the counter area when the office door outside slammed and I heard soft footsteps approaching. I darted beside a shelf as the senior librarian entered. She stopped short at the entrance to the counter and shot an unpleasant look in my direction and at the book in my hand. I smiled gamely and returned to the viewer. I wasn't sure how long it would be before the dragon behind the counter checked that drawer and decided to call for backup.

I tried the 1969 files first. It took some time, even though the *Haven Leader* had been only a weekly newspaper in 1969. There was nothing about any disappearances in the paper. Even in 1969, it seemed that black folks didn't count for much. The paper contained a lot about church socials, history society lectures, and local weddings. There was some minor crime stuff, mostly traffic offenses and drunk-and-disorderlies, but nothing that might lead a casual reader to suppose that children were disappearing in the town of Haven.

Then, in a November issue, I came upon a reference to a man named Walt Tyler. There was a picture of Tyler beside the piece, a good-looking man being led away in handcuffs by a white deputy. *Man Held in Sheriff Attack*, read the headline above the picture. The details contained in the piece below were sketchy but it seemed Tyler had come into the Sheriff's Office and started busting the place up before taking a swing at the sheriff himself. The only indication of a reason for the attack came in the last paragraph.

"Tyler was among a number of Negroes questioned by the Sheriff's Office in connection with the disappearance of his daughter and two other children. He was released without charge."

The 1970 files were more productive. On the night of February 8, 1970, Amy Demeter had disappeared after heading out to a friend's house to deliver a sample of her mother's jam. She never made it to the house and the jar was found broken on a sidewalk about five hundred yards from her home. A picture of her was printed beside the story, along with details of what she had been wearing and a brief history of the family: father Earl an accountant, mother Dorothy a housewife and a schoolteacher, younger sister Catherine a well-liked child with some artistic potential. The story ran for the next few weeks: *Search Goes On for Haven Girl; Five More Questioned in Demeter Mystery;* and, finally, *Little Hope Left for Amy.*

I spent another half hour going back and forth through the *Haven Leader* but there was nothing more on the killings or their resolution, if any. The only indication was a report of the death of Adelaide Modine in a fire four months later, with a reference to her brother's death buried in the piece. There was no description of the circumstances of the death of either, but there was one hint, once again in the last paragraph. "The Haven Sheriff's Office had been anxious to talk to both Adelaide and William Modine in their ongoing investigation into the disappearance of Amy Demeter and a number of other children."

It didn't take a genius to read between the lines and see that either Adelaide Modine or her brother William, or possibly both, had been the main suspects. Local newspapers don't necessarily print all the news; there are some things everyone knows already and sometimes the local press merely prints enough to throw outsiders off the scent. The old librarian was giving me the evil eye so I finished printing off copies of the relevant articles, then gathered them and left.

A Haven County Sheriff's Office cruiser, a brown-and-yellow Crown Victoria, was pulled up in front of my car and a deputy, wearing a clean, well-pressed uniform, was leaning against my driver's door, waiting. As I drew closer I could see the long muscles beneath his shirt. His eyes were dull and lifeless. He looked like an asshole. A fit asshole.

"This your car?" he asked in a Virginia drawl, his thumbs tucked inside a gun belt that glittered with the spotless tools of his trade. On his chest, the name *Burns* stood out on his perfectly straight identity badge.

"Sure is," I said, mimicking his accent. It was a bad habit I had. His jaw tightened, if it was actually possible for it to tighten more than it was already.

"Hear you were looking up some old newspapers?"

"I'm a crossword fan. They were better in the old days."

"You another writer?"

Judging from his tone I didn't think he read much, at least nothing that didn't have pictures or a message from God. "No," I said. "You get a lot of writers around here?"

I don't think he believed I wasn't a writer. Maybe I looked bookish to him or maybe anyone with whom he wasn't personally acquainted was immediately suspected of covert literary leanings. The librarian had sold me out, believing me to be simply another hack trying to make a buck out of the ghosts of Haven's past.

"I'm escorting you to the town line," he said. "I've got your bag." He moved to the patrol car and took my traveling bag from the front seat. I was starting to get very tired of Deputy Burns.

"I'm not planning on leaving just yet," I said, "so maybe you could put it back in my room. By the way, when you're unpacking, I like my socks on the left side of the drawer."

He dropped the bag on the road and started toward me. "Look," I began, "I have ID." I reached into the inside pocket of my jacket. "I'm—"

It was a dumb thing to do but I was hot and tired and pissed at Deputy Burns, and I wasn't thinking straight. He caught one flash of the butt of my gun and his own piece was in his hands. Burns was quick. He probably practiced in front of the mirror. Within seconds I was up against his car, my gun was gone, and Deputy Burns's shiny cuffs were biting into my wrists.

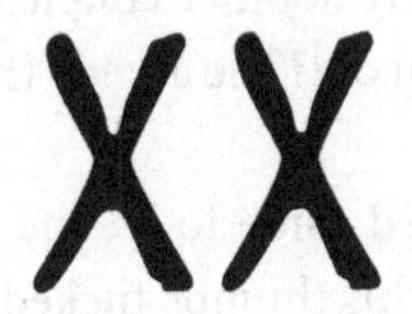

CHAPTER XX

I was left cooling my heels in a cell for what I reckoned to be three or four hours, since the careful Deputy Burns had taken my watch along with my gun, my wallet and ID, my notes, and my belt and laces, in case I decided to hang myself in a fit of remorse for annoying the librarians. These had been entrusted to the safe care of Deputy Wallace, who made some passing reference to Burns of my involvement in the previous night's incident in the bar.

Still, the cell was just about the cleanest one I had ever visited in my life—even the can looked like it could safely be used without needing a course of penicillin later. I passed the time by mulling over what I had learned from the library microfiche, trying to fit the pieces of the puzzle into some recognizable picture and refusing to let my mind drift to the Traveling Man and what he might be doing.

Eventually there was a noise outside and the cell door opened. I looked up to see a tall black man in a uniform shirt watching me. He looked to be in his late thirties but something about the way he walked and the light of experience in his eyes told me he was older. I guessed he might have boxed at one time, probably middle to light-heavy, and he moved gracefully on his feet. He looked smarter than Wallace and Burns put together, although no one was likely to hand out gold stars for that particular feat. This, I guessed, was Alvin Martin. I didn't rush to get up, in case he thought I didn't like his nice, clean cell.

"You want to stay there another couple of hours, or you waiting for someone to carry you out?" he asked. The voice wasn't Southern; Detroit, Chicago maybe.

I stood and he moved aside to let me pass. Wallace waited at the end of the corridor, his thumbs tucked into his belt to take the weight off his shoulders.

"Give him back his things, Deputy."

"Even his gun?" asked Wallace, not making a move to do as he was told. Wallace had that look about him, the look that told you he wasn't used to taking orders from a black guy and didn't like it when he had to. It struck me that he might have more in common with the Rat and his friends than was really wise for a conscientious lawman.

"Even his gun," replied Martin calmly but wearily, giving Wallace the eye. Wallace shoved off from the wall like a particularly ugly ship setting out to sea and steamed behind the counter, surfacing eventually with a brown envelope and my gun. I signed and Martin nodded me toward the door.

"Get in the car, please, Mr. Parker." Outside, the light was starting to fade and there was a cool wind blowing from the hills. A pickup rattled by on the road beyond, a covered shotgun rack on the back guarded by a mangy hound.

"Back or front?" I asked.

"Get in the front," he replied. "I trust you."

He started the cruiser and we drove for a time in silence, the a/c blasting cool air into our faces and onto our feet. The town limits receded behind us and we entered woods thick with trees, the road twisting and winding as it followed the contours of the land. Then, in the distance, a light shone. We pulled up in the parking lot of a white diner, topped by a green neon sign blinking *Green River Eatery* on the road beyond.

We took a booth at the rear, far away from the handful of other patrons, who cast curious glances at us before returning to their food. Martin took off his hat, ordered coffee for both of us, then sat back and looked at me. "It's usually considered good manners for an unlicensed investigator packing a pistol to drop into the local lawmen and state his business, at least before he goes around beating up pool players and stealing library files," he said.

"You weren't around when I called," I said. "Neither was the sheriff, and your friend Wallace wasn't too keen on offering me cookies and swapping race jokes."

The coffee arrived. Martin added creamer and sugar to his. I stuck with milk.

"I made some calls about you," said Martin, stirring his coffee. "A guy called Cole vouched for you. That's why I'm not kicking your ass out of town, least not yet. That and the fact that you weren't afraid to whip some cracker ass in the bar last night. Shows you got a sense of civic pride. So maybe now you'd like to tell me why you're here."

"I'm looking for a woman named Catherine Demeter. I think she might have come to Haven in the last week."

Martin's brow furrowed.

"She anything to Amy Demeter?"

"Sister."

"I figured. Why do you think she might be here?"

"The last call she made from her apartment was to the home of Sheriff Earl Lee Granger. She made a number of calls to your office as well the same night. Since then, there's been no sign of her."

"You hired to find her?"

"I'm just looking for her," I replied neutrally.

Martin sighed.

"I came here from Detroit six months ago," he said after about a minute of silence. "Brought my wife and child. My wife's an assistant librarian. I think you may have met her."

I nodded.

"The governor decided there weren't enough blacks in the police force here and that relations between the local minority population and the cops might not be the best. So, a post came up here and I applied, mainly to get my kid away from Detroit. My father came from Gretna, just a ways from here. I didn't know about the killings before I came here. I know more now.

"This town died along with those kids. No new people came to live here and anyone with an ounce of sense or ambition got the hell out. Now the gene pool here's so shallow you couldn't drown a rat in it.

"In the last month or two there's been signs that something might happen to change that. There's a Japanese firm interested in locating around half a mile out of town. They do research and development of computer software, I hear, and they like the idea of privacy and a quiet little backwater they can call Nippon. They'd bring a lot of money to this town, a lot of jobs for locals, and maybe a chance to put the past to rest. Frankly, the people here don't much care for the idea of working for the Japanese but they know they're sucking shit as it is, so they'll work for anyone as long as he's not black.

"The last thing they want is someone sniffing around ancient history, digging up the past to come up with the bones of dead children. They may be dumb in a lot of cases. They may also be racists and shit kickers and wife beaters, but they're desperate for a second chance and they'll mess up anyone who gets in their way. If they don't do it, Earl Lee will."

He raised a finger and waved it purposefully in my face. "Do you understand what I'm saying here? Nobody wants questions asked about child killings that took place thirty years ago. If Catherine Demeter came back here, and frankly I don't know why she would since she ain't got no one here to come back to, then she wouldn't be welcome either. But she ain't here, because if she had come back it would be all over this town like shit on a shoe."

He took a sip of his coffee and gritted his teeth. "Damn, it's cold." He gestured to the waitress and called for a fresh mug.

"I don't want to stay here any longer than I have to," I said. "But I think Catherine Demeter may have come back here, or tried to come back here. She certainly wanted to talk to the sheriff and I want to talk to him too. So where is he?"

"He took a couple of days' leave to get out of town for a while," said Martin, twisting the brim of his hat so that the hat spun on the vinyl seat. "He's due back—well, he was due back today but he may leave it until tomorrow. We don't have too much crime here beyond drunks and domestics and the usual shit that goes with a place like this. But he may not be too pleased to see you waiting for him when he returns. I'm not so pleased to see you myself, no offense meant."

"None taken. I think I'll wait around for the sheriff anyway." I was also going to have to find out more about the Modine killings, whether Martin liked it or not. If Catherine Demeter had reached into her past, then I was going to have to reach into that past too, or I would understand nothing about the woman for whom I was searching.

"I'll also need to talk to someone about the killings. I need to know more."

Martin closed his eyes and ran his hand over them in weariness. "You're not listening to me . . . ," he began.

"No, *you're* not listening. I'm looking for a woman who may be in trouble and who may have turned to someone here for help. Before I leave town I'm going to find out whether or not she's here, even if it means rattling every cage in this godforsaken dump and scaring your Japanese saviors back to Tokyo. But if you help me, then this can all be done quietly and I'll be out of your hair in a couple of days."

We were both tensed now, leaning toward each other across the table. Some of the other diners were staring at us, their food ignored. Martin looked around at them, then turned back to me again. "Okay," he said. "Most of the people who were around then and might know something useful have either left, or died, or won't talk about it for love or money. There are two who might, though. One is the son of the doc who was around at that time. His name's Connell Hyams and he has a law office in town. You'll have to approach him yourself.

"The other is Walt Tyler. His daughter was the first to die and he lives outside town. I'll talk to him first and maybe he'll see you." He stood up to leave. "When you've got your business done you'd better leave, and I never want to see your face again, understand?"

I said nothing and followed him toward the door. He stopped and turned toward me, placing his hat on his head as he did so. "One more thing," he said. "I've had a word with those boys from the bar, but remember, they ain't got no reason to like you. Frankly, I can see a lot of people thinking the same way once they know why you're here. And they're going to find out. So, you'd best step lightly while you're in town."

"I noticed one of them, I think his name was Gabe, had a Klan shirt on," I said. "You got much of that around here?"

Martin blew breath heavily from puffed cheeks. "There's no klavern, but in a poor town, the dumb ones always look for someone to blame for being poor."

"There was one guy—your deputy called him Clete—who didn't look so dumb."

Martin eyed me from under his hat brim. "No, Clete's not dumb. He sits on the council, says the only way anyone's gonna get him off it is with a gun barrel. Whipping you could be good for another twenty, thirty votes, if he had a mind to do it. Shit, maybe he'll send you a campaign badge.

"But as for the Klan, this ain't Georgia or North Carolina, or even Delaware. Don't go reading too much into this. You can pay for the coffee."

I left a couple of bucks at the till and walked out toward the car, but Martin was already pulling away. I noticed that he'd taken his hat off again inside the car. The man just didn't seem comfortable with that damn hat. I went back into the diner, called Haven's only cab operator, and ordered another coffee.

CHAPTER

It was after six when I got back to the motel. Connell Hyams's office and home address were listed but when I drove by his office all the lights were out. I called Rudy Fry at the motel and got directions for Bale's Farm Road, where not only Hyams but also Sheriff Earl Lee Granger had homes.

I drove cautiously along the winding roads, looking for the concealed entrance Fry had mentioned and still glancing occasionally in my mirror for any sign of the red jeep. There was none. I passed the entrance to Bale's Farm Road once without seeing it and had to go back over my tracks again. The sign was semiobscured by undergrowth and pointed toward a winding, rutted track heavy with evergreens, which eventually opened out on a small but well-kept row of houses with long yards and what looked like plenty of space out back. Hyams's home was near the end, a large, two-story white wooden house. A lamp blazed by a screen door, which shielded a solid oak front door with a fan of frosted glass near the top. There was a light on in the hallway.

A gray-haired man, wearing a red wool cardigan over gray slacks and a striped, open-necked shirt, opened the inner door as I pulled up and watched me with mild curiosity.

"Mr. Hyams?" I said as I approached the door.

"Yes?"

"I'm an investigator. My name's Parker. I wanted to talk to you about Catherine Demeter."

He paused for a long time in silence with the screen door between us.

"Catherine, or her sister?" he inquired eventually.

"Both, I guess."

"May I ask why?"

"I'm trying to find Catherine. I think she may have come back here."

Hyams opened the screen door and stood aside to let me enter. Inside, the house was furnished in dark wood, with large, expensive-looking mats on the floors. He led me into an office at the back of the house, where papers were strewn over a desk on which a computer screen glowed.

"Can I offer you a drink?" he asked.

"No. Thank you."

He took a brandy glass from his desk and gestured me toward a chair at the other side before seating himself. I could see him more clearly now. He was grave and patrician in appearance, his hands long and slim, the nails finely manicured. The room was warm and I could smell his cologne. It smelled expensive.

"That all took place a long time ago," he began. "Most people would rather not talk about it."

"Are you 'most people'?"

He shrugged and smiled. "I have a place in this community and a role to play. I've lived here almost all my life, apart from the time I spent in college and in practice in Richmond. My father spent fifty years practicing here and kept working until the day he died."

"He was the doctor, I understand."

"Doctor, counselor, legal adviser, even dentist when the resident dentist wasn't around. He did everything. The killings hit him particularly hard. He helped perform the autopsies on the bodies. I don't think he ever forgot it, not even in his sleep."

"And you? Were you around when they took place?"

"I was working in Richmond at the time, so I was back and

forth between Haven and Richmond. I knew of what took place here, yes, but I'd really rather not talk about it. Four children died and they were terrible deaths. Best to let them rest now."

"Do you remember Catherine Demeter?"

"I knew the family, yes, but Catherine would have been much younger than I. She left after graduating from high school, as I recall, and I don't think she ever came back, except to attend the funerals of her parents. The last time she returned was probably ten years ago at the very least and her family home has been sold since then. I supervised the sale. Why do you believe she might have come back now? There's nothing here for her, nothing good at any rate."

"I'm not sure. She made some calls to here recently and hasn't been seen since."

"It's not much to go on."

"No," I admitted, "it's not."

He twisted the glass in his hand, watching the amber liquid swirl. His lips were pursed in appraisal but his gaze went through the glass and rested on me.

"What can you tell me about Adelaide Modine and her brother?"

"I can tell you that, from my point of view, there was nothing about them that might have led one to suspect that they were child killers. Their father was a strange man, a philanthropist of sorts, I suppose. He left most of his money tied up in a trust when he died."

"He died before the killings?"

"Five or six years before, yes. He left instructions that the interest on the trust fund should be divided among certain charities in perpetuity. Since then, the number of charities receiving donations has increased considerably. I should know, since it is my duty to administer the trust, with the assistance of a small committee."

"And his daughter and son? Were they provided for?"

"Very adequately, I understand."

"What happened to their money, their property, when they died?"

"The state brought an action to take over the property and assets. We contested it on behalf of the townspeople and eventually an agreement was reached. The land was sold and all assets absorbed into the trust, with a portion of the trust used to fund new developments in the town. That is why we have a good library, our own modern sheriff's office, a fine school, a top-class medical center. This town doesn't have much, but what it does have comes from the trust."

"What it has, good or otherwise, comes from four dead children," I replied. "Can you tell me anything more about Adelaide and William Modine?"

Hyams's mouth twitched slightly. "As I've said, it was a long time ago and I really would prefer not to go into it. I had very little to do with either of them; the Modines were a wealthy family, their children went to a private school. We didn't mix very much, I'm afraid."

"Did your father know the family?"

"My father delivered both William and Adelaide. I do remember one curious thing, but it will hardly be of any great help to you: Adelaide was one of twins. The male twin died in the womb and their mother died from complications shortly after the birth. The mother's death was surprising. She was a strong, domineering woman. My father thought she'd outlive us all." He took a long sip from his glass and his eyes grew sharp with a remembered perception. "Do you know anything about hyenas, Mr. Parker?"

"Very little," I admitted.

"Spotted hyenas frequently have twins. The cubs are extremely well developed at birth: they have fur and sharp incisor teeth. One cub will almost invariably attack the other, sometimes while still in the amniotic sac. Death is usually the result. The victor is also typically female and, if she is the daughter of a dominant female, will in turn become the dominant female in the pack. It's a matriarchal culture. Female spotted hyena fetuses have higher levels of testosterone than adult males, and the females have masculine characteristics, even in the womb. Even in adulthood the sexes can be difficult to differentiate."

He put his glass down. "My father was an avid amateur naturalist. The animal world always fascinated him and I think he liked to find points of comparison between the animal world and the human world."

"And he found one in Adelaide Modine?"

"Perhaps, in some ways. He was not fond of her."

"Were you here when the Modines died?"

"I returned home the evening before Adelaide Modine's body was found and I attended the autopsy. Call it gruesome curiosity. Now, I'm sorry, Mr. Parker, but I have nothing more to say and a great deal of work to do."

He led me to the door and pushed open the screen to let me out.

"You don't seem particularly anxious to help me find Catherine Demeter, Mr. Hyams."

He breathed in heavily. "Who suggested that you talk to me, Mr. Parker?"

"Alvin Martin mentioned your name."

"Mr. Martin is a good, conscientious deputy and an asset to this town, but he is still a comparatively recent arrival," said Hyams. "The reason why I am reluctant to talk is a matter of client confidentiality. Mr. Parker, I am the only lawyer in this town. At some point, nearly everyone who lives here, regardless of color, income, religious or political belief, has passed through the door of my office. That includes the parents of the children who died. I know a great deal about what happened here, Mr. Parker, more than I might wish to know and certainly much more than I plan to share with you. I'm sorry, but that's the end of the matter."

"I see. One more thing, Mr. Hyams."

"Yes?" he asked, wearily.

"Sheriff Granger lives on this road too, doesn't he?"

"Sheriff Granger lives next door, the house on the right here. This house has never been burgled, Mr. Parker, a fact that is surely not unconnected. Good night."

He stood at the screen door as I drove away. I cast a glance at the sheriff's house as I passed but there were no lights within and there was no car in the yard. As I drove back to Haven, raindrops began to strike the windshield and by the time I reached the outskirts of the town it had turned into a harsh, ceaseless downpour. The lights of the motel appeared through the rain. I could see Rudy Fry standing at the door, staring out into the woods and the gathering darkness beyond.

By the time I had parked, Fry had resumed his position behind the reception desk.

"What do folks do around here for fun, apart from trying to run other folks out of town?" I asked.

Fry grimaced as he tried to separate the sarcasm from the substance of the question. "There ain't much to do around here outside of drinking at the Inn," he replied, after a while.

"I tried that. Didn't care for it."

He thought for a little while longer. I waited for the smell of smoke but it didn't come.

"There's a restaurant in Dorien, 'bout twenty miles east of here. Milano's, it's called. It's Italian." He pronounced it *Eye-talian,* in a tone that suggested Rudy Fry was not overfond of any Italian food that didn't come in a box with grease dripping from the vents. "Never eaten there myself." He sniffed, as if to confirm his suspicion of all things European.

I thanked him, then went to my room, showered, and changed. I was getting tired of the unrelenting hostility of Haven. If Rudy Fry didn't like somewhere, then that was somewhere I probably wanted to be. I checked the parking lot carefully before I stepped out and then I was leaving Haven behind and heading for Dorien.

Dorien wasn't much bigger than Haven but it had a bookstore and a couple of restaurants, which made it a cultural oasis of sorts. I bought a typescript copy of e. e. cummings in the bookstore and wandered into Milano's to eat.

Milano's had red-and-white check tablecloths and candles set in miniatures of the Colosseum, but it was almost full and the food looked pretty good. A slim maitre d' in a red bow tie bustled over and showed me to a table in the corner where I wouldn't scare the other diners. I took out the copy of cummings to reassure them and read "somewhere i have never traveled" while I waited for a menu, enjoying the cadence and gentle eroticism of the poem.

Susan had never read cummings before we met, and I sent her copies of his poems during the early days of our relationship. In a sense, I let cummings do my courting for me. I think I even incorporated a line of cummings into the first letter I sent her. When I look back on it, it was as much a prayer as a love letter, a prayer that Time would be gentle with her, because she was very beautiful.

A waiter strolled over and I ordered bruschetta and a carbonara from the menu, with water. I cast a glance around the restaurant but no one seemed to be paying me much attention, which was fine with me. I had not forgotten the warning Angel and Louis had given to me, or the couple in the red jeep.

The food, when it arrived, was excellent. I was surprised at my appetite, and while I ate, I turned over in my mind what I had learned from Hyams and the microfiche, and I remembered the handsome face of Walt Tyler, surrounded by police.

And I wondered, too, about the Traveling Man, before forcing him from my mind along with the images that came with him. Then I got back in my car and returned to Haven.

CHAPTER XXII

My grandfather used to say that the most terrifying sound in the world was the sound of a shell being loaded into a pump-action shotgun, a shell that was meant for you. It woke me from my sleep in the motel as they came up the stairs, the hands of my watch glowing the time at 3:30 A.M. They came through the door seconds later, the sound of the explosions deafeningly loud in the silence of the night as shot after shot was fired into my bed, sending feathers and shreds of cotton into the air like a cloud of white moths.

But by then I was already on my feet, my gun in my hand. The sound of the shots was blocked slightly by the closed connecting door, just as the sound of the door opening into the hall was blocked from them, even when the firing had stopped and their ears sang with the hard notes of the gun. The decision not to make myself an easy target by sleeping in my assigned room had paid off.

I came into the hall quickly, turned, and aimed. The man from the red jeep stood in the hall, the barrel of the Ithaca 12 gauge pump close to his face. Even in the dim hall light I could see that there were no shell casings on the ground at his feet. It had been the woman who fired the shots.

Now he spun toward me as the woman swore from inside the

room. The barrel of the shotgun came down as he turned in my direction. I fired one shot and a dark rose bloomed at his throat and blood fell like a shower of petals on his white shirt. The shotgun dropped to the carpet as his hands clutched for his neck. He folded to his knees and fell flat on the floor, his body thrashing and jerking like a fish on dry ground.

The barrel of a shotgun appeared from behind the doorjamb and the woman fired indiscriminately into the hall, plaster leaping from the walls. I felt a tug at my right shoulder and then sharp white pain through my arm. I tried to hold on to my gun but I lost it on the ground as the woman continued firing, deadly shot zinging through the air and exploding into the walls around me.

I ran down the hall and through the door leading to the fire stairs, tripping and tumbling down the steps as the shooting stopped. I knew she would come after me as soon as she had made certain that her partner was dead. If there had been any chance of him surviving, I think she might have tried to save him, and herself.

I made it to the second floor but I could hear her steps pounding on the stairs above me. The pain in my arm was intense and I felt certain she would reach me before I got to the ground level.

I slipped through the door into the hallway. Plastic sheeting lay upon the ground and two stepladders stood like steeples at either wall. The air was heavy with the smell of paint and thinner. Twenty feet from the door was a small alcove, almost invisible until you were upon it, which contained a fire hose and a heavy, old-fashioned water-based extinguisher. There was an identical alcove near my own room. I slipped into it, leaning against the wall and trying to control my breathing. Lifting the extinguisher with my left hand, I tried to hold it underneath with my right in a vain effort to use it as a weapon, but my arm, bleeding heavily by now, was useless and the extinguisher was too awkward to be effective. I heard the woman's steps slowing and the door sighed softly as she moved into the hall. I listened to her steps on the plastic. There was a loud bang as she kicked open the door of the first room on the floor, then a second bang as she repeated the exercise at the next door. She was almost upon me now, and though she walked softly, the plastic betrayed her. I could feel blood pouring down my arm and dripping from the ends of my fingers as I unwound the hose and waited for her to come.

She was almost level with the alcove when I swung the hose forward like a whip. The heavy brass nozzle caught her in the middle of her face and I heard bone crunch. She staggered back, harmlessly loosing off a blast from the shotgun as she raised her left hand instinctively to her face. I swung the hose again, the rubber glancing against her outstretched hand while the nozzle connected with the side of her head. She moaned and I slipped from the alcove as quickly as I could, the brass nozzle of the hose now in my left hand, and wrapped the rubber around her neck like the coils of a snake.

She tried to move her hand on the shotgun, the stock against her thigh, in an effort to pump a cartridge as blood from her battered face flowed between the fingers of her right hand. I kicked hard at the gun and it fell from her hands as I pulled her tightly against my body, bracing myself against the wall, one leg entwined with hers so she could not pull away, the other holding the hose pipe taut. And there we stood like lovers, the nozzle now warm with blood in my hand and the hose tight against my wrist, as she struggled and then went limp in my grip.

When she stopped moving I released her and she slumped to the ground. I unwound the hose from her neck, and, taking her by the hand, I pulled her down the stairs to ground level. Her face was reddish purple and I realized I had come close to killing her, but I still wanted her where I could see her.

Rudy Fry lay gray on the floor of his office, blood congealing on his face and around the dent in his fractured skull. I called the sheriff's office and, minutes later, heard the sirens and saw the red-and-blue glow of the lights spinning and reflecting around the darkened lobby, the blood and the lights reminding me once again of another night and other deaths. When Alvin Martin entered with his gun in his hand I was nauseous with shock and barely able to stand, the red light like fire in my eyes.

"YOU'RE A LUCKY MAN," said the elderly doctor, her smile a mixture of surprise and concern. "Another couple of inches and Alvin here would have been composing a eulogy."

"I bet that would have been something to hear," I replied.

I was sitting on a table in the emergency room of Haven's small but well-equipped medical center. The wound in my arm was minor but had bled heavily. Now it had been cleaned and bandaged, and my good hand clutched a bottle of painkillers. I felt like I'd been sideswiped by a passing train.

Alvin Martin stood beside me. Wallace and another deputy I didn't recognize were down the hall, guarding the room in which the woman was being kept. She had not regained consciousness, and from what I had heard of the doctor's hurried conversation with Martin, I believed that she might have lapsed into a coma. Rudy Fry was also still unconscious, although he was expected to recover from his injuries.

"Anything on the shooters?" I asked Martin.

"Not yet. We've sent photos and prints to the feds. They're going to send someone from Richmond later today." The clock on the wall read 6:45 A.M. Outside the rain continued to fall.

Martin turned to the doctor. "Could you give us a minute or two in private, Elise?"

"Certainly. Don't strain him, though." He smiled at her as she left, but when he turned back to me the smile was gone. "You came here with a price on your head?"

"I'd heard a rumor, that's all."

"Fuck you and your rumor. Rudy Fry almost died in there and I've got an unidentified corpse in the morgue with a hole in his neck. You know who called out the hit?"

"I know who did it."

"You gonna tell me?"

"No, not yet anyway. I'm not going to tell the feds, either. I need you to keep them off my back for a while."

Martin almost laughed. "Now, why am I gonna do that?"

"I need to finish what I came down here to do. I need to find Catherine Demeter."

"This shooting have anything to do with her?"

"I don't know. It could have but I don't see where she fits in. I need your help."

Martin bit his lip. "The town council's running wild. They reckon if the Japanese get wind of this they'll open up a plant in White Sands before they come here. Everyone wants you gone. In fact, they want you arrested, beaten, then gone."

A nurse entered the room and Martin stopped talking, preferring instead to seethe quietly as she spoke. "There's a call for you, Mr. Parker," she said. "A Lieutenant Cole from New York."

I winced at the pain in my arm as I rose, and she seemed to take pity on me. I wasn't above accepting pity at that point.

"Stay where you are," she said with a smile. "I'll bring in an extension and we can patch the call through."

She returned minutes later with the phone and plugged the jack into a box on the wall. Alvin Martin hovered uncertainly for a moment beside me and then stomped out, leaving me alone.

"Walter?"

"A deputy called. What happened?"

"Two of them tried to take me out in the motel. A man and a woman."

"How badly are you hurt?"

"A nick on the arm. Nothing too serious."

"The shooters get away?"

"Nope. The guy's dead. The woman's in a coma, I think. They're patching in the pics and the prints at the moment. Anything at your end? Anything on Jennifer?" I tried to block out the image of her face but it hung at the edge of my consciousness, like a figure glimpsed at the periphery of one's vision.

"The jar was spotless. It was a standard medical storage jar.

We've tried checking the batch number with the manufacturers but they went out of business in nineteen ninety-two. We'll keep trying, see if we can access old records, but the chances are slim. The wrapping paper must be sold in every damn gift shop in the country. Again, no prints. The lab is looking at skin samples to see if we can pick up anything from them. Technical guys figure he bounced the call—no other way the cell phone could have shown a callbox number—and there's probably no way we can trace it. I'll let you know if there's anything further."

"And Stephen Barton?"

"Nothing there either. The amount I know, I'm starting to think that I may be in the wrong business. He was knocked unconscious by a blow to the head, like the ME said, and then strangled. Probably driven to the parking lot and tipped into the sewer."

"The feds still looking for Sonny?"

"I haven't heard otherwise but I assume they're out of luck too."

"There doesn't seem to be much luck around at the moment."

"It'll break."

"Does Kooper know what happened here?"

I could hear what sounded like a choked laugh at the other end of the line. "Not yet. Maybe I'll tell him later in the morning. Once the name of the trust is kept out of it he should be okay, but I don't know how he feels about the hired help whacking people outside motel rooms. I don't imagine it's happened before. What's the situation at your end?"

"The natives aren't exactly greeting me with open arms and leis. No sign of her so far, but something isn't sitting right here. I can't explain it, but everything feels wrong."

He sighed. "Keep in touch. Anything I can do here?"

"I guess there's no way you can keep Ross off my back?"

"None whatsoever. Ross couldn't dislike you more if he heard that you screwed his mother and wrote her name on the wall of the men's room. He's on his way."

Walter hung up. Seconds later, there was a click on the line. I kind of guessed Deputy Martin might be the cautious sort. He came back in after allowing enough time to elapse so that it didn't look like he'd been listening. The expression on his face had changed, though. Maybe it hadn't been such a bad thing that Martin heard what he did.

"I need to find Catherine Demeter," I said. "That's why I'm here. When that's done, I'll be gone."

He nodded.

"I had Burns call some of the motels in the area earlier," he said. "There's no Catherine Demeter checked in at any of them."

"I checked before I left the city. She could be using another name."

"I thought of that. If you give me a description, I'll send Burns around to talk to the desk clerks."

"Thanks."

"Believe me, I ain't doing this out of the kindness of my heart. I just want to see you gone from here."

"What about Walt Tyler?"

"If we get time, I'll drive out there with you later." He went to check with the deputies guarding the shooter. The elderly doctor appeared again and checked the dressing on my arm.

"Are you sure you won't rest up here for a while?" she asked.

I thanked her for the offer but turned her down.

"I partly guessed as much," she said. She nodded toward the vial of painkillers. "They may make you drowsy."

I thanked her for the warning and slipped them in my pocket as she helped me to put on my jacket over my shirtless chest. I had no intention of taking the painkillers. Her expression told me that she knew that as well.

Martin drove me to the sheriff's office. The motel had been sealed up and my clothes had been moved to a cell. I showered, wrapping my bandaged arm with plastic first, and then slept fitfully in the cell until the rain stopped falling.

TWO FEDERAL AGENTS ARRIVED shortly after midday and questioned me about what had taken place. The questioning was perfunctory, which surprised me until I remembered that Special Agent Ross was due to fly in later that evening. The woman had still not regained consciousness by 5:00 P.M., when Martin came into the Haven Diner.

"Did Burns turn up anything on Catherine Demeter?"

"Burns has been tied up with the feds since this afternoon. He said he'd check some of the motels before calling it a day. He'll let me know if there's any sign of her. You still want to see Walt Tyler, we'd better get going now."

CHAPTER

XXIII

Walt Tyler lived in a dilapidated but clean white clapboard house, against one side of which leaned a teetering pile of car tires that were, according to a sign on the road, *For Sale.* Other items of varying degrees of sellability that rested on the gravel and the well-trimmed lawn included two semirestored mowers, various engines and parts of engines, and some rusting gym equipment, including a full set of bars and weights.

Tyler himself was a tall, slightly stooped man with a full head of gray hair. He had been handsome once, as his picture had suggested, and he still held himself with a kind of loose-limbed grace, as if unwilling to admit that those looks were now largely gone, lost to cares and worries and the never-ending sorrow of a parent who has lost an only child.

He greeted Alvin warmly enough, although he shook my hand less cordially and seemed reluctant to invite us in. Instead he suggested that we sit on the porch, despite the prospect of further rain. Tyler sat in a comfortable-looking wicker chair and Martin and I on two ornate metal lawn chairs, the lost elements of a more complete set and also, according to the sign hung from the back of mine, *For Sale.*

Without Tyler making any effort to ask for it, coffee was brought out in clean china cups by a woman younger than he by maybe ten years. She, too, had been more beautiful once, although in her the beauty of youth had matured into something perhaps more attractive yet, the calm elegance of a woman for whom old age held no fears and in whom lines and wrinkles would alter but not erase her looks. She cast a glance at Tyler, and for the first time since we arrived, he smiled slightly. She returned the smile and went back into the house. We didn't see her on the porch again.

The deputy began to speak but Tyler stopped him with a slight movement of his hand. "I know why you're here, Deputy. There's only one reason why you'd bring a stranger to my home." He looked hard at me, his eyes yellowing and rimmed with red but with an interested, almost amused, look in them.

"You the fella been shooting up folks in the motel?" he asked, and the smile flickered briefly. "Excitin' life you lead. Your shoulder hurt?"

"A little."

"I was shot once, in Korea. Shot in the thigh. Hurt more'n a little. Hurt like hell." He winced exaggeratedly at the memory and then was quiet again. I heard thunder rumble above us, and the porch seemed to grow dark for a time, but I could still see Walt Tyler looking at me and now the smile was gone.

"Mr. Parker's an investigator, Walt. He used to be a detective," said Alvin.

"I'm looking for someone, Mr. Tyler," I began. "A woman. You probably remember her. Her name is Catherine Demeter. She's Amy Demeter's younger sister."

"I knew you weren't no writer. Alvin wouldn't bring one o' them"—he searched for the word—"*leeches* here." He reached for his coffee and sipped long and quietly, as if to stop himself from saying more on the subject and, I thought, to give him time to consider what I had said. "I remember her, but she ain't been back since her pappy died and that's better'n ten years. She ain't got no reason to come back here."

That statement was taking on the sensation of an echo. "Still, I think she did, and I think it can only be connected with what happened before," I replied. "You're one of the only ones left, Mr. Tyler, you and the sheriff and one or two others, the only ones involved with what took place here."

I think it had been a long time since he had spoken of it aloud, yet I knew that no long period went by without him returning to it in his thoughts or without him being dimly or acutely aware of it, like an old ache that never fades but that is sometimes forgotten in the throes of some other activity and then returns in the forgetting. And I thought that each return had etched a line in his face, and so a once handsome man could lose his looks like a fine marble statue being slowly chipped away to a memory of its former self.

"I still hear her sometimes, y'know. Can hear her step on the porch at night, can hear her singing in the garden. At first, I used to run out when I heard her, not knowing but I was sleeping or waking. But I never saw her and after a while I stopped running, though I still waked to her. She don't come as often now."

Perhaps he saw something in my face, even in the slow-darkening evening, that led him to understand. I do not know for certain, and he gave no sign that he knew or that there was anything more between us than a need to know and a desire to tell, but he stopped for a moment in the telling and in that pause we all but touched, like two travelers who pass on a long, hard road and offer comfort to each other in the journey.

"She was my only child," he continued. "She disappeared on the way back from town on a fall day and I never saw her alive again. Next I saw her, she was bone and paper and I didn't know her. My wife—my late wife—she reported her missing to the police, but nobody came for a day or two and in that time we searched the fields and the houses and anywhere we could. We walked from door to door, knocking and asking, but nobody could tell us where she was or where she might have been. And then, three days after she went, a deputy came and arrested me and accused me of killing my child. They held me for two days, beat me, called me a rapist, an abuser of children, but I never said anything but what I knew to be true, and after a week they let me go. And my little girl never appeared."

"What was her name, Mr. Tyler?"

"Her name was Etta Mae Tyler and she was nine years old."

I could hear the trees whispering in the wind and the boards of the house creaking and settling. In the yard, a child's swing moved back and forth as the wind caught it. It seemed that there was movement all around us as we spoke, as if our words had awoken something that had been asleep for a long time.

"Two other children disappeared three months later, black children both, one within a week of the other. Cold it was. Folks thought the first child, Dora Lee Parker, might have fallen through some ice while playing. She was the very devil for ice, that child. But all the rivers were searched, all the ponds dredged, and they didn't find her. The police, they came and questioned me again, and for a while even some of my own neighbors looked at me kinda funny. But then the police's interest all died away again. These were black children and they saw no reason to go connectin' the two vanishings.

"The third child didn't come from Haven, he came from Otterville, about forty miles away. 'Nother black child, little boy named"—he stopped and put the palm of his hand to his forehead, pressing lightly, his eyes closed tight—"Bobby Joiner," he finished quietly, nodding slightly. "By then, people was getting scared and a deputation was sent to the sheriff and the mayor. People started keeping their children inside, specially after dark, and the police, they questioned every black man for miles around, and some white folks too, poor men they knew to be homosexuals, mostly.

"I think then there was a waiting period. Those people waited for the black folks to breathe easy again, to get careless, but they did not. It went on and on, for months, till early in nineteen seventy. Then the little Demeter girl disappeared and everything changed. The police, they questioned people for miles around, took statements, organized searches. But nobody saw a thing. It was like the little girl had disappeared into thin air.

"Things got bad then for black folks. The police figured there might be a connection between the disappearances after all and they called in the FBI. After that, black men walking around town after dark were liable to get arrested or beaten, or both. But those people . . ." He used the phrase again and there was a kind of mental shake of the head in his voice, a gesture of horror at the ways of men. "Those people had a taste for what they were doing, and couldn't stop. The woman tried to snatch a little boy in Batesville but she was alone and the boy fought and kicked and scratched her face and ran away. She chased after him, too, but then she gave up. She knew what was coming.

"The boy was a sharp one. He remembered the make of the car, described the woman, even recalled some of the numbers on the license plate. But it wasn't till the next day that someone else recalled the car and they went looking for Adelaide Modine."

"The police?"

"No, not the police. A mob of men, some from Haven, others from Batesville, two or three from Yancey Mill. The sheriff, he was out of town when it happened and the FBI men had left. But Deputy Earl Lee Granger, as was, he was with them when they arrived at the Modine house, but she was gone. There was only the brother there and he shut himself in the basement, but they broke in."

He was silent then and I heard him swallow in the gathering dark, and I knew that he had been with them. "He said he didn't know where his sister was, didn't know nothing about no dead children. So they hanged him from a beam in the roof and called it suicide. Got Doc Hyams to certify it, though that basement was fourteen feet from floor to ceiling and there was no way that boy could have gotten up there to hang hisself 'less he could climb walls. Folks after used to joke that the Modine boy wanted to hang hisself real bad to get up without help."

"But you said the woman was alone when she tried to snatch the last child," I said. "How did they know the Modine boy was involved?"

"They didn't, at least they weren't sure. But she needed someone to help her do what she did. A child is a hard thing to take sometimes. They struggle and kick and cry for help. That's why she failed the last time, because she had nobody to help her. At least, that's what they figured."

"And you?"

The porch was quiet again. "I knew that boy and he wasn't no killer. He was weak and . . . soft. He was a homosexual—he'd been caught with some boy back in his private school and they asked him to leave. My sister heard that when she was cleaning for white folks in the town. It was hushed up, though there were stories about him. I think maybe some people had suspected him for a while, just for that. When his sister tried to take the child, well, folks just decided he must have known. And he must have, I guess, or maybe suspected at least. I don't know but . . ."

He glanced at Deputy Martin and the deputy stared right back at him. "Go on, Walt. There's some things I know myself. You won't say anything I haven't thought or guessed."

Tyler still looked uneasy but nodded once, more to himself than to us, and went on. "Deputy Earl Lee, he knew the boy wasn't involved. He was with him the night Bobby Joiner was taken. Other nights too."

I looked at Alvin Martin, who stared at the floor nodding slowly. "How did you know?" I asked.

"I saw 'em," he said simply. "Their cars were parked out of town, under some trees, on the night Bobby Joiner was taken. I used to walk the fields sometimes, to get away from here, though it was dangerous given all that was happenin'. I saw the cars parked and crept up and saw them. The Modine boy was . . . down . . . on the sheriff and then they got in the back and the sheriff took him."

"And you saw them together after that?"

"Same place, couple of times."

"And the sheriff let them hang the boy?"

"He wasn't going to say nothin'," Tyler spat, "case someone found out about him. And he watched them hang that boy."

"And his sister? What about Adelaide Modine?"

"They searched for her too, searched the house and then the fields, but she was gone. Then someone saw a fire in the shell of an old house on the East Road about ten miles from town and pretty soon the whole place was ablaze. Thomas Becker, he used to store old paint and inflammables there, away from the children. And when the fire was out, they found a body, badly burned, and they said it was Adelaide Modine."

"How did they identify her?"

Martin answered. "There was a bag near the body, with the remains of a lot of money, some personal papers, bank account details mostly. Jewelry she was known to have was found on the body, a gold and diamond bracelet she always wore. It was her mother's, they said. Dental records matched too. Old Doc Hyams produced her chart; he shared a surgery with the dentist, but the dentist was out of town that week.

"Seems she had holed up, maybe waiting for her brother or someone else to come to her, and fell asleep with a cigarette in her hand. She'd been drinking, they said, maybe to try to keep warm. The whole place went up. Her car was found nearby, with a bag of clothes in the trunk."

"Do you remember anything about Adelaide Modine, Mr. Tyler? Anything that might explain . . ."

"Explain what?" he interrupted. "Explain why she did it? Explain why someone helped her to do what she did? I can't explain those things, not even to myself. She had somethin', sure enough, somethin' strong inside her, but it was a dark thing, a vicious thing. I'll tell you somethin', Mr. Parker: Adelaide Modine was as close to pure evil as I've met on this earth, and I've seen brothers hanged from trees and burned while they were hangin'. Adelaide Modine was worse than the people who did the hangin' because, try as I might, I can't see any reason for the things she did. They're beyond explainin', 'less you believe in the Devil and Hell. That's the only way I can explain her. She was a thing out of Hell."

I stayed silent for a while, trying to sort and balance what I had been told. Walt Tyler watched while these thoughts went through my head and I think he knew what I was thinking. I couldn't blame him for not telling what he knew of the sheriff and the Modine boy. An allegation like that could get a man killed and it didn't provide conclusive proof that the Modine boy wasn't directly involved in the killings, although if Tyler's character assessment was right, then William Modine was an unlikely child killer. But the knowledge that someone involved in the death of his child might have eluded capture must have tortured Tyler all these years.

One part of the story still remained.

"They found the children the next day, just as the search had begun," concluded Tyler. "A boy out hunting took shelter in an abandoned house on the Modine estate and his dog started scraping at the cellar door. It was built into the floor, like a trapdoor. The boy shot the lock off and the dog went down and he followed. Then he ran home and called the police.

"There were four bodies down there, my little girl and the three others. They . . ." He stopped and his face creased but he did not cry.

"You don't have to go on," I said softly.

"No, you gotta know," he said. Then louder, like the cry of a wounded animal: "You've gotta *know* what they did, what they did to those children, to my child. My little girl, all her fingers were broken, crushed, and the bones pulled away from the sockets." He was crying openly now, his large hands open before him like a supplicant before God. "How could they do those things, to children? How?" And then he seemed to retreat into himself and I thought I saw the woman's face at the window, and her fingertips brushing the pane.

We sat with him for a while and then stood up to leave. "Mr. Tyler," I said gently, "just one more thing: where is the house where the children were found?"

"About three, four miles up the road from here. The old Modine estate starts there. There's a stone cross at the start of the track leading up to it. The house is pretty much gone now. There's just a few walls, part of a roof. State wanted to knock it down but some of us protested. We wanted to remind them of what had happened here, so the Dane house still stands."

We left him then, but as I was going down the porch steps I heard his voice behind me.

"Mr. Parker." The voice was strong again and there was no quaver in it, although there was the lingering sound of grief in its tones. I turned to look at him. "Mr. Parker, this is a dead town. The ghosts of dead children haunt it. You find the Demeter girl, you tell her to go back where she came from. There's only grief and misery for her here. You tell her that, now. You tell her that when you find her, y'hear?"

At the margins of his cluttered garden the whispering grew in the trees and it seemed that just beyond the line of vision, where the darkness became almost too dark to penetrate, there was movement. Figures drifted back and forth, skipping just outside the light from the house, and there was childish laughter in the air.

And then there were only the limbs of evergreens fanning the darkness and the empty jangling of a chain in the wreckage of the yard.

CHAPTER XXIV

On the Casuarina Coast of Indonesian New Guinea lives a tribe called the Asmat. They are twenty thousand strong and the terror of every other tribe near them. In their language Asmat means "the people, the human beings," and if they define themselves as the only humans, then all others are relegated to the status of nonhuman, with all that that entails. The Asmat have a word for these others: they call them *manowe*. It means "the edible ones."

Hyams had no answers that would have indicated why Adelaide Modine behaved as she did, and neither did Walt Tyler. Maybe she, and others like her, had something in common with the Asmat. Maybe they, too, saw others as less than human so that their suffering ceased to matter, was below notice apart from the pleasure it gave.

I RECALLED A CONVERSATION with Woolrich, after the meeting with *Tante* Marie Aguillard. Back in New Orleans, we walked in silence down Royal Street, past Madame Lelaurie's old mansion, where slaves were once chained and tortured in the attic until some firefighters found them and a mob ran Madame Lelaurie out of town. We ended up at Tee Eva's on Magazine, where Woolrich ordered sweet potato pie and a Jax beer. He ran his thumb down the side of the bottle, clearing a path through the moisture, and then rubbed his damp thumb along his upper lip.

"I read a Bureau report last week," he began. "I guess it was a 'state of the nation' address on serial killers, on where we stand, where we're goin'."

"And where are we going?"

"We're goin' to Hell is where we're goin'. These people are like bacteria spreading and this country is just one big petri dish to them. The Bureau reckons we could be losing a couple of thousand victims a year to them. The folks watching Oprah and Jerry Springer, or subscribin' to Jerry Falwell, they don't wanna know that. They read about them in the crime mags or see them on the TV, but that's only when we catch one of them. The rest of the time, they don't have the least idea what's goin' on around them."

He took a deep swig of Jax. "There are at least two hundred of these killers operating at the present time. *At least* two hundred." He was reeling off the numbers now, emphasizing each statistic with a stab of the beer bottle. "Nine out of ten are male, eight out of ten are white, and one in five is never goin' to be found. Never.

"And you know what the strangest thing is? We've got more of them than anywhere else. The good old U.S. of A. is breedin' these fuckers like fuckin' Elmo dolls. Three-quarters of them live and work in this country. We're the world's leading producer of serial killers. It's a sign of sickness, is what it is. We're sick and weak and these killers are like a cancer inside us: the faster we grow, the quicker they multiply.

"And you know, the more of us there are, the more distant from each other we become. We're practically livin' on top of each other but we're further away from each other in every other way than we've ever been before. And then these guys come in, with their knives and their ropes, and they're even further removed than the rest of us. Some of them even have cop's instincts. They can sniff each other out. We found a guy in Angola in February who was communicating with a suspected killer in Seattle using biblical codes. I don't know how these two freaks found each other, but they did.

"Strange thing is, most of them are even worse off than the rest of humanity. They're inadequate—sexually, emotionally, physically, whatever—and they're taking it out on those they see around them. They have no"—he shook his hands in the air, searching for the word—"no vision. They have no larger vision of what they're doing. There's no purpose to it. It's just an expression of some kind of fatal flaw.

"And the people they're killing, they're so dumb that they can't understand what's happening around them. These killers should be a wake-up call, but nobody's listening, and that widens the gap even more. All they see is the distance, and they reach across it and pick us off, one by one. All we can do is hope that, if they do it often enough, we'll spot the pattern and put together a link between us and them, a bridge across the distance." He finished his beer and raised the bottle up, calling for another.

"It's the distance," he said, his eyes on the street but his gaze beyond it, "the distance between life and death, Heaven and Hell, us and them. They have to cross it to get close enough to us to take us but it's all a matter of distance. They love the distance."

AND IT SEEMED TO me, as rain poured down on the window, that Adelaide Modine, the Traveling Man, and the others like them who roamed the country were all united by this distance from the common crowd of humanity. They were like small boys who torture animals or take fish from tanks to watch them squirm and gasp in their death throes.

Yet Adelaide Modine seemed even worse than so many of the others, for she was a woman and to do what she had done not only went against law and morality and whatever other titles we give to the common bonds that hold us together and prevent us from tearing each other apart; it went against nature, too. A woman who kills a child seems to bring out something in us that exceeds revulsion or horror. It brings a kind of despair, a lack of faith in the foundations upon which we have built our lives. For we believe that women should not take the life of a child. Just as Lady Macbeth begged to be unsexed so as to kill the old king, so also a woman who killed a child appeared to be denatured, a being divorced from her sex. Adelaide Modine was like Milton's night hag, "lured with the smell of infant blood."

I cannot countenance the death of children. The killing of a child seems to bring with it the death of hope, the death of the future. I recall how I used to listen to Jennifer breathe, how I used to watch the rise and fall of my infant daughter's chest, how I felt a sense of gratitude, of relief, with every inhalation and exhalation. When she cried, I would lull her to sleep in my arms, waiting for the sobs to fade into the soft rhythms of rest. And when she was at last quiet, I would bend down slowly, carefully, my back aching from the strain of the position, and lay her in her crib. When she was taken from me it was like the death of a world, an infinite number of futures coming to an end.

I felt a weight of despair upon me as the motel drew closer. Hyams had said that he had seen nothing in the Modines that would have indicated the depths of evil that existed within them. Walt Tyler, if what he had said was true, saw that evil only in Adelaide Modine. She had lived among these people, had grown up with them, perhaps even played with them, had sat with them in church, had watched them marry, have children, and then had preyed upon them, and no one had suspected her.

I think that what I wanted was a power I could not have: the power to perceive evil, the ability to look at the faces in a crowded room and see the signs of depravity and corruption. The thought sparked a memory of a killing in New York State some years before, in which a thirteen-year-old-boy had killed a younger kid in the woods, beating him to death with rocks. It was the words of the killer's grandfather that had stayed with me. "My God," he said. "I should have been able to see, somehow. There should have been something to see."

"Are there any pictures of Adelaide Modine?" I asked eventually.

Martin's brow furrowed. "There may be one in the files of the original investigation. The library may have some stuff too. There's a kind of town archive stored in its basement, y'know, yearbooks, photos from the paper. There may be something in there. Why d'you ask?"

"Curiosity. She was responsible for so much of what happened to this town but I find it hard to picture her. Maybe I want to see what her eyes looked like."

Martin shot me a puzzled look. "I can get Laurie to look in the library archives. I'll try to get Burns to look through our own files, but it could take a while. They're all packed in boxes and the filing system is pretty obscure. Some of the files aren't even in date order. It's a lot of work to satisfy your idle curiosity."

"I'd appreciate it anyway."

Martin made a sound in his throat but didn't say anything else for a while. Then, as the motel appeared on our right, he pulled over to the side of the road. "About Earl Lee," he said.

"Go on."

"The sheriff's a good man. He held this town together after the Modine killings, from what I hear, him and Doc Hyams and a couple of others. He's a fair man and I've no complaints about him."

"If what Tyler said is true, maybe you should have."

Martin nodded. "That's as may be. If he's right, then the sheriff's got to live with what he's done. He's a troubled man, Mr. Parker, troubled by the past, by himself. I don't envy him anything but his strength." He spread his hands wide and shrugged slightly. "Part of me figures that you should stay here and talk to him when he comes back, but another part of me, the smart part, tells me that it would be better for all of us if you finished up your business as quickly as you can and then got out."

"Have you heard from him?"

"No, I haven't. He had some leave coming to him and maybe he's a little overdue on returning, but I ain't gonna hold that against him. He's a lonely man. A man who likes the company of other men ain't gonna find much comfort here."

"No," I said, as the neon light of the Welcome Inn flickered beyond us. "I guess not."

THE CALL CAME THROUGH almost as soon as Martin pulled away from the curb. There had been a death at the medical center: the unidentified woman who had tried to kill me the previous night.

When we arrived two cruisers were blocking the entrance to the parking lot and I could see the two FBI men talking together at the door. Martin drove us through and as we got out of the car the two agents moved toward me in unison, their guns drawn.

"Easy! Easy!" shouted Martin. "He was with me the whole time. Put them away, boys."

"We're detaining him until Agent Ross arrives," said one of the agents, whose name was Willox.

"You ain't detaining or arresting nobody, not until we find out what's going on here."

"Deputy, I'm warning you, you're out of your league here."

Wallace and Burns came out of the medical center at that point, alerted by the shouts. To their credit, they moved to Martin's side, their hands hanging close by their guns.

"Like I said, let it go," said Martin quietly. The feds looked like they might push the issue but then they holstered their weapons and moved back.

"Agent Ross is going to hear of this," hissed Willox to Martin, but the deputy just walked by.

Wallace and Burns walked with us to the room in which the woman had been kept.

"What happened?" asked Martin.

Wallace turned bright red and started blabbering. "Shit, Alvin, there was a disturbance outside the center and—"

"What kind of disturbance?"

"A fire in the engine of a car, belonged to one of the nurses. I couldn't figure it out. There weren't nobody in it and she hadn't used it since she got in this morning. I only left the door here for maybe five minutes. When I got back, she was like this . . ."

We arrived at the woman's room. Through the open door I could see the pale, waxy pallor of her skin and the blood on the pillow beside her left ear. Something metal, ending in a wooden handle, glinted in the ear. The window through which the killer had entered was still open and the glass had been shattered in order to unhook the latch. A small sheet of sticky brown paper lay on the floor, with glass adhering to it. Whoever had killed the woman had taken the trouble to stick it to the window before breaking the glass, in order to muffle the sound and to ensure that the glass didn't make any noise when it hit the floor.

"Who's been in here, apart from you?"

"The doctor, a nurse, and the two feds," said Wallace. The elderly doctor called Elise appeared behind us. She looked shaken and weary.

"What happened to her?" said Martin.

"A blade of some kind—I think it's an ice pick—was thrust through her ear and into her brain. She was dead when we got to her."

"Left the pick in her," mused Martin.

"Clean and easy," I said. "Nothing to tie the killer to what happened if he—or she—gets picked up."

Martin turned his back on me and began consulting the other deputies. I moved away as they talked and made my way toward the men's washroom. Wallace looked back at me and I made a gagging expression. He looked away with contempt in his eyes. I spent five seconds in the washroom and then slipped out of the center through the rear exit.

Time was running out for me. I knew Martin would try to grill me on the source of the hit. Agent Ross wasn't far behind. At the very least, he'd hold me until he got the information he wanted, and any hope I might have of finding Catherine Demeter would disappear. I made my way back to the motel, where my car was still parked, and drove out of Haven.

CHAPTER XXV

The road to the ruin of the Dane house was little more than two mud tracks and the car moved along them only with a great effort, as if nature itself was conspiring against my approach. It had started to rain heavily again, and the wind and rain combined to render the wipers almost useless. I strained my eyes for the stone cross and took the turning opposite. I missed the house the first time, realizing my mistake only when the road turned into a mass of mud and fallen, rotting trees, forcing me to reverse slowly back the way I had come, until I spotted two small ruined pillars to my left and, between them, the almost roofless walls of the Dane house briefly silhouetted against the dark sky.

I pulled up outside the empty eyes of the windows and the gaping mouth of what was once the door, pieces of its lintel strewn on the ground like old teeth. I took the heavy Maglite from under my seat and climbed out, the rain painful on my head as I ran for what little shelter the interior of the ruin could offer.

Over half of the roof was gone, and in the flashlight beam what remained still showed blackened and charred. There were three rooms: what had once been a kitchen and eating area, identifiable from the remains of an ancient stove in one corner; the main bedroom, now empty except for a stained mattress around which old prophylactics were scattered like the discarded skins of snakes; and a smaller room, which might have served as a children's bedroom once but was now a mass of old timber and rusting metal bars dotted with paint tins, left there by someone too lazy to haul them to the municipal dump. The rooms smelled of old wood, of long-extinct fires, and human excrement.

An old couch stood in one corner of the kitchen, its springs flowering through the rotting cushions. It formed a triangle with the corners of the wall, upon which the remains of some faded floral wallpaper hung tenaciously. I shined the flashlight over the back of the couch, my hand resting on the edge. It felt damp but not wet, for the remains of part of the roof still sheltered it from the worst of the elements.

Behind the couch and almost flush with the corners of the house was what appeared to be a trapdoor some three feet at each side. It was locked and its edges seemed filthy and choked with dirt. Its hinges were bloodied with rust, and pieces of wood and old metal covered most of its surface.

I pulled back the couch to take a closer look and started as I heard a rat scurry across the floor at my feet. It melted into the darkness in a far corner of the room and then was still. I squatted down to examine the lock and bolt, using my knife to scrape away some of the filth from around the keyhole. New steel shone through beneath the dirt. I ran the blade of the knife along the bolt, exposing a line of steel that shone like molten silver in the darkness. I tried the same experiment with the hinge but only flakes of rust greeted me.

I examined the bolt more closely. What had appeared at first sight to be rust now looked more like varnish, carefully applied so that it would blend in with the door. The bolt's battered look could easily have been achieved by dragging it behind a car for a while. It wasn't a bad job, designed as it was to fool only necking teenagers seeking a thrill in a house of the dead, or children daring each other to tempt the ghosts of other children long gone.

I had a crowbar in the car but I was reluctant to brave the driving rain again. As I shined the flashlight around the room, a steel bar some two feet long was caught in the beam. I picked it up, felt its weight, inserted it in the U of the lock, and jimmied. For a moment it seemed the bar might bend or fracture under the strain, and then there was a sharp crack as the lock broke. I pulled it free, released the bolt, and raised the door on its complaining hinges.

A rich, heady stench of decay rose from the cellar, causing my stomach to churn. I covered my mouth and moved away, but seconds later I was vomiting by the couch, my nostrils filled with my own smell and the odor from the cellar below. When I had recovered and breathed in some fresh air outside the house, I ran to the car and took the window rag from the dashboard. I sprayed it with defogger from the glove compartment and tied it around my mouth. The defogger made my head reel but I stuck it in the pocket of my coat in case I needed it again and re-entered the house.

Even though I breathed through my mouth, tasting the spray, the smell of putrefaction was overpowering. I descended the wooden stairs carefully, my strong left hand on the rail and the Maglite in my right with the beam shining at my feet. I didn't want to trip on a ruined step and plunge into the darkness below.

At the base of the steps the flashlight beam caught a glint of metal and blue-gray material. A heavy-set man in his sixties lay near the steps, his knees curled beneath him and his hands cuffed behind his back. His face was gray-white and there was a wound on his forehead, a ragged hole like a dark, exploding star. For a moment, as I shined the flashlight upon it, I thought it was an exit wound, but moving the light to the back of his head, I saw the hole in his skull gape, saw the decaying matter within and the white totem of his spine.

The gun had probably been pressed right against his head. There was some gunpowder smudging around the forehead wound and the star-shaped rip had been caused by the gases shooting under the skin next to the bone, expanding and tearing open the forehead as they exploded. The bullet had exited messily, taking most of the back of his skull with it. The contact wound also explained the unusual position of the body: he had been shot while kneeling, looking up into the muzzle of the gun as it approached and falling sideways and back when the bullet entered. Inside his jacket was a wallet, with a driver's license identifying him as Earl Lee Granger.

Catherine Demeter lay slumped against the far wall of the basement, nearly opposite the stairs. Granger had probably seen her as he walked or was pushed down. She was slumped like a doll at the wall, her legs spread out before her and her hands resting palms up on the floor. One leg was bent at an unnatural angle, broken below the knee, and I guessed that she had been thrown down the cellar stairs and dragged to the wall.

She had been shot once in the face at close range. Dried blood, brain tissue, and bone fragments surrounded her head like a bloody halo on the wall. Both bodies had begun to decay rapidly in the cellar, which seemed to stretch the length and breadth of the house.

There were blisters on Catherine Demeter's skin, and fluid leaked from her nose and eyes. Spiders and millipedes scuttled across her face and slipped through her hair, hunting the bugs and mites that were already feeding on the body. Flies buzzed. I guessed she had been dead for two or three days. I took a quick look around the cellar but it was empty apart from bundles of rotting newspaper, some cardboard boxes filled with old clothes, and a pile of warped timbers, the detritus of lives lived long before and now no more.

A scuffling noise on the floor above me, the sound of wood shifting despite careful footsteps, made me turn quickly and run for the stairs. Whoever was above me heard me, for the steps now moved quicker with no regard for any noise that might be made. As my feet hit the first stairs the sound of the trapdoor hinges greeted me and I saw the patch of star-studded sky begin to shrink as the door came down. Two shots were fired randomly through the gap and I heard them impact on the wall behind me.

The trapdoor was almost to the floor when I jammed the Maglite into the gap. There was a grunt from above and then I felt the flashlight being kicked repeatedly so that I had to grip it firmly to prevent it being wrenched from my hand. Still the bell-shaped end held firm, but my injured right shoulder ached from the strain of pushing up and holding the flashlight.

Above me, the entire weight of my assailant was on the trapdoor as he continued to aim kicks at the flashlight. Below, I thought I heard the sound of rats scurrying in alarm, but faced with the prospect of being trapped in that cellar, I thought it might be something else. I felt that I might yet hear the sound of Catherine Demeter dragging her shattered leg across the floor and up the wooden steps, that her white fingers might grip my leg and pull me down to her.

I had failed her. I could not protect her from the violent end in this cellar where four young children before her had met muffled, terrified deaths. She had returned to the place where her sister had perished, and in a strange circularity, she had reenacted a death that she had probably replayed many times in her mind before that day. In the moments before she died, she gained an insight into her sister's awful end. And so she would keep me company, console me for my weakness and my helplessness in the face of her passing, and lie beside me as I died.

As I breathed through gritted teeth, the stench of decay felt like a dead hand over my mouth and nostrils. I felt vomit rising once again and forced it down, for if I stopped pushing even for a moment I felt sure I would die in this cellar. Momentarily the pressure above me eased and I pushed upward with all my remaining strength. It was an error that my opponent exploited to the full. The torch was kicked once, hard, and slipped through the enlarged gap. The trapdoor slammed shut like the door of my tomb, its echo mocking me from the walls of the cellar. I groaned in despair and began to press futilely against the door once again, when there was an explosion from above and the pressure eased entirely, the trapdoor shooting upward and coming to rest flat on the floor.

I flung myself out, my hand inside my jacket reaching for my gun and the flashlight beam casting wild shadows on the ceilings and walls as I landed awkwardly and painfully on the floor.

The beam caught the lawyer Connell Hyams leaning against the wall just beyond the rim of the trapdoor, his left hand to his wounded shoulder while his right hand tried to raise his gun. His suit was soaked and his clean white shirt clung to his body like a second skin. I held him in the flashlight beam, my gun outstretched in the other hand.

"Don't," I said, but the gun was rising now and his mouth curled into a snarl of fear and pain as he brought it up to fire. Two shots sounded. Neither of them was from Hyams. He jerked as each bullet hit, and his gaze moved from me to a place over my shoulder. As he fell I was already turning, the gun still following the beam of the flashlight. Through the glassless window I caught a glimpse of a thin besuited figure fading into the dark, its limbs like sheathed blades and a scar running across its narrow, cadaverous features.

MAYBE I SHOULD HAVE called Martin then and let the police and the FBI handle the rest. I was sick and weary inside, and an almost overpowering sense of loss tore through me and threatened to unman me. The death of Catherine Demeter was like a physical pain, so that I lay for a moment on the ground, the body of Connell Hyams slumped opposite, and clutched my stomach in agony. I could hear the sound of a car as Bobby Sciorra drove away.

It was that sound that caused me to scramble to my feet. It had been Sciorra who had killed the assassin in the medical center, probably under orders from the old man in case she implicated Sonny in the hit. Yet I couldn't understand why he had killed Hyams and why he had let me live. I staggered to my car, my shoulder aching, and started to drive toward Hyams's house.

CHAPTER

XXVI

As I drove, I tried to piece together what had taken place. Catherine Demeter had returned to Haven in an effort to contact Granger, and Hyams had intervened. Maybe he had learned of Catherine's presence here by chance; the other possibility was that someone had informed him that she was coming and had urged him to ensure that she never spoke to anyone when she got here.

Hyams had killed Catherine and Granger, that much seemed certain. At a guess, I reckoned that he had watched for the sheriff's return and followed him into his house. If Hyams had a key to the sheriff's house—which, since he was a neighbor and a trusted citizen, was a likely possibility—Hyams could have listened to the messages on the sheriff's machine himself and, through that, could have learned of Catherine Demeter's location. Catherine Demeter had been dead before the sheriff returned. The proof: Granger's body had not decayed to the same extent as Demeter's.

Hyams might even have erased the messages, but he couldn't be certain that Granger had not picked them up by remote contact through a Touch-Tone phone. Either way, Hyams couldn't take any chances and acted, probably knocking the sheriff unconscious before cuffing him and then taking him to the Dane house, where he had already killed Catherine Demeter. The sheriff's car, his own

Dodge, had probably been dumped or driven to another town and left somewhere it wouldn't attract undue attention, at least for the time being.

The use of the Dane house pointed to another part of the puzzle: Connell Hyams was almost certainly Adelaide Modine's accomplice in the killings, the man for whom William Modine had been hanged. That raised the question of why he had been forced to act now, and I believed that I was close to an answer to that too, although it was a possibility that made me sick to my stomach.

HYAMS'S HOUSE WAS DARK when I arrived. There was no other car parked nearby, but I kept my gun in my hand as I approached the door. The thought of facing Bobby Sciorra in the darkness made my skin crawl, and my hands shook as I used the keys I had taken from Hyams's body to open the door.

Inside, the house was silent. I went from room to room, my heart pounding, my finger on the trigger of the gun. The house was empty. There was no sign of Bobby Sciorra.

I went through to Hyams's office, pulled the curtains, and turned on the desk light. His computer was password protected but a man like Hyams would have to keep hard copies of all his documents. I wasn't even sure what I was looking for, except that it was something that would connect Hyams to the Ferrera family. The connection seemed almost absurd and I was tempted to give up the search and return to Haven and explain it all to Martin and Agent Ross. The Ferreras were many things, but they were not the consorts of child killers.

The key to Hyams's filing cabinets was also on the set I had taken from his body. I worked fast, ignoring local files and others that seemed irrelevant or unrelated. There were no files for the trust, which seemed extraordinary until I remembered his office in town and my heart sank. If the trust files were not kept in the house, there was a possibility that other files were not here either. If that was the case, the search could prove fruitless.

In the end, I almost passed over the link and only some half-remembered Italian phrases caused me to stop and consider it. It was a rental agreement for a warehouse property in Flushing, Queens, signed by Hyams on behalf of a company called Circe. The agreement was over five years old and had been made with a firm called Mancino Inc. *Mancino,* I remembered, meant "left-handed" in Italian. It derived from another word, meaning "deceitful." It was Sonny Ferrera's idea of a joke: Sonny was left-handed and Mancino Inc. was one of a number of paper companies established by Sonny in the early part of the decade when he had not yet been reduced to the level of a sick, dangerous joke in the Ferrera operation.

I left the house and started driving. As I reached the town limits, I saw a pickup by the side of the road. Two figures sat in the back, drinking beer from cans enclosed in brown paper bags, while a third stood leaning against the cab with his hands in his pockets. The headlights identified the standing man as Clete and one of the seated figures as Gabe. The third was a thin, bearded man whose face I didn't recognize. I caught Clete's eye as I passed and saw Gabe lean toward him and start talking, but Clete just raised a hand. As I drove away I could see him staring after me, caught in the headlights of the pickup, a dark shadow against the light. I felt almost sorry for him: Haven's chances of becoming Little Tokyo had just taken a terminal beating.

I DIDN'T CALL MARTIN until I reached Charlottesville.

"It's Parker," I said. "Anybody near you?"

"I'm in my office and you're in deep shit. Why'd you run out like that? Ross is here and wants all our asses, but your ass especially. Man, when Earl Lee gets back there's gonna be hell to pay."

"Listen to me. Granger's dead. So is Catherine Demeter. I think Hyams killed them."

"Hyams?" Martin almost shrieked the name. "The lawyer? You're out of your mind."

"Hyams is dead too." It was starting to sound like a sick joke, except I wasn't laughing. "He tried to kill me out at the Dane house. The bodies of Granger and Catherine Demeter were dumped in the cellar there. I found them and Hyams tried to lock me in. There was some shooting and Hyams died. There's another player, the guy who took out the woman in the medical center." I didn't want to bring Sciorra's name into it, not yet.

Martin was silent for a moment. "You gotta come in. Where are you?"

"It's not finished. You've got to hold them off for me."

"I ain't holding anyone off. This town is turning into a morgue because of you and now you're a suspect in I don't know how many murders. Come in. You got enough trouble coming to you already."

"I'm sorry, I can't do that. Listen to me. Hyams killed Demeter to prevent her contacting Granger. I think Hyams was Adelaide Modine's accomplice in the child killings. If that's the case, if he escaped, then she could have escaped too. He could have rigged her death. He had access to her dental records through his father's office. He could have switched a set of records from another woman, maybe a migrant worker, maybe someone snatched from another town, I don't know. But something made Catherine Demeter run. Something sent her back here. I think she saw her. I think she saw Adelaide Modine because there's no other reason why she would have come back here, why she would have contacted Granger after all these years away."

There was silence at the other end of the phone. "Ross looks like a volcano in a linen suit. He's going to be onto you. He got your plates from your motel registration."

"I need your help."

"You say Hyams was involved?"

"Yes. Why?"

"I had Burns check our files. Didn't take as long as I thought it would. Earl Lee has . . . *had* the file relating to the killings. He used to check it out every so often. Hyams came looking for it, day before yesterday."

"My guess is that, if you find it, any photos will be gone. I think Hyams probably searched the sheriff's house for it. He had to eliminate any traces of Adelaide Modine, anything that might link her to her new identity."

It is hard to disappear. A trail of paper, of public and private records, follows us from birth. For most of us, they define what we are to the state, the government, the law. But there are ways to disappear. Obtain a new birth certificate, maybe from a death index or by using someone else's birth name and DOB, and age the cert by carrying it around in your shoe for a week. Apply for a library card and, from that, obtain a voter's registration card. Head for the nearest DMV clerk, flash the birth certificate and the VRC, and you now have a driver's license. It's a domino effect, each step based on the validity of the documents obtained in the preceding step.

The easiest way of all is to take on another's identity, someone who won't be missed, someone from the margins. My guess was that, with Hyams's help, Adelaide Modine took on the identity of the girl who burned to death in a Virginia ruin.

"There's more," said Martin. "There was a separate file on the Modines. The photos from that are all gone as well."

"Could Hyams have got access to those files?"

I could hear Martin sigh at the other end of the phone.

"Sure," he said eventually. "He was the town lawyer. He was trusted by everyone."

"Check the motels again. I reckon you'll find Catherine Demeter's belongings in one of them. There might be something there."

"Man, you gotta come back here, sort this out. There's a lot of bodies here and your name is connected with all of them. I can't do any more than I've done already."

"Just do what you can. I'm not coming in."

I hung up and tried another number. "Yeah," answered a voice.

"Angel. It's Bird."

"Where the fuck have you been? Things are going down here. Are you on the cell phone? Call me back on a landline."

I called him back seconds later from a phone outside a convenience store.

"Some of the old man's goons have picked up Pili Pilar. They're holding him until Bobby Sciorra gets back from some trip. It's bad. He's being held in isolation at the Ferrera place—anyone talks to him and they get it in the head. Only Bobby gets access to him."

"Did they get Sonny?"

"No, he's still out there, but he's alone now. He's gonna have to sort whatever it is out with his old man."

"I'm in trouble, Angel." I explained to him briefly what had taken place. "I'm coming back but I need something from you and Louis."

"Just ask, man."

I gave him the address of the warehouse. "Watch the place. I'll meet you there as soon as I can."

I didn't know how long it would take them to start tracking me. I drove as far as Richmond and parked the Mustang in a long-term parking garage. Then I made some calls. For fifteen hundred dollars I bought silence and a flight on a small plane from a private airfield back to the city.

CHAPTER

XXVII

"You sure you wanna be dropped here?" The cabdriver was a huge man, his hair lank with sweat, which dribbled down his cheeks and over the rolls of fat in his neck, eventually losing itself in the greasy collar of his shirt. He seemed to fill the whole front of the cab. The door looked too small for him to have entered through. He gave the impression that he had lived and eaten in the cab for so long that it was no longer possible for him to leave: the cab was his home, his castle, and his bulk gave the impression that it would be his tomb.

"I'm sure," I replied.

"This is a tough area."

"That's okay. I have tough friends."

The Morelli wine warehouse was one of a number of similar premises that lined one side of a long, ill-lit street west of Northern Boulevard in Flushing. It was a redbrick building, its name reduced to a white, flaking shadow below the edge of its roof. Wire screens covered the windows on both the ground and upper levels. There were no visible lights on the walls; the area between the gate and the main building was in almost total darkness.

On the other side of the street stood the entrance to a large yard filled with storage depots and railroad containers. The ground inside was pitted with ponds of filthy water and discarded pallets. I saw a mongrel dog, its ribs almost bursting through its fur, tearing at something in the dim light of the lot's filthy spotlights.

As I stepped from the cab, headlights flashed briefly from the alleyway by the warehouse. Seconds later, as the cab pulled away, Angel and Louis emerged from the black Chevy van, Angel carrying a heavy-looking training bag, Louis immaculate in a black leather coat, a black suit, and a black polo shirt.

Angel screwed up his face as he drew nearer. It wasn't hard to see why. My suit was torn and covered with mud and dirt from the encounter with Hyams in the Dane house. My arm had begun to bleed again and the right cuff of my shirt was a deep red color. I ached all over and I was tired of death.

"You look good," said Angel. "Where's the dance?"

I looked toward the Morelli warehouse. "In there. Have I missed anything?"

"Not here. Louis just got back from Ferrera's place, though."

"Bobby Sciorra arrived there about an hour ago by chopper," said Louis. "Reckon him and Pili are having a real heart-to-heart."

I nodded. "Let's go," I said.

The warehouse was surrounded by a high brick wall topped with barbed wire and spiked fencing. The gate, inset slightly as the wall curved inward at the entrance, was also wire topped and solid except for a gap where a heavy lock and chain linked its two halves together. While Louis lounged semidiscreetly nearby, Angel removed a small, custom-built drill from his bag and inserted the bit into the lock. He pressed the trigger and a high-pitched grinding sound seemed to fill the night. Instantly, every dog in the vicinity started to bark.

"Shit, Angel, you got a fuckin' whistle built into that thing?" hissed Louis. Angel ignored him and moments later the lock fell open.

We entered and Angel gingerly removed the lock and placed it inside the gate. He replaced the chain so that to a casual observer it would still appear secure if, oddly, locked from the inside.

The warehouse dated from the thirties but would have appeared functional even then. Old doors at the right and left sides had been sealed shut, leaving only one way in at the front. Even the fire exit at the back had been welded in place. The security lights, which might once have lit up the yard, now no longer functioned and the illumination from the streetlights did not penetrate the darkness here.

Angel went to work on the lock with a selection of picks, a small flashlight in his mouth, and less than a minute later we were in, lighting our heavy Mags as we went. A small booth, which was probably once occupied by a security guard or watchman when the building was in use, stood directly inside the door. Empty shelves stretched along the walls of the room, paralleled by similar shelving through the center, creating two aisles. The shelves were separated into alcoves, each sufficient to hold a bottle of wine. The floor was stone. This had originally been the display area where visitors could examine the stock. Below, in the cellars, was where the cases were kept. At the far end of the room stood a raised office, reached by three stairs to the right.

Beside the small flight of stairs up to the office, a larger staircase descended down. There was also an old freight elevator, unlocked. Angel stepped in and pulled the lever, and the lift descended a foot or two. He brought it back to its original level, stepped out again, and raised an eyebrow at me.

We started down the stairs. There were four flights, the equivalent of two stories, but there were no other floors between the shop floor and the cellars. At the base was another locked door, this one wooden with a glass window through which the flashlight beam revealed the cellar's arches. I left Angel to the lock. It took him seconds to open the door. He looked ill at ease entering the cellars. The training bag appeared suddenly heavy in his hand.

"Want me to take that for a while?" asked Louis.

"When I'm that old you'll be feeding me through a straw," replied Angel. Although the cellars were cool, he licked at sweat on his upper lip.

"Practically feeding you through a straw already," muttered the voice from behind us.

In the basement, a series of curved, cavelike alcoves stretched away before us. Each had bars running vertically down from ceiling to floor, with a gate set in the middle. They were the old storage bins for the wine. They were obviously disused, strewn with litter. The flashlight beams caught the edge of the floor of one bin that differed from the others. It was the one nearest us on the right, bare earth showing where the cement floor had been removed. Its gate stood ajar.

Our footsteps echoed around the stone walls as we approached. Inside, the floor was clean and the dirt neatly raked. In one corner was a green metal table with two slits on either side through which ran leather restrainers. In another corner stood a large, industrial-sized roll of what appeared to be plastic sheeting.

Two layers of shelving ran around the walls. They were empty except for a bundle, tightly wrapped in plastic, that had been tucked in against the far wall. I walked toward it and the beam of the flashlight caught denim and a green check shirt, a pair of small shoes and a mop of hair, a discolored face whose skin had cracked and burst, with a pair of open eyes, the corneas milky and cloudy. The smell of decay was strong, but dulled somewhat by the plastic. I recognized the clothing. I had found Evan Baines, the child who had disappeared from the Barton estate.

"Sweet Jesus," I heard Angel say. Louis was silent.

I drew closer to the body, checking the fingers and face. Apart from natural decay, the body was undamaged and the boy's clothing appeared undisturbed. Evan Baines had not been tortured before he died but there was some heavier discoloration at his temple and there was dried blood in his ear.

The fingers of his left hand were splayed against his chest but his small right hand had formed into a tightly closed fist.

"Angel, come here. Bring the bag."

He stood beside me and I saw the anger and despair in his eyes.

"It's Evan Baines," I said. "Did you bring the masks?"

He bent down and took out two dust masks and a bottle of Aramis aftershave. He sprinkled the aftershave on each mask, handed one to me, and put the other one on himself. Then he handed me a pair of plastic gloves. Louis stood farther back but didn't take a mask. Angel held the flashlight beam on the body.

I took my pocketknife and sliced through the plastic by the child's right hand. Even through the mask the stench grew stronger and there was a hiss of escaping gas.

I took the blunt edge of the knife and pried at the boy's fist. The skin broke and a nail came loose.

"Hold the light steady, dammit," I hissed. I could see something small and blue in the boy's grip. I pried again, heedless now of the damage I was causing. I had to know. I had to find the answer to what had happened here. Eventually, the object came loose and fell to the floor. I bent to pick it up and examined it by the light of my own flashlight. It was a shard of blue china.

Angel had begun scanning the far corners of the room with his flashlight as I examined the shard and then had left the room. As I clutched the piece of china, I heard the sound of his drill and then his voice calling us from above. We went back up the stairs and found him in a small room, little bigger than a closet, almost directly above the room where the boy lay. Three linked videocassette recorders were stacked one above the other on some shelving and a thin cable snaked through a hole at the base of the wall and disappeared into the floor of the warehouse. On one of the VCRs the seconds ticked off inexorably until Angel stilled them.

"In the corner of that cellar there's a tiny hole, not much bigger than my fingernail but big enough to take a fish-eye and a motion sensor," he said. "An ordinary Joe couldn't have found them unless he knew they were there and he knew where to look. I reckon the wire follows the ventilation system. Someone wanted to record what went on in that room anytime it was entered."

Someone, but not whoever went to work on the children in that room. A regular video camera set up in the room would give better-quality pictures. There was no reason for concealment unless the viewer didn't want to be noticed.

There was no monitor in the room, so whoever was responsible either wanted to watch the tapes in the comfort of his or her own home or wanted to be sure that whoever picked them up couldn't sample what was on them before handing them over. I knew a lot of people who could put together a deal like that, and so did Angel, but I had one in particular in mind: Pili Pilar.

We went back down to the basement. I took the folding spade from Angel's bag and began to break the earth. It didn't take long for me to hit something soft. I dug wider and then began to scrape away the earth, Angel beside me using a small garden trowel to help. A film of plastic was revealed, and through it, barely discernible, I could see brown, wrinkled skin. We scraped away the rest of the dirt until the child's body was visible, curled in a fetal position with its head hidden by its left arm. Even in decay, we could see the fingers had been broken, although I couldn't tell if it was a boy or a girl without moving it.

Angel looked slowly around the floor of the cellar and I knew what he was thinking. It was probably worse than that. This child had been buried barely six inches beneath the ground, which meant there were probably others below. This room had been in use for a long time.

Louis slipped into the room, his finger pressed to his lips. He glanced once at the child, then he pointed slowly above us with his right hand. We stayed still, hardly breathing, and I heard the sound of soft steps on the stairs. Angel retreated into the shadows beside the shelves, clicking off the flashlight as he went. Louis was already gone when I stood up. I moved to take up a position at the other side of the door and was reaching for my gun when a flashlight beam hit me in the face. The voice of Bobby Sciorra simply said, "Don't," and I withdrew my hand slowly.

He had moved quickly, surprisingly so. He emerged from the shadows, the ugly Five-seveN in his right hand and his flashlight focused on me as he neared the open gate. He stopped about ten feet away from me and I could see his teeth shining as he smiled.

"Dead man," he said. "Dead as the kids in the room behind you. I was gonna kill you back in that house but the old man wanted you left alive, 'less there was no other option. I just ran out of options."

"Still doing Ferrera's dirty work," I replied. "Even you should have scruples about this."

"We all have our weaknesses." He shrugged. "Sonny's is short-eyes. He likes looking, you know. Can't do nothing else with his limp dick. He's a sick fuck but his daddy loves him and now his daddy wants the mess cleaned up."

And so it was Sonny Ferrera who had recorded the death agonies of these children, who had watched while Hyams and Adelaide Modine tortured them to death, their screams echoing around the walls as the silent unblinking eye of the camera took it all in to spew out again into his living room. He must have known who the killers were, must have watched them kill again and again, yet he did nothing because he liked what he was seeing and didn't want it to end.

"How did the old man find out?" I asked, but I already knew the answer. I knew now what had been in the car with Pili when he crashed, or thought I knew. It turned out that I was as wrong in that as I had been in so much else.

There was a scuffle of movement in the corner of the alcove and Sciorra reacted with the swiftness of a cat. The flashlight beam widened and he stepped back, the gun moving minutely from me to the corner.

The beam caught the bowed head of Angel. He glanced up into Bobby Sciorra's eyes and smiled. Sciorra looked puzzled for a moment and then his mouth opened in slow-dawning realization. He was already turning to try to locate Louis when the darkness seemed to come alive around him and his eyes widened as he realized, too late, that death had come for him too.

Louis's skin gleamed in the light and his eyes were white as his left hand clamped tight over Sciorra's jaw. Sciorra seemed to tighten and spasm, his eyes huge with pain and fear. He rose up on his toes and his arms stretched wide at either side. He shook hard once, twice, then the air seemed to leave him and his arms and body sagged, yet his head remained rigid, his eyes wide and staring. Louis pulled the long, thin blade from the back of Sciorra's head and pushed him forward, and he fell to the ground at my feet, small shudders running through his body until they stopped entirely.

Angel emerged from the darkness of the room behind me.

"I always hated that fucking spook," he said, looking at the small hole at the base of Sciorra's skull.

"Yeah," said Louis. "I like him a whole lot better now." He looked at me. "What do I do with him?"

"Leave him. Give me his car keys."

Louis frisked Sciorra's body and tossed me the keys.

"He's a made guy. Is that gonna be a problem?"

"I don't know. Let me handle it. Stay close to here. At some point, I'm going to call Cole. When you hear the sirens, disappear."

Angel bent down and gingerly lifted the FN from the ground using the end of a screwdriver.

"We gonna leave this here?" he asked. "That's some gun, what you say is true."

"It stays," I said. If I was right, Bobby Sciorra's gun was the link between Ollie Watts, Connell Hyams, and the Ferrera family, the link between a set of child killings that spanned thirty years and a mob dynasty that was more than twice as old again.

I stepped over Sciorra's body and ran from the warehouse. His black Chevy was pulled into the yard, its trunk facing the warehouse, and the gates had been closed behind it. It looked a lot like the car that had taken out Fat Ollie Watts's killer. I reopened the gates and drove away from the Morelli warehouse and Queens itself. Queens, a mass of warehouses and cemeteries.

And sometimes both together.

CHAPTER XXVIII

I was close now, close to an end, a termination of sorts. I was about to witness the cessation of something that had been happening for over three decades and that had claimed enough young lives to fill the catacombs of an abandoned warehouse. But no matter what the resolution might be, it was insufficient to explain what had taken place. There would be an ending. There would be a closure. There would be no solution.

I wondered how many times each year Hyams had traveled up to the city in his neat lawyer's clothes, clutching an expensive yet understated overnight bag, in order to tear another child apart. As he boarded the train in front of the ticket collector, or smiled at the girl behind the airline check-in desk, or passed the woman at the toll booth in his Cadillac, the interior redolent with the scent of leather, had there been anything in his face that might have caused them to pause, to reconsider their assessment of this polite, reserved man with his trim gray hair and his conservative suit?

And I wondered also at the identity of the woman who had burned to death in Haven all those years ago, for it was not Adelaide Modine.

I remembered Hyams telling me that he had returned to Haven the day before the body was found. It was not difficult to put together a chain of events: the panicked call from Adelaide Modine;

the selection of a suitable victim from the files of Doc Hyams; the alteration of the dental files to match the body; the planting of the jewelry and purse beside the corpse; and the flickering of the first flames, the smell like roasting pork, as the body began to burn.

And then she disappeared back into the darkness to hibernate, to find time to reinvent herself so the killing could continue. Adelaide Modine was like a dark spider squatting in the corner of a web, rushing out when a victim wandered into her sphere of influence and cocooning it in plastic. She had moved unhindered through thirty long years, presenting one face to the world and revealing another to the children. She was a figure glimpsed only by the young, a bogeyman, the creature waiting in the darkness when all the world was asleep.

I believed I could see her face now. I believed also that I understood why Sonny Ferrera had been hunted by his own father, why I had been tracked to Haven by Bobby Sciorra, why Fat Ollie Watts had fled in fear of his life and died in the roar of a gun in a street soaked in late summer sunlight.

THE STREETLIGHTS FLASHED BY like pistol flares. There was dirt beneath my fingernails as I clutched the wheel and I had an almost irresistible desire to pull into a gas station and wash them clean, to take a wire brush and to scrub my skin until it bled, scraping away all the layers of filth and death that seemed to have adhered to me in the past twenty-four hours. I could taste bile in my mouth and I swallowed back hard, focusing on the road ahead, on the lights of the car in front, and, just once or twice, on the careless dusting of stars in the black skies above.

When I arrived at the Ferrera house, the gates were open, and there was no sign of the feds who had watched the house earlier in the week. I drove Bobby Sciorra's car up the driveway and parked in the shadows beneath some trees. My shoulder ached badly now and bouts of nauseous sweating racked my body.

The front door of the house was ajar and I could see men

moving inside. Beneath one of the front windows a dark-suited figure sat slouched with his head in his hands, his automatic lying discarded beside him. I was almost on top of him when he saw me.

"You ain't Bobby," he said.

"Bobby's dead."

He nodded to himself, as if this was no more than he expected. Then he stood up, frisked me, and took my gun. Inside the house, armed men stood in corners talking in hushed tones. The place had a funereal air, a sense of barely suppressed shock. I followed him to the old man's study. He left me to open the door for myself, standing back to watch me as I did so.

There was blood and gray matter on the floor and a dark, black-red stain on the thick Persian carpet. There was blood also on the tan pants of the old man as he cradled his son's head in his lap. His left hand, its fingers red, toyed with Sonny's lank, thinning hair. A gun hung limply from the right, its barrel pointing at the floor. Sonny's eyes were open and in his dark pupils I could see the light of a lamp reflected.

I guessed that he had shot Sonny as he held his head in his lap, as his son knelt beside him pleading for . . . what? For help, for a reprieve, for forgiveness? Sonny, with his mad-dog eyes, dressed in a cheap cream suit and an open-necked shirt, gaudy with gold even in death. The old man's face was stern and unyielding, but when he turned to look at me, his eyes were huge with guilt and despair, the eyes of a man who has killed himself along with his son.

"Get out," said the old man, softly but distinctly, but he wasn't looking at me now. A slight breeze blew in through the open French windows from the garden beyond, bringing with it some petals and leaves and the sure knowledge of the end of things. A figure had appeared, one of his own men, an older soldier whose face I recognized but whose name I did not know. The old man raised the gun and pointed it at him, his hand shaking now.

"Get out!" he roared, and this time the soldier moved, pulling the windows closed instinctively as he departed. The breeze simply blew them open again and the night air began to make the

room its own. Ferrera kept the gun trained there for a few seconds longer and then it wavered and fell. His left hand, stilled by the appearance of his man, returned to its methodical stroking of his dead son's hair with the soothing, insane monotony of a caged animal stalking its pen.

"He's my son," he said, staring into a past that was and a future that might have been. "He's my son but there's something wrong with him. He's sick. He's bad in the head, bad inside."

There was nothing for me to say. I stayed silent.

"Why are you here?" he said. "It's over now. My son is dead."

"A lot of people are dead. The children . . ." For an instant the old man winced. "Ollie Watts . . ."

He shook his head slowly, his eyes unblinking. "Fucking Ollie Watts. He shouldn't have run. When he ran, we knew. Sonny knew."

"What did you know?"

I think that if I had entered the room only minutes later the old man would have had me killed instantly, or would have killed me himself. Instead, he seemed to seek some sort of release through me. He would confess to me, unburden himself to me, and that would be the last time he would bring himself to speak it aloud.

"That he'd looked in the car. He shouldn't have looked. He shoulda just walked away."

"What did he see? What did he find in the car? Videos? Pictures?"

The old man's eyes closed tightly, but he couldn't hide from what he had seen. Tears squeezed themselves from wrinkled corners and ran down the sides of his cheeks. His mouth formed silent words. No. No. More. Worse. When he opened his eyes again, he was dead inside. "Tapes. And a child. There was a child in the trunk of the car. My boy, my Sonny, he killed a child."

He turned to look at me again but this time his face was moving, twitching almost, as if his head could not contain the enormity of what he had seen. This man, who had killed and tortured and who had ordered others to kill and torture in his name, had found in his own son a darkness that was beyond naming, a lightless place where slain children lay, the black heart of every dead thing.

Watching had no longer been enough for Sonny. He had seen the power these people had, the pleasure they took in tearing the life slowly from the children, and wanted to experience it too.

"I told Bobby to bring him to me but he ran, ran as soon as he heard about Pili." His face hardened. "Then I told Bobby to kill them all, all the rest, every one of them." And then he seemed to be talking to Bobby Sciorra again, his face red with fury. "Destroy the tapes. Find the kids, find where they are, and then put them somewhere they'll never be found. Dump them at the bottom of the fucking ocean if you can. I want it like it never happened. It never happened." Then he seemed to remember where he was and what he had done, at least for a time, and his hand returned to its stroking.

"And then you came along, trailing the girl, asking questions. How could the girl know? I let you go after her, to get you away from here, to get you away from Sonny."

But Sonny had come after me through his hired killers and they had failed. Their failure forced his father to act. If the woman lived and was forced to testify, Sonny would be cornered again. And so Sciorra had been dispatched, and the woman had died.

"But why did Sciorra kill Hyams?"

"What?"

"Sciorra killed a lawyer in Virginia, a man who was trying to kill me. Why?"

For a moment, Ferrera's eyes grew wary and the gun rose. "You wearing a wire?" I shook my head wearily and painfully ripped open the front of my shirt. The gun fell again.

"He recognized him from the tapes. That's how he found you, in the old house. Bobby's driving through the town and suddenly he sees this guy driving in the opposite direction and it's the guy in the video, the guy who . . ." He stopped again and rolled his tongue in his mouth, as if to generate enough saliva to keep talking. "All the traces had to be wiped out, all of them."

"But not me?"

"Maybe he should've killed you too, when he had the chance, no matter what your cop friends would have done."

"He should have," I said. "He's dead now."

Ferrera blinked hard.

"Did you kill him?"

"Yes."

"Bobby was a made guy. You know what that means?"

"You know what your son did?"

He was silent then, as the enormity of his son's crime swept over him once more, but when he spoke again there was a barely suppressed fury in his voice and I knew that my time with him was drawing to a close.

"Who are you to judge my son?" he began. "You think because you lost a kid that you're the patron saint of dead children. Fuck. You. I've buried two of my sons and now, now I've killed the last of them. You don't judge me. You don't judge my son." The gun rose again and pointed at my head.

"It's all over," he said.

"No. Who else was on the tapes?"

His eyes flickered. The mention of the tapes was like a hard slap to him.

"A woman. I told Bobby to find her and kill her too."

"And did he?"

"He's dead."

"Do you have the tapes?"

"They're gone, all burned."

He stopped, as he remembered again where he was, as if the questions had briefly taken him away from the reality of what he had done and of the responsibility he bore for his son, for his crimes, for his death.

"Get out," he said. "If I ever see you again, you're a dead man."

No one stood in my way as I left. My gun was on a small table by the front door and I still had the keys to Bobby Sciorra's car. As I drove away from the house it looked silent and peaceful in the rearview, as if nothing had ever happened.

CHAPTER

XXIX

Each morning after the deaths of Jennifer and Susan, I would wake from my strange, disordered dreams, and for an instant, it seemed that they would still be near me, my wife sleeping softly by my side, my child surrounded by her toys in a room nearby. For a moment they still lived and I experienced their deaths as a fresh loss with each waking, so that I was unsure whether I was a man waking from a dream of death or a dreamer entering a world of loss, a man dreaming of unhappiness or a man waking to grief.

And amid all, there was the constant aching regret that I had never really known Susan until she was gone and that I loved a shadow in death as in life.

The woman and the child were dead, another woman and child in a cycle of violence and dissolution that seemed unbreakable. I was grieving for a young woman and a boy whom I had never encountered when they were alive, about whom I knew almost nothing, and through them I grieved for my own wife and child.

The gates of the Barton estate stood open; either someone had entered and planned to leave quickly or someone had already gone. There were no other cars in sight as I parked on the gravel drive and walked toward the house. Light was visible through the glass above the front door. I rang the bell twice but there was no answer, so I moved to a window and peered in.

The door into the hallway was open, and in the gap I could see a woman's legs, one foot bare, the other with a black shoe still clinging to its toes. The legs were bare to the tops of the thighs, where the end of a black dress still covered her buttocks. The rest of her body was obscured. I shattered the glass with the butt of my gun, half expecting to hear an alarm, but there was only the sound of the glass tinkling on the floor inside.

I reached in carefully to open the latch and climbed through the window. The room was illuminated by the hallway lights. I could feel my blood pounding through my veins, could hear it in my ears as I opened the door wider, sensed it tingling at the tips of my fingers as I stepped into the hall and looked at the body of the woman.

Blue veins marbled the skin on her legs, and the flesh at the thighs was dimpled and slightly flabby. Her face had been pounded in, and strands of gray hair adhered to the torn flesh. Her eyes were still open and her mouth was dark with blood. Only the stumps of teeth remained within; she was almost unrecognizable. There was only the gold, emerald-studded necklace, the deep red nail varnish, and the simple yet expensive de la Renta dress to suggest the body was that of Isobel Barton. I touched the skin at her neck. There was no pulse—I hardly expected any—but she was still warm.

I stepped into the study where we had first met and compared the shard of china I had taken from Evan Baines's hand with the single blue dog on the mantelpiece. The pattern matched. I imagined Evan had died quickly when the damage was discovered, the victim of a fit of rage at the loss of one of Adelaide Modine's family heirlooms.

From the kitchen down the hall came a series of uneven clicking sounds and I could smell a faint odor of burning, like a pot left on a stove for too long. Above it, almost unnoticed until now, was the faint hint of gas. No light showed around the edge of the closed door as I approached, although the acrid smell grew more definite, more intense, and the odor of gas was stronger now. I opened the door carefully and stepped back and to one side. My finger rested gently on the trigger, but even as I noticed the pressure, I was aware that the gun was useless if there was gas leaking.

There was no movement from within but the smell was very strong now. The strange, irregular clicking was loud, with a low drone above it. I took a deep breath and flung myself into the room, my useless gun attempting to draw a bead on anything that moved.

The kitchen was empty. The only illumination came from the windows, the hall, and the three large, industrial microwave ovens side by side in front of me. Through their glass doors I could see blue light dance over a range of metal objects inside: pots, knives, forks, pans, all were alive with tiny flickers of silver-blue lightning. The stench of gas made my head swim as the tempo of the clicks increased. I ran. I had the front door open when there was a dull *whump* from the kitchen, followed by a second, louder bang, and then I was flying through the air as the force of the explosion hurled me to the gravel. There was the sound of glass breaking and the lawn was set aglow as the house burst into flames behind me. As I stumbled toward my car I could feel the heat and see the dancing fire reflected in the windows.

At the gate to the Barton estate, a pair of red brake lights glowed briefly and then a car turned into the road. Adelaide Modine was covering her tracks before disappearing into the shadows once again. The house was ablaze, the flames escaping to scale the outside walls like ardent lovers, as I pulled into the road and followed the rapidly receding lights.

She drove fast down the winding Todt Hill Road and in the silence of the night I could hear the shriek of her brakes as she negotiated the bends. I took her at Ocean Terrace, as she headed for the Staten Island Expressway. To the left, a steep slope dense with trees fell down to Sussex Avenue below. I gained on her, mounted the verge at Ocean and swung hard to the left, the weight of the Chevy forcing the BMW closer and closer to the verge, the tinted windows revealing nothing of the driver within. Ahead of me, I saw Todt Hill Road curve viciously to the right, and I pulled away to stay with the curve just as the BMW's front wheels left the road and the car plunged down the hill.

The BMW rolled on garbage and scree, striking two trees before coming to a stop halfway down the leaf-strewn slope, its progress arrested by the dark mass of a young beech. The roots of the tree were partially yanked from the ground and it arched backward, its branches eventually coming to rest unsteadily against the trunk of another tree farther down the slope.

I pulled my car onto the verge, its headlights still on, and ran down the slope, my feet slipping on the grass so that I was forced to steady myself with my good arm.

As I approached the BMW the driver's door opened and the woman who was Adelaide Modine staggered out. A huge gash had opened in her forehead and her face was streaked with blood so that amid the woods and the leaves, in the bleak reflected light of the heads, she seemed a strange, feral being, her clothes inappropriate trappings to be shed as she returned to her ferocious natural state. She was hunched over slightly, clutching her chest where she had slammed into the steering column, but she straightened painfully as I approached.

Despite her pain, Isobel Barton's eyes were alive with viciousness. Blood flowed from her mouth when she opened it and I saw her test something within with her tongue and then release a small bloodied tooth onto the ground. I could see the cunning in her face, as if, even now, she was seeking a means of escape.

There was evil still in her, a foulness that went far beyond the limited viciousness of a cornered beast. I think concepts of justice, of right, of recompense were beyond her. She lived in a world of pain and violence where the killing of children, their torture and mutilation, were like air and water to her. Without them, without the muffled cries and the futile, despairing twistings, existence had no meaning and would come to an end.

And she looked at me and seemed almost to smile. "Cunt," she said, spitting the word out.

I wondered how much Ms. Christie had known or suspected before she died in that hallway. Not enough, obviously.

I was tempted to kill Adelaide Modine then. To kill her would be to stamp out one part of that terrible evil that had taken my own child along with the lives of the children in the cellars, the same evil that had spawned the Traveling Man and Johnny Friday and a million other individuals like them. I believed in the devil and pain. I believed in torture and rape and vicious, prolonged death. I believed in hurt and agony and the pleasure they gave to those who caused them, and to all these things I gave the name evil. And in Adelaide Modine I saw its red, sputtering spark exploded into bloody flame.

I cocked the pistol. She didn't blink. Instead, she laughed once and then grimaced at the pain. She was now curled over again, almost fetal near the ground. I could smell gasoline on the air as it flowed from the ruptured tank.

I wondered what Catherine Demeter had felt when she saw this woman in De Vries's department store. Had she glimpsed her in a mirror, in the glass of a display case? Had she turned in disbelief, her stomach tightening as if in the grip of a fist? And when their eyes met, when she knew that this was the woman who had killed her sister, did she feel hatred, or anger, or simply fear, fear that this woman could turn on her as she had once turned on her sister? For a brief moment, had Catherine Demeter become a frightened child again?

Adelaide Modine might not have recognized her immediately, but she must have seen the recognition in the eyes of the other woman. Maybe it was that slight overbite that gave it away, or perhaps she looked into the face of Catherine Demeter and was instantly back in that dark cellar in Haven, killing her sister.

And then, when Catherine could not be found, she had set about finding a resolution to the problem. She had hired me on a pretext and had killed her own stepson, not only so that he could not give the lie to her story but as the first step in a process that would lead to the eventual death of Ms. Christie and the destruction of her home as she covered the traces of her existence.

Maybe Stephen Barton bore some blame for what happened, for only he could have provided a link between Sonny Ferrera, Connell Hyams, and his stepmother, when Hyams was seeking somewhere to take the children, a property owned by someone who wouldn't ask too many questions. I doubt if Barton ever really knew what was taking place, and that lack of understanding killed him in the end.

And I wondered when Adelaide Modine had learned of the death of Hyams and realized that she was now alone, that the time had come to move on, leaving Ms. Christie as a decoy just as she had left an unknown woman to burn in her place in Virginia.

But how would I prove all this? The videos were gone. Sonny Ferrera was dead, Pilar was certainly dead. Hyams, Sciorra, Granger, Catherine Demeter, all gone. Who would remember a child killer from three decades ago? Who would recognize her in the woman before me? Would the word of Walt Tyler be enough? She had killed Christie, true, but even that might never be proved. Would there be enough forensic evidence in the wine cellars to prove her guilt?

Adelaide Modine, curled in a ball, unraveled like a spider that senses a shift in its web and sprang toward me, the nails of her right hand digging into my face, scratching for my eyes, while the left sought the gun. I struck her in the face with the heel of my hand, pushing her back simultaneously with my knee. She came at me again and I shot her, the bullet catching her above the right breast.

She stumbled back against the car, supporting herself on the open door, her hand clutching at the wound in her chest.

And she smiled.

"I know you," she said, forcing the words out through the pain. "I know who you are."

Behind her, the tree shifted slightly as the weight of the car forced its roots up from the ground. The big BMW moved forward a little. Adelaide Modine swayed before me, blood pouring now from the wound in her chest. There was something bright in her eyes, something that made my stomach tighten.

"Who told you?"

"I know," she said, and smiled again. "I know who killed your wife and child."

I moved toward her as she tried to speak again but her words were swallowed by the sound of grinding metal from the car as the tree finally gave way. The BMW shifted on the slope and then plummeted down the hill. As it rolled, impacting on trees and stones, the rending metal sparked and the car burst into flame. And as I watched, I realized that it was always meant to end this way.

Adelaide Modine's world exploded into yellow flame as the gasoline around her ignited; and then she was enveloped, her head back and her mouth wide for an instant before she fell, striking feebly at the flames as she toppled, burning, into the darkness. The car was blazing at the bottom of the slope, thick black smoke ascending in plumes into the air. I watched it from the road, the heat searing my face. Farther down the hill, in the wooded dark, a smaller pyre burned.

CHAPTER

I sat in the same police interview room with the same wooden table with the same wooden heart carved into its surface. My arm was freshly bandaged and I had showered and shaved for the first time in over two days. I had even caught a few hours' sleep stretched across three chairs. Despite Agent Ross's best effort, I was not in a jail cell. I had been interrogated comprehensively, first by Walter and another detective, then by Walter and the assistant chief, and finally, by Ross and one of his agents, with Walter in attendance to make sure they didn't beat me to death out of frustration.

Once or twice I thought I caught glimpses of Philip Kooper striding around outside, like a corpse that had exhumed itself to sue the undertaker. I guessed that the trust's public profile was about to take a terminal hammering.

I told the cops nearly everything. I told them about Sciorra, about Hyams, about Adelaide Modine, about Sonny Ferrera. I did not tell them that I had become involved in the case at Walter Cole's instigation. The other gaps in my story I left them to fill in for themselves. I told them simply that I had taken some leaps of the imagination. Ross almost had to be forcibly restrained at that point.

Now there was only Walter and me and a pair of coffee cups.

"Have you been down there?" I asked eventually, breaking the silence.

Walter nodded. "Briefly. I didn't stay."

"How many?"

"Eight so far, but they're still digging."

And they would continue digging, not just there but in scattered locations across the state and maybe even farther afield. Adelaide Modine and Connell Hyams had been free to kill for thirty years. The Morelli warehouse had been rented for only a portion of that time, which meant that there were probably other warehouses, other deserted basements, old garages, and disused lots that contained the remains of lost children.

"How long had you suspected?" I asked.

He seemed to think I was asking about something else, maybe a dead man in the toilet of a bus station, because he started and turned to me. "Suspected what?"

"That someone in the Barton household was involved in the Baines disappearance?"

He almost relaxed. Almost. "Whoever took him had to know the grounds, the house."

"Assuming he was taken at the house and hadn't wandered."

"Assuming that, yes."

"And you sent me to find out."

"I sent you."

I felt culpable for Catherine Demeter's death, not only because of my failure to find her alive but because, unwittingly, I might have brought Modine and Hyams to her.

"I may have led them to Catherine Demeter," I said to Walter after a while. "I told Ms. Christie I was going to Virginia to follow a lead. It might have been enough to give her away."

Walter shook his head. "She hired you as insurance. She must have alerted Hyams as soon as she was seen. He was probably on the lookout for her already. If she didn't turn up in Haven, then they were relying on you to find her. As soon as you did, I think you'd both have been killed."

I had a vision of Catherine Demeter's body slumped in the basement of the Dane house, her head surrounded by a circle of blood. And I saw Evan Baines wrapped in plastic, and the decayed body of a child half covered in earth, and the other corpses still to be discovered in the Morelli basement, and elsewhere.

And I saw my own wife, my own child in all of them.

"You could have sent someone else," I said.

"No, only you. If Evan Baines's killer was there, I knew you'd find out. I knew you'd find out because you're a killer yourself."

The word hung in the air for a moment, then tore a rift between us, like a knife cutting through our past together. Walter turned away.

I stayed silent for a time and then, as if he had never spoken, I said: "She told me that she knew who killed Jennifer and Susan."

He seemed almost grateful for the break in the silence. "She couldn't have known. She was a sick, evil woman and that was her way of trying to torture you after she died."

"No, she knew. She knew who I was before she died, but I don't think she knew when she hired me. She would have suspected something. She wouldn't have taken the chance."

"You're wrong," he said. "Let it go."

I didn't say anything more but I knew that, somehow, the dark worlds of Adelaide Modine and the Traveling Man had come together.

"I'm considering retirement," said Cole. "I don't want to look at death anymore. I've been reading Sir Thomas Browne. You ever read Thomas Browne?"

"No."

"*Christian Morals:* 'Behold not Death's Heads til thou doest not see them, nor look upon mortifying objects til thou overlook'st them.'" His back was to me but I could see his face reflected in the window and his eyes seemed far away. "I've spent too long looking at death. I don't want to force myself to look any longer."

He sipped his coffee. "You should go away from here, do something to put your ghosts behind you. You're no longer what you once were, but maybe you can still step back, before you lose yourself forever."

A film was forming on my untouched coffee. When I didn't respond, Walter sighed and spoke with a sadness in his voice that I had never heard before. "I'd prefer it if I didn't have to see you again," he said. "I'll talk to some people, see if you can go."

Something had changed within me, that much was true, but I was not sure that Walter could see it for what it was. Maybe only I could really understand what had happened, what Adelaide Modine's death had unlocked within me. The horror of what she had done through the years, the knowledge of the hurt and pain she had inflicted on the most innocent among us, could not be balanced in this world.

And yet it had been brought to an end. I had brought it to an end.

All things decay, all things must end, the evil as well as the good. What Adelaide Modine's death had done, in its brutal, flame-red way, was to show me that this was true. If I could find Adelaide Modine and could bring her to an end, then I could do the same with others. I could do the same with the Traveling Man.

And somewhere, in a dark place, a clock began to tick, counting off the hours, the minutes, the seconds, before it would toll the end for the Traveling Man.

All things decay. All things must end.

AND AS I THOUGHT of what Walter had said, of his doubts about me, I thought too of my father and the legacy he left me. I have only fragmented memories of my father. I remember a large, red-faced man carrying a Christmas tree into the house, his breath rising into the air like the puffs of steam from an old train. I remember walking into the kitchen one evening to find him caressing my mother and her laughter at their shared embarrassment. I remember him reading to me at night, his huge fingers following the words as he spoke them to me so that they might be familiar to me when I returned to them again. And I remember his death.

His uniform was always freshly pressed and he kept his gun oiled and cleaned. He loved being a policeman, or so it seemed. I did not know then what it was that drove him to do what he did. Maybe Walter Cole gained some knowledge of it when he looked upon the bodies of those dead children. Maybe I, too, have knowledge of it. Maybe I have become like my father.

What is clear is that something inside him died and the world appeared to him in different, darker colors. He had looked upon death's heads for too long and become a reflection of what he saw.

The call had been a routine one: two kids fooling around in a car late at night on a patch of urban wasteland, flashing the lights and sounding the horn. My father had responded and found one of the local boys, a petty criminal well on the road to graduating into felonies, and his girlfriend, a middle-class girl who was flirting with danger and enjoying the sexual charge it brought.

My father couldn't recall what the boy said to him as he tried to impress his girl. Words were exchanged and I can imagine my father's voice deepening and hardening in warning. The boy made mocking movements toward the inside pocket of his jacket, enjoying the effect on my father's nerves and bathing in the ripples of laughter from the young woman beside him.

Then my father drew his gun and the laughter stopped. I can see the boy raising his hands, shaking his head, explaining that there was no weapon there, that it was all just fun, that he was sorry. My father shot him in the face, blood streaking the interior of the car, the windows, the face of the girl in the passenger seat, his mouth wide in shock. I don't think she even screamed before my father shot her too. Then he walked away.

Internal Affairs came for him as he stripped in the locker room. They took him before his brother officers, to make an example of him. No one got in their way. By then, they all knew, or thought they knew.

He admitted everything but could not explain it. He simply shrugged his shoulders when they asked. They took his gun and his badge—his backup, the one I now hold, remained back in his bedroom—and then they drove him home under the NYPD rule that prevented a policeman from being questioned about the possible commission of a crime until forty-eight hours had elapsed. He looked dazed when he returned and wouldn't speak to my mother. The two Internal Affairs men sat outside in their car, smoking cigarettes, while I watched from my bedroom window. I think they knew what would happen next. When the gunshot sounded, they didn't leave their car until the echoes of the shot had faded into the cool night air.

I am my father's son, with all that entails.

THE DOOR OF THE interview room opened and Rachel Wolfe entered. She was dressed casually in blue jeans, high-top sneakers, and a black hooded cotton top by Calvin Klein. Her hair was loose, hanging over her ears and resting on her shoulders, and there was a sprinkling of freckles on her nose and at the base of her neck.

She took a seat across from me and gave me a look of concern and sympathy. "I heard about the death of Catherine Demeter. I'm sorry."

I nodded and thought of Catherine Demeter and how she looked in the basement of the Dane house. They weren't good thoughts.

"How do you feel?" she asked. There was curiosity in her voice, but tenderness too.

"I don't know."

"Do you regret killing Adelaide Modine?"

"She called it. There was nothing else I could do." I felt numb about her death, about the killing of the lawyer, about the sight of Bobby Sciorra rising up on his toes as the blade entered the base of his skull. It was the numbness that scared me, the stillness inside me. I think that it might have scared me more, but for the fact that I felt something else too: a deep pain for the innocents who had been lost, and for those who had yet to be found.

"I didn't know you did house calls," I said. "Why did they call you in?"

"They didn't," she said, simply. Then she touched my hand, a strange, faltering gesture in which I felt—I hoped?—that there was something more than professional understanding. I gripped her hand tightly in mine and closed my eyes. I think it was a kind of first step, a faltering attempt to reestablish my place in the world. After all that had taken place over the previous two days, I wanted to touch, however briefly, something positive, to try to awaken something good within myself.

"I couldn't save Catherine Demeter," I said at last. "I tried and maybe something came out of that attempt. I'm still going to find the man who killed Susan and Jennifer."

She nodded slowly and held my gaze. "I know you will."

RACHEL HAD BEEN GONE for a short time when the cell phone rang.

"Yes?"

"Mista Parker?" It was a woman's voice.

"This is Charlie Parker."

"My name is Florence Aguillard, Mista Parker. My mother is *Tante* Marie Aguillard. You came to visit us."

"I remember. What can I do for you, Florence?" I felt the tightening in my stomach, but this time it was born of anticipation, born of the feeling that *Tante* Marie might have found something to identify the figure of the girl who was haunting us both.

In the background I could hear the music of a jazz piano and the laughter of men and women, thick and sensual as treacle. "I been tryin' to get you all afternoon. My momma say to call you. She say you gotta come to her now." I could hear something in her voice, something that conspired to trip her words as they tumbled from her mouth. It was fear and it hung like a distorting fog around what she had to say.

"Mista Parker, she say you gotta come now and you gotta tell no one you comin'. No one, Mista Parker."

"I don't understand, Florence. What's happening?"

"*I don't know,*" she said. She was crying now, her voice wracked by sobs. "But she say you gotta come, you gotta come *now.*" She regained control of herself and I could hear her draw a deep breath before she spoke again.

"Mista Parker, she say the Travelin' Man comin'."

THERE ARE NO COINCIDENCES, only patterns we do not see. The call was part of a pattern, linked to the death of Adelaide Modine, which I did not yet understand. I said nothing about the call to anyone. I left the interrogation room, collected my gun from the desk, then headed for the street and took a cab back to my apartment. I booked a first-class ticket to Moisant Field, the only ticket left on any flight leaving for Louisiana that evening, and checked in shortly before departure, declaring my gun at the desk, my bag swallowed up in the general confusion. The plane was full, half of the passengers tourists who didn't know better heading for the stifling August heat of New Orleans. The stewards served ham sandwiches with potato chips and a packet of dried raisins, all tossed in the sort of brown paper bag you got on school trips to the zoo.

There was darkness below us when the pressure began building in my nose. I was already reaching for a cocktail napkin when the first drops came, but quickly the pressure became pain, a ferocious, shooting pain that caused me to jerk back in my seat.

The passenger beside me, a businessman who had earlier been cautioned about using his laptop computer while the plane was still on the runway, stared at me in surprise and then shock as he saw the blood. I watched his finger pressing repeatedly to summon the steward, and then my head was thrown back, as if by the force of a blow. Blood spurted violently from my nose, drenching the back of the seat in front of me, and my hands shook uncontrollably.

Then, just as it seemed that my head was going to explode from the pain and the pressure, I heard a voice, the voice of an old, black woman in the Louisiana swamps.

"Chile," said the voice. "Chile, he's here."

And then she was gone and my world turned black.

3

The concavities of my body are like another hell for their capacity.

Sir Thomas Urquhart, "Rabelais' *Gargantua*"

CHAPTER

XXXI

There was a loud thud as the insect hit the windshield. It was a large dragonfly, a "mosquito hawk."

"Shit, that thing must have been big as a bird," said the driver, a young FBI agent named O'Neill Brouchard. Outside, it was probably in the high nineties, but the Louisiana humidity made it seem much hotter. My shirt felt cold and uncomfortable where the air-conditioning had dried it against my body.

A smear of blood and wings lay across the glass and the wipers struggled to remove it. The blood matched the drops that still stained my shirt, an unnecessary reminder of what had happened on the plane since my head still ached and the bridge of my nose felt tender to the touch.

Beside Brouchard, Woolrich remained silent, intent upon loading a fresh clip into his SIG Sauer. The assistant SAC was dressed in his usual garb of cheap tan suit and wrinkled tie. Beside me, a dark Windbreaker marked with the agency's letters lay crumpled on the seat.

I had called Woolrich from the satellite phone on the plane but couldn't get a connection. At Moisant Field, I left a number with his message service telling him to contact me immediately, then hired a car and set out toward Lafayette on I-10. Just outside Baton Rouge, the cell phone rang.

"Bird?" said Woolrich's voice. "What the hell are you doing down here?" There was concern in his voice. In the background, I could hear the sound of a car engine.

"You get my message?"

"I got it. Listen, we're already on our way. Someone spotted Florence out by her house, with blood on her dress and a gun in her hand. We're going to meet up with the local cops at exit one-twenty-one. Wait for us there."

"Woolrich, it may be too late . . ."

"Just wait. No hotdogging on this one, Bird. I got a stake in this too. I got Florence to think about."

In front of us I could see the taillights of two other vehicles, patrol cars out of the St. Martin Parish Sheriff's Office. Behind us, its headlights illuminating the inside of the FBI Chevy and the blood on the windshield, was an old Buick driven by two St. Martin detectives. I knew one of them, John Charles Morphy, vaguely, having met him once before with Woolrich in Lafitte's Blacksmith Shop on Bourbon, as he swayed quietly to the sound of Miss Lily Hood's voice.

Morphy was a descendant of Paul Charles Morphy, the world chess champion from New Orleans who retired in 1859 at the grand old age of twenty-two. It was said that he could play three or four games simultaneously while blindfolded. By contrast, John Charles, with his hard bodybuilder's frame, never struck me as a man much given to chess. Power lifting competitions, maybe, but not chess. He was a man with a past, according to Woolrich: a former detective in the NOPD who had left the force in the shadow of an investigation by the Public Integrity Division over the killing of a young black man named Luther Bordelon near Chartres two years earlier.

I looked over my shoulder and saw Morphy staring back at me, his shaven head glowing in the Buick's interior light, his hands tight on the wheel as he negotiated the rutted track through the bayou. Beside him, his partner, Toussaint, held the Winchester Model 12 pump upright between his legs. The stock was pitted and scratched, the barrel worn, and I guessed that it wasn't regulation issue but Toussaint's own. It had smelled strongly of oil when I spoke to Morphy through the window of the car back where the Bayou Courtableau intersected with I-10.

The lights of the car caught the branches of palmetto, tupelo, and overhanging willows, huge cypress heavy with Spanish moss, and, occasionally, the stumps of ancient trees in the swamps beyond. We turned into a road that was dark as a tunnel, the branches of the cypress trees above us like a roof against the starlight, and then we were rattling over the bridge that led to the house of *Tante* Marie Aguillard.

Before us, the two sheriff's office cars turned in opposing directions and parked diagonally, the lights of one shining out into the dark undergrowth that led down to the swamp banks. The lights of the second hit the house, casting shadows over the tree trunks that raised it from the ground, the building's overlapping boards, the steps leading up the screen door, which now stood open on the porch, allowing the night creatures easy access to the interior of the house.

Woolrich turned around as we pulled up. "You ready for this?"

I nodded. I had my Smith & Wesson in my hand as we stepped from the car into the warm air. I could smell rotting vegetation and a faint trace of smoke. Something rustled through the vegetation to my right and then splashed lightly into the water. Morphy and his partner came up beside us. I could hear the sound of a shell being jacked into the pump.

Two of the deputies stood uncertainly beside their car. The second pair advanced slowly across the neat garden, their guns drawn.

"What's the deal?" said Morphy. He was six feet tall with the V shape of a lifter, his head hairless and a circle of mustache and beard around his mouth.

"No one enters before us," said Woolrich. "Send those two jokers around the back but tell them to stay out of the house. The other two stay at the front. You two back us up. Brouchard, stay by the car and watch the bridge."

We moved across the grass, stepping carefully around the discarded children's toys on the lawn. There were no lights on in the house, no sign of any occupants. I could hear the blood pumping in my head and the palms of my hands were slick with sweat. We were ten feet from the porch steps when I heard a pistol cock and the voice of the deputy to our right.

"Ah, sweet Jesus," he said. "Sweet Jesus Lord, this can't be . . ."

A DEAD TREE, LITTLE more than an extended trunk, stood about ten yards from the water's edge. Branches, some no more than twigs, others as thick as a man's arm, commenced some three feet up the trunk and continued to a height of eight or nine feet.

Against the tree trunk stood Tee Jean Aguillard, the old woman's youngest son, his naked body glistening in the flashlight beam. His left arm was hooked around a thick branch so that his forearm and empty hand hung vertically. His head rested in the crook of another branch, his ruined eyes like dark chasms against the exposed flesh and tendons of his flayed face.

Tee Jean's right arm was also wrapped around a branch but this time his hand was not empty. In his fingers he grasped a flap of his own skin, a flap that hung like an opened veil and revealed the interior of his body from his exposed ribs to the area above his penis. His stomach and most of the organs in his abdomen had been removed. They lay on a stone by his left foot, a pile of white, blue, and red body parts in which coils of intestine curled like snakes.

Beside me, I heard one of the deputies begin to retch. I turned to see Woolrich grabbing him by the collar and hauling him to the water's edge some distance away. "Not here," he said. "Not here." He left the deputy on his knees by the water and turned toward the house.

"We've got to find Florence," he said. His face looked sickly and pale in the flashlight beam. "We gotta find her."

Florence Aguillard had been seen standing at the bridge to her house by the owner of a local bait shop. She had been covered in blood and held a Colt Service revolver in her hand. When the bait shop owner stopped, Florence raised the gun and fired a single shot through the driver's window, missing the bait shop owner by a fraction of an inch. He had called the St. Martin cops from a gas station and they, in turn, had called Woolrich, acting on his notice to the local police that any incident involving *Tante* Marie should be reported immediately to him.

Woolrich took the steps up the porch at a run and was almost at the door when I reached him. I put my hand on his shoulder and he spun toward me, his eyes wide.

"Easy," I said. The wild look disappeared from his eyes and he nodded slowly. I turned back to Morphy and motioned him to follow us into the house. Morphy took the Winchester pump from Toussaint and indicated that he should hang back with the deputy, now that his partner was indisposed.

A long central hallway led, shotgun style, to a large kitchen at the rear of the house. Six rooms radiated off the central artery, three on either side. I knew that *Tante* Marie's was the last door on the right and I was tempted to make straight for it. Instead we progressed carefully, taking a room at a time, the flashlight beams cutting a swath through the darkness, dust motes and moths bobbing in the beams.

The first room on the right, a bedroom, was empty. There were two beds, one made and the second, a child's bed, unmade, the blanket lying half on the floor. The living room opposite was also empty. Morphy and Woolrich each took a room as we progressed to the second set of doors. Both were bedrooms. Both were empty.

"Where are all the children, the adults?" I said to Woolrich.

"Eighteenth birthday party at a house two miles away," he replied. "Only Tee Jean and the old lady supposed to be here. And Florence."

The door opposite *Tante* Marie's room stood wide open and I could see a jumble of furniture, boxes of clothes, and piles of children's toys. A window was open and the curtains stirred slightly in the night air. We turned to face the door of *Tante* Marie's bedroom. It was slightly ajar and I could see moonlight within, disturbed and distorted by the shadows of the trees. Behind me, Morphy had the shotgun raised and Woolrich had the SIG held double-handed close to his cheek. I put my finger on the trigger of the Smith & Wesson, flicked open the door with the side of my foot, and dived low into the room.

A BLOODY HANDPRINT LAY on the wall by the door and I could hear the sound of night creatures in the darkness beyond the window. The moonlight cast drifting shadows across a long sideboard, a huge closet filled with almost identically patterned dresses, and a long, dark chest on the floor near the door. But the room was dominated by the giant bed that stood against the far wall, and by its occupant, *Tante* Marie Aguillard.

Tante Marie: the old woman who had reached out to a dying girl as the blade began to cut her face; the old woman who had called out to me in my wife's voice when I last stood in this room, offering me some kind of comfort in my sorrow; the old woman who had, in turn, reached out to me in her final torment.

She sat naked on the bed, a huge woman undiminished by death. Her head and upper body rested against a mountain of pillows, stained dark by her blood. Her face was a red-and-purple mass. Her jaw hung open, revealing long teeth stained yellow with tobacco. The flashlight caught her thighs, her thick arms, and the hands that reached toward the center of her body.

"God have mercy," said Morphy.

Tante Marie had been split from sternum to groin and the skin pulled back to be held in place by her own hands. As with her son, most of her internal organs had been removed and her stomach was a hollow cavern, framed by ribs, through which a section of her spine gleamed dully in the light. Woolrich's flashlight moved lower, toward her groin. I stopped it with my hand.

"No," I said. "No more."

Then a shout came from outside, startling in the silence, and we were running together toward the front of the house.

FLORENCE AGUILLARD STOOD SWAYING on the grass in front of her brother's body. Her mouth was curled down at either side, the bottom lip turned in on itself in grief. She held the long-barreled Colt in her right hand, the muzzle pointing toward the ground. Her white dress was patterned with blue flowers, obscured in places by her mother's blood. She made no noise, although her body was racked by silent cries.

Woolrich and I came down the steps slowly; Morphy and a deputy stayed on the porch. The second pair of deputies had come from the back of the house and stood facing Florence, Toussaint slightly to the right of them. To Florence's left, I could see the figure of Tee Jean hanging on the tree and, beside him, Brouchard with his unholstered SIG.

"Florence," said Woolrich softly, putting his gun back in his shoulder holster. "Florence, put the gun down."

Her body shook and her left hand wrapped itself tightly around her waist. She bent over slightly and shook her head slowly from side to side.

"Florence," repeated Woolrich. "It's me."

She turned her head toward us. There was misery in her eyes, misery and hurt and guilt and rage all vying for supremacy in her troubled mind.

She raised the gun slowly and pointed it in our direction. I saw the deputies bring their weapons up quickly. Toussaint had already assumed a sharpshooter's stance, his arms in front of his body, his gun unwavering.

"No!" shouted Woolrich, his right hand raised. I saw the cops look toward him in doubt and then toward Morphy. He nodded and they relaxed slightly, still keeping their weapons trained on Florence.

The Colt moved from Woolrich to me, and still Florence Aguillard shook her head slowly. I could hear her voice, soft in the night, repeating Woolrich's word like a mantra—"No no no no no"—and then she turned the gun toward herself, placed the barrel in her mouth, and pulled the trigger.

The explosion sounded like a cannon's roar in the night air. I could hear the sound of birds' wings flapping and small animals hurtling through the undergrowth as Florence's body crumpled to the ground. Woolrich stumbled to his knees beside her and reached out to touch her face with his left hand, his right reaching instinctively, futilely, for the pulse in her neck. Then he lifted her and buried her face in his sweat-stained shirt, his mouth open in pain.

In the distance, red lights shone. Farther away, I could hear the sound of a helicopter's blades scything at the darkness.

CHAPTER XXXII

The day dawned heavy and humid in New Orleans, the smell of the Mississippi strong in the morning air. I left my guest house and skirted the Quarter, trying to clear the tiredness from my head and my bones. I eventually ended up on Loyola, the traffic adding to the oppressive warmth. The sky overhead was gray and overcast with the threat of rain, and dark clouds hung over the city, seeming to lock in the heat. I bought a copy of the *Times-Picayune* from a vending machine and read it as I stood before City Hall. The newspaper was so heavy with corruption that it was a wonder the paper didn't rot: two policemen arrested on drug trafficking charges, a federal investigation into the conduct of the last Senate elections, suspicions about a former governor. New Orleans itself, with its run-down buildings, the grim shopping precinct of Poydras, the Woolworth store with its *Closing Down* notices, seemed to embody this corruption, so it was impossible to tell whether the city had infected the populace or if some of its people were dragging down the city with them.

Chep Morrison had built the imposing City Hall shortly after he returned from the Second World War to dethrone the millionaire Mayor Maestri and drag New Orleans into the twentieth century. Some of Woolrich's cronies still remembered Morrison with fondness, albeit a fondness arising from the fact that police corruption had flourished under him, along with numbers rackets, prostitution, and gambling. More than three decades later, the police department in New Orleans was still trying to deal with his legacy. For almost two decades, the Big Sleazy had been top of the league table of complaints about police misconduct, numbering over one thousand complaints per year.

The NOPD had been founded on the principal of "the cut": like the police forces in other southern cities—Savannah, Richmond, Mobile—it had been formed in the eighteenth century to control and monitor the slave population, with the police receiving a portion of the reward for capturing runaways. In the nineteenth century, members of the force were accused of rapes and murders, lynchings and robberies, of taking graft to allow gambling and prostitution to continue. The fact that police had to stand for election annually meant that they were forced to sell their allegiance to the two main political parties. The force manipulated government elections, intimidated voters, even participated in the massacre of moderates at the Mechanics Institute in 1866.

New Orleans's first black mayor, Dutch Morial, tried to clean up the department at the start of the nineteen eighties. If the independent Metropolitan Crime Commission, which had a quarter of a century's start on Morial, couldn't clean up the department, what hope did a black mayor have? The predominantly white police union went on strike and the Mardi Gras was cancelled. The national guard had to be called out to maintain order. I didn't know if the situation had improved since then. I hoped that it had.

New Orleans is also homicide central, with about four hundred Code 30s—NOPD code for a homicide—each year. Maybe half get solved, leaving a lot of people walking the streets of New Orleans with blood on their hands. That's something the city fathers prefer not to tell the tourists, although maybe a lot of the tourists would still come anyway. After all, when a city is so hot that it offers riverboat gambling, twenty-four-hour bars, strippers, prostitution, and a ready supply of drugs, all within a few blocks of one another, there's got to be some kind of downside to it all.

I walked on, eventually stopping to sit on the edge of a potted tree outside the pink New Orleans Center, the tower of the Hyatt rising behind it, while I waited for Woolrich to show. In the midst of the previous night's confusion, we had arranged a meeting for breakfast. I had considered staying in Lafayette or Baton Rouge, but Woolrich indicated that the local cops might not like having me so close to the investigation, and as he pointed out, he himself was based in New Orleans.

I gave him twenty minutes, and when he didn't arrive, I began to walk down Poydras Street, its canyon of office buildings already thronged with businesspeople and tourists heading for the Mississippi.

At Jackson Square, La Madeleine was packed with breakfasters. The smell of baking bread from its ovens seemed to draw people in like cartoon characters pulled along by a visible, snakelike scent. I ordered a pastry and coffee and finished reading the *Times-Picayune.* It's next to impossible to get the *New York Times* in New Orleans. I read somewhere that the New Orleans citizenry bought fewer copies of the *New York Times* than any other city in the United States, although they made up for it by buying more formal wear than anywhere else. If you're going out to formal dinners every evening, you don't get much time to read the *New York Times.*

Amid the magnolia and banana trees of the square, tourists watched tap dancers and mimes and a slim black man who maintained a steady, sensual rhythm by hitting his knees with a pair of plastic bottles. There was a light breeze blowing from the river, but it was fighting a losing battle with the morning heat and contented itself with tossing the hair of the artists hanging their paintings on the square's black iron fence and threatening the cards of the fortune-tellers outside the cathedral.

I felt strangely distant from what I had seen at *Tante* Marie's house. I had expected it to bring back memories of what I had seen in my own kitchen, the sight of my own wife and child reduced to flesh, sinew, and bone. Instead, I felt only a heaviness, like a dark, wet blanket over my consciousness.

I flicked through the newspaper once again. The killings had made the bottom of the front page, but the details of the mutilations had been kept from the press. It was hard to tell how long that would last; rumors would probably begin to circulate at the funerals.

Inside, there were pictures of two bodies, those of Florence and Tee Jean, being taken across the bridge toward waiting ambulances. The bridge had been weakened by the traffic and there were fears that it might collapse if the ambulances tried to cross. Mercifully, there were no pictures of *Tante* Marie being transported on a special gurney to her ambulance, her huge bulk seeming to mock mortality even as it lay shrouded in black.

I looked up to see Woolrich approaching the table. He had changed his tan suit for a light gray linen; the tan had been covered in Florence Aguillard's blood. He was unshaven and there were black bags beneath his eyes. I ordered him coffee and a plate of pastries and stayed quiet as he ate.

He had changed a great deal in the years I had known him, I thought. There was less fat on his face, and when the light caught him a certain way, his cheekbones were like blades beneath his skin. It struck me for the first time that he might be ill, but I didn't raise the topic. When Woolrich wanted to talk about it, he would.

While he ate, I recalled the first time that I had met him, over the body of Jenny Ohrbach. She had been pretty once, a thirty-year-old woman who had kept her figure through regular exercise and a careful diet and who had, it emerged, lived a life of considerable luxury without any obvious means of support.

I had stood over her in an Upper West Side apartment on a cold January night. Two large bay windows opened out on to a small balcony overlooking Seventy-ninth Street and the river, two blocks from Zabar's deli on Broadway. It wasn't our territory, but Walter Cole and I were there because the initial MO looked like it might have matched two aggravated burglaries we were investigating, one of which had led to the death of a young account executive, Deborah Moran.

All of the cops in the apartment wore coats, some with mufflers dangling around their necks. The apartment was warm and nobody was in any great hurry to head back out into the cold, least of all Cole and I, despite the fact that this seemed to be a deliberate homicide rather than an aggravated burglary. Nothing in the apartment appeared to have been touched and a purse containing three credit cards and over seven hundred dollars in cash was found undisturbed in a drawer under the television set. Someone had brought coffee from Zabar's and we sipped from the containers, our hands cupped around them, enjoying the unaccustomed feeling of warmth on our fingers.

The coroner had almost finished his work and an ambulance team was standing by to remove the body when an untidy figure shambled into the apartment. He wore a long brown overcoat the color of beef gravy, and the sole of one of his shoes had come adrift from the upper. Through the gap, a red sock and an exposed big toe revealed themselves. His tan pants were as wrinkled as a two-day-old newspaper and his white shirt had given up the struggle to keep its natural tones, settling instead for the unhealthy yellow pallor of a jaundice victim. A fedora was jammed on his head. I hadn't seen anyone wear a fedora at a crime scene since the last film noir revival at the Angelika.

But it was the eyes that attracted the most attention. They were bright and amused and cynical, trailing lines like a jellyfish moving through water. Despite his ramshackle appearance, he was clean shaven and his hands were spotless as he took a pair of plastic gloves from his pocket and pulled them on.

"Cold as a whore's heart out there," he remarked, squatting down and placing a finger gently beneath Jenny Ohrbach's chin. "Cold as death."

I felt a figure brush my arm and turned to see Cole standing beside me.

"Who the hell are you?" he asked.

"I'm one of the good guys," responded the figure. "Well, I'm FBI, so whatever that makes me in your eyes." He flicked his ID at us. "Special Agent Woolrich."

He rose, sighed, and pulled the gloves from his hands, then thrust both gloves and hands deep into the pockets of his coat.

"What brings you out on a night like this, Agent Woolrich?" I asked. "Lose the keys to the Federal Building?"

"Oh, the witty NYPD," said Woolrich, with a half smile. "Lucky there's an ambulance standing by in case my sides split." He turned his head to one side as he took in the body again. "You know who she is?" he asked.

"We know her name, but that's it," said a detective I didn't recognize. I didn't even know her name at that point. I knew only that she had been pretty once and now she was pretty no longer. She had been beaten around the face and head with a piece of hollow-centered coaxial cable, which had been dumped beside her body. The cream carpet around her head was stained a deep, dark red and blood had splashed on the walls and the expensive, and probably uncomfortable, white leather furniture.

"She's Tommy Logan's woman," said Woolrich.

"The garbage collection guy," I said.

"The very same."

Tommy Logan's company had clinched a number of valuable garbage collection contracts in the city over the previous two years. Tommy had also expanded into the window cleaning business. Tommy's boys cleaned the windows in your building or you didn't have any windows left to clean, and possibly no building either. Anyone with those kinds of contacts had to be connected.

"Racketeering interested in Tommy?" It was Cole.

"Lots of people interested in Tommy. Lot more than usual, if his girlfriend is lying dead on the carpet."

"You think maybe someone's sending him a message?" I asked.

Woolrich shrugged. "Maybe. Maybe someone should have sent him a message telling him to hire a decorator whose eyesight didn't give out the year Elvis died."

He was right. Jenny Ohrbach's apartment was so retro it should have been wearing flares and a goatee. Not that it mattered to Jenny Ohrbach any more.

No one ever found out who killed her. Tommy Logan seemed genuinely shocked when he was told that his girlfriend was dead, so shocked he even stopped worrying that his wife might find out about her. Maybe Tommy decided to be more generous to his business partners as a result of Jenny Ohrbach's death, but if he did, their arrangement still didn't last much longer. One year later, Tommy Logan was dead, his throat cut and his body dumped by the Borden Bridge in Queens.

But Woolrich I saw more of. Our paths crossed on occasion; we went for a drink once or twice before I returned home and he went back to his empty apartment in Tribeca. He produced tickets to a Knicks game; he came to the house for dinner; he gave Jennifer an enormous stuffed elephant as a birthday present; he watched, but did not judge or interfere, as I drank myself away shot by shot.

I have a memory of him at Jenny's third birthday party, a cardboard clown's hat jammed on his head and a bowl of Ben & Jerry's Cherry Garcia ice cream in his hand. He looked embarrassed, sitting there in his crumpled suit surrounded by three- and four-year-olds and their adoring parents, but also strangely happy as he helped small children blow up balloons or drew quarters from behind their ears. He did farmyard impressions and taught them how to balance spoons on their noses. When he left, there was a sadness in his eyes. I think he was recalling other birthdays, when his child was the center of attention, before he lost his way.

When Susan and Jennifer died, he followed me to the station and waited outside for four hours until they had finished questioning me. I couldn't go back to the house, and after that first night when I found myself crying in a hospital lobby, I couldn't stay with Walter Cole, not only because of his involvement in the investigation but because I did not want to be surrounded by a family, not then. Instead, I went to Woolrich's small, neat apartment, the walls lined with books of poetry: Marvell, Vaughan, Richard Crashaw, Herbert, Jonson, and Ralegh, whose "Passionate Man's Pilgrimage" he sometimes quoted. He gave me his bed. On the day of the funeral, he had stood behind me in the rain and let the water wash over him, the drops falling from the brim of his hat like tears.

"HOW YOU DOING?" I asked eventually.

He puffed his cheeks and breathed out, his head moving slightly from side to side like a nodding-dog figure on the backseat of a car. Gray was seeping through his hair from silver pools over his ears. There were lines like the cracks in fine china spreading from his eyes and the corners of his mouth.

"Not so good," he said. "I got three hours' sleep, if you can call waking up every twenty minutes to flashes of red 'sleep.' I keep thinking of Florence and the gun and the way it looked as it slid into her mouth."

"Were you still seeing her?"

"Not so much. On and off. We got together a coupla times and I was out at the house a few days back to see if everything was okay. Jesus, what a mess."

He pulled the newspaper toward him and scanned its coverage of the killings, his finger moving along the sides of each paragraph so that it became dark with print. When he had finished reading, he looked at his blackened fingertip, rubbed his thumb lightly across it, then wiped them both on a paper napkin.

"We got a fingerprint, a partial print," he said, as if the sight of his own lines and whorls had only just reminded him of it.

Outside, the tourists and the noise seemed to recede into the distance and there was only Woolrich and his soft eyes. He drained the last of his coffee then dabbed at his mouth with the napkin.

"That's why I was delayed. Confirmed it just an hour ago. We've compared it against Florence's prints, but it's not her. There are traces of the old woman's blood in it."

"Where did you find it?"

"Underside of the bed. He may have tried to steady himself as he cut, or maybe he slipped. Doesn't look like there was an attempt to erase it. We're comparing it against local files and our master fingerprint identification records. If he's in the system, we'll find him." As well as criminals, the files covered federal employees, aliens, military personnel, and those individuals who had requested that their prints be retained for identification purposes. Over the next twenty-four hours, the print found at the scene would be checked against about two hundred million others on record.

If it turned out to be the Traveling Man's print, then it would be the first real break since the deaths of Susan and Jennifer, but I wasn't holding my breath. A man who took the time to clean my wife's fingernails after he killed her was unlikely to be so careless as to leave his own fingerprint at a crime scene. I looked at Woolrich and knew he thought the same thing. He raised his hand for more coffee as he looked out at the crowds on Jackson Square and listened to the snorting of the ponies hitched to the touring carriages pulled up on Decatur.

"Florence'd been shopping in Baton Rouge earlier in the day, then returned home to change for some birthday party, one of her second cousins. She called you from some juke joint in Breaux Bridge, then went back to the house. She stayed there until maybe eight-thirty, then went to a cousin's birthday party at Breaux Bridge at about nine. According to witness statements taken by the local cops, she was distracted and didn't stay for long—seems that her momma insisted that she go, that Tee Jean could take care of her. She stayed one hour, maybe ninety minutes, then came back. Brennan, the bait shop owner, spotted her maybe thirty minutes after that. So we're looking at a window of one to two hours, no more, for the killings."

"Who's dealing with the case?"

"Morphy's bunch, in theory. In practice, a lot of it is likely to devolve mainly to us, since it matches the MO on Susan and Jennifer, and because I want it. Brillaud is going to hook up your phone, in case our man calls. It'll mean hanging around your hotel room for a while, but I don't see what else we can do." He avoided my eyes.

"You're cutting me out."

"You can't be too involved in this, Bird. You know that. I've told you before and I'm telling you again: we'll decide the extent of your involvement."

"Limited."

"Damn yes, limited. Look, Bird, you're the link to this guy. He's called once, he *will* call again. We wait, we see." He spread his hands wide.

"She was killed because of the girl. Are you going to look for the girl?"

Woolrich rolled his eyes in frustration. "Look where, Bird? The whole fucking bayou? We don't even know that she existed. We have a print, we'll run with that and see where it takes us. Now pay the check and let's get out of here. We've got things to do."

I WAS STAYING IN a restored Greek Revival house, the Flaisance House, on Esplanade, a white mansion filled with dead men's furniture. I had opted for a room in the converted carriage house at the rear, partly for the seclusion but also because it contained a natural alarm in the form of two large dogs who prowled the courtyard beneath and growled at anyone who wasn't a guest, according to the guy manning the night desk. In fact, the dogs just seemed to sleep a lot in the shade of an old fountain. My large room had a balcony, a brass ceiling fan, two heavy leather armchairs, and a small refrigerator, which I filled with bottled water.

When we reached the Flaisance, Woolrich turned on an early morning game show and we waited, unspeaking, for Brillaud to arrive. He knocked on the door about twenty minutes later, long enough for a woman from Tulsa to win a trip to Maui. Brillaud was a small, neatly dressed man with receding hair, through which he ran his fingers every few minutes as if to reassure himself that there was still some there. Behind him, two men in shirtsleeves awkwardly carried an array of monitoring equipment on a metal trolley, carefully negotiating the wooden external stairway that led up to the four carriage house rooms.

"Get cooking, Brillaud," said Woolrich. "I hope you brought something to read." One of the men in shirtsleeves waved a sheaf of magazines and some battered paperbacks that he had removed from the base of the trolley.

"Where will you be if we need you?" asked Brillaud.

"The usual place," said Woolrich. "Around." And then he was gone.

I HAD ONCE VISITED, through Woolrich, an anonymous room in the FBI's New York office. This was the tech room, where the squads engaged in long-term investigations—organized crime, foreign counterintelligence—monitored their wiretaps. Six agents sat before a row of reel-to-reel voice-activated tape recorders, logging the calls whenever the recorders kicked in, carefully noting the time, the date, the subject of the conversation. The room was almost silent, save for the click and whir of the machines and the sound of pens scratching on paper.

The feds do love their wiretaps. Back in 1928, when the FBI was called the Bureau of Investigation, the Supreme Court allowed almost unrestricted access to wiretaps of targets. In 1940, when the attorney general, Andrew Jackson, tried to end wiretapping, Roosevelt twisted his arm and extended taps to cover "subversive activities." Under Hoover's interpretation, "subversive activities" covered anything from running a Chinese laundry to screwing someone else's wife. Hoover was the god of wiretaps.

Now the feds no longer have to squat by junction boxes in the rain trying to protect their notebooks from the elements. Judicial approval, followed by a call to the telephone company in order to have the signal diverted, is usually enough. It's even easier when the subject is willing to cooperate. In my case, Brillaud and his men didn't even have to sit in a surveillance van, smelling one another's sweat.

I excused myself for five minutes while Brillaud worked to hook up both my own cell phone and the room phone, telling him that I was just heading for the kitchen of the main house. I left the Flaisance and strolled through the courtyard, attracting a bored glance from one of the dogs huddled in the shadows. I walked down to a telephone by a grocery store one block away. From there, I called Angel's number. The machine was on. I left a message telling him the situation and advising him not to call me on the cell phone.

Technically, the feds are supposed to engage in minimization on wiretapping or surveillance duties. In theory, this means that the agents hit the pause button on the recorder and tune out of the conversation, apart from occasional checks, if it becomes apparent that it's a private call unconnected with the business at hand. In practice, only a moron would assume that his private business would remain private on a tapped line and it seemed unwise for me to have conversations with a burglar and an assassin while the FBI was listening. When I had left the message, I picked up four coffees in the grocery store, reentered the Flaisance, and went up to my room, where an anxious-looking Brillaud was waiting by the door.

"We can order coffee up, Mr. Parker," he said disapprovingly.

"It never tastes the same," I replied.

"Get used to it," he concluded, closing the door behind me.

THE FIRST CALL CAME at 4 P.M., after hours of watching bad TV and reading the problem pages in back issues of *Cosmo*. Brillaud rose quickly from the bed and clicked his fingers at the technicians, one of whom was already tugging at his headphones. He counted down from three with his fingers and then signaled me to pick up the cell phone.

"Charlie Parker?" It was a woman's voice.

"Yes?"

"It's Rachel Wolfe."

I looked up at the FBI men and shook my head. There was the sound of breath being released. I put my hand over the mouthpiece. "Hey, minimization, remember?" There was a click as the recorder was turned off. Brillaud went back to lying on my clean sheets, his fingers laced behind his head and his eyes closed.

Rachel seemed to sense that there was something happening at the other end of the line.

"Can you talk?"

"I have company. Can I call you back?"

She gave me her home number and told me she planned to be out until 7:30 P.M. I could call her then. I thanked her and hung up.

"Lady friend?" asked Brillaud.

"My doctor," I replied. "I have a low tolerance syndrome. She hopes that within a few years I'll be able to cope with idle curiosity."

Brillaud sniffed noisily but his eyes stayed closed.

THE SECOND CALL CAME at six. The humidity and the sound of the tourists had forced us to close the balcony window, and the air was sour with male scent. This time, there was no doubt about the caller.

"Welcome to New Orleans, Bird," said the synthesized voice, in deep tones that seemed to shift and shimmer like mist.

I paused for a moment and nodded at the FBI men. Brillaud was already paging Woolrich. On a computer screen by the balcony, I could see maps shifting and I could hear the Traveling Man's voice coming thinly through the headphones of the FBI men.

"No point in welcoming your FBI friends," said the voice, this time in the high, lilting cadences of a young girl's voice. "Is Agent Woolrich with you?"

I paused again before responding, conscious of the seconds ticking by and the "number withheld" message on the cell phone display.

"Don't fuck with me, Bird!" Still the child's voice, but this time in the petulant tones of one who has been told that she can't go out and play with her friends, the swearing rendering the effect even more obscene than it already was.

"No, he's not here."

"Thirty minutes." Then the connection ended.

Brillaud shrugged. "He knows. He won't stay on long enough to get a fix." He lay back down on the bed to wait for Woolrich.

WOOLRICH LOOKED EXHAUSTED. HIS eyes were red rimmed from lack of sleep and his breath smelled foul. He shifted his feet constantly, as if they were too big for his shoes. Five minutes after he arrived, the phone rang again. Brillaud counted down and I picked up the phone.

"Yes."

"Don't interrupt, just listen." It sounded like a woman's voice, the voice of someone who was about to tell her lover one of her secret fantasies, but distorted, inhuman. "I'm sorry about Agent Woolrich's lover, but only because I missed her. She was supposed to be there. I had something special planned for her, but I suppose she had ideas of her own."

Woolrich blinked hard once, but gave no other indication that he was disturbed by what he heard.

"I hope you liked my presentation," continued the voice. "Maybe you're even beginning to understand. If you're not, don't worry. There's plenty more to come. Poor Bird. Poor Woolrich. United in grief. I'll try to find you some company."

Then the voice changed again. This time it was deep and menacing.

"I won't be calling again. It's rude to listen in on private conversations. The next message you get from me will have blood on it." The call ended.

"Fuck," said Woolrich. "Tell me you got something."

"We got nothing," said Brillaud, tossing his headphones on the bed. "Number keeps changing. He knows."

I LEFT THE FBI men to pack away their equipment in a white Ford van and walked down through the Quarter to the Napoleon House to call Rachel Wolfe. I didn't want to use the cellular. For some reason, it seemed soiled by its role as the means of contact with a killer. I also wanted the exercise, after being cooped up in my room for so long.

She picked up on the third ring.

"It's Charlie Parker."

"Hi . . ." She seemed to struggle for a time as she tried to decide what to call me.

"You can call me Bird."

"Well spotted."

There was an awkward pause, then: "Where are you? It sounds incredibly noisy."

"It is. It's New Orleans." And then I filled her in as best I could on what had taken place. She listened in silence, and once or twice, I heard a pen tapping rhythmically against the phone at the other end of the line.

"Any of those details mean anything to you?" I asked, when I had finished.

"I'm not sure. I seem to recall something from my time as a student but it's buried so far back that I'm not sure that I can find it. I think I may have something for you arising out of your previous conversation with this man. It's a little obscure, though." She was silent for a moment. "Where are you staying?"

I gave her the number of the Flaisance. She repeated the name and the number to herself as she wrote them down.

"Are you going to call me back?"

"No," she said. "I'm going to make a reservation. I'm coming down."

I looked around the Napoleon after I hung up. It was packed with locals and vaguely bohemian looking visitors, some of them tourists staying in the rooms above the dimly lit bar. A classical piece I couldn't identify was playing over the speakers and smoke hung thick in the air.

Something about the Traveling Man's calls bothered me, although I wasn't sure what. He knew I was in New Orleans when he made his calls. He knew where I was staying, too, since he was aware of the presence of the feds, and that awareness meant that he was familiar with police procedures and was monitoring the investigation, which matched Rachel's profile.

He had to have been watching the crime scene as we arrived, or shortly after. His reluctance to stay on the line was understandable, given the feds' surveillance, but that second call . . . I played it back in my mind, trying to discern the source of my unease, but it yielded nothing.

I was tempted to stay in the Napoleon House, to breathe in the sense of life and gaiety in the old bar, but instead I returned to the Flaisance. Despite the heat I walked to the large windows, opened them, and stepped out onto the balcony. I looked out at the faded buildings and wrought iron balconies of the upper Quarter and breathed deeply of the smells of cooking coming from a restaurant nearby, mingled with smoke and exhaust fumes. I listened to the strains of jazz music coming from a bar on Governor Nicholls, the shouts and laughter of those heading for the rip-off joints on Bourbon Street, the singsong accents of the locals blending with the voices of the out-of-towners, the sound of human life passing beneath my window.

And I thought of Rachel Wolfe, and the way her hair rested on her shoulders, and the sprinkling of freckles across her white neck.

CHAPTER XXXIII

That night, I dreamed of an amphitheater, with rising aisles filled with old men. Its walls were hung with damask, and two high torches illuminated its central rectangular table, with its curved edges and legs carved like bones. Florence Aguillard lay on the table, the exterior of her womb exposed while a bearded man in dark robes tore at it with an ivory-handled scalpel. Around her neck and behind her ears was the mark of a rope burn. Her head lay at an impossible angle on the tabletop.

When the surgeon cut her, eels slithered from her uterus and tumbled to the floor and the dead woman opened her eyes and tried to cry out. The surgeon stifled her mouth with a burlap sack, then continued to cut until the light went from her eyes.

Figures watched from a twilight corner of the amphitheater. They came to me from the shadows, my wife and child, but now they were joined by a third, one who stayed farther back in the dimness, one who was barely a silhouette. She came from a cold, wet place and brought with her a dense, loamy smell of rotting vegetation, of flesh bloated and disfigured by gas and decay. The place where she lay was small and cramped, its sides unyielding, and sometimes the fish bumped against it as she waited. I seemed to smell her in my nostrils when I woke and could still hear her voice . . .

help me
as the blood rushed in my ears
I'm cold, help me
and I knew that I had to find her.

I WAS AWAKENED BY the sound of the telephone in my room. Dim light lanced through the curtains and my watch glowed the time at 8:35 A.M. I picked up the phone.

"Parker? It's Morphy. Get your ass in gear. I'll see you at La Marquise in an hour."

I showered, dressed, and walked down to Jackson Square, following the early morning worshipers into St. Louis Cathedral. Outside the cathedral, a huckster tried to attract worshipers to his fire-eating act while a group of black nuns crowded beneath a yellow-and-green parasol.

Susan and I had attended mass here once, beneath the cathedral's ornately decorated ceiling depicting Christ among the shepherds and, above the small sanctuary, the figure of the Crusader king Louis IX, Roi De France, announcing the Seventh Crusade.

The cathedral had effectively been rebuilt twice since the original wooden structure, designed in 1724, burned down during the Good Friday fire of 1788, when over eight hundred buildings went up in flames. The present cathedral was less than one hundred and fifty years old, its stained-glass windows, overlooking the Place Jean-Paul Deux, a gift from the Spanish government.

It was strange that I should have remembered the details so clearly after so many years. Yet I remembered them less for their own intrinsic interest than for their connections to Susan. I remembered them because she had been with me when I learned them, her hand clasped in mine, her hair pulled back and tied with an aquamarine bow.

For a brief moment it seemed that, by standing in the same place and remembering the same words spoken, I could reach back to that time and feel her close beside me, her hand in my hand, her taste still on my lips, her scent on my neck. If I closed my eyes, I could imagine her sauntering down the aisle, her hand in mine, breathing in the mingled smells of incense and flowers, passing beneath the windows, moving from darkness to light, light to darkness.

I knelt at the back of the cathedral, by the statue of a cherub with a font in its hands and its feet upon a vision of evil, and I prayed for my wife and child.

MORPHY WAS ALREADY AT La Marquise, a French-style patisserie on Chartres. He was sitting in the rear courtyard, his head freshly shaved. He wore a pair of gray sweatpants, Nike sneakers, and a Timberland fleece top. A plate of croissants and two cups of coffee stood on the table before him. He was carefully applying grape jelly to one half of a croissant as I sat down across from him.

"I ordered coffee for you. Take a croissant."

"Coffee's fine, thanks. Day off?"

"Nah, just avoided the dawn patrol." He took the half croissant and stuffed it into his mouth, using his finger to cram in the last part. He smiled, his cheeks bulging. "My wife won't let me do this at home. Says it reminds her of a kid hogging food at a birthday party."

He swallowed and set to work on the remaining half of the croissant. "St. Martin's been frozen out of the picture, 'part from running around looking under rocks for bloody clothes," he said. "Woolrich and his boys have pretty much taken over the investigation. We don't have a helluva lot to do with it anymore, legwork excepted."

I knew what Woolrich would be doing. The killings of *Tante* Marie and Tee Jean now confirmed the existence of a serial killer. The details would be passed on to the FBI's Investigative Support Unit, the hard-pressed section responsible for advising on interrogation techniques and hostage negotiation, as well as dealing with VICAP, ABIS—the arson and bombing program—and, crucially for this case, criminal profiling. Of the thirty-six agents in the unit, only ten worked on profiling, buried in a warren of offices sixty feet below ground in what used to be the FBI director's fallout shelter at Quantico.

And while the feds sifted through the evidence, trying to build up their picture of the Traveling Man, the police on the ground continued to search for physical traces of the killer in the area around *Tante* Marie's house. I could picture them already, the lines of cops moving through the undergrowth, warm green light shedding down upon them from the trees above. Their feet would be catching in the mud, their uniforms snagging on briars, as they searched the ground before them. Others would be working through the green waters of Atchafalaya, swatting at no-see-ums and sweating heavily through their shirts.

There had been a lot of blood at the Aguillard house. The Traveling Man must have been awash with it by the time his work was done. He must have worn overalls, and it would be too risky for him to hold on to them. They had either been dumped in the swamp, or buried, or destroyed. My guess was that he had destroyed them, but the search had to go on.

"I don't have a helluva lot to do with it anymore, either," I said.

"I hear that." He ate some more croissant and finished off his coffee. "You finished, we'll get going." He left some money on the table and I followed him outside. The same battered Buick that had followed us to *Tante* Marie's was parked half a block away, a hand-lettered cop-on-duty sign taped to the dashboard with duct tape. A parking ticket flapped beneath the wiper.

"Shit," said Morphy, tossing the ticket in a trash can. "Nobody got respect for the law no more."

WE DROVE TO THE Desire projects, a harsh urban landscape where young blacks lounged by rubbish-strewn lots or shot hoops desultorily in wire-rimmed courts. The two-story blocks were like barracks, lining streets with bad-joke names like Piety, Abundance, and Humanity. We pulled in near a liquor store, which was barricaded like a fortress, causing young men to skip away from us at the smell of cop. Even here, Morphy's trademark bald head appeared to be instantly recognizable.

"You know much about New Orleans?" said Morphy after a time.

"Nope," I replied. Beneath his fleece top, I could see the trademark bulge of his gun. The palms of his hands were callused from gripping dumbbells and barbells, and even his fingers were thickly muscled. When he moved his head, muscles and tendons stood out on his neck like snakes moving beneath his skin.

Unlike most bodybuilders, there was an air of suppressed danger about Morphy, a sense that the muscle wasn't just for show. I knew that he had killed a man once in a bar in Monroe, a pimp who had shot up one of his girls and the john she was with in a hotel room in Lafayette. The pimp, a two-hundred-and-twenty-pound Creole who called himself Le Mort Rouge, had stabbed Morphy in the chest with a broken bottle and then tried to choke him on the ground. Morphy, after trying punches to the face and body, had eventually settled for a grip on Le Mort's neck, and the two men had remained like that, locked in each other's grip, until something burst in Le Mort's head and he fell sideways against the bar. He was dead by the time the ambulance arrived.

It had been a fair fight, but sitting beside Morphy in the car, I wondered about Luther Bordelon. He had been a thug, that much was certain. He had a string of assaults stretching back to his years as a juvenile and he was suspected of the rape of a young Australian tourist. The girl had failed to identify Bordelon in a lineup and no physical evidence of the rapist had been left on the girl's body because her assailant had used a condom and then made her wash her pubic region with a bottle of mineral water, but the NOPD cops knew it was Bordelon. Sometimes, that's just the way things are.

On the night he died, Bordelon had been drinking in an Irish bar in the Quarter. He was wearing a white T-shirt and white Nike shorts, and three customers in the bar, with whom he had been playing pool, later swore statements that Bordelon had not been armed. Yet Morphy and his partner, Ray Garza, reported that Bordelon had fired on them when they attempted to routinely question him and that he had been killed in their return of fire. A gun, an old S&W Model 60 that was at least twenty years old, was found by his side with two shots fired. The serial number of the gun had been filed away from the frame under the cylinder crane, making the gun difficult to identify, and Ballistics reported that it was clean and had not been previously used in the commission of a crime in the city of New Orleans.

The gun looked like a throwdown and the NOPD's Police Integrity Division clearly felt that was the case, but Garza and Morphy stuck by their story. One year later Garza was dead, stabbed to death while trying to break up a brawl in the Irish Channel, and Morphy had transferred to St. Martin, where he had bought a house. That was it. That was how it ended.

Morphy gestured toward a group of young blacks, the asses of their jeans around their knees and oversized trainers slapping the sidewalk as they walked. They returned our gaze unflinchingly, as if daring us to make a move on them. From a boom box they carried came the sound of the Wu-Tang Clan, music to kick start the revolution. I felt a kind of perverse pleasure from recognizing the music. Charlie Parker, honorary homeboy.

Morphy grimaced. "That is the worst goddamn racket I ever heard. Shit, these people invented the blues. Robert Johnson heard that crap, he'd know for sure that he'd sold his soul to the devil and gone straight to hell." He turned on his car radio and flicked through the channels with an unhappy look. Resignedly, he pushed in a tape and the warm sound of Little Willie John filled the car.

"I grew up in Metairie, before the projects really took hold in this city," he began. "I can't say any of my best friends were black or nothing—most of the blacks went to public schools, I didn't—but we got along together.

"But when the projects went up, that was the end. Desire, Iberville, Lafitte, those were places you didn't want to end up, 'less you were armed to the teeth. Then fucking Reagan came along and the place got worse. You know, they say there's more syphilis now than there was fifty years ago. Most of these kids ain't even been immunized against measles. If ya have a house in the inner city, might as well abandon it and let it rot. It ain't worth shit." He shook his head and slapped the steering wheel.

"When you got that kind of poverty, a man can make a lot of money from it if he puts his mind to it. Lot of people fighting for a slice of the projects, fighting for a slice of other things too: land, property, booze, gambling."

"Like who?"

"Like Joe Bonanno. His crew's been running things down here for the past decade or so, controlling the supply of crack, smack, whatever. They been trying to expand into other areas too. There's talk that they want to open a big leisure center between Lafayette and Baton Rouge, maybe build a hotel. Maybe they just want to dump some bricks and mortar there and write it off as a tax loss, launder money through it."

He cast an appraising eye around the projects. "And this is where Joe Bones grew up." He said this with a sigh, as if he could not understand how a man would set out to undermine the place in which he had grown and matured. He started the car again, and as he drove, he told me about Joe Bones.

Salvatore Bonanno, Joe's father, had owned a bar in the Irish Channel, standing up against the local gangs who didn't believe that an Italian had any place in an area where people named their children after Irish saints and an "oul sod" mentality still prevailed. There was nothing particularly honorable about Sal's stance; it was simply born out of pragmatism. There was a lot of money to be made in Chep Morrison's postwar New Orleans, if a man was prepared to take the knocks and grease the right palms.

Sal's bar was to be the first in a string of bars and clubs that he acquired. He had loans to pay off, and the income from a single bar in the Irish Channel wasn't going to satisfy his creditors. He saved and bought a second bar, this time in Chartres, and from there his little empire grew. In some cases, only a simple financial transaction was required to obtain the premises he wanted. In others, some more forceful encouragement had to be used. When that didn't work, the Atchafalaya Basin had enough water to hide a multitude of sins. Gradually, he built up his own crew to take care of business, to make sure the city authorities, the police, the mayor's office were all kept happy, and to deal with the consequences when those lower down the food chain tried to better themselves at Sal's expense.

Sal Bonanno married Maria Cuffaro, a native of Gretna, east of New Orleans, whose brother was one of Sal's right-hand men. She bore him one daughter, who died of TB at the age of seven, and a son, who died in Vietnam. She died herself in '58, of breast cancer.

But Sal's real weakness was a woman named Rochelle Hines. Rochelle was what they called a high yellow woman, a Negress whose skin was almost white following generations of interbreeding. She had, as Morphy put it, a complexion like butter oil, although her birth certificate bore the words "black, illegitimate." She was tall, with long dark hair framing almond eyes and lips that were soft and wide and welcoming. She had a figure that would stop a clock and there were rumors that she might once have been a prostitute, although, if that was the case, Sal Bonanno quickly put an end to those activities.

Bonanno bought her a place in the Garden District and began introducing her as his wife after Maria died. It probably wasn't a wise thing to do. In the Louisiana of the late 1950s, racial segregation was a day-to-day reality. Even Louis Armstrong, who grew up in the city, could not perform with white musicians in New Orleans because the state of Louisiana prohibited racially integrated bands from playing in the city.

And so, while white men could keep black mistresses and consort with black prostitutes, a man who introduced a black woman, no matter how pale her skin, as his wife was just asking for trouble. When she gave birth to a son, Sal insisted that he bear his name and he took the child and his mother to band recitals in Jackson Square, pushing the huge white baby carriage across the grass and gurgling at his son.

Maybe Sal thought that his money would protect him; maybe he just didn't care. He made sure that Rochelle was always protected, that she didn't walk out alone, so that no one could come at her. But in the end, they didn't come at Rochelle.

One hot July night in 1964, when his son was five years old, Sal Bonanno disappeared. He was found three days later, tied to a tree by the shore of Lake Cataouatche, his head almost severed from his body. It seems likely that someone decided to use his relationship with Rochelle Hines as an excuse to move in on his operation. Ownership of his clubs and bars was transferred to a business consortium with interests in Reno and Vegas.

As soon as her "husband" was found, Rochelle Hines vanished with her son and a small quantity of jewelry and cash before anyone could come after them. She resurfaced one year later in the area that would come to be called Desire, where a half sister rented a property. The death of Sal had destroyed her: she was an alcoholic and had become addicted to morphine.

It was here, among the rising projects, that Joe Bones grew up, paler yet than his mother, and made his stand against both blacks and whites since neither group would accept him as its own. There was a rage inside Joe Bones and he turned it on the world around him. By 1990, ten years after his mother's death in a filthy cot in the projects, Joe Bones owned more bars than his father had thirty years before, and each month, planeloads of cocaine flew in from Mexico, bound for the streets of New Orleans and points north, east, and west.

"Now Joe Bones calls himself a white man, and don't nobody differ with him," said Morphy. "Anyway, how's a man gonna talk with his balls in his mouth? Joe got no time for the brothers now." He laughed quietly. "Ain't nothin' worse than a man who can't get on with his in-laws."

We stopped at a gas station and Morphy filled the tank, then came back with two sodas. We sipped them by the pumps, watching the cars go by.

"Now there's another crew, the Fontenots, and they got their eyes on the projects too. Two brothers, David and Lionel. Family was out of Lafayette originally, I think—still got ties there—but came to New Orleans in the twenties. The Fontenots are ambitious, violent, and they think maybe Bonanno's time has come. All of this has been coming to a head for about a year now, and maybe the Fontenots have a piece of work planned for Joe Bones."

The Fontenots were not young men—they were both in their forties—but they had gradually established themselves in Louisiana and now operated out of a compound in Delacroix guarded by wire and dogs and armed men, including a hardcore of Cajuns from back in Acadiana. They were into gambling, prostitution, some drugs. They owned bars in Baton Rouge, one or two others in Lafayette. If they could take out Joe Bones, it was likely that they would muscle in on the drugs market in a big way.

"You know anything about the Cajuns?" asked Morphy.

"No, not beyond their music."

"They're a persecuted minority in this state and in Texas. During the oil boom, they couldn't get any work because the Texans refused to employ coon asses. Most of them did what we all do when times are tough: they knuckled down and made the best of things. There were clashes with the blacks, because the blacks and the Cajuns were competing for the same few jobs, and some bad things went down, but most people just did what they could to keep body and soul together without breaking too many laws.

"Roland Fontenot—that's the grandfather—he left all that behind when he came to New Orleans, following some other obscure branch of the family. But the boys, they never forgot their roots. When things were bad in the seventies, they gathered a pretty disaffected bunch around them—a lot of young Cajuns, some blacks—and somehow kept the mixture from blowing up in their faces." Morphy drummed his fingers on the dashboard. "Sometimes I think maybe we're all responsible for the Fontenots.

They're a visitation on us, because of the way their people were treated. I think maybe Joe Bones is a visitation too, a reminder of what happens when you grind a section of the population into the dirt."

Joe Bones had a vicious streak, said Morphy. He once killed a man by slowly burning him with acid over the space of an afternoon and was thought by some to be missing part of his brain, the part that controlled unreasonable actions in most men. The Fontenots were different. They killed, but they killed like businessmen closing down an unprofitable or unsatisfactory operation. They killed joylessly, but professionally. In Morphy's view, the Fontenots and Joe Bones were all bad. They just had different ways of expressing it.

I finished my soda and trashed the can. Morphy wasn't the type to spin a yarn for its own sake. All of this was leading up to something.

"What's the point, Morphy?" I asked.

"The point is, the fingerprint that was found at *Tante* Marie's belongs to Tony Remarr. He's one of Joe Bones's men." I thought about that as he started the car and pulled into the street, trying to match the name to any incident that might have occurred back in New York, anything that might connect me to Remarr. I found nothing.

"You think he did it?" Morphy asked.

"Do you?"

"No, no way. At first I thought, yeah, maybe. You know, the old woman, she owned that land. Wouldn't have taken much drainage work to make something of it."

"If a man was considering opening a big hotel and building a leisure center."

"Exactly, or if he wanted to convince someone he was serious enough about it to dump some bricks there. I mean, swamp's swamp. Assuming he could get permission to build, who wants to share the warm evening air with critters even God regrets making?

"Anyway, the old woman wouldn't sell. She was shrewd. Her

people have been buried out there for generations. The original landowner, an old Southern type who traced his ancestry back to the Bourbons, died in sixty-nine. He stipulated in his will that the land should be offered for sale at a reasonable rate to the existing tenants.

"Now most of the tenants were Aguillards and they bought that land with all the money they had. The old woman, she made all the decisions for them. Their ancestors are there and they have a history with that land going back to the time when they wore chains around their ankles and dug channels through the dirt with their bare hands."

"So Bonanno had been putting pressure on her to sell up, but she wouldn't, so he decided to take things a step further," I said.

Morphy nodded. "I figure maybe Remarr was sent out to put more than pressure on her—maybe he's going to threaten the girl or some of the children, maybe even kill one of them—but when he arrives she's already dead. And maybe Remarr gets careless from the shock, thinks he hasn't left any traces, and heads off into the night."

"Does Woolrich know all this?"

"Most of it, yeah."

"You bringing Bonanno in?"

"Brought him in last night and let him go an hour later, accompanied by a fancy lawyer called Rufus Thibodeaux. He ain't movin', says he ain't seen Remarr for three or four days. Says he wants to find Remarr as much as anyone, something about money from some deal out in West Baton Rouge. It's bullshit, but he's sticking with the story. I think Woolrich is going to try to put some pressure on his operations through Anti-Racketeering and Narcotics, put the squeeze on him to see if he can change his mind."

"That could take time."

"You got a better idea?"

I shrugged. "Maybe."

Morphy's eyes narrowed. "You don't be fuckin' with Joe Bones, now, y'hear? Joe ain't like your boys back in New York, sittin' in social clubs in Little Italy with their fingers curled around the handles of espresso cups, dreaming about the days when everyone respected them. Joe don't got no time for that. Joe don't want folks to respect him; Joe wants folks to be scared to death of him."

We turned onto Esplanade. Morphy signaled and pulled in about two blocks from the Flaisance. He stared out the window, tapping the index finger of his right hand against the steering wheel to some internal rhythm in his head. I sensed he had something more to say. I decided to let him say it in his own time.

"You've spoken to this guy, the guy who took your wife and kid, right?"

I nodded.

"It's the same guy? The same guy who did Tee Jean and the old woman?"

"He called me yesterday. It's him."

"He say anything?"

"The feds have it on tape. He says he's going to do more."

Morphy rubbed the back of his neck with his hand and squeezed his eyes shut tightly. I knew he was seeing *Tante* Marie in his head again.

"You going to stay here?"

"For a while, yes."

"Could be the feds ain't gonna like it."

I smiled. "I know."

Morphy smiled back. He reached beneath his seat and handed me a long brown envelope. "I'll be in touch," he said. I slipped the envelope under my jacket and stepped from the car. He gave a small wave as he drove away through the midday crowd.

I OPENED THE ENVELOPE in my hotel room. Inside were a set of crime scene pictures and photocopied extracts of the police reports, all stapled together. Stapled separately was a copy of the coroner's report. One section had been emphasized with a luminous yellow felt tip.

The coroner had found traces of ketamine hydrochloride in the bodies of *Tante* Marie and Tee Jean, equivalent to a dosage of one milligram per two pounds of weight. According to the report, ketamine was an unusual drug, a special type of anesthetic used for some minor surgical procedures. No one was too clear on its precise mode of action apart from the fact that it was a PCP analogue and worked on sites in the brain, affecting the central nervous system.

It was becoming the drug of choice in the clubs of New York and L.A. while I was still on the force, usually in capsules or tabs made by heating the liquid anesthetic to evaporate the water, leaving ketamine crystals. Users described a ketamine trip as "swimming in the K pool" since it distorted the perception of the body, creating a feeling that the user was floating in a soft yet supportive medium. Other side effects included hallucinations, distortions in the perception of space and time, and out-of-body experiences.

What the coroner did note was that ketamine could be used as a chemical restrainer on animals, since it induced paralysis and dulled pain while allowing the normal pharyngeal-laryngeal reflexes to continue. It was for this purpose, he surmised, that the killer had injected both *Tante* Marie and Tee Jean Aguillard with the drug.

When they were flayed and anatomized, the report concluded, *Tante* Marie and her son had been fully conscious.

CHAPTER

XXXIV

When I had finished reading the coroner's report, I put on my sweats and running shoes and did about four miles on Riverfront Park, back and forth past the crowds lining up to take a trip on the Natchez paddle steamer, the sound of its wheezing calliope sending tunes like messengers across the Mississippi. I was thick with sweat when I was done, and my knees ached. Even three years ago, four miles wouldn't have troubled me to such a degree. I was getting old. Soon, I'd be looking at wheelchairs and feeling impending rain in my joints.

Back at the Flaisance, Rachel Wolfe had left a message to say that she would be flying in later that evening. The flight number and the arrival time were listed at the bottom of the message slip. I thought about Joe Bones and decided then that Rachel Wolfe might like some company on the flight down to New Orleans.

I called Angel and Louis.

THE AGUILLARD FAMILY COLLECTED the bodies of *Tante* Marie, Tee Jean, and Florence later that day. A firm of Lafayette undertakers placed *Tante* Marie's coffin into a wide-back hearse. Tee Jean and Florence lay side by side in a second.

The Aguillards, led by the eldest son, Raymond, and accompanied by a small group of family friends, followed the hearses in a trio of pickup trucks, dark-skinned men and women seated on pieces of sackcloth amid machine parts and farm tools. I stayed behind them as they slipped from the highway and made their way down the rutted track, past *Tante* Marie's, where the police tape fluttered lightly in the breeze, and on to the house of Raymond Aguillard.

He was a tall, large-boned man in his late forties or early fifties, running to fat now but still an imposing figure. He wore a dark cotton suit, a white shirt, and a slim black tie. His eyes were red rimmed from crying. I had seen him briefly at *Tante* Marie's the night the bodies were found, a strong man trying to hold his family together in the face of violent loss.

He spotted me as the coffins were unloaded and carried toward the house, a small group of men struggling with *Tante* Marie. I stood out, since I was the only white face in the crowd. A woman, probably one of *Tante* Marie's daughters, shot me a cold look as she passed by, a pair of older women at each shoulder. When the bodies had been carried into the house, a raised, slatted-wood building not unlike the home of *Tante* Marie herself, Raymond kissed a small cross around his neck and walked slowly toward me.

"I know who you are," he said, as I extended my hand. He paused for a moment before taking it in a short, firm grip.

"I'm sorry," I said, "sorry about it all."

He nodded. "I know that." He walked on, past the white fence at the boundary of the house, and stood by the side of the road, staring out at the empty stretch of track. A pair of mallards flew overhead, their wing beats slowing as they approached the water below. Raymond watched them with a kind of envy, the envy that a man deeply grieving feels for anything untouched by his sorrow.

"Some of my sisters, they think maybe you brought this man with you. They think you got no right to be here."

"Is that what you think?"

He didn't answer. Then: "She felt him comin'. Maybe that's why she sent Florence to the party, to get her away from him. And that's why she sent for you: she felt him comin' and I think she knowed who he was. Deep down, I think she knowed." His voice sounded thick in his throat.

He fingered the cross gently, rubbing his thumb back and forth along its length. I could see that it had originally been ornately carved—it was still possible to discern some details of spirals at its edges—but for the most part it had been rubbed smooth by the action of this man's hand over many years.

"I don't blame you for what happened to my momma and my brother and sister. My momma, she always done what she believed was right. She wanted to find that girl and to stop the man that killed her. And that Tee Jean . . ." He smiled sadly. "The policeman said that he'd been hit three, maybe four times from behind, and there were still bruises on his knuckles where he tried to fight this man."

Raymond coughed and then breathed deeply through his mouth, his head tipped back slightly like a man who has run a great distance in pain.

"He took your woman, your child?" he said. It was as much a statement as a question, but I answered it anyway.

"Yes, he took them. Like you said, *Tante* Marie believed that he took another girl too."

He dug the thumb and forefinger of his right hand into the corners of his eyes and blinked out a tear.

"I know. I seen her."

The world around me seemed to grow silent as I shut out the noise of the birds, the wind in the trees, the distant sound of water splashing on the banks. All I wanted to hear was Raymond Aguillard's voice.

"You saw the girl?"

"That's what I said. Down by a slough in Honey Island, three nights ago. Night before my momma died. Seen her other times too. My sister's husband, he got hisself some traps down there." He shrugged. Honey Island was a nature reserve. "You a superstitious man, Mista Parker?"

"I'm getting there," I replied. "You think that's where she is, down in Honey Island?"

"Could be. My momma'd say she didn't know where she was, just *that* she was. She knew the girl was out there somewhere. I just don't know how, Mista Parker. I never did understand my momma's gift. But then I seen her, a figure out by a cypress grove and a kinda darkness over her face, like a hand was coverin' it, and I knowed it was her."

He looked down and, with the toe of his shoe, began picking at a stone embedded in the dirt. When he eventually freed it, sending it skidding into the grass, tiny black ants scurried and crawled from the hole, the entrance to their nest now fully exposed.

"Other people seen her too, I hear, folks out fishin' or checking the hooch they got distillin' in a shack somewheres." He watched as the ants swarmed around his foot, some of them climbing onto the rim of his sole. Gently, he lifted his foot, shook it, and moved it away.

There were seventy thousand acres of Honey Island, Raymond explained. It was the second-biggest swamp in Louisiana, forty miles long and eight miles wide. It was part of the floodplain of the Pearl River, which acts as a boundary line between Louisiana and Mississippi. Honey Island was better preserved than the Florida Everglades: there was no dredging allowed, no draining or timber farming, no development and no dams, and parts of Honey Island weren't even navigable. Half of it was state owned; some was the responsibility of the Nature Conservancy. If someone was trying to dump a body in a place where it was unlikely to be discovered, then, tourist boats apart, Honey Island sounded like a good place to do it.

Raymond gave me directions to the slough and drew a rough map on the back of an opened-out Marlboro pack.

"Mista Parker, I know you're a good man and that you're sorry for what happened, but I'd be grateful to you if you didn't come out here no more." He spoke softly, but there was no mistaking the force in his voice. "And maybe you'd be kind enough not to turn up at the burial. My family, it's gonna take us a long time to get over this."

Then he lit the last cigarette from the pack, nodded a good-bye, and walked back to his house trailing smoke behind him.

I watched him as he walked away. A woman with steel-gray hair came out to the porch and placed her arm around his waist when he reached her. He put a big arm around her shoulders and held her to him as they walked into the house, the screen door closing gently behind them. And I thought of Honey Island and the secrets that it held beneath its green waters as I drove away from the Aguillard house, the dust rising behind me.

As I drove, the swamp was already preparing to reveal its secrets. Honey Island would yield a body within twenty-four hours, but it would not be the body of a girl.

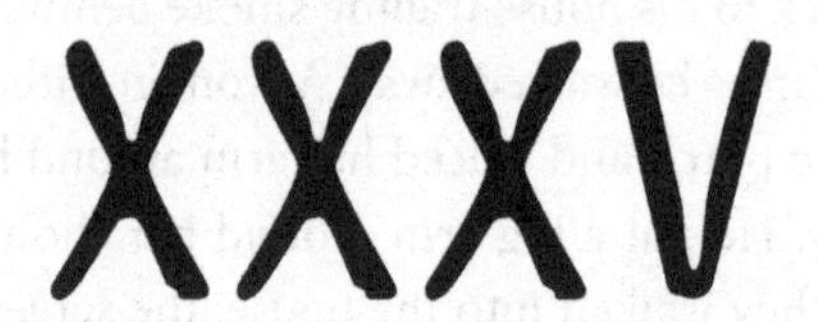

CHAPTER XXXV

I arrived early at Moisant Field so I browsed around the bookstore for a while, taking care to avoid tripping over the piles of Anne Rice novels. I had been sitting in the arrivals terminal for about an hour when Rachel Wolfe walked through the gates. She was wearing dark blue jeans, white sneakers, and a red-and-white Polo Sport top. Her red hair hung loose on her shoulders and her makeup had been so carefully applied that it was almost indiscernable.

The only luggage she carried herself was a brown leather shoulder bag. The rest of what I took to be her belongings was being toted by Angel and Louis, who walked slightly self-consciously at either side of her, Louis in a cream double-breasted suit with a snow white dress shirt open at the neck, Angel in jeans, battered Reebok high-tops, and a green check shirt that had not felt an iron since it left the factory many years before.

"Well, well," I said, as they stood before me. "All human life is here."

Angel raised his right hand, from which dangled three thick piles of books, tied together by string. The ends of his fingers were turning purple. "We brought half the New York Public Library with us as well," he groaned. "Tied with string. I ain't seen books tied with string since *Little House on the Prairie* stopped reruns."

Louis, I noticed, was carrying a lady's pink umbrella and a cosmetics case. He had the look of a man who is trying to pretend that a dog isn't screwing his leg. "Don't say a word, man," he warned. "Not a word."

Between them, the two men also carried two suitcases, two leather traveling bags, and a suit carrier. "Car's parked outside," I said as I walked with Rachel to the exit. "Might be just enough room for the bags."

"They paged me at the airport," whispered Rachel. "They were very helpful." She giggled and glanced over her shoulder. Behind us, I heard the unmistakable sound of Angel tripping on a bag and swearing loudly.

WE DITCHED THE LUGGAGE at the Flaisance, despite Louis's stated preference for the Fairmont at University Place. The Fairmont was where the Republicans usually stayed when they hit New Orleans, which was part of its appeal for Louis. He was the only gay, black, Republican criminal I knew.

"Gerald Ford stayed at the Fairmont," he lamented as he surveyed the small suite he was to share with Angel.

"So?" I countered. "Paul McCartney stayed at the Richelieu and you don't hear me demanding to stay there." I left the door open and headed back to my own room for a shower.

"Paul *who*?" said Louis.

WE ATE IN THE Grill Room of the Windsor Court on Gravier Street, in deference to Louis's wishes, its marbled floors and heavy Austrian drapes strangely uncomfortable for me after the informal setting of the smaller eateries in the Quarter. Rachel had changed into dark pants and a black jacket over a red top. It looked fine but the hot night air had taken its toll on her and she was still pulling the damp cloth of her top away from her body as we waited for the main courses.

As we ate, I explained to them about Joe Bones and the Fontenots. They would be a matter for Angel, Louis, and me. Rachel remained silent for much of our conversation, interjecting occasionally to clarify things that had been said by Woolrich or Morphy. She scribbled notes in a small, wire-bound notebook, her handwriting neat and even. At one point her hand brushed my bare arm lightly and she left it there for an instant, her skin warm against mine.

I watched Angel pulling at his lip as he considered what I had said. "This Remarr must be pretty dumb, dumber than our guy at least," he said eventually.

"Because of the print?" I said.

He nodded. "Careless, very careless." He wore the dissatisfied look of a respected theologian who has seen someone bring his calling into disrepute by identifying Jesus as an alien.

Rachel spotted the look. "It seems to bother you a lot," she commented. I glanced at her. She had an amused expression on her face, but her eyes were calculating and slightly distant. She was playing over in her mind what I had told her, even as she engaged Angel in a conversation that he would usually have avoided. I waited to see how he would respond.

He smiled at her and tilted his head. "I have a certain professional interest in these things," he admitted. He cleared a space in front of him and held up his hands before us.

"Anyone doing a B&E job—that's breaking and entering, for the benefit of our more respectable listener—needs to take certain precautions," began Angel. "The first and most obvious is to make sure that he—or she, B&E being an equal opportunity profession—doesn't leave any fingerprints. So what do you do?"

"You wear gloves," said Rachel. She leaned forward now, enjoying the lesson and putting aside any other thoughts.

"Right. Nobody, no matter how dumb, enters a place he shouldn't be without wearing gloves. Otherwise, you leave visuals, you leave latents, you pretty much sign your name and confess to the crime."

Visuals are the visible marks left on surfaces by a dirty or bloody hand, latents the invisible marks left by natural secretions of the skin. Visuals can be photographed or lifted using adhesive tape, but latents need to be dusted, typically with a chemical reagent like iodine vapor or ninhydrin solution. Electrostatic and fluorescence techniques are also useful, and in the search for latents on human skin, specialized X-ray photography can be used.

But if what Angel had said was correct, Remarr was too much of a professional to risk a job without gloves and then to leave not merely a latent, but a visual. He must have been wearing gloves, but something had gone wrong.

"You working it through in your head, Bird?" smirked Angel.

"Go on, Sherlock, baffle us with your brilliance," I responded.

His smirk widened to a grin, and he continued. "It's possible to get a fingerprint from *inside* a glove, assuming you have the glove. Rubber or plastic gloves are best for obtaining prints: your hands get sweaty under them.

"But what most people don't know is that the exterior surface of a glove can act like a fingerprint as well. Say it's a leather glove, then you got wrinkles, you got holes, you got scars, you got tears, and no two leather gloves are gonna be the same. Now, in the case of this guy Remarr, what we have is a print and no gloves. Unless Remarr can't tie his shoelaces without falling over, we know that he was probably wearing gloves, but he still manages to leave a print. It's a mystery." He made a small, exploding gesture with his hands, like a magician making a rabbit disappear in a puff of smoke, then his face became serious.

"My guess is that Remarr was wearing only a single pair of gloves, probably latex. He imagined this was going to be an easy job: either he was gonna off the old lady and her son, or he was gonna put the frighteners on her, maybe leave a calling card in the house. Since the son, from what I hear, wasn't the kind of guy to let anyone frighten his momma, I'd say Remarr went in there thinking that he might have to kill someone.

"But when he arrives, they're either dead or they're in the process of being killed. Again, my guess is they were already dead: if Remarr stumbled in on the killer, Remarr would be dead as well.

"So Remarr is going in, his one pair of gloves on, and maybe he spots the kid and it throws him. He probably starts to sweat. He goes into the house and finds the old lady. Bam! Second shock, but he goes to take a closer look, steadying himself as he leans over her. He touches blood and maybe considers wiping it away, but he figures wiping it away will only attract more attention to it and, anyway, he's got his gloves.

"But the problem with latex gloves is that one pair isn't enough. You wear them for too long and your prints start coming through. You get thrown, you start to sweat, the prints are gonna come through faster. Could be Remarr has been eating before he came out, maybe some fruit or some kind of pasta with vinegar. That causes extra moisture on the skin, so now Remarr is in real trouble. He's left a print he doesn't even know about, and now the cops, the feds, and difficult people like our good selves want to ask him about it. Ta-da!" He gave a small bow from the waist. Rachel gave him a round of applause. Louis just raised an eyebrow in resignation.

"Fascinating," said Rachel. "You must read a lot of books." Her tone was heavily ironic.

"He does, then Barnes and Noble gonna be grateful that their stolen stock being put to good use," remarked Louis.

Angel ignored him. "Maybe I dabbled in these things, in my younger days."

"Did you learn anything else, in your 'younger' days?" Rachel smiled.

"Lot of things, some of them hard lessons," said Angel with feeling. "Best thing I ever learned: don't hold on to nothin'. If you don't have it, can't nobody prove you took it.

"And I *have* been tempted. There was this figure of a knight on a horse once. French, seventeenth century. Gold inlaid with diamonds and rubies. About this tall." He held the palm of his hand flat about six inches above the table. "It was the most beautiful thing I ever saw." His eyes lit up at the memory. He looked like a child.

He sat back in his chair. "But I let it go. In the end, you have to let things go. The things you regret are the things you hold on to."

"So is nothing worth holding on to?" asked Rachel.

Angel looked at Louis for a while. "Some things are, yeah, but they ain't made of gold."

"That's so romantic," I said. Louis made choking noises as he tried to swallow his water.

Before us, the remains of our coffee lay cold in the cups. "Do you have anything to add?" I asked Rachel when Angel had finished playing to the gallery.

She glanced back through her notes. Her brow furrowed slightly. She held a glass of red wine in one hand and the light caught it, reflecting a streak of red across her breast like a wound.

"You said you had pictures, crime scene pictures?" she asked.

I nodded.

"Then I'd like to hold off until I've had a chance to see them. I have an idea based on what you told me over the phone, but I'd prefer to keep it to myself until I've seen the pictures and done a little more research. I do have one thing, though." She took a second notebook from her bag and flicked through the pages to where a yellow Post-it note stuck out. " 'I lusted for her, but that has always been a weakness of my kind,' " she read. " 'Our sin was not pride, but lust for humanity.' "

She turned to me, but I already recognized the words. "They were the words this Traveling Man said to you when he called," she said. I was aware of Angel and Louis moving forward in their chairs.

"It took a theologian in the archbishop's residence to track down the reference. It's pretty obscure, at least if you're not a theologian." She paused, then asked, "Why was the devil banished from Heaven?"

"Pride," said Angel. "I remember Sister Agnes telling us that."

"It was pride," said Louis. He glanced at Angel. "I remember *Milton* telling us that."

"Anyway," said Rachel pointedly, "you're right, or partially right.

From Augustine onward, the devil's sin is pride. But before Augustine, there was a different viewpoint. Up until the fourth century, the Book of Enoch was considered to be part of the biblical canon. Its origins are a matter of dispute—it may have been written in Hebrew or Aramaic, or a combination of both—but it does seem to have provided a basis for some concepts that are still found in the Bible today. The Last Judgment may have been based on the Similitudes of Enoch. The fiery Hell ruled by Satan also appears for the first time in Enoch.

"What is interesting for us is that Enoch takes a different view of the devil's sin." She turned a page of her notebook and began to read again.

" 'And it came to pass, when men began to multiply on the face of the earth, and daughters were born unto them, that the sons of God saw the daughters of men that they were fair; and they took them wives of all which they chose . . .' "

She looked up again. "Now that's from Genesis, which derives from a similar source as Enoch. The 'sons of God' were the angels, who gave in to sexual lust against the will of God. The leader of the sinning angels, the devil, was cast into a dark hole in the desert and his accomplices were thrown into the fire for their punishment. Their offspring, 'evil spirits upon the earth,' went with them. The martyr Justin believed that the children of the union between angels and human women were responsible for all evil on the earth, including murder.

"In other words, lust was the sin of the devil. Lust for humanity, the 'weakness of our kind.' " She closed the notebook and permitted herself a small smile of triumph.

"So this guy believes he's a demon," said Angel eventually.

"Or the offspring of an angel," added Louis. "Depends on how you look at it."

"Whatever he is, or thinks he is, the Book of Enoch is hardly likely to turn up on Oprah's book choice," I said. "Any idea what his source might have been?"

Rachel reopened the notebook. "The most recent reference I

could find is a nineteen eighty-three New York edition: *The Old Testament Pseudepigrapha: Enoch,* edited by a guy called Isaac, appropriately enough," she said. "There's also an older translation from Oxford, published in nineteen thirteen by R. H. Charles."

I noted the names. "Maybe Morphy or Woolrich can check with the University of New Orleans, see if anyone local has been expressing an interest in the obscure end of biblical studies. Woolrich might be able to extend the search to the other universities. It's a start."

We paid the bill and left. Angel and Louis headed off toward the lower Quarter to check out the gay night life while Rachel and I walked back to the Flaisance. We didn't speak for a time, both of us conscious that we were on the verge of some intimacy.

"I get the feeling that I shouldn't ask what those two currently do for a living," said Rachel, as we paused at a crossing.

"Probably not. It's best to view them as independent operators and leave it at that."

She smiled. "They seem to have a certain loyalty to you. It's unusual. I'm not sure that I understand it."

"I've done things for them in the past, but if there ever was a debt, it was paid a long time ago. I owe them a lot."

"But they're still here. They still help when they're asked."

"I don't think that's entirely because of me. They do what they do because they like it. It appeals to their sense of adventure, of danger. In their own separate ways, they're both dangerous men. I think that's why they came: they sensed danger and they wanted to be part of it."

"Maybe they see something of that in you."

"I don't know. Maybe they do."

We walked through the courtyard of the Flaisance, stopping only to pat the dogs. Her room was three doors down from mine. Between our rooms were the room shared by Angel and Louis and one unoccupied single room. She opened the door and stood at the threshold. From inside, I could feel the coolness of the air-conditioning and could hear it pumping at full power.

"I'm still not sure why you're here," I said. My throat felt dry and part of me was not certain that it wanted to hear an answer.

"I'm still not sure either," she said. She stood on her toes and kissed me gently, softly on the lips, and then she was gone.

I WENT TO MY room, took a book of Sir Walter Ralegh's writings from my bag, and headed back out to the Napoleon House, where I took a seat by the portrait of the Little Corporal. I didn't want to lie on my bed, conscious of the presence of Rachel Wolfe so near to me. I was excited and troubled by her kiss, and by the thought of what might follow.

Almost until the very end, Susan and I had enjoyed an incredible intimacy together. When my drinking truly began to take its toll on us, that intimacy had disintegrated. When we made love it was no longer totally giving. Instead, we seemed to circle each other warily in our lovemaking, always holding something back, always expecting trouble to rear its head and cause us to spring back into the security of our own selves.

But I had loved her. I had loved her until the end and I still loved her now. When the Traveling Man had taken her he had severed the physical and emotional ties between us, but I could still feel the remains of those ties, raw and pulsing at the very extremity of my senses.

Maybe this is common to all those who lose someone whom they have loved deeply. Making contact with another potential partner, another lover, becomes an act of reconstruction, a building not only of a relationship but also of oneself.

But I felt myself haunted by my wife and child. I felt them, not only as an emptiness or a loss, but as an actual presence in my life. I seemed to catch glimpses of them at the edges of my existence, as I drifted from consciousness to sleep, from sleep to waking. Sometimes, I tried to convince myself that they were simply phantoms of my guilt, creations born of some psychological imbalance.

Yet I had heard Susan speak through *Tante* Marie, and once, like a memory from a delirium, I had awakened in the darkness to feel her hand on my face and I had caught a trace of her scent beside me in the bed. More than that, I saw traces of Susan and Jennifer in every young wife, in each female child. In a young woman's laughter, I heard the voice of my wife. In the footsteps of a little girl, I heard the echo of my daughter's shoes.

I felt something for Rachel Wolfe, a mixture of attraction and gratitude and desire. I wanted to be with her but only, I thought, when my wife and child were at peace.

CHAPTER

XXXVI

David Fontenot died that night. His car, a vintage Jensen Interceptor, was found on 190, the road that skirts Honey Island and leads down to the shores of the Pearl. The front tires of the car were flat and the doors were hanging open. The windshield had been shattered and the interior was peppered with 9 millimeter holes.

The two St. Tammany cops followed a trail of broken branches and flattened scrub to an old trapper's shack made of bits of salvaged wood, its tin roof almost obscured by overhanging Spanish moss. It overlooked a bayou lined with gum trees, its waters thick with lime green duckweed and ringing with the sound of mallards and wood ducks.

The shack had been abandoned for a long time. Few people now trapped in Honey Island. Most had moved farther out into the bayous, hunting beaver, deer, and in some cases, alligators.

There were noises coming from the shack as the party approached, sounds of scuffling and thudding and heavy snorting drifting through the open door.

"Hog," said one of the deputies.

Beside him, the local bank official who had called them in flicked the safety on his Ruger rifle.

"Shit, that won't do no good against no hog," said the second deputy. The local, a thick-set, balding man in a Tulane Green Wave T-shirt and an almost unused hunting jacket, reddened. He was carrying a 77V with a telescopic sight, what they used to call in Maine a "varmint rifle." It was good for small game and some police forces even used it as a sniper rifle, but it wouldn't stop a feral hog first time unless the shot was perfect.

They were only a few feet away from the shack when the hog sensed them. It erupted from the open door, its tiny, vicious eyes wild and blood dripping from its snout. The man with the Ruger dived into the bayou waters to avoid it as it came at him. The hog spun, cornered at the water's edge by the party of armed men, then lowered its head and charged again.

There was an explosion in the bayou, then a second, and the hog went down. Most of the top of its head was gone and it twitched briefly on the ground, pawing at the dirt, until eventually it ceased to move. The deputy blew smoke theatrically from the long barrel of a Colt Anaconda, ejected the spent .44 Magnum cartridges with the ejector rod, then reloaded.

"Jesus," said the voice of his partner. He was standing in the open doorway of the shack, his gun by his side. "Hog sure got at him, but it's Dave Fontenot all right."

The hog had ruined most of Fontenot's face and part of his right arm was gnawed away, but even the damage caused by the hog couldn't disguise the fact that someone had forced David Fontenot from his car, hunted him through the trees, and then cornered him in the shack, where he was shot in the groin, the knees, the elbows, and the head.

"Mon," said the hog killer, exhaling deeply. "When Lionel hears about this, there's gonna be hell to pay."

I LEARNED MOST OF what had taken place during a hurried telephone conversation with Morphy and a little more from WDSU, the local NBC affiliate. Afterward, Angel, Louis, and I breakfasted at Mother's on Poydras Street. Rachel had barely worked up the energy to answer the phone when we called her room, and had decided to sleep on and eat later in the morning.

Louis, dressed in an ivory-colored linen suit and a white T-shirt, shared my bacon and homemade biscuits, washed down with strong coffee. Angel opted for ham, eggs, and grits.

"Old folks eat grits, Angel," said Louis. "Old folks and the insane."

Angel wiped a white grit trail from his chin and gave Louis the finger.

"He's not so eloquent first thing in the morning," said Louis. "Rest of the day, he don't have no excuse."

Angel gave Louis the finger again, scraped the last of the grits from the bowl, and pushed it away.

"So, you figure Joe Bones took a preemptive strike against the Fontenots?" he said.

"Looks that way," I replied. "Morphy figures he used Remarr to do the job—pulled him out of hiding, then squirreled him away again. He wouldn't entrust a job like that to anyone else. But I don't understand what David Fontenot was doing out by Honey Island without any backup. He must have known that Joe Bones would take a crack at him if the opportunity arose."

"Could be one of his own people set him up, hauled him out there on some dead-end pretext, and let Joe Bones know he was coming?" said Angel.

It sounded plausible. If someone had drawn Fontenot out to Honey Island, then it must have been someone he trusted enough to make the trip. More to the point, that someone must have been offering something that Fontenot wanted, something to make him risk the drive to the reserve late at night.

I said nothing to Angel or Louis, but I was troubled that both Raymond Aguillard and David Fontenot had, in their own different ways, drawn my attention to Honey Island in a period of less than one day. I thought that, after I had spoken to Joe Bones, I might have to disturb Lionel Fontenot in his time of grief.

My cell phone rang. It was the desk clerk from the Flaisance, informing us that a delivery addressed to a Mr. Louis had arrived and a courier was waiting for us to sign. We took a taxi back to the hotel. Outside, a black transit van was parked with two wheels on the curb.

"Courier," said Louis, but there were no markings on the van, nothing to identify it as a commercial vehicle.

In the lobby, the desk clerk sat nervously watching a huge black man who was squeezed into an easy chair. He was shaven-headed and wearing a black T-shirt with *Klan Killer* written in jagged white writing across the chest. His black combat trousers were tucked into nine-hole army boots. At his feet lay a long steel container, locked and bolted.

"Brother Louis," he said, rising. Louis took out his wallet and handed over three hundred-dollar bills. The man tucked the money into the thigh pocket of his combats, removed a pair of Ray-Ban sunglasses from the same pocket, and put them on before strolling out into the sunlight.

Louis motioned to the container. "If you gentlemen would like to take that up to the room," he said. Angel and I took an end each and followed him up to the suite. The case was heavy and something inside rattled as we walked.

"Those UPS couriers are sure getting bigger," I said, as I waited for him to open the door.

"It's a specialized service," said Louis. "There are some things the airlines just wouldn't understand."

When he had closed and locked the door behind us, he took a set of keys from the pocket of his suit and opened the case. It was separated into three layers, which opened up like those in a tool kit. On the first layer were the constituent parts of a Mauser SP66, a three-round heavy-barreled sniper rifle with a combined muzzle brake and flash hider. The parts were packed in a removable case. Beside it, a SIG P226 pistol and a shoulder holster lay in a fitted compartment.

In the second compartment sat two Calico M-960A minisubs, made in the good old U.S. of A., each handheld sub fitted with a short barrel that extended less than an inch and a half beyond the fore end. With the stock retracted, each gun measured a little over two feet in length and, empty, weighed just under five pounds. They were exceptionally lethal little guns, with a rate of fire of seven hundred and fifty rounds per minute. The third compartment contained an array of ammunition, including four one-hundred-round magazines of 9 millimeter Parabellum for the subs.

"Christmas present?" I asked.

"Yup," said Louis, loading a fifteen-round magazine into the butt of the SIG. "I'm hoping to get a rail gun for my birthday."

He handed Angel the case containing the Mauser, slipped on the holster, and inserted the SIG. He then relocked the case and went into the bathroom. As we watched, he removed the paneling from beneath the sink with a screwdriver and shoved the case into the gap before replacing the panel. When he was satisfied that it was back in place, we left.

"You think Joe Bones will be pleased to see a bunch of strangers show up on his doorstep?" asked Angel, as we walked to my rental.

"We ain't strangers," said Louis. "We're just friends he ain't met yet."

JOE BONES OWNED THREE properties in Louisiana, including a weekend house at Cypremort Point, where his presence must have made the more respectable weekenders, with their expensive holiday houses bearing jokey names like Eaux-Asis and End of the Trail, distinctly uneasy.

His city residence lay across from Audubon Park, almost opposite the bus stop for the shuttle bus that took tourists to the New Orleans Zoo. I had taken a trip on the St. Charles streetcar to inspect the house, a brilliantly white confection adorned with black wrought iron balconies and a cupola topped with a gold weather vane. Finding Joe Bones inside a place like that was like finding a cockroach in a wedding cake. In the carefully maintained garden, a flower I couldn't identify bloomed lushly. Its scent was sickly and heavy, its flower so large and red that it seemed more rotten than blooming, as if the flowers themselves might suddenly burst and send thick fluid down the branches of the plant, poisoning the aphids.

Joe Bones had deserted the house for the summer in favor of a restored plantation house out in West Feliciana Parish, over one hundred miles north of New Orleans. As impending hostilities with the Fontenots grew more and more likely, the decision to remain in West Feliciana allowed him to defend the country house with more force than he could in the city.

It was a white, eight-columned mansion set on about forty acres, bordered at two sides by an expanse of river flowing south toward the Mississippi. Four large windows looked out on a wide gallery, and the house was topped by two dormer windows set into its roof. An avenue of oaks led from a black iron gate through grounds set with camellias and azaleas until the trees stopped before a wide expanse of lawn. On the lawn, a small group of people stood around a barbecue or lounged on iron lawn furniture.

I spotted three security cameras within ten feet of the gate when we drew up, side-on. We had dropped Angel about half a mile back after cruising by the house once, and I knew he was already making for the stand of cypress that stood opposite the gate. In the event of anything going down with Joe Bones, I decided that I had a better chance of dealing with it with Louis rather than Angel by my side.

A fourth camera overlooked the gate itself. There was no intercom and the gate remained resolutely closed, even when Louis and I leaned against the car and waved.

After two or three minutes a converted golf cart came from behind the house and hummed down the oak-lined avenue toward us. Three men in chinos and sports shirts stepped from it. They made no attempt to hide their Steyr machine pistols.

"Hi," I said. "We're here to see Joe Bones."

"There ain't no Joe Bones here," said one of the men. He was tanned and short, no more than five-six. His hair was braided tightly against his scalp, giving him a reptilian appearance.

"How about Mr. Joseph Bonanno, is he there?"

"What are you, cops?"

"We're concerned citizens. We were hoping Mr. Bones would make a donation to the David Fontenot funeral fund."

"He already gave," said the guy by the golf cart, a fatter version of the Lizard Man. His colleagues at the gate laughed fit to burst a gut.

I moved closer to the gate. Lizard Man's gun came up quickly.

"Tell Joe Bones that Charlie Parker is here, that I was in the Aguillard house on Sunday night, and that I'm looking for Remarr. You think funny man back there can remember all that?"

He stepped back from the gate and, without taking his eyes off us, relayed what I had said to the guy by the golf cart. He took a walkie-talkie from the rear seat, spoke into it for a moment, and then nodded at Lizard Man. "He says let 'em through, Ricky."

"Okay," said Ricky, taking a remote signaler from his pocket, "step back from the gate, turn around, and put your hands against the car. You packing, then tell me now. I find anything you haven't told me about, I put a bullet in your head and feed you to the 'gators."

We owned up to a Smith & Wesson and a SIG between us. Louis threw in an ankle knife for good measure. We left the car at the gate and walked behind the golf cart toward the house. One man sat in the back with his pistol pointing at us while Ricky walked behind us.

As we neared the lawn I could smell shrimp and chicken cooking on the barbecue. An iron table held an assortment of spirits and glasses. Abita and Heineken lay in a steel cooler packed with ice.

From the side of the house came a low growl, deep with viciousness and menace. At the end of a strong chain, which was anchored to a bolt set in concrete, was a huge animal. It had the thick coat of a wolf, flecked with the coloring of an Alsatian. Its eyes were bright and intelligent, which rendered its obvious savagery all the more threatening. It looked like it weighed at least one hundred and eighty pounds. Each time it tugged at its chain, it threatened to wrench the bolt from the ground.

I noticed that it seemed to be directing most of its attention at Louis. Its eyes focused on him intently and at one point it raised itself up on its hind legs in its efforts to strike at him. Louis looked at it with the detached interest of a scientist finding a curious new type of bacteria growing in his Petri dish.

Joe Bones speared a piece of spiced chicken with a fork and placed it on a china plate. He was only slightly taller than Ricky, with long dark hair swept back from his forehead. His nose had been broken at least once and a small scar twisted his upper lip on the left side. His white shirt was open to the waist and hung over a pair of Lycra running shorts. His stomach was hard and muscular, his chest and arms slightly overdeveloped for a man of his height. He looked mean and intelligent, like the animal on the chain, which probably explained how he had lasted for ten years at the top of the heap in New Orleans.

He placed some tomatoes, lettuce, and cold rice mixed with peppers beside the chicken and handed the plate to a woman seated nearby. She was older than Joe, I guessed, probably in her early or mid-forties. There was no darkness at her blond roots and she wore little or no makeup, although her eyes were obscured by a pair of Wayfarers. She wore a short-sleeved silk robe over a white blouse and white shorts. Like Joe Bones, she was barefoot. To one side of them stood two more men in shirts and chinos, each armed with a machine pistol. I counted two more on the balcony and one sitting beside the main door to the house.

"You want something to eat?" asked Joe Bones. His voice was low, with only a faint trace of Louisiana in it. He looked at me until I responded.

"No, thanks," I said. I noticed that he didn't offer any to Louis. I think Louis noticed too.

Joe Bones helped himself to some shrimp and salad, then motioned to the two guards to help themselves to what was left. They took turns to do so, each eating a breast of chicken with his fingers.

"Those Aguillard murders. A terrible thing," said Joe Bones. He waved me toward the only empty seat left after he sat down. I exchanged a look with Louis, shrugged, and sat.

"Excuse me for presuming on an intimacy with you," he continued, "but I hear that the same man may have been responsible for the deaths of your family." He smiled almost sympathetically. "A terrible thing," he repeated. "A terrible thing."

I held his gaze. "You're well informed about my past."

"When someone new comes to town and starts finding bodies in trees, I like to make it my business to find out about them. They might be good company." He picked a piece of shrimp from his plate and examined it briefly before starting to eat.

"I understand you had an interest in purchasing the Aguillards' land," I said.

Joe Bones sucked at the shrimp and placed the tail carefully to one side of his plate before responding. "I have a lot of interests, and that wasn't Aguillard land. Just because some senile fuck decides to make up for a bad life by slipping land to the niggers doesn't make it nigger land." He spat the word "nigger" each time. His shell of courtesy had proved remarkably fragile and he seemed intent upon deliberately provoking Louis. It was an unwise course of action, even with guns around him.

"It seems that one of your men, Tony Remarr, may have been in the house the night that the Aguillards died. We'd be interested in talking to him."

"Tony Remarr is no longer part of my operation," said Joe Bones, returning to his formal mode of speech after the burst of profanity. "We agreed a mutual parting of the ways and I haven't seen him in weeks. I had no idea he was in the Aguillard house until the police told me."

He smiled at me. I smiled back.

"Did Remarr have anything to do with David Fontenot's death?"

Joe Bones's jaw tensed but he kept smiling. "I have no idea. I heard about David Fontenot on the news this morning."

"Another terrible thing?" I suggested.

"The loss of a young life is always terrible," he responded. "Look, I'm sorry about your wife and kid, I truly am, but I can't help you. And frankly, now you're getting rude, so I'd like you to take your nigger and get the fuck off my property."

The muscles in Louis's neck rippled, the only sign he gave that he had heard Joe Bones. Joe Bones leered at him, picked up a piece of chicken, and tossed it toward the beast on the chain. It ignored the tidbit until his owner snapped his fingers, when it fell on the chicken and devoured it in a single bite.

"You know what that is?" asked Joe Bones. He spoke to me, but his body language was directed at Louis. It expressed utter contempt. When I didn't respond, he continued.

"It's called a *boerbul.* A man named Peter Geertschen, a German, developed it for the army and antiriot squads in South Africa by crossing a Russian wolf with an Alsatian. It's a white man's watchdog. It sniffs out niggers." He turned his gaze on Louis and smiled.

"Careful," I said. "He might get confused and turn on you." Joe Bones jerked in his chair as if he had been hit by a jolt of electricity. His eyes narrowed and searched my face for any indication that I was aware of a double meaning in what I had said. I stared right back at him.

"You better leave now," said Joe Bones, with quiet, obvious menace. I shrugged and stood up, Louis moving close to me as I did so. We exchanged a look.

"Man got us on the run," said Louis.

"Maybe, but if we leave like this he won't respect us."

"Without respect, a man got nothing," agreed Louis.

He picked a plate from the stack on the table and held it above his head. It exploded in a shower of china fragments as the .300 Winchester cartridge impacted and buried itself in the wood of the house behind. The woman in the chair dived to the grass, the two goons moved to cover Joe Bones, and three men appeared running from the side of the house as the shot echoed in the air.

Ricky, the Lizard Man, was the first to reach us. He raised the pistol and his finger tightened on the trigger, but Joe Bones struck out at his gun arm, pushing it upward.

"No! You dumb fuck, you want to get me killed?" He scanned the treeline beyond his property, then turned back to me.

"You come in here, you shoot at me, you scare my woman. The fuck do you think you're dealing with here?"

"You said the N-word," said Louis quietly.

"He's right," I agreed. "You did say it."

"I hear you got friends in New Orleans," said Joe Bones, his voice threatening. "I got enough troubles without the feds crawling on me, but I see you or your"—he paused, swallowing the word—"friend anywhere near me again and I'll take my chances. You hear?"

"I hear you," I said. "I'm going to find Remarr, Joe. If it turns out that you've been holding out on us and this man gets away because of it, I'll come back."

"You make us come back, Joe, and we gonna have to hurt your puppy," said Louis, almost sorrowfully.

"You come back and I'll stake you out on the grass and let him feed on you," snarled Joe Bones.

We backed away toward the oak-lined avenue, watching Joe Bones and his men carefully. The woman moved toward him to comfort him, her white clothes stained with grass. She kneaded gently at his trapezius with her carefully manicured hands, but he pushed her away with a hard shove to the chest. There was spittle on his chin.

Behind us, I heard the gate open as we retreated beneath the oaks. I hadn't expected much from Joe Bones, and had got less, but we had succeeded in rattling his cage. My guess was that he would contact Remarr and that might be enough to flush him from wherever he was holed up. It seemed like a good idea. The trouble with good ideas is that nine times out of ten someone has had the same idea before you.

"I didn't know Angel was such a good shot," I said to Louis as we reached the car. "You been giving him lessons?"

"Uh-huh," said Louis. He sounded genuinely shocked.

"Could he have hit Joe Bones?"

"Uh-uh. I'm surprised he didn't hit me."

Behind us, I heard the door open as Angel slid into the back seat, the Mauser already back in its case.

"So, we gonna start hangin' out with Joe Bones, maybe shoot some pool, whistle at girls?"

"When did you ever whistle at girls?" asked Louis, bemused, as we pulled away from the gate and headed toward St. Francisville.

"It's a guy thing," said Angel. "I can do guy things."

CHAPTER XXXVII

It was late afternoon when we got back to the Flaisance, where there was a message waiting from Morphy. I called him at the Sheriff's Office and got passed on to a cell phone.

"Where you been?" he asked.

"Visiting Joe Bones."

"Shit, why'd you do a thing like that?"

"Making trouble, I guess."

"I warned you, man. Don't be screwing with Joe Bones. You go alone?"

"I brought a friend. Joe didn't like him."

"What'd your friend do?"

"He got born to black parents."

Morphy laughed. "I guess Joe is kind of sensitive about his heritage, but it's good to remind him of it now and then."

"He threatened to feed my friend to his dog."

"Yeah," said Morphy, "Joe sure does love that dog."

"You got something?"

"Maybe. You like seafood?"

"No."

"Good, then we'll head out to Bucktown. Great seafood there, best shrimp around. I'll pick you up in two hours."

"Any other reason for seeing Bucktown other than seafood?"

"Remarr. One of his exes has a pad there. Might be worth a visit."

BUCKTOWN WAS PRETTY IN a quaint sort of way, as long as you liked the smell of fish. I kept the window up to try to limit the damage but Morphy had his rolled right down and was taking deep, sinful breaths. All in all, Bucktown seemed an unlikely place for a man like Remarr to hole up, but that in itself was probably reason enough for him to choose it.

Carole Stern lived in a small camelback house, a single-story at the front against a two-story rear, set in a small garden a few blocks off Bucktown's main street. According to Morphy, Stern worked in a bar on St. Charles but was currently serving time for possession of coke with intent to supply. Remarr was rumored to be keeping up the rental payments until she got out. We parked around the corner from the house and we clicked off the safeties of our guns in unison as we stepped from the car.

"You're a little out of your territory here, aren't you?" I asked Morphy.

"Hey, we just came out here for a bite to eat and decided to check on the off chance," he said, with an injured look. "I ain't steppin' on no toes."

He motioned me toward the front of the house while he took the back. I walked to the front door, which stood on a small raised porch, and peered carefully through the glass. It was caked with dirt, in keeping with the slightly run-down feel of the house itself. I counted five and then tried the door. It opened with a gentle creak and I stepped carefully into the hall. At the far end, I heard the tinkle of glass breaking and saw Morphy's hand reach in to open the rear door.

The smell was faint, but obvious, like meat that has been left in the sunlight on a warm day. The downstairs rooms were empty and consisted only of a kitchen, a small room with a sofa and an old TV, and a bedroom with a single bed and a closet. The closet contained women's clothes and shoes. The bed was covered only by a worn mattress.

Morphy took the stairs first. I stayed close behind, both of us with our guns pointing toward the second floor. The smell was stronger here now. We passed a bathroom with a dripping showerhead, which had stained the ceramic bath brown. On a sink unit beneath a small mirror stood some shaving foam, blades, and a bottle of Boss aftershave.

Three other doors stood partially open. On the right was a woman's bedroom. It had white sheets on the bed, potted plants, which had begun to wither, and a series of Monet prints on the walls. There were cosmetics on a long dressing table and a white fitted closet ran the length of one wall. A window opposite looked out on a small, overgrown garden. There were more women's clothes in the closet, and more shoes. Carole Stern was obviously funding some kind of shopping addiction by selling drugs.

The second door provided the source of the smell. A large open pot sat on a camper stove by a window facing on to the street. It contained scummy water in which a stew of some kind was cooking on a low heat. From the stench, the meat had been allowed to simmer for some time, probably most of the day. It smelled foul, like offal. Two easy chairs stood in the room on a new red carpet. A portable TV with a coat-hanger aerial sat blankly on a small table.

The third room was also at the front of the house facing onto the street, but its door was almost closed. Morphy took one side of the door. I took the other. He counted three and then nudged the door open with his foot and went in fast to the right-hand wall. I moved in low to the left, my gun level with my chest, my finger resting on the trigger.

The setting sun cast a golden glow over the contents of the room: an unmade bed, a suitcase open on the floor, a dressing table, a poster on the wall advertising a concert by the Neville Brothers in Tipitina's, with the brothers' signatures scrawled loosely across their images. The carpeted floor felt damp beneath my feet.

Most of the plaster had been removed from the ceiling and the roof beams lay exposed. I guessed Carole Stern had been considering some sort of remodeling before her prison sentence put her plans temporarily on hold. At the far end of the room, a series of what looked like climbing ropes had been strung over the beams and used to hold Tony Remarr in position.

His remains glowed with a strange fire in the dying sunlight. I could see the muscles and veins in his legs, the tendons in his neck, the yellow mounds of fatty deposits seeping at his waist, the muscles in his stomach, the shriveled husk of his penis. Huge masonry nails had been driven into the far wall of the room and he hung partially on them, one beneath each arm, while the ropes took the main weight of his body.

As I moved to the right I could see a third nail in the wall behind his neck, holding his head in place. The head faced to the right, in profile, supported by another nail beneath his chin. In places, his skull gleamed whitely through the blood. His eye sockets were almost empty and his gritted teeth were white against his gums.

Remarr had been totally flayed, carefully posed, and hung against the wall. His left hand stretched diagonally outward and down from his body. A long-bladed knife, like a butcher's filleting tool but wider, heavier, hung from his hand. It looked like it had been glued in place.

But the viewer's gaze was drawn, like Tony Remarr's own blind stare, to the figure's right hand. It stood at a right angle to his body until it reached the elbow. From there, the forearm was raised vertically, pulled upward by a rope around the wrist. In the fingers of his right hand and draped over his right arm, Tony Remarr held his own flayed skin. I could see the shape of the arms, the legs, the hair of his scalp, the nipples on his chest. Beneath the scalp, which hung almost at his knees, there were bloody edges where the face had been removed. The bed, the floor, the wall, all were shaded in red.

I looked to my left to see Morphy cross himself and softly say a prayer for the soul of Tony Remarr.

WE SAT AGAINST MORPHY'S car drinking coffee from paper cups as the feds and the New Orleans police milled around the Stern house. A crowd of people, some local, some on their way to eat in Bucktown's seafood joints, hung around the edges of the police cordon waiting to see the body being removed. They were likely to be disappointed: the crime scene was highly organized by the killer, and both the police and the feds were anxious to document it fully before allowing the body to be taken away.

Woolrich, his tan suit now restored to its former tarnished glory, came over to us and offered us the remains of a bag of donuts from his suit pocket. Behind the cordon, I could see his own Chevy, a red '96 model that shone like new.

"Here, you must be hungry." Both Morphy and I declined the offer. I still had visions of Remarr in my head and Morphy looked pale and ill.

"You speak to the locals?" asked Woolrich.

We both nodded. We had given lengthy statements to a pair of Homicide detectives from Orleans Parish, one of whom was Morphy's brother-in-law.

"Then I guess you can go," said Woolrich. "I'll want to talk to both of you again, though." Morphy wandered around to the driver's side of his car. I moved to open the passenger door but Woolrich held my arm.

"You okay?" he asked.

"I think so."

"It was a good hunch that Morphy followed, but he shouldn't have brought you along. Durand's gonna be on my back when he finds out that you were first on another crime scene." Durand was the FBI's special agent in charge in New Orleans. I had never met him but I knew what most SACs were like. They ruled their field offices like kingdoms, assigning agents to squads and giving the go-ahead to operations. The competition for SAC posts was intense. If nothing else, Durand was a tough customer.

"You're still at the Flaisance?"

"Still there."

"I'll drop by. There's something I want to bounce off you."

He turned and walked back toward the Stern house. On his way through the gate, he handed the bag of crushed donuts to a pair of patrolmen sitting in their car. They took the bag reluctantly, holding it like it was a bomb. When Woolrich had entered the house, one of them climbed out of the car and threw the donuts in a trash can.

Morphy dropped me at the Flaisance. Before he left, I gave him my cell phone number. He wrote it in a small black notebook, bound tightly with a rubber band. "If you're free tomorrow, Angie's cooking dinner. It's worth the trip. You taste her cooking and you won't regret it." The tone of his voice changed. "Besides, there's some things I think we need to discuss."

I told him it sounded okay, although part of me wanted never to see Morphy, Woolrich, or another cop again. He was about to pull away when I patted the roof of the car with my palm. Morphy leaned over and rolled down the window.

"Why are you doing this?" I asked. Morphy had gone to considerable lengths to involve me, to keep me posted on what was happening. I needed to know why. I think I also needed to know if I could trust him.

He shrugged. "The Aguillards died on my beat. I want to get the guy who killed them. You know something about him. He's come at you, at your family. The feds are conducting their own investigation and are telling us as little as they can. You're all I got."

"Is that it?" I could see something more in his face, something that was almost familiar.

"No. I got a wife. I'm starting a family. You know what I'm sayin'?"

I nodded and let it go, but there was something else in his eyes, something that resonated inside me. I patted the roof of the car once again in farewell and watched as he drove away, wondering how badly Morphy wanted absolution for what he might have done.

CHAPTER XXXVIII

As I returned to my room at the Flaisance I felt an overpowering sense of decay, which seemed to creep into my nostrils, almost stopping my breathing. It lodged itself beneath my nails and stained my skin. I felt it in the sweat on my back and saw it in the weeds breaking through the cracks in the pavement beneath my feet. It was as if the city were corroding around me. I went to my room and showered under a hot jet until my skin was red and raw, then changed into a sweater and chinos, called Angel and Louis in their room, and arranged to meet them in Rachel's room in five minutes.

She answered the door with an ink-stained hand. She had a pencil tucked behind her ear, and a pair of pencils held her red hair back in a bun. There were dark rims under her eyes, which were red from reading.

Her room had been transformed. A Macintosh PowerBook stood open on the room's only table, surrounded by a mass of paper, books, and notes. On the wall above it were diagrams, yellow Post-it notes, and a series of what appeared to be anatomy sketches. A pile of faxes lay on the floor by her chair, beside a tray of half-eaten sandwiches, a pot of coffee, and a stained cup.

I heard a knock on the door behind me. I opened it to admit Angel and Louis. Angel looked at the wall in disbelief. "Guy on the desk already thinks you're crazy, with all the shit that's been comin' in on his fax. He sees this, he's gonna call the cops."

Rachel sat back in her chair and pulled the pencils from her bun, releasing her hair. She shook her tresses out with her left hand and then twisted her neck to ease her knotted muscles.

"So," she said, "who wants to start?"

I told them about Remarr, and instantly, the tiredness went from Rachel's face. She made me detail the position of the body twice and then spent a couple of minutes shuffling papers on her desk.

"There!" she said, handing me a sheet of paper with a flourish. "Is that it?"

It was a black-and-white illustration, marked at the top of the page, in old lettering: TAB. PRIMERA DEL LIB. SEGVNDO. At the bottom of the page, in Rachel's handwriting, was written "Valverde 1556."

The illustration depicted a flayed man, his left foot on a stone, his left hand holding a long knife with a hooked hilt, his right holding his own flayed skin. The outline of his face was visible on the skin and his eyes remained in his sockets, but with those exceptions, the illustration was profoundly similar to the position in which Remarr had been found. The various parts of the body were each marked with Greek letters.

"That's it," I said quietly as Angel and Louis peered silently over my shoulder. "That's what we found."

"The *Historia de la composición del cuerpo humano,*" said Rachel. "It was written by the Spaniard Juan de Valverde de Hamusco in 1556 as a medical textbook. This drawing"—she took the page and held it up so we could all see it—"is an illustration of the Marsyas myth. Marsyas was a satyr, a follower of the goddess Cybele. He was cursed when he picked up a bone flute discarded by Athene. The flute played itself, because it was still inspired by Athene, and its music was so beautiful that the peasants said it was greater even than that of Apollo himself.

"Apollo challenged Marsyas to a competition to be judged by the Muses, and Marsyas lost because he couldn't play the flute upside down and sing at the same time.

"And so Apollo took his revenge on Marsyas. He flayed him alive and nailed his skin to a pine. According to the poet Ovid, at his moment of death Marsyas cried out, *"Quid me mihi detrahis?"*—which can be roughly translated as: "Who is it that tears me from myself?" The artist Titian painted a version of the myth. So did Raphael. My guess is that Remarr's body will reveal traces of ketamine. To fulfill the myth, the flaying would have to be carried out while the victim was still alive—it's hard to create a work of art if the subject keeps moving."

Louis interrupted. "But in this picture he looks like he flayed himself. He's holding the knife *and* the skin. Why did the killer choose this depiction?"

"This is just a guess, but maybe it's because, in a sense, Remarr did flay himself," I said. "He was at the Aguillard house when he shouldn't have been. I think the Traveling Man was concerned at what he might have seen. Remarr was somewhere he shouldn't have been, so he was responsible for what happened to him."

Rachel nodded. "It's an interesting point, but there may be something more to it, given what happened to Tee Jean Aguillard." She handed me a pair of papers. The first was a photocopy of the crime scene photo of Tee Jean. The second was another illustration, this time marked DE DISSECT. PARTIVM. At the bottom of the page, the date "1545" had been handwritten by Rachel.

The illustration depicted a man crucified against a tree, with a stone wall behind it. His head was cradled by the branches of the tree, his arms spread by further branches. The skin below his chest had been flayed, revealing his lungs, kidneys, and heart. Some unidentified organ, probably his stomach, lay on a raised platform beside him. His face was intact, but once again, the illustration matched the posture of Tee Jean Aguillard's body.

"Marsyas again," said Rachel. "Or at least an adaptation of the myth. That's from Estienne's *De dissectione partium corporis humani,* another early textbook."

"Are you saying that this guy is killing according to a Greek myth?" asked Angel.

Rachel sighed. "It's not that simple. I think the myth has resonances for him, for the basic reason that he's used it twice. But the Marsyas theory breaks down with *Tante* Marie, and Bird's wife and child. I found the Marsyas illustrations almost by accident, but I haven't found a match yet for the other deaths. I'm still looking. The likelihood is that they are also based on early medical textbooks. If that's the case, then I'll find them."

"It raises the possibility that we're looking for someone with a medical background," I said.

"Or a knowledge of obscure texts," said Rachel. "We already know that he has read the Book of Enoch, or some derivative of it. It wouldn't take a great deal of medical knowledge to carry out the kind of mutilation we've found on the bodies so far, but an assumption of some surgical skills, or even some mild familiarity with medical procedures, might not be totally amiss."

"What about the blinding and the removal of the faces?" I asked. I pushed a flashing image of Susan and Jennifer to the back of my mind. "Any idea where they fit in?"

Rachel shook her head. "I'm still working on it. The face appears to be some form of token for him. Jennifer's was returned because she died before he could start working on her, I'd guess, but also because he wanted to shock you personally. The removal could also indicate the killer's disregard for them as individuals, a sign of his disregard for their own status as people. After all, when you remove a person's face, you take away the most immediate representation of their individuality, their main physical distinguisher.

"As for the eyes, there is a myth that the image of the killer stays on the retina of the victim. There were lots of myths like that attached to the body. Even at the start of the last century, some scientists were still examining the theory that a murder victim's body bled when it was in the same room as its killer. I need to do more work on it, then we'll see."

She stood up and stretched. "I don't mean to sound callous, but now I want to take a shower. Then I want to go out and get something decent to eat. After that, I want to sleep for twelve hours."

Angel, Louis, and I started to leave but she held up her hand to stop us. "There's just one more thing. I don't want to give the impression that this is just some freak copying violent images. I don't know enough about this to make that kind of judgment and I want to consult some people who are more experienced in this area than I am. But I can't help feeling that there's some underlying philosophy behind what he's doing, some pattern that he's following. Until we find out what that is, I don't think we're going to catch him."

I had my hand on the door handle when there was a knock at the door. I opened it slowly and blocked the view of the room with my body while Rachel cleared away her papers. Woolrich stood before me. In the light from the room, I noticed a thin growth of beard was forming on his face. "Clerk told me you might be here if you weren't in your own room. Can I come in?"

I paused for a moment, then stepped aside. I noticed that Rachel was standing in front of the material on the wall, obscuring it from view, but Woolrich wasn't interested in her. His eyes had fixed on Louis.

"I know you," he said.

"I don't think so," said Louis. His eyes were cold.

Woolrich turned to me. "You bringing your hired killers to my town, Bird?"

I didn't reply.

"Like I said, man, I think you're making a mistake," said Louis. "I'm a businessman."

"Really? And what kind of business would you be in?"

"Pest control," said Louis.

The air seemed to crackle with tension, until Woolrich turned around and walked from the room. He stopped in the hall and gestured to me. "I need to talk to you. I'll wait for you in the Café du Monde."

I watched him go, then looked at Louis. He raised an eyebrow. "Guess I'm more famous than I thought."

"Guess you are," I said, and went after Woolrich.

I CAUGHT UP WITH him on the street but he said nothing until we were seated and he had a beignet in front of him. He tore off a piece, sprinkling powdered sugar on his suit, then took a long gulp of coffee, which half drained the cup and left a brown stain along its sides. "C'mon, Bird," he said. "What are you trying to do here?" He sounded weary and disappointed. "That guy, I know his face. I know what he is." He chewed another piece of beignet.

I didn't reply. We stared at each other until Woolrich looked away. He dusted sugar from his fingers and ordered another coffee. I had hardly touched mine.

"Does the name Edward Byron mean anything to you?" he said eventually, when he realized that Louis was not going to be a topic of discussion.

"It doesn't ring any bells. Why?"

"He was a janitor in Park Rise. That's where Susan had Jennifer, right?"

"Right." Park Rise was a private hospital on Long Island. Susan's father had insisted that we use it, arguing that its staff were among the best in the world. They were certainly among the best paid. The doctor who delivered Jennifer earned more in a month than I made in a year.

"Where's this leading?" I asked.

"Byron was let go—quietly—following the mutilation of a corpse earlier this year. Someone performed an unauthorized autopsy on a female body. Her abdomen was opened and her ovaries and Fallopian tubes removed."

"No charges were pressed?"

"The hospital authorities considered it, then decided against it. Surgical gloves with traces of the dead woman's blood and tissue on them were found in a bag in Byron's locker. He argued that someone was trying to frame him. The evidence wasn't conclusive—theoretically, someone could have planted that stuff in his locker—but the hospital let him go anyway. No court case, no police investigation, nothing. The only reason we have any record of it is because the local cops were investigating the theft of drugs from the hospital around the same time, and Byron's name was noted on the report. Byron was dismissed after the thefts began and they pretty much ceased, but he had an alibi each time there were found to be drugs missing.

"That was the last anyone heard of Byron. We have his Social Security number, but he hasn't claimed unemployment, paid tax, dealt with state government, or visited a hospital since he was dismissed. His credit cards haven't been used since October nineteenth, ninety-six."

"What brings his name up now?"

"Edward Byron is a native of Baton Rouge. His wife—his ex-wife, Stacey—still lives there."

"Have you spoken to her?"

"We interviewed her yesterday. She says she hasn't seen him since last April, that he owes her six months' alimony. The last check was drawn on a bank in East Texas but his old lady thinks he may be living in the Baton Rouge area, or somewhere nearby. She says he always wanted to come back here, that he hated New York. We've also put out photos of him, taken from his employee record at Park Rise."

He handed me a blown-up picture of Byron. He was a handsome man, his features marred only by a slightly receding chin. His mouth and nose were thin, his eyes narrow and dark. He had dark brown hair, swept from left to right. He looked younger than thirty-five, his age when the picture was taken.

"It's the best lead we've got," said Woolrich. "Maybe I'm telling you because I figure you have a right to know. But I'm telling you something else as well: you keep away from Mrs. Byron. We've told her not to talk to anyone in case the press get wind of it. Secondly, stay away from Joe Bones. His guy Ricky was caught on one of our taps swearing blue hell about some stunt you pulled today, but you won't get away with it a second time."

He laid some money on the table. "Your little team back there got anything that might help us?"

"Not yet. We figure a medical background, maybe a sexual pathology. If I get anything more, I'll let you know. I've got a question for you, though. What drugs were taken from Park Rise?"

He tilted his head to one side and twisted his mouth slightly, as if debating with himself whether or not to tell me.

"Ketamine hydrochloride. It's related to PCP." I gave no indication that I already knew about the drug. The feds would tear Morphy a new asshole if they knew he had been feeding me details like that, although they must have already had their suspicions. Woolrich paused for a moment and then went on. "It was found in the bodies of *Tante* Marie Aguillard and her son. The killer used it as a form of anesthetic."

He spun his coffee cup on its saucer, waiting until it came to rest with the handle pointing in my direction.

"Are you scared of this guy, Bird?" he asked quietly. "Because I sure am. You remember that conversation we had about serial killers, when I brought you to meet *Tante* Marie?"

I nodded.

"Back then, I thought I'd seen it all. These killers were abusers and rapists and dysfunctionals who had crossed some line, but they were so pathetic that they were still recognizably human. But this one . . ."

He watched a family pass by in a carriage, the driver urging the horse on with the reins while he gave them his own history of Jackson Square. A child, a small, dark-haired boy, was seated at the edge of the family group. He watched us silently as they passed by, his chin resting on his bare forearm.

"We were always afraid that one would come who was different from the others, who was motivated by something more than a twisted, frustrated sexuality or wretched sadism. We live in a culture of pain and death, Bird, and most of us go through life without ever really understanding that. Maybe it was only a matter of time before we produced someone who understood that better than we did, someone who saw the world as just one big altar on which to sacrifice humanity, someone who believed he had to make an example of us all."

"And do you believe that this is him?"

"'I am become Death, the destroyer of worlds.' Isn't that what the Bhagavadgita says? 'I am become Death.' Maybe that's what he is: pure Death."

He moved toward the street. I followed him, then remembered my slip of paper from the previous night. "Woolrich, there is one more thing." He looked testy as I gave him the references for the Book of Enoch.

"What the fuck is the Book of Enoch?"

"It's part of the Apocrypha. I think he may have some knowledge of it."

Woolrich folded the paper and put it in the pocket of his pants.

"Bird," he said, and he almost smiled, "sometimes I'm torn between keeping you in touch with what's happening and not telling you anything." He grimaced, then sighed as if to indicate that this was something that just wasn't worth arguing about. "Stay out of trouble, Bird, and tell your friends the same." He walked away, to be swallowed up by the evening crowds.

I KNOCKED ON RACHEL'S door, but there was no reply. I knocked a second time, harder, and I heard some noises from inside the room. She answered the door with a towel wrapped around her body and her hair hidden by a second, smaller towel. Her face was red from the heat of the shower and her skin glowed.

"Sorry," I said. "I forgot that you'd be showering."

She smiled and waved me in.

"Take a seat. I'll get dressed and let you buy me dinner." She took a pair of gray pants and a white cotton shirt from the bed, picked some matching white underwear from her case, and stepped back into the bathroom. She didn't close the door fully behind her so that we could talk while she dressed.

"Should I ask what that exchange was about?" she said.

I walked to her balcony window and looked out on the street below.

"What Woolrich said about Louis is true. It's not as simple as that, maybe, but he has killed people in the past. Now, I'm not so sure. I don't ask, and I'm not in a position to pass judgment on him. But I trust both Angel and Louis. I asked them to come because I know what they're good at."

She came out of the bathroom buttoning her shirt, her damp hair hanging. She dried her hair with a travel dryer, then applied a little makeup. I had seen Susan do the same things a thousand times, but there was a strange intimacy in watching Rachel perform them in front of me. I felt something stir inside me, a tiny yet significant shift in my feelings toward her. She sat on the edge of the bed and slipped her bare feet into a pair of black slingbacks, her finger moving inside each one to ease the progress of her heel. As she leaned foward, moisture glistened on the small of her back. She caught me looking at her and smiled cautiously, as if afraid of misinterpreting what she had seen. "Shall we go?" she said.

I held the door open for her as we left, her shirt brushing my hand with a sound like water sizzling on hot metal.

WE ATE IN MR. B's on Royal Street, the big mahogany room cool and dark. I had steak, tender and luscious, while Rachel ate blackened redfish, the spices causing her to gasp at the first bite. We talked of little things, of plays and films, of music and reading. It emerged that we had both attended the same performance of *The Magic Flute* at the Met in '91, both of us alone. I watched her as she sipped her wine, the reflected light playing on her face and dancing in the darkness of her pupils like moonlight seen from a lakeshore.

"So, you often follow strange men to distant lands?"

She smiled. "I bet you've been waiting to use that line all your life."

"Maybe I use it all the time."

"Oh *puh*-lease. Next thing you'll be wielding a club and asking the waiter to step outside."

"Okay, guilty as charged. It's been a while."

I felt myself redden and caught something playful but uncertain in her glance—a kind of sadness, a fear of hurting and being hurt. Inside me, something twisted and stretched its claws, and I felt a little tear in my heart.

"I'm sorry. I know almost nothing about you," I said quietly.

She reached out gently and brushed along the length of my left hand, from the wrist to the end of the little finger. She followed the curves of my fingers, delicately tracing the lines and whorls of my fingerprints, her touch soft as a leaf. At last, she let her hand rest on the table, the tips of her fingers resting on top of my own, and began to speak.

She was born in Chilson, near the foothills of the Adirondacks. Her father was a lawyer, her mother taught kindergarten. She liked basketball and running, and her prom date got the mumps two days before the prom, so her best friend's brother went with her instead and tried to feel her breast during "Only the Lonely." She had one brother of her own, Curtis, ten years her elder. For five of his twenty-eight years, Curtis had been a cop. He was two weeks short of his twenty-ninth birthday when he died. "He was a detective with the State Police, newly promoted. He wasn't even on duty the day he was killed." She spoke without hesitation, not too slowly, not too quickly, as if she had gone over the story a thousand times, examining it for flaws, tracing its beginning, its resolution, cutting all extraneous detail from it until she was left with the gleaming core of her brother's murder, the hollow heart of his absence.

"It was a quarter after two, a Tuesday afternoon. Curtis was visiting some girl in Moriah—he always had two or three girls trailing him at any one time. He just broke their hearts. He was carrying a bunch of flowers, pink lilies bought in a store five doors from the bank. He heard some shouting and saw two people come running from the bank, both armed, both masked, a man and a woman. There was another man sitting in a car, waiting for them to come out.

"Curtis was drawing his gun when they saw him. They both had sawed-offs and they didn't hesitate. The man emptied both barrels into him and then, while he lay dying on the ground, the woman finished him off. She shot him in the face, and he was so handsome, so lovely."

She stopped talking and I knew that this was a story she had told only in her mind, that it was something not to be shared, but to be safeguarded. Sometimes, we need our pain. We need it to call our own.

"When they caught them, they had three thousand dollars. That was all they got from the bank, all that my brother was worth to them. The woman had been released from an institution the week before. Someone decided that she no longer posed a threat to the community."

She lifted her glass and drained the last of her wine. I signaled for more and she remained silent as the waiter refilled her glass.

"And here I am," she said at last. "Now I try to understand, and sometimes I get close. And sometimes, if I'm lucky, I can stop things from happening to other people. Sometimes."

I found that her hand was now gripped tightly in mine, and I could not recall how that had happened. Holding her hand, I spoke for the first time in many years about leaving New York and the move to Maine with my mother.

"Is she still alive?"

I shook my head. "I got in trouble with a local big shot named Daddy Helms," I said. "My grandfather and my mother agreed that I should go away to work for the summer, until things quieted down. A friend of his ran a store in Philly, so I worked there for a while, stocking shelves, cleaning up at night. I slept in a room above the store.

"My mother began taking physiotherapy for a trapped nerve in her shoulder, except it turned out that she had been misdiagnosed. She had cancer. I think she knew, but she chose not to say anything. Maybe she thought that if she didn't admit it to herself, she could fool her system into giving her more time. Instead, one of her lungs collapsed as she left the therapist's office.

"I came back two days later on a bus. I hadn't seen her in two months and when I tried to find her in the hospital ward, I couldn't. I had to check the names on the ends of the beds because she had changed so much. She lasted six weeks after that. Toward the end, she became lucid, even with the painkillers. It happens a lot, I believe. It can fool you into thinking they're getting better. It's like the cancer's small joke. She was trying to draw a picture of the hospital the night before she died, so she would know where she was going when it was time to leave."

I sipped some water. "I'm sorry," I said. "I don't know why all those things should have come back to me."

Rachel smiled and I felt her hand tighten again on mine.

"And your grandfather?"

"He died eight years ago. He left me his house in Maine, the one I'm trying to fix up." I noticed that she didn't ask me about my father. I guessed that she knew all there was to know.

Later, we walked slowly back through the crowds, the music from the bars blending together into one blast of sound in which familiar tunes could sometimes be identified. When we came to the door of her room we held each other for a while, then kissed softly, her hand on my cheek, before we said good night.

Despite Remarr and Joe Bones and my exchanges with Woolrich, I slept peacefully that night, my hand still holding the specter of her own.

CHAPTER

XXXIX

It was a cool, clear morning and the sound of the St. Charles streetcar carried on the air as I ran. A wedding limousine passed me on its way to the cathedral, white ribbons rippling on its hood. I jogged west along North Rampart as far as Perdido, then back through the Quarter along Chartres. The heat was intense, like running with my face in a warm, damp towel. My lungs struggled to pull in the air and my system rebelled, struggling to reject it, but still I ran.

I was used to training three or four times each week, alternating circuits for a month or so with a split bodybuilding workout. After a few days outside my training regimen I felt bloated and out of condition, as if my system was full of toxins. Given the choice between exercise and colon cleansers, I opted for exercise as the less uncomfortable option.

Back at the Flaisance I showered and changed the dressing on my wounded shoulder; it still ached a little, but the wounds were closing. Finally, I left a batch of clothes at the local laundry, since I hadn't figured on staying quite so long in New Orleans and my underwear selection was becoming pretty limited.

Stacey Byron's number was in the phone book—she hadn't reverted to her maiden name, at least not as far as the phone company was concerned—so Angel and Louis volunteered to take a trip to Baton Rouge and see what they could find out from her, or about her. Woolrich wouldn't be pleased, but if he wanted her left in peace then he shouldn't have said anything at all.

Rachel e-mailed details of the kind of illustrations she was seeking to two of her research students at Columbia and Father Eric Ward, a retired professor in Boston who had lectured at Loyola in New Orleans on Renaissance culture. Instead of hanging around waiting for a response, she decided to come with me to Metairie, where David Fontenot was due to be buried that morning.

We were silent as we drove. The subject of our growing intimacy and what it might imply had not come up between us, but it seemed that we were both acutely aware of it. I could see something of it in Rachel's eyes when she looked at me. I thought that she could probably see the same in mine.

"So what else do you want to know about me?" she asked.

"I guess I don't know too much about your personal life."

"Apart from the fact that I'm beautiful and brilliant."

"Apart from that," I admitted.

"By personal, do you mean sexual?"

"It's a euphemism. I don't want to seem pushy. If it makes you happier you can start with your age, since you didn't tell me last night. The rest will seem easy by comparison."

She gave me a twisted grin and the finger. I chose to ignore the finger.

"I'm thirty-three but I admit to thirty, if the lighting is right. I have a cat and a two-bedroom apartment on the Upper West Side, but no one to share it with currently. I do step aerobics three times a week and I like Chinese food, soul music, and cream ale. My last relationship ended six months ago and I think my hymen may be growing back."

I arched an eyebrow at her and she laughed. "You do look shocked," she said. "You need to get out more."

"Sounds like you do, too. Who was the guy?"

"A stockbroker. We'd been seeing each other for over a year and we agreed to live together on a test basis. He had a one-bed, I had a two-bed, so he moved in with me and we used the second bedroom as a shared study."

"Sounds idyllic."

"It was. For about a week. It turned out that he couldn't stand the cat, he hated sharing a bed with me because he said I kept him awake by turning over all the time, and all my clothes started to smell of his cigarettes. That clinched it. Everything stank: the furniture, the bed, the walls, the food, the toilet paper, even the cat. Then he came home one evening, told me he was in love with his secretary, and moved to Seattle with her three months later."

"Seattle's nice, I hear."

"Fuck Seattle. I hope it falls into the sea."

"At least you're not bitter."

"Very funny." She looked out of her window for a while and I felt an urge to reach out and touch her, an urge enhanced by what she said next. "I still feel reluctant to ask you too many questions," she said, gently. "After what happened."

"I know." Slowly, I extended my right hand and touched her lightly on the cheek. Her skin was smooth and slightly moist. She leaned her head toward me, increasing the pressure against my hand, and then we were pulling up outside the entrance to the cemetery and the moment was gone.

Branches of the Fontenots had lived in New Orleans since the late nineteenth century, long before the family of Lionel and David had moved to the city, and the Fontenots had a large vault in Metairie Cemetery, the largest of the city's cemeteries, at Metairie Road and Pontchartrain Boulevard. The cemetery covered one hundred and fifty acres and was built on the old Metairie racecourse. If you were a gambling man, it was an appropriate final resting place, even though it proved that, in the end, the odds are always stacked in favor of the house.

New Orleans cemeteries are strange places. While most cemeteries in big cities are carefully manicured and encourage discreet headstones, the dead citizens of New Orleans rested in ornate tombs and spectacular mausoleums. They reminded me of Père

Lachaise in Paris, or the Cities of the Dead in Cairo, where people still lived among the bodies. The resemblance was echoed by the Brunswig tomb at Metairie, which was shaped like a pyramid and guarded by a sphinx.

It was not simply the funerary architecture of Spain and France that had caused the cemeteries to develop the way they did. Most of the city was below sea level, and until the development of modern drainage systems, graves dug in the ground had rapidly filled with water. Aboveground tombs were the natural solution.

The Fontenot funeral had already entered the cemetery when we arrived. I parked away from the main body of vehicles and we walked past the two police cruisers at the gate, their occupants' eyes masked by shades. We followed the stragglers past the four statues representing Faith, Hope, Charity, and Memory, at the base of the long Moriarity tomb, until we came to a Greek Revival tomb marked with a pair of Doric columns. FONTENOT was inscribed on the lintel above the door.

It was impossible to tell how many Fontenots had come to rest in the family vault. The tradition in New Orleans was to leave the body for a year and a day, after which the vault was reopened, the remains moved to the back, and the rotting casket removed to make way for the next occupant. A lot of the vaults in Metairie were pretty crowded by this point.

The wrought iron gate, inlaid with the heads of angels, stood open and the small party of mourners had surrounded the vault in a semicircle. A man I guessed to be Lionel Fontenot towered above them. He was wearing a black, single-breasted suit and a thick black tie. His face had been weathered to a reddish brown, and deep lines etched his forehead and snaked out from the corners of his eyes. His hair was dark but streaked with gray at the temples. He was a big man, certainly six-three at least and weighing close to two hundred and forty pounds, maybe two-fifty. His suit seemed to struggle to contain him.

Beyond the mourners, ranged at intervals around the vaults and tombs, or standing beneath trees scanning the cemetery, were four hard-faced men in dark jackets and trousers. Their pistols caused the jackets to bulge slightly. A fifth man, a dark overcoat hanging loosely on his shoulders, turned at an old cypress and I caught a glimpse of the telltale sights of an M16-based submachine gun concealed beneath its folds. Two others stood at either side of Lionel Fontenot. The big man wasn't taking any chances.

The mourners, both black and white, young white men in snappy black suits, old black women wearing black dresses gilded with lace at the neckline, grew silent as the priest began to read the rites of the dead from a tattered prayer book with gold-edged pages. There was no wind to carry away his words and they hung in the air around us, reverberating from the surrounding tombs like the voices of the dead themselves.

"Our Father, who art in Heaven . . ."

The pallbearers moved forward, struggling awkwardly to fit the casket through the narrow entrance to the vault. As it was placed inside, a pair of New Orleans policemen appeared between two round vaults about eighty feet west of the funeral party. Two more emerged from the east and a third pair moved slowly down past a tree to the north. Rachel followed my glance.

"An escort?"

"Maybe."

"Thy kingdom come, thy will be done on earth . . ."

I felt uneasy. They could have been sent to ensure that Joe Bones wasn't tempted to disturb the mourners, but something was wrong. I didn't like the way they moved. They looked uncomfortable in the uniforms, as if their shirt collars were too tight and their shoes pinched.

"Forgive us our trespasses . . ."

Fontenot's men had spotted them too, but they didn't look too concerned. The policemen's arms hung loosely by their sides and their guns remained in their holsters. They were about thirty feet away from us when something warm splashed my face. An elderly moonfaced woman in a tight black dress, who had been sobbing quietly beside me, spun sideways and tumbled to the ground, a dark hole in her temple and a damp glistening in her hair. A chip of marble flew from the vault, the area around it stained a vivid red. The sound of the shot came almost simultaneously, a dull subdued noise like a fist hitting a punching bag.

"But deliver us from evil . . ."

It took the mourners a few seconds to realize what was happening. They looked dumbly at the fallen woman, a pool of blood already forming around her head as I pushed Rachel into the space between two vaults, shielding her with my body. Someone screamed and the crowd began to scatter as more bullets came, whining off the marble and stone. I could see Lionel Fontenot's bodyguards rush to protect him, pushing him to the ground as the bullets bounced from the tomb and rattled its iron gate.

Rachel covered her head with her arms and crouched to try to make herself a smaller target. Over my shoulder, I saw the two cops to the north separate and pick up machine pistols concealed in the bushes at either side of the avenue. They were Steyrs, fitted with sound suppressors: Joe Bones's men. I saw a woman try to run for the cover of the outspread wings of a stone angel, her dark coat whipping around her bare legs. The coat puffed twice at the shoulder and she sprawled face forward on the ground, her hands outstretched. She tried to drag herself forward but her coat puffed again and she was gone.

Now there were pistol shots and the rattle of a semiautomatic as Fontenot's men returned fire. I drew my own Smith & Wesson and joined Rachel as a uniformed figure appeared in the gap between the tombs, the Steyr held in a two-handed grip. I shot him in the face and he crumpled to the ground.

"But they're cops!" said Rachel, her voice almost drowned by the exchange of fire around us.

I reached out and pushed her down further. "They're Joe Bones's men. They're here to take out Lionel Fontenot." But it was more than that: Joe Bones wanted to sow chaos and to reap blood and fear and death from the consequences. He didn't simply want Lionel Fontenot dead. He also wanted others to die—women, children, Lionel's family, his associates—and for those left alive to remember what had taken place and to fear Joe Bones more because of it. He wanted to break the Fontenots and he would do it here, beside the vault where they had buried generations of their dead. This was the action of a man who had moved beyond reason and passed into a dark, flame-lit place, a place that blinded his vision with blood.

Behind me, there was a scuffling, tumbling sound and one of Fontenot's men, the overcoated man with the semiautomatic, fell to his knees beside Rachel. Blood bubbled from his mouth and I heard her scream as he fell forward, his head coming to rest by her feet. The M16 lay on the grass beside him. I reached for it but Rachel got to it first, a deep, unquenchable instinct for survival now guiding her actions. Her mouth and eyes were wide as she fired a burst over the prone frame of the bodyguard.

I flung myself to the end of the tomb and aimed in the same direction, but Joe Bones's man was already down. He lay on his back, his left leg spasming and a bloody pattern etched across his chest. Rachel's hands were shaking as the adrenaline coursed through her system. The M16 began to fall from her fingers. Its strap became entangled in her arm and she shook herself furiously to release it. Behind her, I could see mourners running low through the avenues of tombs. Two white women dragged a young black man by his arms over the grass. The belly of his white shirt was smeared with blood.

I figured that there must have been a fourth set of Joe Bones's men who approached from the south and fired the first shots. At least three were down: the two killed by Rachel and me and a third who lay sprawled by the old cypress. Fontenot's man had taken one of them out before he was hit himself.

I helped Rachel to her feet and moved her quickly to a grimy vault with a corroded gate. I struck at the lock with the butt of the M16 and it gave instantly. She slipped inside and I handed her my Smith & Wesson and told her to stay there until I came back for her. Then, gripping the M16, I ran east past the back of the

Fontenot tomb, using the other vaults as cover. I didn't know how many shots were left in the M16. The selector switch was set for three-round bursts. Depending on the magazine capacity, I might have anything between ten and twenty rounds left.

I had almost reached a monument topped by the figure of a sleeping child when something hit me on the back of the head and I stumbled forward, the M16 slipping from my grasp. Someone kicked me hard in the kidneys, the pain lancing through my body as far as the shoulder. I was kicked again in the stomach, which forced me on to my back. I looked up to see Ricky standing above me, the reptilian coils of his hair and his small stature at odds with the NOPD uniform. He had lost his hat and the side of his face was cut slightly where he had been hit by splinters of stone. The muzzle of his Steyr pointed at my chest.

I tried to swallow but my throat seemed to have constricted. I was conscious of the feel of the grass beneath my hands and the glorious pain in my side, sensations of life and existence and survival. Ricky raised the Steyr to point it at my head.

"Joe Bones says hello," he said. His finger tightened on the trigger in the same instant as his head jerked back, his stomach thrusting forward and his back arching. A burst of fire from the Steyr raked the grass beside my head as Ricky fell to his knees and then toppled sideways, his body lying prone across my left leg. There was a jagged red hole in the back of his shirt.

Behind him, Lionel Fontenot stood in a marksman's stance, the pistol in his hand slowly coming down. There was blood on his left hand and a bullet hole in the upper left arm of his suit. The two bodyguards who had stood beside him at the cemetery walked quickly from the direction of the Fontenot tomb. They glanced at me, then turned their attention back to Fontenot. I could hear the sound of sirens approaching from the west.

"One got away, Lionel," said one. "The rest are dead."

"What about our people?"

"Three dead, at least. More injured."

Beside me, Ricky stirred slightly and his hand moved feebly. I could feel his body move against my leg. Lionel Fontenot walked over and stood above him for a moment before shooting him once in the back of the head. He looked at me curiously once more, then picked up the M16 and tossed it to one of his men.

"Now go help the wounded," he said. He cradled his injured left arm with his right hand and walked back toward the Fontenot tomb.

MY RIB ACHED AS I returned to where I had left Rachel, after kicking Ricky's corpse from my leg. I approached carefully, conscious of the Smith & Wesson I had left with her. When I reached the tomb, Rachel was gone.

I found her about fifty yards away, crouching beside the body of a young girl who was barely beyond her teens. As I approached, Rachel reached for the gun by her side and spun toward me.

"Hey, it's me. You okay?"

She nodded and returned the gun to its resting place. I noticed that she had kept her hand pressed on the young girl's stomach for the entire exchange.

"How is she?" I asked, but as I looked over her shoulder, I knew the answer. The blood oozing from the gunshot wound was almost black. Liver shot. The girl, shivering uncontrollably, her teeth gritted in agony, was not going to live. Around us, mourners were emerging from hiding, some sobbing, some trembling with shock. I saw two of Lionel Fontenot's men running toward us, both with pistols, and I took hold of Rachel's arm.

"We have to go. We can't afford to wait for the cops to arrive."

"I'm staying. I'm not leaving her."

"Rachel." She looked at me. I held her gaze and we shared our knowledge of the girl's impending death. "We can't stay."

The two Fontenots were beside us now. One of them, younger than the other, dropped to his knee beside the girl and took her hand. She gripped it tightly and he whispered her name. "Clara," he said. "Hold on, Clara, hold on."

"Please, Rachel," I repeated.

She took the younger man's hand and pressed it against Clara's stomach. The girl cried out as the pressure was reapplied.

"Keep your hand there," hissed Rachel. "Don't take it away until the medics get here."

She picked up the gun and handed it to me. I took it from her, slipped the safety, and put it back in my holster. We made our way from the focus of the mayhem, until the shouting had diminished, then I stopped and she reached out and held me tightly. I cradled her in my arms and kissed the top of her head and breathed in the scent of her. She squeezed me and I gasped as the pain in my ribs increased dramatically.

Rachel pulled back quickly. "Are you hurt?"

"I took a kick, nothing else." I held her face in my hands. "You did all that you could for her."

She nodded but her mouth trembled. The girl had an importance to her that went beyond the simple duty to save her life. "I killed that man," she said.

"He would have killed us both. You had no choice. If you hadn't done it, you'd be dead. Maybe I'd be dead too." It was true, but it wasn't enough, not yet. I held her tightly as she cried, the pain in my side inconsequential beside her own suffering.

CHAPTER XL

I had not thought of Daddy Helms in many years, not until I spoke of him to Rachel the previous night and recalled the part he played in my absence during my mother's lingering death.

Daddy Helms was the ugliest man I had ever seen. He ran most of Portland from the late sixties to the early eighties, building up a modest empire that had started with Daddy Helms boosting liquor warehouses and moved on to take in the sale of drugs over three states.

Daddy Helms weighed over three hundred pounds and suffered from a skin ailment that had left him with raised bumps all over his body, but most visible on his face and hands. They were a deep red color and formed a kind of scaly skin over his features, blurring them so that the observer always seemed to be seeing Daddy Helms through a red mist. He wore three-piece suits and Panama hats and always smoked Winston Churchill cigars, so you smelled Daddy Helms before you saw him. If you were smart enough, this usually gave you just enough time to be somewhere else before he arrived.

Daddy Helms was mean, but he was also a freak. If he had been less intelligent, less bitter, and less inclined toward violence, he would probably have ended up living in a little house in the woods of Maine and selling Christmas trees door-to-door to sympathetic citizens. Instead, his ugliness seemed to be an outward manifestation of some deeper spiritual and moral blight within himself, a corruption that made you think that Daddy Helms's skin might not be the worst thing about him. There was a rage inside him, a fury at the world and its ways.

My grandfather, who had known Daddy Helms since he was a young boy and was generally a man who empathized with those around him, even the criminals he was forced to arrest when he served as a sheriff's deputy, could see nothing but evil in Daddy Helms. "I used to think maybe it was his ugliness that made him what he is," he said once, "that the way he behaves is because of the way he looks, that he's finding a way to strike back at the world he sees around him." He was sitting on the porch of the house that he shared with my grandmother, my mother, and me, the house in which we had all lived since my father's death. My grandfather's basset hound, Doc—named after the country singer Doc Watson for no reason other than that my grandfather liked his rendition of the song "Alberta"—lay curled at his feet, his ribs expanding in deep sleep and small yelps occasionally erupting from his jowls as he enjoyed dog dreams.

My grandfather took a sip of coffee from a blue tin mug and then laid it down by his feet. Doc stirred slightly, opened one bleary eye to make sure he wasn't missing anything interesting, and then went back to his dreams.

"But Daddy Helms isn't like that," he continued. "Daddy Helms just has something wrong with him, something I can't figure. Only thing I wonder is what he might have made of himself if he weren't so damn ugly. I reckon he could have been the president of the United States, if he'd wanted to be and if people could have beared to look at him, 'cept he would've been more like Joe Stalin than John Kennedy. You oughta have stayed outta his way, boy. You learned a hard lesson yesterday, a hard lesson at the hands of a hard man."

I had come from New York with the idea that I was a tough guy, that I was smarter and faster and, if it came down to it, harder than those I would come up against in the Maine boondocks. I was wrong. Daddy Helms taught me that.

Clarence Johns, a kid who lived with his drunk father near Maine Mall Road, learned that lesson too. Clarence was amiable but dumb, a natural sidekick. We had been hanging out together for about a year, firing off his air rifle on lazy summer afternoons, drinking beers stolen from his old man's stash. We were bored and we let everybody know it, even Daddy Helms.

He had bought an old, run-down bar on Congress Street and was slowly working to transform it into what he imagined would be a pretty high-class establishment. This was before the refurbishment of the port area, before the arrival of the T-shirt stores, the craft shops, the art house cinema, and the bars that serve free nibbles to the tourist crowd between five and seven. Maybe Daddy Helms had a vision of what was to come, for he replaced all of the old windows in the bar, put a new roof on the place, and bought up furnishings from some old Belfast church that had been deconsecrated.

One Sunday afternoon, when Clarence and I were feeling particularly at odds with the world, we sat on the wall at the back of Daddy Helms's half-finished bar and broke just about every goddamned window in the place, flinging stones with pinpoint accuracy at the new panes. Eventually, we found an old abandoned septic tank, and, in a final act of vandalism, we hoisted it through the large arched window at the back of the premises, which Daddy Helms had intended would span the bar itself like a fan.

I didn't see Clarence for a few days after that and thought nothing of the consequences until one night, as we walked down St. John with an illicitly bought six-pack of beer, three of Daddy Helms's men caught us and dragged us toward a black Cadillac Eldorado. They cuffed our hands and put duct tape over our mouths and tied dirty rags over our eyes, then dumped us in the trunk and closed it. Clarence Johns and I lay side by side as we were carried away and I was conscious of the sour, unwashed smell from him, until I realized that I probably smelled the same.

But there were other smells in that trunk beyond oil and rags and the sweat of two teenage boys. It smelled of human excrement and urine, of vomit and bile. It smelled of the fear of impending death and I knew, even then, that a lot of people had been brought for rides in that Cadillac.

Time seemed to fade away in the blackness of the car, so that I couldn't tell how far we had traveled until it ground to a halt. The trunk was opened and I could hear waves crashing to my left and could taste the salt in the air. We were hauled from the trunk and dragged through bushes and over stones. I could feel sand beneath my feet, and, beside me, I heard Clarence Johns start to whimper, or maybe it was my own whimperings I heard. Then we were thrown facedown on the sand and there were hands at my clothes, my shoes. My shirt was ripped from me and I was stripped from the waist down, kicking frantically at the unseen figures around me until someone punched me hard with his knuckles in the small of the back and I stopped kicking. The rag was pulled away from my eyes and I looked up to see Daddy Helms standing above me. Behind him, I could see the silhouette of a large building: the Black Point Inn. We were on Western Beach at Prouts Neck, part of Scarborough itself. If I had been able to turn, I would have seen the lights of Old Orchard Beach, but I was not able to turn.

Daddy Helms held the butt of his cigar in his deformed hand and smiled at me. It was a smile like light flashing on a blade. He wore a white three-piece suit, a gold watch chain snaking across his vest, and a red-and-white spotted bow tie arranged neatly at the collar of his white cotton shirt. Beside me, Clarence Johns's shoes scuffled in the sand as he tried to gain enough purchase to raise himself up, but one of Daddy Helms's men, a blond-haired savage called Tiger Martin, placed the sole of his foot on Clarence's chest and forced him back on to the sand. Clarence, I noticed, was not naked.

"You Bob Warren's grandson?" Daddy Helms asked after a while. I nodded. I thought I was going to choke. My nostrils were filled with sand and I couldn't seem to get enough air into my lungs.

"You know who I am?" asked Daddy Helms, still looking at me.

I nodded again.

"But you can't know who I am, boy. You knew me, you wouldn'ta done what you did to my place. 'Less you're a fool, that is, and that's worse than not knowin'."

He turned his attention briefly to Clarence, but he didn't say anything to him. I thought I caught a flash of pity in his eyes as he looked at Clarence. Clarence was dumb, there was no doubt about that. For a brief instant, I seemed to be looking at Clarence with new eyes, as if he alone was not part of Daddy Helms's gang and all five of us were about to do something terrible to him. But I was not with Daddy Helms and the thought of what was about to happen brought me back again. I felt the sand beneath my skin and I watched as Tiger Martin came forward, carrying a heavy-looking black garbage bag in his arms. He looked to Daddy Helms, Daddy Helms nodded, and then the bag was tipped upside down and the contents poured over my body.

It was earth, but something else too: I sensed thousands of small legs moving on me, crawling through the hairs on my legs and groin, exploring the crevasses of my body like tiny lovers. I felt them on my tightly closed eyes and shook my head hard to clear them away. Then the biting started, tiny pinpoints of pain on my arms, my eyelids, my legs, even my penis, as the fire ants began to attack. I felt them crawling into my nostrils, and then the biting started there as well. I twisted and writhed, rubbing myself on the sand in an effort to kill as many of them as I could, but it was like trying to remove the sand itself, grain by grain. I kicked and spun and felt tears running down my cheeks and then, just as it seemed that I couldn't take any more, I felt a gloved hand on my ankle and I was dragged through the sand toward the surf. My wrists were freed and I plunged into the water, ripping the tape from my mouth, ignoring the pain as it tore my lips in my desire to rub and scratch myself. I submerged my head as the waves crashed above me, and still it seemed that I felt threadlike legs moving on me and felt the final bites of the insects before they drowned. I was shouting in pain and panic and then I was crying too, crying in shame and hurt and anger and fear.

For days afterward, I found the remains of ants in my hair. Some of them were longer than the nail on my middle finger, with barbed pincers that curved forward to embrace the skin. My body was covered in raised bumps, almost an imitation of those of Daddy Helms himself, and the inside of my nose felt tender and swollen.

I pulled myself from the water and staggered onto the sand. Daddy Helms's men had gone back to the car, leaving only Clarence and me on the beach with Daddy Helms himself. Clarence was untouched. Daddy Helms saw the realization in my face and he smiled as he puffed on his cigar.

"We found your friend last night," he said. He placed a thick, melted-wax hand on Clarence's shoulders. Clarence flinched, but he didn't move. "He told us everything. We didn't even have to hurt him."

The pain of betrayal superseded the bites and the itching, the lingering sensation of movement on my skin. I looked at Clarence Johns with new eyes, adult eyes. He stood on the sand, his arms wrapped around his body, shivering. His eyes were filled with a pain that sang out from the depths of his being. I wanted to hate him for what he had done, and Daddy Helms wanted me to hate him, but instead I felt only a deep emptiness and a kind of pity.

And I felt a kind of pity, too, for Daddy Helms, with his ravaged skin and his mounds and folds of heavy flesh, forced to visit this punishment on two young men because of some broken glass, punishing them not only physically but by severing the bonds of their friendship.

"You learned two lessons here tonight, boy. You learned not to fuck with me, ever, and you learned something about friendship. In the end, the only friend you got is yourself, 'cause all the others, they'll let you down in the end. We all stand alone, in the end." Then he turned and waddled through the marram and dunes, back to his car.

They left us to walk back to Route 1, my clothes torn and

soaked through from the seawater. We said nothing to each other, not even when we parted at the gate to my grandfather's property and Clarence headed off into the night, his cheap plastic shoes slapping on the road. We didn't hang out together after that and I largely forgot Clarence until he died in a failed robbery attempt at a computer warehouse on the outskirts of Austin twelve years later. Clarence was working as a security guard. He was shot by the raiders as he tried to defend a consignment of PCs.

When I entered my grandfather's house I took some antiseptic from the medicine cabinet, then stripped and stood in the bath, rubbing the liquid into the bites. It stung. When I had finished, I sat in the empty bath and wept, and that was where my grandfather found me. He said nothing for a while, then disappeared and came back with a red bowl containing a paste made from baking soda and water. He rubbed it painstakingly across my shoulders and chest, my legs and arms, then poured a little into my hand so I could rub it into my groin. He wrapped me in a white cotton sheet and sat me down in a chair in the kitchen, before pouring us each a large glass of brandy. It was Remy Martin, I remember, XO, the good stuff. It took me some time to finish it, but neither of us spoke a word. As I stood to go to bed, he patted me lightly on the head.

"A HARD MAN," REPEATED my grandfather, draining the last of his coffee. He stood and the dog rose with him.

"You want to walk the dog with me?"

I declined. He shrugged his shoulders and I watched him as he walked down the porch steps, the dog already running ahead of him, barking and sniffing and looking back to make sure the old man was following, then running on farther again.

Daddy Helms died two years later of stomach cancer. When he died, it was estimated that he had been involved, directly or indirectly, with over forty killings, some of them as far south as Florida. There was no more than a handful of people at his funeral.

I thought of Daddy Helms again as Rachel and I made our way from the killings in Metairie. I don't know why. Maybe I felt there was something of his rage in Joe Bonanno, a hatred of the world that stemmed from something rotten inside him. I remembered my grandfather, I remembered Daddy Helms, and I recalled the lessons they had tried to teach me, lessons that I still had not yet fully learned.

CHAPTER XLI

Outside the main cemetery gate, the New Orleans police were corralling witnesses and clearing the way for the injured to be carried to waiting ambulances. TV crews from WWDL and WDSU were trying to talk with survivors. I stayed close to one of Lionel Fontenot's men, the one who had been entrusted with the care of the M16, as we approached the gates at an angle. We followed him until he arrived at a portion of ruptured fencing by the highway, then made his way through it to a waiting Lincoln. As he drove away, Rachel and I climbed over the fence and walked back toward our car, unspeaking, approaching it from the west. It was parked away from the main center of activity and we were able to slip off without attracting any attention.

"How did that happen?" asked Rachel in a quiet voice as we drove back into the city. "There should have been police. There should have been someone to stop them . . ." Her voice trailed away and she remained silent as we drove back to the Quarter, her hands clasped across her upper body. I didn't disturb her.

One of a number of things had happened. Someone in charge could have screwed up by assigning insufficient police to Metairie, believing that Joe Bones would never try to take out Lionel Fontenot at his brother's funeral in front of witnesses. The guns had been stashed either late the previous night or early that morning, and the cemetery had not been searched. It could also have been the case that Lionel warned off the cops, just as he had warned off the media, anxious not to turn his brother's funeral into a circus. The other possibility was that Joe Bones had paid off or threatened some or all of the cops at Metairie and they had turned their backs while his men went about their business.

When we reached the hotel, I took Rachel to my room—I didn't want her surrounded by the images she had pinned to the walls of her own room. She went straight to the bathroom and closed the door behind her. I could hear the sound of the shower starting up. She stayed there for a long time.

When she eventually emerged, she had a big white bath towel draped around her from her breasts to her knees and was drying her hair with a smaller towel. Her eyes were red as she looked at me, then her chin trembled and she began to cry again. I held her, kissing the top of her head, then her forehead, her cheeks, her lips. Her mouth was warm as she responded to the kiss, her tongue darting around my teeth and entwining with my own tongue. I pressed hard against her, pulling the towel from her as I did. Her fingers fumbled at my belt and my zipper, then reached inside and held me tightly. Her other hand worked at the buttons on my shirt as she kissed my neck and ran her tongue across my chest and around my nipples.

I kicked off my shoes and leaned over awkwardly to try to take off my socks. Damn socks. She smiled a little as I almost fell over while removing the left one and then I was on top of her as she pushed down my pants and shorts.

Her breasts were small, her hips slightly wide, the small triangle of hair at their center a deep, fiery red. She tasted sweet. When she came, her back arched high and her legs wrapped around my thighs, I felt like I had never been held so tightly, or loved so hard.

Afterward, she slept. I slipped from the bed, put on a T-shirt and jeans, and took the key to her room from her bag. I walked barefoot down the gallery to the room, closed the door behind me, and stood for a time before the pictures on the wall. Rachel had bought a large draftsman's pad on which to work out patterns and ideas. I took two sheets from it, taped them together, and added them to the images on the wall. Then, surrounded by pictures of the anatomized Marsyas and photocopies of the crime-scene photos of *Tante* Marie and Tee Jean, I took a felt-tip and began to write.

In one corner I wrote the names of Jennifer and Susan, a kind of pang of regret and guilt hitting me as I wrote Susan's name. I tried to put it from my mind and continued writing. In another corner I put the names of *Tante* Marie, Tee Jean, and slightly to one side, Florence. In the third corner I wrote Remarr's name and in the fourth I placed a question mark and the word "girl" beside it. In the center I wrote "Trav Man" and then, like a child drawing a star, I added a series of lines emanating from the center and tried to write down all that I knew, or thought I knew, about the killer.

When I had finished, the list included a voice synthesis program or unit; the Book of Enoch; a knowledge of Greek myths / early medical texts; a knowledge of police procedures and activities, based on what Rachel had said following the deaths of Jennifer and Susan, the fact that he had known that the feds were monitoring my cell phone, and the killing of Remarr. Initially I thought that if he had seen Remarr at the Aguillard house, then Remarr would have died there and then, but I reconsidered on the basis that the Traveling Man would have been reluctant to remain at the scene or to engage an alert Remarr, and had decided to wait for another chance. The other option was that the killer had found out about the fingerprint and, somehow, the killer had also later found Remarr.

I added other elements based on standard assumptions: white, male killer, probably somewhere between his twenties and forties; a Louisiana base from which to strike at Remarr and the Aguillards; a change of clothing, or coveralls worn over his own clothes, to protect him from the blood; and access to and knowledge of ketamine.

I drew another line from Trav Man to the Aguillards, since

the killer knew that *Tante* Marie had been talking, and a second line connecting him to Remarr. I added a dotted line to Jennifer and Susan, and wrote Edward Byron's name with a question mark beside it. Then, on impulse, I added a third dotted line and wrote David Fontenot's name between those of the Aguillards and Remarr, based only on the Honey Island connection and the possibility that, if the Traveling Man had lured him to Honey Island and tipped off Joe Bones that David Fontenot would be there, then the killer was someone known to the Fontenot family. Finally, I wrote Edward Byron's name on a separate sheet and pinned it beside the main diagram.

I sat on the edge of Rachel's bed and breathed in the scent of her in the room as I looked at what I had written, shifting the pieces around in my head to see if they would match up anywhere. They didn't, but I made one more addition before I returned to my own room to wait for Angel and Louis to return from Baton Rouge: I drew a light line between David Fontenot's name and the question mark representing the girl in the swamp. I didn't know it then, but by drawing that line I had made the first significant leap into the world of the Traveling Man.

I returned to my own room and sat by the balcony, watching Rachel in her uneasy sleep. Her eyelids moved rapidly and once or twice she let out small groans and made pushing movements with her hands, her feet scrambling beneath the blankets. I heard Angel and Louis before I saw them, Angel's voice raised in what seemed to be anger, Louis responding in measured tones with a hint of mockery beneath them.

Before they could knock, I opened the door and indicated that we should talk in their room. They hadn't heard about the shootings at Metairie since, according to Angel, they hadn't been listening to the radio in the rental car. His face was red as he spoke and his lips were pale. I don't think that I had ever seen him so angry.

In their room, the bickering started again. Stacey Byron, a bottle blonde in her early forties who had kept her figure remarkably well for a woman of her age, had apparently come on to

Louis in the course of their interrogation of her. Louis had, in a manner, responded.

"I was pumping her for information," he explained, his mouth twitching in amusement as he looked sideways at Angel. Angel was unimpressed.

"Sure you wanted to pump her, but the only information you were after was her bra size and the dimensions of her ass," he spat. Louis rolled his eyes in exaggerated bafflement and I thought, for a moment, that Angel was going to strike him. His fists bunched and he moved forward slightly before he managed to restrain himself.

I felt sorry for Angel. While I didn't believe there was anything in Louis's courting of Edward Byron's wife, beyond the natural response of any individual to the favorable attentions of another and Louis's belief that, by leading her on, she might give away something about her ex-husband, I knew how much Louis mattered to Angel. Angel's history was murky, Louis's more so, but I remembered things about Angel, things that I sometimes felt Louis forgot.

When Angel was sent down to Rikers Island, he attracted the attentions of a man named William Vance. Vance had killed a Korean shopkeeper in the course of a botched robbery in Brooklyn and that was how he ended up in Rikers, but there were other things suspected of him: that he had raped and killed an elderly woman in Utica, mutilating her before she died; that he may have been linked to a similar killing in Delaware. There was no proof, other than rumor and conjecture, but when the opportunity came to put Vance away for the killing of the Korean, the DA, to his credit, seized it.

And for some reason, Vance decided that he wanted Angel dead. I heard that Angel had dissed him when Vance had tried to get it on with him, that he had knocked out one of Vance's teeth in the showers. But there was no telling with a man like Vance: the workings of his mind were obscure and confused by hatred and strange, bitter longing. Now Vance didn't just want to rape Angel: he wanted to kill him, and kill him slowly. Angel had pulled three to five. After one week in Rikers, the odds of him surviving his first month had plummeted.

Angel had no friends on the inside and fewer still outside, so he called me. I knew that it pained him to do so. He was proud and I think that, under ordinary circumstances, he would have tried to work out his problems for himself. But William Vance, with his tattoos of bloodied knives on his arms and a spider's web over his chest, was far from ordinary.

I did what I could. I pulled Vance's files and copied the transcripts of his interrogation over the Utica killing and a number of similar incidents. I copied details of the evidence assembled against him and the account of an eyewitness who later retracted after Vance made a call and threatened to fuck her and her children to death if she gave evidence against him. Then I took a trip to Rikers.

I spoke to Vance through a transparent screen. He had added an india ink tattoo of a tear below his left eye, bringing the total number of tattooed tears to three, each one representing a life taken. A spider's silhouette was visible at the base of his neck. I spoke to him softly for about ten minutes. I warned him that if anything happened to Angel, anything at all, I would make sure that every con in the place knew that he was only a hair's breadth away from sexual homicide charges involving old, defenseless women. Vance had five years left to serve before he became eligible for parole. If his fellow inmates found out what he was suspected of doing, there were men who could ensure that he would have to spend those five years in solitary to avoid death. Even then, he would have to check his food every day for powdered glass, would have to pray that a guard's attention didn't wander for an instant while he was being escorted to the yard for his hour's recreation, or while he was being brought to the prison doctor when the stress began to take its toll on his health.

Vance knew all this and yet, two days after we spoke, he tried to castrate Angel with a shank. Only the force of Angel's heel connecting with Vance's knee saved him, although Angel still needed twenty stitches across his stomach and thigh after Vance slashed wildly at him as he fell to the ground.

Vance was taken in the shower the next morning. Persons unknown held him down, used a wrench to hold his mouth open, and then pumped water mixed with detergent into his body. The poison destroyed his insides, tearing apart his stomach and almost costing him his life. For the remainder of his life in prison he was a shell of a man, racked by pains in his gut that made him howl in the night. It had taken one telephone call. I live with that too.

After he was released, Angel hooked up with Louis. I'm not even sure how these two solitary creatures met, exactly, but they had now been together for six years. Angel needed Louis, and in his way, Louis needed Angel too, but I sometimes thought that the balance of the relationship hinged on Angel. Men and men, men and women, whatever the permutation, in the end one partner always feels more than the other and that partner usually suffers for it.

It emerged that they hadn't learned much from Stacey Byron. The cops had been watching the house from the front but Louis and Angel, dressed in the only suit he owned, had come in from the back. Louis had flashed his fitness club membership and his smile as he told Mrs. Byron that they were just conducting a routine search of her garden and they spent the next hour talking to her about her ex-husband, about how often Louis worked out, and in the end, whether or not he'd ever had a white woman. It was at that point that Angel had really started to get annoyed.

"She says she hasn't seen him in four months," said Louis. "Says that last time she saw him, he didn't say much, just asked after her and the kids and took some old clothes from the attic. Seems he had a carrier bag from some drugstore in Opelousas and the feds are concentrating their search there."

"Does she know why the feds are looking for him?"

"Nope. They told her that he might be able to assist them with information on some unsolved crimes. She ain't dumb, though, and I fed her a little more to see if she'd bite. She said that he always had an interest in medical affairs; seems he might have had ambitions to be a doctor at one time, although he didn't have the education to be a tree surgeon."

"Did you ask her if she thought he could kill?"

"I didn't have to. Seems he threatened to kill her once, while they were arguing over the terms of the divorce."

"Did she remember what he said?"

Louis nodded deeply, once.

"Uh-huh. He said he'd tear her fucking face off."

ANGEL AND LOUIS PARTED on bad terms, with Angel retiring to Rachel's room while Louis sat on the balcony of their room and took in the sounds and smells of New Orleans, not all of them pleasant.

"I was thinking of getting a bite to eat," he said. "You interested?"

I was surprised. I guessed that he wanted to talk but I had never spent time with Louis without Angel being present as well.

I checked on Rachel. The bed was empty and I could hear the shower running. I knocked gently on the door.

"It's open," she said.

When I entered, she had the shower curtain wrapped around her. "Suits you," I said. "Clear plastic is in this season."

The sleep hadn't done her any good. There were dark rings under her eyes and she still looked shaky. She made a halfhearted effort to smile, but it was more like a grimace of pain than anything else.

"You want to go out and eat?"

"I'm not hungry. I'm going to do some work, then take two sleeping pills and try to sleep without dreaming."

I told her that Louis and I were heading out, then went to tell Angel. I found him flicking through the notes Rachel had made. He motioned to my chart on the bedroom wall. "Lot of blank spaces on that."

"I still have one or two details to work out."

"Like who did it and why." He gave me a twisted grin.

"Yeah, but I'm trying not to get too hung up on minor problems. You okay?"

He nodded. "I think this whole thing is gettin' to me, all this . . ." He waved an arm at the illustrations on the wall.

"Louis and I are heading out to eat. You wanna come?"

"Nah, I'd only be the lemon. You can have him."

"Thanks. I'll break the bad news of my sexual awakening to the *Swimsuit Illustrated* models tomorrow. They'll be heartbroken. Look after Rachel, will you? This hasn't been one of her better days."

"I'll be right along the hall."

LOUIS AND I SAT in Felix's Restaurant and Oyster Bar on the corner of Bourbon and Iberville. There weren't too many tourists there; they tended to gravitate toward the Acme Oyster House across the street, where they served red beans and savory rice in a hollowed-out boat of French bread, or a classier French Quarter joint like Nola. Felix's was plainer. Tourists don't care much for plain. After all, they can get plain at home.

Louis ordered an oyster po'boy and doused it in hot sauce, sipping an Abita beer between bites. I had fries and a chicken po'boy, washed down with mineral water.

"Waiter thinks you're a sissy," commented Louis as I sipped my water. "The ballet was in town, he'd hit on you for tickets."

"Shows what he knows," I replied. "You're confusing things by not conforming to the stereotype. Maybe you should mince more."

His mouth twitched and he raised his hand for another Abita. It came quickly. The waiter performed the neat trick of making sure we weren't left waiting for anything while trying to spend as little time as possible in the vicinity of our table. Other diners chose to take the scenic route to their tables rather than pass too close to us and those forced to sit near us seemed to eat at a slightly faster pace than the rest. Louis had that effect on people. It was as if there was a shell of potential violence around him, and something more: the sense that, if that violence erupted, it would not be the first time that it had done so.

"Your friend Woolrich," he said as he drained the Abita halfway with one mouthful. "You trust him?"

"I don't know. He has his own agenda."

"He's a fed. They only got their own agendas." He eyed me over the top of the bottle. "I think, if you were climbing a rock with your friend and you slipped, found yourself dangling on the end of the rope with him at the other end, he'd cut the rope."

"You're a cynic."

His mouth twitched again. "If the dead could speak, they'd call all cynics realists."

"If the dead could speak, they'd tell us to have more sex while we can." I picked at my fries. "The feds have anything on you?"

"Suspicions, maybe; nothing more. That's not really what I'm getting at."

His eyes were unblinking and there was no warmth in them now. I think that, if he had believed Woolrich was close to him, he would have killed him and it would not have cost him another thought afterward.

"Why is Woolrich helping us?" he asked, eventually.

"I've thought about that too," I said. "I'm not sure. Part of it could be that he empathizes with the need to stay in touch with what's going on. If he feeds me information, then he can control the extent of my involvement."

But I knew that wasn't all. Louis was right. Woolrich had his own agenda. He had depths to him that I only occasionally glimpsed, as when the different shifting colors on the surface of the sea hint at the sharp declivities and deep spaces that lie beneath. He was a hard man to be with in some ways: he conducted his friendship with me on his own terms, and in the time I had known him, months had gone by without any contact from him. He made up for this with a strange loyalty, a sense that, even when he was absent from their lives, he never forgot those closest to him.

But as a fed, Woolrich played hardball. He had progressed to assistant SAC by making collars, by attaching his name to high-profile operations, and by fixing other agents' wagons when they got in his way. He was intensely ambitious and maybe he saw the Traveling Man as a way of reaching greater heights: SAC, assistant director, a deputy directorship, maybe even to eventually becoming the first agent to be appointed directly to the post of director. The pressure on him was intense, but if Woolrich were to be responsible for bringing an end to the Traveling Man, he would be assured a bright, powerful future within the Bureau.

I had a part to play in this, and Woolrich knew it and felt it strongly enough that he would use whatever friendship existed between us to bring about an end to what was taking place. "I think he's using me as bait," I said at last. "And he's holding the line."

"How much you think he's holding back?" Louis finished his beer and smacked his lips appreciatively.

"He's like an iceberg," I replied. "We're only seeing the ten percent above the surface. Whatever the feds know, they're not sharing it with the local cops and Woolrich sure isn't sharing it with us. There's something more going on here, and only Woolrich and maybe a handful of feds are privy to it. You play chess?"

"In my way," he replied dryly. Somehow, I couldn't see that way including a standard board.

"This whole thing is like a chess game," I continued. "Except we only get to see the other player's move when one of our pieces is taken. The rest of the time, it's like playing in the dark."

Louis raised a finger for the check. The waiter looked relieved.

"And our Mr. Byron?"

I shrugged. I felt strangely distant from what was happening. Part of it was because we were players on the periphery of the investigation, but part of it was also because I needed that distance to think. In one way, what had taken place with Rachel that afternoon, and what it meant to my feelings of grief and loss about Susan, had given me some of that distance.

"I don't know." We were only beginning to construct a picture of Byron, like a figure at the center of a jigsaw puzzle around which other pieces might interlock. "We'll work our way toward him. First, I want to find out what Remarr saw the night *Tante* Marie and Tee Jean were killed. And I want to know why David Fontenot was out at Honey Island alone."

It was clear now that Lionel Fontenot would move against Joe Bones. Joe Bones knew that too, which was why he had risked an assault at Metairie. Once Lionel was back in his compound, he would be out of the reach of Joe Bones's men. The next move was Lionel's.

The check arrived. I paid and Louis left a deliberately overgenerous twenty-dollar tip. The waiter looked at the bill like Andrew Jackson was going to bite his finger when he tried to lift it.

"I think we're going to have to talk to Lionel Fontenot," I said as we left. "And Joe Bones."

Louis actually smiled. "Joe ain't gonna be too keen on talking to you, seeing as how his boy tried to put you in the ground."

"I kinda figured that," I replied. "Could be that Lionel Fontenot might help us out there."

We walked back to the Flaisance. The streets of New Orleans aren't the safest in the world but I didn't think that anyone would bother us.

I was right.

CHAPTER XLII

I slept late the next morning. Rachel had returned to her own room to sleep. When I knocked, her voice sounded harsh with tiredness. She told me she wanted to stay in bed for a while, and when she felt better, she would go out to Loyola again. I asked Angel and Louis to watch out for her, then drove from the Flaisance.

The incident at Metairie had left me shaken, and the prospect of facing Joe Bones again was unappealing. I also felt a crushing sense of guilt for what had happened to Rachel, for what I had drawn her into and for what I had forced her to do. I needed to get out of New Orleans, at least for a short time. I wanted to clear my head, to try to see things from a different angle. I ate a bowl of chicken soup in the Gumbo Shop on St. Peter and then headed out of the city.

Morphy lived about four miles from Cecilia, a few miles northwest of Lafayette. He had bought and was refurbishing a raised plantation home by a small river, a budget version of the classic old Louisiana houses that had been built at the end of the nineteenth century, a blend of French Colonial, West Indian, and European architectural influences.

The house presented a strange spectacle. Its main living quarters were on top of an aboveground basement area, which had once been used for storage and as protection from flooding. This section of the house was brick and Morphy had reworked the arched openings with what looked like hand-carved frames. The living quarters above, which would usually have been weatherboard or plaster-covered, had been replaced with timber slats. A double-pitched roof, which had been partially reslated, extended over the gallery.

I had called ahead and told Angie I was on my way. Morphy had just got home when I arrived. I found him in the yard at the rear of the house, benching two hundred in the evening air.

"What do you think of the house?" he asked as I approached, not even pausing in his reps as he spoke.

"It's great. Looks like you still have some way to go before it's finished."

He grunted with the effort of the final rep as I acted as spotter, slotting the bar back onto its rest. He stood up and stretched, then looked at the back of his house with barely concealed admiration.

"It was built by a Frenchman in eighteen eighty-eight," he said. "He knew what he was doing. It's built on an east-west axis, with principal exposure to the south." He pointed out the lines of the building as he spoke. "He designed it the way the Europeans designed their houses, so that the low angle of the sun in winter would heat the building. Then, in the summer, the sun would only shine on it in the morning and evening. Most American houses aren't built that way, they just put 'em up whatever way suits 'em, throw a stick in the air and see where it lands. We were spoiled by cheap energy. Then the Arabs came along and hiked up their prices and people had to start thinking again about the layout of their houses."

He smiled. "Don't know how much good an east-west house does around here, though. Sun shines all the goddamn time anyway."

When he had showered, we sat at a table in the kitchen with Angie and talked as she cooked. Angie was almost a foot smaller than her husband, a slim, dark-skinned woman with auburn hair that flowed down her back. She was a junior high school teacher, but she did some painting in her spare time. Her canvases, dark, impressionistic pieces set around water and sky, adorned the walls of the house.

Morphy drank a bottle of Breaux Bridge and I had a soda. Angie sipped a glass of white wine as she cooked. She cut four chicken breasts into about sixteen pieces and set them to one side as she set about preparing the roux.

Cajun gumbo is made with roux, a glutinous thickener, as a base. Angie poured peanut oil into a cast iron skillet over a high flame, added in an equal amount of flour, and beat it with a whisk continuously so it wouldn't burn, gradually turning the roux from blond to beige and through mahogany until it reached a dark chocolate color. Then she took it off the heat and allowed it to cool, still stirring.

While Morphy looked on, I helped her chop the trinity of onion, green pepper, and celery and watched as she sweated them in oil. She added a seasoning of thyme and oregano, paprika and cayenne, onion and garlic salt, then dropped in thick pieces of chorizo. She added the chicken and more spices, until their scent filled the room. After about half an hour, she spooned white rice onto plates and poured the thick rich gumbo over it. We ate in silence, savoring the flavors in our mouths.

When we had washed and dried the dishes, Angie left us and went to bed. Morphy and I sat in the kitchen and I told him about Raymond Aguillard and his belief that he had seen the figure of a girl at Honey Island. I told him of *Tante* Marie's dreams and my feeling that, somehow, David Fontenot's death at Honey Island could be linked to the girl.

Morphy didn't say anything for a long time. He didn't sneer at visions of ghosts, or at an old woman's belief that the voices she heard were real. Instead, all he said was: "You sure you know where this place is?"

I nodded.

"Then we'll give it a try. I'm free tomorrow, so you better stay here tonight. We got a spare room you can use." I called Rachel at the Flaisance and told her what I intended to do the next day and where in Honey Island we were likely to be. She said that she would tell Angel and Louis, and that she felt a little better for her sleep. It would take her a long time to get over the death of Joe Bones's man.

IT WAS EARLY MORNING, barely ten before seven, when we prepared to leave. Morphy wore heavy steel-toed Caterpillar work boots, old jeans, and a sleeveless sweatshirt over a long-sleeved T-shirt. The sweat was dappled with paint and there were patches of tar on the jeans. His head was freshly shaved and smelled of witch hazel.

While we drank coffee and ate toast on the gallery, Angie came out in a white robe and rubbed her husband's clean scalp, smirking at him as she took a seat beside him. Morphy acted like it annoyed the hell out of him, but he doted on her every touch. When we rose to go, he kissed her deeply with the fingers of his right hand entwined in her hair. Her body instinctively rose from the chair to meet him, but he pulled away laughing and she reddened. It was only then that I noticed the swelling at her belly: she was no more than five months gone, I guessed. As we walked across the grass at the front of the house, she stood on the gallery, her weight on one hip and a light breeze tugging at her robe, and watched her husband depart.

"Been married long?" I asked, as we walked toward a cypress glade that obscured the view of the house from the road.

"Two years in January. I'm a contented man. Never thought I would be, but that girl changed my life." There was no embarrassment as he spoke and he acknowledged it with a smile.

"When is the baby due?"

He smiled again. "Late December. Guys held a party for me when they found out, to celebrate the fact that I was shooting live ones."

An old Ford truck was parked in the glade, with a trailer attached on which a wide, flat-bottomed aluminum boat lay covered in tarpaulin, its engine tilted forward so that it rested on the bed. "Toussaint's brother dropped it over late last night," he explained. "Does some hauling on the side."

"Where's Toussaint?"

"In bed with food poisoning. He ate some bad shrimp, least that's how he tells it. Personally, I think he's just too damn lazy to give up his morning in bed."

In the back of the truck, beneath some more tarpaulin, were an axe, a chain saw, two lengths of chain, some strong nylon rope, and a cooler. There was also a dry suit and mask, a pair of waterproof flashlights, and two air tanks. Morphy added a flask of coffee, some water, two sticks of French bread, and four chicken breasts coated in K-Paul's Cajun spices, all contained in a waterproof bag, then climbed into the driver's seat of the truck and started her up. She belched smoke and rattled a bit, but the engine sounded good and strong. I climbed in beside him and we drove toward Honey Island, a Clifton Chenier tape on the truck's battered stereo.

We entered the reserve at Slidell, a collection of shopping malls, fast food joints, and Chinese buffets on the north shore of Lake Pontchartrain named for the Democratic senator John Slidell. In the 1844 federal election, Slidell arranged for two steamboats to carry a bunch of Irish and German voters from New Orleans to Plaquemines Parish to vote. There was nothing illegal about that; what was illegal was letting them vote at all the other polling stations along the route.

A mist still hung over the water and the trees as we unloaded the boat at the Pearl River ranger station, beside a collection of run-down fishing shacks that floated near the bank. We loaded the chains, rope, chain saw, the diving gear, and the food. In a tree beside us, the early morning sun caught the threads of a huge, intricate web, at the center of which lay, unmoving, a golden orb spider. Then, with the sound of the motor blending with the noise of insects and birds, we moved onto the Pearl.

The banks of the river were lined with high tupelo gum, water birch, willows, and some tall cypress with trumpet creeper vines, their red flowers in bloom, winding up their trunks. Here and there trees were marked with plastic bottles, signs that catfish lines had been sunk. We passed a village of riverside homes, most of them down-at-the-heel, with flat-bottomed pirogues tied up outside them. A blue heron watched us calmly from the branches of a cypress; on a log beneath him, a yellow-bellied turtle lay soaking up the sun.

I still had Raymond Aguillard's map but it took us two attempts to find the trevasse, the trappers' channel that he had marked. There was a stand of gum trees at its entrance, their swollen buttresses like the bulbs of flowers, with a sole green ash leaning almost across the gap. Further in, branches weighed down with Spanish moss hung almost to the surface of the water and the air was redolent with the mingled scents of growth and decay. Misshapen tree trunks surrounded by duckweed stood like monuments in the early morning sun. East, I could see the gray dome of a beaver lodge, and as we watched, a snake slithered into the water not five feet from us.

"Diamondback," said Morphy.

Around us, water dripped from cypress and tupelo, and birdsong echoed in the trees.

"Any chance of 'gators here?" I asked.

He shrugged. "Maybe. Don't bother people much, though, unless people bother them. There's easier pickings in the swamps. If you see any while I'm down there, fire a shot to let me know what's happening."

The bayou started to narrow until it was barely wide enough to allow the boat passage. I felt the bottom scrape on a tree trunk resting below us. Morphy killed the engine and we used our hands and a pair of wooden paddles to pull ourselves through.

It seemed then that we might somehow have made a mistake in our map reading, because we were faced with a wall of wild rice, the tall, green stalks like blades in the water. There was only one narrow gap visible, big enough for a child to pass through. Morphy shrugged and restarted the engine, aiming us for the gap. I used the paddle to beat back the rice stalks as we moved forward. Something splashed close by us and a dark shape, like a large rat, sliced through the water.

"Nutria," said Morphy. I could see the big rodent's nose and whiskers now as it stopped beside a tree trunk and sniffed the air inquisitively. "Taste worse than 'gators. I hear we're trying to sell their meat to the Chinese since no one else wants to eat it."

The rice blended into sharp-edged grass that cut at my hands as I worked the paddle, and then the boat was free and we were in a kind of lagoon formed by a gradual accumulation of silt, its banks surrounded mainly by gum and willows that dragged the fingers of their branches in the water. There was some almost firm ground at the eastern edge, near some arrowroot lilies, with wild pig tracks in the dirt, the animals attracted by the promise of the arrowroot at the lilies' base. Further in, I could see the rotting remains of a T-cutter, probably one of the craft that had originally cut the channel. Its big V-8 engine was gone, and there were holes in its hull.

We tied the boat up at a sole red swamp maple that was almost covered with resurrection fern, waiting for the rains to bring it back to life. Morphy stripped down to a pair of Nike cycling shorts, rubbed himself down with grease, and put the dry suit on. He added the flippers, then strapped on the tank and tested it. "Most of the waters around here are no more than ten, maybe fifteen feet deep, but this place is different," he said. "You can see it in the way the light reflects on the water. It's deeper, twenty feet or more." Leaves, sticks, and logs floated on the water, and insects flitted above the surface. The water looked dark and green.

He washed the mask in the swamp water then turned to me. "Never thought I'd be looking for swamp ghosts on my day off," he said.

"Raymond Aguillard says he saw the girl here," I replied. "David Fontenot died up the river. There's something here. You know what you're looking for?"

He nodded. "Probably a container of some sort, heavy, sealed."

Morphy flicked on the flashlight, slipped on his mask, and began sucking bottled air. I tied one end of the climbing rope to his belt and another to the trunk of the maple, yanked it firm, then patted him on the back. He raised a thumb and waded into the water. Two or three yards out, he began to dive and I started to feed the rope out through my hands.

I had had little experience of diving, beyond a few basic lessons taken during a holiday with Susan on the Florida Keys. I didn't envy Morphy, swimming around in that swamp. During my teens, we went swimming in the Saco River, south of the Portland city limits, during the summer. Long, lean pike dwelt in those waters, vicious things that brought a hint of the primeval with them. When they brushed your bare legs, it made you think of stories you had heard about them biting small children or dragging swimming dogs down to the bottom of the river.

The waters of Honey Island swamp were like another world compared to the Saco. With its glittering snakes and its cowens, the name the Cajuns give to the swamp's snapping turtles, Honey Island seemed so much more feral than the backwaters of Maine. But there were alligator gar here too, and scaled shortnoses, as well as perch and bass and bowfins. And 'gators.

I thought of these things as Morphy disappeared below the surface of the bayou, but I also thought of the young girl who might have been dumped in these waters, where creatures she couldn't name bumped and clicked against the side of her tomb while others searched for rust holes through which to get at the rotting meat inside.

Morphy surfaced after five minutes, indicated the short, northeastern bank, and shook his head. Then he submerged again and the line on the ground snaked south as he swam. After another five minutes the rope began to pull out quickly. Morphy broke the surface again, but this time some distance from where the rope entered the water. He swam back to the bank, removed the mask and mouthpiece, and breathed in short gasps as he gestured back toward the southern end of the bayou.

"We got a couple of metal boxes, maybe four feet long, two feet wide, and eighteen inches deep, dumped down there," he said. "One's empty, the other's locked and bolted. Maybe a hundred yards away there's a bunch of oil barrels marked with red fleurs-de-lys. They belong to the old Brevis Chemical Company, used to operate out of West Baton Rouge until a big fire in eighty-nine put it out of business. That's it. Nothing else down there."

I looked out toward the edge of the bayou, where thick roots lay obscured beneath the water.

"Could we pull in the box using the rope?" I asked.

"Could do, but that box is heavy and if we bust it open while hauling it in we'll destroy whatever's inside. We'll have to bring the boat out and try to haul it up."

It was getting very warm now, although the trees on the bank provided some shade from the sun. Morphy took two bottles of still mineral water from the cooler and we drank them sitting on the bank. Then Morphy and I got into the boat and took it out to his marker.

Twice the box caught on some obstacle on the bottom as I tried to pull it up, and I had to wait for Morphy to signal before I could start hauling it in again. Eventually, the gray metal box broke the surface of the water, Morphy pushing up from beneath before he went back down to tie the marker rope to one of the oil barrels in case we had to search them.

I brought the boat back to the landing and dragged the box up onto the shore. The chain and lock securing it were old and rusted, probably too old to yield anything of any use to us. I took the axe and struck at the rusty lock that held the chain in place. It broke as Morphy walked onto the bank. He knelt beside me, the air tank still on his back and the mask pushed up on his forehead as I pulled at the lid of the box. It was stuck fast. I took the blunt head of the axe and struck upward along the edges until the lid lifted.

Inside was a consignment of breech-loading Springfield .50 caliber rifles and the bones of what seemed to be a small dog. The butts of the rifles had almost rotted but I could still see the letters *LNG* on the metal butt plates.

"Stolen rifles," said Morphy, pulling one free and examining it. "Maybe eighteen seventy or eighteen eighty. The authorities probably issued a stolen arms proclamation after these were taken and the thief dumped them or left them there with the intention of coming back."

He prodded at the dog's skull with his fingers. "The bones are an indicator of some kind. Pity nobody been seein' the Hound of the Baskervilles out here, else we'd have the whole mystery cleared up." He looked at the rifles, then back out toward the oil drums. He sighed, then began to swim out to the marker.

Hauling in the drums was a laborious process. The chain slipped off three times as we tried to pull in the first drum. Morphy came back for a second chain and wrapped it, parcel style, around the drum. The boat almost overturned when I tried to open the barrel while I was still on the water, so we were forced to bring it back to dry land. When we eventually got it to the bank, brown and rusting, it contained only stale oil. The drums had a hole for loading and pouring the oil, but the entire lid could also be pried off. When we opened the second drum it didn't even contain oil, just some stones that had been used to weigh the barrel down.

By now, Morphy was exhausted. We stopped for a time to eat some of the chicken and bread, and drink some of the coffee. It was now past midday and the heat in the bayou was heavy and draining. After we had rested, I offered to do some of the diving. Morphy didn't refuse, so I handed him my shoulder holster, then suited up and strapped on the spare tank.

The water was surprisingly cool as I slipped into it. As it reached my chest, it almost took my breath away. The chains were heavy across my shoulder as I guided myself along the marker rope with one hand. When I reached the spot where the rope entered the water, I slipped the flashlight from my belt and dived.

The water was deeper than I expected and very dark, the duckweed above me blocking out the sunlight in patches. At the periphery of my vision, fish twisted and spun. The barrels, of which five remained, all piled in a heap, were gathered around the submerged trunk of an ancient tree, its roots buried deep in the bottom of the bayou. Any boat that might have been using the bayou bank to land on would have avoided the tree, which meant that the barrels were in no danger of being disturbed. The water at the base of the tree was darker than the rest, so that without the flashlight the barrels would have been invisible.

I wrapped the top barrel in chains and yanked once to test its weight. It tumbled from the top of the pile, yanking the rope from my grasp as it headed for the bottom. The water muddied, and dirt and vegetation obscured my vision, and then everything went black as oil began to leak from the drum. I was kicking back to get into clearer water when I heard the dull, echoing sound of a gunshot from above me. For a moment, I thought that Morphy might be in trouble until I remembered what the gunshot was supposed to signal and realized that it was I, not Morphy, who was in trouble.

I was breaking for the surface when I saw the 'gator. It was small, maybe only six feet long, but the flashlight beam caught the wicked-looking teeth jutting out along its jaws and its light-colored underbelly. It was as disoriented by the oil and dirt as I was, but it seemed to be angling toward my flashlight. I clicked it off and instantly lost sight of the 'gator as I made a final kick for the surface.

When I broke the water the marker rope was fifteen feet in front of me, Morphy beside it.

"Come on!" he shouted. "There's no other landing around you."

I splashed hard as I swam to him, all the time aware of the reptile cruising beneath me. As I splashed, I spotted it on the surface to my left, about twenty feet away from me. I could see the scales of its back, its hungry eyes and the line of its jaw pointed in my direction. I turned on my back so I could keep the 'gator in my sight and kicked out, sometimes using the rope to pull myself along, at other times using my hands.

I was still five feet from the boat when the 'gator moved, working its way swiftly through the water in my direction. I spat the mouthpiece out.

"Shoot it, goddammit," I shouted. I heard the boom of a gun and a spume of water kicked up in front of the 'gator, then a second. The creature stopped short and then a sprinkling of pink and white fell to my right and it turned in that direction. It reached the objects just as a second shower fell, farther away to the right, and I felt the boat against my back and Morphy's hands helping me to haul myself up. We turned for the bank as Morphy sent a third handful of marshmallows into the air. When I looked at him, he was grinning as he popped a last marshmallow into his mouth. Out on the bayou, the 'gator was snapping at the last of the candy.

"Scared you, huh?" Morphy smiled as I shrugged off the air tank and lay flat on the bottom of the boat.

I nodded and kicked off a flipper.

"I think you're going to have to get your dry suit cleaned," I said.

WE SAT ON A log and watched the 'gator for a while. It cruised the bayou looking for more marshmallows, eventually settling for a wait-and-see policy, which consisted of it lying partially submerged near the marker rope. We sipped coffee from tin cups and finished off the last of the chicken.

"You should have shot it," I said.

"This *is* a nature reserve and there are laws about killing 'gators," responded Morphy testily. "Not much point in having a nature reserve if people can come in when they please and shoot all the wildlife."

We sipped the coffee some more, until I heard the sound of a boat coming our way through the rice and grass.

"Shit," said a familiar Brooklyn drawl as the prow of the boat broke the grass, "it's the Donner Party."

Angel emerged first, then Louis behind him, controlling the rudder. They moved steadily toward us and tied up at the maple.

Angel splashed into the water, then followed our gaze out to the 'gator. He caught one sight of the partially submerged reptile and ran awkwardly onto the bank, his knees high and his elbows pumping.

"Man, what is this, Jurassic Park?" he said. He turned to Louis, who jumped from his boat to ours and then onto the bank. "Hey, didn't you tell your sister not to be swimmin' in no strange ponds?"

Angel was dressed in his usual jeans and battered sneakers, with a denim jacket over a Doonesbury T-shirt that depicted Duke and the motto *Death Before Unconsciousness.* Louis was wearing crocodile-skin boots, black Levi's, and a white collarless Liz Claiborne shirt.

"We dropped by to see how you were," said Angel, casting anxious glances out at the 'gator after I had introduced him to Morphy. He held a bag of donuts in his hand.

"Our friend's gonna be real upset if he sees you wearing one of his relatives, Louis," I said.

Louis sniffed and approached the water's edge. "Is there a problem?" he asked at last.

"We were diving and then Wally Gator appeared and we weren't diving anymore," I explained.

Louis sniffed again. "Hmm," he said. Then he drew his SIG and blew the tip of the 'gator's tail off. The reptile thrashed in pain and the water around it turned bright red. Then it turned and headed off into the bayou, trailing blood behind it. "You should have shot it," he said.

"Let's not get into it," I responded. "Roll up your sleeves, gentlemen, we're going to need some help."

I STILL HAD THE dry suit on so I offered to keep diving.

"Trying to prove to me that you ain't chicken?" grinned Morphy.

"Nope," I said, as we untied the boat. "Trying to prove it to myself."

We rowed out to the marker rope and then I dived down with

the hook and chains, leaving Angel topside with Morphy and his gun in case the 'gator showed up again. Louis joined us in the second boat. A thick black film of oil had formed on the surface of the water and hung in the depths below. The barrels had scattered when the topmost drum fell. I checked the ruptured barrel with the flashlight but it appeared to contain nothing except the oil that remained.

It was laborious work, tying the barrel and hauling it up each time, but with two boats it meant that we could transport two barrels at a time to the bank. There was probably an easier way to do it, but we hadn't figured it out.

The sun was growing low and the waters were bathed in gold when we found her.

CHAPTER XLIII

It seems to me now that when I touched the barrel for the first time to attach the chains, something coursed through my system and tightened in my stomach like a fist. I felt a jolt. A blade flashed before my eyes and the depths were colored by a fountain of blood, or perhaps it was simply the dying sun on the water above reflected on my mask. I closed my eyes for a moment and felt movement around me, not just the water of the bayou or the fish in its depths but another swimmer who twisted around my body and legs. I thought I felt her hair brush my cheek but when I reached out I caught only swamp weed in my hand.

This barrel was heavier than the others, weighed down, as we would discover, with masonry bricks that had been split neatly in half. It would need the combined efforts of Morphy and Angel to pull it up.

"It's her," I said to Morphy. "We've found her." And then I swam down to the barrel and maneuvered it slowly over the rocks and tree trunks at the bottom as we brought it up. We all seemed to handle this barrel more gently than the rest, as if the girl inside was merely sleeping and we didn't want to disturb her, as if she was not long decayed but had been laid within it only yesterday. On the bank, Angel took the crowbar and carefully applied it to the rim of the lid, but it refused to move. He examined it more closely.

"It's been sealed," he said. He scraped the crowbar over the surface of the barrel and checked the mark left. "The barrel's been treated with something as well. That's why it's in better condition than the others."

It was true. The barrel had hardly rusted and the fleur-de-lys on its side was as clear and bright as if it had been painted only days before.

I thought for a moment. We could use the chain saw to cut it, but if I was right and the girl was inside, I didn't want to damage the remains. We could also have called for assistance from the local cops, or even the feds. I suggested it, more out of duty than desire, but even Morphy declined. He might have been concerned at the embarrassment that would be caused if the barrel was empty, but when I looked in his eyes I could see that wasn't the case. He wanted us to take it as far as we could.

In the end, we tested the barrel by gently tapping along its length with the axe. From the difference in sound, we judged as best we could where we could safely cut. Morphy carefully made an incision near the sealed end of the barrel, and using a combination of chain saw and crowbar, we cut an area that was roughly half the circumference, then pushed it up with the crowbar and shined a flashlight inside.

The body was little more than bones and shreds of material, the skin and flesh entirely rotted away. She had been dumped in head-first and her legs had been broken to fit her into the space. When I shined the beam to the far end of the barrel, I glimpsed bared teeth and strands of hair. We stood silently beside her, surrounded by the lapping water and the sounds of the swamp.

IT WAS LATE THAT night when I got back to the Flaisance. While we waited for the Slidell police and the rangers, Angel and Louis departed, with Morphy's agreement. I stayed on to give my statement and back up Morphy's version of what had taken place. On Morphy's advice, the locals called the FBI. I didn't wait around. If Woolrich wanted to talk, he knew where to find me.

The light was still on in Rachel's room as I passed, so I stopped and knocked. She opened the door wearing a pink Calvin Klein nightshirt, which stopped at mid-thigh level.

"Angel told me what happened," she said, opening the door wider to let me enter. "That poor girl." She hugged me and then ran the shower in the bathroom. I stayed in there for a long time, my hands against the tiles, letting the water roll over my head and back.

After I had dried myself, I wrapped the towel around my waist and found Rachel sitting on the bed, leafing through her papers. She cocked an eyebrow at me.

"Such modesty," she said, with a little smile.

I sat on the edge of the bed and she wrapped her arms around me from behind. I felt her cheek and her warm breath against my back. "How are you feeling?" I asked.

Her grip tightened a little. "Okay, I think."

She turned me around so that I was facing her. She knelt on the bed before me, her hands clasped between her legs, and bit her lip. Then she reached out and gently, almost tentatively, ran her hand through my hair.

"I thought you psychology types were supposed to be good at all this," I said.

She shrugged. "I get just as confused as everybody else, except I know all the terminology for my confusion." She sighed. "Listen, what happened yesterday . . . I don't want to put pressure on you. I know how hard all this is for you, because of Susan and—"

I held my hand against her cheek and rubbed her lips gently with my thumb. Then I kissed her and felt her mouth open beneath mine. I wanted to hold her, to love her, to drive away the vision of the dead girl.

"Thanks," I said, my mouth still against her, "but I know what I'm doing."

"Well," she said, as she eased back slowly on the bed, "at least one of us does."

THE FOLLOWING MORNING, THE remains of the girl lay on a metal table, curled fetally by the constriction of the barrel as if to protect herself for eternity. On the instructions of the FBI, she had been brought to New Orleans, weighed and measured, X-rayed, and fingerprinted. The body bag in which she had been removed from Honey Island had been examined for debris that might have fallen from her while she was being transported.

The clean tiles, the shining metal tables, the glinting medical instruments, the white lights hanging above them all seemed too harsh, too relentless in their mission to expose, to examine, to reveal. It seemed a final indignity, after the terrors of her final moments, to display her here in the sterility of this room, with these men looking upon her. A part of me wanted to cover her with a shroud and carry her carefully, gently, to a dark hole beside flowing water, where green trees would shade the ground under which she lay and where no one would disturb her again.

But another part of me, the rational part, knew that she deserved a name, that she needed an identity to put an end to the anonymity of her sufferings and, perhaps, to close in on the man who had reduced her to this. And so we stood back as the gowned coroner and his assistants moved in with their tapes and their blades and their white-gloved hands.

The pelvis is the most easily recognizable distinguishing feature between the male and female skeletons. The greater sciatic notch, situated behind the inominate bone—which itself consists of the hip, the ischium, the ilium, and the pubis—is wider in the female, with a subpubic angle roughly the size of that between the thumb and forefinger. The pelvic outlet is also larger in the female but the thigh sockets are smaller, the sacrum wider.

Even the female skull is different from that of the male, a reflection in miniature of the physical differences between the two sexes. The female skull is as smooth and rounded as the female breast, yet smaller than the male skull; the forehead is higher and more rounded; the eye sockets, too, are higher and the edges less sharply defined; the female jaw, palate, and teeth are smaller.

The skeletal remains before us conformed to the general pelvic and skull rules governing the female body. In estimating the age of the body at the time of death, the ossification centers, or areas of bone formation, were examined, as were the teeth. The femur of the girl's body was almost completely fused at the head, although there was only partial joining of the collarbone to the top of the breastbone. After an examination of the sutures on her skull, the coroner estimated her age at twenty-one or twenty-two. There were marks on her forehead, the base of her jaw, and on her left cheekbone, where the killer had cut through to the bone as he removed her face.

Her dental features were recorded, a process known as forensic odontology, to be checked against missing persons files, while samples of bone marrow and hair were removed for possible use in DNA profiling. Then Woolrich, Morphy, and I watched as the remains were wheeled away, covered in a plastic wrap. We exchanged a few words before we each went our separate way, but to be honest, I don't recall what they were. All I could see was the girl. All I could hear was the sound of water in my ears.

If the DNA profiling and the dental records failed to reveal her identity, Woolrich had decided that facial reconstruction might prove valuable, using a laser reflected from the skull to establish the contours, which could then be compared against a known skull of similar dimensions. He decided to contact Quantico to make the initial arrangements as soon as he had had time to wash and grab a cup of coffee.

But facial reconstruction proved unnecessary. It took less than two hours to identify the body of the young woman in the swamp. Although she had been lying in the dark waters for almost seven months, she had been reported missing only three months before.

Her name was Lutice Fontenot. She was Lionel Fontenot's half sister.

CHAPTER XLIV

The Fontenot compound lay five miles east of Delacroix. It was approached via a raised private road, newly built, which wound through swamps and decaying trees until it reached an area that had been cleared of all vegetation and was now only dark earth. High fencing, topped with razor wire, enclosed two or three acres, at the center of which lay a low, single-story, horseshoe-shaped concrete building. A black convertible and three black Explorers were parked in a line in the concrete lot created by the arms of the building. To the rear was an older house, a standard single-story wooden dwelling with a porch and what looked like a series of parallel linked rooms. No one seemed to be around as I pulled the rented Taurus up to the compound gate, Louis in the passenger seat beside me. Rachel had taken the other rental with her on a final visit to Loyola University.

"Maybe we should have called ahead," I said as I looked at the silent compound.

Beside me, Louis raised his hands slowly above his head and gestured in front of him with his chin. Two men, dressed in jeans and faded shirts, stood before us pointing Heckler & Koch HK53s with retracted stocks. I caught two more in the rearview mirror and a fifth, wearing an axe in his belt, opposite the passenger window. They were hard, weathered-looking men, some of them with beards already tinged with gray. Their boots were muddy and their hands were the hands of manual laborers, scarred in places.

I watched as a man of medium height, dressed in a blue denim shirt, jeans, and work boots, walked toward the gate from the main compound building. When he reached the gate he didn't open it but stood watching us through the fencing. He had been burned at some point: the skin on the right of his face was heavily scarred, the right eye useless, and the hair hadn't grown back on that side of his scalp. A fold of skin hung over his dead eye, and when he spoke, he did so out of the left side of his mouth.

"What you want here?" The voice was heavily accented: Cajun stock.

"My name's Charlie Parker," I replied through the open window. "I'm here to see Lionel Fontenot."

"Who this?" He motioned at Louis with a finger.

"Count Basie," I said. "The rest of the band couldn't make it."

Pretty Boy didn't crack a smile, or even a half smile. "Lionel don't see no one. Get yo' ass outta here 'fo you get hurt." He turned and walked back toward the compound.

"Hey," I said. "You accounted for all of Joe Bones's goons at Metairie yet?"

He stopped and turned back to us.

"What you say?" He looked like I'd just insulted his sister.

"I figure you have two bodies at Metairie that no one can account for. If there's a prize, I'd like to claim it."

He seemed to consider this for a moment, then: "You a joker? You are, I don't think you funny."

"You don't think I'm funny?" I said. There was an edge to my voice now. His left eyelid flickered and an H&K ended up two inches from my nose. It smelled like it had been used recently. "Try this for funny: I'm the guy who hauled Lutice Fontenot from the bottom of Honey Island swamp. You want to tell Lionel that, see if he laughs?"

He didn't reply, but pointed an infrared signaler at the compound gate. It opened almost noiselessly.

"Get outta the car," he said. Two of the men kept our hands in view and their guns trained on us as we opened the car doors, then two others came forward and frisked us against the car, looking for wires and weapons. They handed Louis's SIG and knife and my S&W to the scarred guy, then checked the interior of the car for concealed weapons. They opened the hood and trunk and checked under the car.

"Man, you like the Peace Corps," whispered Louis. "Make friends wherever you go."

"Thanks," I replied. "It's a gift."

When they were satisfied that it was clean, we were allowed to drive slowly up to the compound with one of Fontenot's men, the axe man, in the back. Two men walked alongside the car. We parked beside the jeeps and were escorted up to the older house.

On the porch, waiting for us with a china cup of coffee in his hand, was Lionel Fontenot. The burn victim went up to him and spoke a few words in his ear, but Lionel stopped him with a raised hand and turned the hard stare on us. I felt a raindrop fall on my head and within seconds we were standing in a downpour. Lionel left us in the rain. I was wearing my blue linen Liz Claiborne suit and a white shirt with a blue silk-knit tie. I wondered if the dye would run. The rain was heavy and the dirt around the house was already turning to mud when Lionel ordered his men to leave, took a seat on the porch, and indicated with a nod of his head that we should come up. We sat on a pair of wooden chairs with woven seats while Lionel took a wooden recliner. The burn victim stood behind us. Louis and I moved our chairs slightly as we sat so that we could keep him in view.

An elderly black maid, with a face that I recognized from the Metairie funeral party, emerged from the house with a silver coffeepot and sugar and cream in a matching set, all on an ornate silver tray. There were three china cups and saucers on the tray. Multicolored birds chased one another's tails around the rim of the cups, and a heavy silver spoon with a sailing ship at the end lay neatly positioned beneath the handle of each one. The maid placed the tray on a small wicker table and then left us.

Lionel Fontenot was wearing a pair of black cotton pants and a white shirt with an open collar. A matching black jacket lay over the back of his chair and his brogues were newly polished. He leaned over the table and poured three cups of coffee, added two sugars to one, and then handed it wordlessly to the burn victim.

"Cream and sugar?" he asked, looking to Louis and me in turn.

"Black's fine," I said.

"Likewise," said Louis.

Lionel handed us each a cup. It was all very polite. Above us, the rain hammered on the porch roof.

"You want to tell me how you came to be looking for my sister?" Lionel said at last. He looked like someone who finds a strange guy cleaning the windshield of his car and can't decide whether to tip him a buck or hit him with a tire iron. He held his cup with his little finger cocked while he sipped his coffee. I noticed that the burn victim did the same.

I told Lionel some of what I knew then. I told him about *Tante* Marie's visions and her death and about the stories of the ghost of a girl at a Honey Island slough. "I think the man who killed your sister killed *Tante* Marie Aguillard and her son. He also killed my wife and my little girl," I said. "That's how I came to be looking for your sister."

I didn't say that I was sorry for his pain. He probably knew that anyway. If he didn't, then it wasn't worth saying.

"You take out two men at Metairie?"

"One," I answered. "Someone else killed the other."

Lionel turned to Louis. "You?"

Louis didn't reply.

"Someone else," I repeated.

Lionel put his cup down and spread his hands. "So why are you here now? You want my gratitude? I'm going to New Orleans now to take away my sister's body. I don't know that I want to thank you for that." He turned his face away. There was pain in his eyes, but no tears. Lionel Fontenot didn't look like a man with well-developed tear ducts.

"That's not why I'm here," I said quietly. "I want to know why Lutice was reported missing only in the last three months. I want to know what your brother was doing out at Honey Island on the night he was killed."

"My brother," he said. Love and frustration and guilt chased one another in his voice like the birds on his pretty cups. Then he seemed to catch himself. I think he was about to tell me to go to Hell, to keep out of his family's business if I wanted to stay alive, but I held his gaze and for a while he said nothing.

"I got no reason to trust you," he said.

"I can find the man who did this," I said. My voice was low and even. Lionel nodded, more to himself than to me, and appeared to make his decision.

"My sister left at the end of January, start of February," he began. "She didn't like"—he waved his left hand gently at the compound—"all this. There was trouble with Joe Bones, some people got hurt." He paused and chose his next words carefully. "One day she closed her bank account, packed a bag, and left a note. She didn't tell us to our faces. David wouldn't have let her leave anyways.

"We tried to trace her. We looked up friends in the city, even people she knew in Seattle and Florida. There was nothing, not a trace. David was real cut up about her. She was our half sister. When my momma died, my father married again. Lutice came out of that marriage. When my father and her momma died—that was in nineteen eighty-three, in an automobile accident—we took care of her, David especially. They were real close.

"Few months back, David started having dreams about Lutice. He didn't say nothing at first, but he got thinner and paler and his nerves started to play at him. When he told me, I thought he was going crazy and told him so, but the dreams just kept comin'. He dreamed of her underwater, he said, heard her banging against metal in the night. He was sure that something had happened to her.

"But what could we do? We had searched half of Louisiana. I'd even made approaches to some of Joe Bones's men, to see if there was something that maybe needed to be sorted out. There was nothing. She was gone.

"Next thing I knew, he reported her missing and we had the cops crawling over the compound. Mon, I nearly killed him that day, but he insisted. He said something had happened to Lutice. He was beyond reason by then, and I had to take care of things on my own, with Joe Bones hangin' over me like a sword 'bout to fall."

He looked to the burn victim.

"Leon here was with him when the call came. He wouldn't say nothin' about where he was goin', just took off in his damned yellow car. When Leon tried to stop him, he pulled a gun on him."

I glanced at Leon. If he felt any guilt about what had happened to David Fontenot, he kept it well hidden.

"Any idea who made the call?" I asked.

Lionel shook his head.

I put my cup on the tray. The coffee was cold and untasted.

"When are you going to hit Joe Bones?" I asked. Lionel blinked like he had just been slapped, and out of the corner of my eye, I saw Leon step forward.

"The hell you talkin' about?" said Lionel.

"You've got a second funeral coming up, at least as soon as the police release your sister's body. Either you won't have too many mourners or the funeral will be overrun with police and media. Whatever happens, I figure you'll try to take out Joe Bones before then, probably at his place in West Feliciana. You owe him for David, and anyway, Joe won't rest easy until you're dead. One of you will try to finish it."

Lionel looked at Leon. "They clean?" Leon nodded.

Lionel leaned forward. There was menace in his voice. "The fuck does any of this have to do with you?"

I wasn't fazed by him. The threat of violence was in his face, but I needed Lionel Fontenot.

"You heard about Tony Remarr's death?"

Lionel nodded.

"Remarr was killed because he was out at the Aguillard place after *Tante* Marie and her son were murdered," I explained. "His fingerprints were found in *Tante* Marie's blood, Joe Bones heard about it, and told Remarr to lie low. But the killer found out—I don't know how yet—and I think he used your brother to lure Remarr into making the hit so he could take him out. I want to know what Remarr told Joe Bones."

Lionel considered what I had said. "And you can't get to Joe Bones without me."

Beside me, Louis's mouth twitched. Lionel caught the movement.

"That's not entirely true," I said. "But if you're going to be calling on him anyway, we might tag along."

"I go calling on Joe Bones, his fucking place is gonna be real fucking quiet by the time I leave," said Lionel softly.

"You do what you have to do," I replied. "But I need Joe Bones alive. For a while."

Lionel stood and buttoned the top of his shirt. He took a wide black silk tie from the inside pocket of his jacket and began to put it on, using his reflection in the window to check the knot.

"Where you staying?" he asked. I told him, and gave Leon the number of my phone. "We'll be in touch," said Lionel. "Maybe. Don't come out here again."

Our discussions appeared to be at an end. Louis and I were almost at the car when Lionel spoke again. He pulled on his jacket and adjusted the collar, then smoothed down the lapels.

"One thing," he said. "I know Morphy out of St. Martin was there when Lutice was found. You got cop friends?"

"Yeah. I got federal friends too. That a problem?"

He turned away. "Not as long as you don't make it one. If you do, the crabs gonna be feeding on you and your buddy."

Louis fooled around with the car radio until he found a station that seemed to be playing back-to-back Dr. John. "This is music, right?" he said.

The music segued uneasily from "Makin' Whoopee" to "Gris

Gris Gumbo Ya-Ya" and John's throaty rumble filled the car. Louis flicked the presets again, until he found a country station playing three in a row from Garth Brooks.

"This be the devil's music," mumbled Louis. He turned the radio off and tapped his fingers on the dash.

"You know," I said, "you don't have to hang around if you don't want to. Things could get difficult, or Woolrich and the feds could decide to make them difficult for you." I knew that Louis was what Angel diplomatically referred to as semiretired. Money, it appeared, was no longer an issue. The "semi" indicated that it might have been replaced by something else, although I wasn't sure yet what that was.

He looked out the window, not at me. "You know why we're here?"

"Not entirely. I asked, but I wasn't sure that you'd come."

"We came because we owe you, because you'd look out for us if we needed it, and because someone has to look out for you after what happened to your woman and your little girl. More than that, Angel thinks that you're a good man. Maybe I think so too and maybe I think that what you brought to an end with the Modine bitch, what you're trying to bring to an end here, they're things that should be brought to an end. You understand me?"

It was strange to hear him talk this way, strange and affecting. "I think I understand," I replied quietly. "Thank you."

"You *are* going to end this thing here?" he said.

"I think so, but we're missing something, a detail, a pattern, something." I kept catching glimpses of it, like a rat passing under streetlights. I needed to find out more about Edward Byron. I needed to talk to Woolrich.

RACHEL MET US IN the main hall of the Flaisance House. I guessed that she had been watching for the car. Angel lounged beside her eating a Lucky Dog, which looked like the business end of a baseball bat topped with onion, chili, and mustard.

"The FBI came," said Rachel. "Your friend Woolrich was with them. They had a warrant. They took everything: my notes, the illustrations, everything they could find." She led the way to her room. The walls had been stripped of their notes. Even the diagram I had drawn was gone.

"They searched our room too," remarked Angel to Louis. "And Bird's." My head jerked up as I thought of the case of guns. Angel spotted the move. "We ditched them soon as your FBI friend put the stare on Louis. They're in a storage depot on Bayonne. We both have keys."

I noticed that Rachel seemed more irritated than upset as we followed her to her room. "Am I missing something here?"

She smiled. "I said they took everything they could *find.* Angel saw them coming. I hid some of the notes in the waistband of my jeans, under my shirt. Angel took care of most of the rest."

She took a small pile of papers from under her bed and waved them with a small flourish. She kept one separate in her hand. It was folded over once.

"I think you might want to see this," she said, handing the paper to me. I unfolded it and felt a pain in my chest.

It was an illustration of a woman seated naked on a chair. She had been split from neck to groin and the skin on each side had been pulled back so that it hung over her arms like the folds of a gown. Across her lap lay a young man, similarly opened but with a space where his stomach and other internal organs had been removed. Apart from the detail of the anatomization and the alteration in the sex of one of the victims, it resembled in its essence what had been done to Jennifer and Susan.

"It's Estienne's *Pietà,*" said Rachel. "It's very obscure, which is why it took so long to track down. Even in its day, it was regarded as excessively explicit and, more to the point, blasphemous. It bore too much of a resemblance to the figure of the dead Christ and Mary for the liking of the church authorities. Estienne nearly burned for it."

She took the illustration from me and looked at it sadly, then placed it on her bed with the other papers. “I know what he's doing,” she said. “He's creating memento mori, death's-heads.” She sat on the edge of the bed and put her hands together beneath her chin, as if in prayer.

“He's giving us lessons in mortality.”

4

He had a mind to be acquainted with your inside, Crispin.

Edward Ravenscroft, The Anatomist

CHAPTER XLV

In the medical school of the Complutense University of Madrid there is an anatomical museum, founded by King Carlos III. Much of its collection derives from the efforts of Dr. Julián de Velasco in the early to mid-nineteenth century. Dr. Velasco was a man who took his work seriously. He was reputed to have mummified the corpse of his own daughter, just as William Harvey was assisted in his discovery of circulation by his decision to autopsy the bodies of his own father and sister.

The long rectangular hall is arrayed with glass cases of exhibits: two giant skeletons, the wax model of a fetal head, and at one point, two figures labeled *despellejados*. They are the "flayed men," who stand in dramatic poses, displaying the movement of the muscles and the tendons without the white veil of the skin to hide it from the eye of the beholder. Vesalius, Valverde, Estienne, their forebears, their peers, their successors, worked in the knowledge of this tradition. Artists such as Michelangelo and Leonardo da Vinci created their own *écorchés*, as they termed their drawings of flayed figures, basing their work on their own participation in dissections.

And the figures they created were more than merely anatomical specimens: they served, in their way, as reminders of the flawed nature of our humanity, a reminder of the body's capacity for pain and, eventually, mortality. They warned of the futility of the pursuits of the flesh, the reality of disease and pain and death in this life, and the promise of something better in the next.

In eighteenth-century Florence, the practice of anatomical modeling reached its peak. Under the patronage of the Abbot Felice Fontana, anatomists and artists worked side by side to create natural sculptures from beeswax. Anatomists exposed the cadavers, the artists poured the liquid plaster, and molds were created. Layers of wax were placed into them, with pig fat used to alter the temperature of the wax where necessary, allowing a process of layering that reproduced the transparency of human tissue.

Then, with threads and brushes and fine point, the lineaments and striations of the body were reproduced. Eyebrows and eyelashes were added, one by one. In the case of the Bolognese artist Lelli, real skeletons were used as a frame for his wax creations. The emperor of Austria, Joseph II, was so impressed by the collection that he ordered 1,192 models, to promote medical teaching in his own country. By contrast, Frederik Ruysch, professor of anatomy at the Atheneum Illustre in Amsterdam, used chemical fixatives and dyes to preserve his specimens. His house contained an exhibition of the skeletons of infants and children in various poses, reminders of the transience of life.

Yet nothing could compare to the reality of the actual human body exposed to view. Public demonstrations of anatomization and dissection attracted huge crowds, some of them in carnival disguise. Ostensibly, they were there to learn. In reality, the dissection was little more than an extension of the public execution. In England, the Murder Act of 1752 provided a direct link between the two events by permitting the bodies of murderers to be anatomically dissected, and postmortem penal dissection became a form of further punishment for the criminal, who would now be denied a proper burial. In 1832, the Anatomy Act extended the deprivation of the poor into the next life by allowing the confiscation of the bodies of dead paupers for dissection.

So death and dissection walked hand in hand with the extension of scientific knowledge. But what of pain? What of the Renaissance disgust with the workings of the female body, which led to a particularly morbid fascination with the uterus? In the acts of flaying and anatomization, the realities of suffering, sex, and death were not far away.

The interior of the body, when revealed, speaks to us of mortality. But how many of us can ever bear witness to our own interiors? We see our own mortality only through the prism of the mortality of others. Even then, it is only in exceptional circumstances, in cases of war, or violent accidental death, or murder, when the viewer is a witness to the act itself or its immediate consequences, that mortality in all its deep red reality is made clear to us.

In his violent, pain-filled way, Rachel believed, the Traveling Man was trying to break down these barriers. In killing his victims in this way, he was making them aware of their own mortality, exposing to them their own interiors, introducing them to the meaning of true pain; but they also served as a reminder to others of their own mortality and the final, dreadful pain that would someday find them.

The Traveling Man crisscrossed the boundaries between torture and execution, between intellectual and physical curiosity and sadism. He was part of the secret history of mankind, the history recorded in the thirteenth-century *Anatomia Magistri Nicolai Physici,* which observed that the ancients practiced dissection upon both the living and the dead, binding condemned criminals hand and foot and gradually dissecting them, beginning with their legs and arms and moving on to their internal organs. Celsus and Augustine made similar allegations about live dissections, still contested by medical historians.

And now the Traveling Man had come to write his own history, to offer his own blending of science and art, to make his own notes on mortality and to create a Hell within the human heart.

ALL THIS RACHEL EXPLAINED as we sat in her room. Outside, it had grown dark and the strains of music floated on the air.

"I think the blinding may be related to ignorance, a physical representation of a failure to understand the reality of pain and death," she said. "But it indicates just how far the killer himself is removed from ordinary humanity. We all suffer, we all experience death in various ways before we die ourselves. He believes that only he can teach us this."

"That, or he believes we've lost sight of it and need to be reminded, that it's his role to tell us just how inconsequential we are," I added. Rachel nodded her assent.

"If what you say is true, then why was Lutice Fontenot dumped in a barrel?" It was Angel. He sat by the balcony, staring out on to the street below.

"'Prentice work," said Rachel. Louis cocked an eyebrow but stayed silent.

"This Traveling Man believes he's creating works of art: the care he takes in displaying the bodies, their relation to old medical texts, the links with mythology and artistic representations of the body all point in that direction. But even artists have to start somewhere. Poets, painters, sculptors all serve an apprenticeship of sorts, formal or otherwise. The work they create during their apprenticeships may go on to influence their later work, but it's usually not for public display. It's a chance to make mistakes without criticism, to see what you can and cannot achieve. Maybe that's what Lutice Fontenot was to him: 'prentice work."

"But she died after Susan and Jennifer," I added softly.

"He took Susan and Jennifer because he wanted to, but the results were unsatisfactory. I think he used Lutice to practice again before he returned to the public arena," she answered, not looking at me. "He took *Tante* Marie and her son for a combination of reasons, out of both desire and necessity, and this time he had the time he needed to achieve the effect for which he was searching. He then had to kill Remarr, either because of what he actually saw or the mere possibility that he might have seen something, but again he created a memento mori out of him. He's practical, in his way: he's not afraid to make a virtue out of necessity."

Angel looked unhappy with the thrust of Rachel's words. "But what about the way most of us react to death?" he began. "It makes us want to live. It even makes us want to *screw.*"

Rachel glanced at me, then returned to her notes.

"I mean," continued Angel, "what does this guy want us to do? Stop eating, stop loving, because he's got a thing about death and he thinks the next world is going to be something better?"

I picked up the illustration of the *Pietà* again and examined the detail of the bodies, the carefully labeled interiors, and the placid expressions on the faces of the woman and the man. The faces of the Traveling Man's victims had looked nothing like this. They were contorted in their final agonies.

"He doesn't give a damn about the next world," I said. "He's only concerned with the damage he can do in this one."

I stood and joined Angel at the window. Beneath us, the dogs scampered and sniffed in the courtyard. I could smell cooking and beer and imagined that, beneath it all, I could smell the mass of humanity itself, passing us by.

"Why hasn't he come after us? Or you?" It was Angel. His words were directed at me, but it was Rachel who answered.

"Because he wants us to understand," she said. "Everything he's done is an attempt to lead us to something. All of this is an effort to communicate, and we're the audience. He doesn't want to kill us."

"Yet," said Louis softly.

Rachel nodded once, her eyes locked on mine. "Yet," she agreed quietly.

I ARRANGED TO MEET Rachel and the others later in Vaughan's. Back in my room, I called Woolrich and left a message on his machine. He returned the call within five minutes and told me he'd meet me at the Napoleon House within the hour.

He was as good as his word. Shortly before ten he appeared, dressed in off-white chinos and carrying a matching jacket over his arm, which he put on as soon as he entered the bar.

"Is it chilly in here, or is it just the reception?" There was sleep caked at the corners of his eyes and he smelled sour and unwashed. He was no longer the assured figure I recalled from Jenny Orbach's apartment, wresting control of the room from a group of vaguely hostile cops. Instead he looked older, more uncertain. Taking Rachel's papers in the way he did was out of character for him; the old Woolrich would have taken them anyway, but he would have asked for them first.

He ordered an Abita for himself and another mineral water for me.

"You want to tell me why you seized materials from the hotel?"

"Don't look on it as a seizure, Bird. Consider it as borrowing." He sipped at his beer and looked at himself in the mirror. He didn't seem to like what he saw.

"You could just have asked," I said.

"Would you have given it to me?"

"No, but I'd have discussed what was there."

"I don't think that Durand would have been too impressed with that. Frankly, I wouldn't have been too impressed either."

"Durand called it? Why? You have your own profilers, your own agents on it. Why were you so sure that we could add something?"

He spun around on his stool and leaned close to me, close enough that I could smell his breath. "Bird, I know you want this guy. I know you want him for what he did to Susan and Jennifer, to the old woman and her son, to Florence, to Lutice Fontenot, maybe even to that fuck Remarr. I've tried to keep you in touch with what's been going down and you've walked all over this case like a fucking child in new boots. You've got an assassin staying in the room next door, God alone knows what his pal does, and your lady friend is collecting graphic medical imagery like box tops. You ain't given me shit, so I did what I had to do. You think I'm holding back on you? With the shit you're pulling, you're lucky I don't put you back on a plane to Noo Yawk."

"I need to know what you know," I said. "What are you holding back about this guy?"

We were almost head to head now. Then Woolrich grimaced and leaned back.

"Holding back? Jesus, Bird, you're unbelievable. Here's something: Byron's wife? You want to know what she majored in when she was at college? Art. Her thesis was on Renaissance art and depictions of the body. You think that might have included medical representations, that maybe that was where her ex got some of his ideas?"

He took a deep breath and a long swig of beer. "You're bait, Bird. You know it, and I know it. And I know something else too." His voice was cold and hard. "I know you were at Metairie. There's a guy in the morgue with a bullet hole in his head and the cops have the remains of a ten millimeter Smith & Wesson bullet that was dug out of the marble behind him. You want to tell me about that, Bird? You want to tell me if you were alone in Metairie when the killing started?"

I didn't reply.

Then: "You screwing her, Bird?"

I looked at him. There was no mirth in his eyes and he wasn't smiling. Instead, there was hostility and distrust. Whatever I needed to know about Edward Byron and his ex-wife, I would have to find out myself. If I had hit him then, we would have hurt each other badly. I didn't waste any more words on him and I didn't look back as I left the bar.

I TOOK A CAB to Bywater and stopped off right outside Vaughan's Lounge on the corner of Dauphine and Lesseps. I paid the five-dollar cover at the door. Inside, Kermit Ruffins and the Barbecue Swingers were lost in a rhapsody of New Orleans brass and there were plates of red beans scattered on the tables. Rachel and Angel were dancing around chairs and tables while Louis looked on with a long-suffering expression. As I approached, the tempo of the music slowed a little and Rachel made a grab for me. I moved with her for a while as she stroked my face, and I closed my eyes and let her. Then I sipped a soda and thought my own thoughts until Louis moved from his seat and sat beside me.

"You didn't have much to say back in Rachel's room," I said.

He nodded. "It's bullshit. All this stuff, the religion, the medical drawings, they're all just trappings. And maybe he believes them and maybe he don't. Sometimes it's nothing to do with mortality, it's to do with the beauty of the color of meat."

He took a sip of beer.

"And this guy just likes red."

BACK AT THE FLAISANCE, I lay beside Rachel and listened to her breathing in the dark.

"I've been thinking," she said. "About our killer."

"And?"

"I think the killer may not be male."

I raised myself up on my elbows and looked at her. I could see the whites of her eyes, wide and bright.

"Why?"

"I'm not sure, exactly. There just seems to be something almost feminine about the sensibility of whoever is committing these crimes, a . . . *sensitivity* to the interconnectedness of things, to their potential for symbolism. I don't know. I guess I'm thinking out loud, but it's not a sensibility typical of a modern male. Maybe 'female' is wrong—I mean, the hallmarks, the cruelty, the capacity to overpower, all point to a male—but it's as close as I can get, at least for now."

She shook her head and then was silent again.

"Are we becoming a couple?" she asked at last.

"I don't know. Are we?"

"You're avoiding the question."

"No, not really. It's not one that I'm used to answering, or that I ever thought that I'd have to answer again. If you're asking if I want us to stay together, then the answer is yes, I do. It worries me a little, and I'm bringing in more baggage than the handlers at JFK, but I want to be with you."

She kissed me softly.

"Why did you stop drinking?" she asked, adding: "Since we're having this heart-to-heart."

I started at the question. "Because if I took one drink now, I'd wake up in Singapore with a beard a week later," I replied.

"It doesn't answer the question."

"I hated myself and that made me hate others, even the people closest to me. I was drinking the night Susan and Jennifer were killed. I'd been drinking a lot, not just that night but other nights too. I drank because of a lot of things, because of the pressure of the job, because of my failings as a husband, as a father, and maybe other things as well, things from way back. If I hadn't been a drunk, Susan and Jennifer might not have died. So I stopped. Too late, but I stopped."

She didn't say anything else. She didn't say, "It wasn't your fault," or, "You can't blame yourself." She knew better than that.

I think I wanted to say more, to try to explain to her what it was like without alcohol, about how I was afraid that, without alcohol, each day would now leave me with nothing to look forward to. Each day would simply be another day without a drink. Sometimes, when I was at my lowest ebb, I wondered if my search for the Traveling Man was just a way to fill my days, a way to keep me from going off the rails.

Later, as she slept, I lay on the bed, on top of the sheets, and thought about Lutice Fontenot and bodies turned into art, before I, too, faded into sleep.

CHAPTER XLVI

I slept badly that night, wound up by my conversation with Woolrich and troubled by dreams of dark water. The next morning, I had breakfast alone after tracking down what seemed to be the only copy of the *New York Times* in Orleans Parish, over at Riverside News, by the Jax Brewery. Later, I met Rachel at Café du Monde and we walked through the French Market, wandering between the stalls of T-shirts and CDs and cheap wallets, and on to the fresh produce at the Farmers' Market. There were pecans like dark eyes, pale, shrunken heads of garlic, melons with dark red flesh that held the gaze like a wound. White-eyed fish lay packed in ice beside crawfish tails; headless shrimp rested by racks of "'gator on a stick" and murky tanks in which baby alligators lay on display. There were stalls loaded with eggplants and militones, sweet onions and elephant toe garlic, fresh Roma tomatoes and ripe avocadoes.

Over a century before, this had been a two-block stretch of Gallatin Street on the riverfront docks between Barracks and Ursuline. Outside of maybe Shanghai and the Bowery, it was one of the toughest places in the world, a strip of brothels and lowlife gin mills where hard-faced men mixed with harder women and anyone without a weapon had taken a wrong turning somewhere that he was bound to regret.

Gallatin is gone now, erased from the map, and instead tourists mix with Cajun fishermen from Lafayette and beyond, come to sell their wares surrounded by the thick, heady smell of the Mississippi. The city was like that, it seemed: streets disappeared; bars opened and, a century later, were gone; buildings were torn down or burned to the ground and others rose to take their place. There was change, but the spirit of the city remained the same. On this muggy summer morning, it seemed to brood beneath the clouds, feeling the people as a passing infection that it would cleanse from itself with rain.

The door of my room was slightly ajar when we returned through the courtyard. I motioned Rachel against the wall and drew my Smith & Wesson, keeping to the sides of the wooden stairway so that the steps wouldn't creak. The noise of Ricky's Steyr sending bullets raking past my ear had stayed with me. *"Joe Bones says hello."* I figured that if Joe Bones tried to say hello again, I could spare enough powder to blow him back to Hell.

I listened at the door but no sounds came from inside. If it had been the maid in my room, she'd have been whistling and bumping, maybe listening to a blues station on her tinny portable radio. If there was a maid in my room now, she was either asleep or levitating.

I hit the door hard with my shoulder and entered fast, my gun at arm's length, scanning the room with the sight. It came to rest on the figure of Leon sitting in a chair by the balcony, flicking through a copy of *GQ* that Louis had passed on to me. Leon didn't look like the kind of guy who bought much on *GQ*'s recommendation, unless the *Q* had made a big play for the JCPenney contract. Leon glanced at me with even less interest than he gave to *GQ*. His damaged eye glistened beneath its fold of skin like a crab peering out of a shell.

"When you're finished, there are hairs in the shower and the closet door sticks," I said.

"Room falls down around your ears, I could give a fuck," he replied. That Leon, what a kidder.

He threw the magazine on the floor and looked past me to Rachel, who had followed me into the room. His eyes didn't register any interest there either. Maybe Leon was dead and no one had worked up the guts to tell him.

"She's with me," I said. Leon looked like he could have keeled over from apathy.

"Ten tonight, at the nine-sixty-six junction at Starhill. You *et ton ami noir.* Anyone else, Lionel cornhole you both with a shotgun."

He stood to leave. As I moved aside to let him pass, I made a pistol of my finger and thumb and fired it at him. There was a flash of steel in each of his hands and two barb-edged knives appeared inches from each of my eyes. I could see the tops of the spring loaders in his sleeves. That explained why Leon didn't seem to feel the need to carry a gun.

"Impressive," I said, "but it's only funny until someone loses an eye." Leon's dead right eye seemed to gaze into my soul, as if to rot it and turn it to dust, then he left. I couldn't hear his footsteps as he walked down the gallery.

"A friend of yours?" asked Rachel.

I walked out of the room and looked down at the already empty courtyard. "If he is, I'm lonelier than I thought."

WHEN LOUIS AND ANGEL returned from a late breakfast, I went to their door and knocked. A couple of seconds went by before there was a response.

"Yeah?" shouted Angel.

"It's Bird. You two decent?"

"Jeez, I hope not. C'mon in."

Louis sat upright in bed, reading the *Times-Picayune.* Angel sat beside him outside the sheets, naked but for a towel across his lap.

"The towel for my benefit?"

"I'm afraid you might become confused about your sexuality."

"Might take away what little I have."

"Very witty for a man screwing a psychologist. Why don't you just pay your eighty bucks an hour like everyone else?"

Louis gave us both bored looks over the top of his newspaper. Maybe Leon and Louis were related way back.

"Lionel Fontenot's boy just paid me a visit," I said.

"The beauty queen?" asked Louis.

"None other."

"We on?"

"Tonight at ten. Better get your stuff out of hock."

"I'll send my boy." He kicked Angel in the leg from beneath the sheets.

"The ugly queen?"

"None other," said Louis.

Angel continued to watch his game show. "It's beneath my dignity to comment."

Louis returned to his paper. "You got a lot of dignity for a guy with a towel on his dick."

"It's a big towel," sniffed Angel.

"Waste of a lot of good towel space, you ask me."

I left them to it. Back in my room, Rachel was standing by the wall, her arms folded and a fierce expression on her face.

"What happens now?" she asked.

"We go back to Joe Bones," I said.

"And Lionel Fontenot kills him," she spat. "He's no better than Joe Bones. You're only siding with him out of expediency. What will happen when Fontenot kills him? Will things be any better?"

I didn't answer. I knew what would happen. There would be a brief disturbance in the drug trade, as Fontenot renegotiated existing deals or ended them entirely. Prices would go up and there would be some killing, as those who felt strong enough to challenge him for Joe Bones's turf made their play. Lionel Fontenot would kill them; of that I had no doubt.

Rachel was right. It was only expediency that made me side with Lionel. Joe Bones knew something about what had happened the night *Tante* Marie died, something that could bring me a step closer to the man who had killed my wife and child. If it took Lionel Fontenot's guns to find out what that was, then I would side with the Fontenots.

"And Louis will stand beside you," said Rachel quietly. "My God, what have you become?"

LATER, I DROVE TO Baton Rouge, Rachel accompanying me at my insistence. We were uneasy together, and no words were exchanged. Rachel contented herself with looking out of the window, her elbow resting against the door, her right hand supporting her cheek. The silence between us remained unbroken until we reached exit 166, heading for LSU and the home of Stacey Byron. Then I spoke, anxious that we should at least try to clear the air between us.

"Rachel, I'll do what I have to do to find whoever killed Susan and Jennifer," I said. "I need this, else I'm dead inside."

She did not reply immediately. For a while, I thought she was not going to reply at all.

"You're already dying inside," she said at last, still staring out the window. I could see her eyes, reflected in the glass, following the landscape. "The fact that you're prepared to do these things is an indication of that."

She looked at me for the first time. "I'm not your moral arbiter, Bird, and I'm not the voice of your conscience. But I am someone who cares about you, and I'm not sure how to deal with these feelings right now. Part of me wants to walk away and never look back, but another part of me wants, needs, to stay with you. I want to stop this thing, all of it. I want it all to end, for everybody's sake." Then she turned away again and left me to deal with what she had said.

Stacey Byron lived in a small white clapboard house with a red door and peeling paint, close to a small mall with a big supermarket, a photo shop, and a twenty-four-hour pizzeria. This area by the LSU campus was populated mainly by students, and some of the houses now had stores on their first floor, selling used CDs and books or long hippie dresses and overwide straw hats. As we drove by Stacey Byron's house and pulled into a parking space in front of the photo shop, I spotted a blue Probe parked close by. The two guys sitting in the front seats looked bored beyond belief. The driver had a newspaper folded in four resting on the wheel and was sucking on a pencil as he tried to do the crossword. His partner tapped a rhythm on the dashboard as he watched the front door of Stacey Byron's house.

"Feds?" asked Rachel.

"Maybe. Could be locals. This is donkey work."

We watched them for a while. Rachel turned on the radio and we listened to an AOR station: Rush, Styx, Richard Marx. Suddenly, the middle of the road seemed to be running straight through the car, musically speaking.

"Are you going in?" asked Rachel.

"May not have to," I replied, nodding at the house.

Stacey Byron, her blond hair tied back in a ponytail and her body encased in a short white cotton dress, emerged from the house and walked straight toward us, a straw shopping basket over her left arm. She nodded at the two guys in the car. They tossed a coin and the one in the passenger seat, a medium-sized man with a small belly protruding through his jacket, got out of the car, stretched his legs, and followed her toward the mall.

She was a good-looking woman, although the short dress was a little too tight at the thighs and dug slightly into the fat below her buttocks. Her arms were strong and lean, her skin tanned. There was a grace to her as she walked: when an elderly man almost collided with her as she entered the supermarket, she spun lightly on her right foot to avoid him.

I felt something soft on my cheek and turned to find Rachel blowing on it.

"Hey," she said, and for the first time since we left New Orleans there was a tiny smile on her lips. "It's rude to lech when you're with another woman."

"It's not leching," I said, as we climbed from the car, "it's surveillance."

I wasn't sure why I had come here, but Woolrich's remarks about Stacey Byron and her interest in art made me want to see her for myself, and I wanted Rachel to see her as well. I didn't know how we might get to talk to her but I figured that these things had a habit of working themselves out.

Stacey took her time browsing in the aisles. There was an aimlessness about her shopping as she picked up items, glanced at the labels, and then discarded them. The cop followed about ten feet behind her, then fifteen, before his attention was distracted by some magazines. He moved to the checkout and took up a position where he could see down two aisles at once, limiting his care of Stacey Byron to the occasional glance in her direction.

I watched a young black man in a white coat and a white hat with a green band stacking prepackaged meat. When he had emptied the tray and marked off its contents on a clipboard, he left the shop floor through a door marked *Staff Only.* I left Rachel to watch Byron and followed him. I almost hit him with the door as I went through, since he was squatting to pick up another plastic tray of meat. He looked at me curiously.

"Hey, man," he said, "you can't come in here."

"How much do you earn an hour?" I asked.

"Five twenty-five. What's it to you?"

"I'll give you fifty bucks if you lend me your coat and that clipboard for ten minutes."

He thought it over for a few seconds, then said: "Sixty, and anyone asks I'll say you stole it."

"Done," I said, and counted out three twenties as he took off the coat. It fitted a bit tightly across the shoulders, but no one would notice as long as I left it unbuttoned. I was stepping back onto the shop floor when the young guy called me.

"Hey, man, 'nother twenty, you can have the hat."

"For twenty bucks, I could go into the hat business myself," I replied. "Go hide in the men's room."

I found Stacey Byron by the toiletries, Rachel close by.

"Excuse me, ma'am," I said, as I approached, "can I ask you some questions?"

Up close, she looked older. There was a network of broken veins beneath her cheekbones and a fine tracery of lines surrounded her eyes. There were tight lines, too, around her mouth, and her cheeks were sunken and stretched. She looked tired and something else: she looked threatened, maybe even scared.

"I don't think so," she said, with a false smile, and started to step around me.

"It's about your ex-husband."

She stopped then and turned back, her eyes searching for her police escort. "Who are you?"

"An investigator. What do you know about Renaissance art, Mrs. Byron?"

"What? What do you mean?"

"You studied it in college, didn't you? Does the name Valverde mean anything to you? Did your husband ever use it? Did you?"

"I don't know what you're talking about. Please, leave me alone." She backed away, knocking some cans of deodorant to the floor.

"Mrs. Byron, have you ever heard of the Traveling Man?"

Something flashed in her eyes and behind me I heard a low whistle. I turned to see the fat cop moving down the aisle in my direction. He passed Rachel without noticing her and she began moving toward the door and the safety of the car, but by then I was already heading back to the staff area. I dumped the coat and walked straight through and on to the back lot, which was crowded with trucks making deliveries, before slipping around the side of the mall where Rachel already had the car started. I stayed low as we drove off, turning right instead of passing Stacey Byron's house again. In the side mirror I could see the fat cop looking around and talking into his radio, Byron beside him.

"And what did we achieve there?" asked Rachel.

"Did you see her eyes when I mentioned the Traveling Man? She knew the name."

"She knows something," agreed Rachel. "But she could have heard it from the cops. She looked scared, Bird."

"Maybe," I said. "But scared of what?"

THAT EVENING, ANGEL REMOVED the door panels of the Taurus and we strapped the Calicos and the magazines into the space behind them, then replaced the panels. I cleaned and loaded my Smith & Wesson in the hotel room while Rachel watched.

I put the gun in my shoulder holster and wore a black Alpha Industries bomber jacket over my black T-shirt and black jeans. With my black Timberlands, I looked like the doorman at a nightclub.

"Joe Bones is living on borrowed time. I couldn't save him if I wanted to," I told her. "He was dead from the moment the Metairie hit went wrong."

Rachel spoke. "I've decided. I'm leaving in a day or two. I don't think I can be part of this any longer, the things you're doing, the things I've done." She wouldn't look at me and there was nothing that I could say. She was right, but she wasn't simply preaching. I could see her own pain in her eyes. I could feel it every time we made love.

Louis was waiting by the car, dressed in a black sweat top and black denim jacket over dark jeans and Ecco boots. Angel checked the door panels one last time to make sure they slipped off without any trouble, then stood beside Louis.

"You don't hear anything from us by three A.M., you take Rachel and clear out of the hotel. Book into the Pontchartrain and get the first plane out in the morning," I said. "I don't want Joe Bones trying to even up scores if this turns bad. Handle the cops whatever way you think is best."

He nodded, exchanged a look with Louis, and went back into the Flaisance. Louis put an Isaac Hayes tape into the stereo and we rolled out of New Orleans to the strains of "Walk On By."

"Dramatic," I said.

He nodded. "We the men."

LEON LOUNGED BY A gnarled oak, its trunk knotted and worn, as we reached the Starhill intersection. Louis's left hand was hanging loosely by his side, the butt of the SIG jutting from beneath the passenger seat. I had slipped the Smith & Wesson into the map compartment on the driver's door as we approached the meeting place. Seeing Leon alone against the tree didn't make me feel any better.

We slowed and turned onto a small side road that ran past the oak tree. Leon didn't seem to register our presence. I killed the engine and we sat in the car, waiting for him to make a move. Louis had his hand on the SIG now and drew it up so that it lay along his thigh.

We looked at each other. I shrugged and got out of the car, leaning against the open door with the Smith & Wesson within reach. Louis climbed from the passenger side, stretched slightly to show Leon that his hands were empty, and then rested against the side of the car, the SIG now on the seat beside him.

Leon hauled himself from the tree and walked toward us. Other figures emerged from the trees around us. Five men, H&Ks hanging from their shoulders, long-bladed hunting knives at their belts, surrounded the car.

"Up against the car," said Leon. I didn't move. From around us came the sound of safeties clicking.

"Don't move, you die now," he said. I held his gaze, then turned and put my hands on the roof of the car. Louis did the same. As he stood behind me, Leon must have seen the SIG on the passenger seat but he didn't seem concerned. He patted my chest, beneath my arms, and checked my ankles and thighs. When he was satisfied that I wasn't wearing a wire, he did a similar check on Louis, then stepped back.

"Leave the car," he instructed. Headlights shone as engines started up around us. A brown Dodge sedan and a green Nissan Patrol burst through from behind the treeline, followed by a flatbed Ford pickup with three pirogues lashed down on the bed. If the Fontenot compound was under surveillance, then whoever was responsible needed his eyesight tested.

"We got some stuff in the car," I said to Leon. "We're gonna take it out." He nodded and watched as I removed the minisubs from behind the door panels. Louis took two magazines and handed one to me. The long cylinder stretched over the rear end of the receiver as I checked the safety at the front edge of the trigger guard. Louis placed a second magazine inside his jacket and tossed me a spare.

As we climbed into the back of the Dodge, two men drove our car out of sight and then jumped into the Nissan. Leon sat in the passenger seat of the Dodge beside the driver, a man in his fifties with long gray hair tied back in a ponytail, and indicated to him to move off. The other vehicles followed at a distance, so that we wouldn't look like a convoy to any passing cops.

We drove along the border of East and West Feliciana, Thompson Creek to our right, until we came to a turnoff that led down to the riverbank. Two more cars, an ancient Plymouth and what looked like an even older Volkswagen Beetle, were pulled up at the bank, and two more pirogues lay beside them. Lionel Fontenot, dressed in blue jeans and a blue work shirt, stood by the Edsel. He cast an eye over the Calicos but didn't say anything.

There were fourteen of us in all, most armed with H&Ks, two carrying M16 rifles, and we split three to a pirogue, with Lionel and the driver of the Dodge taking the lead in a smaller boat. Louis and I were separated and each handed a paddle, then we moved off upriver.

We rowed for twenty minutes, staying close to the western bank, before a darker shape appeared against the night sky. I could see lights flickering in windows and then, through a stand of trees, a small jetty against which a motorboat lay moored. The grounds of Joe Bones's house were dark.

There was a low whistle from in front of us and hands were raised in the pirogues to indicate that we should stop rowing. Sheltered by the trees, which hung out over the water, we waited in silence. A light flashed on the jetty, and briefly, the face of a guard was illuminated as he lit a cigarette. I heard a low splash somewhere in front of me, and high on the bank, an owl hooted. I could see the guard moving against the moon-haunted water, could hear the sound of his boots scuffing against the wooden jetty. Then a dark shape rose up beside him and the pattern of the moonlight on the water was disturbed. A knife flashed and the red ember of the cigarette tumbled through the night air like a signal of distress as the guard crumpled to the ground. He made hardly a sound as he was lowered into the water.

The ponytailed man stood waiting at the jetty as we paddled by, moving as close as we could to the grass bank beyond before we climbed from the pirogues and dragged them onto dry land. The bank rose up to join an expanse of green lawn, undisturbed by flowers or trees. It rolled uphill to the back of the house, where steps led up to a patio overlooked by two French windows at ground level and a gallery on the second floor, which mirrored the one on the front of the house. I caught a movement on the gallery and heard voices from the patio. Three guards at least, probably more at the front.

Lionel raised two fingers and singled out two men to my left. They moved forward cautiously, keeping low against the ground as they moved toward the house. They were about twenty yards in front of us when the house and grounds were suddenly illuminated with bright white light. The two men were caught like rabbits in headlights as shouts came from the house and automatic fire burst from the gallery. One of them spun like an ice skater who has missed his jump, blood bursting forth from his shirt like red flowers opening. He fell to the ground, his legs twisting, as his partner dived for the cover of a metal table, part of a lawn set that stood, semiobscured, by the riverbank.

The French windows opened and dark figures spilled out onto the patio. On the gallery, the guard was joined by two or three others, who raked the grass in front of us with heavy fire. From the sides of the house, muzzles flashed as more of Joe Bones's men inched their way around.

Close to where I lay, Lionel Fontenot swore. We were partly protected by the slope of the lawn as it curved down to meet the river, but the guards on the gallery were angling for clear shots at us. Some of Fontenot's men returned fire, but each time they did so, they exposed themselves to the guards at the house. One, a sharp-faced man in his forties with a mouth like a paper cut, grunted as a bullet hit him in the shoulder. He kept firing, even as the blood turned his shirt red.

"It's fifty yards from here to the house," I said. "There are guards moving in from the sides to cut us off. We don't move now, we're dead." A spray of earth kicked up by Fontenot's left hand. One of Joe Bones's men had progressed almost to the bank by approaching from the front of the house. Two bursts of M16 fire came from behind the metal lawn table and he tumbled sideways, rolling along the grass into the river.

"Tell your men to get ready," I hissed. "We'll cover you." The message was passed down the line.

"Louis!" I shouted. "You ready to try these things out?" A figure two men down from me responded with a wave and then the Calicos burst into life. One of the guards on the gallery bucked and danced as the 9 millimeter bullets from Louis's gun tore into him. I pushed the selector on the trigger guard fully forward and sent a burst of automatic fire across the patio. The French windows exploded in a shower of glass and a guard tumbled down the steps and lay unmoving on the lawn. Lionel Fontenot's men sprang from their cover and raced across the lawn, firing as they did so. I switched to single shot firing and concentrated on the eastern end of the house, sending wood splinters shooting into the air as I forced the men there to take cover.

Fontenot's men were almost at the patio when two fell, hit by fire from behind the ruined French windows. Louis sent a burst into the room beyond and Fontenot's men moved to the patio and entered the house. Exchanges of fire were coming from within as Louis and I rose and ran across the lawn.

To my left, the guy behind the lawn table abandoned his cover to join us. As he did so, something huge and dark appeared out of the shadows and launched itself from the grass with a deep, ferocious growl. The *boerbul* struck him on the chest, knocking him to the ground with its enormous weight. He shouted once, his hands pounding at the creature's head, and then the huge jaws closed on his neck and the *boerbul*'s head shook as he tore the man's throat apart.

The animal lifted its head and its eyes gleamed in the darkness as it found Louis. He was turning the Calico in its direction when it bounded from the dead body and sprang into the air. Its speed was astonishing. As it moved toward us, its dark form blotted out the stars in the sky above. It was at the apex of its jump when Louis's Calico sang and bullets ripped into it, causing it to spasm in midair and land with a crunch on the grass not two feet from us. Its paws scrambled for purchase and its mouth worked in biting motions, even as blood and froth spilled from between its teeth. Louis pumped more rounds into it until it lay still.

My eye caught movement at the western corner of the house as we neared the steps. A muzzle flashed and Louis yelled in pain. The Calico dropped to the ground as he leaped for the steps, cradling his injured hand. I fired three shots and the guard dropped. Behind me, one of Fontenot's men fired single shots from his M16 as he advanced toward the house, then let the gun hang from its shoulder strap as he reached the corner. I saw moonlight catch the blade of his knife as he stood waiting. The short muzzle of a Steyr appeared, followed by the face of one of Joe Bones's men. I recognized him as the one who had driven the golf cart to the plantation gates on our first visit here, but the flash of recognition became one with the flash of the knife as it struck across his neck. A crimson jet flew into the air from his severed artery, but even as he fell Fontenot's man raised the M16 once again and fired past him as he moved toward the front of the house.

Louis was examining his right hand as I reached him. The bullet had torn across the back of the hand, leaving a bad gash and damaging the knuckle of his forefinger. I tore a strip from the shirt of a dead guard who lay sprawled across the patio and wrapped it around Louis's hand. I handed him the Calico and he worked the strap over his head, then fitted his middle finger into the trigger guard. With his left hand he freed his SIG, then nodded to me as he rose. "We better find Joe Bones."

Through the patio doors lay a formal dining room. The dining table, which could seat at least eighteen people comfortably, was splintered and pitted by shots. On the wall, a portrait of a Southern gentleman standing by his horse had sustained a large hole through the horse's belly and a selection of antique china plates lay shattered in the remains of their glass-fronted display cabinet. There were two bodies in the room. One of them was the ponytailed man who had driven the Dodge.

The dining room led out into a large carpeted hallway and a white chandeliered reception area, from which a staircase wound up to the next floor. The other doors at ground level stood open, but there were no sounds coming from inside. There was sustained firing on the upper levels as we made our way to the stairs. At their base, one of Joe Bones's men lay in a pair of striped pajama bottoms, blood pooling from an ugly head wound.

From the top of the stairs, a series of doors stretched left and right. Fontenot's men seemed to have cleared most of the rooms, but they had been pinned down in the alcoves and doorways by gunfire from the rooms at the western end of the house, one on the river side to the right, its panels already pockmarked by bullets, and the other facing out to the front of the house. As we watched, a man in blue overalls carrying a short-handled axe in one hand and a captured Steyr in the other moved quickly from his hiding place to within one doorway of the front-facing room. Shots came through the door on the right and he fell to the ground, clutching his leg.

I leaned into an alcove in which the remains of long-stemmed roses lay in a pool of water and shattered pottery and fired a sustained burst at the door on the front-facing side. Two of Fontenot's men moved forward at the same time, keeping low on the ground as they did so. Across from me, Louis fired shots at the semiclosed river-side door. I stopped firing as Fontenot's men reached the room and rushed the occupant. There were two more shots, then one of them emerged wiping his knife on his trousers. It was Lionel Fontenot. Behind him was Leon.

The two men took up positions at either side of the last room. Six more of his men moved forward to join him.

"Joe, it's over now," said Lionel. "We gon' finish this thing."

Two shots burst through the door. Leon raised his H&K and appeared to be about to fire, but Lionel raised his hand, looking past Leon to where I stood. I advanced forward and waited behind Leon's back as Lionel pushed open the door with his foot, then pressed himself flat against the wall as two more shots rang out, followed by the click of a hammer on an empty chamber, a sound as final as the closing of a tomb.

Leon entered the room first, the H&K now replaced by his knives. I followed him, with Lionel behind me. The walls of Joe Bones's bedroom were marked with holes and the night air entered through the shattered window and sent the white curtains swirling in the air like angry ghosts. The blonde who had lunched with Joe on his lawn earlier in the week lay dead against the far wall, a red stain on the left breast of her silk nightgown.

Joe Bones stood before the window in a red silk dressing gown. The Colt in his hand hung uselessly at his side but his eyes glowed with anger and the scar on his lip seemed painfully pinched and white against his skin. He dropped the gun.

"Do it, you fuck," he hissed at Lionel. "Kill me, you got the fucking guts."

Lionel closed the bedroom door behind us as Joe Bones turned to look at the woman.

"Ask him," said Lionel.

Joe Bones didn't seem to hear. His face seemed consumed with a look of terrible grief as his eyes traced the contours of the dead woman's face. "Eight years," he said softly. "Eight years she was with me."

"Ask him," repeated Lionel Fontenot.

I stepped forward and Joe Bones sneered as he turned, that look of sadness now gone. "The fucking grieving widower. You bring your trained nigger with you?"

I slapped him hard and he took a step back.

"I can't save you, Joe, but if you help me maybe I can make it quicker for you. Tell me what Remarr saw the night the Aguillards died."

He wiped blood from the corner of his mouth, smearing it across his cheek. "You have no idea what you're dealing with, no fucking idea in the world. You're so out of your fucking depth, the fucking pressure should be making your nose bleed."

"He kills women and children, Joe. He's going to kill again."

Joe Bones twisted his mouth into the semblance of a grin, the scar distorting his full lips like a crack in a mirror. "You killed my woman and now you're gonna kill me, no matter what I say. You got nothing to bargain with," he said.

I glanced at Lionel Fontenot. He shook his head almost imperceptibly, but Joe Bones caught it. "See, nothing. All you can offer is a little less pain, and pain don't hold no surprises for me."

"He killed one of your own men. He killed Tony Remarr."

"Tony left a print at the nigger's house. He was careless and he paid the price. Your guy, he saved me the trouble of killing the old bitch and her brood myself. I meet him, I'll shake his hand."

Joe Bones smiled a broad smile like a flash of sunshine through dark, acrid smoke. Haunted by visions of tainted blood flowing through his veins, he had moved beyond ordinary notions of humanity and empathy, love and grief. In his shimmering red robe, he looked like a wound in the fabric of space and time.

"You'll meet him in Hell," I said.

"I see your bitch there, I'll fuck her for you." His eyes were bland and cold now. The smell of death hung around him like old cigar fumes. Behind me, Lionel Fontenot opened the door and the rest of his men walked quietly into the room. It was only now, seeing them all together in the ruined bedroom, that the resemblance between them became clear. Lionel held the door open for me.

"It's a family thing," he said as I left. Behind me, the door closed with a soft click like the knocking of bones.

After Joe Bones died, we gathered the bodies of the Fontenot dead on the lawn in front of the house. The five men lay side by side, crumpled and torn as only the dead can be. The gates to the plantation were opened and the Dodge, the VW and the pickup sped in. The bodies were loaded gently but quickly into the trunks of the cars, the injured helped into the rear seats. The pirogues were doused in gasoline, set on fire, and left to float down the river.

We drove from the plantation and kept driving until we reached the rendezvous point at Starhill. The three black Explorers I had seen at the Delacroix compound stood waiting, their motors idling, their lights dimmed. As Leon sprayed gasoline into the cars and the pickup, the bodies of the dead were removed, wrapped in tarps, and placed in the backs of two of the jeeps. Louis and I watched it all in silence.

As the jeeps roared into life and Leon threw lighted rags into the discarded vehicles, Lionel Fontenot walked over to us and stood with us as they burned. He took a small green notebook from his pocket, scribbled a number on a sheet, and tore it out.

"This guy will look after your friend's hand. He's discreet."

"He knew who killed Lutice, Lionel," I said.

He nodded. "Maybe. He wouldn't tell, not even at the end." He rubbed his index finger along a raw cut on the palm of his right hand, picking dirt from the wound. "I hear the feds are looking for someone around Baton Rouge, used to work in a hospital in New York."

I stayed silent and he smiled. "We know his name. Man could hide out in the bayou for a long time, he knew his way around. Feds might not find him, but we will." He gestured with his hand, like a king displaying his finest troops to his worried subjects. "We're looking. We find him, it'll end there."

Then he turned and climbed into the driver's seat of the lead jeep, Leon beside him, and they disappeared into the night, the red taillights like falling cigarettes in the darkness, like burning boats floating on black water.

I called Angel as we drove back to New Orleans. At an all-night drugstore I picked up antiseptic and a first-aid kit so we could work on Louis's hand. There was a sheen of sweat on his face as I drove and the white rags binding his fingers were stained a deep red. When we arrived back at the Flaisance, Angel cleansed the wound with the antiseptic and tried to stitch it with some surgical thread. The knuckle looked bad and Louis's mouth was stretched tight with pain. Despite his protests, I called the number we had been given. The bleary voice that answered the phone on the fourth ring shook the sleep from its tones when I mentioned Lionel's name.

Angel drove Louis to the doctor's office. When they had gone, I stood outside Rachel's door and debated whether or not to knock. I knew she wasn't asleep: Angel had spoken to her after I called, and I could sense her wakefulness. Still, I didn't knock, but as I walked back toward my own room her door opened. She stood in the gap, a white T-shirt reaching almost to her knees, and waited for me. She stood carefully aside to let me enter.

"You're still in one piece, I see," she said. She didn't sound particularly pleased.

I felt tired and sick from the sight of blood. I wanted to plunge my face into a sink of ice-cold water. I wanted a drink so badly my tongue felt swollen inside my mouth and only a bottle of Abita, ice frosting on its rim, and a shot of Redbreast whiskey could restore it to its normal size. My voice sounded like the croak of an old man on his deathbed when I spoke.

"I'm in one piece," I said. "A lot of others aren't. Louis took a bullet across the hand and too many people died out at the house. Joe Bones, most of his crew, his woman."

Rachel turned her back and walked to the balcony window. Only the bedside lamp lit the room, casting shadows over the illustrations that she had kept from Woolrich and that were now restored to their places on the walls. Flayed arms and the face of a woman and a young man emerged from the semidarkness.

"What did you find out, for all that killing?"

It was a good question. As usual with good questions, the answer didn't live up to it.

"Nothing, except that Joe Bones was happier to die painfully than to tell us what he knew."

She turned then. "What are you going to do now?"

I was getting tired of questions, especially questions as difficult as these. I knew she was right and I felt disgusted at myself. It felt as if Rachel had become tainted through her contact with me. Maybe I should have told her all of those things then, but I was too tired and too sick and I could smell blood in my nostrils; and, anyway, I think she already knew most of it.

"I'm going to bed," I said. "After that, I'm winging it." Then I left her.

CHAPTER XLVII

The next morning I awoke with an ache in my arms from toting the Calico, exacerbated by the lingering pain of the gunshot wound inflicted in Haven. I could smell powder on my fingers, in my hair, and on my discarded clothes. The room stank like the scene of a gunfight, so I opened the window and let the hot New Orleans air slip heavily into the room like a clumsy burglar.

I checked on Louis and Angel. Louis's hand had been expertly bound after the doctor picked the shards of bone from the wound and padded the knuckle. Louis barely opened his eyes as I exchanged a few quiet words with Angel at the door. I felt guilty for what had happened, although I knew that neither of them blamed me.

I sensed, too, that Angel was anxious now to return to New York. Joe Bones was dead, and the police and the feds were probably closing in on Edward Byron, despite Lionel Fontenot's doubts. Besides, I didn't believe that it would take long for Woolrich to connect us to what had happened to Joe Bones, especially if Louis was walking around with a bullet crease on his hand. I told Angel all of this and he agreed that they would leave as soon as I returned, so that Rachel would not be left alone. The whole case seemed to have ground to a kind of halt for me. Elsewhere, the feds and the Fontenots were hunting Edward Byron, a man who still seemed as distant from me as the last emperor of China.

I left a message for Morphy. I wanted to see what his people had on Byron; I wanted to add flesh to the figure. As things stood, he was as shorn of identity as the faceless figures of the slain that the feds believed he had left behind. The feds might well have been right. With the local police, they could conduct a better search than a bunch of visitors from New York with delusions of adequacy. I had hoped to work my way toward him from a different direction, but with the death of Joe Bones that path seemed to have come to an end in a tangle of dark undergrowth.

I took my phone and my book of Ralegh's writings and headed for Mother's on Poydras Street, where I drank too many cups of coffee and picked at some bacon and brown toast. When you reach one of life's dead ends, Ralegh is good company. "*Go soul . . . since I needs must die / And give the world the lie.*" Ralegh knew enough to take a stoical attitude to adversity, although he didn't know enough to avoid getting his head cut off.

Beside me, a man ate ham and eggs with the concentrated effort of a bad lover, yellow egg yolk tingeing his chin like sunlight reflected from a buttercup. Someone whistled a snatch of "What's New?" then lost his thread in the complicated chord changes of the song. The air was filled with the buzz of late morning conversation, a radio station easing into neutral with a bland rock song and the low, aggravated hum of distant, slow-moving traffic. Outside, it was another humid New Orleans day, the kind of day that leads lovers to fight and makes children sullen and grim.

An hour passed. I rang the detective squad in St. Martin and was told that Morphy had taken a day's leave to work on his house. I had nothing better to do now, so I paid my bill, put some gas in the car, and started out once again toward Baton Rouge. I found a Lafayette station playing some scratchy Cheese Read, followed by Buckwheat Zydeco and Clifton Chenier, an hour of classic Cajun and zydeco, as the DJ put it. I let it play until the city fell away and the sound and the landscape became one.

A sheet of plastic slapped dryly in the early afternoon wind as I pulled up outside Morphy's place. He was replacing part of the exterior wall on the west side of the house, and the lines holding the plastic in place over the exposed joints sang as the wind tried to yank them from their moorings. It tugged at one of the windows, which had not been fastened properly, and made the screen door knock at its frame like a tired visitor.

I called his name but there was no reply. I walked to the rear of the house, where the back door stood open, held in place by a piece of brick. I called again but my voice seemed to echo emptily through the central hallway. The rooms on the ground level were all unoccupied and no sounds came from upstairs. I drew my gun and climbed the stairs, newly planed in preparation for treating. The bedrooms were empty and the bathroom door stood wide open, toiletries neatly arranged by the sink. I checked the gallery and then went back downstairs. As I turned back toward the rear door, cold metal touched the base of my neck.

"Drop it," said a voice.

I let the gun slip from my fingers.

"Turn around. Slowly."

The pressure was removed from my neck and I turned to find Morphy standing before me, a nail gun held inches from my face. He let out a deep breath of relief and lowered the gun.

"Shit, you scared the hell out of me," he said.

I could feel my heart thumping wildly in my chest. "Thanks," I said. "I really needed that kind of adrenaline rush on top of five cups of coffee." I sat down heavily on the bottom step.

"You look terrible, mon. You up late last night?"

I looked up to see if there was an edge to what he had said, but he had turned his back.

"Kind of."

"You hear the news? Joe Bones and his crew were taken out last night. Someone cut Joe up pretty bad before he died, too. Police weren't even sure it was him until they checked the prints." He walked down to the kitchen and came back with a beer for himself and a soda for me. I noticed it was caffeine-free cola. Under his arm he held a copy of the *Times-Picayune.*

"You see this today?"

I took the paper from him. It was folded into quarter size, the bottom of the front page facing up. The headline read: POLICE HUNT SERIAL KILLER IN RITUAL MURDERS. The story below contained details of the deaths of *Tante* Marie Aguillard and Tee Jean that could only have come from the investigation team itself: the display of the bodies, the manner of their discovery, the nature of some of the wounds. It went on to speculate on a possible link between the discovery of Lutice Fontenot's body and the death of a man in Bucktown, known to have links with a leading crime figure. Worst of all, it said that police were also investigating a connection to a similar pair of murders in New York earlier this year. Susan and Jennifer were not named, but it was clear that the writer—anonymous beneath a "*Times-Picayune* Journalists" byline—knew enough about the murders to be able to put a name on the victims.

I put the paper down wearily. "Did the leak come from your guys?" I asked.

"Could have done, but I don't think so. The feds are blaming us: they're all over us, accusing us of sabotaging the investigation." He sipped his beer before saying what was on his mind.

"One or two people maybe felt that it could have been you who leaked the stuff." He was obviously uncomfortable saying it, but he didn't look away.

"I didn't do it. If they've got as far as Jennifer and Susan, it won't be too long before they connect me to what's happening. The last thing I need is the press crawling all over me."

He considered what I said, then nodded. "I guess you're right."

"You speak to the editor?"

"He was contacted at home when the first edition came out. We got freedom of the press and the protection of sources coming out our ass. We can't force him to tell but"—he rubbed at the tendons on the back of his neck—"it's unusual for something like this to happen. The papers are real careful about jeopardizing investigations. I think it had to come from someone close to all this."

I thought about it. "If they felt okay about using this stuff, then it must be cast iron and the source impeccable," I said. "It could be that the feds are playing their own game on this." It seemed to reaffirm our belief that Woolrich and his team were holding back, not only from me but probably from the police investigating team as well.

"It wouldn't be anything new," said Morphy. "Feds wouldn't tell us what day it is, they thought they could get away with it. You think they might have planted the story?"

"Somebody did."

Morphy finished his beer and crushed the can beneath his foot. A small stain of beer spread itself on the bare wood. He picked up a tool belt from where it hung on a hat stand near the door and strapped it on.

"You need any help?"

He looked at me. "Can you carry planks without falling over?"

"No."

"Then you're perfect for the job. There's a spare pair of work gloves in the kitchen."

For the rest of the afternoon I worked with my hands, hoisting and carrying, hammering and sawing. We replaced most of the wood on the west side, a gentle breeze spraying sawdust and shavings around us as we worked. Later, Angie returned from a shopping trip to Baton Rouge, carrying groceries and boutique bags. While Morphy and I cleaned up, she grilled steaks with sweet potatoes, carrots, and Creole rice, and we ate them in the kitchen as the evening drew in and the wind wrapped the house in its arms.

Morphy walked me out to my car. As I put the key in the ignition, he leaned in the window and said softly: "Someone tried to get to Stacey Byron yesterday. Know anything about it?"

"Maybe."

"You were there, weren't you? You were there when they took Joe Bones?"

"You don't want to know the answer to that," I replied. "Just like I don't want to know about Luther Bordelon."

As I drove away, I could see him standing before his uncompleted house. Then he turned away and returned to his wife.

WHEN I ARRIVED BACK at the Flaisance, Angel and Louis were packed and ready to go. They wished me luck and told me that Rachel had gone to bed early. She had booked a flight for the next day. I decided not to disturb her and went to my own room. I don't even remember falling asleep.

The luminous dial on my watch read 8:30 A.M. when the pounding came at my door. I had been in deep sleep and I pulled myself slowly into wakefulness like a diver struggling for the surface. I had got as far as the edge of the bed when the door exploded inward and there were lights shining in my face and strong arms hauled me to my feet and pushed me hard against the wall. A gun was held to my head as the main light came on in the room. I could see NOPD uniforms, a couple of plainclothesmen, and directly to my right, Morphy's partner Toussaint. Around me, men were tearing the room apart.

And I knew then that something had gone terribly, terribly wrong.

THEY ALLOWED ME TO pull on a tracksuit and a pair of sneakers before cuffing me. I was marched through the hotel, past guests peering anxiously from their rooms, to a waiting police car. In a second car, her face pale and her hair matted from sleep, sat Rachel. I shrugged helplessly at her before we were driven in convoy from the Quarter.

I was questioned for three hours, then given a cup of coffee and grilled again for another hour. The room was small and brightly lit. It smelled of cigarette smoke and stale sweat. In one corner, where the plaster was broken and worn, I could see what looked like a bloodstain. Two detectives, Dale and Klein, did most of the questioning, Dale assuming the role of aggressive interrogator, threatening to dump me in the swamp with a bullet in the head for killing a Louisiana cop, Klein taking the part of the reasonable, sensitive man trying to protect me while ensuring that the truth was told. Even with other cops as the object of their attentions, the good cop–bad cop thing never went out of fashion.

I told them all I could, again and again and again. I told them of my visit to Morphy, the work on the house, the dinner, the departure, all of the reasons why my prints were all over the house. No, Morphy hadn't given me the police files found in my room. No, I couldn't say who did. No, only the night porter saw me re-enter the hotel, I didn't speak to anyone else. No, I didn't leave my room again that night. No, there was no one to confirm that fact. No. No. No. No. No.

Then Woolrich arrived and the merry-go-round started all over again. More questions, this time with the feds in attendance. And still, no one told me why I was there or what had happened to Morphy and his wife. In the end, Klein returned and told me I could go. Behind a slatted-rail divider, which separated the detective squadroom from the main corridor, Rachel sat with a mug of tea while the detectives around her studiously ignored her. In a cage ten feet behind her, a skinny white man with tattooed arms whispered obscenely to her.

Toussaint appeared. He was an overweight, balding man in his early fifties, with straggly white curls around his pate like the top of a hill erupting from out of a mist. He looked red eyed and nauseous and was as out of place here as I was.

A patrolman motioned to Rachel. "We'll take you back to your hotel now, ma'am." She stood. Behind her, the guy in the cage made sucking noises and grabbed his crotch in his hand.

"You okay?" I asked as she passed by.

She nodded dumbly, then: "Are you coming with me?"

Toussaint was at my left hand. "He'll follow later," he said. Rachel looked over her shoulder at me as the patrolman led her away. I gave her a smile and tried to make it look reassuring, but my heart wasn't in it.

"Come on, I'll drive you back and buy you a coffee on the way," said Toussaint, and I followed him from the building.

We ended up in Mother's, where less than twenty-four hours before I had sat waiting for Morphy's call and where Toussaint would tell me how John Charles Morphy and his wife, Angela, had died.

Morphy had been due to work a special early duty that morning and Toussaint had dropped by to pick him up. They alternated pickup duties as it suited. That day, it happened to be Toussaint's turn.

The screen door was closed, but the front door behind stood open. Toussaint called Morphy's name, just as I had the afternoon before. He followed in my footsteps through the central hallway, checking the kitchen and the rooms to the right and left. He thought Morphy might have slept in, although he had never been late before, so he called up the stairs to the bedroom. There was no reply. He recalled that his stomach was already tightening as he worked his way up the stairs, calling Morphy's name, then Angie's, as he advanced. The door of their bedroom was partially open, but the angle obscured their bed.

He knocked once, then slowly opened the door. For a moment, the merest flashing splinter of a second, he thought he had disturbed their lovemaking, until the blood registered and he knew that this was a parody of all that love stood for, of all that it meant, and he wept then for his friend and his wife.

Even now, I seem to recall only snatches of what he said, but I can picture the bodies in my head. They were naked, facing each other on what had once been white sheets, their bodies locked together at the hips, their legs intertwined. From the waist, they leaned backward at arm's length from each other. Both had been cut from neck to stomach. Their rib cages had been split and pulled back, and each had a hand buried in the breast of the other. As he neared, Toussaint saw that each was holding the other's heart in the palm of a hand. Their heads hung back so that their hair almost touched their backs. Their eyes were gone, their faces removed, their mouths open in their final agony, their moment of death like an ecstasy. In them, love was reduced to an example to other lovers of the futility of love itself.

As Toussaint spoke, a wave of guilt swept over me and broke across my heart. I had brought this thing to their house. By helping me, Morphy and his wife had been marked for a terrible death, just as the Aguillards too seemed to have been tainted by their contact with me. I stank of mortality.

And in the midst of it all, some lines of verse seemed to float into my head and I could not recall how I had resurrected them, or who had given them to me in the first place. And it seemed to me that their source was important, although I could not tell why, except that in the lines there seemed to be echoes of what Toussaint had seen. But as I tried to remember a voice speaking them to me, it slipped away, and try as I might, I could not bring it back. Only the lines remained. Some metaphysical poet, I thought. Donne, perhaps. Yes, almost certainly Donne.

If th'unborne
Must learne, by my being cut up, and torne:
Kill, and dissect me, Love; for this
Torture against thine owne end is,
Rack't carcasses make ill Anatomies.

Remedium amoris, wasn't that the term? The torture and death of lovers as a remedy for love.

"He helped me," I said. "I involved him in this."

"He involved himself," Toussaint said. "He wanted to do it. He wanted to bring this guy to an end."

I held his gaze.

"For Luther Bordelon?"

Toussaint looked away. "What does it matter now?"

But I couldn't explain that in Morphy I saw something of myself, that I had felt for his pain, that I wanted to believe he was better than me. I wanted to know.

"Garza called the Bordelon thing," said Toussaint at last. "Garza killed him and then Morphy supplied the throwdown. That's what he said. Morphy was young. Garza shouldn't have put him in that situation, but he did, and Morphy's been paying for it ever since." And then he caught himself using the present tense and went silent.

Outside, people were living another day: working, touring, eating, flirting still continued despite all that had taken place, all that was happening. It seemed, somehow, that it should all have come to a halt, that the clocks should have been stopped and the mirrors covered, the doorbells silenced and the voices reduced to a respectful, hushed volume. Maybe if they had seen the pictures of Susan and Jennifer, of *Tante* Marie and Tee Jean, of Morphy and Angie, then they would have stopped and considered. And that was what the Traveling Man wanted: to provide, in the deaths of others, a reminder of the deaths of us all and the worthlessness of love and loyalty, of parenthood and friendship, of sex and need and joy, in the face of the emptiness to come.

As I stood to leave, something else came to me, something awful that I had almost forgotten, and I felt a deep, violent ache in my gut, which spread through my body until I was forced to lean against the wall, my hand scrabbling for purchase.

"Ah, God, she was pregnant."

I looked at Toussaint and his eyes briefly fluttered closed.

"He knew, didn't he?"

Toussaint said nothing, but there was despair in his eyes. I didn't ask what the Traveling Man had done to the unborn child, but in that instant, I saw a terrible progression over the last months of my life. It seemed that I had moved from the death of my own child, my Jennifer, to the deaths of many children, the victims of Adelaide Modine and her partner, Hyams, and now, finally, to the deaths of all children. Everything this Traveling Man did signified something beyond itself: in the death of Morphy's unborn child, I saw all hope for the future reduced to tattered flesh.

"I'm supposed to bring you back to your hotel," said Toussaint at last. "The New Orleans PD will make sure you get on the evening flight back to New York."

But I hardly heard him. All I could think was that the Traveling Man had been watching us all along and that his game was still going on around us. We were all participants, whether we wanted to be or not.

And I recalled something that a con man named Saul Mann had once told me back in Portland, something that seemed important to me yet I couldn't recall why.

You can't bluff someone who isn't paying attention.

CHAPTER XLVIII

Toussaint dropped me at the Flaisance. Rachel's door was half open when I reached the carriage house. I knocked gently and entered. Her clothes had been thrown across the bedroom floor and the sheets from her bed were tossed in an untidy pile in the corner. All of her papers were gone. Her suitcase sat open on the bare mattress. I heard movement from the bathroom and she emerged carrying her cosmetics case. It was stained with powder and foundation and I guessed that the cops had broken some of its contents during their search.

She was wearing a faded blue Knicks sweat top, which hung down over her dark blue denims. She had washed and showered and her damp hair clung to her face. Her feet were bare. I had not noticed before how small they were.

"I'm sorry," I said.

"I know." She didn't look at me. Instead, she started to pick up her clothes and fold them as neatly as she could into her suitcase. I bent down to pick up a pair of socks, which lay in a ball by my feet.

"Leave it," she said. "I can do it."

There was another knock at the door and a patrolman appeared. He was polite, but he made it clear that we were to stay in the hotel until someone arrived to take us to the airport.

I went back to my room and showered. A maid came and made

up the room and I sat on my clean sheets and listened to the sounds from the street. I thought about how badly I had screwed up, and how many people had been killed because of it. I felt like the Angel of Death; if I stood on a lawn, the grass would die.

I must have dozed for a while, because the light in the room had changed when I awoke. It seemed that it was dusk, yet that could not have been the case. There was a smell in the room, an odor of rotting vegetation and water filled with algae and dead fish. When I tried to take a breath, the air felt warm and humid in my mouth. I was conscious of movement around me, shapes shifting in the shadows at the corners of the room. I heard whispered voices and a sound like silk brushing against wood and, faintly, a child's footsteps running through leaves. Trees rustled and there came a flapping of wings from above me, beating unevenly as if the bird was in distress or pain.

The room grew darker, turning the wall facing me to black. The light through the window frame was tinged with blue and green and shimmered as seen through a heat haze.

Or through water.

They came from out of the dark wall, black shapes against green light. They brought with them the coppery scent of blood, so strong that I could taste it on my tongue. I opened my mouth to call out something—even now, I am not sure what I could have called, or who would have heard—but the dank humidity stilled my tongue like a sponge soaked in warm, filthy water. It seemed that a weight was on my chest, preventing me from rising, and I had trouble taking air into my lungs. My hands clasped and unclasped until they too were still and I knew then how it felt to have ketamine coursing through one's veins, stilling the body in preparation for the anatomist's knife.

The figures stopped at the edge of the darkness, just beyond the reach of the window's dim light. They were indistinct, their edges forming and reforming like figures seen through frosted glass, or a projection losing and then regaining its focus.

And then the voices came,

birdman

soft and insistent,

birdman

fading and then strong again,

birdman

voices that I had never heard and others that had called out to me in passion,

bird

in anger, in fear, in love.

daddy

She was the smallest of them all, linked hand in hand with another who stood beside her. Around them, the others fanned out. I counted eight in all and, behind them, other figures, more indistinct, women, men, young girls. As the pressure built on my chest and I struggled to draw the shallowest of breaths, it came to me that the figure that had haunted *Tante* Marie Aguillard, that Raymond believed he had seen at Honey Island, the girl who seemed to call out to me through dark waters, might not have been Lutice Fontenot.

chile

Each breath felt like my last, none getting farther than the back of my throat before it was choked in a gasp.

chile

The voice was old and dark as the ebony keys on an ancient piano singing out from a distant room.

wake up, chile, his world is unraveling

And then my last breath sounded in my ears and all was stillness and quiet.

I WOKE TO THE sound of a tapping on my door. Outside, daylight had passed its height and was ebbing toward evening. When I opened the door, Toussaint stood before me. Behind him, I could see Rachel waiting. "It's time to go," he said.

"I thought the New Orleans cops were taking care of that."

"I volunteered," he replied. He followed me into the room as I threw my shaving gear loosely into my suit carrier, folded it over, and attached the clasps. It was London Fog, a present from Susan.

Toussaint nodded to the NOPD patrolman.

"You sure this is okay?" said the cop. He looked distracted and uncertain.

"Look, New Orleans cops got better things to be doing than baby-sitting," replied Toussaint. "I'll get these people to their plane; you go out and catch some bad guys, okay?"

We drove in silence to Moisant Field. I sat in the passenger seat, Rachel sat in the back. I waited for Toussaint to take the turn to the airport but he continued straight on 10.

"You missed your turn," I said.

"No," said Toussaint. "No, I didn't."

WHEN THINGS START TO unravel, they unravel fast. We got lucky that day. Everybody gets lucky some time.

On a junction of the Upper Grand River, southeast of 10 on the road to Lafayette, a dredging operation to remove silt and junk from the bottom of the river got some of its machinery caught up on a batch of discarded barbed wire that was rusting away on the riverbed. They eventually freed it and tried to haul it up, but there were other things caught in the wire as well: an old iron bedstead; a set of slave irons, more than a century and a half old; and, holding the wire to the bottom, an oil drum marked with a fleur-de-lys.

It was almost a joke to the dredging crew as they worked to free the drum. The report of the discovery of a girl's body in a fleur-de-lys drum had been all over the news bulletins and it had taken up ninety lines below the fold on the *Times-Picayune* on the day of its discovery.

Maybe the crew joshed one another morbidly as they worked the barrel out of the water in order to get at the wire. Perhaps they went a little quieter, barring the odd nervous laugh, as one of them worked at the lid. The drum had rusted in places and the lid had not been welded shut. When it came off, dirty water, dead fish, and weeds flowed out.

The legs of the girl, partially decayed but surrounded by a strange, waxy membrane, emerged from the open lid as well, although her body remained jammed, half in, half out of the drum. The river life had fed on her but when one man shined his flashlight to the end of the drum he could see the tattered remains of skin at the forehead and her teeth seemed to be smiling at him in the darkness.

ONLY TWO CARS WERE at the scene when we arrived. The body had been out of the water for less than three hours. Two uniformed cops stood by with the dredging crew. Around the body stood three men in plain clothes, one of them wearing a slightly more expensive suit than the rest, his silver hair cut short and neat. I recognized him from the aftermath of Morphy's death: Sheriff James Dupree of St. Martin Parish, Toussaint's superior.

Dupree motioned us forward as we stepped from the car. Rachel hung back slightly but still moved toward the body in the drum. It was the quietest crime scene at which I had ever been present. Even when the coroner appeared later, it remained restrained.

Dupree pulled a pair of plastic gloves from his hands, making sure that he didn't touch their exterior with his exposed fingers. His nails were very short and very clean, I noticed, although not manicured.

"You want to take a closer look?" he asked.

"No," I said. "I've pretty much seen all I want to see."

There was a rotten, pungent odor coming from the mud and silt dredged up by the crew, stronger even than the smell from the girl's body. Birds hovered over the detritus, trying to target dead or dying fish. One of the crew lodged his cigarette in his mouth, bent to pick up a stone, and hurled it at a huge gray rat that scuttled in the dirt. The stone hit the mud with a wet, thudding sound like a piece of meat dropped on a butcher's slab. The rat scurried away.

Around it, other gray objects burst into activity. The whole area was alive with rodents, disturbed from their nests by the actions of the dredging crew. They bumped and snapped at one another, their tails leaving snaking lines in the mud. The rest of the crew now joined in, casting stones in a skimming motion close to the ground. Most of them had better aims than their friend.

Dupree lit a cigarette with a gold Ronson lighter. He smoked Gitanes, the only cop I had ever seen do so. The smoke was acrid and strong and the breeze blew it directly into my face. Dupree apologized and turned so that his body partially shielded me from the smoke. It was a peculiarly sensitive gesture and it made me wonder, once again, why I was not sitting at Moisant Field.

"They tell me you tracked down that child killer in New York, the Modine woman," said Dupree eventually. "After thirty years, that's no mean feat."

"She made a mistake," I said. "In the end, they all do. It's just a matter of being in the right place at the right time to take advantage of the situation."

He tilted his head slightly to one side, as if he didn't entirely agree with what I had said but was prepared to give it a little thought in case he'd missed something. He took another long drag on his cigarette. It was an upmarket brand, but he smoked it the way I had seen longshoremen on the New York docks smoke, the butt held between the thumb and the first two fingers of the hand, the ember shielded by the palm. It was the sort of hold you learned as a kid, when smoking was still a furtive pleasure and being caught with a cigarette was enough to earn you a smack across the back of the head from your old man.

"I guess we all get lucky sometimes," said Dupree. He looked at me closely. "I'm wondering if maybe we've got lucky here."

I waited for him to continue. There seemed to be something fortuitous in the discovery of the girl's body, or perhaps I was still remembering a dream in which shapes came out of my bedroom wall and told me that a thread in the tapestry being woven by the Traveling Man had suddenly come loose.

"When Morphy and his wife died, my first instinct was to take you outside and beat you to within an inch of your life," he said. "He was a good man, a good detective, despite everything. He was also my friend.

"But he trusted you, and Toussaint here seems to trust you too. He thinks maybe you provide a linking factor in all this. If that's true, then putting you on a plane back to New York isn't going to achieve anything. Your FBI friend Woolrich seemed to feel the same way, but there were louder voices than his shouting for you to be sent home."

He took another drag on his cigarette. "I reckon you're like gum caught in someone's hair," he continued. "The more they try to pry you out, the more you get stuck in, and maybe we can use that. I'm risking a storm of shit by keeping you here, but Morphy told me what you felt about this guy, how you believed he was observing us, manipulating us. You want to tell me what you make of this, or do you want to spend the night at Moisant sleeping on a chair?"

I looked at the bare feet and exposed legs of the girl in the drum, the strange yellow accretion like a chrysalis, lying in a pool of filth and water on a rat-infested stretch of a river in western Louisiana. The coroner and his men had arrived with a body bag and a stretcher. They positioned a length of plastic on the ground and carefully maneuvered the drum onto it, one of them supporting the girl's legs with a gloved hand. Then slowly, gently, the coroner's hands working inside the drum, they began to free her.

"Everything we've done so far has been dogged and predicted by this man," I began. "The Aguillards learned something, and they died. Remarr saw something, and he was killed. Morphy tried to help me, and now he's dead as well. He's closing off the options, forcing us to follow a pattern that he's already set. Now someone's been leaking details of the investigation to the press. Maybe that person has been leaking things to this man as well, possibly unintentionally, possibly not."

Dupree and Toussaint exchanged a look. "We've been considering that possibility as well," said Dupree. "There are too many damn people crawling over this for anything to stay quiet for long."

"On top of all that," I continued, "the feds are keeping something back. You think Woolrich has told you everything he knows?"

Dupree almost laughed. "I know as much about this guy Byron as I know about the poet, and that's sweet FA."

From inside the drum came a scraping sound, the sound of bone rubbing on metal. Gloved hands supported the girl's naked, discolored body as it was freed from the confines of the drum.

"How long can we keep the details quiet?" I asked Dupree.

"Not long. The feds will have to be informed, the press will find out." He spread his hands in a gesture of helplessness. "If you're suggesting that I don't tell the feds . . ." But I could see in his face that he was already moving in that direction, that the reason why the coroner was examining the body so soon after its discovery, the reason why there were so few police at the scene, was to keep the details limited to the minimum number of people.

I decided to push him. "I'm suggesting you don't tell *anyone* about this. If you do, the man who did this will be alerted and he'll cut us off again. If you're put in a position where you have to say something, then fudge it. Don't mention the barrel, obscure the location, say you don't believe the discovery is connected to any other investigation. Say nothing until the girl is identified."

"Assuming that we can identify her," said Toussaint mournfully.

"Hey, you want to rain someplace else?" snapped Dupree.

"Sorry," said Toussaint.

"He's right," I said. "We may not be able to identify her. That's a chance we'll have to take."

"Once we exhaust our own records, we'll have to use the feds," said Dupree.

"We'll burn that bridge when we come to it," I responded. "Can we do this?"

Dupree shuffled his feet and finished his cigarette. He leaned through the open window of his car and put the butt into the ashtray.

"Twenty-four hours max," he said. "After that, we'll be accused of incompetence or deliberately impeding the progress of an investigation. I'm not even sure how far we'll get in that time, although"—he looked at Toussaint, then back to me—"it may not come to that."

"You want to tell me," I said, "or do I have to guess?"

It was Toussaint who answered.

"The feds think they've found Byron. They're going to move on him by morning."

"In which case, this is just a backup," said Dupree. "The joker in our pack."

But I was no longer listening. They were moving on Byron, but I would not be there. If I tried to participate, then a sizable portion of the Louisiana law enforcement community would be used to put me on a plane to New York or to lock me in a cell.

THE CREW WERE LIKELY to be the weakest link. They were taken aside and given cups of coffee, then Dupree and I were as honest with them as we felt we could be. We told them that if they didn't keep quiet about what they had seen for at least one day, then the man who had killed the girl would probably get away and that he would kill again. It was at least partly true; cut off from the hunt for Byron, we were continuing the investigation as best we could.

The crew was made up of hardworking local men, most of them married with children of their own. They agreed to say nothing until we contacted them and told them that it was okay to do so. They meant what they said, but I knew that some of them would tell their wives and their girlfriends as soon as they got home, and word of what had happened would spread from there. A man who says he tells his wife everything is either a liar or a fool, my first sergeant used to say. Unfortunately, he was divorced.

Dupree had been in his office when the call came through and had picked pairs of deputies and detectives whom he trusted implicitly. With the addition of Toussaint, Rachel, and me, along with the coroner's team and the dredging crew, maybe twenty people knew of the discovery of the body. It was nineteen people too many to keep a secret for long, but that couldn't be helped.

After the initial examination and photography, it was decided to bring the body to a private clinic outside Lafayette, where the coroner sometimes consulted, and he agreed to commence his work almost immediately. Dupree prepared a statement detailing the discovery of a woman of unspecified age, cause of death unknown, some five miles from the actual location of the discovery. He dated it, timed it, then left it under a sheaf of files on his desk.

By the time we both arrived at the autopsy room, the remains had been X-rayed and measured. The mobile cart that had brought the body in had been pushed into a corner, away from the autopsy table on its cylindrical tank, which delivered water to the table and collected the fluids that drained through the holes on the table itself. A scale for the weighing of organs hung from a metal frame, and beside it, a small-parts dissection table on its own base stood ready for use.

Only three people, apart from the coroner and his assistant, attended the autopsy. Dupree and Toussaint were two. I was the third. The smell was strong and only partly masked by the antiseptic. Dark hair hung from her skull, and the skin that was left was shrunken and torn. The girl's remains were almost completely covered by the yellow-white substance.

It was Dupree who asked the question. "Doc, what is that stuff on the body?"

The examiner's name was Dr. Emile Huckstetter, a tall, stocky man in his early sixties with a ruddy complexion. He ran a gloved finger over the substance before he responded.

"It's a condition called adipocere," he said. "It's rare—I've seen maybe two or three cases at most, but the combination of silt and water in that canal seems to have resulted in its development here."

His eyes narrowed as he leaned toward the body. "Her body fats broke down in the water and they've hardened to create this substance, the adipocere. She's been in the water for a while. This stuff takes at least six months to form on the trunk, less on the face. I'm taking a stab here, but I figure she's been in the water for less than seven months, certainly no more than that."

Huckstetter detailed the examination into a small microphone attached to his green surgical scrubs. The girl was seventeen or eighteen, he said. She had not been tied or bound. There was evidence of a blade's slash at her neck, indicating a deep cut across her carotid artery as the probable cause of death. There were marks on her skull where her face had been removed and similar marks in her eye sockets.

As the examination drew to a close, Dupree was paged, and minutes later, he arrived back with Rachel. She had checked into a Lafayette motel, storing both her own baggage and mine, then returned. She recoiled initially at the sight of the body, then stood beside me and, without speaking, took my hand.

When the coroner was done, he removed his gloves and commenced scrubbing. Dupree took the X rays from the case envelope and held them up to the light, each in turn. "What's this?" he said, after a time.

Huckstetter took the X ray from his hand and examined it himself. "Compound fracture, right tibia," he said, pointing with his finger. "Probably two years old. It's in the report, or it will be as soon as I can compile it."

I felt a falling sensation and an ache spreading across my stomach. I reached out to steady myself and the scales jangled as I glanced against their frame. Then my hand was on the autopsy table and my fingers were touching the girl's remains. I pulled my hand back quickly, but I could still smell her on my fingers.

"Parker?" said Dupree. He reached out and gripped my arm to steady me. I could still feel the girl on my fingers.

"My God," I said. "I think I know who she is."

IN THE EARLY MORNING light, near the northern tip of Bayou Courtableau, south of Krotz Springs and maybe twenty miles from

Lafayette, a team of federal agents, backed up by St. Landry Parish sheriff's deputies, closed in on a shotgun house that stood with its back to the bayou, its front sheltered by overgrown bushes and trees. Some of the agents wore dark rain gear with *FBI* in large yellow letters on the back, others helmets and body armor. They advanced slowly and quietly, their safeties off. When they spoke, they did so quickly and with the fewest possible words. Radio contact was kept to a minimum. They knew what they were doing. Around them, deputies armed with pistols and shotguns listened to the sound of their breathing and the pumping of their hearts as they prepared to move on the house of Edward Byron, the man they believed to be directly responsible for the deaths of their colleague, John Charles Morphy, his young wife, and at least five other people.

The house was run down, the slates on the roof damaged and cracked in places, the roof beams already rotting. Two of the windows at the front of the house were broken and had been covered with cardboard held in place by duct tape. The wood on the gallery was warped and, in places, missing altogether. On a metal hook to the right of the house hung the carcass of a wild pig, newly skinned. Blood dripped from its snout and pooled on the ground below.

On a signal from Woolrich, shortly after 6 A.M., agents in Kevlar body armor approached the house from the front and the rear. They checked the windows at either side of the front door and adjoining the rear entrance. Then, simultaneously, they hit the doors, moving into the central hallway with maximum noise, their flashlights burning through the darkness of the interior.

The two teams had almost reached each other when a shotgun roared from the back of the house and blood erupted in the dim light. An agent named Thomas Seltz plunged forward as the shot ripped through the unprotected area of his armpit, the vulnerable point in upper-body armor, his finger tightening in a last reflex on the trigger of his machine pistol as he died. Bullets raked across the wall, ceiling, and floor as he fell, sending dust and splinters through the air and injuring two agents, one in the leg and one in the mouth.

The firing masked the sound of another shell being pumped into the shotgun. The second shot blasted wood from the frame of an interior door as agents hit the ground and began firing through the now empty rear door. A third shot took out an agent moving fast around the side of the house. A mass of logs and old furniture, destined for firewood, lay scattered on the ground, dispersed when the shooter broke from his hiding place beneath it. The sound of small-arms fire directed into the bayou reached the agents as they knelt to tend to their injured colleagues or ran to join the chase.

A figure in worn blue jeans and a white-and-red check shirt had disappeared into the bayou. The agents followed warily, their legs sinking almost to the knee at times in the muddy swamp water, dead tree trunks forcing them to deviate from a straight advance, before they reached firm ground. Using the trees as cover, they moved slowly, their guns at their shoulders, sighting as they went.

There was the roar of a shotgun from ahead. Birds scattered from the trees and splinters shot out at head height from a huge cypress. An agent screamed in pain and stumbled into view, impaled in the cheek by the shards of wood. A second blast rang out and shattered the femur in his left leg. He collapsed on the dirt and leaves, his back arched in agony.

Automatic fire raked the trees, shattering branches and blasting foliage. After four or five seconds of concentrated firing, the order went out to cease fire and the swamp was quiet once again. The agents and police advanced once more, moving quickly from tree to tree. A shout went up as blood was found by a willow, its broken branches white as bone.

From behind came the sounds of dogs barking as the tracker, who had been kept in reserve three miles away, was brought in to assist. The dogs were allowed to sniff around Byron's clothing and the area of the woodpile. Their handler, a thin, bearded man with his jeans tucked into muddy boots, let them smell the blood by the willow as soon as he caught up with the main party. Then, the dogs straining at their leashes, they moved on cautiously.

But no more shots came at them from Edward Byron, because the lawmen were not the only ones hunting him in the swamp.

WHILE THE HUNT CONTINUED for Byron, Toussaint, two young deputies, and I were in the sheriff's office in St. Martinville, where we continued our trawl through Miami's dentists, using emergency numbers from answering machines where necessary.

Rachel provided the only interruption, when she arrived with coffee and hot Danishes. She stood behind me and gently laid a hand on the back of my neck. I reached around and clasped her fingers, then pulled them forward and lightly kissed their tips.

"I didn't expect you to stay," I said. I couldn't see her face.

"It's almost at an end, isn't it?" she asked quietly.

"I think so. I feel it coming."

"Then I want to see it out. I want to be there at the end."

She stayed for a little longer, until her exhaustion became almost contagious. Then she returned to the motel to sleep.

It took thirty-eight calls before the dental assistant at Erwin Holdman's dental surgery at Brickell Avenue found the name of Lisa Stott on her records, but she declined even to confirm if Lisa Stott had attended during the last six months. Holdman was on the golf course and didn't like being disturbed, the assistant said. Toussaint told her that he didn't give a good goddamn what Holdman liked or didn't like and she gave him a cell phone number.

She was right. Holdman didn't like being disturbed on the golf course, especially when he was about to make a birdie on the fifteenth. After some shouting, Toussaint requested Lisa Stott's dental records. The dentist wanted to seek the permission of her mother and stepfather. Toussaint handed the phone to Dupree and Dupree told him that, for the present, that wasn't possible, that they only wanted the records in order to eliminate the girl from their inquiries and it would be unwise to disturb the parents unnecessarily.

When Holdman continued to refuse to cooperate, Dupree warned him that he would ensure that all his records were seized and his tax affairs subjected to microscopic examination.

Holdman cooperated. The records were kept on computer, he said, along with copies of X rays and dental charts that had been scanned in. He would send them on as soon as he returned to his office. His dental assistant was new, he explained, and wouldn't be able to send on the records electronically without his password. He would just finish his round . . .

There was some more shouting and Holdman decided to suspend his golfing activities for that day. It would take him one hour, traffic permitting, to get back to his surgery. We sat back to wait.

BYRON HAD MADE IT about a mile into the swamp. The cops were closing and his arm was bleeding badly. The bullet had shattered the elbow of his left arm and a steady current of pain was coursing through his body. He paused in a small clearing and reloaded the shotgun by tensing the stock against the ground and pumping awkwardly with his good hand. The barking was closer now. He would take the dogs as soon as they came in sight. Once they were gone, he would lose the lawmen in the swamp.

It was probably only when he rose that he first became aware of the movement in front of him. The pack couldn't have got around him already, he reasoned. The waters were deeper to the west. Without boats, they would not have been able to make it into the swamp from the road. Even if they had, he would have heard them coming. His senses had become attuned to the sounds of the swamp. Only the hallucinations threatened to undo him, but they came and went.

Byron crooked the shotgun awkwardly beneath his right arm and moved forward, his eyes moving constantly. He advanced slowly toward the treeline, but the movement seemed to have stopped. Maybe he shook his head then to clear his sight, fearing the onset of the visions, but they didn't come. Instead, death came for Edward Byron as the woods came alive around him and he was surrounded by dark figures. He loosed off one shot before the gun was wrenched from his grip and he felt a pain shoot across his chest as the blade opened his skin from shoulder to shoulder.

The figures surrounded him—hard-faced men, one with an M16 slung over his shoulder, the others armed with knives and axes, all led by a huge man with reddish brown skin and dark hair streaked with gray. Byron fell to his knees as blows rained down on his back and arms and shoulders. Dazed with pain and exhaustion, he looked up in time to see the big man's axe scything through the air above him.

Then all was darkness.

WE WERE USING DUPREE'S office, where a new PC sat ready to receive the dental records Holdman was sending. I sat in a red vinyl chair that had been repaired so often with tape that it was like sitting on cracking ice. The chair squeaked as I shifted in it, my feet on the windowsill. Across from me was the couch on which I had earlier caught three hours of uncomfortable sleep.

Toussaint had gone off to get coffee thirty minutes before. He still hadn't come back. I was starting to get restless when I heard the sound of voices raised from the squad room beyond. I passed through the open door of Dupree's office and into the squad room, with its rows of gray metal desks, its swivel chairs, and hat stands, its bulletin boards and coffee cups, its half-eaten bagels and donuts.

Toussaint appeared, talking excitedly to a black detective in a blue suit and open-collar shirt. Behind him, Dupree was talking to a uniformed patrolman. Toussaint saw me, patted the black detective on the shoulder, and walked over to me.

"Byron's dead," he said. "It was messy. The feds lost two men, couple more injured. Byron broke for the swamp. When they found him, someone had cut him up and split his skull with an axe. They've got the axe and a lot of boot prints." He fingered his chin. "They think maybe Lionel Fontenot decided to finish things his way."

Dupree ushered us into his office, but didn't close the door. He stood close to me and touched my arm gently.

"It's him. Things are still confused, but they've got sample jars matching the one in which your daughter's"—he paused, then rephrased it—"the jar that you received. They've got a laptop computer, the remains of some kind of homemade speaker attachment, and scalpels with tissue remains, most of it found in a shed at the back of the property. I talked to Woolrich, briefly. He mentioned something about old medical texts. Said to tell you that you were right. They're still searching for the faces of the victims, but that could take some time. They're going to start digging around the house later today."

I wasn't sure what I felt. There was relief, a sense of a weight being lifted and taken away, a sense that it had all come to a close. But there was also something more: I felt disappointment that I had not been there at the end. After all that I had done, after all the people who had died, both at my hands and the hands of others, the Traveling Man had eluded me right until the end.

Dupree left and I sat down heavily in the chair, the sunlight filtering through the shades on the window. Toussaint sat on the edge of Dupree's desk and watched me. I thought of Susan and Jennifer and of days spent in the park together. And I remembered the voice of *Tante* Marie Aguillard, and I hoped that she was now at peace.

A low, two-note signal beeped from Dupree's PC at regular intervals. Toussaint hauled himself from the desk and walked around to where he could see the screen of the PC. He tapped some keys and read what was on-screen.

"It's Holdman's stuff coming through," he said.

I joined him at the screen and watched as Lisa Stott's dental records appeared, detailed in words, then as a kind of two-dimensional map of her mouth with fillings and extractions marked, and then in the form of a mouth X ray.

Toussaint called up the coroner's X ray from a separate file and set the two images side by side.

"They look the same," he said.

I nodded. I didn't want to think of the implications if they were.

Toussaint called up Huckstetter, told him what we had, and asked him to come over. Thirty minutes later, Dr. Emile Huckstetter was running through Holdman's file, comparing it with his own notes and the X-ray images he had taken from the dead girl. At last, he pushed his glasses up on his forehead and pinched the corners of his eyes.

"It's her," he said.

Toussaint let out a long, jagged breath and shook his head in sorrow. It was the Traveling Man's last jest, it seemed, the old jest. The dead girl was Lisa Stott, or, as she once was known, Lisa Woolrich, a young girl who had become an emotional casualty of her parents' bitter divorce, who had been abandoned by a mother anxious to start a new life without the complication of an angry, hurt teenage daughter, and whose father was unable to provide her with the stability and support she needed.

She was Woolrich's daughter.

CHAPTER XLIX

The voice on the telephone was heavy with tiredness and tension.

"Woolrich, it's Bird." I spoke as I drove; a St. Martin's deputy had retrieved the rented car from the Flaisance.

"Hey." There was no life to the word. "What have you heard?"

"That Byron's dead, some of your men too. I'm sorry."

"Yeah, it was a mess. They call you in New York?"

"No." I debated whether or not to tell him the truth and decided not to. "I missed the flight. I'm heading toward Lafayette."

"*Lafayette?* Shit, what you doin' in Lafayette?"

"Hanging around." With Toussaint and Dupree, it had been decided that I should talk to Woolrich. Someone had to tell him that his daughter had been found. "Can you meet me?"

"Shit, Bird, I'm on my last legs here." Then, resignedly: "Sure, I'll meet you. We can talk about what happened today. Give me an hour. I'll meet you in the Jazzy Cajun, off the highway. Anyone will tell you where it is." I could hear him coughing at the other end of the phone.

"Your lady friend go home?"

"No, she's still here."

"That's good," he said. "It's good to have someone with you at times like this." Then he hung up.

THE JAZZY CAJUN WAS a small dark bar annexed to a motel, with pool tables and a country music jukebox. Behind the bar, a woman restocked the beer while Willie Nelson played over the speakers.

Woolrich arrived shortly after I began drinking my second coffee. He was carrying a canary yellow jacket and the armpits of his shirt were stained with sweat. The shirt itself was marked with dirt on the back and sleeves, and one elbow was torn. His tan trousers were dark with mud at the cuffs and hung over mud-encrusted, ankle-high boots. He ordered a bourbon and a coffee, then took a seat beside me near the door. We didn't say anything for a time, until Woolrich drained half of his bourbon and began sipping at his coffee.

"Listen, Bird," he began. "I'm sorry for what went down between us this last week or so. We were both trying to bring this to an end our own way. Now that it's done, well . . ." He shrugged and tipped his glass at me before draining it and signaling for another. There were black stains beneath his eyes and I could see the beginnings of a painful boil at the base of his neck. His lips were dry and cracked and he winced as the bourbon hit the inside of his mouth. He noticed my look. "Mouth ulcers," he explained. "They're a bitch." He took another sip of coffee. "I guess you want to hear what happened."

I shook my head. I wanted to put off the moment, but not like that.

"What are you going to do now?" I asked.

"Sleep," he said. "Then maybe take some time off, go down to Mexico and see if I can't rescue Lisa from these goddamn religious freaks."

I felt a pain in my heart and stood suddenly. I wanted a drink as badly as I had ever wanted anything before in my life. Woolrich didn't seem to notice my lack of composure, or even register that I was walking toward the men's room. I could feel sweat on my forehead and my skin felt hypersensitive, as if I was about to come down with a fever.

"She's been asking after you, Birdman," I heard him say, and I stopped dead.

"What did you say?" I didn't turn around.

"She asks after you," he repeated.

I turned then. "When did you hear from her last?"

He waved the glass. "Couple of months back, I suppose. Two or three."

"You sure?"

He stopped and stared at me. I hung by a thread over a dark place and watched as something small and bright separated from the whole and disappeared into the blackness, never to be found again. The surroundings of the bar fell away and there was only Woolrich and me, alone, with nothing to distract either of us from the other's words. There was no ground beneath my feet, no air above me. I heard a howling in my head as images and memories coursed through my mind.

Woolrich standing on the porch, his finger on the cheek of Florence Aguillard.

"I call this my metaphysical tie, my George Herbert tie."

A couplet from Ralegh, from "The Passionate Man's Pilgrimage," the poem from which Woolrich so loved to quote: *"Blood must be my bodies balmer/No other balme will there be given."*

The second phone call I had received in the Flaisance, the one during which the Traveling Man had allowed no questions, the one during which Woolrich was in attendance.

"They have no vision. They have no larger view of what they're doing. There's no purpose to it."

Woolrich and his men seizing Rachel's notes.

"I'm torn between keeping you in touch and telling you nothing."

Cops throwing a bag of donuts he had touched into a trash can.

"Are you fucking her, Bird?"

You can't bluff someone who isn't paying attention.

Adelaide Modine. *"They can sniff each other out."*

And a figure in a New York bar, fingering a Penguin volume of metaphysical verse and quoting verses from Donne.

"Rack't carcasses make ill Anatomies."

A metaphysical sensibility: that was what the Traveling Man had, what Rachel had tried to pinpoint only days before, what united the poets whose works had lined the shelves of Woolrich's East Village apartment on the night he took me back there to sleep, on the night after he killed my wife and child.

"Bird, you okay?" His pupils were tiny, like little black holes sucking the light from the room.

I turned away. "Yeah, just a moment of weakness, that's all. I'll be back."

"Where are you going, Birdman?" There was doubt in his voice, and something else: a note of warning, of violence, and I wondered if my wife had heard it as she tried to escape, as he came after her, as he broke her nose against the wall.

"I have to go to the john," I said.

I am still not certain why I turned away. Bile was rising in my throat, threatening to make me gag and vomit on the floor. A fierce, burning pain dug at my stomach and clawed at my heart. It was as if a veil had been pulled aside at the moment of my death, revealing only a cold, black emptiness beyond. I wanted to turn away. I wanted to turn away from it all, and when I returned, everything would be normal again. I would have a wife and a child who looked like her mother. I would have a small, peaceful home and a patch of lawn to tend and someone who would stand by me, even to the end.

The toilet was dark and smelled of stale urine from the unflushed bowl, but the tap worked. I splashed cold water on my face, then reached into my jacket pocket for my phone.

It wasn't there. I had left it on the table with Woolrich. I wrenched the door open and moved around the bar, my right hand drawing my pistol, but Woolrich was already gone.

I CALLED TOUSSAINT BUT he had left the office. Dupree had gone home. I convinced the switchboard operator to ring Dupree's home number and to ask him to call me back. Five minutes later he did. His voice was bleary.

"This had better be good," he said.

"Byron isn't the killer," I said.

"What?" He was wide awake instantly.

"He didn't kill them," I repeated. I was outside the bar, gun in hand, but there was no sign of Woolrich. I stopped two black women passing with a child between them, but they backed off as soon as they saw the gun. "Byron wasn't the Traveling Man. Woolrich was. He's running. I caught him out with a lie about his daughter. He said he had spoken to her two or three months back. You and I both know that's not possible."

"You could have made a mistake."

"Dupree, listen to me. Woolrich set Byron up. He killed my wife and daughter. He killed Morphy and his wife, *Tante* Marie, Tee Jean, Lutice Fontenot, Tony Remarr, and he killed his own daughter too. He's running, do you hear me? He's running."

"I hear you," said Dupree. His voice was dry with the realization of how wrong we had been.

ONE HOUR LATER, THEY hit Woolrich's apartment in Algiers, on the south bank of the Mississippi. It lay on the upper floor of a restored house on Opelousas Avenue, above an old grocery store, approached by a flight of cast iron stairs, girded with gardenias, that led up to a gallery. Woolrich's apartment was the only one in the building, with two arched windows and a solid oak door. The New Orleans police were backed up by six FBI men. The cops led, the feds taking up positions at either side of the door. There was no movement visible in the apartment through the windows. They had not expected any.

Two cops swung an iron battering ram with *Hi, Y'all* painted in white on its flat head. It took one swing to knock the door open. The FBI men poured into the house, the police securing the street and the surrounding yards. They checked the tiny kitchen, the unmade bed, the lounge with the new television, the empty pizza cartons and beer cans, the Penguin poetry editions which sat in a milk crate, the picture of Woolrich and his daughter smiling from on top of a nest of tables.

In the bedroom was a closet, open and containing an array of wrinkled clothes and two pairs of tan shoes, and a metal cabinet sealed with a large steel lock.

"Break it," instructed the agent in charge of the operation, Assistant SAC Cameron Tate. O'Neill Brouchard, the young FBI man who had driven me to *Tante* Marie's house centuries before, struck at the lock with the butt of his machine pistol. It broke on the third attempt and he pulled the doors open.

The explosion blew O'Neill Brouchard backward through the window, almost tearing his head off in the process, and sent a hailstorm of glass shards into the narrow confines of the bedroom. Tate was blinded instantly, glass embedding itself in his face, neck, and his Kevlar vest. Two other FBI men sustained serious injuries to the face and hands as part of Woolrich's store of empty glass jars, his laptop computer, a modified H3000 voice synthesizer, a smaller, portable voice changer with the capacity to alter pitch and tone, and a flesh-colored mask, used to obscure his mouth and nose, were blown to pieces. And amid the flames and the smoke and the shards of glass, burning pages fluttered to the ground like black moths, a mass of biblical apocrypha disintegrating into ash.

AS O'NEILL BROUCHARD WAS dying, I sat in the detective squad room in St. Martinville as men were pulled in from holidays and days off to assist in the search. Woolrich had switched off his cell phone but the phone company had been alerted. If he used it, they would try to pinpoint a location.

Someone handed me a cup of coffee in an alligator cup, and while I drank it, I tried Rachel's room at the motel again. On the tenth ring the desk clerk interrupted.

"Are you . . . Do they call you the Birdman?" he said. He sounded young and uncertain.

"Yes, some people do."

"I'm sorry, sir. Did you call before?"

I told him that this was my third call. I was aware of an edge in my voice.

"I was grabbing lunch. I have a message for you, from the FBI."

He said the three letters with a sort of wonder in his voice. Nausea bubbled in my throat.

"It's from Agent Woolrich, Mr. Birdman. He said to tell you that he and Ms. Wolfe were taking a trip, and that you'd know where to find them. He said he wanted you to keep it to just the three of you. He doesn't want anyone else to spoil the occasion. He told me to tell you that especially, sir."

I closed my eyes and his voice grew further away.

"That's the message, sir. Did I do okay?"

TOUSSAINT, DUPREE AND I laid the map across Dupree's desk. Dupree took out a red felt-tip and drew a circle around the Crowley-Ramah area, with the two towns acting as the diameters of the circle and Lafayette as its center.

"I figure he's got a place in there somewhere," said Dupree. "If you're right and he needed to be close to Byron, if not to the Aguillards as well, then we're looking at an area as far as Krotz Springs to the north and, damn, maybe as far as Bayou Sorrel to the south. If he took your friend, that probably delayed him a little: he needed time to check motel reservations—not much, but enough if he was unlucky with the places he called—and he needed time to get her out. He won't want to stay on the roads, so he'll hole up, maybe in a motel or, if it's close enough, his own place."

He tapped the pen in the center of the circle. "We've alerted the locals, the feds, and the state troopers. That leaves us—and you."

I had been thinking of what Woolrich had said, that I would know where to find them, but so far nothing had come to me.

"I can't pin anything down. The obvious ones, like the Aguillard house and his own place in Algiers, are already being checked, but I don't think he's going to be at either of those places."

I put my head in my hands. My fears for Rachel were obscuring my reasoning. I needed to pull back. I took my jacket and walked to the door.

"I need space to think. I'll stay in touch."

Dupree seemed about to object, but he said nothing. Outside, my car was parked in a police space. I sat in it, rolled down the windows, and took my Louisiana map from the glove compartment. I ran my fingers over the names: Arnaudville, Grand Coteau, Carencro, Broussard, Milton, Catahoula, Coteau Holmes, St. Martinville itself.

The last name seemed familiar from somewhere, but by that point all the towns seemed to resonate with some form of meaning, which left them all meaningless. It was like repeating your name over and over and over again in your head, until the name itself lost its familiarity and you began to doubt your own identity. I started to drive out of town toward Lafayette.

Still, St. Martinville came back to me again. Something about New Iberia and a hospital. A nurse. Nurse Judy Neubolt. Judy the Nut. As I drove, I recalled the conversation that I had had with Woolrich when I'd arrived in New Orleans for the first time after the deaths of Susan and Jennifer. Judy the Nut. *"She said I murdered her in a past life."* Was the story true, or did it mean something else? Had Woolrich been toying with me, even then?

The more I thought about it, the more certain I became. He had told me that Judy Neubolt had moved to La Jolla on a one-year contract after their relationship broke up. I doubted that Judy had ever got as far as La Jolla.

Judy Neubolt wasn't in the current directory, or the previous year's directory either. I found her in an old directory in a gas station—her phone had since been disconnected—and figured I could get more directions in St. Martinville. Then I called Huckstetter at home, gave him Judy Neubolt's address, and asked him to contact Dupree in an hour if he hadn't heard from me. He agreed, reluctantly.

As I drove, I thought of David Fontenot and the call from Woolrich that had almost certainly brought him to Honey Island, a promise of an end to the search for his sister. He couldn't have known how close he was to her resting place when he died.

I thought of the deaths I had brought on Morphy and Angie; the echo of *Tante* Marie's voice in my head as he came for her; and Remarr, gilded in fading sunlight. I think I realized, too, why the details had appeared in the newspaper: it was Woolrich's way of bringing his work to a larger audience, a modern-day equivalent of the public anatomization.

And I thought of Lisa: a small, heavy, dark-eyed girl, who had reacted badly to her parents' separation, who had sought refuge in a strange Christianity in Mexico, and who had returned at last to her father. What had she seen to force him to kill her? Her father washing blood from his hands in a sink? The remains of Lutice Fontenot or some other unfortunate floating in a jar?

Or had he simply killed her because the pleasure he took in disposing of her, in mutilating his own flesh and blood, was as close as he could come to turning the knife on his own body, to enduring his own anatomization and finding at last the deep red darkness within himself?

CHAPTER L

Neat lawns mixed with thick growths of cypress as I drove back along the blacktop of 96 to St. Martinville, past a *God Is Pro-Life* sign and the warehouselike structure of Podnuh's nightclub. At Thibodeaux's Café, on the neat town square, I asked for directions to Judy Neubolt's address. They knew the house, even knew that the nurse had moved to La Jolla for a year, maybe longer, and that her boyfriend was maintaining the house.

Perkins Street started almost opposite the entrance to Evangeline State Park. At the end of the street was a T-junction, which disappeared on the right into a rural setting, with houses scattered at distant intervals. Judy Neubolt's house was on this street, a small, two-story dwelling, strangely low despite the two floors, with two windows on either side of a screen door and three much smaller windows on the upper level. At the eastern side, the roof sloped down, reducing it to a single story. The wood of the house had been newly painted a pristine white, and damaged slates on the roof had been replaced, but the yard was overgrown with weeds and the woods beyond had begun to make inroads on the boundaries of the property.

I parked some way from the house and approached it through the woods, stopping at their verge. The sun was already falling from its apex and it cast a red glow across the roof and walls. The rear door was bolted and locked. There seemed to be no option but to enter from the front.

As I moved forward, my senses jangled with a tension I had not felt before. Sounds, smells, and colors were too sharp, too overpowering. I felt as if I could pick out the component parts of every noise that came to me from the surrounding trees. My gun moved jerkily, my hand responding too rapidly to the signals from my brain. I was conscious of the firmness of the trigger against the ball of my finger and every crevice and rise of the grip against the palm of my hand. The sound of the blood pumping in my ears was like an immense hand banging on a heavy oak door, my feet on the leaves and twigs like the crackling of some huge fire.

The drapes were pulled on the windows, top and bottom, and across the inner door. Through a gap in the drapes on the door I could see black material, hung to prevent anyone from peering through the cracks. The screen door opened with a squeak of rusty hinges as I eased it ajar with my right foot, my body shielded by the wall of the house. I could see a thick spider's web at the upper part of the door frame, the brown, drained husks of trapped insects shivering in the vibrations from the opening door.

I reached in and turned the handle on the main door. It opened easily. I let it swing to its fullest expanse, revealing the dimly lit interior of the house. I could see the edge of a sofa, one half of a window at the other side of the house, and to my right, the beginning of a hallway. I took a deep breath, which echoed in my head like the low, pained gasp of a sick animal, then moved quickly to my right, the screen door closing behind me.

I now had a full, uninterrupted view of the main room of the house. The exterior had been deceptive. Judy Neubolt, or whoever had decided on the design of the house's interior, had removed one floor entirely so that the room reached right to the roof, where two skylights, now encrusted with filth and partly obscured by black drapes stretched beneath them, allowed thin shafts of sunlight to penetrate to the bare boards below. The only illumination came from a pair of dim floor lamps, one at each end of the room.

The room was furnished with a long sofa, decorated with a red-and-orange zigzag pattern, which stood facing the front of the house. At either side of it were matching chairs, with a low coffee table in the center and a TV cabinet beneath one of the windows facing the seating area. Behind the sofa was a dining table and six chairs, with a fireplace to their rear. The walls were decorated with samples of Indian art and one or two vaguely mystical paintings of women with flowing white dresses standing on a mountain or beside the sea. It was hard to make out details in the dimness.

At the eastern end was a raised wooden gallery, reached by a flight of steps to my left, which led up to a sleeping area with a pine bed and a matching closet.

Rachel hung upside down from the gallery, a rope attached from her ankles to the rail above. She was naked and her hair stretched to within two feet of the floor. Her arms were free and her hands hung beyond the ends of her hair. Her eyes and mouth were wide open, but she gave no indication that she saw me. A needle, attached to the plastic pipe of a drip, was taped to her left arm. The drip bag hung from a metal frame, allowing the ketamine to seep slowly and continuously into her system. On the floor beneath her was stretched an expanse of clear plastic sheeting.

Beneath the gallery was a dark kitchen area, with pine cupboards, a tall refrigerator, and a microwave oven beside the sink. Three stools stood empty by a breakfast nook. To my right, on the wall facing the gallery, hung an embroidered tapestry with a pattern similar to the sofa and chairs. A thin patina of dust lay over everything.

I checked the hallway behind me. It led into a second bedroom, this one empty but for a bare mattress on which lay a military green sleeping bag. A green knapsack lay open beside the bed and I could see some jeans, a pair of cream trousers, and some men's shirts inside. The room, with its low, sloping roof, took up about half the width of the house, which meant that there was a room of similar size on the other side of the wall.

I moved back toward the main room, all the time keeping Rachel in sight. There was no sign of Woolrich, although he could have been standing hidden in the hallway at the other side of the house. Rachel could give me no indication of where he might be. I began moving slowly along the tapestried wall to the far wall of the house.

I was about halfway across when a movement behind Rachel caught my attention and I spun, my gun raised to shoulder level as I instinctively assumed a marksman's stance.

"Put it down, Birdman, or she dies now." He had been waiting in the darkness behind her, shielded by her body. He stood close to her now, most of his body still hidden by her own. I could see the edge of his tan pants, the sleeve of his white shirt, and a sliver of his head, nothing more. If I tried to shoot, I would almost certainly hit Rachel.

"I have a gun pointing at the small of her back, Bird. I don't want to ruin such a beautiful body with a bullet hole, so *put the gun down.*"

I bent down and placed the gun gently on the ground.

"Now kick it away from you."

I kicked it with the side of my foot and watched it slide across the floor and spin to rest by the foot of the nearest chair.

He emerged from the shadows then, but he was no longer the man that I had known. It was as if, with the revelation of his true nature, a metamorphosis had occurred. His face was more gaunt than ever and the dark shadows beneath his eyes gave him a skeletal look. But those eyes: they shone in the semidarkness like black jewels. As my eyes grew more accustomed to the light, I saw that his irises had almost disappeared. His pupils were large and dark and fed greedily on the light in the room.

"Why did it have to be you?" I said, as much to myself as to him. "You were my friend."

He smiled then, a bleak, empty smile that drifted across his face like snow.

"How did you find her, Bird?" he asked, his voice low. "How did you find Lisa? I gave you Lutice Fontenot, but how did you find Lisa?"

"Maybe she found me," I replied.

He shook his head in slow disappointment. "It doesn't matter," he said softly. "I don't have time for those things now. I got a whole new song to sing."

He was fully in view now. In one hand he held what looked like a modified, wide-barreled air pistol, in the other a scalpel. A SIG was tucked into the waistband of his pants. I noticed that they still had mud on the cuffs.

"Why did you kill her?"

Woolrich twisted the scalpel in his hand. "Because I could."

Around us, the light in the room changed, darkening as a cloud obscured the slivers of sunlight filtering through the skylights above us. I moved slightly, shifting my weight, my eye on my gun where it lay on the floor. My movement seemed exaggerated, as if, faced with the potential of the ketamine, everything shifted too quickly by comparison. Woolrich's gun came up in a single fluid moment.

"Don't, Bird. You won't have long to wait. Don't rush the end."

The room brightened again, but only marginally. The sun was setting fast. Soon there would only be darkness.

"It was always going to end this way, Bird, you and me in a room like this. I planned it, right from the start. You were always going to die this way. Maybe here, or maybe later, in some other place." He smiled again. "After all, they were going to promote me. It would have been time to move on again. But, in the end, it was always going to come down to this."

He moved forward, one step, the gun never wavering.

"You're a little man, Bird. Do you have any idea how many little people I've killed? Trailer park trash in penny-ass towns from here to Detroit. Cracker bitches who spent their lives watching Oprah and fucking like dogs. Addicts. Drunks. Haven't you ever hated those people, Bird, the ones you know are worthless, the ones who will never amount to anything, will never do anything, will never contribute anything? Have you ever thought that you might be one of them? I showed them how worthless they were, Bird. I showed them how little they mattered. I showed your wife and your daughter how little they mattered."

"And Byron?" I asked. "Was he one of the little people, or did you turn him into one of them?" I wanted to keep him talking, maybe work my way toward my gun. As soon as he stopped, he would try to kill both Rachel and me. But more than that, I wanted to know why, as if there could ever be a why that would explain all of this.

"Byron," said Woolrich. He smiled slightly. "I needed to buy myself some time. When I cut up the girl at Park Rise, everyone believed the worst of him and he ran, all the way back to Baton Rouge. I visited him, Bird. I tested the ketamine on him and then I just kept giving it to him. He tried to run once, but I found him. In the end, I find them all."

"You warned him that the feds were coming, didn't you? You sacrificed your own men to ensure that he would lash out at them, to ensure that he died before he could start raving to them. Did you warn Adelaide Modine too, after you sniffed her out? Did you tell her I was coming after her? Did you make her run?"

Woolrich didn't answer. Instead, he ran the blunt edge of the scalpel down Rachel's arm. "Have you ever wondered how skin so thin . . . can hold so much blood in?" He turned the scalpel and ran the blade across her scapula, from the right shoulder to the space between her breasts. Rachel did not move. Her eyes remained open, but something glittered and a tear trickled from the corner of her left eye and lost itself in the roots of her hair. Blood flowed from the wound, running along the nape of her neck and pooling at her chin before it fell on her face, drawing red lines along her features.

"Look, Bird," he said. "I think the blood is going to her head."

His head tilted. "And then I drew you in. There's a circularity to this which you should appreciate, Bird. After you die, everybody is going to know about me. Then I'll be gone—they won't find me, Bird, I know every trick in the book—and I'll start again."

He smiled slightly.

"You don't look very appreciative," he said. "After all, Bird, I gave you a gift when I killed your family. If they had lived, they'd have left you and you would have become just another drunk. In a sense, I kept the family together. I chose them because of you, Bird. You befriended me in New York, you paraded them in front of me, and I took them."

"Marsyas," I said quietly.

Woolrich glanced at Rachel. "She's a smart lady, Bird. Just your type. Just like Susan. And soon she'll be just another of your dead lovers, except this time you won't have long to grieve over her."

His hand flicked the scalpel back and forth, tearing fine lines across Rachel's arm. I don't think he even realized what he was doing, or the manner in which he was anticipating the acts to come.

"I don't believe in the next world, Bird. It's just a void. This is Hell, Bird, and we are in it. All the pain, all the hurt, all the misery you could ever imagine, you can find it here. It's a culture of death, the only religion worth following. The world is my altar, Bird.

"But I don't think you'll ever understand. In the end, the only time a man really understands the reality of death, of the final pain, is at the moment of his own. It's the flaw in my work, but somehow, it makes it more human. Look upon it as my conceit." He turned the scalpel in his hand, dying sunlight and blood mingling on the blade. "She was right all along, Bird. Now it's time for you to learn. You're about to receive, and become, a lesson in mortality.

"I'm going to recreate the *Pietà* again, Bird, but this time with you and your lady friend. Can't you see it? The most famous representation of grief and death in the history of the world, a potent symbol of self-sacrifice for the greater good of humanity, of hope, of resurrection, and you're going to be a part of it. Except this is the anti-resurrection we're creating, darkness made flesh."

He moved forward again, his eyes terrifyingly bright.

"You're not going to come back from the dead, Bird, and the only sins you're dying for are your own."

I was already moving to the right when the gun fired. I felt a sharp, stinging pain in my left side as the aluminum-bodied syringe struck and I heard the sound of Woolrich's footsteps approaching across the wooden floor. I lashed out at it with my left hand, dislodging the needle painfully from my flesh. It was a huge dose. I could already feel it taking effect as I reached for my gun. I gripped the butt hard and tried to draw a bead on Woolrich.

He killed the lights. Caught in the center of the floor, away from Rachel's body, he moved to the right. I found a shape moving past the window and I loosed off two shots. There was a grunt of pain and the sound of glass breaking. A finger of sunlight lanced into the room.

I worked my way backward until I reached the second hallway. I tried to catch a glimpse of Woolrich but he seemed to have disappeared into the shadows. A second syringe whacked into the wall beside me and I was forced to dive to my left. My limbs were heavy now, my arms and legs propelling me with difficulty. I felt as if there was a pressure on my chest and I knew I would not be able to support my own weight if I tried to rise.

I kept moving backward, every movement a huge effort, but I felt certain that if I stopped, I would never be able to move again. The creaking of boards came from the main room and I heard Woolrich breathing harshly. He barked out a short laugh and I could hear the pain in it.

"Fuck you, Bird," he said. "*Shit,* that hurts." He laughed again. "I'm going to make you pay for that, Bird, you and the woman. I'm going to tear your fucking souls apart."

His voice came to me as if through a heavy fog that distorted the sound and made it difficult to tell distances or direction. The walls of the hallway rippled and fragmented, and black gore oozed from the cracks. A hand reached out to me, a slim, female hand with a narrow gold loop on its wedding finger. I saw myself reach out to touch it, although I could still feel my hands on the floor beneath me. A second female hand appeared, flailing blindly.

bird

I backed away, shaking my head to try to clear the vision. Then two smaller hands emerged from the darkness, delicate and child-like, and I closed my eyes tightly and gritted my teeth.

daddy

"*No*," I hissed. I dug my nails into the floor until I heard one crack, and pain coursed through the index finger of my left hand. I needed the pain. I needed it to fight off the effects of the ketamine. I pressed down hard on the injured finger and the pain made me gasp. There were still shadows moving along the wall, but the figures of my wife and child had gone.

I was conscious now of a reddish glow bathing the hallway. My back struck something cold and heavy, which moved slowly as I pressed against it. I was leaning against a half-open reinforced steel door, with three bolts on its left side. The central bolt was a monster, easily an inch in diameter with a huge open brass lock hanging from it. Red light seeped out from the crack in the door.

"Birdman, it's almost over now," said Woolrich. His voice sounded very close now, although I still could not see him. I guessed he was standing at the very edge of the corner, waiting for me to finally stop moving. "The drug is going to stop you soon. Throw the gun away, Bird, and we can get started. The sooner we start, the sooner we finish."

I leaned back harder on the door and felt it give fully. I pushed back with my heels once, twice, a third time, until I came to rest against a set of shelving that reached from ceiling to floor. The room was lit by a single red bulb, which hung unshaded from the center of the ceiling. The windows had been bricked up, the brick-work left uncovered. There was no natural light to illuminate the contents of the room.

Opposite me, to the left of the door, was a row of metal shelving, perforated bars holding the shelves in place with screws. On each shelf sat a number of glass jars, and in each jar, glowing in the dim red light, lay the remains of a human face. Most were beyond recognition. Lying in the formaldehyde, some had sunken in on themselves. Eyelashes were still visible on some, lips bleached almost white on others, the skin at their edges tattered and torn.

On the lowest shelf, two dark faces lay almost upright against the glass, and even though they had been violated in this way, I recognized the faces of *Tante* Marie Aguillard and her son. I counted maybe fifteen bottles in front of me. Behind me, the shelving moved slightly and I heard the sound of glass knocking against glass and the slick movement of liquid.

I raised my head. Row upon row of bottles reached up to the ceiling, each bearing its faint, white, human remains. Beside my left eye, a face leaned against the front of a jar, its empty eyes gaping, as if trying to peer into eternity.

And I knew that somewhere among these faces, Susan lay preserved.

"What do you think of my collection, Bird?" The dark bulk of Woolrich moved slowly down the hallway. In one hand, I could see the outline of the pistol. In the other, he rubbed his thumb along the clean line of the scalpel.

"Wondering where your wife is? She's on the middle shelf, third from the left. Shit, Bird, you're probably sitting beside her right now."

I didn't move. I didn't blink. My body lay slumped against the shelves, surrounded by the faces of the dead. My face would be there soon, I thought, my face and Rachel's and Susan's, side by side forever.

Woolrich came forward until he stood in the doorway. He raised the air pistol.

"Nobody ever lasted this long before, Bird. Even Tee Jean, and he was a strong kid." His eyes glowed redly. "I gotta tell you, Bird: in the end, this is going to hurt."

He tightened his finger on the pistol and I heard the sharp crack as the hypo shot from the barrel. I was already raising my gun as the sharp pain struck my chest, my arm achingly heavy, my vision blurred by the shadows moving across my eyes. I tightened my finger on the trigger, willing it to increase the pressure. Woolrich sprang forward, alive to the danger, the scalpel raised to slash at my arm.

The trigger moved back slowly, infinitesimally slowly, and the world slowed down with it. Woolrich seemed to hang in space, the blade curving down in his hand as if through water, his mouth wide and a sound like a wind howling in a tunnel coming from his throat. The trigger moved back another tiny measure and my finger froze as the gun boomed loudly in the enclosed space. Woolrich, barely three feet from me now, bucked as the first shot took him in the chest. The next eight shots seemed to come together, the sound of their firing joining together as the bullets tore into him, the 10 millimeter rounds ripping through cloth and flesh before the gun locked empty. Glass shattered as the bullets exited and the floor became awash with formaldehyde. Woolrich fell backward and lay on the floor, his body shaking and spasming. He rose once, his shoulders and head lifting from the ground, the light already dying in his eyes. Then he lay back and moved no more.

My arm gave in under the weight of the gun and it fell to the floor. I could hear liquid dripping, could feel the presence of the dead as they crowded around me. From a distance, there came the sound of approaching sirens and I knew that, whatever happened to me, Rachel at least would be safe. Something brushed my cheek with a touch light as gossamer, like the last caress of a lover before the time to sleep, and a kind of peace came over me. With a final act of will, I closed my eyes and waited for the stillness to come.

EPILOGUE

I turn left at the Scarborough intersection, down the steep hill, past the Maximillian Kolbe Catholic church and the old cemetery, the fire department on my right, the late evening sun shining bleakly on the expanse of marshland to the east and west of the road. Soon it will be dark and lights will appear in the houses of the locals, but the summer houses on Prouts Neck Road will not be lit.

The sea rolls in gently at Prouts Neck, washing slowly over sand and stone. The season is over now and behind me the bulk of the Black Point Inn looms darkly, its dining room deserted, its bar quiet, the screen doors of the staff dormitories locked down. In the summer, the old and wealthy from Boston and upstate New York will come to stay, eating buffet lunches by the pool and dressing for dinner, the candlelight reflecting on their heavy jewelry and dancing around the table like golden moths.

Across the water, I can see the lights of Old Orchard Beach. A chill wind is coming in over the sea, tossing and buffeting the last of the gulls. I pull my coat tightly around me and stand on the sand, watching the grains swirl and twist before me. They make a sound like a mother hushing her child as the wind raises them from the dunes and lifts them like the shapes of old ghosts before laying them to rest again.

I am standing near the spot where Clarence Johns stood all those years ago, as he watched Daddy Helms's man pour dirt and ants over my body. It was a hard lesson to learn, harder still to learn it twice. I recall the look on his face as he stood shivering before me, the desolation, the realization of what he had done, of what he had lost.

And I want to put my arm around the shoulders of Clarence Johns and tell him that it's all right, that I understand, that I bear him no malice for what he did. I want to hear the soles of his cheap shoes slapping on the road. I want to watch him skim a stone over the water and know that he is still my friend. I want to walk the long walk home beside him and hear him whistling the only three bars he knows of some tune that he can't get out of his head, a tune that returns again and again to haunt him as he makes his way along the road.

But instead I will climb back in my car and return to Portland in the waning autumn light. I have a room at the Inn at St. John, with big bay windows and clean white sheets and a separate bathroom two doors down the hall. I will lie on my bed as the traffic passes beneath my window, as the Greyhound buses arrive and depart from the terminal across the street, as the street people push their shopping carts filled with bottles and cans down the sidewalk and the taxi drivers wait silently in their cabs.

And in the gathering darkness I will call Rachel's number in Manhattan. The phone will ring—once, twice—and then her machine will kick in: "Hi, no one can come to the phone right now, but . . ." I have heard the same message again and again since she left the hospital. Her receptionist says that she cannot tell me where Rachel is. She has canceled her college lectures. And from my hotel room, I will talk to the machine.

I could find her, if I chose. I found the others, but they were dead when I found them. I do not want to chase her down.

It is not supposed to end this way. She should be beside me now, her skin perfect and white, not scarred by Woolrich's knife; her eyes bright and inviting, not wary and haunted by the visions that torment her in the night; her hands reaching for me in the darkness, not raised to ward me off, as if even my touch might cause her pain. We will both reach an accommodation with the past, with all that has taken place, but, for now, we will each do so alone.

In the morning, Edgar will have the radio playing and there will be orange juice and coffee on the table in the lobby, and muffins wrapped in plastic. From there, I will drive out to my grandfather's house and start working. A local man has agreed to help me fix my roof and mend my walls, so that the house can be made habitable for the winter.

And I will sit on my porch as the wind takes the evergreens in hand, pressing and molding their branches into new shapes, creating a song from their leaves. And I will listen for the sound of a dog barking, its paws scraping on the worn boards, its tail moving lazily in the cool evening air; or the tap-tap-tap on the rail as my grandfather prepares to tamp the tobacco into his pipe, a glass of whiskey beside him warm and tender as a familiar kiss; or the rustle of my mother's dress against the kitchen table as she lays out plates for the evening meal, blue on white, older than she is, old as the house.

Or the sound of plastic-soled shoes fading into the distance, disappearing into the darkness, embracing the peace that comes at last to every dead thing.

ACKNOWLEDGMENTS

A number of books proved particularly valuable in the course of researching this novel. Chief among them was *The Body Emblazoned* (Routledge, 1995), Jonathan Sawday's brilliant study of dissection and the human body in Renaissance culture. Other works to which I returned included F. Gonzalez-Crussi's *Suspended Animation* (Harcourt Brace & Co., 1995); Denis C. Rousey's *Policing the Southern City* (Louisiana State University Press, 1996); Luther Link's *The Devil* (Reaktion Books, 1995); Lyall Watson's *Dark Nature* (Hodder & Stoughton, 1995); and the *Crime Classification Manual* (Simon & Schuster, 1993) by Ressler, Douglas, Burgess, and Burgess.

On a more personal note, I wish to thank my agent, Darley Anderson, without whom *Every Dead Thing* would not have seen the light of day. I also wish to acknowledge the faith, advice, and encouragement of my editor at Hodder & Stoughton, Sue Fletcher, as well as Bob Mecoy and Emily Bestler, my editors at Simon & Schuster in New York.

Read on for the newest chilling installment in the Charlie Parker series by bestselling author John Connolly

A SONG OF SHADOWS

Available online and wherever books are sold in Fall 2015

The Hurricane Hatch stood at the end of a strip of land midway between Jacksonville and St. Augustine on the Florida coast, far enough away from the real tourist traps to ensure that it retained a degree of local custom while still attracting enough business of any stripe to sustain it. A man named Skettle owned 90 percent of the Hurricane Hatch, but he rarely frequented it, preferring to leave the running of the place to its chief bartender and ten percent shareholder, Lenny Tedesco. Skettle liked to keep quiet about the fact that he had a big piece of the Hurricane Hatch. His family, from what Lenny knew of them, contained a high percentage of Holy Rollers, the kind who visited the Holy Land Experience down in Orlando a couple of times a year, and regarded the Goliath Burger at the theme park's Oasis Palms Café as damn fine dining, although Lenny doubted if they would have used that precise term to describe it. Lenny Tedesco had never been to the Holy Land Experience, and had zero intention of ever visiting it. He reckoned that a Christian theme park wasn't really the place for a Jew, not even a nonobservant Jew like himself, and he didn't care if it did boast a recreation of a Jerusalem street market.

Then again, the Hurricane Hatch was about as authentic in Florida bar terms as the Holy Land Experience was as an accurate reflection of the spiritual makeup of Jerusalem in the first century AD. It looked like what a classic Florida beach bum's bar was supposed to look like—wood, stuffed fish, a picture of Hemingway—but had only been built at the start of the nineties, in anticipation of a housing development named Ocean Breeze Condos which never got further than a series of architect's plans, a hole in the ground, and a tax write-off. The Hurricane Hatch remained, though, and had somehow managed to prosper, in large part because of Lenny and his wife, Pegi, who was a good fry cook of the old school. She prepared fried oysters that could make a man weep, the secret ingredients being creole seasoning, fine yellow cornmeal, and Diamond Crystal—*kosher*—salt. Neither did Skettle evince too much concern about making a large profit, just as long as the Hatch didn't lose money. Lenny figured that Skettle, who didn't drink alcohol and appeared to subsist primarily on chicken tenders and chocolate milk, just enjoyed secretly giving the finger to his holier-than-thou, pew-polishing relatives by owning a bar. Lenny's wife, however, claimed that Skettle's sister Lesley, a Praise Jesus type of the worst stripe, was not above polishing other things too, and could give a pretty accurate description of half the motel ceilings between Jacksonville and Miami, giving rise to her nickname of Screw-Anything-Skettle.

Lenny was alone in the bar. Entirely alone. This was one of Pegi's nights off, and Lenny had sent the replacement cook, Fran, home early, because he knew she'd have better luck selling fried oysters in an abandoned cemetery than in the Hurricane Hatch on this particular evening. Midweeks were always quiet, but lately they had been quieter than usual, and even weekend business was down from previous years. There just wasn't as much money around as before, but the Hatch was surviving.

Lenny glanced at his watch. It was nine thirty. He'd give it until ten, maybe ten thirty, then call it a night. Anyway, he was in no hurry to go home—not that he didn't love his wife, because he did, but sometimes he thought that he loved the Hatch more. He was at peace there, regardless of whether it was empty or full. In fact, on evenings like this, with the wind blowing gently outside, and the boards creaking and rattling, and the sound of the waves in the distance, visible as the faintest of phosphorescent glows, and the TV on, and a soda water and lime on the bar before him, he felt that he would be quite content just to stay this way forever. The only blot on his happiness—if blot was a sufficient word for it, which he doubted—was the subject of the TV news report currently playing in front of him. He watched the footage of the two old men being transported by United States Marshals into the holding facility somewhere in New York City: Engel and Fuhrmann, with almost two centuries of life clocked up between them, Engel barely able to walk unaided, Fuhrmann stronger, his gaze fixed somewhere in the distance, not even deigning to notice the men and women who surrounded him, the cameras and the lights, the protestors with their signs, as if all of this was a show being put on for another man, and the accusations leveled against him were somehow beneath his regard. The men disappeared from the screen, to be replaced by an attorney from the Human Rights and Special Prosecutions Section, the arm of the Justice Department entrusted with investigating assorted human rights violations and, particularly, Nazi war criminals. The attorney was a pretty young woman, and Lenny was surprised by the passion with which she spoke. She didn't have a Jewish name, or Demers didn't sound like one. Not that this was a requirement for justice under the circumstances. Perhaps she was just an idealist, and God knew the world needed as many of those as it could find.

Engel and Fuhrmann, she said, had been fighting the US government's decision to rescind their citizenship, but that process had now been exhausted. The delivery of the arrest warrant for Fuhrmann from the Bavarian state public prosecutor's office in Munich a week earlier meant that his extradition could now proceed immediately, and Engel's deportation would follow shortly after for breaches of immigration law, regardless of whether or not charges were filed against him in his native land. Soon, she said, Engel and Fuhrmann would be banished from American soil forever.

Deportation didn't sound like much of a punishment to Lenny, whose family had lost an entire branch at Dachau. He hadn't understood why they couldn't be put on trial here in the United States until Bruno Perlman explained to him that the US Constitution precluded criminal prosecutions committed abroad before and during World War II, and the best that the United States could do was send war criminals back to countries that did have jurisdiction, in the hope that proceedings might be taken against them there. Not that Perlman was happy about the situation either. He would tell Lenny admiringly about the activities of the TTG, the Tilhas Tizig Gesheften, a secret group within the Jewish Brigade Group of the British Army who, after the German surrender, took it upon themselves to hunt down and assassinate *Wehrmacht* and SS officers believed to have committed atrocities against Jews; and of the Mossad killers who trapped the Latvian Nazi collaborator Herberts Cukurs, "the Butcher of Riga," in a house in Montevideo in 1965, beating him with a hammer before shooting him twice in the head and leaving his body to rot in a trunk until the Uruguayan police found him, drawn by the smell. The gleam in Perlman's eye as he spoke of such matters disturbed Lenny, but he supposed that the end met by such foul men was no more than they deserved. Lately, though, that light in Perlman's eyes had grown brighter, and his talk of vengeance had taken a personal turn. Lenny worried for him. Perlman had few friends. Obsessives rarely did.

"How do they even know it's really them?" said a voice. "Old men like that, they could be anyone."

A man was seated at the far end of the bar, close to the door. Lenny had not heard him enter. Neither had he heard a car pull into the lot. The visitor's face was turned slightly away from the television, as though he could not bear to watch it. He wore a straw fedora with a red band. The hat was too large for his head, so that it sat just above his eyes. His suit jacket was brown, worn over a yellow polo shirt. The shirt was missing two buttons, exposing a network of thin white scars across the man's chest, like a web spun by a spider upon his skin.

"Sorry, I didn't hear you come in," said Lenny, ignoring the question. "What can I get you?"

The man didn't respond. He seemed to be having trouble breathing. Lenny looked past him to the parking lot outside. He could see no vehicle.

"You got milk?" the man rasped.

"Sure."

"Brandy and milk." He rubbed his stomach. "I got a problem with my guts."

Lenny prepared the mix. The milk was cold enough to create beads of condensation on the glass, so he wrapped it in a napkin before placing it on the bar. The man exuded a sour, curdled odor, the rankness of untold brandy-and-milk combinations. He raised the glass and drank it half-empty.

"Hurts," he said. "Hurts like a motherfucker."

He lowered the glass, raised his left hand, and removed the hat from his head. Lenny tried not to stare before deciding that it was easier just to look away entirely, but the image of the man's visage remained branded on Lenny's vision like a sudden flare of bright, distorted light in the dimness of the bar.

His bare skull was misshapen, as pitted with concave indentations as the surface of the moon. His brow was massively overdeveloped, so that his eyes—tiny dark things, like drops of oil in snow—were lost in its shadow, and his profile was suggestive of one who had slammed his forehead into a horizontal girder as a child, with the soft skull retaining the impression of the blow as it hardened. His nose was very thin, his mouth the barest slash of color against the pallor of his skin. He breathed in and out through his lips with a faint, wet whistle.

"What's your name?" he asked.

"Lenny."

"Lenny what?"

"Lenny Tedesco."

"This your place?"

"I got a share in it. Skettle owns the rest."

"I don't know any Skettle. You're a bitch to find. You ought to put up a sign."

"There is a sign."

"I didn't see none."

"Which way did you come?"

The man waved a hand vaguely over his shoulder—north, south, east, west: what did any of it matter? The only issue of consequence was that he was here at last.

"Tedesco," he said. "That's a Sephardic name. Some might mistake it for Italian, but it's not. It means 'German,' but you most likely had Ashkenazi forbears. Am I right?"

Lenny wished that the bar had remained empty. He didn't want to engage in this discussion. He wanted this vile man with his pungent stink to be gone.

"I don't know," he said.

"Sure you do. I read once that the word 'Nazi' comes from 'Ashkenazi.' What do you think of that?"

Lenny worked on polishing a glass that didn't need a cloth taken to it. He rubbed so hard that the glass cracked under the pressure. He tossed it in the trash and moved on to another.

"I've never heard that before," he replied, and hated himself for responding. "My understanding is that it refers to National Socialism."

"Ah, you're probably right. Anything else is just the frothings of ignorant men. Holocaust deniers. Fools. I don't give no credit to it. As though so much slaughter could be ascribed to Jew-on-Jew violence."

Lenny felt the muscles in his neck cramp. He clenched his teeth so hard that he felt something come loose at the back of his mouth. It was the way the man spoke the word "Jew."

On the television screen, the news report had moved on to a panel discussion about Engel and Fuhrmann, and the background to their cases. The volume was just low enough for the content to remain intelligible. Lenny moved to change the channel, but that same voice told him to leave it be. Lenny glanced at the glass of brandy and milk. A curl of red lay upon the surface of the remaining liquid. The man saw it at the same time as Lenny did. He dipped a finger and swirled the blood away, then drained the glass dry.

"Like I said, I got a problem with my guts. Got problems all over. I shit nails and piss broken glass."

"Sorry to hear that."

"Hasn't killed me yet. I just don't care to think about what my insides might look like."

Couldn't be any worse than what's outside, Lenny thought, and those dark eyes flicked toward him, as though that unspoken wisecrack had found form above Lenny's head.

"You got another of these?"

"I'm closing up."

"Won't take you much longer to make than it'll take me to drink."

"Nah, we're done."

The glass slid across the bar.

"Just the milk then. You wouldn't deny a man a glass of milk, would you?"

Oh, but Lenny wanted to. He wanted to so badly, yet still he poured three fingers of milk into the glass. He was grateful that there was no more left in the carton.

"Thank you."

Lenny said nothing, just tossed the empty container in the trash.

"I don't want you to get me wrong," said the man. "I got no problem with Jews. When I was a boy, I had a friend who was a Jew. Jesus, it's been a long time since I thought about him. I can hardly remember his name now."

He put the thumb and forefinger of his right hand to the bridge of his nose and squeezed hard, his eyes closed as he tried to pull the name from the pit of his memory.

"Asher," he said at last. "Asher Cherney. That was his name. Damn, that was hard. I called him Ash. I don't know what anyone else called him, because no one else palled around with him much. Anyway, I'd hang out with Ash when none of the other boys were there to see. You had to be careful. The people I grew up with, they didn't care much for Jews. Niggers neither. Fuck, we didn't even like Catholics. We stuck with our own, and it wasn't good to be seen making friends outside your own circle. And Ash, you see, he had a deformity, which made it worse for him. You listen to Kiss?"

Lenny, who had somehow been drawn into the tale despite himself, was puzzled. Following the man's thought processes was like trying to keep track of a ricochet in a steel room.

"What, the band?"

"Yeah, the band. They're shit, but you got to have heard of them."

"I know them," said Lenny.

"Right. Well, their singer has the same thing that Ash had. They call it microtia. It's a deformity of the ear. The cartilage doesn't grow right, so you have a kind of stump. Makes you deaf too. They say it usually occurs in the right ear, but Ash, he had it in his left, so he was strange even among other people like him. Now they can do all kinds of grafts or implants, but back then you just had to live with it. Ash would grow his hair long to try to hide it, but everybody knew. If his life didn't suck already, being a Jew in a town that didn't care much for anyone who wasn't in some white-bread church, he had to deal with the ignorance and bile of kids who spent their lives just looking for some physical defect to hone in on.

"So I felt sorry for Ash, though I couldn't show it, not in public. But if I was alone, and I saw Ash, and *he* was alone, then I'd talk to him, or walk with him, maybe skim stones by the river if the mood took us. He was okay, Ash. You never would have known he was a Jew, unless he told you his name. That microtia, you think it's a Jew thing?"

Lenny said that he didn't know. He felt as though he were watching some terrible accident unfold, a catastrophic collision of bodies that could only result in injury and death, yet was unable to tear his eyes away from it. He was hypnotized by this man's awfulness, the depth of his corruption only slowly revealing itself by word and intonation.

"Because," the man went on, "there are diseases that Jews are more likely to carry than other races. You, being Ashkenazi from way back, are more likely to get cystic fibrosis. I mean, there are others, but that's the one that sticks in my mind. Cystic fibrosis is a bitch. You don't want to get that. Anyhow, I don't know if this microtia thing is like it. Could be. Doesn't matter, I suppose. Unless you have it, and don't want to pass it on to your kids. You got kids?"

"No."

"Well, if you're thinking about having them, you ought to get checked out. You don't want to be transmitting shit to your kids. Where was I? Oh yeah: Ash. Ash and his fucked-up ear. So, me and Ash would do stuff together, and we'd talk, and I got to like him. Then, one day, this kid, a degenerate named Eddie Tyson, he saw us together, and next thing you know they were saying I was queer for Ash, and me and Ash were doing things under bridges and in his mom's car, and Eddie Tyson and a bunch of his buddies caught me alone on my way home and beat the living shit out of me, all on account of how Ash Cherney was my friend.

"So you know what I did?"

Lenny could barely speak, but he found the strength to say the word "no."

"I went around to Ash's house, and I asked if he wanted to go down to the river with me. I told him what had happened, because I looked like hell after what they'd done to me. So me and Ash went down to the river, and I got a stone, and I hit Ash with it. I hit him so hard in the face that I was sure I'd knocked his nose into his brain. I thought I'd killed him, but somehow he stayed conscious. Then I threw the stone away and used my fists and feet on him, and I left him by the river in a pool of his own blood, spitting teeth, and I never heard from him again, because he never came back to school, and his parents moved away not long after."

He sipped his milk.

"I guess me and Ash weren't such good friends after all, huh?"

The television was showing black-and-white footage of emaciated men and women standing behind wire fences, and holes filled with bones.

"You ever wonder what would make men do such things?"

He wasn't looking at the screen, so Lenny didn't know if he was still speaking of what he had done to Ash Cherney, or about the evidence of atrocities committed decades before. Lenny was cold. His fingertips and toes hurt. He figured that it didn't matter what the man was referring to. It was all part of one great mass of viciousness, a cesspit of black, human evil.

"No," said Lenny.

"Course you do. We all do. Wouldn't be human if we didn't. There are those who say that all crimes can be ascribed to one of two motives—love or money—but I don't believe that. In my experience, everything we do is predicated on one of two other things: greed or fear. Oh, sometimes they get mixed up, just like my brandy and milk, but mostly you can keep them separated. We feel greed for what we don't have, and fear because of what we might lose. A man desires a woman who isn't his wife, and takes her—that's greed. But, deep down, he doesn't want his own wife to find out because he wants to keep what he has with her, because it's different, and safe. That's fear. You play the markets?"

"No."

"You're wise. It's a racket. Buying and selling, they're just other names for greed and fear. I tell you, you understand that, and you understand all there is to know about human beings and the way the world works."

He sipped his milk.

"Except, of course, that isn't all. Look at those pictures from the camps. You can see fear, and not just in the faces of the dying and the dead. Take a look at the men in uniform, the ones they say were responsible for what happened, and you'll see fear there too. Not so much fear of what might happen if they didn't follow orders. I don't hold with that as an excuse, and from what I've read the Germans understood that killing naked Jews and queers and Gypsies wasn't for every man, and if you couldn't do it then they'd find someone who would, and send you off to shoot at someone who could shoot back.

"But there's still fear in those faces, no matter how well they try to hide it: fear of what will happen to them when the Russians or the Americans arrive and find out what they've done; fear of looking inside themselves to see what they've become; maybe even fear for their immortal souls. There will also be those who feel no fear of that at all, of course, because sometimes men and women do terrible things just because they gain pleasure from the act, but those ones are the exceptions, and exceptions make bad law. The rest, they just did what they did because they were told to do it and they couldn't see much reason not to, or because there was money in gold teeth and rendered human fat. I guess some of them did it out of ideology, but I don't have much time for ideologies either. They're just flags of convenience."

The man's voice was very soft, and slightly sibilant, and held a note of regret that most of the world could not see itself as clearly as he did, and this was his cross to bear.

"You hear that woman on the TV?" he continued. "She's talking about evil, but throwing around the word 'evil' like it means something don't help anyone. Evil is the avoidance of responsibility. It doesn't explain. You might even say that it excuses. To see the real terror, the real darkness, you have to look at the actions of men, however awful they may appear, and call them human. When you can do that, then you'll understand."

He coughed hard, spattering the milk with droplets of blood.

"You didn't answer my question from earlier," he said.

"What question was that?" said Lenny.

"I just can't figure out how they know that those two old men are the ones they were looking for. I seen the pictures of the ones they say did all those things, the photographs from way back, and then I see those two old farts and I couldn't swear that it's the same men sixty, seventy years later. Jesus, you could show me a picture of my own father as a young man, and I wouldn't know him from the scarecrow he was when he died."

"I think there was a paper trail of some kind," said Lenny. To be honest, he didn't know how Engel and Fuhrmann had been traced. He didn't much care either. They had been found at last, and that was all that mattered. He just wanted this conversation to reach its end, but that was in the hands of the man at the bar. There was a purpose to his presence here, and all Lenny could do was wait for it to be revealed to him, and hope that he survived the adumbration.

"I can't even say that I've heard of the camps that they're supposed to have done all that killing in," said the man. "I mean, I heard of Auschwitz, and Dachau, and Bergen-Belsen. I suppose I could name some others, if I put my mind to it, but what's the place that Fuhrmann was at, or the one they claim is Fuhrmann. Ball Sack? Is that even a place?"

"Belsec," said Lenny softly. "It's called Belsec."

"And the other?"

"Lubsko."

"Well, you have been paying attention, I'll give you that. You had people there?"

"No, not there."

"So it's not personal, then."

Lenny had had enough. He killed the TV.

"I don't want you to mistake me," said the man, not even commenting upon the sudden absence of light and sound from the screen. "I got no problem with any race or creed: Jews, niggers, spics, white folks, they're all the same to me. I do believe, though, that each race and creed ought to keep to itself. I don't think any one is better than the other, but only trouble comes when they mix. The South Africans, they had it right with apartheid, except they didn't have the common sense, the basic human fucking decency, to give every man the same privileges, the same rights. They thought white was superior to black, and that's not the case. God made all of us, and he didn't put one above another, no matter what some might say. Even your own folk, you're no more chosen than anyone else."

Lenny made one final effort to save himself, to force this thing away. It was futile, but he had to try.

"I'd like you to leave now," he said. "I'm all done for the night. Have the drinks on me."

But the man did not move. All this was only the prelude. The worst was yet to come. Lenny felt it. This creature had brought with him a miasma of darkness, of horror. Maybe a small chance still remained, a chink in the wall that was closing in around him through which he might escape. He could not show weakness, though. The drama would play out, and each would accept the role that had been given to him.

"I haven't finished my milk yet."

"You can take it with you."

"Nah, I think I'll drink it here. Wouldn't want it to spill."

"I'm going to be closing up around you," said Lenny. "You'll have to excuse me."

He moved to take the drawer from the register. Usually he counted the takings before he left, but on this occasion he'd leave that until the morning. He didn't want to give this man any cause to linger.

"I'm no charity case," said the visitor. "I'll pay my own way, just as I always have."

He reached into his jacket pocket.

"Well, what do you think this is?"

Lenny couldn't help but look to see what had drawn the other's attention. He glimpsed something small and white, apparently drawn from the man's own pocket.

"Jesus, it's a tooth." He pronounced it "toot." He held the item in question up to the light, like a jeweler appraising a gemstone. "Now where do you suppose that came from? It sure ain't one of mine."

As if to put the issue beyond doubt, he manipulated his upper row of teeth with his tongue, and his dentures popped out into his left palm. The action caused his mouth to collapse in upon itself, rendering his appearance stranger still. He smiled, nodded at Lenny, and replaced his appliance. He then laid the single tooth on the surface of the bar. A length of reddish flesh adhered to the root.

"That's certainly something, isn't it?" he said.

Lenny backed off. He wondered if he could get away for long enough to call the cops. There was no gun on the premises, but the back office had a strong door and a good lock. He could seal himself inside and wait for the police to come. Even if he could make it to a phone, what would he tell the operator—that a man had produced a tooth for his inspection? Last he heard, that wasn't a crime.

Except, except . . .

Like a conjuror, the customer reached into his pocket again and produced a second tooth, then a third. Finally, he seemed to tire of the whole business, rummaged for a final time, and scattered a full mouth's worth of teeth on the bar. Some were without roots. At least one appeared to have broken during extraction. A lot of them were still stained with blood, or trailed tails of tissue.

"Who are you?" asked Lenny. "What do you want from me?"

The gun appeared in the man's hand. Lenny didn't know from guns, but this one looked big and kind of old.

"You stay where you are now," said the man. "You hear me?"

Lenny nodded. He found his voice.

"We got next to nothing in the register," he said. "It's been quiet all day."

"I look like a thief to you?"

He sounded genuinely offended.

"I don't know what you look like," said Lenny, and he regretted the words as soon as they left his mouth.

"You got no manners," said the man. "You know that, you fucking kike?"

"I'm sorry," said Lenny. He had no pride now, only fear.

"I accept your apology. You know what this is?"

He gave the weapon a little jerk.

"No. I don't know much about guns."

"There's your first error. It's not a gun, it's a *pistol*: a Mauser C96 military pistol, made in long nine millimeter, which is rare. Some people call it a Broomhandle Mauser on account of the shape of the grip, or a Red 9 after the number carved into the grip. Consider that an education. Now move away from the door. You pay attention to me and what I say, and maybe this won't go as bad for you as it might."

Lenny knew that wasn't true—men who planned to let other men live didn't point guns at them without first concealing their faces—yet he found himself obeying. The man reached into his pocket again. This time his hand emerged holding a pair of cuffs. He tossed them to Lenny and instructed him to attach one to his right wrist, then put his hands close together behind his back and place them on the bar. If he tried to run away, or pull a fast one, he was assured that he would be shot in the back. Once more, Lenny did as he was told. When he turned his back and put his hands on the bar, the second cuff was quickly cinched tight around his left wrist.

"All done," said the man. "Now come around here and sit on the floor."

Lenny moved from behind the bar. He thought about running for the door, but knew that he wouldn't get more than a few feet without being shot. He gazed out into the night, willing a car to appear, but none came. He walked to the spot indicated by the man, and sat down. The TV came on again, blazing into life at the gunman's touch on the remote. It continued to show images of the camps, of men and women climbing from trains, some of them still wearing ordinary clothing, others already dressed in the garb of prisoners. There were so many of them, and they outnumbered their captors. As a boy, Lenny would wonder why they didn't try to overcome the Germans, why they didn't fight to save themselves. Now he thought that he knew.

The man leaned against the bar, the pistol leveled at Lenny.

"You asked me who I am," he said. "You can call me Steiger. It doesn't matter much. It's just a name. Might as well have plucked it from the air. I can give you another, if you don't like that one."

And again Lenny felt a glimmer of hope warm the coldness of his insides. Perhaps, just perhaps, this night might not end in his death. Could it be that, if he was withholding his true name, this freakish individual planned to return to the hole from which he had emerged and leave Lenny alive? Or was all this a ruse, just one more way to torment a doomed man before the inevitable bullet brought all to an end?

"You know where these teeth came from?"

"No."

"Your wife. They came from her mouth."

Steiger grabbed a handful of the teeth from the bar and threw them on the floor before Lenny. One landed in his lap.

For a moment Lenny was unable to move. His vomit reflex activated, and he tasted sourness in his throat. Then he was moving, trying to rise to his feet, but a bullet struck the floor inches from the soles of his shoes, and the noise as much as the sight of the splintered mark upon the floor stilled him.

"Don't do that again," said Steiger. "If you try, the next one will take out a kneecap, or maybe your balls."

Lenny froze. He stared at the tooth stuck to his jeans. He didn't want to believe that it had once been his wife's.

"I'll tell you something," said Stegner. "Working on your wife's teeth gave me a renewed admiration for the skill of dentists. I used to believe that they were just like failed doctors, because, I mean, how difficult can it be to work on teeth, all the nerves and stuff apart. I hated going to the dentist as a kid. Still do.

"Anyway, I always thought extractions would be the easy part. You get a grip, and you yank. But it's harder to get a good grip on a tooth than you might think, and then you have to twist, and sometimes—if there's a weakness—the tooth just breaks. You'll see that some of your wife's teeth didn't emerge intact. I like to think that it was a learning experience for both of us.

"If you doubt me, and are trying to convince yourself that they're not your wife's teeth," said Steiger, "I can tell you that she was wearing jeans and a yellow blouse, with green—no, blue—flowers. It was hard to tell in the dark. She also has a mark here, on her left forearm, like a big freckle. That would bother me, I have to say. She's a nice-looking woman, but I'd always have been aware of that mark, like a reminder of all that's wrong inside, because we all have things wrong with us inside. That sound like your wife? Pegi, right? Spelled with an *i*. Short for Margaret. That's what she said, while she could still speak.

"No, no, don't go getting all upset now. You'll move, or you'll try to lash out, and this will all get a whole lot worse for you both. Yeah, that's right: she's still alive, I swear to you. And—listen to me, now, just listen—there are worse things than losing your teeth. They can do all kinds of miracles with implants now. She could have teeth that are better than her old ones. And if that's too expensive, or just doesn't work out because of the damage—because, to remind you, I'm no professional—then there's always dentures. My mother wore dentures, just like I do, and I thought that they made her look younger, because they were always clean and even. You ever see old people with their own teeth? They look like shit. Nothing you can do about old age. It's pitiless. It ravages us all."

He squatted before Lenny, still careful to remain just beyond his reach should Lenny's anger overcome his fear, but he needn't have worried. Lenny was weeping.

"Here's how it will go," said Steiger. "If you're straight with me, and answer my questions, I'll let her live. She's all dosed up on painkillers, so she's not feeling much of anything right now. Before I leave, I'll call an ambulance for her, and she'll be looked after. I promise you that.

"As for you, well, I can't promise anything other than, if you're honest, you won't be aware of your own dying, and you'll have saved your wife in the process. Are we clear?"

Lenny was now sobbing loudly. Steiger reached out and slapped him hard across the side of the head.

"I said, are we clear?"

"Yes," said Lenny. "We're clear."

"Good. I have only two questions for you. What did the Jew named Perlman tell you, and who else knows?"

WHEN THE QUESTIONS WERE answered at last, and Lenny Tedesco was dead, Steiger removed from the dishwasher the glasses that he had used and placed them in a bag. He also emptied the register for appearances' sake. He had been careful to touch as few surfaces as possible, but he went over them once again with some bleach that he found behind the bar. Some traces of his presence would still remain, but they would be useless without a suspect, or a record against which to check them, and Steiger was a ghost. He traced the hard drive for the bar's security camera, and removed it. He turned off the lights in the Hurricane Hatch before he left, and closed the door behind him. Lenny's car was parked behind the bar, and would not be noticed unless someone came looking for it.

Steiger walked for five minutes to where his car was parked, out of sight of both the bar and the road, then drove to the Tedescos' small, neat home. He opened the door with Pegi Tedesco's key, and went upstairs to the main bedroom, where he had left her tied to the bed. Beside her were the tools with which he had removed all of her teeth, along with some others for which he had not yet found a use. The painkillers were wearing off, and Pegi was moaning softy against the gag.

Steiger sat down beside her on the bed, and brushed the hair from her face.

"Now," he said, "where were we?"

IF *EVERY DEAD THING* GAVE YOU CHILLS, DON'T MISS THE OTHER BOOKS IN JOHN CONNOLLY'S THRILLING CHARLIE PARKER SERIES...

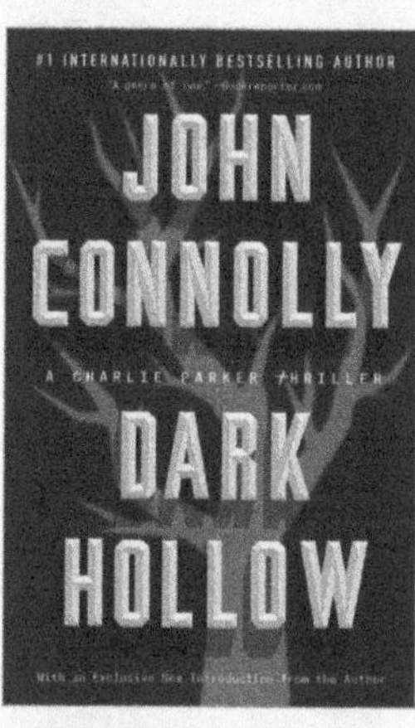

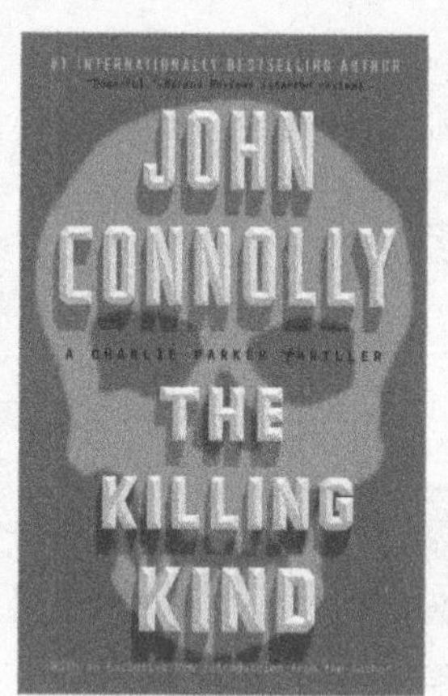

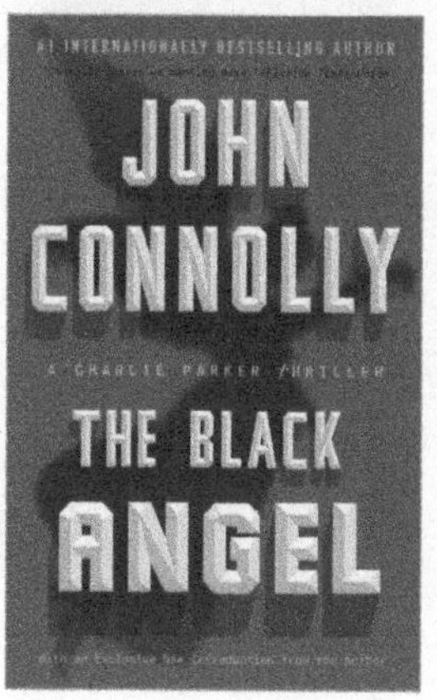

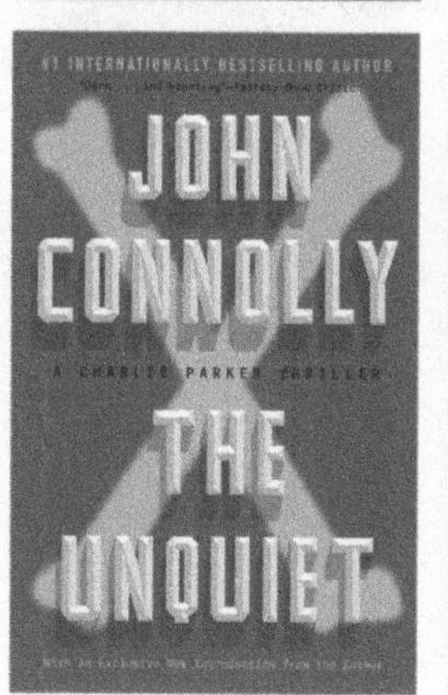

#1 INTERNATIONALLY BESTSELLING AUTHOR
JOHN CONNOLLY
A CHARLIE PARKER THRILLER
THE REAPERS

Pick up or download your copies today!

PART ONE

• I

I was the only passenger on the ferry crossing to Grand Manitou Island. As I stood on deck holding tight to the railing while we dipped and tumbled on the green, roiling waves, I understood why tourist season grinds to a halt when the November winds blow.

I was called to the tiny island in the middle of the Great Lakes by a dead woman. I traveled there at an unwelcoming time of year to learn the story of her life, hoping to discover my own story as well. A few whitecaps and swells wouldn't keep me away.

A summons from the dead is a strange way to begin a tale, but, as I have since learned, it's really no stranger than any other story in my family. As it turns out, I come from a long line of people who hover on the edge of reality. My family history isn't merely a chronicle of births and deaths and weddings and accomplishments, though it includes those things. No, the stories of my relatives sound more like fairy tales—Grimm's, unfortunately—with witches, hauntings, and malevolence all wrapped up in regrettable and sometimes bloody mishaps.

Until recently, I knew nothing of this. Growing up, I had an altogether different notion of who I was and where I came from. Then the truth began to reveal itself, as it always does. Truth seeks the light of day, needs it just like we need air, and so it finds ways to seep out of the sturdiest, most skillfully hidden boxes—even those buried deeply in the hearts of the dead.

My truth took its first breath one foggy autumn morning, nearly a thousand miles away from where I stood on the tossing ferry. That particular day didn't begin with anything out of the ordinary. Isn't that always the way? Life is thrown into chaos while you're making your way through mundane everyday tasks—an accident on the way to the grocery store takes your beloved, a heart attack interrupts a lazy Sunday morning, or, in my case, life-altering news arrives with the morning mail.

I awoke in my little bungalow overlooking Puget Sound and lay in bed awhile, listening to the barking of the seals. Then I pulled on a sweatsuit and sneakers and headed outside for my usual morning walk. I had already crossed the street and started up the hill before I noticed the fog settling in, dulling the edges of the world around me.

Some people find the sound of a foghorn romantic, evoking images of travel to faraway places with strange-sounding names. But I've never liked the fog. It obscures reality with what seems to be sinister intent, erasing all that is not within arm's reach. Anything could be out there, beyond.

I knew it was silly, being unnerved by fog in a seaside town, so I continued to walk my usual route, listening to the tinkling of the wind chimes—*tubular bells*—that were hanging from the eaves of various houses along the way.

I can't explain why—did I sense what was coming?—but the back of my neck began to tingle with a thousand tiny pinpricks. I paused, holding my breath, dread seeping off the cold pavement into the bottoms of my feet and working its way up my legs. Then something convinced me to hurry home, and I arrived at my door just in time to see the mailman materialize out of the fog.

"Pea soup," he said, shaking his head as he handed me a stack of mail.

"You be careful out there, Scooter." I smiled at him. "I couldn't see you until you were on my front step."

"Don't you worry about me, Ms. James. I'm old friends with this fog."

I watched him disappear into the whiteness and took the mail inside, where hot coffee was waiting, and poured myself a cup as I sorted through the stack. Along with the usual assortment of letters, bills, and catalogs was a large manila envelope labeled ARCHER & SON, ATTORNEYS-AT-LAW. I noticed the postmark: Grand Manitou Island, a popular tourist destination in one of the Great Lakes, halfway across the country from my home.

I sat at my kitchen table sipping coffee, turning the envelope over and over in my hands. What was this about? What did this lawyer want with me? Finally, I took a deep breath and tore it open to face whatever it contained.

I found two letters inside. One bore my name and address handwritten on the front of a thick creamy envelope, the back flap sealed with crimson wax. It was old-fashioned and lovely, reminding me of an invitation from another time and place. (As it turned out, that's exactly what it was.) The other was a white business-sized no-nonsense envelope. I opened that one first.

Dear Ms. James,

It is with deep regret that I inform you of Madlyn Crane's death. I am Ms. Crane's attorney and the executor of her will.

Please contact me at your earliest convenience.

Respectfully yours,
William Archer
Attorney-at-law

Madlyn Crane. The name sounded familiar, but I couldn't quite place it. Why did this lawyer regret to inform me of her death? A feeling of undefined, unexplainable apprehension began to cling to me as I picked up the second letter. Why was my heart pounding so? Why were my hands shaking? I broke the seal on the back of the envelope, unfolded the letter, and began reading. It was dated almost one month ago.

Dear Hallie,

Thirty years ago, my daughter and my husband were killed in a boating accident near our island home. Imagine my surprise to find that they—you and your father—are very much alive.

I don't quite know how to continue this letter. What do I say to my only child, for whom I have grieved all these years?

I'll start here. When I learned that you were alive, I was as stunned as you must be now. I had the impulse to pick up the phone and call you immediately, but then it hit me: I could not do that. I had no idea what you had been told.

Did you believe I was dead? Did you believe I had abandoned you? Your father could have told you anything. But now you're a grown woman. If you had any inkling I was alive, you would have found a way to contact me. I came to the conclusion that you and I must have been told the same lie, each believing the other was dead. We were both deceived.

How does a mother rise from the dead and enter her child's life? I thought of coming to see you, but simply showing up on your doorstep did not seem wise. A letter seemed like the gentlest way to turn your world upside down.

I know you must have many questions, as do I. I'll tell you a little about myself now, but really, can one sum up a lifetime in a few words? My name is Madlyn Crane. I still live in the house where you were born on Grand Manitou Island. You may recognize my name. I am a photographer. You may have seen my work in various magazines.

I imagine you grew up grieving for me, wishing to have a mother to shepherd you through the heaven that is childhood and the purgatory that is adolescence. I'm so sorry that I was not there for you. But Hallie, every time you wished for a mother's love, you had it. I loved you before you were born, I loved you during the empty years when I thought you were dead, and I love you now. That will never change. Although you did not know it, you have always had a mother who loved you more than anything.

I know you must be wondering what to think about this—a letter from a stranger who is alleging to be your mother. Is it true? I'm sure it flies in the face of everything you have believed about your life for the past thirty years.

I'm sorry to create such a tempest for you; believe me, I considered staying "dead" to spare you this confusion, but I concluded that the truth, no matter how painful, must be told.

By way of authentication, please look at the photograph I am enclosing. It is you and your father, a few days before you "died." I took it myself. I also offer this—an invitation. Come back to Grand Manitou Island. So much time has been wasted already.

Love from your mother,
Madlyn Crane

The photograph fluttered out as I let the letter drop to the ground. It was a small, square, black-and-white print with a white border. I saw a little girl with a strange sheen in her eyes. Was it me? It certainly looked like me, but I couldn't really be sure. It might have been any dark-haired girl. But there was no mistaking my father—younger, thinner, with more hair, but unquestionably him. This was the man who put me to bed and dried my tears and took me ice-skating. I had no doubt.

I picked up Madlyn Crane's letter and read the words over and over again, until they blurred into meaningless symbols. I don't know how long I sat there, staring at it: a letter from a ghost.

· 2

The drive from my house usually took twelve minutes. On this day I did it in six, a lifetime of questions and more than a few accusations flying through my mind.

My mother's name was Annie James, and she died in a fire when I was five, or so my father had told me. He said he carried me out of our burning house and tried to go back to save her, but the flames were too intense. The house was engulfed before the firefighters arrived. That's why there were no pictures of her, no records, no mementos of our life together as a family. He was hailed as a hero at the time, but he certainly didn't feel like one. Annie James had no other family, he told me. No grandparents, aunts, uncles, or cousins from her side. I had no surviving grandparents on his side, either, so we were alone in the world, just he and I.

Even as a child, I realized that the story of my mother's death was a tidy little tale, with no loose ends for a girl's questions to unravel. When I asked my dad about her—*What was she like? Did she have hair like mine?*—I could see his grief, as tangible and blinding as a snowstorm. *Please don't ask, Hallie. Put it out of your mind. She's gone.*

As I sped through yellow lights, my questions morphed into a mix of anger and defensiveness. Over the years I had created a tangible mother in my mind—brown hair, brown eyes, medium build. She had a sort of Jackie Kennedy quality. She liked those colorful pantsuits that were so popular in the 1970s, but we wore mother-daughter dresses to important events. She was kind but firm, loving but playful. Graceful. Elegant. If this letter was true—which it couldn't be—it would negate the only mother I had ever known. I wasn't about to let a stranger kill off my mother in a few short paragraphs.

Not to mention the fact that, if this letter was true, Madlyn Crane was accusing my father of something horrible. I loved my dad with the fierce feelings of protection common to children of single parents. How dare this woman, this stranger, flutter into my life and call my father—*my dad*—a liar? She accused him of faking our deaths and whisking me off across the country. She was basically saying I was an abducted child, someone whose photo might have appeared on a milk carton.

Where did she get off? Men like my dad don't abduct children from their mothers and assume new identities. Men like my mathematician father find rational solutions to problems. It was absurd and insulting, the whole thing. I couldn't imagine what would motivate this woman to make up such a cruel pack of lies.

But wasn't it a little odd that there were no photographs of my mother? No relatives? No friends who could talk about our life together? What if it wasn't grief but fear that I had seen in my dad's eyes when I mentioned my mother? What if he had lived for thirty years afraid that every day would be the day his abandoned wife, my abandoned mother, would show up on our doorstep? That would certainly explain his reluctance to talk about her.

Funny thing is, I remember the fire. I can see the flames and the smoke, hear the screaming and the roar of the fire trucks, feel the spray from the hoses. Was this nothing but a shadow of what never was, a memory deliberately implanted by years of storytelling? That's how powerful stories are. They can actually create the past if told often enough.

Janine, the day nurse, looked up as I walked in. Her smile faded when she saw my expression. "What's the matter?" she asked, but I put a hand up, as if to stop her words in midair. I walked by the nurses' station toward the recreation room, where I knew my father would be sitting.

I found him in front of the window, where he spent most of his days. He loved to watch the birds at the feeder. Their movements entranced him, or perhaps he was simply fascinated by those strange, flitting bits of color hovering in the air outside. It was impossible to know. I pulled up a chair and took his hands in mine.

"Dad?" I said gently. "Dad, it's Hallie."

He turned his head carefully. His deliberate slow-motion movements reminded me of a fetus in the womb, floating in another dimension, one with a thicker, viscous atmosphere, suspended there awaiting the time when he would enter a new world. He looked at me, a mix of innocence and confusion in his eyes.

"Did you bring my lunch?"

My conflicted emotions melted into the sorrow and grief

that always overcame me when I visited my father these days. The great man, the profound thinker, reduced to this. I smiled sadly at him. "Janine will bring your lunch in a little while, Dad."

What was I doing here? I wanted answers, but he was clearly unable to provide them. I sighed and squeezed his hands, the love and loss filling my throat.

"Hallie?" My father's voice brought me back into the moment. A smile crept onto his face.

It was to be one of *those* days, then. I had been hoping for it. Most of the time, my father didn't recognize me, his eyes expressionless, his spark extinguished. It was as though his spirit was submerged deep inside his body, exploring some hidden world within. I often wondered where his spirit had gone and what it was doing while the husk that looked like my father sat motionless in his chair, staring at birds.

Every so often, though, he would have moments of lucidity. His eyes would become clear and bright as he rose to the surface, animating the lifeless features with his familiar spark. He would know me again. He would smile and say, "Come to see your old dad, eh?" And we'd be able have a conversation, albeit a brief one. Soon enough, I'd lose him as he descended back into the depths of his being. The doctors told me that was typical of Alzheimer's patients.

"I've come to ask about Mom."

"Your mother?" He frowned at me, confused.

I knew I didn't have much time, so I dove right in. "Did you take me away from her on purpose, Dad?" I couldn't believe I had even said the words. They sounded so idiotic, so untrue.

He leaned in and put a finger to his lips. "I saw your mother yesterday," he admitted, his eyes darting back and forth, making sure nobody was listening. "I looked out of my bedroom window and there she was, walking in the courtyard."

I was silent for a moment. "You saw Mom?"

He slowly nodded his head. "She was wearing that long purple dress she used to like so much." A smile, then. "I think she's come for me this time, Hallie."

His earnestness gave me a chill. "Dad." I held his hand. "I got a letter today from somebody claiming to be Mom."

"Madlyn wrote to you?"

I took a sharp breath. *He said Madlyn, not Annie.* "Did you do it?" I managed to ask. "Why, Dad? Why did you take me away from her?"

He smiled, his eyes brimming with tears as he stroked my cheek. "I had to save my little girl."

"Save me from what?"

The tears spilled onto his face. "From that place, Hallie. It would have destroyed you."

And that was it. My window of time was gone, at least for that day. He turned back to the birds. I held my hand to his cheek, as if I were trying to transfuse all the love I felt for him into his veins.

"And I thought he was having such a good morning." It was his nurse, there with his lunch tray.

"He was, Janine. It's just. . . ." My words trailed off into a long sigh. I looked up at her in silence.

"I know, honey, I know. It never gets any easier. For us or for them."

I hugged my father tight as I got up to leave. "I love you, Dad," I said, hoping, wherever he was within that shell of a body, he heard me.

The next morning I got the call.

"Did he say anything?" I choked, the emotion shredding my voice to a rasp. "Did he ask for me?"

"I've seen a lot of death in my years here, honey," Janine told me softly. "They almost never have any last words. Dying is too hard."

· 3

Before I lost my father, I never understood all the rituals surrounding funerals: the wake, the service itself, the reception afterward, the dinners prepared by well-meaning friends and delivered in plastic containers, even the popular habit of making poster boards filled with photos of the dear departed. But now I know why we do those things. It's busywork, all of it. I had so much to take care of, so many arrangements to make, so many people to inform, I didn't have a moment to be engulfed by the ocean of grief that was lapping at my heels. Instead, I waded through the shallows, performing task after task, grateful to have duties to propel me forward.

Three hundred people, maybe more, crammed into our small church for my dad's funeral. His colleagues and former students came, as did my friends and their spouses and parents. Old pals I hadn't seen since high school—the entire flute section of the band I marched with in tenth grade—my colleagues at the newspaper, town restaurant owners, and shopkeepers and fishermen. Most of the stores on the main street closed for the afternoon with signs on their doors: GONE TO THE JAMES FUNERAL. No matter what else he had done, my dad was beloved in this town; all these people standing with me in my grief were proof of that. Simply by being there, they were telling me what a good man my father had been, and I desperately needed to hear it, in light of what I now knew.

Midway through the service, the minister nodded in my direction. It was time. I stood up and made my way to the front of the church to deliver my father's eulogy, my steps achingly slow, as if I were treading through quicksand. It took an eternity for me to reach the lectern, but, finally there, I took a deep breath and looked out onto the sea of stricken faces, friends, neighbors, and colleagues, many dabbing at their eyes or blowing their noses.

I could see their emotion hanging in the air. Grief covered the room like a black shroud, but I also saw relief, wispy and white, swirling around friends whose parents were still vibrant and living; it was not yet their turn to bury the most important person in their lives. Fear radiated from some of the mourners, a hazy almost colorless thread that wrapped around their throats, pulled their gazes to the ground, and twined around their hands. But it was the intense sadness that moved me the most, a blue mist that fell throughout this congregation like gentle Seattle rain, pooling on heads and laps and pews and trickling through the aisles. Somehow, I saw all this as I stood before them—I had a long history of seeing peculiar sights that nobody else seemed to notice—and I felt comforted.

I cleared my throat as I fumbled with the sheets of paper

in front of me, but when I looked down to begin reading the eulogy I had written, I saw that my sadness had slipped onto the words, transforming them into vibrating, watery symbols with no real meaning. I had no choice but to speak from the heart.

"My father was a wonderful man," I began, my voice sounding strange and foreign to my own ears. Was it really me speaking? Was my father *really* the one being eulogized? *How can this be happening?*

"I never knew my mother, so my dad was all I had. While most of us would probably agree that it's difficult enough to bring up children with two parents in the household, my dad did a spectacular job of being both mother and father to me. It was his life's mission. He made sure I never missed out on anything because I didn't have a mom—he even took me to the mother-daughter picnics at school, which amused my teachers no end."

A slight chuckle rumbled through the congregation.

"He took me whale watching even though he hated the water; he went shopping with me for my prom dress. And he made hot chocolate on damp winter nights, when we'd sit up talking about everything from the beauty of the universe to small-town politics to the latest dramas in my life, whatever they happened to be. He was always there with his mathematician's mind, making sense of the nonsensical, calmly explaining that there had to be a reason for even the most absurd event. In these ways and countless others, my dad protected me from the harshness of the world, as he also tried to do with many of the students he mentored. I felt safe when I was with him; I knew he could ward off any impending storm."

More nods and smiles from the crowd.

"And now he's gone ahead to prepare the way, for me and for everyone in this room. When it's our time to go, he'll be there to greet us with hot chocolate, helping us make sense out of the unfathomable reality of death and what comes next."

I looked out across the room, and although it was probably the tears welling up in my eyes and clouding my vision, I could've sworn I saw my dad standing in the back of the church, smiling. *Good job, Peanut,* I heard him say softly, in my ear. *Thanks for the kind words. I love you, too.*

After the service and the reception were over, after my friends had put the last plate in the dishwasher and turned it on, packed the remainder of the food into the freezer, and left, I heard a knock at the door. I didn't have to open it to know who was standing on the other side.

He was just as I had last seen him, black overcoat, slightly rumpled hair, electric blue eyes. He smelled of salt air and memories, pain and forgiveness. We didn't say anything for a moment, and then I flew into his arms.

"God, I'm so sorry, Hallie," my ex-husband whispered into my hair. "I know how much you loved him. I loved him, too."

Finally the tears came. I burst into sobs, there in Richard Blake's arms, crying for my father and for a little girl who had lost the only parent she had ever known—and the one she hadn't known—in the space of a few days. The crushing sadness I felt at the passing of my dad mixed with confusion and rage. I had been grieving for my mother my whole life, and she apparently was *there all the time,* while she spent a lifetime mourning the loss of a child who was very much alive. All because of the man whose death now left a gaping hole inside me.

Richard led me to the living-room sofa, my body shaking with the force of the grief running through it. I don't know how long I lay there, my head in his lap, as he stroked my hair. When I finally dried my eyes, he got up and opened a bottle of wine for both of us. "I think you could use this." He smiled sadly, handing me a glass, the rhythm of his accent reminding me of our years together in London. It seemed like a lifetime ago.

A mouthful of cold, oaky chardonnay slipped down my throat. "You came all this way. I can't believe it."

"Of course I came," he said softly. "Where else would I be?"

I could think of a thousand places, none of which was at my side. "You might have just sent a card." I took his hand.

He squeezed back. "What other chance would I have to travel halfway around the world from one depressingly rainy city to another?"

I suddenly ached for the lack of his wicked sense of humor in my life. I was grieving every loss now, it seemed. "Did Ethan come with you?" I asked, referring to Richard's new husband. The man who was once the love of my life had sealed a union with the love of his as soon as they were able to do so in London. I hadn't gone to the ceremony—I *was* invited—but I did send a place setting of their china. What else was I to do? The battle had been lost long ago, when I realized it was never really mine to win.

He nodded. "He's got friends in Seattle and is staying with them. I rented an utterly dreadful car and drove up here alone. I thought you'd rather . . ." He didn't finish this thought. He was right; I was grateful he hadn't brought Ethan, but I didn't want to get into that conversation just now.

I grinned at him instead. "You *drove*? In America?"

"Apart from everyone else driving on the wrong side of the road, it went fine," he replied, sighing and slumping into a chair. Both of us were trying to lighten the mood, but it wasn't catching fire. "Seriously, I missed the funeral, didn't I? I didn't get here in time."

I shook my head. "Don't worry about it. I was in a daze anyway. The last few days have been a blur. But I'm so glad you're here now. I didn't know what I was going to do with myself, after it was all over and everyone had gone home and I was alone."

"You're not alone," he said gently. "'Ain't no river wide enough.' Isn't that what they say?"

I held his gaze for a long time, both of us, I think, remembering how much we loved each other, until I broke our silence. "And what do *you* say, Rich? Dinner? More wine?"

"Both would be lovely. And then let's sit and reminisce about your dad for a while."

Later, after we had laughed and cried, remembering my father, I handed Richard the envelope that had flung my entire existence into the abyss a few days earlier. "I haven't told anybody else about this." I fidgeted in my chair, eyeing him as he began reading the letter from Madlyn Crane.

He looked up at me with wide eyes. "Good Lord. Is this true?"

I nodded, shrugging. "I asked my dad about it the day before he died. I told him I got a letter from someone claiming to be my mother, and he said her name. *Madlyn wrote to you?* he asked. That was all the confirmation I needed."

Richard took my hands and held them tightly. "But why?" His eyes were searching mine for answers I didn't have. "Why the devil would he do something like that? I know your dad. He wouldn't—"

"I have no idea. He said something about saving me. That's all I know."

Richard let out a sigh and leaned against the back of his chair, staring at Madlyn's letter as if trying to will the words to reveal their secrets. "I can't believe Madlyn Crane is your mother," he murmured. "I mean, of all people."

"You say that as if you know her."

"Well, I don't *know* her, but I know *of* her. So do you. I've got one of her books on my coffee table. You've seen it a million times."

An image shot into my mind: Richard and me, sitting with cups of tea in our flat, looking through a book of photographs of London.

"Where's your laptop?" he asked, and I pointed up the stairs. In moments he was back with it, sitting next to me at the table and typing her name into the search engine.

I watched as page after page of hits came up on my screen.

Time, Travel & Leisure, National Geographic, Vanity Fair, Vogue, and many more, all having published her work. Madlyn Crane was famous.

"Let's go to her website," I suggested, and I held my breath as it loaded.

A list of headings ran down the left side of the screen: WATER, ANIMALS, PORTRAITS. Richard clicked on them, one by one. We found photos of celebrities dressed in finery or in nothing at all, ordinary people in sidewalk cafés or on street corners, children playing in foreign lands. I could not look away from these photos, because somehow I could see beyond the subject's façade. It was as though their inner thoughts were captured there on film. It sounds absurd, but I thought I could hear those people whispering to me.

Behind one celebrity's eyes, I saw an impending divorce. In the next photo, intense fear of failure. Cancer was lurking deep within the esophagus of the third. I cannot explain how I knew these things just by looking at their portraits, but I am quite certain they were there. I felt hypnotized, as though I could, at any time, be sucked into the world captured on film by Madlyn Crane.

And then we found something that caused my own spirit to catch in my throat. Richard clicked on a heading called LOVE and there was only one photo, the black-and-white image of a child. She was jumping off a swing attached to the limb of an enormous oak tree. The photographer had captured her at just the right moment, the midair flight before hitting the ground. Her eyes were looking right into the camera—she obviously knew someone was taking her picture—and she had an enormous smile on her face, radiating the sheer thrill of being airborne. But behind those sparkling eyes and exuberant smile, I could sense something else. That little girl whispered to me: *Help me. I'm afraid.*

Then I saw the name under the photograph: HALCYON CRANE, 1974–1979.

"It's you, my dear," Richard said. We looked at each other in silence, neither knowing what else to say.

Hours later, with Richard snoring in the guest room, I padded back downstairs and opened the laptop again, its bright screen glaring in the darkness. I'm not quite sure what I was looking for—more information about her? A way to know her better somehow? What I found was this article on the *Chicago Sun Times* website:

"SOUL CAPTURER" DIES OF HEART ATTACK

Photographer Madlyn Crane died in her home on Grand Manitou Island on Thursday of an apparent heart attack, said William Archer, Ms. Crane's attorney.

In four decades as one of this nation's preeminent photographers, Ms. Crane shot travel pieces, newsmakers and landscapes, but she was best known for her haunting portraits. Whether she was shooting celebrities for a magazine layout, people she met on her travels, or animals, Ms. Crane had a reputation for illuminating a subject's inner being, thus earning her the nickname of "Soul Capturer," which, as it happens, was also the title of one of her books. As her fame grew, many celebrities refused to allow Ms. Crane to photograph them during times of personal strife or distress, for fear of showing too much to Ms. Crane's eerily penetrating eye.

Ms. Crane leaves no survivors.

"Apparently, she did," I said to myself. I retrieved William Archer's letter from the drawer in the kitchen where I had stuffed it and dialed the number on the letterhead. I'd only reach his voice mail at this late hour, but I wanted to call immediately, while I still had the nerve to set something in motion that I might think better of in the light of day.

"This is Hallie James," I said, to Mr. Archer's machine. "I got your package, and I'm calling to let you know I plan to travel to Grand Manitou Island on Monday. Please get in touch with me tomorrow to confirm the date."

I put the phone down and sighed in the darkness of my kitchen. And then I crept up to my empty bed, where I tossed and turned all night long. The next morning, early, the phone rang.

"Is this Miss James?"

"I can't remember the last time anyone called me that, but yes." I smiled into the receiver. "I'm Hallie."

"Hallie, I'm William Archer," he said. "I'm calling about your visit to this island next week. I was very well acquainted with Madlyn, and I want to assure you that everything you say to me will be kept in the strictest confidence."

"Thank you, but I'm not sure—" He interrupted me.

"If I may? A couple of factors are in play here that I suggest would best be discussed in person, when you arrive. Suffice it to say that one of them is Miss Crane's sizable estate and the other is the rather delicate nature of—well, if I may be blunt here—your actual existence."

"I'm not sure what you mean." I began to get a knot in my stomach. Maybe this wasn't such a good idea after all.

"Hallie, I'm aware of the fact that you're Madlyn's daughter. But nobody else on the island knows, not to my knowledge anyway. That's because certain events surrounded your . . . departure so many years ago. I was just a child myself when it happened, but the circumstances are well known here."

Well known? "Can you tell me more? I feel like I'm totally in the dark."

"It's better spoken of in person," he said quickly. "I'm only bringing it up now because of the fact that you and your father are alive—"

I interrupted, choking on the words. "My father passed away. His funeral was yesterday."

"Oh." Silence for a moment. "I'm so sorry for your loss, and for . . . well, the timing couldn't be worse. I thought it was difficult when Madlyn died before she contacted you. But your dad dying, too? This puts a whole new level of awful into the mix."

His kindness touched me. "I'm getting through it," I said, fighting back the tears. "What doesn't kill you makes you stronger; isn't that what they say?"

"I've always thought that was a load of crap," he said softly. It made me smile. "Are you sure you want to come here now? The island isn't going anywhere. We can wait."

"I think it'll do me good," I told him, understanding fully for the first time myself. "Getting away, seeing a new place.

It'll take my mind off the emptiness that has settled around me here."

"Okay, then," he said. "But I need to ask one thing. Please wait until you speak with me before divulging the true nature of your visit to anyone here on the island. Believe me, it'll be easier that way. You don't want to be answering questions before you have all the facts." He went on to give me a list of practical things I should pack for my visit—sweaters, jeans, hiking boots, a warm waterproof coat—and even offered to make reservations for me on the ferry and at a local inn. "I'll have you picked up at the ferry dock as well."

And it was done. I was really going. "Thank you, Mr. Archer. I appreciate everything you're doing on my behalf."

"I'm looking forward to seeing you on Monday," he said, and I hung up the phone.

I stood there holding the receiver for a few moments, wondering what I had just talked myself into. I hadn't noticed Richard standing behind me.

"Going somewhere?" he asked, raising his eyebrows and pouring some steaming coffee into a mug.

I opened the refrigerator and handed him the skim milk. "Sugar's in the tin on the counter."

"Nice deflection, but I asked you a question." He smiled as he stirred his coffee. "You're going to Grand Manitou Island, aren't you?"

I poured myself a cup and sank into a chair at the table. "I'm flying out on Monday," I admitted.

"Are you sure that's wise right now? After all you've been through? She's not there anymore, Hallie."

"I know that. But she lived there all these years. *I* lived there, Richard; so did my dad. Maybe . . ." I didn't know what else to say. The truth was, I wasn't quite sure why I was going.

He reached across the table and took my hand. "If you're determined to do this, I'll go with you. I can change my plans."

"It's tempting." I smiled at him, wanting what I knew I couldn't have. "But I think I need to do this alone. I have no idea who I really am, Rich. Everything I was told about my childhood has been a lie. Maybe this trip will help me find out the truth. I won't ever meet my mother, but by going to the place where she lived, I'll get to know her a little. I'll see her house and her town and where she bought her groceries. I'll walk the streets she walked and meet her friends. I know it's not much, but it's something."

He took a long sip of coffee, looking at me over the rim with concern in his eyes.

"There's another reason for me to go," I went on. "What was so terrible about our life with Madlyn Crane on Grand Manitou Island that pushed Dad to take me away and move all the way out here? There may still be some people on the island who know. That's what I'm hoping, anyway."

"Be careful what you wish for," Richard warned, wagging a finger at me. "You might not like what you unearth. Whatever the reason was, it's not going to be pleasant."

I sighed. "It might not be pleasant, but at least it will be the truth."

It sounded convincing enough, but the tightness in my stomach told me I wasn't so sure this was the right thing to do. And as I stirred my coffee, I thought I saw storm clouds forming in the cup.

4

After an exhausting day of travel—two hours of driving with Richard to the airport in Seattle, the long flight to Minneapolis, the white-knuckle ride on a puddle jumper to Saint Barnabas, a small mainland town across the lake from Grand Manitou, and finally the taxi to the ferry dock—I arrived with just moments to spare. As soon as the ferry shoved off, I stumbled out onto the deck to get a whiff of Great Lakes air, but the icy burst of spray hitting my cheeks made me wish that I hadn't. I held on tight to the railing as the boat dipped and tossed from side to side. As I was inching my way back toward the cabin, something in the distance caught my eye.

A wide expanse of open water lay ahead, but as the ferry turned, the island appeared, seeming to rise from beneath the surface of the lake. It looked like a great turtle's nose poking into the air above the waterline, followed by the hump of its shell. Somewhere in the dark recesses of my brain, cells that hadn't been called upon in decades sputtered and choked at the sight. Yes, I had seen this before, been here before. I couldn't quite capture the full memory, though. It hung just out of reach, like a carrot in front of a horse, drawing me forward.

"Miss?" I turned and saw a man in uniform, his gray hair blowing in the stiff wind. His weathered face spoke of years of exposure to the elements, but kindness radiated from his eyes. "Why don't you come up into the pilothouse? Your bags are safe here. The view from there is just as clear and you won't be so cold."

A very good idea. I followed him upstairs.

"We don't get many tourists this time of year," he began, as he ushered me into the cramped cabin, looking at me too hard, too long. I pulled my purse into my lap and encircled it with my arms as I settled into one of the high chairs.

"I'm not a tourist. Not exactly." He waited for me to continue. "I'm seeing William Archer on a legal matter." It was, in fact, the truth.

"Ah. Good lawyer, that one."

He stroked his beard and looked at me deeply. There was that uncomfortable feeling again. One thing I didn't want, as the only woman on this ferry in the middle of an angry lake, was to be the object of intense interest. This captain seemed nice enough, but I had no idea who he was.

"You know I won't be making a return run to the island until Friday?"

I nodded. "I've planned to stay until then."

"First time on the island?" He turned his gaze out toward the water.

"No," I replied, fidgeting in my chair. "I was there as a child, but I don't remember much about it. I'm anxious to look around. Again."

He smiled, finally. "It's a beautiful place. Pity you couldn't have seen it in summer, with everything in bloom. Tourists flock to Grand Manitou in the spring and summer, but after Halloween things die down considerably. Do you know why they call it Grand Manitou?"

"It's got to be a Native American word, right?"

He nodded. "Means *great spirit*. They believed that the Great Spirit himself, the creator, lived here. This was the gateway into his world."

"Sort of like the Mount Olympus of the Great Lakes?"

"Something like that, yes." He chuckled. Then he pointed out the window. "Look, you can see the town coming into view now."

We chugged slowly past the shoreline. Even though I had seen photographs of this place and read about it in a guidebook, I was not prepared for what I saw: Enormous Victorian-era houses with grand front porches and turreted roofs lined a high cliff that gave way to a rocky shore. Each house was more magnificent than the next, each porch larger, each yard more meticulously manicured.

"Before the turn of the last century, wealthy people from Chicago and Detroit and Minneapolis built these 'shacks' as vacation homes," my de facto tour guide told me. I had the feeling he had given this speech many times before. "They came for the clean air and the cool summers."

I couldn't imagine having the kind of money it would take to build one of those grand homes at all, let alone as a summer place. "Are these houses mostly inns now?" William Archer had made arrangements for me to stay in one of the island inns. Perhaps it was one of the houses I was seeing.

"Some of them are," he told me, nodding, "but some are still in private hands."

The captain took the helm then, guiding the ferry into the dock. I prepared to gather up my bags, wondering what I would find when I set foot in my mother's world.

"Is Will meeting you at the dock, then, miss, or are you needing a ride?" the captain wanted to know. "I can arrange a cab for you before shoving off for the mainland."

"Thank you so much for the offer, but Mr. Archer is sending a car for me," I called over my shoulder, dragging my heavy bags down the ramp and onto the dock as the ferry workers scrambled to unload the rest of the cargo. I noticed that several people, along with horses pulling flat wagons, had arrived to pick up food deliveries, mail, and other supplies brought by this twice-weekly ferry. It struck me as odd: horses? Then I remembered. I had read in the guidebook that—like its counterpart, Mackinac Island—Grand Manitou did not allow motorized vehicles, with the exception of an ambulance and a fire truck or two for emergencies. Tourists parked their cars at the mainland ferry dock and got around the island either on bikes, on foot, or in horse-drawn carriages that served as taxis. Residents did the same. Even the police were on horseback.

The gray November sky hung low and the wind swirled around me, so I buttoned my jacket all the way up to the neck to ward off the chill. An unsettling emptiness permeated the air. Apart from the bustle of the ferry dock, I didn't see another soul. I looked up and down the main street but heard no sound—no cars backfiring, no radios blaring, no people talking—only the wind whispering in my ears. Used to city noises as I was, it seemed deathly quiet.

This was the town where I was born, where I lived until I was five years old, and yet nothing seemed familiar. Both sides of the street were lined with buildings, some wooden and painted in bright colors, others red brick, none more than two stories high. A slightly raised wooden sidewalk ran in front of all the buildings as far as I could see. Colorful shingles swayed in the wind, advertising the businesses, many of them no doubt closed for the season: a fudge shop, an ice-cream parlor, a bakery. Like a movie set, nothing was amiss; there was no garbage on the street, no paint peeling from the walls of any of the buildings, nothing faded or bleak, only the perfection that might result from careful stagehands touching up the entire town between scenes. It was like Main Street at Disney World come to life—old-fashioned, idyllic, quaint.

Behind me, I heard a soft *clop, clop, clop* coming down the street, and I turned to see a horse and carriage approaching. It wasn't the open-air type you see in New York's Central Park but rather a more sensible enclosed vehicle, the likes of which you might imagine passengers using in their daily travels around the turn of the last century. Mr. Archer had said he would send a taxi for me, and here it was. Even though I knew there was no motorized traffic on the island, I stupidly had had the idea in my head that I'd be met by the kind of taxi with four wheels and an engine.

Perception and reality collided when the two chestnut-brown Clydesdales stopped in front of me and the coachman, an elderly man with a shock of white hair, said, "I assume you're Miss James. I'm here to take you to the Manitou Inn."

He groaned as he clambered down from his seat to gather up my bags.

"I'm supposed to be meeting William Archer at his office."

He reached into his pocket and pulled out a small envelope, which he held out in my direction. "I'm to give you this by way of explanation," he said. I opened the envelope and read the note inside.

Dear Hallie,

Please forgive this change in plans. A last-minute urgent business matter cropped up just about the time your ferry pulled in. Rather than meeting at my office as we discussed, I've instructed Henry, the coachman, to take you to the inn.

I've taken the liberty of rescheduling our appointment for 9 a.m. tomorrow. If this doesn't work for you, please phone me from the inn and let me know a better time.

Again, please accept my apologies for any inconvenience this might cause.

Most sincerely,
William Archer

A handwritten *note*? Why hadn't he just called my cell with the change in plans? "I'll just give him a buzz to confirm," I mumbled, fishing my phone out of my purse. As I stared at the NO SERVICE message on my phone's display, I realized why Mr. Archer hadn't made the call.

Henry shrugged. He was probably thinking: *Tourist.*

I dropped the useless phone back into my purse. "I guess

I'm going to the inn, then." I smiled as he held out his hand to help me up the two steps into the carriage.

"This is the first time I've ever ridden in something like this," I said to Henry, who hadn't heard me. I settled in, and with a slight shaking motion we were off. The soft sound of the hoofbeats was mesmerizing: *clop, clop, clop.* I looked out the window at the town passing by—a diner, the bank, a bar, yet another fudge shop—settled back against the carriage seat, and exhaled. A feeling of peace washed over me. I supposed it came from the lack of anything motorized—no cars, no buses, no exhaust fumes, no booming car stereos, no cell phones—to interfere with the quiet beating of my own heart.

We turned from the main street and began climbing a long hill lined with more Victorian-era houses, not quite as opulent as the mansions I saw from the ferry but certainly nice enough, each with a front porch and a well-maintained lawn. Had my mother lived in one of these houses? Had I? I tried to search the closed compartments in my brain for any hint of recognition, any flare of familiarity. I had walked these streets as a child, played here, lived here; surely there must be some imprint left, some ghostly residue of my life. Yet it was as if I were seeing it all with entirely new eyes.

Up the hill we went, finally stopping in front of a massive yellow wooden house with a porch that snaked from the front all the way around to the back. A brightly painted sign swung noisily from the eaves: MANITOU INN.

As Henry retrieved my bags, I climbed the steps toward the front door but stopped in my tracks because of the view in front of me. From the porch, I could see across the wide expanse of water in all directions, the island's rocky coast, and even the mainland on the opposite shore. In the distance, I could make out the ferry chugging along on its return trip; from this vantage point it looked like a tiny toy boat. I held my breath. I could easily imagine why wealthy people from the past built their summer homes on this spot.

"It's quite something, isn't it?" Henry was grinning broadly.

"It really is," I agreed. "I could stand here all day."

The door opened and out came a woman wearing jeans and a cream-colored fisherman's-knit sweater, bright red bifocals hanging around her neck on a silver chain. Long graying hair softened her angular face; I couldn't tell if she was about my age and prematurely gray or a phenomenal-looking sixty. The innkeeper, I assumed. I knew she was expecting me—Mr. Archer had made arrangements for me to stay here—yet she just stood there in the doorway for a moment, eyeing me with what seemed to be suspicion mixed with surprise. I didn't quite know what to make of the cool reception, so I broke the silence between us.

"Hi!" I smiled the brightest smile I could muster, extending my hand. "I'm Hallie James. I believe I have a reservation?"

She nodded, her suspicious glance melting into a grin as she took my hand. "You sure do, Hallie. Welcome, welcome! I don't know what's wrong with me. Come in, for heaven's sake, out of this wind." She turned and called her thanks to the coachman before ushering me inside.

The house had a comforting, welcoming aura. Its shining wood floors were covered with oriental rugs; colorful oil paintings of island scenes hung on the walls; photographs lined the fireplace mantel in the living room. The overstuffed couch and love seat looked like inviting places to curl up and read. Through a doorway, I could see a study with floor-to-ceiling bookshelves.

"I'm Mira Finch," she said, leading me up the stairs to the second floor. "Your room's up here."

"I was so glad to learn that you're still open for business." I was chattering, nervously. "I understand most inns are closed this time of year."

She opened the first door at the top of the stairs. "It's true, the weather can get pretty nasty here in November," she said, nodding. "I don't have any other guests, haven't for weeks. But I'm a year-round resident, so I'm happy to put you up for as long as you plan to stay. This is your room, the Mainland Suite."

"Wow," I murmured, looking at the enormous bay window. Its cushioned seat was covered with multicolored pillows; a couple of afghans were folded in the corner next to the wall. I saw the same view as from the front porch: the great expanse of choppy water below and the flickering lights of the mainland beyond. A king-sized bed held a down comforter, and a wood fire crackled in the corner fireplace. "This is absolutely beautiful."

"It'll do." Mira's smile broadened, warming somewhat. "Your keys are on the nightstand. One opens the front door—which you'll rarely find locked—the other is for your room. Coffee and some sort of breakfast—muffins, scones, eggs, whatever—will be available in the kitchen after seven o'clock, but I'm usually up earlier if you want something before then."

"Hey, please don't trouble yourself on my account," I told her. "Coffee and a little something to munch on would be great, but I'm not expecting the full treatment, it being off-season and all. You've got no other guests; I really don't want to be a bother."

Mira patted my arm; I was grateful to be melting her somewhat icy exterior. "How about we say this: I'll make coffee in the morning. After that, the kitchen's open. I've got cereal, oatmeal, bagels, eggs. Help yourself to whatever you'd like."

"That sounds perfect," I said, lugging my bags to a settee at the foot of the bed.

I could tell she was taking a moment to decide whether or not to say something further. Finally she added, "I was just planning on sitting down for some tea when you arrived. Join me after you get settled, if you'd like."

I had imagined I would spend my first hours on this island discussing wills and mothers and deaths with Mr. Archer, but this was infinitely nicer. "I'd love that, thank you! Is it okay if I clean up a little first? I've been traveling since early this morning, and I feel the grime of several states is covering me from head to toe."

She laughed. "Take your time getting settled. I'll be downstairs whenever you're ready." And she left me alone, closing the door behind her.

I slid my pajamas out of my suitcase but left the rest of my clothes where they were. Then I took my travel kit into the bathroom, which to my delight was round. Located in one of the inn's turrets, no doubt. It contained an enormous tiled shower and a Jacuzzi, facing another window overlooking the lake. Fluffy white towels sat in a stack on the counter, along with candles, soap, shampoo, and lotions.

Instead of unpacking further, I snuggled into the window seat, pulled one of the afghans over my legs, and stared out across the water. Back home, Puget Sound was my safe haven, the barking of the seals and the lapping of the waves like a sedative to me. Any problems in my life—from high school angst to college uncertainty to my divorce to my dad's illness—were solved on the seashore, pounded out of existence by the relentless beating of the surf. I got a similar feeling here, looking out over this great lake. There were no seals or whales, but the peacefulness was the same.

I took a moment to catch my breath, and the enormity of it all hit me—I was actually on my mother's island, looking at my mother's lake! This was the place from which my father had fled with me, all those years ago.

My mind swam with a jumble of thoughts. If I had only been here a few weeks earlier, I'd have met her. If she had just called instead of sending a letter. If she had flown out to see me. If.

Tears were stinging my eyes. I went into the bathroom, peeled off my clothes, and turned on the tap. A shower would do me good. I tried not to break down, but as I stepped under the stream of water the tears began to flow. I stood there sobbing as I let the water wash away the miles between me and my home, the lies between me and my father, and the regret I felt about my mother.

Finally, I toweled off, ran a brush through my hair, pulled on a shirt and jeans, and made my way downstairs. I found Mira in the living room with a plate of cheese and crackers, veggies and dips, and some assorted meats. When she spied me coming down the stairs, she poured me a cup of tea and topped off her own.

She looked at my puffy eyes and splotchy complexion with concern. "Everything okay?"

"Long day. Long week. Long month."

"I hear you." She smiled. "I thought you'd probably be hungry after your trip so I've got a chicken in the oven, but let's dig into this for now."

She had made dinner for me? I hadn't realized how famished I was. That handful of peanuts on the plane wasn't much of a lunch. And I hadn't even thought about finding dinner on an island where most everything was closed up tight for the season.

"Thank you so much, Mira," I said, taking a sip of my tea. "I certainly didn't expect you to do anything like this, but it's wonderful and much appreciated."

"Hey, I'm an innkeeper." She grinned, clinking her cup with mine. "It's what I do. I should also give you the particulars of life on the island during the off season."

I folded myself into the armchair next to hers.

"The first thing you should know: Most shops and restaurants are closed for the season."

"So I've heard," I said, taking another sip of tea. It tasted comforting and warm. "Is anything still open?"

"There's the grocery store, the wine bar on Main Street, the diner where just about everyone congregates for breakfast and lunch, and the Lodge on the other side of the island. There's Jonah's Coffee Shop and—let's see—the library's open, too. But that's about it."

"That's more than I was expecting, actually."

Mira dug into the cheese and crackers. "So, what brings you to our little island during the gales of November?"

William Archer had given me express instructions not to discuss my circumstances with anyone. Still, after a somewhat chilly reception, Mira seemed friendly and welcoming. On the other hand, he knew I was staying at this inn; he had even made the reservation for me. If he thought I could take Mira into my confidence, he would've said so. He had alluded to a "situation" that had occurred around the time my father left with me all those years ago, something the islanders who were living here then had not forgotten. Now was not the time to find out if Mira was one of them. She was the only innkeeper still open on this island. If she threw me out for claiming to be Madlyn Crane's long-dead daughter, I'd be without a place to stay.

"I'm seeing William Archer on a legal matter."

She looked at me, a mix of interest and curiosity in her eyes. "Oh?" Clearly, she wanted to hear more. "It's really none of my business. It's the innkeeper's curse; we're naturally inquisitive."

"No, it's perfectly all right," I said to her, hesitating. "I'm here to talk with Mr. Archer about Madlyn Crane's will."

Mira stared at me for a moment and my mind raced, trying to think of a plausible way to backpedal away from an explanation.

"Oh, I'm so sorry," she said slowly. "I didn't think Madlyn had any living relatives."

I had succeeded in digging myself into a nice little hole.

Should I admit who I was? Keep silent? Saying as much as I already had was clearly foolish.

"I'm not exactly—" I began, and then stopped and started again. I didn't want to tell an outright lie. Too many lies had been told already. "I really don't know much right now. I got a letter from Mr. Archer requesting me to meet with him about the will. I didn't know Madlyn Crane. I knew her work, obviously, but beyond that—"

She squinted at me. "You've never met the woman?"

"I don't remember ever meeting her, no." It was technically the truth.

She raised her eyebrows. "You've come all this way at this time of year to talk about the will of a woman you didn't know." A statement.

I was starting to get more than a little uncomfortable with her intrusion into my personal business. What did she care why I was here? Why was she grilling me like this? "Actually, if you must know, I've been dealing with quite a lot at home lately, and when I received Mr. Archer's letter I was grateful for the chance to get away for a few days."

"If you *must* know," wielded correctly, always turns the tide. I watched as her suspicion melted into concern mixed with what might have been a good dose of chagrin.

"I'm sorry," she said softly. "I understand. Everyone can use a getaway now and then, even in November."

"In any case, I'll learn more tomorrow when I see Mr. Archer. I'm curious to find out about all of this, too."

The conversation turned to other things, and we spent the rest of the evening quite amicably. After all, she had prepared dinner for me and was doing everything she could to make me feel at home. Still, I couldn't shake the feeling that had crept up my spine when I mentioned Madlyn Crane's name. It was as though Mira's suspicion and mistrust had worked its way into my body and was taking root, reminding me to be on guard.

When I finally retreated to my room I climbed beneath the thick down comforter, but I couldn't shake the cold.

· 5

I awoke with a start, a silent scream catching in my throat. Someone had touched my face; I was sure of it. I sat up fast. Was somebody here, watching me as I slept? Mira?

Moonlight streamed in from the bay window, illuminating the room with an eerie whiteness. My heart was pounding in my chest as I looked around: my bags, the television, the armoire, the window seat. Nothing seemed amiss.

I slipped out of bed and poked my head into the bathroom. Empty. So was the closet. Nobody was under my bed, either. After checking the lock on my door—bolted, the chain fastened—I exhaled, not realizing I had been holding my breath all the while.

It had been a dream, then. *Silly.*

I tried settling back down under the covers, but the adrenaline rush had pushed sleep away. I tossed and turned for an hour or so, trying to coax slumber back from wherever it had gone, but my thoughts ran wild, from my mother to William Archer's letter to Mira's suspicious eyes. The numbers on the clock glowed 4:15. I finally gave in; there would be no more sleep tonight. I slipped on my robe and padded over to the window seat, covering my legs with an afghan as I leaned back against the pillows.

There wasn't the whisper of a wave; the lake was so calm it seemed as though a thin sheet of ice were covering its surface. Moonlight sparkled on the inky water in a long column that stretched as far as I could see. There were a few lights still blinking on the mainland at this hour; most everyone else, apparently, was sensible enough to be in bed.

Curled up in the window seat, I used the water to calm my racing thoughts, breathing in and out, trying to become as still as its glassy surface. Then, not far offshore, a splash.

I squinted and saw, plain as day, an arm slowly coming up out of the water. A human arm. Then another. More splashing. Then a head, a face gasping for air. A person was in trouble out there! I jumped to my feet. But that was impossible, wasn't it? I had been sitting in the window seat for several minutes—maybe longer than that—and I hadn't seen a boat or a swimmer or . . . anything. That lake had been as still as the grave.

It didn't matter. Impossible or not, I knew what I had seen. I fumbled with the bolt on my door, flew out of my room, and pounded down the stairs. "Mira! Call nine-one-one!" I shouted, as I flung open the front door and ran outside to get a better look at what was happening. I hurried down the steps and ran to the edge of the cliff, the chill from the ground stinging my bare feet.

Mira was beside me almost instantly, portable phone in hand. "Hallie! What the hell—"

My eyes were frozen on the lake. Instead of the glassy,

serene surface I had seen from my window just minutes earlier, the water was now rough and angry. Whitecaps were being whipped up by the stiff wind; the huge waves crashed violently onto the rocky shore below. *How could that be?*

"Hallie!" Mira shook me by the arm, as if to wake me from a dream. "What are you doing out here?"

I didn't respond.

"Let's get you back inside. You'll catch your death." She led me back to the house, closing the front door behind her.

"I saw—"

"What, Hallie?"

I walked over to the window. "I saw a person out there. In the lake."

"In a boat?"

"No, in the water. About a hundred yards offshore. Maybe more."

She looked at me, questioning, shaking her head. "That's impossible. You must've been dreaming."

"No, really," I insisted. "I was wide awake. I couldn't sleep, so I was sitting on the window seat in my room. And all of a sudden I saw a person out there, in the water, trying to come up for air. He seemed to be drowning, Mira. I feel like we should call the police or the Coast Guard or somebody. Only . . ." My words trailed off. I was beginning to doubt what I had seen with my own eyes.

"Only, what?"

"When I was looking at the lake from my room, the surface of the water was like glass. It was completely still. And then I went outside . . ." I looked into Mira's eyes, wanting some sort of explanation for what had just occurred, some confirmation that winds blow up here in an instant. But she just shook her head.

"The gales have been blowing all night long. Haven't you heard it? The whole house has been shaking. I was worried it would keep you up."

I didn't know what to think. "But that person—"

"Hallie." She took my hand gently. "There's no way somebody could have been swimming. Even in summer you can't swim out there. The water temperature is too cold. People fall off their sailboats and get hypothermia *in August*. At this time of year? Nobody could survive for long in water that cold."

It took a moment for her words to take root in my mind. She was right, of course, it must've been a dream. Now it was my turn to apologize. "I feel like such an idiot, waking you up in the middle of the night and running outside like a crazy woman."

She smiled. "Don't sweat it. There's something about this island that does things to people. I should've mentioned it to you earlier. I think it's the combination of the horse-and-carriage thing and the rhythm of the lake itself, but people's imaginations get thrown into high gear when they're here. We get a lot of writers and artists who come specifically for inspiration.

"And it's not only that," she went on, leading me up the steps. "You may very well have seen a ghost."

I stopped. "You're kidding, right?"

"Oh, not at all." She winked at me. "I lead ghost tours around this island for visitors during high season. There is definitely something here, Hallie. The old-timers say it has something to do with ancient legends about the island being a sort of gateway to the spirit world. This place is chock-full of ghosts. I'm not surprised you picked up on it."

Back in my room, I noticed the first hint of light appearing in the eastern sky. Early as it was, I turned on the shower and stood under the hot water for a long time, trying to wash the image of that drowning person out of my mind.

After drying off, I figured I might as well dress for the day. What to wear for my meeting with a lawyer? A pair of comfortable jeans and a cotton sweater? Combined with a tweed jacket, it would have to do. I got the impression most people didn't dress formally here, anyway. I hunted in my suitcase for my hair dryer and found that the steam from the shower was still hanging in the air, like fog. It made me think of that foggy day back home, when this all began. As I ran a brush through my hair, the reflection in the bathroom mirror made me catch my breath: A hand print was on the outside of the steamy glass shower door. It was clear as daylight.

I felt exactly the same way I felt that day in the fog; fear was seeping up off the floor into my body. Did I make that hand print as I got out of the shower? Or had someone been in that steamy bathroom, standing there, watching me? I fervently hoped it was the former, but really, how often do you make a full hand print on the shower door?

I checked the bedroom. In all the excitement, I must've forgotten to flip the dead bolt when I came back to my room. Somebody could've come in here and lurked outside my shower. But who, Mira? Nobody else—that I knew of—was in the house.

6

I hitched a ride into town with Mira in her carriage behind two enormous Clydesdales. It was too early for my meeting, but I figured it was wise, here on the island, to take advantage of the opportunity for a ride whenever it presented itself. A chill wind wrapped around us from off the lake, and dark clouds hung low and threatening in the sky. I buttoned up my jacket and was thankful for my warm sweater.

Mira dropped me at the coffee shop on Main Street, Jonah's, armed with directions to William Archer's office. "See you later!" she called over her shoulder, as she clopped away. "Good luck with your meeting!" I looked at my watch and found I had just over an hour to kill.

I pushed open the door of the coffee shop and saw a group of people, all of them about my dad's age, sitting at a table by the window: a woman in a red fleece vest and jeans, a couple of men in flannel shirts, another woman in a fisherman's-knit sweater. Locals, obviously.

I heard their laughter and chatter as I came in, but all conversation stopped when I entered the room. Those people silenced themselves mid-laugh, mid-story, mid-sip, and every head turned in my direction. Had they been looking at me with curiosity and friendliness, it would have been one thing. But this—I felt as if I had just stumbled into a secret-society enclave. I was every inch the trespasser, thoroughly scrutinized. My skin was crawling with the force of their stares. What was their problem? Just a few weeks ago, this town had been awash with tourists. Now, suddenly, these people were stunned by the sight of a stranger in their midst?

I cleared my throat in an effort to let the man behind the counter know I was standing there. He finally saw me and broke the uncomfortable silence.

"Let me guess." He winked at me, deliberately talking loudly enough for the gang in the corner to hear. "You're in, of all places, a coffee shop, for a latte." The group got the message and reluctantly turned back to their own conversation, their eyes, mercifully, off my back.

"That's amazing." I grinned. "You must be psychic. I am indeed here for a latte. Skim. With a half shot of almond and a half shot of chocolate." Why not treat myself on such a day?

As he heated the milk for my drink, I remembered the name I saw above the door as I came in. "You must be Jonah?"

"I am indeed." He handed me the steaming mug. "And you?"

"I'm Hallie James, a stranger in these parts."

Jonah let out a laugh, which caused several heads to turn

in my direction again. "Drink's on me. Welcome to the island, Hallie James."

"Are you sure?" I asked him, fishing a twenty out of my purse and brandishing it in his direction.

"Absolutely." He nodded. "Island tradition. The first out-of-season visitor of the year gets a free coffee."

Jonah was about my age, maybe a few years younger, with shoulder-length blond hair and a sunny disposition to match. His face exuded a warmth I was grateful for.

"Thanks." I smiled, grabbed the newspaper that was sitting on the counter, and headed to a table as far as I could get from the locals.

Windows looking out onto the harbor lined the back wall of the shop. As I buried my face in the headlines, I imagined it must be quite a sight here in the summertime, sipping iced coffee while the ferries chugged into port and colorful sailboats floated languidly by. The picture it painted in my mind was so real and vivid, it was almost as though I had seen it before. That thought caught in my throat. Maybe I had! I wondered how long this coffee shop had been in business.

Roughly two minutes had passed since the last time I checked my watch. I tried to immerse myself in last week's news (the paper was old), but I couldn't quiet my racing thoughts enough to read. What would I learn at my meeting with William Archer?

The local welcome wagon pushed their chairs away from the table and began to drift out of the shop. As some of them called their goodbyes to Jonah, one woman stopped at my table, smiling. She looked as though she were baring her teeth. "I'm so sorry we all stopped and stared when you came in," she said. "It must have made you terribly uncomfortable. It's just that we don't get many tourists this time of year and—well, you looked so familiar, it took us all aback." I nodded, not knowing how to respond. She added, still smiling that oddly aggressive smile, "I'm afraid we were quite rude." She waited, then, for me to say something.

"No offense taken."

She thrust her hand in my direction. "I'm Isabel Stroud."

I took her palm in mine. "Hallie James." I managed a smile.

"So, Hallie," she began, "what brings you to Grand Manitou in the off-season?"

These are exactly the people Mr. Archer was warning me against, I thought, *those who might have some objection to me being—well, me.* "I'm here on business. I'll be here all week, actually."

"Wonderful." She was still smiling. "We'll see you around town, then."

I was sure she would. I got the distinct feeling that she and her cronies would be watching me closely, and not with a neighborly eye. As the door shut behind her, it was as though a burst of fresh air entered in her stead.

Jonah busied himself wiping down tables, saying, over his shoulder, "I'm sorry about that. It's the curse of living in a small town, I'm afraid."

"A small *island* town. After tourist season."

"Everybody's got to know your business."

Funny. Just because he'd said that, I wanted to tell him mine. "I'm here for a meeting with William Archer this morning. After that, I might have some further business to attend to, here on the island."

Jonah stopped wiping the tables. "How come Archer always finagles the meetings with pretty women? I don't get it."

My cheeks flushed. Was he actually flirting with me? It had been a long time since anyone had. He poured himself a cup of coffee and walked up to my table. "Mind if I join you?"

I wasn't sure if I wanted him to join me or not. But without waiting for my answer, he sat down in the chair opposite. "So," I said, trying to think of small talk. "I gather now's your downtime here."

Jonah nodded. "Now and through the winter. People don't like to be out on the lake when there are twenty-foot waves."

"Sissies." I took a sip of coffee. "Have you had your shop long?"

"I opened it about ten years ago," he told me. "I thought about leaving the island, finding a job on the mainland. But there's something about this place, for the right kind of person. It grabs you and won't let go."

A tingling climbed up my spine just then and I, too, felt caught. Maybe it was the way his blue eyes were shining, like steel. Maybe it was the cloud that seemed to drape itself over his sunny disposition when he said it. Was he trying to tell me something?

I didn't have time to find out, because I saw it was nearly nine o'clock. "Oh," I said. "Time for my meeting."

"I hope you'll be back soon, Hallie James," he said. All

traces of whatever had clouded his face were erased by his smile, which looked familiar and safe.

"I'm sure I will." I smiled back at him, warmth flowing through me.

I pushed the door open and walked out onto Main Street, fishing the address of William Archer's office out of my purse, and began making my way down the empty street, looking into the windows of the businesses I passed. Each one was dark and closed up tight. It was like a ghost town.

And then I heard it: a whispering on the wind. A faint noise, a child's voice, singing softly, deep within my ear and yet all around me at the same time.

Say, say, oh, playmate, come out and play with me.

I whirled around to look behind me: There was nothing but the empty street.

And bring your dollies three. Climb up my apple tree.

I knew this song. I remembered it from my childhood. I could almost see myself sitting on the ground facing a playmate, playing patty-cake, singing, clapping hands in rhythm to the words. But this wasn't the happy childhood tune I remembered. It was the same melody but morphed into a minor key. And the singing was slow and deliberate.

Slide down my rain barrel. Into my cellar door.

The cold wind was inside me now, holding fast to my throat, almost as if it were pulling the words out of my mouth. I sang along in a whisper.

And we'll be jolly friends, forevermore.

Suddenly, the song was over. I looked up and down the street, but nobody was there. I was alone. I hurried along to

William Archer's office. I wanted very much to be inside with someone.

On the next block, I saw the shingle swaying back and forth in the stiff wind: ARCHER & SON, ATTORNEYS AT LAW. The slight creaking noise, coupled with what had just happened in the complete emptiness of the street, suddenly made me think I was the only person alive on the island. Everyone else here—the people in the coffee shop, Jonah, even Mira—were ghosts from another time. But of course that was a silly notion. I pushed it out of my mind as I opened the door.

The office was empty: a reception desk, several chairs, a bookshelf, but no receptionist, no other clients, and no William Archer. This constant emptiness was really beginning to unnerve me.

"Hello?" I called out. A man came walking out of a back office, carrying a cup of coffee. All of a sudden, the eerie feeling that had gripped me vanished, dissipated by the warmth of the man standing before me.

"Hallie James?"

I extended my hand. "You must be William Archer."

He took my hand and smiled. "You're right on time."

William Archer was not at all what I had expected. When I had spoken to him on the phone, the conversation was so formal that I got the impression of a buttoned-down conservative lawyer much older than myself. But in front of me stood a man in jeans and a soft plaid flannel shirt worn open over a T-shirt. He had the trim build of an athlete and seemed to be about my age. His dark wavy hair hung to his shoulders; his blue eyes were deep and bright and were, in a way, familiar to me. He looked more like an artist or an environmental activist than a lawyer.

We stood there for a minute, taking each other in, each reconciling the image we had in our minds with the reality before us.

"I'm sorry I couldn't meet you at the ferry yesterday," he said, taking a sip of his coffee.

"Quite all right," I said quickly. I could feel myself blush. *What am I, thirteen years old? Get it together, Hallie.*

"Why don't we go in here?" he gestured toward his office.

I felt the need to fill the silence that hung in the room between us—an annoying habit I wish I could break—so I resorted to meaningless small talk. "Are you the Archer or the Son?" I asked him, referring to his shingle.

"This was my dad's law practice," he explained. "I came to work with him one summer when I was just out of law school and never left. He's been retired for several years, but I haven't wanted to change the name on the door, even though it's just one Archer now."

He walked around his desk and sat down, motioning me to sit as well, and I realized it was time to get down to the reason for this meeting. I folded my hands in my lap and took a deep breath. It was like sitting in the doctor's office after a biopsy, knowing you're about to hear life-changing news. I managed a shaky smile. "I'm very nervous. You may have already figured that out."

"I know," he said, nodding and looking at me with real compassion in his eyes. "This is heavy stuff."

"Where do we start?"

"Instead of just diving into the will, let me give you a bit of background first," he began, reaching into his desk drawer. He pulled out a framed photograph. "Madlyn Crane tended to stay behind the camera, so I don't know if you've ever seen a picture of her from her younger days. I brought this from the house."

She looked nothing like the Jackie Kennedy mother I had imagined. It was not quite my own face but very close to it. Madlyn Crane had long wavy auburn hair like mine, which in this photograph was blowing in an unseen breeze. Her hazel eyes (like mine) sparkled with mischief. She was looking directly at the photographer and smiling, as though she were gazing into the eyes of someone she loved. She held a camera in one hand and had the other on her hip. A long, brightly colored scarf was wound around her neck. She wore a cream-colored sweater and shorts, and long earrings that dangled past her chin.

"You look just like her," he said softly. "It struck me when you walked in. There's no doubt in my mind now that this is all true. You're Halcyon Crane."

I tried to form a response, but the words caught in my throat. At least it explained why everyone had looked at me so oddly, from the ferry captain, to Mira, to the people in the coffee shop. Even Jonah. I was a dead ringer for a dead woman. It was a lot to take in.

"I wasn't convinced any of this was true when I got your letter," I admitted, clearing my throat. "I didn't buy into this right away. Who would? I wasn't about to reject everything my father had ever told me about my life on the basis of one letter from a stranger."

"What convinced you?"

I told him about the photograph my mother had sent along with her letter, and the one of me on her website. I told him about my father saying her name before he died. And now, looking at this photo, there was no denying that I was this woman's daughter.

"Can you tell me a little bit about her?" I managed to ask.

As he spoke, I sat perfectly still, barely breathing, as though any movement on my part would break the spell he was weaving with his words.

"Everyone on the island knew Madlyn Crane," Mr. Archer began. "She was our most famous resident. Tourists came here specifically to catch a glimpse of her—although she didn't often make time for fans, which, I suppose, made her all the more alluring."

He told me she was a woman with a big personality, a fiery temper, strong opinions, and a generous heart.

"When she wasn't traveling the world shooting portraits of celebrities, animals in the wild, or nature scenes, she often could be found in her gallery here in town," he went on. "She displayed her own work, of course, but also the work of other local artists: painters, jewelers, and potters. Fans were delighted on the rare occasions when she worked there as a sales clerk.

"Let me see, what else can I tell you about her? She loved kayaking, rowing, her dogs, and her horses. She was a third-generation islander and lived in a home built more than a century ago by her grandfather. She was proud of that house and even more proud of her heritage here on the island."

I had been longing for this kind of information all my

life and now, finally hearing it, I had a difficult time gathering the words to respond. He waited quietly, understanding.

"I'm just sick that I didn't have the chance to know her," I began. "She wrote me one letter and died before I had a chance to read it. I can't get over that. What are the odds, finding a child you thought was dead and then dying yourself before . . ." I couldn't continue.

"The irony is heartbreaking," he said softly. "It's a damn shame."

We sat there awhile, neither of us saying anything.

"So, she had a heart attack? That's what I read in an obituary I found online. Is that right?" I asked finally.

William nodded. "It was a surprise to everyone on the island. Most of all to her, I imagine." He looked at me hesitantly, as though he was considering saying more.

"And?" I prodded.

"It happened in the barn. Her neighbors came over and found her when the dogs wouldn't stop howling. It took several police officers to get them—Madlyn's dogs—away from her. From her body, I mean. They didn't want to let her go."

"Loyal friends," I said, the words catching in my throat.

"Madlyn loved her animals."

"How did she find out about me?" I asked him. "She wasn't searching all these years, was she?"

William shook his head. "Everyone, including Madlyn, thought you were dead, until very recently." He pulled an envelope from his desk drawer and handed it to me. Inside, I found a newspaper clipping.

THOMAS JAMES HONORED AS TEACHER OF THE DECADE

It was a local award given to my dad by the school district just a few months before he died. Along with a short article, there was a photograph. My dad was smiling broadly for the camera, holding the plaque they'd given him. He was in the grip of the disease at that time, but he knew what was happening and was proud to be honored by his peers. I was standing next to him, also beaming.

As I held the photo in my hands and looked up at William, the question was apparently evident in my eyes.

"One of Madlyn's friends, a colleague she knew through her work, happens to live in Seattle," he explained. "She saw this article in the paper and was struck by the resemblance, which is really remarkable. So she called Madlyn and asked about it, saying that the woman in the photo looked enough like her to be her daughter. As soon as Madlyn saw it, she knew."

"But why didn't she just get on a plane? Or call me? If only she had . . ."

"She told me she hired a private investigator to do some nosing around first," he said. "She found out your father was in a nursing home and was concerned about the effect her showing up out of the blue would have on you. She wasn't quite sure how to handle such a delicate situation and decided a letter was the best approach."

I sighed and slumped a little lower in my chair.

"I know," he said, in sympathy. "I wish she had lived long enough to mail it."

I closed my eyes and covered them with my hands, afraid tears would begin. As if to pull me back from the precipice of grief that I was teetering on, William cleared his throat and said, "We should really talk about the will, Hallie. Are you ready to do that?"

"Of course," I told him. "I don't have any idea what she might have left to me, but it will be nice to have some token of who she was."

He smiled sadly, picked up a sheet of paper that had been sitting on his desk, face down, this whole time—the will, I assumed—and said, "I'll just read this aloud."

I braced myself for what I was about to hear.

" 'I, Madlyn Crane, being of sound mind and body, do hereby leave all my worldly goods to my daughter, Halcyon Crane, also known as Hallie James.' "

I gasped.

" 'I do have one stipulation, however. The house is not to be sold. Hallie, you are a fourth-generation islander. You were born in that house. Your great-grandfather built it and he would want it to stay in the family as much as I do. Come and go as you wish, use my money to maintain it, but do not sell it. Raise your family here as I intended to raise mine.' "

He stopped. "There's a bit more, but it's just legal stuff. We changed her will almost immediately after she found out you were alive. She had planned to divide her estate to endow several arts foundations, but the fact of your existence changed her mind about that. Madlyn was a very family-oriented woman."

I was silent for a moment. "I can't believe she left everything to me."

"Of course you're shocked. This is so unexpected. You have just inherited a fortune from a woman you didn't even know."

"What do you mean, a fortune?"

"Madlyn was a wealthy woman," he said. "Her death has quite literally changed your life."

He handed me a stack of bank statements, investment reports, and other financial documents I didn't recognize. I looked through them, dumbly, not really knowing what I was seeing. But I do know one thing: There were a lot of zeroes. Madlyn Crane was worth millions. And now, unbelievably, so was I.

My mind was spinning. It raced from the goodbye letter I'd send to my boss, to finally being able to pay off all my creditors, to taking that trip back to Europe I'd always dreamed of. I had never in my life been financially secure, and now, in an instant, I was *wealthy.* After a moment, though, I felt ashamed. "I wish I could trade all that money for the childhood I was supposed to have had here."

William's eyes met mine. He gave me a slight smile and shrugged.

"What do I do now?" I asked him.

"You have a house and a couple of dogs waiting for you."

The enormity of that statement had not yet hit me. A house? Dogs? It didn't feel real. But then again, nothing had, from the moment I read Madlyn's letter.

"I've got the keys right here," he continued. "I thought you'd probably want to head out there after you heard they were yours." He stood up and reached for a brown leather jacket hanging on the coat rack in the corner. "I'll take you, if you'd like."

"Really? Do you have the time? I mean, what about your other clients?"

He looked around the empty room. "Everyone here can just wait until we get back." He laughed and then explained that his business, like everyone else's, slowed to a crawl when the seasonal residents packed up and went home.

"I've always meant to go south for the winter like so many people here do, my parents included," he said, pulling on his jacket, "but I never quite manage to do it. There's something about this island in winter that intrigues me. I love the solitude. It's like the whole place exists just for me."

"I've been feeling exactly the same way," I told him. "Like I've walked onto my own deserted movie set."

"You get it, then."

I nodded. But I didn't get it, not really. To me, the emptiness was more than a little unsettling, as if I were wandering alone in a graveyard. I felt it encircle me as we walked out the door and into the wind. The scent of rain was hanging in the air.

"My car's out back," he said, leading me around the building.

Car? As we rounded the corner, I saw what he meant. An enormous white horse—the kind of animal that I imagined had pulled fire trucks in the past—stood tied to a railing. Behind it stood a contraption that could only be described as a buggy. It had two wheels, a seat designed for two, and a canopy over the top. Looking up at the heavy gray sky, I wished for a real car—or at least an enclosed carriage like Henry's.

"This is Tinkerbelle," he said to me, reaching up to scratch the horse's nose.

It struck me funny, such a dainty name for such a massive, muscular horse. "I had a very tiny cat named Tinkerbelle once," I teased him. "It suited *her.*"

He laughed, held out his hand to help me into the vehicle, and glanced upward at the rain clouds. "I hope we make it before the downpour."

I heard a rumble of thunder in the distance and hoped so, too. "How far do we have to go?"

"Only a couple of miles." He untied the horse, hopped into the driver's seat, took the reins, and made a clicking sound with his tongue. "Let's go, Belle."

And we were off. At a snail's pace. Belle was in no hurry to deliver me to my past and seemed unconcerned about the impending rain. I, on the other hand, couldn't get to the house quickly enough. "You know, I could run faster than this," I said, giving William a sidelong glance.

"You're free to lope ahead of the buggy any time the mood hits you. But don't lag behind. It can get quite unpleasant in back of a horse."

I laughed. "Hey, you must have a whole staff of people who do nothing but clean up after horses. I haven't seen any—evidence—the whole time I've been here."

"We do indeed," he said. "It's the most glamorous job on the island. We usually save it for the spoiled children of wealthy seasonal residents."

I was grateful for the bit of levity. As we got closer and closer to the house, the reality of my past life here was looming larger. I felt almost suffocated by it, but somehow the sound of Belle's hooves on the cobblestones, along with the swaying of the buggy, had a calming, almost hypnotizing effect. It was the heartbeat of this place.

"I love that sound," I murmured, referring to the hoofbeats. "It's a sound from the past, isn't it? Our ancestors heard it constantly as part of their daily lives, but now it's almost nonexistent in our world."

"It's funny you picked up on that. I always imagine what it might've been like in New York or Chicago a century ago: no cars, people coming and going in carriages, business deliveries being made by horse-drawn wagons. Hoofbeats everywhere. That sound was the constant din of traffic back then. They probably didn't even hear it or register it, because it was always there, every time they went out in the street. We've replaced it with engines and motors."

"And radios."

"And most recently the constant chatter of people on cell phones. That's my pet peeve, by the way, the privilege of listening to somebody else's conversation."

"I know. I can't stand it."

"Another reason to love the island," William said. "No cell service."

I snuck a glance at his ring finger—empty. Why? He was an eligible, presumably well-off lawyer. You'd think he'd have to beat women off with a stick. Living in Seattle, he certainly would have.

"So, William—" I began.

He interrupted. "Call me Will. Everybody else does."

"Will." I smiled, forgetting what I had intended to say. We rode in silence for a while, the swaying of the buggy and Belle's hoofbeats calming me. My eyelids felt heavy. For the first time that day, the adrenaline that had been stirred up the night before seemed to dissipate, leaving my body. Tired from too little sleep, I might have nodded off if a rumble of thunder hadn't pealed through the sky.

"We're almost there," Will said to me. "We'll make it before the rain starts. Madlyn lives just up the hill on the cliff." And then, quietly: "Lived."

It occurred to me for the first time that he was grieving for her, too. "Did you know her well?"

"Quite well, actually." He sighed. "Not only was I her lawyer, Madlyn and my mother were the best of friends. They grew up together."

Suddenly, it clicked. How could I have been such an idiot? The ease I felt with this man, roughly my age, whose mother and mine had known each other so well . . .

"Will." I looked deeply at him, trying to spark any hint of memory. "Did we know each other, before?"

He grinned broadly but stared straight ahead. "I was wondering if you'd remember."

"We were friends?"

"We played together all the time when we were kids. I practically lived at your house."

I didn't know what to say. I was five years old when my father took me away from this place—still a child, yes, but plenty old enough to remember a friend, a mother, a home. But a huge expanse of nothingness existed in my brain where those memories should've been. I felt empty, my entire childhood covered by a dark shroud. Who or what had draped it there?

"I don't remember anything, not one thing," I said, shaking my head. "It's crazy. The only memories I have of my childhood involve me and my father in our little town north of Seattle, just the two of us. Why can't I remember this place? My mother? You? It's not like I was a baby when—"

My words evaporated in the air. We had turned into the driveway of the house where I was born, just as fat raindrops began to fall. I could swear I saw my mother, long auburn hair, fisherman's-knit sweater, colorful scarf, and all, standing on the front porch, waving.

7

The sky opened up and the rain fell to earth with a fury, beating down so hard it was difficult to see much past the rim of Will's buggy.

"You run up to the house, and I'll put Belle and this contraption in the stable," he directed.

I did as I was told. I jumped out of the buggy and hurried up a set of steps onto a covered front porch, where I paused to catch my breath and look around. Rain pounded down behind me, but the porch was dry. It was difficult to make out the view, in all the rain and fog, but I could tell this much: The house sat on top of a cliff overlooking the water.

My entire body was humming with electricity. This had been my home. It had not been destroyed by fire then, all those years ago, as my father had told me. My one clear memory of that time, the fire, was a lie.

Will hurried up the steps to the porch, shaking the rain off a large umbrella.

"You had an umbrella all along!"

"I found it in the stable." He laughed. "Sorry." He pointed out into the rain. "You can't tell now, but the view from this house is incredible. You can see downtown, the harbor, and the lake beyond it. I think it's the best view on the whole island, and that's saying something."

I turned, catching a glimpse of a porch swing swaying back and forth in the wind, as though an unseen rocker were admiring the view.

"Shall we go inside?" Will suggested.

"Not just yet," I said, not realizing how heavily I had been breathing until I settled onto the swing. "This is a lot to process at once. Can we sit here for a minute?"

He sat down next to me and we swayed back and forth in silence for a while. I noticed containers filled with wilting autumn plants and flowers—black-eyed Susans (my favorite), mums, and several other kinds I didn't recognize—scattered here and there on the porch. The welcome mat in front of the bright red front door said GO AWAY. That made me smile.

"After you—well . . . died"—William's eyes were on the ground—"I didn't come here for years. I couldn't."

For the second time that day, something obvious occurred to me. This man had lost a friend all those years ago and now she had reappeared, back from the dead. I wasn't the only one having a tough time with this new reality. I wasn't the only one with a lot to take in.

"What did everybody think happened to my father and me?"

"Boating accident," he said quickly. "They found your overturned kayak. The entire island put their boats in the water to search for you, but . . ." His words trailed off into a sigh.

I didn't quite know what to say. "How about we go inside?" I offered, trying to push out of my mind the image of dozens of colorful kayaks, rusting fishing boats, and elegant cruisers all searching for me. Will produced a set of keys from his pocket, unlocked the front door, and held it open as I walked through it into my home.

I found myself standing in a large square foyer, the living room on one side, the dining room on the other, and a grand wooden staircase ascending in the middle.

"Where's the welcoming committee?" Will looked left, right, and up the stairs. "Girls! Tundra! Tika!"

I heard a clatter of toenails on the wood floor, and two enormous dogs burst through the swinging door separating the dining room from what I assumed was the kitchen. They looked like huskies but were much bigger; their thick white and gray fur, bushy tails, long legs, and dark masks around steely golden eyes all hinted at ancient timberwolf ancestors. One was carrying a twisted rope bone in her mouth; the other had a stuffed rabbit. The dogs wiggled and curled around our legs, their great tails wagging, ears pinned back in greeting. Will was scratching and petting them in return, murmuring, "Good girls! Such good, good girls!"

One of them, the bigger of the two, jumped up on me, putting one saucerlike paw on my shoulder and the other on the top of my head. I was afraid to move. "They're friendly, right?"

"Down, Tundra!" Will commanded, and the dog dropped to the floor and sat in front of me. "She loves visitors. They're the highlight of her day. And yes, they're both friendly—but protective, too."

I reached down gingerly to scratch this beast behind the ears. "So these were my mother's dogs."

Will nodded. "Tundra and Tika. They're giant Alaskan malamutes. The breed is traditionally used as sled dogs, though the most work these two do is to walk from the couch to their food dishes. I've been taking care of them at home since Madlyn's death, but I brought them here this morning before going to the office. I knew you'd like to meet them at the very least, even if you don't end up keeping them. The girls belong to you now."

"They're magnificent," I murmured, staring into their fierce golden eyes.

The greeting complete, both dogs settled down, curling up next to each other on the floor. I noticed they didn't take their eyes off Will and me.

"We don't have to stand here in the foyer, you know," Will said, as he shut the front door behind us. "Take a look around."

As I wandered farther into the house, images flashed in my mind like a slide show on fast forward: A little girl dressed in white pounding up the stairs. The same girl, squealing as she slid down the banister. A glowering woman in a long black dress. Was I remembering snippets from a long-buried childhood or just imagining what might have been? I didn't know. It seemed real, but after seeing a person drowning in the water earlier and hearing that singsong tune on the street in front of Will's office, I wasn't certain I trusted my own mind.

In the living room, I ran my hand gently over the back of the sofa as I took a look around. Like those in the Manitou Inn, the floors here were made of gleaming hardwood, and the woodwork around the door frames and windows shone as though it had been freshly waxed. An overstuffed brown leather sofa sat in the middle of the room, along with a love seat and an armchair. Worn rugs were scattered about. A stone fireplace stretching all the way up to the vaulted ceiling stood in one corner, a flat-screen television in the other. Cherrywood paneling lined the walls that did not face the lake.

Photographs were everywhere—on the walls, the coffee tables, the raised stone hearth—as were framed covers of several magazines: *Time, National Geographic, Vanity Fair.* I had already seen many of the shots on Madlyn's website, but several were new to me.

I picked up a photograph here, a candle holder there, fingering the stuff of my mother's world in an attempt to leave my imprint. Dust floated in the air. The energy in the room was electric and alive, as though the house itself were watching me.

Will came over to me. "You okay?"

"I guess I'm a little overwhelmed," I admitted. The truth was, I was a lot overwhelmed. The house was bigger and more opulent than I had expected, and I was having trouble wrapping my mind around two notions: that it was now mine, and that I used to live here.

"Check out the sunporch." William pointed toward a set of sliding doors at the far end of the room. "It won't be sunny out there on a day like this, of course, but you'll get the idea."

I pushed open one of the doors into a room with windows on three sides. It overlooked the lake to the front and the side gardens to the back. Rain was hitting the windows in gusts, mixed with a little icy sleet. Lovely. I heard the thunder again, and then a crack of lightning arced through the sky.

"Wow," I murmured, settling onto a chaise in the corner of the room. "It's great to watch a storm in here."

Along with the chaise, a couch with a muted floral print and an overstuffed striped armchair formed a sitting area, next to a small glass table and an enormous wooden rocking chair. The style could be described as the shabby chic that was popular a few years ago, but this furniture seemed just plain old. Comfortable but old. Magazines were strewn in racks, books sat on end tables. It occurred to me that this was where Madlyn spent much of her time. I could feel her—or something—alive here.

And then I heard it, as clear as crystal: *Hallie! Halcyon Crane! Have you done something with your mother's camera?* It was a female voice, a loud female voice, coming from behind me.

I spun around and onto my knees to look over the back of the chaise. Nobody was there.

"Hallie—" William poked his nose into the room and began to speak but stopped when he saw my expression. "What's the matter?"

I was breathing heavily and could feel my heart pounding in my chest. I rubbed my hands on my jeans. "Nothing. It's just—I thought I heard something."

"The dogs?"

"No, it was a voice. I think it was my mother's voice."

He stood there for a moment, eyeing me carefully. Sizing

up the lunatic, I thought. But then he said, "You know what? Maybe your memories are coming back."

Could that be? A childhood memory of this place? My first one! "I'll bet I played in here a lot as a child," I said, smiling and turning around in a circle. "I love this room."

"You did." He smiled at me. "*We* did."

I imagined a little girl, that same girl in white I had seen in my mind before, playing with toy horses in the corner. I saw her reading a picture book, sprawled out on her stomach, feet kicking up toward the sky.

"What do you say we join the dogs in the kitchen and make ourselves a cup of tea—or something stronger?" he suggested. "With this rain, we might as well settle in for a while."

"You're sure it's okay?" I felt I was trespassing, as though the real owner of the house would come barging in at any moment, demanding to know what we were doing there.

"It still hasn't sunk in. This place is yours, Hallie."

Right. I smiled. "Onward to the kitchen."

He led me back through the living room, the foyer, and the dining room into the kitchen, and I couldn't muffle the squeal of delight that escaped from my lips. Of all the rooms I had seen thus far, I liked this one the best.

The walls were painted a muted red; the windows were framed in dark wood. A long counter was topped with wooden cabinets that stretched all the way to the ceiling. An ancient armoire with glass doors displayed china and glassware, a rack of brightly colored plates stood in a row over the sink, and a small bookshelf was filled with cookbooks. A butcher-block center island was ringed with bar stools, and the mammoth stove sat sentinel beneath a set of copper pots and pans. A long rough-hewn table with chairs all around took up the end of the room by the back door and windows. A chaise sat in the far corner. What a perfect spot for curling up with a cookbook and figuring out what's for dinner!

"Madlyn had a lot of parties," Will explained, as though he were a tour guide through the mystery world my mother had inhabited. "She loved bringing people together for informal meals: professors and artists and bankers and groundskeepers, men and women from all walks of life. She liked the mix of viewpoints, I think. This kitchen got a lot of use."

I had always lived in places with cold utilitarian kitchens, long slim rooms with metal cabinets on one side and a tiny table shoved into a corner. This kitchen had a feeling of life to it, a warmth that seemed to envelop me. It was as though the room itself were matronly and loving, ready to offer me a cup of tea or a freshly baked cookie. For the first time on the island, I felt truly at home.

"All my life I've wished for a big old kitchen," I said, but the words caught in my throat. "Exactly like this." I looked at Will. "When I was wishing for my ideal kitchen, I was actually remembering this one, wasn't I?"

"It's possible," he said, reaching up into one of the cabinets. "It makes sense that your memories are slowly taking shape, the more you see of your old surroundings." He retrieved a couple of teabags, ran some water into a teakettle, and set it on the stove. "Do you want to explore the rest of the house while the water boils?"

"I want to stay right here," I said, climbing onto one of the bar stools.

We sat there for a while, drinking tea and munching on some scones Will found in a tin on the counter, as the dogs circled and sniffed and finally settled back down. We talked a little, about nothing much in particular—where he went to law school, how I liked my home north of Seattle. Mostly we listened to the rain beat on the windowpanes and the thunder growl its warnings . . .

I woke up, confused. It was nearly dark. As my eyes slowly adjusted, I could make out enough to realize that I was lying on the chaise in the sunroom, covered with an afghan. One of the dogs was on the floor next to me, her great head resting near mine. I shook the cobwebs out of my brain. Now I remembered. Will and I had come into the sunroom with our tea. I fell asleep? How idiotic.

Rain was still beating against the windows, but the thunder had subsided. Sitting up, I saw a light on in the next room. I padded through the doorway to find Will on the couch, reading.

"How long have I been out?"

"Not long. Half an hour, maybe." He closed the book, put it in his lap, and smiled at me. "We were watching the rain in the sunroom, and before I knew it . . ." He made a horrible snoring sound.

"That's really attractive." I laughed and settled into the armchair across from him.

"I assumed you succumbed to the day's events."

I rubbed my eyes. "I didn't get a whole lot of sleep last night. I nearly drifted off on the ride out here."

The rain sounded angry and heavy outside. It was just a few degrees away from snow. The thought of riding all the way back into town in Will's buggy made me feel—well, cold. "What do you do when it rains like this? For transportation, I mean?"

"If it's not too bad, I just go. But on days like this, I wait it out until the storm passes. Or I call Henry and take one of his carriages home, trailing Belle behind it. But he won't come all the way up here in this weather, unless it's an emergency."

"So what do we do now?"

Will smiled. "Popcorn and a movie? There's a DVD player and lots of selections. Maybe by the time the movie's over, the rain will have stopped long enough to get you back to the inn."

I wasn't thrilled about being trapped by a storm in the house of a dead woman with a man I barely knew. But as I snuggled deeper into the armchair, Will made a fire in the fireplace, the dogs curled up in front of me, and things soon felt friendly and companionable—as if I were home.

· 8

Riding in a horse-drawn buggy on a rainy evening has none of the turn-of-the-century charm you might expect. It was a cold damp November night, and I could see my breath in front of me as we plodded along the muddy streets.

Earlier we had watched one movie and started a second, before the rain tapered off and Will suggested we make a break for it.

The idea of staying the night had been brought up, of course. I was getting my mind around the idea that it was my house now, after all, and there were enough bedrooms and bathrooms for both of us to have our privacy. But tramping upstairs and choosing a bedroom filled with another woman's things just didn't feel right. Not to mention the fact that I had no intention of spending the night with Will, no matter how far apart our bedrooms were. So we put fresh food and water out for the dogs—Will explained he had asked a neighbor to let them out in the morning—locked up the place, ran out to the stable, and hitched up Belle. Five minutes into the cold, damp ride, I regretted it but didn't say so.

"Hey." A thought popped into my brain. "In the will, my mother said she had horses, too. Where are they?"

"Next door at the Wilsons'," he said, gesturing down the lane. "Charlie and Alice are happy to take care of them until you decide what to do."

I wasn't sure what that would be, especially in regard to the animals. I loved Tundra and Tika already, but I couldn't take them back home with me on the plane.

"That begs the question: What are your plans?" Will asked, as we clopped along down the soggy road.

"I haven't really decided. I'm definitely not going to sell the house; my mother's wishes were crystal clear on that point. Beyond that? I don't know."

My options were, for once in my life, wide open. I knew one thing: Quitting my job would be my first order of business in the morning. I'd call my boss to deliver the bad news. Or maybe just send him an e-mail. Yes, that was better. It made me a little sad to admit that quitting my job was the first thing I would do after being told I had inherited a house and a large sum of money. I had devoted more than a decade to a career I could jettison without a backward glance. I wondered what I might have done with my life instead, where my passions might have led me, if I hadn't worked simply to make money.

Then a rather unpleasant thought occurred to me. I had intended to make this a brief trip to the island—one week, tops—but when it came right down to it, I didn't really have a reason to rush home. My dad was gone. I had friends, sure, but truthfully, since moving back to the States after my divorce, I'd had some trouble reconnecting with many of my oldest ones. I'd been gone for nearly a decade, and during that time most of them had begun to build families of their own. They were busy ferrying children to music lessons and soccer games, while I found myself suddenly single and alone. Our lives had gone on different tracks.

Richard, who in many ways was still my closest friend despite everything, was back in England by now, so there was nobody, not even a pet, whose life was hanging on my return. It seemed unbearably sad, sitting there in Will's damp buggy, that I could have reached a certain age without accumulating any tethers.

I decided, right then and there: "I'm going to stay awhile, at least for a couple of weeks." Madlyn's house—my house now—was a tether, after all. I was tied to this place, if not by a living person then by her memory, and the memories of all the people who had lived here before. Including me.

"That's great." Will smiled sideways at me. "It's been nice getting to know you again today. I'm glad you're not going to hurry up and leave."

I was glad too, suddenly.

"Since you'll be staying a bit, we should talk about the issue of telling everyone who you are," he said.

Ah, yes. I had forgotten, for the moment, that he had specifically warned me about revealing the fact that I was Madlyn Crane's long-dead daughter. What had he said in that first phone call? There was a "situation" concerning the disappearance of my father and me, something islanders still remembered.

"I ran into a group of locals at the coffee shop today who gave me a less-than-royal welcome," I admitted. "It was freaky. They looked at me as though I were a ghost."

Will nodded his head. "Considering the resemblance, can you blame them? There's something else, though. I've been wondering all day about how to bring this subject up. I should've said something earlier, when we were at the house, but I didn't know how."

The air between us thickened. "People aren't going to welcome me with open arms," I said. "I get that."

Will shook his head. "It's not that, not at all. They'll welcome you just fine. It's just . . ." He hesitated. "I'm having trouble finding the right words."

"You're starting to scare me a little, Will. What could be so bad?"

He stared straight ahead. "I think islanders are going to have some trouble digesting the notion that not so much *you* but your *father* was alive all these years."

"You mean, because he . . ." My words were falling apart before I had a chance to say them. I tried again. "Because he took me away from my mother? I know she was a well-loved person here. They'll be—what—outraged on her behalf? If that's what it is, I can understand it, I guess. I agree with them, actually."

Will shook his head. "No, that's not it. Not all of it. I mean, people will certainly feel that way, sure. But what I'm talking about is something else."

Silence, then. I felt a very sharp pain in the pit of my stomach that made me want to jump out of that buggy and run the other way. I almost did it, but I had nowhere to run.

I had to sit and listen to whatever horrible thing Will had to tell me.

"What kind of father was your dad?" he asked me finally.

"The best father anyone ever had," I said, perhaps a bit too defensively. "Okay, all right. I know he *abducted* me. I have no idea why he did what he did, but I'm sure he had his reasons. And I'll tell you this: He gave me an idyllic childhood. He worked hard to be both mother and father to me. I loved him more than you can imagine and, not incidentally, so did everyone he ever met in our town. He was a teacher at the high school. Three hundred people came to his funeral. I have enough casseroles and banana bread in my freezer from the wake to feed me for a year."

Tears stung my eyes at the thought of my dad. Suddenly, I missed him so much. I had been focusing on my mother during this whole trip and had forgotten how alone my dad's death—and, indeed, his illness—had left me. I turned my face away from Will.

"I'm sorry, Hallie," he said. "I'm glad to hear you had such a great father, I really am. And, for the record, I never quite believed what people were saying about him. It just seemed wrong to me."

"What people were *saying*? It was thirty years ago. How could it possibly still matter to people now? I mean, come on. Thirty years is a long time to hold a grudge."

"Not about the murder of a child."

"But I'm *not* dead, Will. Everyone will see—"

"Not you, Hallie," he said softly. "Somebody else. Another child died just before you left the island. She died at your house. You obviously don't remember any of it."

For the rest of my life, I will be able to feel the physical impact those words had on my body. My senses went into overdrive. I became aware of, and felt swallowed by, the intense darkness outside the buggy. I heard the footfalls of an animal creeping its way through the nearby marsh. I could smell the dusty perspiration of the horse in front of us, mixed with the mossy, rainy air. And my whole body was tingling with dread.

I managed to croak out, "What did you say?"

Will sat staring straight ahead, holding Belle's reins and shaking his head. "This is really hard. Even for a lawyer."

I couldn't respond. I was just hoping he would go on anyway. Thankfully, he did.

"Better you hear it from me, right? Better you know everything."

I nodded, staring at him, wide-eyed.

He took a deep breath and cleared his throat. "Okay. I'm just going to say it. A girl died—was murdered—at your house, and all the evidence pointed to your father's having done it."

That's impossible! It's patently false. My dad didn't even like to kill spiders, for God's sake; he'd never kill a person, let alone a child.

He went on. "She fell from a third-floor window."

An image began to form in my mind. A girl with long braids. A white dress. An open window. I was leaning out of it, looking down at the ground. I saw a body there, below. I didn't tell Will about these images, or memories, or whatever they were. I said, "She fell? An accident, obviously. Why did people think it was murder?"

"The police found signs of a struggle in the room she fell from: lamps knocked over, the dresser pushed onto its side, things in disarray. The girl's dress was ripped. And they found your dad's fingerprints on the window and frame and his footprints around the body. And—" He stopped abruptly.

"What?"

"There were marks on her neck consistent with strangulation."

I digested that remark in silence. It was impossible, all of it. My father might have faked our deaths, he might have abducted me and moved me halfway across the country, but he was no child killer.

"People think my father killed this girl?" I couldn't believe I was even saying the words. "That's ridiculous." I was talking louder than I meant to. "Is that what she died of, then? Strangulation? Or did the fall kill her? Because there's no way my father would strangle a child and throw her out a window. It had to have been an accident."

"The fall killed her."

I stared at him silently. He went on. "The police were about to arrest your dad when you two . . . went missing."

I knew by his expression that there was more to the story, but I wasn't sure I wanted to hear it.

"Most people here on the island thought he killed himself *and* you," he said finally. "The way they saw it, his suicide was an admission of guilt."

"Who was the girl?" I managed to say.

"Her name was Julie Sutton," Will said quietly. "She was playing with you at your house that day."

I could feel my lungs expanding, but I couldn't get any air.

Julie Sutton. The sound of her name created a deep black hole in my mind. I knew I should know her, remember her, but the hole swallowed up any memories that might have been there.

"She was a friend of mine?" I whispered.

Will nodded. "And mine."

"Were you there, too?"

He shook his head. "I was on the mainland with my parents that day, or I certainly would have been with you."

"But . . ." I couldn't formulate words for what I was feeling. *A child killed at my house? A friend of mine? I was there?* I managed to say it: "Did I see it?"

"I don't know," he said. "Nobody knew exactly what happened, where you were or where your dad was. But everyone assumed that, yeah, you witnessed the murder."

I shook my head in disbelief. It couldn't be true. It just couldn't. Not my dad.

"Her parents still live here on the island," Will continued. "They, like everyone else here, blame your father for Julie's death. So now you can see why people aren't going to be exactly thrilled to learn he escaped justice for his crime and went on to live the rest of his life in a little town north of Seattle instead of in prison."

We rode in silence for a few minutes. I thought of one Halloween when my dad dressed up like a cowboy to take me, Annie Oakley, trick-or-treating. I thought of the concern in his eyes on the humid night I showed up on his doorstep, suitcases in hand, after I left Richard. I thought of his vacant stare the last time I saw him. And then I thought of my mother, living on this island all these years with neighbors who believed her husband was a murderer.

"How did they treat her? My mother, I mean. After we were gone."

"Truthfully, Hallie, I don't know," Will said to me. "I was just a kid myself. But she stayed, didn't she? It probably has a lot to do with her long family history here. She was an islander. If I had to guess what happened, I'd say that people came around to believing she was just as much a victim as you were."

My stomach contracted suddenly. "Stop!" I cried. "I have to get out. I'm going to be sick."

As Will pulled on Belle's reins, I leaped out of that ridiculous contraption onto the muddy road and ran, blindly, into the dark. After a few steps, I leaned over and vomited, my body shaking with the force of it.

And then Will was there, offering a handkerchief, saying a string of what I presumed to be kind words, but I couldn't hear him. I sank onto the wet grass. My body physically couldn't handle the possibility that my father might have killed that girl and then fled to escape prosecution. I thought my chest might actually rip open, that I might break in two. This is what it is to die of shock, I thought. I'm going to have a heart attack right here.

But I didn't, of course. Will led me back to the buggy and helped me climb in. "Let's get you back to the inn," he said.

I didn't want to go back to Mira's prying questions. I knew she'd be curious about my meeting with Will that day. But I didn't want to go back to Madlyn's house, either. I didn't want to be anywhere on this island. Maybe my coming here was a mistake. I wanted to be the woman I was before this all began. I wanted to be Hallie James, daughter of Thomas James, the best father in the whole world.

9

He did take me back to the inn, of course. I had no other place to go.

"I'm sorry about all this, Hallie," he said, as we pulled up outside the inn. I nodded. I hadn't spoken during the rest of the ride home. "For the record, I never believed your father killed that girl. I knew your dad. I don't think he had it in him."

I didn't know what I believed. I had been searching for a reason for my father's taking me away from here, and now, by God, I had one. It made a disgusting sort of sense. And yet it just didn't connect with the man I knew.

I climbed out of the buggy and stumbled on shaky legs. Within an instant, Will was at my side. "Let me help you inside, at least," he said, wrapping a strong arm around my waist.

I leaned into him and put my head on his shoulder, allowing him to take me up the steps toward the front door.

"Have dinner with me tomorrow?" he asked. "And call me in the morning? Or come by the office. I really want to know that you've gotten through the night."

"Okay," I whispered, and tried to manufacture a smile. I don't think it came off too well.

Will enveloped me in his arms, then, and I sighed into his embrace, closing my eyes and resting my face on his chest. He smelled of rain and kindness. "This is going to be okay," he promised. "You're in a hell of a spot here. People will be shocked, sure. But I'll be by your side, standing between you and anyone on this island who tries to say one word against your father."

I sighed again. Had I ever had as good a friend as this man I barely knew?

"I mean it, Hallie, I want to hear from you in the morning," he said, and went off in his buggy, after waiting on the porch until I was safely inside.

Through what I fully believe was an act of God, Mira was not at home, so I did not have to face the questions I knew she would ask. I found a note saying she had gone out for the evening. The house was blissfully empty. Even nicer than that, a roast was warming in the oven. *Help yourself! See you at breakfast!* God bless her. I was starving. It was just after six o'clock, but it seemed much later. It occurred to me that I hadn't eaten much since breakfast, only the scones and popcorn that we had had at Madlyn's, which had ended up on the ground. I still had a metallic taste in my mouth. Suddenly, dinner sounded like a wonderful idea.

I went to the kitchen, made a sandwich from the roast beef in the oven, and took a bag of salad out of the fridge. Blue cheese dressing, perfect. Then I found a tray. I didn't want a chance meeting with the returning innkeeper, so I decided to eat in my room. I teetered my way up the stairs, hoping I wouldn't drop anything.

I settled the tray down on my bed and switched on the

TV, wanting some mindless companionship with my meal. After I had eaten, I drew a bath and slipped into the steaming water. I was enormously grateful to be able to retreat into the tub that particular night. I've always found a long hot bath to be the cure for almost any problem—or at least a way to release its stress.

But it wasn't long before the tears came yet again. Would I ever stop crying? At the same time, I felt as though every cell in my body were screaming in response to what I had learned. *My dad? My sweet dad?*

I cried for the gentle, level-headed, sensible man whose rock-solid love and support built the foundation for the woman I grew up to be. I cried for all the nights he tucked me into bed with a kiss on the forehead and a wish that I would have sweet dreams. I cried for the man who didn't hide his tears but, instead, wrapped me in his arms, both of us grieving, when we had to put our old dog to sleep. I cried for the shell of a man he became because of his disease, the birds outside the window his only enjoyment.

Could this man also have been a murderer? Could he have murdered the girl they found outside our window that day? What possible reason would my dad—or anyone—have to kill a child? I also felt a pang of disloyalty. My father had taken me and fled this island thirty years ago, and now here I was, stirring up everything he spent his life laying to rest. Maybe I shouldn't be here at all.

I knew one thing: I was immeasurably grateful to Will for warning me, before I came to the island, not to blurt out the fact that I was the long-dead Halcyon Crane. God knows how that ferry captain might have reacted to the news;

certainly he was around when the incident happened. And what about Mira? She was, I estimated, a decade or more older than I and, by her own account, a longtime islander. She must remember the murder or at least have heard of it. What would people do when they learned the truth? What would they think of me?

I toyed with the idea of leaving the island right away, on the next ferry. I would go home to my safe warm house on Puget Sound without facing these people. But then I remembered: It wasn't possible, no matter how much I wanted to run away. I had two whole days to endure on this island before the ferry would come.

I slipped under the surface of the water and floated there awhile, holding my breath. It felt good to be weightless, the rush of the water filling my ears.

Then I heard something: laughter. I opened my eyes and saw the face of a little girl looking down at me. The girl in the white dress. With long braids. The same girl I had imagined seeing earlier at Madlyn's house. She was standing over the tub, watching me. Her mouth didn't move, but I heard the singing all the same: *Say, say, oh, playmate. Come out and play with me.*

I shot up out of the water, sputtering, to find—nobody. I hurried out of the tub, wrapped a towel around me, and padded out into the main room. No one was there. No one had been there. No little girl in a white dress.

My entire body was quivering. Was this girl a figment of my imagination? Was she Julie Sutton, the girl who had died? Was I remembering her?

I pulled on my pajamas, climbed into bed, and found I

could not stop shaking. I switched on the television, wanting to fill the room with voices, and laughter, and ridiculous situations.

I don't remember turning off the television, but I must've done that because I drifted off to sleep. I dreamed of the ferry ride I had taken the day before, only I wasn't alone on deck as I watched the island emerge out of the water. My father came up behind me and wrapped me in his arms.

"Hi, Peanut," he said softly.

"Dad!" I cried, hugging him, and only then did I realize that it wasn't my adult self, there on deck, but myself as a child. He picked me up, and I wrapped my legs around his waist monkey-style, the way small children do.

"I don't want you to go back there, Hallie," my father said to me. "It's not safe for you."

"But I'm already here, Daddy."

"Look," he said, pointing across the water. I turned my head toward the island, which was coming closer and closer. What I saw horrified me: hundreds, maybe thousands, of writhing beings, some in the water, some on land. I believed they were ghosts or spirits of some kind, moving in slow motion, all of them looking at me with empty eyes. They were trying to speak, but their mouths were dark hollow shells.

My father spoke. "You see now, Hallie. This is why I took you away."

I woke with a start, sweating, my legs caught between the damp, twisted sheets. It was only one o'clock. I had another six hours to get through until daylight.

· 10

I opened my eyes to see the sun streaming in through the windows. Glancing at the clock, I bolted awake. Almost ten-thirty! How could I have slept so late?

As I showered and made my way downstairs, I pondered my dilemma. The way I saw it, I had only two choices: I could hide here, staying out of everyone's way until the next ferry, sell the house, and never come back to the island again. Or I could do what my father hadn't done all those years ago: stay and fight.

I found Mira in her office, a tiny room just off the kitchen. I popped my head inside and said hello.

"Hey, Sleeping Beauty!"

"Yeah." I sighed. "I had a rough day. And night."

She looked up from the papers in front of her, lowering the pen poised in her hand. "Hallie, is everything okay?" Her expression was so kind. I wondered how it would change when I told her what I had to say.

"Well," I began, "I got some strange and upsetting news yesterday."

Mira stood up. "Why don't I get you some coffee and a muffin and you can tell me all about it."

My heart was beating so hard in my throat that I was certain it looked like an enormous Adam's apple. And my stomach was beginning to churn. I hoped I wouldn't have a repeat performance of last night's unpleasantness.

Mira had arranged a full pot of coffee, a jug of milk, a few muffins, and two cups on a tray. "Why don't you come into the sunroom?" She beckoned, sitting down in a wicker armchair while I took the rocker across from her.

As she poured the coffee, adding milk to mine, I leaped directly into the fray. "Madlyn Crane left everything she owned to me."

Mira choked on the sip of coffee she had just taken. "But I thought you said you didn't know her."

"I didn't," I said evenly. "But she knew me." Mira was clearly not understanding, so I went on. "I just found out I'm her daughter."

Mira stared at me, confusion all over her face, weighing her disbelief against my uncanny resemblance to my mother.

"Madlyn had another daughter?" she said. "I never knew that. I don't think anyone here knew that."

Another daughter. Mira, apparently, was not the brightest bulb. What did she think, Madlyn had two daughters, both named Hallie?

"I don't know anything about *another* daughter," I said slowly. "Mira, my name is Hallie James. But islanders would know me as Halcyon Crane." My former real name echoed like an incantation inside of my head: Halcyon Crane. Me.

Her face was crimson. "But Halcyon was killed thirty years ago."

"And yet here I am. Believe me when I tell you I'm just as surprised as you are."

"But"—she was searching for words—"the accident. Halcyon survived?" Mira's mind was obviously spinning. "How? I was at her funeral."

I shook my head. "There was no accident. Apparently the whole thing was deliberate. I grew up in Bellingham, Washington, a small town north of Seattle. I lived there all these years with my dad. I grew up thinking my mother was dead, never knowing she was actually very much alive here on the island."

"Bellingham." I could see Mira's mind was racing. She was getting it. "You're Halcyon. Madlyn and Noah's daughter."

Noah. The sound hit me like a thunderbolt. It had never occurred to me that Thomas James wasn't my father's real name, but of course it wasn't. I nodded. "That's right." And then I told her about the morning Madlyn's letter arrived in my mailbox and turned my entire world upside down. "I didn't believe it myself for a while," I said to her. "But she sent photos. Apparently it's all true."

Silence.

"She didn't say anything to me," Mira mused finally, sipping her coffee. "Nothing at all. I wonder how in the world she found you. It's not like she was looking for an abducted child all these years. Everyone thought you were dead."

"A friend of hers who lives in Seattle saw a picture of me and my father in a local newspaper," I explained. "The resemblance was striking enough for her to mention it to Madlyn."

Mira nodded, taking it all in.

"What eats at me most is the timing," I admitted. "I grieved for my mother all my life, and she was right here all the time. She finds me and, *bang*, she's gone. We were so close to finally seeing each other again, and now I'll never know her."

Mira reached over and took my hand. "I could see the resemblance the moment you walked in the door, of course. I thought you were a relative, a cousin maybe . . ." She shook her head. "He escaped. We all thought he was dead. The Suttons—what you must've endured all those years at the hands of that monster. I'm so sorry, Hallie."

I was tempted to play the wounded child card. It was convenient, her feeling sorry for me, but I couldn't betray my dad for the sake of convenience. "He was no monster, Mira. I loved him more than anything. He was a perfect father."

The sympathy in Mira's eyes turned cold. "Perfect father? That's quite a description, considering the man is a murderer who took you away from your mother and made sure everyone thought you were dead."

"Mira, please. You don't know anything about the life I had with my father. He was a good man. I know he was. We were very close."

"Hallie, you have no idea what that man did."

"I know exactly what he did—and what he didn't do," I told her. "I heard about that girl's death for the first time yesterday. And my father *didn't* murder her."

"You don't know that. The police—"

Was this how it was going to go with every islander? Was I going to have to defend my dad's memory in what was tantamount to a street brawl?

"I don't care what the police said. The man who raised me didn't kill anybody."

Mira sniffed. "Tell that to the Suttons."

"I will!" I said indignantly. "I *will* tell that to the Suttons! Bring them on, Mira! I'm sorry their daughter is dead, but my dad didn't kill her. I was there. It was an accident."

Mira's eyes widened. "You saw what happened? We all suspected as much! That's why he killed you—or pretended to."

"I don't remember it." I looked down at my hands, trying to regain my composure. "I wish I could. I don't remember anything about my life here on the island, not one thing. Yes, it looks pretty bad. He took me away from here under false pretenses. He changed our names. I know that now. The only thing I have to go on is what I actually remember—the best father a girl could ever have."

"You can talk all you want about his being a great father, but it's not up to you or me," she said. "This is a police matter, Hallie. There's no statute of limitations on murder. When the police learn he's been alive all these years—"

Then it hit me. She didn't know my dad was dead. "The police aren't going to reopen this case, Mira," I told her softly. "My dad's gone. Remember I said I was having a hard time back home? It was because he died—the day after I got the letter from Madlyn."

"Noah's dead?" Mira's eyes darted back and forth, as if she were looking for something she'd never find. "I . . . this is a lot to digest in one sitting. Noah was alive all these years, but now he's dead? You thought your mother was dead all these years, but she was alive—and now *she's* dead? What you've been through!"

"Yeah, it's been . . . devastating. I guess that's the only way to describe it."

"Hallie, I'm so sorry. I didn't mean to imply anything or to insult his memory. What you've endured these past few weeks I wouldn't wish on anyone. It's just that we've believed, all this time—"

My head was starting to pound. I ran a hand through my hair. "Thank you for that, Mira. But I know what you've believed, and it's not true. It can't be."

"Okay, then," she conceded. "If it's not true, if he didn't kill that poor girl, why did he leave? What other reason could there be?"

"That's what I need to find out. If he was not guilty of murder, and yet all the evidence pointed to him and the police were bearing down on him, it would've been cause enough to run. Or it might have been something else."

"Another woman, maybe?" Mira offered.

"I don't think so," I said slowly. "There was no woman in our lives. My dad never even dated anybody, all those years. When I was in high school, I used to encourage him to see the single mothers of my friends, but he never would. He used to say he had had one true love in his life and that was all he ever needed."

"If that was so, why would he take her child away from her?" she said icily.

Mira had a point. And suddenly I knew, without a doubt, what I was going to do.

"Well, I certainly have the time and the resources to find out," I told her, standing up with an air of finality. "Mira, thank you for your hospitality. I'd appreciate it if you'd put my bill together so I can settle up. Madlyn's house is mine now, and I'm going to move in. Today."

Mira nodded. "If you need any help along the way, Hallie, please don't hesitate to call on me. I want to know the truth about what happened just as much as you do."

I hugged her tight. "Thank you, Mira. I promise I will."

She pulled back and grabbed my hands, squeezing them hard. "Listen. Somebody's going to have to break this news to the Suttons. It's going to devastate them."

The thought of confronting the Suttons made me physically ill. "Mira, would you do it? I don't even know these people. It would be better coming from someone they know and love."

She nodded. "I'll make sure they hear today."

After paying my bill, I arranged with Henry to take my bags to my new house and hurried down the hill toward town at a quick walk. I hadn't had any real exercise since I reached the island. The day was blue and brisk following yesterday's rainstorm, but I didn't mind the cold. It felt like a cool washcloth to the face after an intense bout of crying. I tried to distract myself by imagining what the harbor must look like in summer, filled with ferries and sailboats and yachts. But all I could think of was a father and daughter fleeing together to a new life, while the parents of another daughter grieved in unimaginable horror.

I reached town to discover it was deserted, as usual. Should I go to Will's office? The coffee shop? The harbor? Will put an end to my wondering by poking his head out of his office door.

"Hey!" he called to me. "I saw you coming down the hill. How about some coffee?"

"Sure," I called back, and he emerged onto the street, closing his door behind him.

"How did you sleep?" he asked me.

"Not well," I said, taking off my sunglasses to reveal puffy dark-ringed eyes. "This morning wasn't any better. I told Mira the truth and got an earful in response."

"I'll bet you did." Will flashed me a grin as he opened the door to the coffee shop and we slipped inside, out of the chill. "I want to hear all about it. But first, how do you like your latte?"

"Skim, with a half shot of chocolate and a half shot of almond," Jonah piped up. I looked up to see him standing behind the counter.

"I like a man who remembers how I drink my coffee."

Will looked at Jonah and then at me. "Did I miss something? You guys know each other?"

"I was in here yesterday," I explained quickly.

"How did your meeting with this clown go?" Jonah asked, nodding toward Will as he slid my coffee across the counter.

I grinned. "It went as well as a meeting with a lawyer can go, I suppose."

Jonah chuckled. "One of the gals who was in here yesterday saw you two headed out toward Madlyn Crane's place." He leaned in, giving me a conspiratorial wink.

"Yup, that's where we went." I took a deep breath and continued. "You might as well know. The house belongs to me now, Jonah. She left it to me in her will, among other things."

Jonah squinted at me for a moment. "I knew it!" he exclaimed, slapping a hand on the counter. "I saw the resemblance when you came in yesterday; we all did. But I wasn't sure—"

"Hey, let's give the lady a break from the questioning," Will interjected. "She has a lot to take in right now, and she's not up to another inquisition this morning."

Jonah gave him a sidelong glance. "What do you mean, *another* inquisition?"

"She's staying at the Manitou Inn." Will smiled, and a knowing look came over Jonah's face. Apparently, Mira's reputation as a busybody was well known.

"Enough said," Jonah conceded. "I won't keep you. You guys grab a seat and enjoy that coffee."

We sank into a pair of armchairs by the fire, and in hushed tones I told Will about my confrontation with Mira, my decision to move to the house, and my determination to get to the bottom of what really happened there all those years ago.

"This mystery about the murder, I just can't let it be. I have to try to clear my dad's name." I paused. "But there's something else I want to find out, too, something that's like a thread running through everything."

"What's that?"

"I know nothing of my family history. My great-grandfather built the house I now own, and I don't know the first thing about him, or about anyone else who ever lived there over the years. I want to know them. I want to know what I'm really made of. The good, the bad, and the ugly."

Will chuckled. "Good and bad, maybe. Ugly? Never."

I felt my cheeks heat up. "Will, seriously."

"Seriously, I suspect you'll find a little of all three." Will leaned back in his chair and took a sip of coffee. "That's how family histories usually go. I'm sure you'll find it all at the house. There'll be boxes of old photos and other family memorabilia stashed somewhere."

I nodded. "Henry has already taken my bags over there. After I get settled, I'll dive into the mystery of Julie Sutton's death. Do you think the local police still have their records of the case?" I really had no idea what I'd do with those records, if I even got a chance to see them. The chances of finding any new information after thirty years were slim to none. Still. It was a place to start.

"I'm sure they've got them in some dusty file cabinet somewhere," Will said, finishing his coffee with a slurp. "Listen, I have to get back to the office. How about dinner tonight?"

On the one hand, the thought of being alone in Madlyn's house for the whole evening was less than appealing. But on the other, I didn't want to give Will the wrong idea.

Seeing the hesitation in my eyes, he prodded. "There's a great place on the other side of the island. A girl's gotta eat."

I caved. "Sounds good to me." What could it hurt?

As I gathered up my purse to leave, Jonah called from behind the counter. "Did I hear you right, you're staying awhile?"

"I am indeed," I told him, smiling broadly. "I'm moving into the house today."

He threw a bag of coffee beans my way. "Madlyn was a tea drinker."

I caught the bag with a smile. "Maybe you can come over to help me drink this one day soon."

"I'd like that," he said.

Will threw him a look as he guided me out to the street. "I'd drive you up myself, but I've got some calls to make in a few minutes and they might take a while." He glanced at his watch. "I'll call Henry to come and get you. He usually makes his way downtown around this time anyway."

I walked with Will toward his office and was about to ask him what time he'd pick me up for dinner when I heard the familiar sound of hoofbeats.

"Henry! Right on cue." Will waved him over. I noticed my bags were tied on top of the carriage. "This lady needs to go up to the Crane house."

Henry pulled his horses to a stop and Will held out his hand to help me up into the carriage. "How's six o'clock for dinner?"

"Great." I smiled and clambered up to my seat, and Henry headed off. We were only a few blocks into the ride when he stopped the carriage, hopped down, and poked his head in the window. "I thought you might want to stop at the grocery store to get some provisions. I'll wait here for you."

It hadn't even occurred to me to get groceries. "Thanks. I won't be too long, Henry," I said, as I hurried into the store.

I wasn't quite sure what I needed. Yogurt, eggs, and some fruit. Peanut butter, English muffins, milk. I whipped through the store's deli section, picking up sliced turkey, cheese, and tortillas. I threw a bag of lettuce and some blue cheese dressing into my cart, along with a pound of hamburger, buns, and a couple of low-calorie French bread pizzas. Potato chips and onion dip. Four bottles of wine—*What the hell, I'm under stress*—and I was good to go. I could pick up more provisions later.

The feel of a hand tugging on my sleeve caused me to whirl around in surprise. It was a woman in her early seventies, with curly gray hair and kind brown eyes.

"Is it true?" she asked.

"I'm not quite sure what you mean, ma'am," I said to her quietly. "But if you're asking if I'm the daughter of Noah and Madlyn Crane, the answer is yes. My name is Hallie James."

She shook her head violently, the kindness in her eyes replaced by a simmering fury. "Tell me, Halcyon, how has *your* life been these past thirty years?"

The man behind the deli counter looked up. "You okay there, Mrs. Sutton?"

Mrs. Sutton! I bit my lip and braced for the impact. "I'm . . . I'm so sorry for your loss, Mrs. Sutton," I stammered, "but—"

"But what?" She cut me off. "What could you possibly be intending to say to me?"

I suppose I was intending to say that my father hadn't killed her daughter. But standing there with this sad old woman, her eyes brimming with bitter tears of rage and grief for her long-dead daughter, I was speechless.

"Was my daughter afraid when your father tried to strangle her? Did she cry out for me when he pushed her through that window?" She gripped my arm with her bony hands. I looked up and down the aisle for help, but the shopkeeper had disappeared.

"I'm sorry, Mrs. Sutton, but I can't remember anything about what happened," I told her quickly, trying in vain to free my arm from her grasp. "The first I had ever heard about your daughter's death was yesterday. And for that matter, the first I had ever heard about this island and my whole life here was just a week before that. I believed, all my life, that my mother died in a fire in Seattle when I was five years old; that's all I ever knew." I said all this in one breath, hoping she would realize I wasn't to blame for her loss.

"Well, I know different," she spat back at me, her voice growing louder. "I know my daughter never went to a dance. She never had a boyfriend. She never went to a prom. She never fell in love and got married. She never had children. And all the while, you were alive, doing all those things, raised by the man who killed her."

She was tightening her grip on my arm, a fierce look in her eyes. I had to get away from her immediately. I couldn't bear to hear her grief. More than that, I felt she was a real danger to me. The woman was in a rage; there was no telling what she might do. I finally broke free of her grasp and, abandoning my cart, ran from the store. I heard her calling after me, "How dare you come back to this island? How *dare* you?"

"Thanks so much for waiting," I managed to choke out as I got back into the carriage, my whole body shaking from the force of the encounter I had just experienced.

"No trouble at all, Halcyon." Henry nodded as he gently snapped the reins, easing the carriage into motion. He didn't ask about my lack of groceries; blessedly, he didn't ask about anything at all as we clopped our way home.

When we reached the house, he took my bags from the

carriage and carried them to the front door. "She was a good girl, Madlyn was. Her father and I were friends, back then. He was our local veterinarian, you know."

I smiled into Henry's caring face. "No, I didn't know that. I don't know much about my family history, I'm afraid."

"That'll change, I have a feeling," Henry said. "It's a miracle, you being back here. She grieved for you every day of her life. It's a pity she couldn't have seen what a lovely woman you've become."

Tears welled up and I turned my head with an embarrassed blink. "Thank you." I nodded at him, fumbling with the keys.

"If you need anything, just holler," he said, patting my arm. "I'm just a phone call away."

"You're going to be sorry you said that."

"No, indeed. Night or day."

I waved to him from the porch and then turned inside, pushing my bags in front of me. To hell with the Suttons. At long last, I was finally home.

• 11

Tundra and Tika greeted me like a returning hero—tails wagging, ears back, bodies wiggling round and round—but their enthusiasm did little to abate my uneasiness as I eyed the grand staircase of my childhood home, wondering how I was going to put one foot in front of the other and climb into the unknown. I hadn't ventured up to the second and third floors last night. Why hadn't I explored the whole house with Will by my side?

I got the distinct feeling I didn't belong here, as if I were a trespassing teenager in danger of being caught by the ill-tempered homeowner at any moment. This was my house now, I reminded myself. Madlyn wanted me to have it. *She wanted me here.* I went from room to room on the main floor, repeating it aloud—"This is my house now; this is my house now"—as if to explain my presence to anyone who might be listening.

I stood at the foot of the stairs awhile, looking at the gleaming wood and the soft maroon of the rug running up the center. *Just do it, already.* I took a deep breath and climbed the stairs, chanting *I belong here* with each step. When I reached the top, I found myself in a long hallway containing several doors, all of them closed.

I opened the first door gingerly, and then poked my head into each room in turn. Guest bedrooms, mostly. A guest bath at the end of the hall. The second floor of the house had the same feel as the first—cozy, warm, welcoming. Handmade quilts covered the beds; photos (I assumed they were taken by Madlyn) hung on the walls. Why had I felt so uneasy about coming up here?

I kept hoping my memories would come rushing back, that the act of opening a door would somehow unlock my long-forgotten childhood. Surely I would recognize what had been my own room? But nothing looked familiar. I was seeing it all with new eyes.

Two last doors stood at the end of the hallway. I opened the nearer door and, to my astonishment, found a woman standing beside the bed. I saw her only for a second or two, because I screamed and slammed the door.

In movies you see women shrieking at the top of their lungs all the time, but I always doubted I would—or could—make a noise like that if a truly terrifying circumstance ever arose. Wrong. I screamed like a banshee when I saw that woman in the bedroom and reeled backward, after slamming the door, my back colliding with the opposite wall.

I stood there trembling, trying to catch my breath. I had assumed the dogs were my only companions in the house, so I was completely taken aback by finding someone there. In combination with her rather unsettling appearance, it made for quite a fright. She was wearing a long black dress and sensible shoes, and her wispy gray hair was twisted into a severe bun on top of her head. Her skin was as white as alabaster.

She opened the bedroom door and scowled at me. "May I help you?"

"I—I—"

"I'm Iris Malone, Mrs. Crane's housekeeper," she said. "I'm here to go through her things."

Oh, of course. I was starting to get my wind back.

"And you are . . . ?" she wanted to know. This woman had a haughty air about her, as though she, and not I, belonged there. Technically, I suppose she was correct in that assumption. She was the housekeeper, so it made sense if she felt a certain ownership of the place. And I was a stranger. I might have been anybody—a fan, a looter, or worse—for all she knew.

Still. Those *things* she was going through had been my mother's, and now they belonged to me. I went from frightened idiot to indignant heir in a matter of seconds.

I straightened up. "I guess you haven't heard."

She squinted at me in response.

"There's no need for you to go through Mrs. Crane's things," I proclaimed. "I'm Halcyon Crane, Madlyn's daughter. I believe it's my place to do that."

Watching Iris's face blanch in that moment, I saw that it really is possible for a person to turn a whiter shade of pale. She walked over to me and raised one claw, and for an instant I thought she was going to slap me or scratch my face or God knows what. But she didn't. Placing her hand on my cheek with what I could only assume was as much warmth as she could summon, which wasn't much, she croaked, "So it's true."

I nodded, as much to free my cheek from the touch of her talons as to confirm her statement. "I was just as surprised to learn this as you are."

I don't know if she heard me. She was staring at my face and stroking my hair, her eyes unfocused and hazy, as though she were somewhere else, in another place and time.

"It *is* you, Hallie," she murmured. "We thought you were dead."

Iris wrapped her arms around me, pulling me close. Her embrace felt cold, as though she were trying to transmit her chill into my body. She smelled of decaying roses and dirt. I pulled away after a moment, a little too forcefully, perhaps. This seemed to bring her back into the moment. She shook her head and looked at me with clear pale-blue eyes.

"Yes, it is really me. I'm Hallie, and very much alive. I've met with Madlyn's attorney, who read her will. She has left the house and everything in it to me, her daughter. So, please, I'd like to be the one to go through her things."

"Of course," Iris said, nodding in that efficient yet deferential manner I had always imagined in household servants of the very rich. We stood there for a moment, looking at each other. A standoff, of sorts. I wasn't sure what to do next.

"So. What they're saying is true?" Iris wanted to know.

"If you're talking about the fact that my father has also been alive all these years, the answer is yes. If you hadn't heard the details, we were living in Washington State, where I was a copy editor at the local newspaper and my dad taught math at the high school. He died a few weeks ago." For good measure, I added, "Until very recently, I had no idea that my mother was alive. I had been told she died in a fire when I was a child."

Iris clucked. "And you believed that?"

"Of course I believed it." Who was she to question me about my life? "Now, if you'll excuse me, Iris—"

"Your mother was a wonderful woman," Iris said, with fury in her eyes, as if she thought I needed convincing on that point. She fiddled with her apron, and I could see the tears she was trying desperately to conceal. She withdrew a balled-up Kleenex from her sleeve and dabbed at her eyes. It was a gesture so fragile and vulnerable that my anger began to subside.

"Did you work for her very long?" I asked her.

"I was here before she was born, and I was here the day she died," she said proudly. "I took care of Mrs. Crane for her entire life, and this house for longer than that."

I caught my breath. "You knew me when I was a child."

Iris nodded, and a slight smile slowly cracked across her face. "I was here when you were born and I was here when she got the news that you and your father were dead. I was sitting beside her at your memorial service."

She seemed almost gleeful. I felt an urgent need to get out of the hallway.

"Why don't we go downstairs and have some tea, and you can tell me all about it?" I said, hurrying toward the stairs.

"Oh, no. I couldn't. I should take my leave," she said, and she began to shuffle toward the stairs, one pained, measured step after another.

Guilt crept in. Here was this old hen who had taken care of my mother all her life. Iris was obviously grieving the loss of her employer and, indeed, her whole way of life. I looked at her, standing there in her shabby black dress, holding the tissue every old woman seems to have up her sleeve. What I really wanted was for this creepy old bat to climb on her broomstick and leave me to my house and its secrets. But my mother had employed her all these years. (And yet, oddly enough, left her nothing in her will. I didn't know what to make of that.) I wondered if Iris had enough money set aside to make ends meet, or if my mother's death would put her in the breadline.

We reached the bottom of the stairs, where my bags were sitting in the corner. Iris looked at them pointedly. "You're here to stay?"

"I don't know," I told her. "For the immediate future, yes. I'm going to stay for a few weeks. Long-term, I'm not sure. I don't have any concrete plans."

"I'll come a few times each week to help out while you're here, then." This was not a question but a statement. "I'll tend to the laundry and the cleaning, and do some cooking as well."

"That's really not necess—"

"It's no trouble at all," she said quickly. Maybe she really did need the money. Or at least something to do, a reason to get up in the morning.

I caved. "Great. I'll be glad to have your help, and I'll pay you whatever my mother paid you. I'm sure there are records around here somewhere?"

Iris nodded slowly as we walked into the kitchen. "It

occurs to me, Miss Crane, that given your particular circumstances growing up, you must know little to nothing about your mother and her—your—family. If you'd like, I can fill in the details for you. I've been here through it all."

I looked at her carefully; her clear blue eyes blinked back. "You're absolutely right! The truth is, I'm desperate to learn about my mother and her ancestors. The only thing I really know about Madlyn Crane is what I've read about her work."

At this, Iris smiled. "I'll be happy to tell you all I can."

I hadn't been sure how I was going to learn my family's history. Pictures and records existed, names and important dates. But here was somebody who could tell me about the people themselves. "Hearing those stories will mean the world to me, Iris."

She smiled a self-satisfied smile. "I'll take my leave of you now, miss, so you can settle in," she said, with an air of finality. But as she made her way toward the door, she turned one last time. "Is there anything I can do for you now, before I go?" Her eyes were oddly expectant, almost childlike.

"I can't think of anything, no," I said.

"All right, then. Expect me back on Monday morning." With that, she left through the kitchen door.

It was as though she took the gloom with her and left a fresh breeze in its place. Suddenly, I was parched. I looked into the refrigerator for something to drink and found a single bottle of water. I was mid-gulp when I realized with a shudder that my dead mother had purchased it.

I left the bottle on the counter, grabbed my bags, and headed back upstairs to the master suite where I had discovered Iris. There I found an enormous main room with a fireplace tucked into one corner. On the wall across from the king-sized bed (cherrywood headboard: antique, I assumed) hung a flat-screen television. A nice mix of old and new. It was, in a word, awesome, and I don't use that word lightly. It was a perfect place for me, an Eden. I didn't need any other part of the house; I could've lived right there. I'd had apartments that weren't as big, and none, certainly had been as beautiful. Books were piled on the nightstand: a couple of recent best sellers, a nonfiction work about the discovery of a long-lost book of the Bible, and a crossword puzzle dictionary. I picked them up, one by one, and smiled. Her bedtime reading told me the most I had learned about my mother since I had been here.

A big bay window, bigger than the one at the Manitou Inn, looked out onto the lake. It seemed to be a feature of many of the houses here; the islanders apparently loved their views. Next, I poked my head into the bathroom. I was delighted to see a huge claw-foot tub under one of the windows—a nice view from the bath—and a tiled shower in one corner. This was an old house, but obviously Madlyn had renovated it. *I could get used to this.*

The bedroom opened up to another room, a study. Bookshelves lined the walls; another fireplace stood in a corner; photos in frames were everywhere. Two big overstuffed leather chairs with ottomans stood in front of the fireplace, with a comfy chaise on the opposite wall.

Back in the bedroom, I opened a door to find a walk-in closet, with clothes hanging from long racks on both walls. My mother's clothes. I embraced an armful of blouses and buried my face in the fabrics; they smelled like lilac and herbs and lavender. Behind my closed eyes, I saw my mother's face, smiling. *I love you, Hallie girl.* A memory of her at last. At the realization of this, I slumped down to the floor. I missed her so intensely right at that moment, there among her things.

"Why couldn't you have stayed alive long enough for me to get here?" I asked her, out loud. I sat there awhile, in my mother's closet, until it was time to get myself together and start unpacking.

I pushed some of my mother's things aside to make room for my clothes. Seeing my shirts there, hanging side by side with hers, gave me a feeling of belonging that nothing else had. There we were, my mother and I, together. Her house was my house now, and I felt it, through and through.

I looked at the clock in her bedroom, surprised. Nearly five o'clock already. Will would be here in less than an hour. I wanted to shower and change, so I went looking for towels. I didn't have to look far; there was a linen closet in the bathroom where I found everything I needed: fluffy white towels, shampoo (my favorite brand), body wash, and even a few extra Puffs. I smiled. My mother and I shared the same tastes.

I undressed, placing my necklace and earrings on the vanity, and hopped into the shower; the steaming water promised renewal and optimism. Afterward, I pulled on a white robe that was hanging on the back of the door. Using her things and wearing her robe made me feel so close to my mother. Maybe I could find something of hers to wear for my dinner with Will.

I wasn't sure if the restaurant where we were going was

casual or fancy, but I knew one thing: We'd be riding in an open-air carriage to get there. No short skirts or high-heeled pumps tonight.

I stood there awhile staring into the closet. I didn't want to give Will the wrong impression—this wasn't a date, it was a friendly dinner. How could I convey that, exactly? I found a long black stretchy cotton dress with a scoop neckline—casual enough so I wouldn't look like I was dressed for a prom if Will was in jeans, yet dressy enough if he showed up in a suit. I had a pair of black flats in my suitcase that would go perfectly with the dress.

I pulled on the dress and scrutinized myself in the mirror. It hugged in all the right places and camouflaged the trouble spots. As I stood there gazing at my reflection, a second vision of myself swam into view behind me. The mirror itself was vibrating and swaying, as though someone had thrown a rock into the glassy surface of a pool, and I saw another me, wearing the same black dress, brushing the same hair. Me, but not me. Older. I took a sharp breath. Was I seeing my mother's reflection in her own mirror?

I was afraid to breathe or move or do anything to disturb the image of my mother standing behind me. I watched as, in slow motion, she raised her arms and wrapped them around my shoulders. I felt her gently stroking my hair. After a lifetime of wishing for it, it was finally happening. My mother was embracing me. Hoping to feel what the image in the mirror reflected, I closed my eyes. When I opened them again, she was gone. I turned around and looked behind me, not sure she had been there at all. How could she have been? No,

I reasoned, it was just a fantasy, brought about by standing in my mother's house, wearing my mother's dress, staring in my mother's mirror.

I shook my head to bring me back into the moment. Will would be here soon, and I had to finish getting ready. All I needed now was my jewelry. The necklace was on the vanity where I had left it, but when I went to put on the earrings they were gone.

That's odd. I looked on the floor—maybe they had fallen off the vanity?—but found nothing there. Maybe I had put them into my purse? They weren't there either. I wondered if they had fallen down the sink, but no, the drain was closed. That reminded me: I needed to brush my teeth. I retrieved my toothbrush from my suitcase, came back into the bathroom, and was lifting the brush to my teeth when I saw the earrings. They were on the vanity, just where I had left them.

What was going on? Those earrings were not on the vanity a moment ago. Or were they?

I didn't have long to ponder this mystery, because the doorbell and the barking dogs told me Will had arrived. I slipped my earrings into place, grabbed my purse, and headed down the stairs.

"Hey," he said, as I opened the door. "You look great!"

He looked great, too, in jeans (I was glad I wasn't too dressy), a striped shirt, and a soft brown leather jacket. The bunch of black-eyed Susans in his hand made my stomach do a quick flip.

I flashed a teasing grin. "Did you pull these from the flowerpots on the porch?"

"No, I stopped at the cemetery and took them off a grave."

I couldn't help laughing. "Wherever you found them, thank you. Black-eyed Susans are my favorite." I buried my nose in the deep yellow petals.

A short while later we were in the buggy clopping toward our dinner reservation. Will turned off the main road and headed into the forest, explaining that the restaurant was on the other side of the island, where I hadn't yet been.

"We're about to go through an ancient stand of trees," Will explained, as we jostled along. "The native people who first lived on this island thought these trees were enchanted, that at any time one or all of them could come to life, reach out, and—" He made a grabbing gesture with his hand and chuckled.

Although the night sky was filled with stars, the darkness was inky and dense around us. Tufts of fog drifted here and there like ghosts flitting through the trees. I looked nervously from one side of the carriage to the other. It felt as if a set of eyes was out there, in the woods, watching. Maybe even in the trees themselves. This island's native residents weren't so silly in thinking these woods were enchanted.

I tried to make light of it. "I'm getting a definite Ichabod Crane feeling—" I started, but I choked on the word *Crane*. That I shared the name of a character who had been decapitated in woods like these on an autumn night did nothing to assuage the gnawing in my stomach.

"It does feel a little strange out here at night, I'll give you that." Will chuckled, clearly amused at my nervousness. "Especially since we're about to go by the oldest cemetery on the island." He looked at me wide-eyed, in mock surprise.

"Oh, right." I stifled the urge to pinch him.

"I'm not kidding." He grinned, pointing to the left. There I saw an old wrought-iron fence, decaying gravestones, and dead leaves swirling around like restless spirits.

"I actually sort of like cemeteries, especially very old ones." I chattered away loudly to fill up the dread that was hanging in the air. "Graveyards give a sense of tangible history to a place, names of people, dates when they were born and died."

"Oh, I agree completely. This one is very cool in just that way. You can find gravestones from three hundred years ago. It's amazing."

I was hoping he wasn't intending to give me a tour right then. "Maybe we'll come back sometime during the light of day." I smiled. "High noon. Bright sunshine."

"You know," he mused, "I had an experience in that cemetery not too long ago that I'll never forget."

"Are you going to tell me a ghost story now to further terrify me? I'll pinch you if you do. Hard."

Will laughed. "It's not a ghost story," he said, and then, thinking for a moment, changed his mind. "Well, it might be. Do you still want to hear it?"

"Okay. Yes . . . yes!"

"All right. I was riding my bike along the path that climbs the hill near here, and I got the urge to go into the cemetery and take a look at all those old gravestones," he began. "I hadn't been in there since I was a kid. I was looking around, and I came upon an old, white, crumbling stone. It looked ancient. I read the names: Persephone, Patience, and Penelope Hill. Triplets, apparently. They were born on the same day in 1905 and died on the same day in 1913."

A tendril of chill slithered its way up my spine.

"Of course, I was struck by the fact that they died on the same day and thought about the family that had to bury their three young children," he went on. "But the thing that really got to me? Somebody had been there recently, within a day or so, and placed fresh flowers on the grave."

I shuddered. "That is the creepiest thing I've heard, on a day of hearing very creepy things."

"You haven't heard the creepiest part yet," he continued. "Does the name Hill mean anything to you?"

"No. Should it?"

"It's your family name. On Madlyn's side. Your house? Built by Hills."

I crossed my arms over my chest in a kind of hug. "Was it my mother, tending those graves? It speaks to the enduring nature of grief, doesn't it? I mean, somebody is still thinking about those long-dead girls, even though they couldn't possibly have known them while they were alive."

The forest opened up and revealed a massive Tudor-style building and barn, quite unlike any of the breezy wooden Cape Cod houses that dominated the other side of the island. This looked solid and masculine and regal, like something you might find deep within the forest of a Grimm's fairy tale. We pulled up to the barn, where an attendant loped out to take Belle's reins. I saw the barn was full of similar carriages and horses. Will helped me down, and we walked toward the house.

"Wow," I said, looking around. "This is something."

"I thought you'd like it." He smiled. "It was built as a hunting lodge by an industrialist from Germany in the late seventeen hundreds. It was passed down through the generations but stood empty for almost a century until the current owner bought it and restored it. Now it's an inn and restaurant. The best on the island, to my way of thinking."

We walked through enormous double doors and into a hallway lined with dark wood paneling. A candle chandelier, similar to the one at Madlyn's house, blazed in the foyer, bathing the room in soft flickering light. A bar stood to the left, where several men were enjoying what I assumed were predinner cocktails.

A maître d' wearing a tuxedo greeted us. "Mr. Archer, Miss Crane, so nice to see you both." How lovely to be greeted by name. Will must've told him who I was when he made the reservation. The maître d' smiled over his shoulder and led us into the main dining room. "Right this way."

A massive stone fireplace dominated one wall. Above it hung a boar's head, complete with tusks. Long dark wooden beams lined the ceiling. Candle chandeliers similar to the one in the foyer, along with candles on the tables, provided the only light. The walls were a deep red, and there were several stained-glass windows, although, without sunlight streaming through them, I couldn't see the scenes they depicted.

I was surprised to see every table was occupied; I hadn't thought that so many people were even on the island at this time of year. With everyone talking and laughing, the room should've been very noisy, but the chatter was muted by the high ceiling to a dull, seemingly faraway roar.

Everyone looks so happy, I thought, as the host held a chair for me to sit down. People would catch my eye, one after another, and nod or smile my way. If word about my return had reached these folks, they were certainly not upset about it. The flickering candlelight made the air in the room seem hazy and swirling, made people's faces look slightly out of focus, as though I were looking at them through the lens of an old spyglass.

"What looks good to you?" Will's voice brought me back from my dreamy reverie. "Steaks are good here."

They were. Over dinner, our conversation meandered this way and that, from island life to national politics to favorite movies. We shared our important stories, some funny and some heartbreaking. I told him of my year traveling in Europe and my marriage; he told me of his college days and the time he nearly drowned in a rip current just off the island.

I could feel the air between us changing, morphing into something tangible and electric and real. In an earlier time in my life, this would have been the moment I thought I was falling in love with the man sitting across from me. But I was more cautious now.

When we finished our meals, the waiter brought the check. "Why don't you go to the bar for some hot cognacs to go while I get the buggy?" Will suggested. "That'll take the chill out of a cold ride home."

Hot cognacs *to go*. What a fabulous concept. "A capital idea, Mr. Archer." I smiled and headed to the bar as he walked out the door.

When, cognacs in hand, I pushed my way outside into the night, I was met by a faceful of chill. Will was standing alongside Belle, waiting to help me up. I climbed in and he draped a thick woolen blanket over my lap before jumping up himself. I handed him one of the cups and took a sip of my own, the warm spiciness lighting me up from inside.

"This is one of the benefits of a horse and carriage," he said, as we touched paper cups in a toast. "You can have your nightcap on the drive home."

When Will pulled Belle to a stop in front of the house, I was glad I had left so many lights on—the warm yellow glow from the windows looked inviting and homey.

"Thanks for a lovely time," I said, gathering up my purse and pushing the blanket off my knees.

"Thank *you*," he said softly, reaching up and grasping a lock of my hair, twirling it lightly before letting it fall back into place as he leaned in to kiss me.

I stiffened and pulled back, jumping out of the buggy just in time and calling a hasty farewell as I ran up the steps.

· 12

I've brought you a housewarming gift!" Mira announced the next afternoon. She stood on the porch, holding a wicker picnic basket. "Welcome to the island!"

"Thanks so much, Mira!" I exclaimed, as I took the basket from her arms. It was heavier than I had imagined. "This is really thoughtful."

We stood in the doorway for a moment, smiling awkwardly, and then I said, "Come in, come in!"

We trooped into the kitchen, where I turned the heat on under the kettle and opened the basket. I found it lined with a red-and-white checked tablecloth and filled with gourmet items: fancy mixes for scones and soup and cardamom bread, island-made jams and salsa, a crock of lemon curd—even a bottle of red wine.

It was a very kind thing for Mira to do, to search out these various treats, put them in a basket, and haul it over here, especially considering that our last encounter had been rather chilly.

I handed Mira a cup of tea and she held it aloft in the air between us. "To your new beginning!"

A new beginning. That's exactly what this was for me, wasn't it? I hadn't thought of it that way before. I was so wrapped up in death I had failed to appreciate that I was beginning to build a life, albeit a small one, here on the island. And it wasn't half bad.

"Why don't we go into the sunroom with our tea?" I suggested.

"This is such a gorgeous place," she mused on our way from the kitchen. "It's been years since I was here."

I was sure that was, at least partially, the reason for her visit—to get a look inside Madlyn's home. She also would want to find out if I had made any plans. What was I going to do with the house, turn it into an inn? Live in it? I imagine she wondered about all these things. Still, I didn't care. It was nice to have a visitor, even a gossipy one.

We spent the next hour or so chatting as she told me some island particulars: Thursday was garbage day, the wine bar on Main Street was closed on Sundays, Henry didn't like to drive people to the other side of the island anymore so I shouldn't ask. I told her I wasn't sure about my long-term future, but for the short term I intended to stay.

"Excellent news! It'll be wonderful to have another interesting Crane woman on the island." She grinned.

She left with the promise to meet me for lunch sometime the next week. After her visit, I felt warm inside. I wasn't a stranger on the island anymore. I knew people and they knew me. I would have garbage to put out next Thursday! Little by little, despite the uncertainty surrounding my departure from here thirty years ago, and the ugliness of my encounters with the group of islanders at the coffee shop and with Julie Sutton's mother in the grocery store, I was starting to belong.

The phone rang, startling me out of my reverie. It was the first time the phone had rung since I'd been there, and in the few seconds it took me to cross the room and pick it up I thought of a myriad of practical things I had so far neglected to do. Bills, for example. I didn't even know if Madlyn heated with oil or propane or electricity. I made a mental note to put the utilities in my name and make sure they were paid up. I didn't want to wake up one morning with no lights or heat.

"Hello?" I wondered who might be calling me. I had already talked to Will that morning when he stopped by to tell me he was off to the mainland to tend to some business for a client, and Mira had just left. So who was this?

"Hello, Hallie James. This is Jonah, from the coffee shop."

A grin spread across my face. "Hello, Jonah from the coffee shop."

"I know this is awfully short notice, but I'm just getting ready to close up here, and I started thinking how nice it would be to meet you for drinks at the wine bar on Main Street."

Getting out of the house suddenly seemed like a very good idea. "Sounds like fun."

"Excellent. Meet me in an hour?"

After giving the dogs a jaunt around the property and filling their food dishes, I grabbed my jacket and an umbrella, in case of rain, and set off down the hill. I wasn't sure about Jonah's mode of transportation, but I hoped he could take me home after our drinks. Barring that, I figured I could call Henry.

I got into town just as rain began to fall and hurried into the wine bar, shaking off my umbrella in the doorway. I found a cozy room with booths along the windowed wall facing the street and tables scattered in the center. Black leather-covered bar stools stood in front of an enormous, elaborately carved wooden bar (it looked ancient) accented by a mirror running all the way along the back wall and various bottles stacked to the ceiling, which itself was painted with an ornate mural depicting what I assumed to be life on the island in the early days. Small sconces along the walls gave a soft yellow light, and votive candles flickered on every table and the bar, bathing the room in a cozy glow. Two men I hadn't seen before were sitting at one end of the bar, and when I came in, one turned to me and smiled. Other than those two, I saw no one.

I settled onto a stool at the opposite end of the bar, relieved at the relative solitude of the place. Outside, sleet was hitting the glass in icy bursts. Just then, the door opened and a wave of chilly air rushed into the room along with the stunningly handsome Jonah.

"Hey," he said to me, smiling as he ran a hand through his sandy-blond hair. "Beautiful day out there. I nearly got blown down the street by the wind."

I smiled back at him. "Winnie-the-Pooh would call this a blustery day."

"Ah, but that was on a Windsday," he replied, his eyes shining as he led me over to a booth by the window.

"Pinot, Jonah?" the bartender called out.

Jonah looked at me, raising his eyebrows. That sounded good to me, so I nodded in response. "Make it a bottle, Cal," Jonah replied.

The wine was warm and syrupy, and I felt myself relax as it slid down my throat.

"So, who are you, Hallie James? Where did you come from?"

"Don't you know?" I teased. "I thought everyone on the island was talking about me."

"Well, sure. I know you're Madlyn's daughter, and I've heard what everyone has been saying about you and your father. But that doesn't really tell me anything, does it? You lived half a lifetime between leaving this island and returning to it. That's what I want to hear about."

I wanted to leap across the table and hug this man. What a fabulous thing for him to say. If only more people on the island felt that way.

"So, tell me about Hallie James," he continued. "What was her life like on the wild West Coast?"

We talked all the way through that bottle of pinot and a second one, punctuated by some hot artichoke dip and crusty French bread. I told him about my childhood in Bellingham and what kind of man my father had been. I told him what it was like growing up the daughter of a single dad, and about my beloved seals, whose barking on the rocks of Puget Sound lulled me to sleep. Jonah seemed as interested as though I were telling him the most fascinating story he'd ever heard. It was intoxicating, I must admit.

"How did your dad die, if you don't mind my asking?" he said, leaning toward me and resting his chin on one hand.

"Early-onset Alzheimer's," I said, looking down at my glass. "It took him quickly, within two years. I suppose that's merciful. The funny thing is, I'm mourning his death, of course, but I'd been grieving ever since I had to put him into a nursing home. And even before that, when the signs of the disease were first appearing. My dad was gone a long time ago."

"You must've felt very lonely during those years," Jonah said softly.

"Yeah, I did. I went to see him in the nursing home every day after work"—I sighed, remembering how painful it was to visit a father who no longer knew me—"but that wasn't my dad, not really."

"He was lucky to have such a devoted daughter," Jonah said. But something about the way he said it didn't match the kind words. His face was unchanged and his eyes were still shining, but . . . I can't really explain it. Maybe it was the wine, or maybe I was being paranoid, but his statement sounded the least little bit like an accusation. My father had a devoted daughter and—what, Julie Sutton's father didn't? That's what it sounded like to me. I had to shrug it off because it didn't make any sense. Jonah seemed to be about my age. He certainly wouldn't be one of the islanders holding a grudge against my dad. Nevertheless, a cloud hung in the air between us for a moment and then dissipated as our conversation turned to other matters.

We left the bar much later. Jonah asked if I'd like to come

back to his place for coffee—he lived above his shop on the main street, I learned—but it didn't seem like a good idea to me. I had drunk too much wine with too little food, always a recipe for bad decision-making.

"I think I had better just head home," I told him, hanging on to his arm for support as we walked unsteadily down the street. It had stopped sleeting and the wind had died down, but it was still chilly and damp. I pulled my jacket closed around me. "Can we call Henry from your place?"

Jonah shook his head. "Henry's in bed now, I'm afraid. In the high season there are carriages everywhere at all hours, but now that it's just Henry driving, people need to get where they're going early unless they have their own transportation."

Well, this was very unwelcome news. I had no way to get home. Since Jonah lived downtown, he didn't need to have his own horse and carriage. Will was on the mainland, and I hated to bother Mira at this hour. That meant I was out of options.

"I guess I'll just walk home," I told him, gazing up at the dark hill, an uneasy feeling settling around me. "It's really not that far. And I could use the air."

"I'll walk with you, then," he said. But that didn't seem like a sensible idea either. He'd have to walk two miles up the hill and two miles back down just to see me home.

"I'm a big girl," I told him. "I'll make it back to the house just fine."

He argued a bit but relented when I reminded him of his early wake-up call, and we parted as I headed out of town. I liked Jonah a lot, despite the fact that I got a strange vibe from him. I couldn't quite figure him out, but I knew one thing: There was no chemistry between us. Not anything like what I felt when I was with Will. No, Jonah and I were destined to be friends and nothing more.

It took a while for my eyes to adjust to the darkness after I was out of range of the Main Street lights. I put one foot in front of the other—it's only two miles, I told myself—and just kept moving forward despite the fact that I was becoming more and more uneasy. No stars were visible in the cloudy sky, no moon illuminated the landscape. It was inky black as far as I could see. The dark night seemed to press in around me from all sides.

As I walked along, I was thinking about my date with Jonah. Something hadn't occurred to me when we were sitting in the bar, but it did now, as I trudged through the cool air. Jonah had asked a lot of questions, but he didn't answer many. I had told him my entire life story, but I had learned almost nothing about him. I had been so wrapped up in talking about myself, I hadn't noticed he didn't share anything about his own life. Was that a good or a bad thing? It was the exact opposite of most men I knew, including my ex-husband, who adored nothing better than talking about himself. *Richard.* I made a mental note to call and tell him everything that had transpired. He had made me promise to do so, but I had forgotten.

I was so wrapped up in my own thoughts that I didn't hear the carriage until it was nearly upon me. I turned to see a black horse pulling a two-seater buggy similar to Will's. It was coming up behind me awfully fast; I had just enough time to scramble into the ditch on the side of the road as it thundered by. The driver, a man I vaguely recognized but couldn't quite place, pulled the horse to a stop several yards away from me. I thought he was stopping to make sure I was all right or even to give me a ride. But he wasn't. He turned to me and said, in a low growl, "You shouldn't be walking alone on this road late at night, Halcyon. It's dangerous. Anything might happen out here." And then he went on his way.

I was speechless. What the hell kind of thing was that to say? No offer of a ride? Thanks for nothing! I stood there, watching that carriage roll on into the darkness ahead. *Did that just happen? Did this man actually threaten me?*

I could understand how people here might still be harboring anger and resentment against my father, but what did this guy have against *me*? I was five years old when it all went down, for heaven's sake. I knew I'd be facing some ugliness when people found out the truth about who I was—the incident in the grocery store with Mrs. Sutton was a prime example of that—but I had no idea that someone would actually *threaten* me. I wished Will weren't away on business.

There was nothing left to do, of course, but continue on home. I saw my house, not far away, light shimmering from the downstairs windows. Suddenly I wanted very much to be safe inside. I ran, breathless, until I reached the front door. I slammed it shut, leaned against it, and locked it safely behind me. I checked all the doors and windows before calling the dogs to accompany me to my bedroom, and I locked that door, too, for good measure. But I still couldn't get the man's threatening words out of my mind.

• • •

The next morning, walking the dogs, I decided to go into town. I wanted to talk to Jonah—maybe he knew the man I'd encountered last night or had seen the carriage leaving town—but I didn't want to go alone. As if reading my thoughts, the girls positioned themselves on either side of me as we headed down the hill, and curled up next to the coffee shop door as I burst through it, finding the place empty but for Jonah. I told him the whole story in one long stream.

Jonah put up his hands as if to hold back the tide of my words. "Slow down, Hallie. What man? Who was it?"

"I don't know." I was pacing back and forth in front of the counter. "He looked vaguely familiar, but I couldn't quite place him. He was driving a black horse and a two-seater buggy."

Jonah thought for a moment, squinting as if to get a clear picture in his mind's eye. "I'm sorry. I can't imagine who that might be."

"I'm wondering if I should go to the police," I said to him, rubbing my forehead.

"And say what? That somebody you can't identify tried to run you down?"

He was just standing there, rational and sensible and calm, while I paced like a caged wolf. "I shouldn't tell the police about this? I mean, I think this guy was threatening me."

He shook his head. "All I'm saying is, there's got to be a rational explanation for what happened. You may feel like

"He asked me to tell you how sorry he was."

"I'll bet."

"Anyway, Hallie, the mystery is solved. He wasn't deliberately trying to hurt you. It was an honest mistake. Just drop it and move on."

I wished the islanders would do the same. Would they hate me forever, or was I perceiving their disapproval because of the guilt I felt about somehow being a party to Julie Sutton's death? Did I feel it on my father's behalf?

I didn't mention any of these thoughts to Jonah. Instead, we made small talk for a bit before he ended the conversation with an invitation for me to stop by the shop soon. "I'll buy you a latte," he said, before hanging up.

I heard a crackling coming from the other side of the room and then a voice. "Miss? Lunch is served." I looked around in the direction of the voice and noticed a small intercom on the wall. I hurried over to it and pressed one of the buttons. "Um, thank you?" I said into it, too loudly. "I'll be right down."

As I slipped down the back stairs, I could smell something wonderful wafting from the kitchen. I found a thick stew simmering on the stove and Iris taking a fresh loaf of crusty bread out of the oven. One place was set at the table.

"Won't you join me?" I asked her as I sat down. "You must be hungry after all of your work this morning."

"I've already eaten, miss," she said to me, ladling the stew into a small earthenware crock and setting it, with a basket containing several slices of fresh hot bread and a butter dish, in front of me. "This lunch is for you. But I will join you for a cup of tea. It occurs to me that you might like to hear about

everyone is gossiping about you, and you know what? That's true. You're the best story to hit this island in decades. But it's going to die down soon, trust me. And no matter how much people are talking right now, nobody on this island would threaten you, Hallie. Not one soul. I know everyone who lives here."

"You sound just like my father," I muttered, rubbing my forehead. "Always a rational explanation for things."

He smiled and reached across the counter to take my hand. "There usually is. It was a dark road, after all. Maybe the guy was startled because he didn't see you until it was almost too late."

He had a point, I had to admit. Maybe Jonah was right. Maybe I had misinterpreted the whole thing. I was suddenly embarrassed by the scene I had just made and grateful that nobody but Jonah was in the shop to see it.

"You know what? You're right. I *am* thinking that everyone is whispering about me, and paranoia is obviously setting in. Let's just forget it, can we?" I asked him.

"Don't worry about it," Jonah said, idly wiping down the counter. "You had a fright last night, that's all."

"I'm going to let you get back to work," I said, pushing my way out the door. On my way back up the hill with the dogs, walking the route that had seemed so malevolent and frightening last night but that was now made benign by the light of day, I let it go. There was no reason for that man, or anyone else, to be threatening me. I had done nothing—that I knew of.

. . .

After a quiet weekend spent reading and settling in, Monday dawned gray and blustery. I took the dogs for a quick trip outside, then headed with them upstairs, where I crept back into bed and watched the sleet hitting the windowpanes in icy bursts. It felt good to laze about, warm and snug under the covers, flanked by two enormous dogs, on such a nasty morning. I might have lain there all day if I hadn't remembered that Iris was on her way. I threw back the covers, hopped into the shower, and, to my own astonishment, found myself actually looking forward to seeing her. Maybe we could sit down over coffee and she could tell me about my mother or about my childhood here. It would be a welcome change from the town gossip and the ghostly encounters that had been my lot so far.

Dressed, I went down the back stairs to the kitchen, where the smell of brewing coffee told me Iris had already arrived.

"Morning, miss." She smiled. "I've made scones, started the laundry, and picked up the living room."

Already? How long had she been here? It was a bit odd, knowing she had let herself in and was scurrying around the house while I was sleeping or showering.

But I shrugged it off; it was her job. Besides, one look at the fresh coffee and the plate of warm scones, and I was charmed by the idea of having a housekeeper.

"Thank you for all of this, Iris." I yawned and poured a cup of coffee. "It's wonderful, it really is. Care to join me for some coffee and a scone?"

"Perhaps after I finish my work, miss," she said curtly. "I still have the windows to do."

While Iris shuffled about, dusting, cleaning the windows

with vinegar, sweeping, finishing the wash, and rubbin down the woodwork with Murphy's Oil Soap, I hung aroun feeling guilty. It goes without saying that I had not had th luxury of a housekeeper growing up. Now here I was, an able bodied young woman, sitting around on my ever-widenin rear end while poor decrepit Iris slaved away in her long blac dress and sensible shoes. More than once I tried to give her hand, but I was rebuffed in the iciest of tones.

"This is my job, miss. I've been taking care of thi house for more years than you've been alive. Let me d things my own way."

Fine. I retreated to the master suite. Iris could clean hous all day long if she wanted. I didn't have to watch her.

I started a fire in the bedroom fireplace and spent th morning curled up in the window seat with a good book watching the sleet continue to fall on the angry water. It wa exactly the sort of morning I love best, nothing to do bu indulge myself, the blustery weather preventing me fron doing anything productive like exercise or gardening.

The phone rang. "I found out who your mystery man is, Jonah told me.

"You mean the guy in the carriage who tried to run m down?"

"John Stroud. And he wasn't trying to run you down. H was one of the men here the other morning when you cam in. And he was here this morning, talking about wha happened. He didn't see you in the dark until it was almos too late. You gave him quite a fright, apparently. His bloo pressure went through the roof."

"I gave *him* a fright?"

your family now. I'm the only one left alive to tell you their story. If you don't hear it from me, you won't hear it. And they—the stories of your people—will be lost forever."

As sleet continued to hit the windowpanes behind us, and I lifted a steaming spoonful of stew from its crock, Iris began to tell me a tale.

PART TWO

· 13

When Hannah and Simeon Hill, your great-grandparents, came to this island, it was just after the turn of the last century and they were newly married. Hannah was nothing more than a girl, just seventeen years old; Simeon was thirty, thirty-five, perhaps. Maybe more. They're both buried in the cemetery on the other side of the island. Have you seen it?"

"I have indeed. We drove by it the other day."

Iris went on. "Good. You can find the exact birth and death dates on their headstones, but he was a good deal older than his bride. By the time they married, Simeon was already quite a wealthy man. He had started a logging company with his brothers a decade earlier and now he owned the company outright. Much of what you have inherited was initially earned by Simeon Hill and invested wisely over time."

I looked around the magnificent kitchen and gave silent thanks for my great-grandfather's industrious nature. Iris took a sip of her tea and continued, her eyes hazy and unfocused, staring off into nothingness as she spoke.

"Simeon brought his new bride here to this island, which had been an important fur trading outpost for more than a hundred years. By 1900, most of the trappers had gone and Grand Manitou was fast becoming a playground for the wealthy from Chicago and Minneapolis and elsewhere. Simeon had been here several times on business, fell in love with the island, and built a fine house for his young wife."

"What was the island like back then?" I asked.

"Much the same as it is now," Iris replied. "Grand homes, wealthy people, horses and carriages. Not much has changed in a hundred years. The island is charmed in that way. Time passes here, of course, but not like it does elsewhere."

She cleared her throat, took a long sip of tea, and continued.

"By all accounts, Simeon and Hannah had a good marriage, despite the difference in their ages. It is widely known how devoted they were to each other. He was very handsome—tall, dark-haired, eyes as inky as the lake on a November day—and although Hannah was no great beauty, she possessed a certain air about her that drew people in. It was youth and exuberance, certainly, but she also had the most magnificent head of hair on the island—thick, wavy, and auburn just like your mother's—and she usually wore it long and free instead of piled on top of her head as was the style for most women of the day."

Iris turned her eyes toward mine, squinting. "Can you see them, child? Can you see Hannah and Simeon?"

Could I *see* them? What was that supposed to mean? "I can imagine them, yes," I said, not knowing exactly what she was after.

"Good, good." Iris nodded. "Happy as they were, they didn't have the one thing that would make their family complete: a child. One year passed with no children, then another, and another, and soon tongues began to wag around town, with women providing all sorts of advice for poor Hannah.

"'Eat more salty foods,' a woman whispered to her after church one Sunday.

"'Make sure to go to him when the moon is full,' said another.

"None of these silly remedies had any effect at all, of course, and Hannah was becoming desperate. She knew Simeon was eager to sire a new generation of Hills, a family to take over the house and the business someday. But as more and more time passed with no baby, Hannah grew afraid that Simeon would find another way to produce heirs to the family fortune—a new wife.

"She had seen it herself, right there on the island. Three years earlier she had watched in horror as Sandra Harrington boarded the ferry, bags in hand, a veil covering her face. She never returned. A few months later her husband brought a new young wife to live in the house he had built for Sandra, and they set about the business of starting a family."

"That's horrible!" I said, imagining the humiliation of poor barren Sandra, sent away.

"Believe me, worse has happened to women who couldn't produce heirs." Iris clucked. "Sandra was lucky to wind up with a generous stipend to live on instead of a mysterious death."

I shuddered. "Why couldn't they just adopt?"

"Oh, child, that wasn't done in those days. Wealthy men wanted blood heirs and were not forgiving to women who could not produce them. Hannah wasn't about to let that happen to her—she loved her husband too much—so she decided to take drastic measures."

Iris's tone became low and conspiratorial, as though she were telling me something she shouldn't. "One afternoon when Simeon was away on the mainland, Hannah went to the other side of the island and knocked on the door of a local medicine woman, Martine Bertrand, a French Canadian who had come here fifty years earlier with her fur trader husband.

"According to local legend, Martine was a witch." Iris's eyes sparkled. "The Witch of Summer Glen, the children used to call her. Deep within the cedar forest on the other side of the island is a clearing with a small creek running through it that became known as Summer Glen. This fur trader, Jacques Bertrand, built a small cottage there for himself and his wife. But that was long, long ago, fifty years before Hannah herself came to the island. Martine was now an old woman who had been living alone in Summer Glen for decades.

"Plenty of tales exist about her, local legends made more exciting over time, no doubt. Children would sneak through the woods to get a look at the old woman, despite their terror that she would spirit them away. They say she was a vindictive, evil old witch, casting spells against the high society that had turned her rustic island home into an enclave for the wealthy."

"A witch, Iris? Come on. You're not about to tell me you think she actually was a witch."

Iris smiled. "Of course not, child. All those rumors are nothing but hysterical nonsense. Martine was a healer, a medicine woman, someone who knew how to make potions and poultices with ingredients she found in the earth and the water. She possessed much knowledge, ancient knowledge. Though nobody would readily admit it, and certainly wouldn't talk about it outright, many of the society ladies would steal across the island, wearing cloaks to disguise themselves, and knock on Martine's back door. Some sought love potions for indifferent men, others a cure for a recurring cough. Some wanted the right combination of herbs to break a child's fever; others wanted teas that would ease female complaints. Martine always gave them what they were looking for and never asked for anything in return—no payment, no acknowledgment on the street, not even a kind word.

"Rumor had it, however, that Martine exacted her own price. They say she sometimes laced her potions with malevolence and magic, curing and cursing at the same time. A man would recover from fever only to find his voice mysteriously gone. An always sickly child would become hale and hearty enough to play outside, only to die in a fall from the first tree he ever climbed."

"But that can't be true," I murmured, feeling physically cold at the thought of my great-grandmother going to such a woman for help. This story was beginning to sound suspiciously dark and gloomy. Was it true or was Iris embellishing a local legend?

"I don't know whether to believe those stories or not." Iris eyed me suspiciously, as if reading my thoughts. "I only know what happened to Hannah.

"When all else had failed, when doctors could do nothing but encourage her to pray, and when hope of ever having a child was seeping away, Hannah wrapped her crimson cloak around her, stole out to the stable, saddled her horse—your great-grandmother was an accomplished horsewoman in her day—rode to Summer Glen, and knocked on Martine's back door."

Iris's eyes were deep and dark now, filled with excitement and thrill. "Martine was waiting in the kitchen. She ushered her visitor inside—the doorway was so small your great-grandmother had to stoop to make her way under the lintel. Hannah found herself in a tiny kitchen, dominated by a big cast-iron pot bubbling away on the stove.

"'So you have finally come to Summer Glen, Hannah Hill,' the old woman said to her. 'What is it you want of me?'

"'Please,' Hannah begged in a low whisper. 'All I want is to give my husband a child.'

"'Is that all you want? You want no more than that?'

"Hannah bowed her head. 'Please. I've come to you because of what people say, and I believe you have the power to give me what I seek. I want to be able to give my husband a child.'

"'You do not need me for that,' Martine said to her. 'You are fully capable of giving your husband a child. It is he who cannot give a child to you.'

"Hannah was speechless.

"'But I can help you help him.' Martine smiled slyly and crossed the room. She returned, holding a small cloth bag. She opened it and Hannah saw it contained dried leaves and herbs she could not identify.

"'Your husband is a tea drinker, yes?' she asked. Hannah nodded. Simeon liked freshly brewed tea in the mornings and afternoons, a habit he had picked up from his British mother.

"'Mix a spoonful of this with his tea leaves for three mornings,' Martine instructed. 'He will not be able to smell it or taste it. On the third evening, go to him and you will conceive.'

"Hannah looked at this stooped, gnarled old woman, black shawl around her shoulders, bag of magical herbs in her hand, and suddenly had doubts. Should she be doing this? Wasn't this against God and nature?

"'Is this—witchcraft?' Hannah wanted to know.

"The old woman smiled. 'That depends. I know certain secrets about making cures from what I find here in the glen. If you want to call that witchcraft, so be it. I call it the knowledge to use what God has given us on this earth.'

"Hannah nodded, somewhat calmed by Martine's words. Gingerly, she took the bag from the old woman's hand. 'Are you sure this will not harm my husband in any way?'

"'The only thing these herbs will do for your husband is make it possible for him to father children—not just once but from now until his dying day,' Martine said forcefully. 'The tea will change him forever; he will be fertile like any other man. You will bear as many children as you desire. But it will not otherwise harm or damage or change your husband. On that you have my promise.'

" 'I've wished for a child for so long,' Hannah murmured, eyeing the contents of the bag.

" 'Be careful what you wish for,' Martine warned. 'And listen well to me, Hannah Hill. I said this tea will not harm your husband, and it will not, but you must know this: He is not meant to father children. His line should end with him. By using these herbs, you are calling forth certain *powers* to deliver children to you, against what nature itself has intended. This cannot be undone.'

" 'Yes.' Hannah nodded anxiously. 'That's why I've come.'

" 'But you must understand.' Martine tried again. 'Any child conceived this way, out of—as you call it—witchcraft, can be unpredictable. You might get a demon or an angel or something in between; there is no way of knowing. *Children conceived out of witchcraft are witches themselves, as are their children and their children's children.* Whether they are good or evil depends on their spirit. I cannot control the type of spirit that might come through. Your children, their children, and their children—all will be similarly cursed or gifted.' "

"More talk about witches, Iris?" I said. "This is sounding like the stuff of Grimm's tales."

"And yet it's the story of your own family." She looked me square in the face. "Best listen, child."

I nodded, drawing my arms around me as though I had felt a sudden chill. "I'm sorry. Please go on."

"Hannah listened to what Martine was telling her about cursed or gifted children, but there, in that tiny kitchen, she reasoned that the same uncertainty would surround any child. No mother knew what kind of child she would have, sweet or rebellious, blond or brunette, strong or sickly. That was up to God, or so Hannah believed. Martine was really saying the same thing, wasn't she? In her desperation, Hannah thought so. Hesitating only for a moment, she put the cloth bag in her pocket and got back on her horse.

"Over the next three days, Hannah brewed the herbs and leaves with her husband's morning tea, and, just as Martine predicted, on the third day she did indeed conceive a child. Hannah knew it the moment it occurred, with a jolt that felt to her like an explosion deep within her body. And nine months later, Hannah and Simeon were the parents of triplet girls, Penelope, Persephone, and Patience."

"I heard about them!" I told Iris. "Will Archer found their graves. They died so young. What happened to them?"

Iris smiled ruefully and shook her head. "This is where the story gets a little bit haunting," she said slowly, sipping her tea. "You know what people said about Martine, how she always exacted her price for the cures she doled out? Well, in this case, it was true.

"Simeon and Hannah loved their daughters fiercely, but, truth be told, something about the girls just wasn't right. From a very young age, they were devilish and mischievous, pinching one another in their cribs, pushing one another down the stairs, deliberately frightening their mother by pretending one or another of them was dead."

A shudder crept up my spine.

"They were not like other children of the time, who were,

for the most part, obedient and quiet. You never knew what those triplets might do. They gave Hannah and Simeon quite a time of it.

"They loved playing hide-and-seek in the house and around the grounds, and poor Hannah was forever looking for them." At this, Iris actually chuckled. It was a gurgling, choking sound I didn't care to hear again.

"It wasn't just the disobedience," Iris continued, shaking her head. "It was also their strangeness. It seemed as though the girls were not separate people at all. They never went anywhere alone. They spoke in the same monotone voice, came when you called any one of them, and would stand in front of you with identical looks on their faces. I know it sounds like a fantastic tale, but it seemed as though the girls shared one soul. Of course that could not have been the case."

"Of course," I mumbled.

"One more thing you should know about them," Iris went on, her eyes shining. "They were almost transparent. Their skin was papery thin, so thin you could see blue rivulets of blood rushing through their veins just beneath the surface. Their eyes were the palest of blue, so pale it was nearly not a color at all. And their hair was stark white. It was as though Hannah had given birth to a trio of ghosts."

"Will said the girls died young."

"There was a freak storm when they were eight years old. The townspeople were certain Martine had caused it, but that was, of course, hysteria on their part. Storms brew up out of lake and water wind here on the island when you least expect them. This one happened on an early November day, a beautiful day. The girls were playing outside, right there on the cliff. Hannah was in this very kitchen making supper when the storm descended. Nobody knew it was coming. That's how it was with storms and tornadoes and floods back in those days, with no modern weather forecasting."

My mind sputtered, caught in a hazy fog of remembering. "Are you talking about the 1913 storm? I've heard about that somewhere."

Iris nodded. "It was one of the worst disasters ever to happen here—or anywhere else on the Great Lakes, for that matter." She gathered her thoughts and went on. "It was a relatively mild day, typical of early November, the type of day that lures sailors and fishermen onto the lakes with the promise of calm seas and balmy temperatures, only to turn ugly and murderous once the poor souls are too far from land to return.

"This was the time of year in which the leaves had long since fallen, their abandoned branches now spindly and gnarled, exposed and vulnerable—as, in a way, were the residents themselves—to the wind and snow that would surely come. But that particular day, no snow was on the ground, the sun was high and bright in the sky, and the winds were calm."

"It sounds like the weather now," I offered.

"Exactly like now. People relished those rare November days, riding their bicycles one last time before the snowfall, hanging wash on the line to capture the air's fresh scent, opening their windows to coax that freshness inside the house before closing them for six months of winter.

"That's why Hannah Hill had no objection when her young daughters begged to go outside after school instead of doing their chores. Let the children play out of doors while they can, Hannah decided, glad to have them out of her hair for a few hours. Her husband was scheduled to return from a trip to the mainland that afternoon, and she wanted to make everything right in the house for his arrival.

"It was so balmy, the girls didn't take their coats when they ran off to the cliff, some hundred yards away. Hannah, meanwhile, cleaned and fluffed the living room and turned her attention to dinner. During the off-season, she and her husband gave the servants a liberal amount of free time to visit family on the mainland, and this was one of those days. Hannah was managing on her own—unlike many women of her station, she was a capable cook and housekeeper—and enjoyed the quiet pursuits of making just the right dinner for Simeon and creating a lovely atmosphere for him to find when he returned home. These were acts of love for Hannah.

"She was making a meat pie, a favorite dish of her husband's, wanting him to find a kitchen smelling of care and attention when he got home. She had no idea, as she chopped the onions, potatoes, and carrots, that her life was about to take a horrifying turn. It always happens that way, doesn't it? Destruction descends at a moment's notice, without any warning, when one is caught up in the business of everyday living."

I nodded, thinking of the day this life-altering journey began for me.

"She didn't notice, being inside the warm kitchen with the stove blazing, that the temperature outside had dropped dramatically. Had she realized what was happening, she might have called her daughters in. The four of them might have huddled together by the fire, perfectly safe in the fortress of a home her husband had built, until the storm passed.

"Certainly, if Hannah had had any inkling that a storm had been killing people on the lakes for four full days already—and was rapidly moving eastward, toward the island—she would have acted differently. But as it was, the Hill triplets were playing their favorite game, hide-and-seek, on the cliff while their mother made dinner.

"As two of them hid and called out clues to the searcher, the storm was marching through the Great Lakes, ravaging whatever it touched. Ten-foot snowdrifts engulfed entire towns; hurricane-force winds shattered windows and tore up cobblestones. People lucky enough to be in their houses were trapped there. Those caught unawares on their way home were never seen again.

"The snow and wind were only the half of it, however. This was early November, and none of the lakes had yet frozen, so enormous icy waves, taller than three-story buildings, slammed into shore, destroying docks and piers and seawalls."

I pulled my legs under me. "I can't imagine a storm that fierce."

Iris shook her head. "It was nature's fury unleashed, child, nothing less. Imagine being out on the water with those waves engulfing ships and freezing them solid. Dozens of freighters went down in a single day, not to mention all the small fishing boats and other vessels that were lost. Hundreds upon hundreds of people died, including three little girls who were playing outside when this murderous storm finally reached Grand Manitou Island."

I had been holding my breath for this entire story. I was so cold I felt I, too, was being caught unawares in that dreadful weather.

"The death of the Hill triplets wasn't as simple as just freezing to death, which in the end, of course, they did. Before the girls knew what was happening, the storm was upon them. The temperature dropped dramatically and the wind came. Had they gone inside right away, they would have survived. They would have grown up, married, had children, and finally died. But that didn't happen.

"Persephone spotted it first: a steamer, out of control, being pounded like a toy boat against the rocks just offshore. The horrifying realization hit the girls: Their father was returning home that afternoon, on board that steamer.

"Despite the cold, despite the wind, the three sisters scrambled down a path on the rocky cliffside to the shore; in their young, naïve minds, they believed they could do something to help their father. They were yelling *Papa! Papa!* but their words were swallowed up by the wind and carried away, and they could only watch in abject terror as wave after icy wave bombarded the steamer, encasing it—and all the men aboard—in a solid layer of ice.

"As bad as it was for their father on that steamer, the girls had worse trouble. They were standing on the shoreline, just steps from the water, when the snow bore down on them.

"An ordinary blizzard on the Great Lakes is an awesome and frightening thing, but this was wrath tenfold. Carried on the back of the punishing gale-force wind, the snow began streaming sideways so hard and fast that the girls could not keep their eyes open against its force. It was a complete whiteout—even if they could have opened those pale blue eyes, they would not have seen anything beyond their own noses.

"They stumbled, cold, frightened, frantic, holding onto one another, toward the cliff, but they had no idea where to find the path up to the house. They couldn't make out anything, held as they were in the grip of that blinding white monster. So they huddled together against the rocky cliff, hoping someone would come to their aid.

"But no one came. It didn't take long before the massive waves that had blown the steamer into the rocks reached land—and the three girls. Wave after wave hit the poor sisters, and within minutes they were frozen solid in a block of ice, wrapped in one another's arms.

"Meanwhile, up at the house, a frantic mother was looking for her daughters. Hannah had been working at the stove when she happened to glance out the kitchen window and, in horror, realized that a blizzard had descended upon them. She grabbed her shawl and ran outside into the storm, screaming her daughters' names: 'Persephone! Penelope! Patience!'

"More and more panicked as the minutes passed, she too was soon blinded and confused by the storm. Which way back to the house? Where were the girls? She couldn't see more than an inch in front of her, the snow beating down so hard and fast that it sliced tiny wounds into her exposed face and arms. She had trouble remaining upright in the punishing wind, so she bent low, yet she kept on. She would not leave her girls out there, alone, in the storm. Tears froze on her face, creating a hideous, icy mask of grief."

My own eyes had welled with tears, and as I reached for

my napkin to blot them away, Iris handed me an old lace handkerchief. Like her, it smelled of decaying roses and dust. "I know, child," she said, with a softness on her face that I hadn't before seen. "I know." She waited until I had blown my nose and dried my eyes and then continued her tale.

"Hannah Hill didn't know it, but she was walking directly toward the cliff. She would've stumbled to her death if she hadn't heard voices, soft and low, on the wind behind her. She held her breath and listened.

" 'You're going the wrong way!' The voices seemed to be saying. 'You're cold! You're ice cold!' And then laughter.

"Was it the children playing hide-and-seek? Hannah turned and began walking blindly in the direction of the voices. 'Girls? Where are you?'

"She heard, 'Warmer! You're getting warmer!'

" 'Girls! Stop this game and come inside!'

" 'Warmer, Mama, warmer!' And so Hannah kept going, against the wind, one foot in front of the other, following the sound of those voices—'You're hot! You're burning up!'—until one foot bumped into a stone step. Hannah was astonished to find herself standing at her own back door. She hadn't been able to see the house until she was upon it.

"Hannah stood there for a long while, listening in vain for the voices; she heard only the howling of the wind. Had the voices been there at all? Surely no child could have been playing out in that storm.

"She thought she might rest a moment before heading out to look for her daughters once again. She went inside, closed the door, and lay down on the floor in front of the fire, her face and arms bleeding from the razor-thin cuts made by the icy snow. She would just put her head down for a moment, she thought, and then resume the search. She was so tired."

"Oh, no," I whispered. "Don't tell me—"

Iris nodded. "Yes, child. This is no children's story. It's as real as it gets. Poor Hannah woke up the next day, after the storm had passed. The residents of Grand Manitou Island, including Hannah Hill, knew it was time to look for the dead and do what they could for the living. As they emerged from their homes, they saw a world completely covered in ice. Bright sunshine glinted off shining trees, porches, and fences. Three feet of snow had fallen, drifting to cover second-story windows in some places. It might have seemed beautiful, had it not been so deadly. Hannah tried to make her way from her house to the cliff but could not manage to slog through all that snow. Digging out would have to be the work of hardier souls, those with snowshoes and shovels and spirits that were not in mourning. She went back into her house and slumped in a chair by the fire, waiting for someone to come.

"It was a good thing she was not the one to find the bodies of her daughters, frozen together, their terrified expressions still clearly visible through the inch-thick layer of ice that encased them. But they weren't the only souls frozen to death that day.

"For nearly a week after the storm, Manitou residents watched in horror as the frozen, deathly still bodies of sailors, having perished on steamers and freighters and fishing boats, floated ashore, one after another, in a ghostly parade of the dead."

I thought about the dream I'd had about my father and

knew then where all those lost souls had come from. "And Simeon? Did he survive?"

Iris nodded. "Miraculously enough, he did. Everyone on board his steamer lived to tell the tale. The waves had run the boat aground on an enormous rock, so it didn't sink despite the fact that much of it was torn to shreds. The passengers had huddled together in the pilothouse. After the storm subsided they tried to break out through the doors and windows, using anything they could find. But it was no use. A thick layer of ice covered everything. They were entombed.

"Luckily for them, rescue was on the way. The next day, men from the island made their way to the steamer in fishing boats and were astonished to find everyone alive, trapped within. The rescuers went back to the island, grabbed every pickax and shovel they could find, and returned to the steamer, working furiously to break the icy shell.

"Simeon's gratitude for surviving the storm was short-lived. He came home to find his beloved daughters dead and his wife in a state of catatonic grief. Nature's fury had taken more from him than his own life.

"Time passed, and Hannah slowly came back to herself. She and her husband were resilient and not unaccustomed to death, so they leaned on each other for comfort and support, and in time, they put the enormous pain of their loss behind them. Their lives went on. Simeon and Hannah had a son a few years later.

"But that is not the end of this sad tale. Curiously enough, until the day she died, Hannah Hill was never again caught unawares by a storm as she was on that horrible day."

"What do you mean, Iris? How?"

"Whenever a storm was brewing, whether it was an emotional storm, as when, many years later, Simeon died of a heart attack one afternoon on the golf course, or a dangerous physical storm like the one that took her daughters' lives, Hannah would hear small voices whispering to her, warning her of impending doom."

"How can you possibly know all this, Iris? Did you hear the story from my mother?"

Pridefully, she sat a little straighter. "Child, I was the one who told these stories to your mother and to her father before her. I was here. My mother was Hannah and Simeon's housekeeper. We lived here, on the third floor of this house. I knew the girls and I saw it all. And everything that came after."

"You knew the girls?" I was stunned.

"Of course! I played with them. I was just a girl myself."

Somehow, it was not difficult to imagine the creepy Iris playing with those three bedeviled girls.

"So where were you when the storm hit?"

"I was on the mainland that day, with my mother," she explained. "It was her day off and we went to shop as we oftentimes did. We were stranded in the hotel; the snowdrifts were so high we couldn't see out of the second-floor windows! If I hadn't gone with her, I surely would've been playing with the girls outside that day. My life was spared."

I gazed out the window. I had no idea how much time had passed while Iris was telling her tale, but it seemed to me that the gray day was spilling into a gray evening.

Iris cleared her throat and stood up from the table. "That's enough for one day, I believe," she said. She took her cup and saucer to the sink, gave them a quick wash, and dried them with a towel. "I'll take my leave now, miss, and be back on Wednesday. Perhaps you'd like to pick up where we left off, once I've finished my work. There's much more to tell, and much more for you to see."

"You're a wonderful storyteller," I said to her.

Iris puffed up a little at this compliment, clearly pleased. With that, she pulled on her overcoat and rain bonnet and made her way to the back door. I felt bad about her going out into the rain on her own. I would have offered her a lift home—if I had had the means to give her one.

"Shall I walk with you, Iris? Make sure you get home okay?" I asked, but she just shook her head.

"No need, miss. I've been walking these lanes since long before you were born. I know my way well enough."

I went with her to the door, where I gingerly hugged her brittle frame. "Thank you, Iris. You don't know what it has meant to me, finally hearing about my family."

"Oh, I think I do, child." She smiled. "I think I do." I watched as she made her way down the path toward the driveway and slipped out of sight, into the gloom. Then I closed the door, but I couldn't get rid of the damp feeling that had seeped in from outside.

· 14

Later, as I sat by the fire, I stared into the flames and thought about the story Iris had told me. It was, literally, the first family story I had ever heard. My father never told me anything about his family and he certainly never told me anything about my mother's. Now I had a history—ancestors with names and lives and, in this case, tragedies—Hannah and Simeon Hill, my great-grandparents. As I looked around the room, I thought, *They built this house, began to raise one family here, lost it, and then somehow finished raising another.* And here I was, a woman with the same genes, the same heritage, the same lineage, living here still. Despite the icy reception I had received from some of the townspeople, I at last had a solid feeling of belonging.

Day slipped into night and I crept under the covers of my bed, ready for sleep, when two thoughts seeped into my brain, thoughts strange enough to make me sit upright with a jolt.

Iris said she was a child when the girls died, that she knew them. But they died in 1913. *Just how old was Iris?*

As I was calming down from that idea—okay, she was old

as the hills, so what?—the second thought occurred to me. I heard, as clearly as if I had been standing in a corner of the room when they were first uttered, the words Martine said to Hannah the day she went to seek out a fertility potion:

By using these herbs, you are calling forth certain powers to deliver a child to you. . . . This cannot be undone. Any child conceived this way, out of—as you call it—witchcraft, can be unpredictable. You might get a demon or an angel or something in between; there is no way of knowing.

I had been thinking of Martine as nothing more than a woman who knew enough about the earth and plants and herbs to make poultices and cures for sicknesses and maladies. Women with that type of knowledge were branded as witches back then. But the warning from Martine, and the fact that the girls had indeed been an eerie lot, made me wonder exactly what was in that bag of herbs.

Then Martine's next lines came to mind: *Children conceived out of witchcraft are witches themselves. As are their children and their children's children.*

I took a quick breath. That meant me.

· 15

I awoke with a start. Somebody had touched my face, I was sure of it. I thought in my grogginess: *Iris?* It couldn't be. Why would Iris be creeping about in my house in the middle of the night? Still, my eyes adjusted to the darkness and peered this way and that, half expecting to see her face, white and ashen, at my bedside. I looked at the clock: 3:15 A.M. This was silly, I thought. Iris wouldn't be here in the dead of night.

I was about to close my eyes and fade back into sleep when I realized I had felt the same thing, the same delicate brushing against my face, several nights earlier at the inn. Was that same someone—or something—here in my room now?

I sat up in bed, flipped on the bedside lamp, and looked around. Nothing was amiss that I could see. There was the sweater I had thrown on the chair when I put on my pajamas; there was the book I had been reading before I fell asleep. No ghouls were hiding under the bed, no ghosts floating in the corners of the room.

Still, it wouldn't hurt to give the whole suite a once-over. I swung my legs over the side of the bed, tucked my feet into my slippers, and padded across the floor to the sitting room. I turned on the light and saw that all was just as I had left it: the afghan on the armchair, the water glass on the side table.

Bathroom? I looked in the tub and poked my head into the shower. Nothing but a spider scurrying toward the drain. I was thinking about opening the bedroom door and looking up and down the hallway for good measure, but I decided against it. I was in a little fortress here, safe and protected in my small suite of rooms. There was no need to open up the door and invite the rest of this enormous house into the mix. If I did that, I'd have to explore every room in order to feel secure enough to sleep.

I lay down on my bed, convinced I had been dreaming. I was just closing my eyes when the singing began.

Say, say, oh, playmate.

My eyes shot open. Did I really hear what I thought I heard? It was the same song in the same strange minor key that I had heard a few days before. My heart was beating hard and fast in my chest as I gathered the courage to look once again around my room. I did not want to see Iris there—or someone worse—singing that eerie song in the darkness.

Nobody was there, thank goodness. I was alone in the room. I exhaled.

Come out and play with me.

Oh, no, no. Stop that singing! I don't want to hear more singing. It sounded far away, as though coming from outside. Oh, Lord. Is somebody outside my window, singing? In the middle of the night? How long it would take for this person to find his or her way inside the house? How many paces would it take me to get to the kitchen, where I could at least grab a knife or even a large fork to protect myself? Was this night going to end with me fighting for my life?

And bring your dollies three.

Like hell I will. I flipped off my bedside light, gathered my courage, and walked over to the window. The bright moon was illuminating the grounds and shining on the water. A multitude of stars filled the sky, and slight wispy clouds floated this way and that. The leafless trees stood sentinel on the cliff, their limbs inky and black.

Nobody was there. Only trees and rocks and the lake, just as they should be. I was midway through my sigh of relief when there it was again.

Climb up my apple tree.

I squinted to get a clearer view of the grounds below, trying to spot whoever or whatever was doing this.

There, from behind one gnarled tree branch, I saw something floating through the air. Held aloft by the wind, it danced and swayed in the darkness, its white surface illuminated by the moon's light: a single silk ribbon. All the breath flew from my body in the instant I saw that ribbon, and I sat down hard on the window seat, my heart pounding, my mind grasping at several thoughts at once. And then she stepped out from behind the tree: a girl, with long fair braids, one of them missing a ribbon. She was looking directly up at me, smiling.

I was still as the grave. I could not believe what I was seeing: a little girl, there in my yard, in the middle of the night. My eyes fixed on her smiling face, I watched her open her mouth to speak. As her lips began to move, I heard a small voice whispering directly into my ear, as though she were standing right behind me.

And we'll be jolly friends, forevermore.

I made a noise that emanated from the core of my being, a sound so fierce and terrible and deep that, as I think of it now, it might really have had the power to curdle the blood of any unfortunate soul who happened to be within earshot. As I screamed once, twice, and a third time, I jumped up and whirled around in a circle, first one way, then back again, to make sure nothing was lurking behind me.

Breathing heavily, telling myself, *That didn't just happen, that did* not *just happen*, I ran across the room and turned on the overhead light, bright as day. Then I crept back to the windows and, one after another after another, I pulled down every shade. If she was still out there, I could not see her. And she could not see me.

Now what, call the police? And tell them I had been frightened by a little girl playing with a ribbon? That I had seen a ghost? I'd look like a complete idiot.

I could call Will, Jonah, or Mira, but I didn't think anyone would appreciate being awakened at three in the morning for a nonemergency. Especially not Jonah, who had to get up in a couple of hours himself. I didn't want to jeopardize my seedling friendships with any of them by hysterical calls in the middle of the night. I had already puzzled Mira with my nighttime outburst at the inn, I had already seemed paranoid when I made a scene in Jonah's about the man and his carriage almost running me down as I walked home a few nights earlier. I was rapidly becoming the crazy lady who thinks everyone, living or dead, is out to get her. Despite how frightened I was, I didn't want to further that reputation. I was completely on my own.

Shaking, I crawled back into bed. Why couldn't the dogs be sleeping with me instead of downstairs? I grabbed the remote. Thank goodness for cable. I flipped through the channels until I found an old rerun of a sitcom I used to enjoy. Perfect.

A couple of hours later, I was flipping through the channels again—a World War II documentary, a Weather Channel storm story, a testimonial for a weight-loss drug (mildly intriguing)—when I paused on what looked like a movie. There was something familiar and comforting about the scene: blue sky, laundry flapping on the line, a child rolling in the green grass.

But then the child winced as though she were in pain. "Ouch!" she squealed. "Stop it!' She got up and ran from the clothesline. "Leave me alone!" Crying, she fell backward, as though she had been pushed. "Stop it! I don't like you!"

"Hey, Peanut," a voice called as a man walked into view. "What's the matter with my girl?" He scooped the child into his arms and comforted her, cooing, "It's all right now, honey. It's all right. I'm here now." As they walked out of sight, the girl gazed over the man's shoulder and stuck out her tongue.

The camera panned to the object of the girl's derision: a child. Dressed in white. Long braids tied with white ribbons.

Mid-scream, I realized that I was awake. I had fallen asleep, obviously, and was dreaming about the girl I had seen outside my window. After rubbing my eyes, I caught sight of the time. Nearly eight-thirty. Bright morning sunshine bathed my room in light.

I lay there for a moment deciding whether to get up or slip back into sleep, but when it hit me I shot upright in bed. The windows. I had closed those shades last night; I was sure of it. Now they were open, just as they had been when I went to bed the first time. And the television was turned off, as were the lights.

I tucked my feet into my slippers, hopped out of bed, and gingerly opened the bedroom door, looking up and down the hallway before venturing into it. I made my way down the back stairs to the kitchen, where, to my astonishment, I found fresh coffee brewing. A basket of hot muffins sat on the counter. At my place at the kitchen table, some yogurt and a bowl filled with fruit.

Iris, of course. Had she opened my shades and turned off my television? It was the only explanation—or so it seemed. I went from room to room searching for her, calling her name. However unsettling as Iris was, she was at least a human companion. After the night I had just endured, I needed one. But Iris was nowhere to be found. She had made coffee and breakfast for me and then departed. At least, I hoped it had been Iris. With shaking hands, I poured some coffee and flipped on the morning news. *My house. My coffee.* No ghost was going to scare me away.

My father had taught me to be a practical thinker, but reason couldn't explain away a little girl in a white dress outside my window in the middle of the night, whispering into my ear a strange and unsettling childhood song. Either someone was playing an elaborate hoax on me—but who? to what end?—or something truly otherworldly was happening.

With a sinking feeling, I told myself I knew exactly who that little girl was. Iris was the only person alive who could tell me what the triplets looked like, but she wasn't scheduled to come back to the house until Thursday, and I had no idea how to get in touch with her. But she *had* been to the house and made breakfast today, hadn't she? Maybe she'd come back tomorrow to do the same.

I topped off my coffee and wandered into the living room. Madlyn must have had photos—somewhere—of her relatives and ancestors, especially considering the fact that the Hills had lived in this house for three generations. Old family photos, perhaps an album, had to exist.

I dug around the living room for a while and found a couple of albums, but they mostly consisted of recent photos. Madlyn and friends, Madlyn and celebrities, Madlyn and politicians. I spent a few hours going through them, enthralled by being privy, just a little bit, to my mother's world. I even found a shot of my mother with her arm around a young Will, his tall gawky build suggesting he was about fourteen. Will.

I felt a tightening deep inside. What had he thought of me pulling away from that kiss? I certainly didn't want to alienate him—I needed all the friends I could get on this island—but having sprinted up to the house after what he probably considered a date, I knew I'd have to make the first move if we were to get together again. Maybe he was back from his business on the mainland and we could have lunch. I picked up the phone and dialed his office.

"Hello to you, Miss Crane," he said, surprising me by answering his phone himself. Obviously he had caller ID.

"Don't you have a receptionist?" I laughed, ridiculously happy to hear his voice. It felt good to be talking out loud—to anyone—after the night I'd had.

"The job's open for the season if you want it," he said. "But of course, you're a lady of leisure these days."

"I'll have you know I've been hard at work this morning," I told him.

"Have you now?"

"I have indeed. Care to know what I've been working on?"

"I'm dying to know."

"Lunch plans. Got any?"

"Let me just check my schedule." I heard a great shuffling of papers and then: "You're in luck. By an astonishing coincidence, I have no lunch plans for today. Or any day for the next five months, with the possible exception of a dental appointment in January that I'm already planning to cancel."

"I'm so glad you'll be able to squeeze me in."

"Where would you like to eat? We have all of two choices."

"Actually, I was thinking you could come here for lunch," I told him. "I thought maybe we could have a picnic on the grounds since it's such a nice day." I had cold chicken and salad makings as well as the rest of Iris's bread, cheese, a little fruit, and some wine. And the picnic basket from Mira.

"Hey, what a good idea," Will said. "I'll stop by the deli at the grocery store and bring a little something. And I know a perfect spot for a picnic on the grounds of the house. You know it, too, but you probably don't remember it."

"I do?" Nothing came to mind. "I mean, I don't?"

"I'll refresh your memory when I get there. About noon?"

"Sounds great." I looked at the clock. It was nearing eleven already. I raced upstairs and hopped into the shower.

I wrapped myself and my hair in a couple of thick towels and trotted to the closet, where I began to go through my clothes for just the right outfit. I settled on jeans and a cream fisherman's-knit sweater. I found a long colorful scarf in the closet and wound it around my neck. After drying my hair and putting on some makeup, I gave myself a final once-over in the mirror. Ready as I would ever be.

Only then did I realize I was hearing the quiet drone of the television in the background. I poked my head out of the bathroom and, sure enough, a morning talk show was in full swing.

All the lights were on, too. And the shades were closed. Just as I had left things last night. *Okaaay.* When I woke up this morning, the TV and lights were off and the shades open. Weren't they?

I stood there for a moment, taking in the scene. Somebody—or something—was messing with my head. This was a child's trick. If it had happened in the middle of the night I would've been terrified, but now, in the light of day, it just made me angry.

"Very funny, girls," I shouted into the empty room. "You're not scaring me, if that's what you're trying to do. You're annoying me."

I stalked out of the room, slammed the door, and started down the hallway, stopping short when I heard giggling coming from my room. My breath caught in my throat.

Maybe I wasn't so fearless after all. I ran down the stairs and into the kitchen, not daring to look back over my shoulder. I hurriedly threw together the picnic lunch and hovered near the door and the dogs until I saw Will loping up the drive.

Soon enough, we were sitting together, nibbling on cold chicken salad and sipping white wine as he relayed an account of his past few days, tending to the needs of an extremely fussy and wealthy client.

"That reminds me," I started. "I've been meaning to ask. How did you get back from the mainland? I thought the ferry didn't come back until Friday."

Will nodded. "Exactly right. The only way to get back and forth this time of year is on a private boat, which is what I did. My client sent his for me."

I yawned—not from the conversation but because of the wine in the middle of the day—and looked around. Will had led me to a part of the estate I had never seen. I hadn't done much exploring on the grounds since I had been here—too much of the house itself to explore, I supposed. Through the gardens and a stand of trees, a clearing opened. It was high on the cliff overlooking the water, but the view here was wider than the view from the house. We could see down the shoreline for miles.

I had spread a plastic tarp on the ground first, then a thick blanket, then the lightweight red-and-white tablecloth Mira had given me. And we settled in. It was a bright blue day, crisp enough for a jacket but comfortable in the sun. The dogs lay on the cliff beside us, noses held aloft in the slight breeze.

"And what have you been doing for the past few days?" Will asked.

"Before I tell you, I have a question." I grinned at him over the rim of my wineglass. "What are your feelings about ghosts?"

"You mean, do I believe in them in a literal sense?"

"Well, yes."

"I'm not sure." He took a sip of his wine. "It doesn't seem to be beyond the realm of possibility, but I've never experienced a ghostly encounter personally. Although people say this island is full of them. Why?"

I was already wishing I hadn't brought it up. But the frightening experiences I was having were wearing on me and I couldn't afford to hide in my denial any longer. I had to tell someone. "Strange things have been happening to me ever since I got here," I began. "Truthfully, they started happening before I got here."

He sat up straight and folded his arms. "What kind of things?"

Taking a long sip of wine, I told him the whole story. I told him about my experience at the inn, first seeing the person drowning, then the hand print, then the vision of a girl hovering over me while I bathed. I told him about my jewelry disappearing and appearing the night we went to the restaurant on the other side of the island. Finally, I told him about the girl outside my window.

"She was singing," I told him. "Do you want to know what she sang?"

He smiled. " 'Muskrat Love'?"

I can't explain why—maybe it was a function of how nervous it made me to tell Will about the ghosts, maybe it was because it put that whole horrible incident the night before into an absurd light—but the image of that creepy little ghost girl singing "Muskrat Love" struck me as so funny that I put my head down on the blanket and exploded into laughter. It was one of those unexplainable, unstoppable, breathless bouts of laugh-until-you-cry that keeps feeding on itself. When I could finally catch my breath, I kicked at Will and said, "She was not singing 'Muskrat Love.' "

"What was it, then?"

I sang, minor key and all, softly into his ear. *"Say, say, oh, playmate. Come out and play with me."*

"Whoa!" Will shivered, displaying goose bumps on one arm. "That officially gave me chills. Listen, are you sure you saw what you thought you saw last night? Are you sure you weren't sleeping?"

"Reasonably sure," I said. "So, Mr. Attorney, what's the rational real-world explanation for all the things that have happened to me in the past few days?"

"I don't know what to tell you." Will sighed. "I'd love to be able to say that the little girl who was outside your window last night is a well-known prankster here on the island who makes a career out of scaring newcomers."

"But you can't tell me that, can you?"

Will shook his head. "No, I can't."

"I know this sounds crazy, but I'm wondering if she's one of those dead triplets you told me about. I've been learning about my family history, and I know they died in a blizzard right here on the property. Do you think—"

"I really don't know what to think, Hallie," he interjected. "The only sort of real-world explanation I can offer is the possibility that your imagination is working overtime.

We had the conversation about the triplets the night we went to the restaurant. Maybe it planted a seed in your mind. You had the encounter with this girl last night, right? You'd been asleep. Maybe it was all a dream. Can you be sure it wasn't?"

"Well, no," I admitted. "The thing is, though, I saw the same girl at the inn before we went to the restaurant. Before I even knew about the triplets."

Will nodded. "Right."

I went on. "And what about the fact that I closed the shades and turned *on* the lights and the TV last night, but when I woke up this morning, the shades were open and the lights and TV were *off*?"

He smiled. "That proves it was a dream, though, doesn't it?"

"You'd think so," I told him, excited now. "Except that when I got out of the shower this morning, I found the shades drawn again and the lights and the TV turned back on."

I sat there, looking at him expectantly. When he didn't say anything for a moment, I filled up the silence. "This is the part where you think I'm just fabricating and all of this is in my head, isn't it? You're wondering if you can creep away from the crazy woman slowly and safely."

Will laughed. "I wasn't wondering that, actually. I was wondering what in the hell is going on."

"I can't think of any other explanation. Can you? Other than me being insane."

"Yes, there's that." He laughed. "The old schizophrenia flaring up again. Off your meds?"

I pinched his arm in response.

We chuckled for a few moments, and then he said, "Okay. Let's say you've got a bona fide ghost at the house. What now?"

"I'm not quite sure," I confessed. "If I was watching this in a movie, I'd be screaming at me to get out."

"Yeah, the whole little-girl-ghost thing is about as ghoulish as you can get," Will mused.

We both lay on our backs, looking up at the sky, which was rapidly turning gray.

"So what now?" he asked again.

I sighed. "If only I knew."

· 16

Giant drops of rain began to fall. As we threw the picnic mess back into the basket, a deep rumble of thunder echoed over the hill and we were drenched by the time we burst through the kitchen door, laughing and out of breath. Before I knew what was happening, Will's arms were around me, his mouth on mine. His lips tasted like wine and rain and possibility, and for a moment I almost let myself get carried away in the romance of the moment. But something inside me went cold. All I wanted was to be free of his touch.

I put my hands on his chest and pressed myself back toward the wall, shaking my head. "No, Will."

He looked at me, confusion clouding his eyes. "Hallie," he began.

"I'm sorry," I said weakly, staring at the ground.

"No, *I'm* sorry," he murmured. "I didn't mean . . . Look, I thought—" His words hung in the air. I didn't catch them, I didn't offer a safety net, and I could almost hear the thud as they fell to the ground.

"I should leave," he said softly, turning his eyes to the door. He didn't look at me again. He just walked out of the house and into the storm without a backward glance, and I let him go.

I stood there for a moment, wondering what I had just done.

It rained for the rest of the afternoon. I tried to fill up the time with reading and watching TV and playing with the dogs, but my mind was on Will. The look in his eyes before he left was devastating.

I tried to call him several times but only reached voice mail. Then I took the phone into the living room, made a quick calculation about the time difference, sank into one of the armchairs, and dialed Richard, half a world away.

"Well, it's about bloody time," he said gruffly, and instantly I was filled with the warmth of his humor and his caring. "I've been worried sick about you. Tell me *everything*."

And so I did. I told him about the house and the dogs and Iris, Jonah, and Mira and the island itself. I told him about inheriting everything from my mother, and what little I knew about her. I told him about Iris, laughing about her dour demeanor. I told him about the singsong tune I kept hearing and about my strange experiences here in the house and at the inn. And I told him about Julie Sutton.

"It all sounds quite Gothic," he said. "A huge old house, stuck on an island in bad weather, an unsolved murder, mysterious encounters with ghosts and rude townspeople, even the eerie old maid."

I agreed, laughing. "It does sound rather Gothic. The house is just gorgeous, Rich. You'll have to come someday soon."

A silence, then. I could hear the tiny clink of his spoon against the side of a china teacup. "Hallie." He was still stirring, which he always did to fill time when he wasn't quite sure how to phrase what he wanted to say. "What aren't you telling me? I know there's something you're not saying."

I hesitated for a moment before admitting it. "Okay," I said quickly. "I met someone and I think I just screwed it up."

"Ah. That's the real reason for your call. All this ghost talk was just the preamble."

I felt a twinge of guilt. I should've called him sooner, as I had promised. "I really need somebody to talk to, Rich. Somebody who knows me. Somebody who isn't weirded out by how much I look like a dead woman. To everyone here, I'm just this freak who died thirty years ago."

He chuckled at this. "You really do fit in there among the skulking maids and haunted houses, don't you?"

"Finally, a place where I belong." I laughed, too.

"All right, freaky girl. Go ahead. Tell me about him. Who is he and what did you do?"

"He's a lawyer here on the island," I began. "We were friends when we were kids."

"That's starting off very well. Go on."

"We've spent a lot of time together; he was my mother's lawyer. He's the one who contacted me initially. We get along great. It's like we've known each other forever. He's easy to talk to, and . . ."

"And?"

"Well, he's everything I've ever looked for in a guy," I admitted, both to Richard and to myself. "He's smart, thoughtful, funny, and we like to do the same things. I don't know. He's a real catch. Plus, he's gorgeous."

"Oh. Well, then, I can see why you threw him out, or whatever you did. He sounds perfectly hideous."

A smile crept across my face. "That's the thing. There's nothing wrong with him. It's just—when he tried to kiss me, I froze."

"What do you mean, froze?"

"I mean, I froze. I couldn't respond to him."

"Why ever not?"

I thought about this for a moment. "I'm not sure. We were having such a great time on our picnic. And then it started to rain. We ran into the house—"

"It sounds quite romantic, Hallie."

"It was. It's just . . ."

"What? The right setting, the wrong guy? No chemistry?"

I shook my head. "No, that's not it, not exactly. There's plenty of chemistry between us."

I heard Richard stirring his tea again. "What happened then?"

Poor Will's face swam into my mind. "He seemed really confused and embarrassed and muttered an apology. And then he left. I haven't talked to him since."

More stirring. "I'm going to ask you a question now. You're not going to like it, but I'm going to ask it anyway."

My stomach tightened up. Richard has a way of cutting right to the chase, and he is not known for his gentleness in doing so.

He went on. "What are you afraid of?"

"I'm not sure what you mean by that."

"Well, come on, Hallie. Gorgeous guy. You get along great. He's got no discernible flaws, and you've got chemistry between you. You're both single. Why not give it a go? I mean, really. What's the worst that could happen?"

All of a sudden I realized why I had wanted to talk to Richard. "Well, he could be the love of my life, marry me, and then discover I'm not his type."

Richard sighed. "I wish I were there right now to throw my arms around you, tell you how sorry I am, and make you believe that it's never going to happen to you again."

"I wish you were here, too. I wish a lot of things."

Richard cleared his throat. "I have to ask. Have you dated *anyone* since we broke up?"

"Not really," I admitted. "I've been on a few dates, but—"

He cut me off. "Listen, Hallie. You've got to get back out there. You are a terrific woman, the best I've ever met. You're drop-dead gorgeous, and now you are a woman of means. You deserve to be happy, my darling. You can't cut yourself off from love because of me, you just can't. I cannot have wrecked you. I'd never forgive myself."

"But I believed you," I said. "I trusted you, and then my world came crashing down."

"You're right. That's exactly what happened. But the thing is, Hallie, that wall of protection you've built around yourself isn't going to bring you happiness. It might bring safety, but it's awfully cold and lonely living alone in a fortress. You have to dare to take a risk. You have to risk having your heart broken, again and again and again. That's the only way you'll find happiness, my love. It's the only way."

17

I tossed and turned all night, Richard's words rattling through my brain. Was he right? Had I really built a fortress around myself?

The next morning, I called Will at the office. Still no answer. Obviously, he was avoiding me. Had I destroyed whatever had been happening between us before it even had a chance to start? I toyed with the idea of marching into town to find him, but the rain hadn't let up overnight. It was still pouring outside.

No Iris this morning either, and even the dogs had retreated to parts unknown. I was on my own. I sank into one of the kitchen chairs next to the window, looked out onto the rainy yard, and sighed.

Hours passed. I rattled around the house trying to occupy myself; I watched a DVD, read a bit, but always kept coming back to the kitchen window. Staring out seemed to make the most sense; it seemed like the right thing to do. I desperately wanted to talk to Will, but I wasn't sure what I would say.

Finally, I saw a figure coming up the drive, and a moment

later Will burst through the back door, his clothes soaking wet. "Hallie, I—" he started, the rest of his thought hanging in midair.

"I know," I said, crossing the room in an instant. I brushed a wet tendril of hair off his forehead. "I'm sorry. I've been through so much lately, and I reacted badly."

He grasped my arms in his hands, finally finding his voice. "I understand you've been through the wringer, but you've got to understand something. I'm not your ex-husband. And I'm not your father. What you see is what you get; I'm as uncomplicated as that. I have no secrets, no hidden life, no agenda. It's just me, a man who is scared to death because he's fallen in love with you and you don't seem to be on the same trip."

My heart began pounding. I wanted nothing more than to run out of the door, away from the edge of the cliff. But I didn't do that. With Richard's advice ringing in my ears, I leaped off the precipice, not caring how hard I might hit the ground. I wound my arms around Will's neck and pressed my mouth to his, tasting wind and rain and forever. With thunder growling outside and the lights flickering on and off, we made our way up the back stairs to my bedroom and fell into each other's arms.

Later, Will wrapped himself in a robe and went downstairs to the kitchen to retrieve our wine. We lay in bed together, talking about our dreams, our disappointments, our important stories. But truly, nothing in my past seemed as important as what was happening between us right then.

"I'm sorry about yesterday," I finally said, twisting the sheet between my hands.

Will reached up and brushed a strand of hair from my eyes. "I know it's hard for you to trust me," he said gently. "But I'll never let you down like they did."

I looked deeply into his eyes and knew I was hearing the truth.

"By the way," he asked, as he rolled onto his back and stretched. "When did you have time to make dinner?"

I wasn't sure what he meant. "I didn't."

"Somebody did. There's a pot of something on the stove. I noticed it when I went down to the kitchen to get the wine."

We both pulled on robes and investigated. It was true, there was a big pot of barbecued boneless spareribs simmering on the stove, along with cornbread muffins in the oven. Suddenly, I was famished.

"It looks fabulous," he murmured.

After I had set the table and served us both big plates of ribs, I explained. "Must've been Iris."

"This is the second time you've mentioned her. Who's Iris?" Will wanted to know. It struck me as funny that, on an island this small, he didn't already know her.

"The housekeeper," I explained. "I found her going through Madlyn's things the first day I moved in. She told me she had been keeping house here for decades. Her mother worked here before her, when the first Hills built the house."

"Oh, right," Will said slowly. "I vaguely remember Iris. I haven't seen her in years. But of course I haven't been to the house in years. Madlyn and I would do all our business in my office." He thought a moment. "Iris was old thirty years ago, or she looked old, at any rate. She must be—what—pushing eighty now?"

"More than that, I think," I told him. "She told me she knew the triplets, used to play with them as a child. But that was ninety years ago."

"And she still comes here to clean?"

"She cleans like a tornado." I laughed. "Look at this place, it's spotless. She cooks, too, as you can see."

Will squinted at me. "Don't you think it's time Iris retired, slave mistress?"

"Believe me, I've tried to rip that dust mop from her hands on more than one occasion. I feel guilty every time she's here, working like a dog while I sit around watching soap operas. But she won't let me help and gets offended when I tell her to take it easy."

"She's proud."

"Yes, that's it. She feels a sense of ownership of this place, and rightly so. She grew up here."

We sat in silence for a moment.

"You've got to meet her sometime. I'm telling you, Iris is the eeriest human being alive."

"How so?"

"It's her manner," I mused. "She seems to have taken her persona right out of a Vincent Price film. Dour, ashen-faced. She wears a long black dress and winds her white hair into a tight bun on top of her head. And she comes and goes whenever she wants. I'll get up in the morning and discover she's been creeping around while I slept. She was down here in the kitchen today while we were—upstairs."

Will laughed. "She sounds lovely."

"Hey, at least she leaves food in her wake," I said.

When we had finished eating, we went back upstairs, watched a Woody Allen movie, and then snuggled down in my bed. I slept better in Will's arms than I had during my entire stay on this island: no ghostly visits, no scary dreams, nothing that went bump in the night—except each other.

· 18

The next morning I was sitting at the kitchen table drinking coffee with Will when the phone rang. It was a call for him, oddly enough. He had given my number to his answering service, apparently, and now real life—a client from the mainland—was intruding on our love affair. I had imagined we'd spend the day together.

"Duty calls," he said, kissing me goodbye. "I wasn't expecting this conference call, but I've got to get to the office."

I pouted. "That's what they all say."

He stopped and scooped me into his arms. "Dinner tonight?"

"I'll cook," I said. "I'll make my famous Cornish pasty. You'll love it."

"I knew you'd force me into eating English food sooner or later." He grinned as he made his way out the door.

A short while later I was climbing out of the shower and heard a soft whirring; someone was vacuuming downstairs. I pulled on my clothes and went down to greet Iris.

She scowled at me. "You've had an overnight guest."

I wasn't sure if she was simply making conversation, in

her strange and uneasy way, or if she was passing judgment on the fact that Will had spent the night. In any case, what business was it of hers?

"Yes," I said, a bit too loudly, over the vacuum. "Will Archer. I hope to see a lot more of him."

"Your choice, of course," Iris muttered darkly, and went back to her vacuuming.

I was about to deliver a sermon about minding one's own business when I thought better of it. Perhaps I could coax Iris to sit down with me again today. Maybe she'd tell me another story about the past. I could've sworn I saw a slight smile creep across her face as I walked past her toward the sunroom, as though she knew what power she held.

I whistled for the dogs, and we walked down the hill to the grocery store, to stock up for dinner tonight and for the coming weekend. It felt good to get out of the house and into the bright blue day. The dogs ran ahead, playing and barking and then circling back. They never strayed too far.

I'd learned that the grocery store had a delivery service for residents who didn't have the means to get the bags back to their homes. Just pick out your groceries, pay for them, and they arrive on your doorstep within the hour. I was immensely grateful for this as I walked leisurely through the aisles, finding the ingredients for Cornish pasty and wild rice soup and throwing in some cheeses, fruit, crackers, and wine as well.

When I finished shopping, I went outside and whistled for the dogs. To my horror, there on the other side of the street stood Julie Sutton's parents. I was not up for another confrontation with these people, so I tried to slink around the building into the alley, but then I heard my name called. "Halcyon! Please wait!" *Damn it all.* I turned to find that they were walking across the street in my direction, so I steadied myself and braced for a fight.

I didn't get one.

"Halcyon, I'm Frank Sutton," Julie's father said to me, extending his hand. "I believe you met my wife, June, the other day."

I nodded, wondering where this was going. "That's right."

"I'm just sick about the way I treated you," June Sutton said, her eyes brimming with tears. "I had no right to talk to you the way I did, and I want you to know I'm sorry."

I squeezed her hands. "I can't imagine what you went through back then. I can only tell you that I didn't know anything about it until I got here to the island."

"I know," June said. "I shouldn't have taken it out on you. It's just that, after all these years—"

I could see she was close to losing it again, so I spoke up. "Please, think nothing of it. We'll put it behind us and start fresh."

The Suttons nodded, each suffering the particular hell that only parents who have lost a child can know, and we went our separate ways. I was more determined than ever to learn the truth about what had happened to their daughter, once and for all.

I walked up and down the streets of town, one destination on my mind. Finally, two blocks off Main Street in an old three-story brick building, I found what I was seeking: the police station.

I took a deep breath and pushed open the door to find a

man seated at a desk immersed in paperwork. He looked up as I walked in. "Ah . . . I'd like to inquire about the possibility of gaining access to the police files dealing with a closed case."

He squinted at me. I wasn't sure if he knew who I was or not. "Which case?"

"Well, it's something that happened here on the island thirty years ago, and—"

He cut me off. "You're Halcyon Crane." He was not smiling.

I nodded, putting my hands on the counter. "That's right. I'd like to see the file of the Julie Sutton investigation, please."

"The Sutton *murder*," he corrected me.

"Her death." I could feel tension in the air between us, as though the very mention of the case was making this man angry.

He shook his head. "No can do, I'm afraid."

I knew I couldn't just waltz into the police station and emerge with the file, so I was prepared to fight. "Aren't police records of closed cases, especially ones this old, a matter of public record?" I wasn't sure about this, but I thought I'd seen it on a *Law & Order* episode.

He nodded. "You're right. Closed cases *are* a matter of public record. But this case isn't closed."

"But"—I was confused—"it happened thirty years ago and the suspect is dead. Maybe you hadn't heard that my father died a few weeks ago."

"Dead or alive, his status has no bearing on the case," the policeman told me. "It's an open investigation."

"I don't understand. Are you investigating another suspect?"

The policeman shook his head. "In this state, all murder cases are considered open until they're solved. We haven't looked into this case since your father's death—since he went *missing* thirty years ago. But that doesn't mean the case is solved."

"So there's no way for me to get a look at the file."

"Unfortunately, no." And he went back to his work, or pretended to. Defeated, I gathered up my purse and went outside into the sunshine.

"Lost the battle but not the war," I muttered to myself as I walked up the street.

Back at the house, I saw Iris had already set out some leftovers for lunch—ribs, bread, and a steaming cup of stew from the day before. She was at the stove when the dogs and I burst in through the back door.

"Won't you join me for lunch, Iris?"

"No, miss, I've already eaten. This lunch is for you." She also handed me a cup of tea, steam filling the air in front of me. It was a scent I didn't recognize—a strange herbal concoction of earthy smells: moss, leaves, and autumn. "Your mother's special blend." Iris smiled, remembering, as she sat down at the kitchen table beside me, and I knew it was time for her to continue her story.

"I told you that Hannah recovered from the loss of her girls with strength and courage," Iris began, "but that's not entirely the case. She did go on with her life, and she and Simeon did have another child: your grandfather, Charles Hill. He lived and died in this house. But that's a story for another day."

I took a big bite of the ribs, chewing slowly as she continued.

"Hannah went on with her life after the girls died, it's true, but it was not without suffering and not without foolishness. She was destroyed by the loss of her daughters, as any mother would be. But the difference between Hannah and any other mother was that Hannah knew she had conceived those babies only with the help of the Witch of Summer Glen."

I felt that familiar chill creeping up my spine. Iris's eyes grew dark and cloudy.

"For weeks after the girls' deaths, Hannah was consumed by a sort of madness. She was convinced that the children, while not actually alive—she had been at their funeral, everyone on the island had attended—were still hovering near her. Unexplainable things would happen around the house: a clock falling from the fireplace mantel, glasses shattering, doors opening and closing of their own volition. Hannah came to believe that the girls were causing these things to happen, and she concluded, to her horror, that her precious daughters were someplace between life and their heavenly reward. The girls hadn't made it to heaven, Hannah believed, and she was frantic for their safety."

"What did Simeon think about all of this?" I interrupted.

"Simeon?" She sneered. "He was a good man, to be sure, but an extraordinarily practical one. He put no stock in the otherworldly. Clocks falling, glass shattering, doors opening and closing—these things could be easily explained. This was, and is, a drafty house.

"He had no idea, remember, that Hannah had visited the witch Martine in order to conceive those babies and that his daughters were the direct result of a spell. So he humored his wife. A bereaved mother must be permitted ample time to grieve, after all, no matter what form that grief takes.

"Privately, however, he visited with the minister on the island—a devout missionary with no tolerance for anyone who did not conform to the line of strict church doctrine. He also consulted her doctor, who quietly suggested medication or even committal if Hannah's hysteria didn't resolve itself in short order. So Simeon held his breath and waited, watching his wife closely as he talked to her in the most gentle of tones.

"One afternoon when Simeon had gone to work, she saddled up her horse and rode to the other side of the island. She had questions, and she knew only one person who could answer them."

"Martine."

Iris nodded. "Although it had been nearly nine years since she had last seen her, the witch was waiting. Hannah told Martine the whole tragic story: her daughters had perished in the blizzard but had somehow managed to guide their mother to safety, sparing her their tragic fate.

"'I am convinced they are still with me, there in the house,' Hannah said to the witch.

"'How do you know this?' Martine asked, absently handing Hannah a cup of tea.

"'I can feel it,' Hannah answered, drinking it. 'I feel their presence near me. And things have happened around the house. Glasses break. A clock fell. Doors open and close.'

" 'But they have not contacted you? They have not spoken to you since the day they died?'

" 'No,' Hannah admitted, 'but I am sure they are with me.'

"Hannah began to feel hazy and random, as though her thoughts weren't her own. The edges of reality began to blur, the world disappeared, and she saw nothing except the old witch's face.

" 'What do you want of me, Hannah Hill?'

" 'I want to communicate with my daughters,' Hannah replied. 'I want to tell them I'm all right. I want to know that they're all right.'

" 'Summoning the spirits of the dead is not a thing to be done lightly,' Martine warned. 'Summoning the spirits of the dead who were given life through witchcraft is all the more dangerous.'

" 'Why is that?'

" 'By calling them to you, you're asking them to stay in this world. Are you prepared for that?'

" 'They're my daughters,' Hannah insisted, her head heavy and dull. 'Are they all right? Do they need me to do something for them? I want to know. I need to know.'

" 'Are you certain?' Martine asked.

" 'Yes,' Hannah murmured.

" 'So be it. I will come to you when your husband is away. Together we will summon the girls, and you will have what you desire.' "

As I listened to this part of the tale, something nagged at me. "Iris," I interrupted. "How do you know all these things? How can you possibly know the conversations that took place between Hannah and Martine?"

Iris looked annoyed by the question. "Just listen, Halcyon. It will all become clear in time. Do not interrupt."

I settled back into my chair, murmuring, "Sorry," while Iris cleared her throat, took a sip of tea, and prepared to continue.

"Hannah thanked Martine and left. It was only when she was away from the house, deep in the cool air of the woods, that she realized she had not asked Martine for what she *really* wanted: help in seeing that her girls would get their reward in heaven. No matter. Martine had said she would be able to talk to the girls. She would sort it all out then.

"The minutes dissolved into hours and seeped into days as Hannah anxiously awaited Martine's visit. Every day Simeon left the house for work, Hannah would sit expectantly in the kitchen, at this very table, staring out to the road beyond the house."

Iris pointed an arthritic finger toward the windows behind me. I fidgeted in my seat, imagining my great-grandmother sitting just where I was sitting, waiting for a witch who would contact her dead daughters. I thought of my own ghostly visitors, if that's indeed what they were, and shivered. I sipped my tea, hoping to feel its warmth inside.

"Finally, the day came," Iris continued. "Martine, disguised in a hooded cloak, appeared at Hannah's back door. She was carrying a small velvet bag.

"'You are sure no one else is here?' Martine asked her,

looking around the room furtively. Hannah nodded. But she was not correct. Hannah did not know I was here, along with a young cousin of mine from the mainland. My mother was here as well, doing the wash in the laundry house, which at one time stood where Madlyn's garden is today."

I looked out the window and saw the ghostly outline of a crude wooden building. Iris's mother was carrying loads of white sheets out of its door toward the clothesline. I shook my head. *Am I really seeing what I think I'm seeing?*

Iris interrupted my vision. "Look deeply, child. Deep within yourself."

"I don't understand what you mean."

"You will." Iris smiled. "The visions will solidify. Soon I'll become little more than a narrator for what you're seeing with your own eyes. After that, you won't need me at all."

"Iris, you're not making any sense."

"You'll soon see." Then she continued the story. "I suppose Mrs. Hill was too wrapped up in her desire to talk to her daughters again to have thought about the maid and *her* daughter. My cousin Jane and I were playing outside in the big stand of cedar trees when we saw Martine coming up the drive.

"Of course, when we saw her we ran to the house immediately to get a better look. We had heard tales of the Witch of Summer Glen, but we had been much too afraid to cross the island to spy on her as the other children did. Now, here she was, coming up my very own drive!

"My cousin and I looked through the window and watched as Martine opened the small crimson velvet bag and began setting items from it on the kitchen table: a lace cloth, candles, dried herbs. Then she said, 'I need one personal item from each of the girls.'

"Hannah left the kitchen and returned a few moments later with three satin ribbons. "'They wore these in their hair,' she murmured, clutching the ribbons as though they were sacred talismans."

My breath caught in my throat at this. Satin ribbons?

"Martine nodded her approval silently and gathered the ribbons in the center of the table. She placed the candles around them. Into the flame of one of the lit candles, she sprinkled an herb of some kind, which produced a crimson-colored smoke and a dark musky scent so strong it reached even to our young noses, outside the window. And then Martine began to speak in a language I did not understand. She was saying strange-sounding words, over and over and over—an incantation. She seemed to have slipped into some sort of altered state, a trance, because her eyes began to roll back into her head, exposing the whiteness around them.

"I looked at Hannah, and she was still as the grave. She seemed hypnotized. She was staring into space, not looking at Martine, not looking at us through the window, just staring.

"I, too, began to feel a sort of pull toward oblivion. I tried to move but could not, trapped as I was, right there, at the window, watching this witch cast a spell that would summon the dead.

"Suddenly I understood the words Martine was saying. She had begun to chant the girls' names, over and over again. Persephone, Patience, Penelope; Persephone, Patience, Penelope. She was calling on their spirits to return."

As Iris chanted the girls' names, I felt as though I became

the little child outside the window, peeking in at the scene. Through the hazy windowpane I saw Martine's grizzled face, Hannah's blank stare, the kitchen transformed into how it had been a century earlier—no microwave in the corner, no stainless-steel fridge—just two women sitting at the kitchen table, summoning the dead.

"Persephone, Patience, Penelope," Iris went on, her face contorting into the sort of trancelike mask Martine's face had worn.

I felt the ribbon on my cheek. I wanted to cry out for Iris to stop. Was she was summoning those children just as Martine had done almost a century ago? I didn't want to find out. I tried to tell Iris to stop whatever she was doing, but I couldn't move; I couldn't speak; I was trapped in the web Iris was weaving with her words.

Now the scene shifted. I was no longer the girl outside the window but Hannah. Vaguely, somewhere in the distance, I could see Iris sitting next to me, eyes rolled back in her head, chanting an incantation to three dead children. The clearer, more tangible image before me was that of Martine sitting across the table. I was seeing what my great-grandmother had seen, here in the kitchen, nearly ninety years ago.

A crash from the living room caused the vision to dissipate like steam rising from a teacup. I shook my head to clear my confusion as the kitchen door flew open and slammed closed, again and again and again. This brought Iris out of whatever spell she was weaving as well, and she looked at me with clear, dark eyes.

I jumped up from the table. "What do you think you're doing?" I demanded to know, looking around wildly. Several

"Martine and Hannah did not see my cousin and me, rouched and shivering with fear beneath the kitchen window, but Persephone, Patience, and Penelope did. They homed in on my cousin, the poor thing. I'm still not sure why they left me alone; perhaps because I had been their playmate in life.

"I heard them giggling and whispering as they descended upon my poor cousin Jane. They pushed and jostled and kicked her. They pinched her and tripped her. I should have intervened, should have done something to help, but I was just as terrified as Jane was. I cowered behind a bush and watched as Jane ran screaming from her invisible tormentors. The last I saw, she was tumbling over the cliff."

I sat there staring at Iris in stunned silence for a moment. "What do you mean, the last you saw of her?"

"I mean Jane died that day, Halcyon. They found her body in the exact spot where the girls had died a few months earlier."

glasses had fallen from the shelves and shatt
ter. Thankfully, the doors had quieted dow
accord.

Iris just smiled and shook her head. "I'm mer
finish the story. There is much more to tell."

"I'm not at all sure I want to know the rest, to te
truth," I said, holding fast to the back of my chair. "
look around. Did all those glasses just fling themselv
the shelf?"

"I'll clean them up as soon as we're finished," she said.

"That's not the point. Were you trying to summon thos
girls, just like Martine did?"

She looked at me and said, in a voice not entirely her own, "I do not need to summon Penelope, Patience, and Persephone. They are here. When the witch summoned them that day, she called them to this house from beyond and they have been here ever since."

I sat down hard. It was true, then.

"There is more to the story, child, more you must hear."

I nodded weakly, and Iris went on.

"As Martine chanted the girls' names, glasses began to break, doors began to open and close, and Hannah, when she was able to break free of the spell Martine was wrapping around the table, sprang to her feet and cried, 'Girls! Girls! It's your mother!'

"But the girls weren't bothering with their mother that day. As I said, these girls were not normal children of the day. They were mischievous to the point of viciousness, even in life. It was as though they didn't have souls at all. Nary a conscience among them.

19

I think I know why my father took me away from here," I told Will later that night over dinner.

When he arrived on my doorstep a few hours after Iris had left, I flew into his arms. I had been terrified the rest of the afternoon in the house alone. Hearing the story about Hannah, Martine, and the girls—and poor Jane!—had pushed *me* over some kind of precipice. This had gone beyond a few odd ghostly encounters that would make interesting dinner party conversation. Now I felt as though I had been drawn into a nightmare. I had suddenly become the unlucky sap who happens upon the children of the corn, the traveler whose car breaks down in a town filled with vampires.

I stayed with the dogs in the kitchen until Will got there, not wishing to venture into other parts of the house, areas where three evil little girls could be lurking. I busied myself making dinner. The dogs sensed my uneasiness and kept close, curled up next to me all the while.

Now I was serving Will a slice of Cornish pasty and telling him everything—how Hannah and Martine had summoned the spirits of the girls, how Iris had been watching from the window and saw the whole thing unfold, how poor Jane had been driven to her death by the three spirits.

"That's an incredible story." Will shook his head. "I wonder if any of it's true."

I held my soup spoon in midair. "You think Iris was making it up? Why would she do that?"

Will backpedaled. "I'm not saying she fabricated anything, but it all happened a long, long time ago, when Iris was just a child. An old witch, spells, incantations, summoning dead children—you have to admit, Hallie, that it sounds like a legend. Something straight out of a child's imagination."

"I'd love to believe Iris's story was just her imagination working overtime, but I've seen the girls. One of them, at least."

Will nodded. "Or what you believe to be one of the girls."

"What I *believe*?" I stared at him. "I'm not crazy, Will, if that's what you think."

"I know you're not." He backpedaled again, putting his palms in the air as if to hold back my anger. "Okay. Let's go with the theory that everything Iris told you today is the honest truth; nothing was embellished, nothing overblown. What now?"

"It might explain why my father took me away." Will started to shake his head in disbelief, but I cut him off before he could speak. "Just hear me out. What if my father found out about this story somehow? Maybe he saw the girls himself, just like I have. Maybe . . ." My words trailed off. I hoped Will would pick them up.

"Okay, I'll play along. Maybe the girls were threatening you." He continued my thought. "That's reason enough for a father to resort to drastic measures to save his daughter, certainly."

"It is," I said, suddenly tearing up at the mention of my dad. I wished he were here to make sense of this, to tell me why he had taken me away from this place all those years ago.

Will took my hand. "Have you remembered anything at all from that time?"

I shook my head. "Not a thing."

"That could say something in itself," Will speculated. "I remember a lot about our childhood friendship. You don't. It suggests you might have experienced some kind of trauma that was best forgotten."

This theory had occurred to me while I was cowering in the kitchen, terrified, waiting for Will that day. The intense fear seemed familiar somehow, as though I had felt the same thing in the same place before.

"What do you remember about being here when we were kids?" I asked him.

Will smiled, thinking back. "We had a lot of fun together. We played outside, made tree forts, went swimming."

"Did you ever see . . . you know. The girls?"

Will shook his head. "Not that I can recall. As far as I can remember, we had an altogether normal childhood."

Our conversation was at a dead end. I didn't know what else to say and neither did Will, so I decided to change the subject to a more real-world matter.

"I went to the police station today," I told him.

"Why did you do that?"

"I wanted to see the old file concerning the Sutton case."

He finished the last of his pasty and shook his head. "Let me guess. You got nowhere."

"How did you know?"

"There's not a chance the police would give you that file, Hallie. I told you that."

I sighed. "Then how can I find out more about what happened that day? I'm the only one alive who was there, and I can't remember anything about it. I thought if I could get my hands on that file, it might jog something loose in my brain."

"I said they wouldn't give it to *you*."

"But they'd give it to *you*?"

Will smiled mischievously. "I'm not sure. But this is a very small town and its old records aren't exactly housed in Fort Knox. I'll see if I can get my hands on them."

· 20

"Today you'll hear the story of your grandfather," Iris began, over the next day's morning coffee.

"He was the vet on the island, right?"

"That's right. But before he was a veterinarian, Charles was a little boy. He was born on the second anniversary of the deaths of his sisters," Iris said, her eyes closed in remembrance. "He was a happy baby, chubby and blue-eyed with a full head of blond hair. I was especially fond of Charles because we spent so much time together. I had been given the task of looking after him, you see."

I pictured a young vibrant girl with long hair blowing in the breeze, pushing a baby stroller in the garden, singing to the baby inside it. Iris?

"I was eleven or twelve years old at the time—I had grown up considerably since the girls' deaths—and my mother suggested that I be allowed to take charge of the baby as his nanny. This pleased Hannah, who was rather preoccupied. She never saw Martine after the séance on that horrible day, but not for lack of trying on her part. Martine had disappeared, her cottage on the other side of the island emptied of its contents. Nobody ever knew what happened to the witch, where she went or how she got off the island without even the ferry captain seeing her. As time passed, Hannah came to distrust her own mind and her own memories, wondering if Martine had ever existed at all."

"I know how she felt," I murmured, sipping my coffee. As I swallowed, a vision swam and wavered in the air before me: Charles as a baby, under Iris's watchful eye. I looked at Iris, questioning.

Iris explained: "You've always had the ability to see the spirits beyond the veil, Halcyon. They're showing themselves to you—the important moments in their lives."

"But how—"

Iris cut off my questioning. "You must wait. Yours is a tale for another day. Today we're talking about Charles."

Fair enough. I took another sip as she continued. "Charles was such a good-natured child, sunny and obedient and pleasant, always laughing and cooing and smiling. Perhaps that's the reason nobody thought anything of the fact that, by age two, he had not yet spoken a word."

"Two? That's pretty late to begin talking, isn't it?"

Iris nodded. "It was indeed. After his second birthday, Hannah began to voice some concern about her silent child. I accompanied her on several trips to doctors on the mainland, none of whom ever came up with any sort of diagnosis that would explain his lack of speech. So I decided to try to teach Charles to speak myself. I read to him, teaching him the alphabet and rudimentary mathematics. I'd point to the letters and make the sounds: *aaaay*, *beeee*, *seeee*. Charles did not respond in kind, but I knew he was listening and learning. When he was four years old—"

"Four?" I interrupted. "You mean to say he still wasn't speaking at *four*?"

"That's right. But he did begin wandering out of the kitchen door on his own, much to my consternation. I'd be frantic, searching everywhere—in the garden? on the cliff? But soon I learned to find him in one of two places: the barn or the back lawn."

A watery, wavy image of a young boy formed in the air above the table, a blond-haired blue-eyed child sitting in the grass by the garden with a couple of dogs. A deer stood nearby, curious, and a hawk circled above.

"Animals?" I asked Iris, doubting what I was seeing.

"The boy had an otherworldly connection to animals. That was his gift. It was almost as though he could read their thoughts and understand what they were saying. Charles spoke their language even though he never made a sound. I'd find him lying in the stall with one of the cows, or sitting on the grass with a dozen robins perched around him, or lazily petting a wayward skunk that had found its way onto the grounds.

"I never bothered him during those times," Iris continued. "I can't explain why, but I knew I shouldn't intrude. So I watched, amazed."

"It sounds magical and wonderful, Iris," I murmured, as I envisioned an enormous hawk landing on Charles's tiny outstretched arm.

"It was indeed." Iris smiled at me, a thrilled look in her

eyes. "One day when Charles was five years old, I found him on the back lawn curled up with a cougar!"

I gulped. "I had no idea there were big cats on this island." With all of my wanderings, had I been in danger of meeting one?

"In those days, we had quite a few of them here, but they're long since gone. We all knew what cougars—some used to call them panthers—were capable of, especially if they were hungry. Well, of course I was terrified, so I called out for Hannah, who did nothing but collapse to the floor, screaming at the sight of her child sitting with this big cat. I ran to get Simeon, telling him to come quickly and bring his rifle. He strode out the door toward Charles and the cougar, aiming at the cat's great head.

" 'Don't be afraid, now, son,' Simeon said evenly to Charles. 'Daddy's here. Stay perfectly still.'

"But for once in his life, Charles did not do as he was told. He stood up, positioned himself between his father and the cat, and threw his arms open wide.

" 'Why would you want to shoot this cat, Father?' Charles cried out. 'Bella is here to protect me, taking her turn just as all the animals have done.'

"These were Charles's first words. At the sound of his son's voice, Simeon dropped his gun and sank to his knees.

" 'Don't cry, Father,' Charles said, running up to Simeon and throwing his little arms around his father's neck.

"Simeon picked up the boy and hugged him tight, and as he did so the great cat stood up and padded toward them. Simeon was ready to reach for his gun—I saw the look of terror on his face—when Charles said, 'It's all right, Father. I've told Bella you're not hurting me.' And with that, the cat rubbed against Simeon's legs, just as a housecat would do, before taking her place in the yard again."

"Amazing," I murmured, having seen the whole thing.

Iris nodded. "Nobody could quite believe their eyes. Later on, after dinner, when everyone had gotten over the shock that the mute Charles was sitting at the table chattering away, Simeon asked his son, 'Charles, why haven't you spoken a word before today?'

"Charles looked at him, confused. 'I don't understand, Father.'

"Simeon repeated the question. 'You haven't said one word until today, son. We were wondering if you'd ever speak.'

"Charles just shook his head. 'I've been talking for years, Father. Haven't you been able to hear me?'

"A silence fell around the table. Nobody knew what to say. The boy had been silent as the grave his entire life, of that everyone was certain. Simeon answered his son in the best way he knew how. 'No, Charles, we haven't heard you. I'm so sorry, son. I guess we just weren't listening carefully enough.'

"Charles smiled a great smile, then, and took his father's hand. 'That's all right, Father. I was listening carefully enough for all of us.' "

The compassion in my young grandfather's voice—which I was able to hear as clearly as if he were standing right next to me—was overwhelming. I dabbed at my eyes with a Kleenex. "Charles sounds like a wonderful child."

"He was a magical child, really," Iris said.

"So the animals kept coming around as he grew up?"

"They did indeed," Iris said. "Especially the wolves and

the big cats. None of them ever went after our chickens or cows or even the dogs. They were here for one purpose, to protect Charles."

"Protect him from what?"

A smile spread slowly across Iris's lined face as she shook her head. "Child, were you not listening to my story the other day?"

"Of course I was listening."

"Then what do you suppose Charles needed protection from?"

The answer hit me like an icy wave as an image of three ghostly girls swept through my mind. He needed protection from his dead sisters.

· 21

I decided not to tell Will about Iris's latest tale. I had been enthralled by her storytelling, but when she left for home that day, Will's words echoed in my head and I wondered how much of her story was true. I knew how it sounded: a young mute boy able to forge an otherworldly connection with the animal world? It was the stuff of a children's book.

No, before I could tell Will any more stories, I would need to find some sort of proof. I was burning for it. On Saturday morning, I made my way up to the third floor, determined to find some old family photos that would confirm what Iris had told me.

I hadn't ventured up to the third floor yet. There were many reasons for my reluctance to explore the top of the house, all of them admittedly silly. The third floor was accessible only by the back staircase because, I imagined, it had housed the servants, who needed to come and go from the kitchen and laundry without disturbing the main areas of the house. Even the staircase felt haunted, empty, forbidden, so I could only imagine what the floor itself might feel like.

Also, at the top of those stairs there was a locked door, with no sign of a key in sight.

Well, of course I might have simply asked Iris for it. She certainly had the key or knew where it was stashed, because from time to time I heard her scurrying around up there, cleaning. But I had the overwhelming feeling that I wasn't supposed to go up there, which probably stemmed from my childhood. Whatever happened to my father and Julie Sutton had happened up there. Something about confronting that scene again made me feel queasy.

But on this day, curiosity got the better of me. It's not as if I expected to find a photo of Martine in mid-séance, but I hoped I could find a shot of Charles with some animals, at the very least. Perhaps an old photo of the girls?

I set about finding that key and finally, after nearly an hour of searching, I slipped my hand onto the sill of the high window above the kitchen sink and felt something cool and metallic, an old skeleton key on a chain. That had to be it. I closed my palm around the metal, crept up the back stairs, my heart beating furiously, and slipped the key into the lock. The door opened easily.

I found myself standing in a long hallway similar to the one on the second floor. It was dark, the shutters on the windows at both ends of the hallway drawn tightly closed against the sun. I flicked the light switch—nothing. I opened the shutters at one end of the hallway and then the other, letting bright slim shafts of light stream in through the slats. There was nothing frightening about this third floor. Being servants' quarters, it just wasn't as opulently decorated as the rest of the house. A plain red carpet sat on the hallway floor and the walls were painted a simple cream that had yellowed over time.

I grasped the knob on the first door and turned it to find a small room with a single bed (no sheets or bedding, just a bare mattress) and a little bedside table. A dresser sat against the wall, unused and empty. A small bathroom occupied one end of the hall. I imagined Iris and her mother living in these spartan rooms back when they would've been clean and comfy.

As I neared the doorway at the end of the hall, my pulse began to quicken. Had the incident with Julie Sutton, whatever it was, happened in that room? I held my breath and opened the door.

A set of twin beds, still made up with yellow and red quilts, were pushed to opposite walls; a rocking horse, its paint flaking in spots, sat between them. A rocking chair was positioned in the corner by the shuttered window. The walls were covered with a faded yellow wallpaper on which ducks, geese, and chickens paraded to a barnyard on the opposite side of the room. It was a delightful nursery, even now. I felt very much at home in this room. Had I played here as a child?

In one corner, I spied several boxes, trunks, and suitcases. Success! The boxes were clearly labeled: toys, clothes, coats. I found photos in one of the trunks, album after album, clearly marked and organized. I was about to sit down and begin going through generations of photos when I saw a box labeled NOAH and next to it, one for HALLIE. This stopped me in my tracks. My original reason for exploring the third floor forgotten, I sank to the floor and opened my father's box, finding his things neatly folded and stacked—a few clothes, books, ties, and other personal items—and, what interested me the most, two albums of photographs.

I held my breath as I opened one of them, an ache of longing and loss filling me as I saw my mother and father together for the first time. He looked younger, certainly, but it was the joy in his eyes that struck me most. I flipped through the pages, seeing the two of them on a picnic, at the lakeshore, posing arm in arm at the Grand Canyon (their honeymoon?) and she, in her youth, looking unsettlingly like the reflection I saw in the mirror each day. They had been happy then, in the early years of their relationship. These photos didn't lie.

I pushed my father's box to the side and held my breath as I opened the one with my name on it. A stuffed purple skunk gave off a vague scent of lilac and I knew that was his name, Lilac. A Raggedy Ann doll lay next to a white stuffed dog, who, like the Velveteen Rabbit, had become real as a result of all of the love I had undoubtedly given him during my childhood. His name came to me: Puppy Dog. I unfolded a tiny white sweater and a long white gown that I must have worn on my baptism day. I found a plaid jumper, which evoked the sense of autumn and sharpened number 2 pencils and a walk down the hill, lunchbox in hand, to a kindergarten class. I took a few books out of the box: *The Little Mermaid* (the Hans Christian Andersen version) along with *Hans Brinker and the Silver Skates* and an entire boxed set of *Little House on the Prairie* books, their bindings still stiff and unread. All these things had been mine.

Here, too, were photographs. I had never seen any of my

early childhood—me as an infant and a toddler, happy and laughing and playing. Birthday parties and Christmases and summer celebrations. But as I flipped through these photos, I slowly realized that something seemed a little off; the images weren't entirely happy and carefree. As I aged, the pictures began to evoke a slightly ominous feeling. Guilt and secrecy and even a bit of fear were hiding behind my eyes.

Faced with the artifacts of my forgotten childhood here in this house, things my grieving mother must've put away in remembrance of the husband and daughter she believed to be dead, I was overwhelmed. No wonder she kept that third-floor door locked, I thought. Better to shut away those painful memories.

That's what I wanted to do then, too: get out of the dusty past and back down to the part of the house that lived in the present. I grabbed one box of old family photographs; I'd take them down to the sunroom and look there for the proof I was seeking. At the last second, I stashed Puppy Dog under my arm as well. I locked the hallway door behind me and made my way down the stairs, feeling a little lighter with every step.

I spent most of the the weekend going through those photographs. If it was proof I wanted, I certainly got it. I came upon a grainy shot of a young couple standing on the cliff, her long hair blowing in the breeze, his hat placed at a jaunty angle on his head: a handsome couple. But what struck me about the photo was the fact that I recognized Hannah and Simeon. *I knew their faces.* It hadn't been my imagination, then; I had actually seen them when Iris was weaving her tales. How? I had no idea.

I carefully picked up a small photo of a young boy and immediately knew it was Charles. He was lying in the barn with some animals around him, but I couldn't make out exactly what sort of animals they were. I squinted to get a closer look, and all of a sudden it was as though the photo itself enlarged and opened, pulling me into its black-and-white world. I watched as Charles gathered up his books. "Let's go!" he called to his menagerie, his sweet, cheerful voice filling my heart. I followed as he trotted out of the barn door, putting one foot in front of the other until I saw him again, this time sitting at a desk by the window in what looked to be a one-room schoolhouse. I noticed birds perched on the windowsills, dogs curled up outside the schoolhouse door, deer standing ready in the woods. *They're really guarding him. It's all true, then.*

The scene shifted and I saw children in the classroom teasing Charles—"The Pied Piper's animals are here again!"—and Charles, undaunted, running happily outside into the midst of his mismatched flock.

A flurry of animals—bats, raccoons, squirrels—swept into my vision and out again, and I saw the children, the ones who had been taunting Charles, running home, crying all the way, a squirrel chasing one, a bat diving into the hair of another.

I took it all in, mesmerized by the black-and-white images of my grandfather as a boy, a small Dr. Dolittle. I held my breath hoping the scene wouldn't fade, but soon enough it did, the barn dissolving and re-forming into a church, filled to the last pew with mourners. There was Hannah, dressed in black with a black veil over her face, sitting in the first pew, a dashing and grown-up Charles by her side, and I knew I was seeing the funeral of my great-grandfather Simeon.

In an instant, I was in this house, standing in the kitchen. There, I saw Hannah in her nightdress, her hair wild, her eyes searching, her lips mouthing words that found no sound. I stood at the window, watching her wandering outside in the rain, rubbing her hands together as though washing away blood.

Finally, I saw her stride purposefully toward the cliff: *No, Hannah!* I screamed it out, running toward her, but of course she couldn't hear me. I wasn't part of these scenes, I was only observing them. I could do nothing but watch as she stood on the edge of the cliff and simply leaned forward, falling in slow motion and hitting the ground below with a thud, a slumped and broken form, limbs splayed this way and that, lying in nearly the same spot where they had found her girls, years earlier.

I opened my eyes and found myself lying on the chaise in the sunroom. I sat up and shook my head, trying to make sense of what I had just seen. Photos were strewn about; the box I had been exploring was on its side on the floor. Had I fallen asleep? Had I dreamed everything?

Later, over dinner with Wil', I opened one of the albums. "My grandfather," I told him, showing him a photo of Charles with his animals.

He studied it, a slight smile on his face. "You know, I remember him quite well. Of course he was much older than this."

"He was still alive when we were kids?" This hadn't occurred to me.

Will nodded. "Everybody on the island trusted their horses to your grandfather, in addition to their household pets and livestock."

"Iris said he had a knack for relating to animals, even at a very young age. Apparently he didn't talk until he was five years old, and then one day he just started speaking in complete sentences." I left out the part about the cougar.

Will took my hand. "You're really enjoying hearing all of these stories about your family, aren't you?"

I nodded. He didn't know the half of it. "It means the world to me." I closed the album, then. I could languish in my ancestors' pasts with Iris, but with Will, I desired nothing but the here-and-now.

· 22

Monday morning, after breakfast, Iris appeared at the back door.

"Will Archer says he knew Charles," I announced.

Iris nodded. "Of course. Everyone on the island knew him. But Charles was an old man by that time. There's much more to tell about his life up until then."

With that tease of things to come, Iris set about her cleaning. I knew the story would have to wait until her work was done, around lunchtime, so I pulled on a jacket I found hanging by the back door and made my way outside and down the back stairs to the barn. I hadn't yet been inside it. The horses were still with Madlyn's neighbors; I had felt I had enough to deal with without learning the particulars of caring for horses, too. Now I pushed open the side door, and as it closed behind me I found myself nearly overcome by the sweet smell of hay. The barn was dark, but light was streaming in through the windows above the loft, illuminating the dust floating in the air this way and that. In the corner sat a woman's bicycle with a basket on the handlebars: a few years old, but not ancient. It must have been my mother's, I thought; the tires were still inflated. What a perfect way to get around the island! Deciding to take it for a spin, I wheeled it outside into the sunshine, hopped on the seat, and pedaled out to the main road.

I didn't feel like going down into town—the climb back up the hill to the house would be daunting on a bike—so I turned the opposite way and set off. The houses grew farther and farther apart until they ended altogether, and I found myself riding through the countryside. I love all seasons, but late fall is especially beautiful to me—the leaves have already said their spectacular goodbyes for the year, trees stand ready for the chill to come, everything else is browned and yellowed and dry. It is the time before the death of winter and the rebirth brought by spring.

Soon I rode into a forest of enormous cedar and red pine trees, towering high above my head. I spied an overgrown dirt path leading from the road deeply into the woods and remembered Iris's description—was this possibly the way to Summer Glen? I steered my bike onto the path and pedaled slowly through the sweet-smelling trees, sunshine stubbornly poking its way between their great limbs.

The path opened up into a grassy field ringed by enormous ancient trees and covered with unlikely wildflowers: lupines, daisies, poppies, and tangles of wild rose bushes. What were they doing in bloom here, at this time of year? I noticed overgrown low-lying foliage I couldn't identify, smelled the heady mixture of their perfumes as I set the bike's kickstand on the ground to explore the area on foot. I saw the crumbled remnants of an ancient fireplace, on what seemed to be the flat clearing for a house, and suspected I had indeed found Summer Glen.

This is fantastic, I thought, as I held my breath and walked gingerly through the glen, not wanting to make any noise to stir up the memories that surely resided there. I closed my eyes and tried to use my "gift," as Iris called it, and almost immediately I saw before me the images of wealthy society ladies sneaking their way here, cloaks covering their faces, each hoping Martine would work her magic for them. I thought of my great-grandmother, so desperate for a child that she'd turn to witchcraft to conceive one. My eyes grew wide as the thought hit me: None of us would have been born—not Charles, not my mother, *not me*—if not for the concoction Martine had given Hannah, right here on this spot.

I heard a voice, whispering in my ear: *Children conceived out of witchcraft are witches themselves, as are their children and their children's children.* I thought of Charles's otherworldly way with animals; was that his form of witchcraft? And what about these "visions" of mine?

Suddenly, I felt as though I wasn't alone. Something—no, a lot of somethings—swirled in the air around me, brushing at me, nudging me. It was as if I were in the middle of a tornado of spirits. I ran toward the bike, but the rosebushes grew up to block my path, reaching and grabbing at me with their gnarled branches. I pushed my way through the brambles, the skin on my arms and legs tearing on the thorns until I reached the bike, hopped on, and pedaled away as fast as I could. When I was safely inside the cedar forest, I braked to look at my arms and legs, which I assumed would be ripped raw and bleeding from the thorns. But I didn't find so much as a scratch.

I pedaled toward home, wondering what, if anything, had happened in that glen.

· 23

You've been to the glen," Iris stated, pulling a chicken-and-broccoli casserole out of the oven just as I burst through the back door.

I nodded, bending low to catch my breath. My leg muscles were throbbing and my throat was parched. I filled up a glass with cold water and drank it all in one gulp.

"You mustn't go back there, not yet." Iris had a stern look in her eyes.

"What is it about that place, anyway?" I asked, filling my water glass again and brushing the wet hair from my face. "I felt like . . ." My words trailed off. "I don't know what I felt like." I eyed the casserole, suddenly famished. After what I had just been through, I wanted only to immerse myself in the safety and familiarity of one of Iris's tales. I settled into my chair, took a bite of the steaming casserole, and listened as she cleared her throat and began to speak.

"After Hannah's death, life went on here in the house. We had a very companionable existence for the next few years.

Charles built a thriving business while I ran the household, supervising a staff of three. I'd have breakfast, lunch, and dinner on the table for Charles every day. He had grown into such a fine man.

"Of course, he never stopped mourning his beloved mother and father. I believe that's what drew him to Amelia, the woman who would become your grandmother. I thought she bore a striking resemblance to Hannah; they had the same fiery eyes.

"Amelia's parents—a wealthy Irish couple from Chicago by the name of Fister—had built a vacation home on the island several years earlier. Charles had a bit of contact with the Fister family over the years; he had seen Amelia once or twice and never thought much about her. But the year Hannah died, Amelia came to the island with her parents. Her father, no fool, hoped to interest the handsome, rich, and single veterinarian in his daughter, so he arranged a party where they could be introduced.

"When she came to the house a few days later carrying a sick cat, I tried to send her away. I knew why she was really here. But she was too smart for me. She took it upon herself to find Charles in the barn."

Iris's eyes became black and cloudy at the thought of Amelia, which made me wonder: Had she been in love with Charles all those years? Yes, she had been his nanny, but she was barely a decade older. It was plausible. So I said, "Iris, you haven't said much about yourself in your stories of this family. Did *you* ever marry?"

"Marry?" she spat. "My life was here, in this house, taking

care of the Hill family. There was neither time for nor thought of marriage for me."

"I'm sorry, I shouldn't have—"

"Never mind me. It wasn't long before Charles and Amelia were married. She was a thin, slight woman with short dark hair and deep blue eyes. She liked to wear trousers, something many women of the time didn't do, and she was quite athletic, enjoying golf and tennis and a walk with Charles and whatever animals happened to be on hand in the afternoons. When she came into this house as Charles's wife, I let her know right away that I was head of the household staff. I told her what was what and how the house was run. I was the one who had taken care of him all of these years, I was the one who was here when Simeon died and poor Hannah lost her mind. I was the one who had cooked his meals and washed his clothes."

I saw a fierce determination in Iris's eyes then, and the familiar darkening that shrouded her face when she was angry. She *had* loved him. It sent a chill through me. I did not envy Amelia, coming into this house and facing Iris.

"Of course, everything changed," Iris went on bitterly. "Our quiet, simple existence was obliterated. In the evenings, Charles used to enjoy reading in the study. I would bring him his tea and perhaps sit with him awhile, doing my needlepoint. All this ended when Amelia arrived. She was an overly talkative, grossly exuberant person. Charles became more outgoing than I had ever seen him, always laughing and smiling, especially when she was around. He was in love with her, anyone could see that."

I heard the resignation in Iris's voice.

"It was all a whirlwind of parties, dinners, travel, and people until the day she told him their lives were about to change yet again. I was busying myself making my mother's cabbage rolls for dinner. I remember it plain as day."

I could smell the simmering cabbage as she spoke, a curl of smoke rising from the heat of the stove.

" 'Oh, Iris,' she said to me, as she rushed into the kitchen, breathless. 'Do you know where my husband is?' She was bursting with news, her eyes sparkling in anticipation. Of course, I knew immediately what it was.

" 'You are with child,' I said to her matter-of-factly, stirring the rolls.

"She looked at me with wide eyes. 'Yes! I am! I've just come from the doctor. How did you know?'

"Ridiculous girl. Any fool could've seen it. 'Charles is in the barn,' I told her, and watched her run out the back door. I did not see her fall."

Iris stopped talking while a wicked smile crossed her face for just an instant, replaced quickly by a countenance of concern and caring.

"She fell?" I prodded. "Where, on the way to the barn? But it's just flat ground between here and there."

Iris shook her head as she continued her tale. "Somehow, she found her way to the cliffside."

"You mean to tell me she fell from the cliff? How did that happen?"

"I have no idea," Iris replied. "The last thing I heard, she was on her way to the barn to tell her husband she was with child."

"She died?" Why did Iris's stories, no matter how lovely and benign at the start, always seem to take a sinister turn?

"No," Iris explained. "Remember, child, Amelia was your grandmother, Madlyn's mother. She did not die at the bottom of the cliff that day. Charles found her. She was alive, but the baby had perished.

"After that, Charles treated his wife like a china doll, as you might expect. If I thought he doted on her before, it was nothing compared to the way he became. He expected me, along with the rest of the staff, to wait on her hand and foot. Which of course we did." Iris sniffed at this; I could see her resentment bubbling just under the surface.

"Within a few months, she was on the nest again, so to speak."

"That time, she carried the baby to full term, right? That was Madlyn?" But even as I said it, I knew I was wrong.

Iris shook her head. "All of Charles's attentiveness wasn't enough to stop her from tumbling down the stairs one night."

"You're kidding me. She fell again?"

"She did," Iris confirmed, adding slyly, "It was the middle of the night, and apparently she had been sleepwalking. She fell down the front staircase. Accident-prone, that one."

But I didn't think Amelia was accident-prone. It seemed to me that someone or something had pushed her. *The girls?* As if that wasn't dark enough, a darker thought crossed my mind. I saw an image of Iris creeping about at the top of the darkened stairway.

"Iris, you didn't—" I was too afraid to finish the thought.

She silenced me with a harsh look and continued her tale.

"Amelia did a great deal of crying during those years after losing two babies. It was Charles who gave her the strength to keep going, to keep trying. If he hadn't been so gentle and kind, your mother might never have been born."

Iris set her teacup on the table with an air of finality. "I will come again tomorrow," she said, after studying my face as though she was looking for something. "You were interested in hearing the stories of your great-grandparents and your grandparents, to be sure, but I can see that you are much more anxious to hear about your mother."

She gathered up her things, a tattered old purse and an umbrella, and was gone. It was an hour or so after she left that I realized. Iris had begun her tale where my vision in the sunroom had left off.

· 24

I hopped onto the bike and rode down into town. Once the spell Iris was weaving with her storytelling was broken, I felt like some real-world companionship. I coasted to a stop in front of Jonah's coffee shop.

"Hey." He smiled at me as I walked into the otherwise empty shop. "Glad you're here. I owe you a latte."

"Sounds wonderful," I said, climbing onto a counter stool, looking forward to a quiet chat with Jonah. I didn't get my wish, however, because at that moment, a group of islanders entered the shop, ordered cappuccinos, and announced it was time for their weekly book club. I recognized many faces from the group I had encountered in Jonah's shop my first day on the island. They were friendly to him, of course, but they gave me the same icy reception they had given me that first day: cold stares and whispered comments as they sat down and took out their copies of the latest book club selection.

I truly don't know what it was about that day; perhaps after living with three ghosts, I was unafraid of this lot. I walked over and faced them.

"Hi, ladies," I said, leaning down and putting my hands on their table. "In case there's one person left on this island unaware of who I am, I'm your friend and new neighbor, Halcyon Crane. And I'm just wondering: Are you ever planning to treat me like a neighbor, or are you always going to stop talking and stare and whisper when I come into a room?" Silence from the group, as I expected. I continued. "Because it's getting tiresome. I'm not sure how long I'm staying on this island, but it'll be a while. I suggest you get used to it and start acting like human beings."

With that I walked away from them, grinning from ear to ear.

"Nicely done." Jonah laughed as he handed me a latte. Then he added, under his breath, "Call me after closing time, Hallie. There's something more I've been wanting to tell you since the night we met for drinks, but I wasn't sure . . . Like I said, it's complicated."

I nodded and walked out of the shop with my coffee. After a few steps I ran into Will.

"Hi." He smiled at me and kissed my cheek. "I've just come from dropping some paperwork off at the police station. Care to take a look at what I picked up while I was there?"

He passed me a plastic bag. I peeked into it just long enough to see a folder with SUTTON, JULIE, 1979 written on the front.

"Will—" I started, but he silenced me with a kiss.

"I've gotta run right now, but I'll come by the house later and we'll look at this together." He winked at me and then headed off down the street, toward his office. I put the bag into the basket on my bike and started the long pedal up the hill to home.

I stared at that folder on my kitchen table for the rest of the afternoon, dreading what might be inside, but when Will arrived just before dinner, I knew it was time to face whatever it contained.

Before I opened it, Will shook his finger at me. "I just need to say this: Astonishingly enough, despite the fact that it's sitting right here on this table, I never saw this file. And neither did you."

"Understood," I said, as I took the folder from him. Now was the time. I took a long sip of wine and opened it up.

The first thing I saw was an article reporting my death. On a yellowing tear sheet from the local newspaper, I read the headline under a photo of my father and me.

NOAH CRANE AND DAUGHTER HALCYON PRESUMED DEAD IN KAYAK ACCIDENT

Island mathematics teacher Noah Crane, 37, and his daughter, Halcyon, 5, disappeared during a kayak excursion early Friday and are presumed dead.

Crane left his home on Hill Cliff early Friday with his daughter for a day of kayaking around the island. When they didn't return by late that afternoon, his wife, Madlyn Crane, who is also the girl's mother, became alarmed and alerted local authorities.

Police quickly organized a search party of some three

dozen islanders, all of whom used their own vessels—speedboats, kayaks, canoes—to scour the island shoreline in an attempt to find the missing boaters. The Grand Manitou Ferry Line also participated in the search.

Sheriff Chip Norton reported that islander Mira Finch spotted an overturned kayak near the Ring, a rock formation on the north side of the island that has long been a popular destination for kayakers and boaters. There was no sign of Crane or his daughter.

After searching the island's coastline with no success, rescuers enlisted the aid of the Coast Guard and other vessels to patrol the waters between the island and the mainland. However, as day wore into night, hopes dimmed of finding the boaters alive.

"We believe father and daughter may have been carried into the shipping lanes by the current, which is pretty strong on the north side of the island," Norton stated. "We hoped we'd find them alive, but, after all this time in the water, if those folks haven't drowned by now they've certainly succumbed to hypothermia. As a result, we've changed our focus from rescue to recovery."

"Well, this sort of takes your breath away," I said, after a moment of stunned silence. It's not that I didn't know this information; I knew full well that my father had faked our deaths. But reading it in the newspaper, there in black and white, made it real and tangible in a way it hadn't been before.

"Did Mira ever mention to you that she was the one who found the kayak?" Will asked.

"No, she didn't say anything at all about that day. Not a thing. I wonder why."

Will looked at me and shrugged. "That's a good question."

"It must've been pretty emotional for her, finding that kayak."

"Still, don't you think the moment she discovered who you were she might have said something?" Will went on. "*I was part of the search party that looked for you. I was the one who found your kayak*—or words to that effect."

"You'd think so, wouldn't you?" But I didn't know what to think. Not really.

"The lawyer in me smells more to the story here," he said, then backpedaled a bit. "Of course, the lawyer in me thinks there's more to every story. It could be she just didn't want to dredge up the past."

I put the article aside and looked at the one beneath it. It was a longer story about my dad, Julie's murder, and our deaths, and how the three might be connected.

"I'm not sure I want to read this," I told Will.

"You said you wanted to know everything," he said gently. "This is part of it, unfortunately. Remember, Hallie, it's all in the past. Nothing here can hurt you now."

He was right, of course. So I took a deep breath and began reading.

QUESTIONS SURROUND THE DEATH OF NOAH CRANE, DAUGHTER

The memorial service for Noah and Halcyon Crane took place last week, but questions remain about the exact nature of their deaths. Police have reason to believe the father and daughter died as a result of a murder-suicide.

At the time of his death, Noah Crane was under investigation for the island's only murder in more than 50 years. Julie Sutton, 6, the daughter of island residents Frank and June Sutton, was found dead on the Crane property in July. Police initially believed it was an accident, but soon the evidence began pointing toward foul play.

The girl had apparently fallen from a third-floor window of the Crane home. Noah Crane, upon discovering the body, called the police. When they arrived, their investigation turned up several clues. The room from which the girl fell was in a state of general disarray, lamps broken, furniture knocked over, dishes cracked, indicating a struggle had occurred. The girl's dress had been torn, presumably in the struggle, and there were marks on her neck consistent with strangulation.

"As we began piecing together the evidence of what happened that night, it started to look as though Mr. Crane was involved in this poor girl's death," said Sheriff Chip Norton, who headed up the investigation. Norton explained that Crane's footprints were found around the girl's body and his fingerprints were identified on the windowsill of the room where she fell. Strands of hair believed to be his were found in the girl's closed fist, indicating that she fought with him before she died.

Crane maintained his innocence. The police were not able to bring the investigation of Julie Sutton's murder to a conclusion before Crane's death.

Crane's wife, Madlyn, was off the island on business at the time of the incident. The only other witness to the event was Halcyon Crane, five years old. She never spoke another word

> after that night. Her parents had taken her to psychiatrists on the mainland, but none could determine how or why the girl stopped speaking.
>
> According to the American Psychiatric Association, it is not uncommon for children who have witnessed a crime or have been the victims of physical or emotional abuse to be struck mute as a result of the severe trauma involved.

I looked at Will, incredulous. I had had no idea.

"I know." He took my hand. "It startled me when I read it, too."

"I stopped speaking? Do you remember that?"

"I was thinking back, Hallie, and I don't remember ever seeing you again after the death of that child. I'm not sure about it, but I'll bet my parents never let me come back to your house. I can ask them." He refilled our wineglasses.

I was beginning to think things were starting to make a kind of perverted sense. "That would explain why I don't remember anything of my life here," I mused. "Witnessing the death of a friend is certainly a severe trauma."

"It makes me wonder what you saw that night."

"I wonder, too," I said, and went back to reading the article.

> The final blow to the investigation came with the deaths of Noah and Halcyon Crane. "He was our only suspect in this murder, and we were in the process of building our case against him," Norton confirmed. "His death, and the death of the only witness to the crime, puts an end to that."
>
> Although they acknowledge it's pure speculation, police

> believe that Noah Crane killed himself and his daughter to escape the consequences of his actions.
>
> Madlyn Crane declined to be interviewed for this article, but through her lawyer she issued a strong statement in defense of her husband. "The idea that Noah Crane murdered that child—and his own daughter—is a macabre, disgusting fabrication put forth by an incompetent police force in order to create a murder out of what was clearly an accident in both cases. To accuse my husband of this is a desecration of his memory, and I will not tolerate it."

I laid the article back on the pile and wiped the tears from my eyes. "You gotta love my mother for saying that. I wonder how the islanders treated her."

Will stood up and wrapped his arms around me from behind. "Like I said, I don't remember a whole lot about those days, but my parents tell me people looked at Madlyn as another victim. They didn't blame her, not really."

"What about Frank and June Sutton?" I asked him. "I wonder how she made peace with them. They lived here on this same small island for thirty years with Julie's death hanging between them."

"They had both lost daughters, remember," Will said quietly.

Of course they had.

I began sifting through the police file, which was woefully incomplete. A sketchy incident report described the scene of the crime. My father had made the call to police. I was a witness. My mother had been out of town. Nothing I didn't know there.

The report also included notes of an interview with Frank and June Sutton. June had dropped Julie off at our house that morning to spend the day playing with me. My father was supposed to take her home after dinner. Other than the part about me not speaking again, it was all pretty benign stuff, nothing I didn't know or suspect.

Then I came to a photograph of the crime scene, and everything changed. It was the third-floor nursery, the one in which I had found the boxes of pictures the day before, and the police report was correct. The room was in disarray: lamps knocked over, comforters pulled from the beds, books lying everywhere. Obviously, there had been a fight.

I began to feel something at the moment I saw the photograph: a hand, tightening around my throat. I started coughing, first softly, then violently. Someone was choking me, constricting my airway. I stood up, knocking over my chair as I did so, and stared at Will, wide-eyed.

"Hallie." He stood up and took me by the shoulders. "What's the matter? What's going on?"

I couldn't breathe. I felt a tremendous pressure on my chest, as though I were an undersea diver whose air tank had sprung a leak. I was gasping for air but unable to fill my lungs. I was going to die, right there in my mother's kitchen.

And then, nothing. Everything stopped.

"My God, Hallie," Will said, frantic. "Should I call a doctor?"

I shook my head and sat down. "I felt like my throat was closing up," I croaked. "It was like somebody was strangling me. I couldn't breathe. I literally could not get any air."

Will crossed the kitchen and poured a glass of water for

me. "Here," he said, thrusting it in my direction. "How do you feel now?"

I drank the water in one gulp. "I'm okay. I think."

"You know," Will said, slowly, "you were looking at the photo of the crime scene when your throat closed up."

I nodded.

"Whatever happened there that night, you saw it all, and it traumatized you to the point where you couldn't speak. And now you felt as though your throat was closing. Seeing this photo might have brought some of that back to you. I think we had better just close this file for now."

"No." I shook my head. "Whatever's in here, I have to see it all."

That decision may have been a mistake, because I came upon a photo of the dead girl, taken as her body lay in a heap on the ground beneath that all-important third-floor window. I recognized her.

It was a girl in a white dress. She had long braids, one still tied with a white ribbon.

As I dropped the photo and it fluttered to the floor, I put my hands over my face and turned toward the wall, my mouth open but making no sound. I don't know if I would have simply stayed in that suspended state of reality had Will not been there with me, but he wrapped his arms around me again and held me tight. Somewhere far away, I heard him saying my name.

"Hallie, what is it? What's going on?"

But I could barely say the words. I had been trying so hard to shield Will from all of Iris's fantastic stories, her tall tales, the ghosts. But at that moment I didn't care any longer. "It's her." I said it over and over.

"You recognize Julie. You were a witness to her death. Are you remembering her?"

I shook my head. "No, Will, that's not Julie. That's the girl I saw outside my window the other night. That's the girl I saw at the inn. I'm certain of it, right down to the white hair ribbons."

Will bent down, picked up the photo, and studied it. "What ribbon?"

"Tied to one braid," I said.

He shook his head, holding out the picture. "Hallie, there's no ribbon here. And no braids."

I took it out of his hand, confused. I was looking at the image of a small, vaguely familiar girl—Julie Sutton—who lay on the ground, arms and legs splayed every which way. Her hair was curly and shoulder-length. She was wearing Levi's and a T-shirt. Her eyes were open. Blood was pooling near the back of her head. No white dress. No white ribbon.

I slumped to the floor, holding the photo close to my chest, and began to shake.

25

Will took me upstairs, ran a hot bath, and sat with me as I soaked in the water. I was a mess; there's no other way to describe it. I couldn't stop crying. Seeing that photograph—both of them, really, the shot of the crime scene and the one of the dead girl—had clicked on a switch inside me that had been in the off position for thirty years.

My shoulders shook as I tried to pull myself together. "I don't know what's the matter with me," I blubbered between sobs.

"Shhhh," Will said, rubbing my back. "Don't worry about it. You've had a series of shocks."

I sniffed. "I'm so sorry about this."

"You had an unspeakable trauma when you were a child, so bad you couldn't remember anything about it. And now you're seeing it again. Anyone would be shaken by that."

His voice was soothing and I began to breathe a little easier. He went on.

"Of course you've been seeing that poor little girl's face all over this island ever since you got here. Your memories of that night are coming back on their own."

My mind began to review everything that had happened to me since coming to the island. Could repressed memories really be the explanation for it all?

"You're back here in this house where the trauma occurred. A girl—*your friend*—was killed, on purpose or by accident, and you saw it. It was so horrible, you stopped speaking for a while and blocked it out of your mind. And now here you are, confronted with all this stuff again. I don't think there's any doubt that the girl you've been seeing and the girl who was killed are one and the same."

I must've looked confused, so he continued.

"It's your mind, Hallie. You're remembering bits of what happened, piecing it all together. You're remembering *her*."

"No, Will. The girl I've been seeing isn't Julie Sutton. The girl I initially saw in the photograph . . ." My words trailed off. How could I explain seeing another girl's face in that photo?

He shook his head. "Doesn't it make sense that something psychological is going on here? Flashes of memory coming to the surface as a result of being back, for the first time, at the scene of a crime?"

It did make sense, in a confusing, muddled sort of way. I wasn't sure about any of it. "So what do I do now?" I asked him.

He considered for a while. "You don't have to do anything, not right away. But if it were me, I'd be thinking about seeing someone for a few rounds of regression therapy."

"You mean like hypnosis?"

He nodded. "A psychiatrist can take you back to that night. Uncover what really happened. It might give you a sense of closure. Hey, you might even begin to remember your childhood here on the island and get some bona fide memories of your mother out of the deal."

That sounded good to me.

"We'll have to find a psychiatrist on the mainland who does that sort of thing," Will mused. "Jim Allen—the doctor here on the island—can probably recommend someone."

It was settled, then. Everything that had happened to me since I came to Great Manitou was the result of repressed trauma. I wasn't seeing or hearing ghosts. I didn't have a haunted house. It was just my mind that was haunted, by the spirit of a girl I had seen fall to her death. I put the incongruity of my first and second impressions of the girl in that photograph out of my mind. It didn't matter. A wave of calm came over me, and I sank low into the water, enjoying it.

The feeling did not last long.

After I climbed out of my bath, I went to bed, quickly falling asleep in Will's arms. I awoke with a start to discover myself alone. Groggily, I eyed the clock, its fuzzy symbols slowly jelling into numbers as I squinted. Nearly 2:30. Where was Will? The bathroom, surely. I waited for a few minutes, nearly drifting back into a light sleep. "Will?" I called out softly. No response. I sat up and looked around the room, but he wasn't anywhere in the suite. That's when I noticed the open door.

I crept out into the darkened hallway. "Will?" Again, no response.

Moonlight was streaming onto the wood floor from the windows at the end of the hall, creating a river of light that seemed to vibrate with a life of its own. And then there she was: a little girl, standing in the corner next to the windows. The white dress. The braid tied at the end with a ribbon. And then she dissipated, as though she were nothing more than fog burning off in the midday sun.

Just at that moment, I heard a sickening crash and knew immediately what had happened. I ran down the hallway toward the front stair, screaming Will's name, and saw him lying in a heap at the bottom. I flew down to his side.

"Oh my God, oh my God," I was muttering. "Please be all right, please don't be dead."

Will groaned and clutched his head.

"Thank God!" I said, intensely relieved that he was alive, breathing and groaning. "Are you all right?" I helped him to his feet.

"I'm not sure," he said, groggy. "That was some fall. I hit my head pretty hard."

I helped him into the kitchen, turning on every light as we went, sat him down at the table, and poured him a glass of water. Then I started opening cabinets; I knew I had seen pain reliever around somewhere.

"Take these," I told him, handing him some Motrin. "Should we call the doctor?" I wasn't sure what to do. I was afraid he had had a concussion, but I didn't know the signs or symptoms.

He shook his head. "I didn't pass out or anything. I don't think we need to wake Jim in the middle of the night for this."

"What happened? Why did you get out of bed?"

"I thought I heard something," he told me. "It was the weirdest thing. Something woke me up, I'm not sure what it was. You were fast asleep. Snoring, I might add." He grinned at me. "As I was closing my eyes again, I heard—I know this sounds crazy, but I thought I heard my name."

"Your name," I repeated.

"So I got up," Will continued. "When I got into the hallway I realized nobody was there, but I was still hearing voices. Talking. Chattering."

"What kind of voices?" I asked him, but I already knew the answer.

"Children's voices," he admitted. "I must have been dreaming somehow, still in a sleep state—you know, sleepwalking. My mind was full of that story about the dead girls you told me the other night, and maybe I was dreaming the whole thing. I don't know. But whether I was awake or asleep, I followed the voices to the edge of the stairs and stood there with my hands on the railing, listening. The voices seemed to be coming from the living room."

I did not want to hear the rest of this story. I knew where it was going, and I didn't want it to go there. But it did.

"I started down the stairs," he said. "And Hallie, I know this is going to sound absurd but I swear to you that I was pushed. I don't know if I was dreaming or sleepwalking, but I definitely felt hands on my back."

"Somebody pushed you?"

Will shook his head in amazement. "I think so."

I had fallen asleep believing that the Hill House ghosts were nothing but memories surfacing in my own head, and frankly I liked that notion. But now, Iris's stories were swirling around in my brain, her assertion that the girls had driven her cousin off a cliff, poor Amelia's sudden falls, and now

Will tumbling down the stairs. These certainly weren't products of my imagination.

"I think we should get out of here right now," I said. "Let's go to your place."

Will shook his head. "My place is all the way on the other side of the island. Besides, it's almost morning. Let's just make some coffee and watch the sun come up."

There, with the lights of the kitchen illuminating the darkness, in a house built on secrets and filled with ghosts and murder, I realized that the lines between Iris's stories and my reality were blurring. Were Will and I somehow caught up in my family's grim and bloody fairy tale?

· 26

I asked Will not to go into the office the next day, but he insisted.

"I thought you didn't have anything to do in the off-season." I was terrified that he would collapse alone in the office from the aftereffects of a concussion.

"I don't have *much* to do." He smiled, pulling on jeans and a sweater.

"Then why go in? We could spend the day reading or taking a walk around the grounds."

"I've got a conference call to make—"

"Which you could do here." I wasn't letting this go.

"Yes, I could. And I would, if my files and my computer weren't down at the office. Besides, I have to go into town anyway to get feed for Belle. I won't stay long. I promise."

"Do you want me to come with you?" I yawned.

He smiled and wrapped his arms around me. "Stay here and take a nap. I'll come back after lunch. How's that?"

I relented. "Okay."

"Any thoughts on dinner?" he wondered. I shook my head. "How about if I make us a stir-fry?"

"A great lover who also cooks." I managed a tired smile. "You're too good to be true."

I walked with him down the stairs, saw him out the back door, the cold air snatching away any sleep I might have fallen back into that morning, and watched as he and Belle set off toward town. I pulled on a jacket and sat on the sunporch with a cup of strong coffee, staring out at the angry water and thinking about everything and nothing at all.

"Morning, miss." It was Iris, walking in from the kitchen.

I wanted to ask her whether she thought Will's and Amelia's falls might be connected somehow. I had intended to bring it up right away, but for some reason I can't explain, I didn't. She started in on another of her tales and I found myself fully drawn into the past, the present goings-on receding into the background like one of my wispy visions.

"Madlyn Hill was born on a spring day when the lilacs came into full bloom here on the island. She came into this world feet first and both mother and daughter nearly died during the ordeal, but Amelia finally delivered the girls with Charles—"

I interrupted. "You said *girls,* Iris. Plural."

Iris nodded. "Twins. Maddie was born first, healthy and pink and crying. Only then did the doctor realize he had more work to do, and shortly thereafter he delivered a second girl, Sadie.

"I was tending to Maddie when Sadie was born. Amelia was exhausted and near-delirious from the difficult delivery, but when the nurse rushed into the study to tell Charles that another baby was coming, he was over the moon with excitement. His joy, however, was short-lived. It lasted just long enough for him actually to see the baby."

Iris closed her eyes for a moment, as if to shut out an image too painful to recall, before she continued. "I'll never forget the sight of Sadie, so tiny and blue and delicate, like a newly hatched baby bird. She lived for only a few minutes, her mouth opening and closing like a fish out of water. I could see she did not belong in this world.

"As the doctor explained it, while the twins were in the womb, Madlyn was taking in most of the nutrients. She grew bigger and stronger as her twin withered and starved. A horrible thought, really. It was as though Madlyn ingested her sister's very life. I wish Amelia had not heard the doctor's explanation of how the twins had developed. I wish she had been told only of the death. It might have made things easier, later."

I shuddered at this, closing my eyes to the vision I knew was beginning to form.

"We buried Sadie the next day in the family plot, next to Hannah and Simeon. There was a short service, a few prayers read. Amelia was too weak to attend. And though Charles grieved for his lost daughter, in time he embraced life again. Amelia was a different matter. She was forever haunted by the thought of Sadie's death. Somewhere deep inside, in her darkest, most twisted thoughts, Amelia believed Maddie had killed her sister."

"Killed her? On purpose? That's crazy, Iris."

"You're absolutely right. After the birth, Amelia did sink into a sort of madness."

"Postpartum depression?"

"Worse. Amelia didn't get out of bed for days and days, not to wash, not to eat. She didn't want to see the baby, hold her, or even feed her. She spent most days tossing and turning in her bed and most nights wandering the hallways of the house in her white nightdress, her hair wild and uncombed. Poor Charles would find her in the nursery in the middle of the night, hovering over Maddie's crib, staring, muttering incomprehensible things. One night he caught her carrying the baby down the hall toward the stairs.

"With memories of his mother's madness fresh in his mind, Charles was terrified that he'd have to institutionalize his young wife. So he didn't call the doctor or tell anyone about Amelia's odd behavior. I believed this was a mistake. Amelia was intent on hurting the child, anyone could see that. Charles certainly did. But he decided to handle the situation himself, so what could I say?

"I did what I could, taking it upon myself to protect little Maddie from her mother, stationing myself in a hard-backed chair in the nursery as soon as the sun went down and not leaving again until it rose in the morning. Night after night, Amelia would appear in Maddie's room, wild-eyed, her face white as bone, and I'd order her back to bed. Most of the time, thank goodness, she obeyed me. But some nights I'd have to shove her out of the room."

"Did my grandmother end up in an institution?" I wanted to know.

Iris shook her head. "It took many months, but Amelia came back to herself. It happened suddenly, and nobody was ever sure how or why. One morning she simply got out of bed, bathed, and came downstairs to the kitchen as though she had awakened from a coma or a long sickness. Whatever cloud had descended upon her had dissipated, and Amelia walked out of her room smiling, wanting to know where her husband and daughter were, as though none of the madness had ever happened.

"Charles was overjoyed. He stood there, holding his wife and crying openly, so relieved was he to see her back to herself. I credit much of her recovery to his gentle ways and loving nature. He was so patient with her during those long months.

"But Amelia was never the same as she was before the birth of her children, not quite. As Charles was holding her that day, I noticed a strange new look on her face and in her eyes. I don't want to say it was sinister, exactly, but there was something of an undercurrent to her from that day on. The way she continued to look at her daughter unsettled me quite a bit.

"In no time whatsoever, baby Maddie was crawling, then toddling, then walking and, unlike her father, talking a blue streak from a very early age. However, in a strange development that alarmed her parents and me, little Maddie directed most of her conversation toward one person: her sister.

"Her father brought a toy telephone home for her one afternoon, and Maddie would use it to call her sister. 'Sadie! Time for dinner! Come to the table!' This frightened Charles and Amelia, because of course they had not told young Maddie she had had a twin sister, much less the sister's name. Yet somehow she knew.

'Who are you talking to, dear?' Charles would ask. Maddie would simply answer, 'Sister.'

"There were many whispered and frantic conversations about this odd behavior behind closed doors, but finally Charles came to the decision that they would simply have to live with it. Maddie and Sadie had been twins together in the womb, and somehow Maddie retained the memory. He was sure stranger things had happened at other times to other families. I thought, *Yes, and in this very house*, but of course I did not say it aloud."

I shuddered as I saw my young mother holding conversations with her dead sister.

"Neither Charles nor Amelia ever knew what was really going on with their daughter." Iris smiled, her eyes shining. "But I knew. In the womb, as poor Sadie grew weaker and weaker and Maddie grew ever stronger, the two girls made a pact. Sadie would not live a day in the outside world, so Maddie would live for both of them. And right there in the calm waters of the womb, the girls joined hands and Maddie called Sadie's soul to her."

Iris paused for effect, looking at me expectantly.

I scowled. "What do you mean, she called Sadie's soul?"

"It was a gift she would possess her entire life."

"What do you *mean*, Iris?" I repeated.

"Your mother was called *soul capturer* in her work. It's how she was known professionally."

"I had heard that, yes. But I assumed it was because she had a way of capturing a person's true spirit in her photographs."

"That's exactly what it was." Iris nodded. "The photography came later, of course. But when Madlyn was just a child, she began to collect bits and pieces of people's souls, their spirits, wherever she went. They always stayed with her, hovering around her, until she learned to put them in her photographs, the way other children collect butterflies or frogs."

"I still don't quite get what you're saying."

"It was her special ability, her *gift,*" Iris stressed. "Have you not looked at one of her photographs and known exactly what the person was thinking or feeling?"

I nodded, thinking back to the first time I had found my mother's website. I could clearly see—and sometimes even hear—her subjects' thoughts.

"But I'm getting ahead of my story with all of this talk about Madlyn's photographs. I'll tell you about them, to be sure, but you have more to hear first." Iris looked at her slim watch. "But that's enough for today, miss. I'll come back and continue the story tomorrow."

She stood up and prepared to leave. As I shook the visions out of my head, I remembered I had intended to talk with Iris about Will's fall the previous night.

"Iris, I woke up last night to find Will crumpled at the bottom of the front staircase," I began. "He thought he had heard voices, children's voices, and I know this might sound silly but he felt as though someone had pushed him. With you telling me about Amelia's falls the day before . . ."

Iris stared deeply into my eyes. It made me more than a little uncomfortable. "You're wondering if something or someone in the house caused those falls."

"Well, yes."

"What do you think?"

"I think it's a very strange coincidence that certainly could have a reasonable explanation," I said weakly. It's not what I thought at all.

Iris nodded, smiling. "That's what they all say at the beginning."

I needed answers, not evasions. "Listen, Iris, if you think Will is in any kind of danger—or if I'm in danger—from someone or something in this house, I want to know it right now. Are we safe here?"

"Miss Hallie, you're asking questions for which I have no answers," she said sadly. "I am only this family's storyteller. That is my role. I cannot tell the future. I don't know what will be. None of us does."

I wouldn't let it go. "But, judging from what you've told me about things that have happened in the past—Charles needing protection, Amelia's falls, even your poor cousin—isn't the same thing happening now?"

Iris's smile sent a chill through me. "The girls have never liked strangers," she said, and she turned and went into the kitchen.

Suddenly, I felt the cold. It must've been no more than 40 degrees on that porch, and I had been sitting out there in just a jacket listening to Iris. I found myself wishing for a big pot of the stew she made so often, and oddly enough, when I went back into the house, I found just that. She must've brought it with her when she arrived that morning and left it simmering on the stove when she came to join me. As I ate a few spoonfuls of stew right out of the pot, I wished Will were already home.

An hour later, during which time I had done nothing but stare out of the back window watching for him, the ringing of the phone jarred me out of my trance.

"I know, I know," Will said. "I should be back by now, but I've been caught up in something that's going to take a while."

"How are you feeling? How's your head?"

"I'm fine. Just a headache and a dull one at that."

We hung up after he promised to come for an early dinner. I looked around the kitchen, not knowing quite what to do. I called Mira at the Manitou Inn; I wanted to find out about her being the one to discover my dad's overturned kayak the day we disappeared and thought perhaps we could get together and talk about it. No such luck. Her machine said she had gone to the mainland for a few days.

I rattled around the house for a while, wandering from kitchen to dining room to sunroom, but nothing felt quite right. I began to think about Will, and how he believed Iris's stories sounded too fantastic to be true. She had to be embellishing or outright inventing past events, he said. But now, after his fall, I needed to know the truth. Was I imagining things or was there a ghost on this property that was inclined to push people down staircases . . . ?

It hit me, then. Down staircases and *out of windows.*

· 27

I called the dogs and ran out the back door and into the wind, grabbing a thick cardigan that was hanging over a chair in the kitchen as I went past. I needed to get out of that house. My thoughts were swimming and I wanted to clear my head. I wrapped the sweater around me and made my way down the drive and onto the road, Tundra and Tika following close behind, dirt crunching under my shoes with each step.

Walking through the leafless, stark landscape, I knew only one thing for certain: I was faced with one of two highly undesirable prospects: uncovering some pretty ugly childhood memories in order to get to the bottom of these visions, or exorcising a trio of dead children from my house.

How had I found myself here, exactly? What would I be doing right now if I hadn't received the letters from Will? Maybe I'd be sitting in my living room in Washington drinking tea and listening to the seals bark in Puget Sound. Maybe I'd be wandering through my favorite bookstore.

I walked on, my feet heading in an unknown direction. I was going somewhere, even as it began to mist, the spray wetting my face.

The sight of the island cemetery surprised me. *Of course.* I wanted some proof that what Iris was telling me was real, and it doesn't get more real than gravestones with names and dates on them.

The black wrought-iron gate was rusted and weathered in spots, decaying with age. I swung it open and stepped inside, but the dogs stayed where they were, yowling in warning. I began to wander around, floating from one grave to the next, touching each headstone in reverence.

And then I found what I had been seeking. The sight of it brought me up short: a marble tombstone with the words MADLYN HILL CRANE, *1938–2009. Devoted daughter, wife, and mother.*

I sat down on my mother's grave, wondering why I hadn't visited it before. "Hi, Mom," I said out loud.

And then I leaned my head against her stone and cried, my tears mixing with the icy rain that began to fall. I don't know how long I sat there—minutes, an hour maybe. But at some point the dogs' barking pulled me back into the moment, and I knew I couldn't sit on that sodden ground anymore.

That's when I saw my own marker. HALCYON HILL CRANE, *1973–1979. Beloved child.*

It takes your breath away, seeing your own tombstone. It hadn't occurred to me before this moment, but of course I had one. Everyone thought I was dead. There had been a memorial service.

Next to my stone, my father's: NOAH THOMAS CRANE, *1940–1979. Devoted husband and father.* So that's where he came up with *Thomas.* I wondered where he got *James.*

I was standing on the Hill family plot, obviously, so I looked around at the neighboring gravestones and found them all. Hannah and Simeon. Sadie. Charles—who had died only a few years earlier—and Amelia. And then I saw the names of the three girls, Patience, Persephone, and Penelope. Their stone stark white, crumbling and ancient, almost a century old.

I sat down there, among my ancestors, feeling strangely at home. Thanks to Iris, I knew these people now. I had seen them all through her rich storytelling: Hannah, young and beautiful, when her children were born. Charles, toddling around as a baby, communing silently with animals, now lying only a few miles from where he grew up, having lived more than ninety years. My mother, whispering to her dead twin.

All the Hills had lived on the island; this was where they were born, grew up, and died. And now here I was among them. I felt, for the first time in my life, that I was part of a large family. Yes, they were all dead, but they were my people, my history, my roots. Even seeing my own gravestone there—I don't know, it felt as though ultimately I knew where I would rest. I was home.

I stood up and looked around once more, knowing I'd return to tend these graves often. I might have stayed longer, but I knew it would be an unpleasant walk home in the cold rain.

When I finally walked through my back door, I found Will in the kitchen, phone in his hand. He looked at me, stunned, and then said into the receiver: "Thanks, Jonah, but she just walked in. Sorry to have bothered you." And then, to me: "Where in the *hell* have you been?"

My smile faltered. Except for Richard, when had a man been worried about me? I pushed my dripping hair out of my face and said, "I went for a walk."

This was met with open-mouthed silence from Will. Finally, gesturing toward the window, he said, "In *this*?"

The dogs had followed me inside the warm kitchen and were shaking their fur dry as I took off the sodden sweater I was wearing; nothing smells quite like wet wool or wet dog. "Not the smartest decision I've ever made, although it wasn't raining when I left. I got caught in it a few miles from the house."

"I called everyone I could think of." He was still standing with the phone in his hand. "Jonah, Henry, Mira, the grocery store. I even called the wine bar, wondering if you had ended up there. I couldn't imagine where you had gone." Then his arms were around me and I could feel his heart beating fast, like a bird's. "I was so worried about you," he murmured into my wet hair.

Suddenly I was freezing. Something about coming into the warm kitchen made me acutely aware of how awfully cold I had been.

"You're shivering," he said to me, pulling back from our embrace. "My God, your lips are blue. They're actually blue."

He looked at me for a moment, and I could tell he was running through various scenarios of what to do. First he poured a brandy and handed it to me. It tasted hot and spicy on the way down, warming me from the inside. "Right," he said then, leading me out of the kitchen. "Let's get you upstairs and into the tub."

As he drew a bath, I peeled off my sodden clothes. They smelled of peat and rain and centuries-old dirt. Maybe I'd just throw them away. I left them in a heap on the bathroom floor, climbed into the steaming water, and submerged. I felt safe and protected there, with the sound of the water rushing in my ears.

It wasn't until later, when Will and I were back in the kitchen eating dinner, that he asked me where I had gone. "I know you're a grown woman, but I was really worried when I got here and found you weren't home," he admitted. "After last night, I half expected to find you in a heap at the bottom of the stairs."

"Or lying under the third-floor window."

He looked at me. "Well. That's an interesting thing to say."

I twirled some noodles around my fork and considered how to continue the line of discussion I had just started. I hadn't even worked it out in my own head.

Will jumped into the silence. "Are you saying you think that Julie Sutton's death thirty years ago is connected to what happened to me last night?"

"I'm not sure what I think—about anything."

"Anything?" He poked me with his fork.

I poked him back. "Okay, you I'm sure of." I smiled. "Everything else is up in the air. But the thing is, whether they're fabrications or embellishments or outright lies, Iris told me her cousin was pushed or somehow driven off the cliff—she died, by the way. And my grandmother, Amelia, had several suspicious falls when she was pregnant. She lost two babies, Will!"

The ideas were jelling, becoming more real as I spoke them.

"Then, thirty years ago, we have the death of a child here in the house from being pushed or thrown out of a window. And now, you are pushed—or simply fall—down the stairs. Either we've got an epidemic of clumsiness around here or something else is going on."

"What's the something else?" he wanted to know.

Even as I said this I felt like an idiot, but it had to be said. "A ghost who likes to push people to their deaths."

We ate in silence for a few minutes, digesting, no doubt, the ridiculousness of the conversation we had been having. Then Will said, "Listen. You know how I feel about all this ghost business, but what would be the harm in calling a priest to come here?"

"No harm at all," I said. "A blessing on my new house. Let's do it tomorrow."

More silence.

"I was thinking of going at this another way," I started. "Maybe we should get a medium."

Will raised his eyebrows, as he took a bite off his fork.

"Seriously, Will, this is what these people do for a living—contacting the dead. Maybe we could find out if there's a ghost here and, if so, who it is."

He shook his head. "I don't know."

"What's the difference between a priest exorcizing the house and a medium doing it?"

Will considered this. "Aside from the authority behind the priest, not much, I guess. I'm still not sure this all doesn't have some sort of reasonable explanation. But whatever you want to do, I'll support you."

I squeezed his hand. "I want to get this ball rolling soon. Like tomorrow."

He nodded. "Whatever you want."

I stood up and began to nose around the kitchen. "Do mediums advertise in the phone book? Do I even *have* a phone book for the mainland?"

"Don't need one," he said, smiling. "I know a medium. And so do you."

"If you tell me it's you, I'll hit you very hard."

Will laughed. "No, you dope. Not me. It's Mira."

I stared at him, wondering if he was telling the truth. "You've got to be kidding."

He shook his head. "As I live and breathe. I don't know if she's on the level or not, but Mira bills herself as a—what does she call it?—a *sensitive*." As he said the word, he elongated the syllables and raised his eyebrows in mock fear. I laughed.

"It's true. She has a little cottage business in tourist season doing tarot card readings and giving walking tours of haunted spots on the island. It's quite popular, actually. People tend to get a sort of haunted-house vibe when they come to the island. Mira plays into that."

"But does she really have any ability at all—beyond the nose for a good business opportunity, I mean?"

"That's what I don't know," he said. "I've always thought she was sort of loopy. But at least she'd be a good place to start, if you want to go down that road."

We cleaned up the kitchen and headed upstairs. For now, we had other important things to attend to.

bellished accounts with threads of truth running through them."

A smile crept across Iris's face. "It's the boyfriend doing the wondering, I expect."

"Well . . ." Where was I to go from there?

She nodded and closed her eyes and sat for a bit. "Do you not see them as I tell their stories?" she said, finally.

"I do. I do see them." She had a point. I hadn't told this to Will for fear of how strange it would sound.

"Then you know what I'm saying is true. You're seeing it as it happened." She looked at me deeply. Trying to discern what I believed?

"Okay—well, good, then," I said, awkwardly. "I just wanted to know." What I really wanted was for her to stop staring at me and get on with today's tale.

"I was beginning to tell you of Madlyn's gift," she began, "her ability to capture bits and pieces of the souls of others through her photography. Have you heard that many ancient cultures—and some not so ancient ones—were convinced of the power of mirrors?"

I nodded slowly. "I think so. It sounds familiar."

"Many cultures have believed that mirrors hold the power to predict the future, capture people's souls, and send bad luck to whoever is unfortunate enough to break one."

That last one I *had* heard. "Seven years of bad luck."

"Exactly. Because mirrors capture and contain bits and pieces of a person's soul. In other cultures, they believe mirrors are portals to the spirit world, allowing people and spirits to travel back and forth between the two planes."

"So?" I led her. "What does this have to do with my mother's photography?"

"Cameras, my dear, contain mirrors. And unlike the fleeting image reflected in a mirror, cameras capture images that remain."

"Of *course*," I said. "I've heard that. Many Native Americans refused to be photographed. Crazy Horse never allowed a photo of himself to be taken, even on his deathbed."

Iris smiled like a teacher whose student has finally caught on. "Yes, child. And why?"

"Because the camera would steal a bit of their soul."

"Exactly. They weren't wrong. A camera does have the ability to capture the soul of its subject, just as a mirror does. But it needs to be in the right hands to do so. Your mother had such hands. It was her gift. Oh, she didn't see it right away. Nobody did. But even from a young age, she was drawn to photography. She begged her parents for a camera for her birthday when she was, I believe, about five years old. Of course, Charles could never deny his daughter anything, so he got one for her, believing her interest to be a phase and he would be the one to end up using it.

"But Madlyn was never without that camera. She took it everywhere. When your grandfather got the first set of pictures developed, he was amazed at their quality and clarity. He had expected to see childish snaps: people's heads cut off, fuzzy landscapes. Instead, he found that his little daughter had taken beautiful, haunting portraits of himself, of Amelia, and of people who had visited the house.

"Charles especially loved Maddie's portraits of his animals, the horses in the barn and the dogs. He was astonished to find that they represented these creatures in a way that only Charles knew them.

"As you might imagine, Madlyn never wanted to do anything else. In very short order after she graduated from high school, she was working for major magazines, hired on the strength of the photographs she had taken growing up. She was on her way."

"You've told me a lot about my mother's talents and gifts, Iris, but not much about who she was as a person. I'd like to know that, too."

"Madlyn was a complicated girl," Iris said. "She was at times a delight and at times a terror, not unlike many teenage girls today. She would sink into dark moods in which she would talk to no one except—when she thought nobody was listening—her twin. At those times, it was as though her twin's spirit was attached to her, weighing her down. She continued having these dark moods her whole life, even after she met your father. Sadie never left her. But at other times, as I said, Madlyn was a complete delight. She was Charles's daughter, all smiles and laughter and goodness. Soon enough, she met your father."

I smiled at the thought of my young parents. And then another thought struck me. "Iris, you never mentioned my mother being bothered by the triplets. Charles had animals to protect him; who protected my mother?"

Iris nodded her head. "A very good question, Halcyon. Sadie, of course, was there to stand between the girls and your mother. But it was the camera, and Madlyn's unique ability to capture souls, that really kept the girls at bay. They knew not to get too close. At least, it was that way when Madlyn was young. When she met your father and brought him into this house, things changed somewhat.

"It was the summer of your mother's twentieth year. She was already a photographer of some note, living in New York City and traveling all over the world, working for *National Geographic* and other magazines. But this particular summer, she came home to the island because Amelia was in ill health. It was cancer, but nobody knew it then. She had been growing weaker and weaker, and Charles, frantic and already, I believe, grieving, contacted Madlyn and asked her to come home.

"She was a great solace to Amelia and Charles during this time, as you might expect. And they made the most of it, spending every day together, whether it was simply sitting and reading in the house or taking Amelia, who by now was confined to a wheelchair, out onto the cliff for picnics. It was as though they wanted to extract every bit of togetherness they could out of every moment Amelia had left.

"She died in August of that year." Iris sighed deeply. "Charles grieved for her every day of his life. He never got over losing her, although he did throw himself back into his practice. Tending animals gave him comfort during those first dark days.

"Madlyn, meanwhile, was due back at her New York apartment and her high-powered life the following month, and she was contemplating what she was going to do with her father—take him to New York, perhaps?—when she met Noah Crane."

I smiled, curling my feet up under me. I loved all of Iris's stories, grim though they were, but now we were getting to the best ones.

"Noah was working on the island in one of the hotels for the summer with a few of his friends from the mainland. Your mother met him one evening in a pub downtown. He was drawn to her immediately, of course, as everyone was. But the difference was, she was also drawn to him.

"She knew immediately that she would never be going back to that New York apartment. And he knew he wasn't going to take the teaching job waiting for him in the fall on the mainland. Within a few days of meeting each other, they had both decided to remain on the island and build a life together right here.

"I can see you'd like to know a little about their courtship." Iris eyed me. "They did all the usual things—dinners and dances and picnics and walks. But most of all, Noah and Madlyn talked. They were able to talk more deeply and intimately to each other than to anyone else."

It sounded familiar. It's just how I felt with Will.

Iris went on. "Your father asked about a job at the small local school here on the island. They happened to have an opening for a math teacher, which is what he was, and he didn't have a moment's hesitation in accepting the position. Madlyn, meanwhile, called all the editors at her various client magazines and informed them that her home base would now be Grand Manitou, not New York. She would still go on assignment as she always had.

"Everything fell into place so neatly and nicely, Madlyn always suspected her dead mother had had a hand in it somehow. Of course, that was true. I know for certain that Amelia was whispering in Noah's ear that night in the pub—*Turn around, turn around now*—when Madlyn was about to walk by. If she hadn't done that, my dear, you may well have never been born.

"She was also whispering *Stay, stay on the island* into their ears whenever they were together, planting that seed firmly and deeply. Yes, it was all Amelia's doing that Noah and Madlyn got together and ended up settling down here. She did it all, of course, for her beloved Charles. She was terrified to think of him alone and knew how much he needed his daughter beside him.

"Oh, Amelia was a busy one during those months after her death. But when Madlyn was married to your father and Charles was suitably provided for, she turned toward that ever-present light behind her and saw a tiny figure standing there. Sadie. Amelia ran to her, wrapping her arms around her beloved child for the first time, and the two of them floated away into that light together."

Iris's face was softer and kinder than I had ever seen it, perhaps in response to the fact that I was, and had been for the past several minutes, bawling like a baby.

"That was so beautiful, Iris." I sniffed, wiping my nose with a Kleenex. "But I don't understand. They were so happy. What could have gone so horribly wrong in just five years to make my father steal me away from her?"

Iris's face hardened into her familiar expression, but she grasped my hand as she shook her head. "That, my dear, is a story for another day. It is your story. The tale of Halcyon Crane."

"You can't tell me now?" I was desperate to hear it.

"You have guests coming, miss. You need to prepare for them, and I need to take my leave."

I knew better than to try to stop Iris when she was intent on leaving the house. *Let her go*, I thought. I had a séance to attend.

· 29

I made pasta with chicken, caramelized onions, sun-dried tomatoes, and a Gorgonzola sauce—a recipe pirated from my favorite restaurant back in Seattle. Will brought fresh bread and several bottles of wine (those would definitely be needed) and rattled uncomfortably around the kitchen while I cooked until Mira materialized at the front door, seven o'clock on the dot.

I found her looking—well, just like she always looked. Jeans and a striped shirt, a sweater slung across her shoulders. Funky glasses hanging on a chain around her neck, her hair pulled back in a ponytail. She seemed so—I don't know, normal?—that it startled me. This made her laugh.

"Did you expect me to show up in a velvet cloak?"

I laughed. "Get in here, Madam Mira."

Our dinner conversation covered everything from the weather to my relationship with Will to island gossip. I was skirting one of the issues I wanted to talk about with her and Will could see it, catching my eye every now and then to give me a look that seemed to say, *So? Ask already.*

After a few uncomfortable forays into the subject—"Mira,

I was wondering . . . that is to say, I found out something . . . It got me thinking . . ." I finally choked out the words: "I recently learned that you found our kayak on the day my dad and I disappeared."

Will winked at me across the table. Mira twirled the pasta around her fork, considering her response.

"That was some day," she said finally. "Most everyone on the island was out looking for the two of you. I had the feeling I knew where he had gone—somehow I just *knew*—and sure enough, I was right. Still, the sight of that kayak took my breath away. I wanted to be wrong more than anything." She looked at me with a mixture of regret and anger. "Your father certainly put this island through the wringer with his little stunt."

Mira was baiting me, trying to shift the focus away from her finding the kayak toward my dad's sins. But I refused to play along. "Why didn't you tell me? We've had plenty of opportunities."

"I really don't know why," she said, flustered. "When you first came to the island, I was stunned to find out who you were. Who wouldn't be? You were dead for thirty years, Hallie. And then, as a bit more time went on—I don't know, it didn't seem to matter that I had been part of the search party that day. Everyone on the island helped, not just me."

This made a kind of strange sense. I nodded, ready to change the subject, but Mira leaned toward me and continued, in an almost conspiratorial tone. "The thing is, Hallie, all these years, and especially back then, I had the feeling there was more to the story than we were being told."

This intrigued me. "You did? How so?"

"Julie Sutton's death. Your disappearance shortly thereafter. Everyone, especially the police, believed that Noah committed suicide in the face of those allegations and took you with him because you were the one witness to his crime. I wasn't convinced. If he wanted to end his own life just as the police were bearing down on him, fine, but what would be the point of killing you? He loved you more than you can imagine. And if he *had* committed that horrible crime and somehow killed that girl, the Noah Crane I knew would've stood up and faced his punishment."

"The Thomas James I knew would've done the same thing," I said to her.

"So." Mira changed the subject as I loaded the last of the silverware into the dishwasher. "You've called me here for some ghost busting."

I laughed nervously as we took our wine and moved from the kitchen to the dining room, where I had already lit the candle chandelier. It bathed the dark room in a soft flickering light that danced along the windowpanes. The three of us took seats around the table, and Mira sat up straight and cleared her throat. She was now taking control of the proceedings, a role I sensed she was very comfortable assuming.

"Why don't we begin by you telling me exactly what's been happening in the house," she directed.

I took a deep breath and told her everything: the sightings of the girl in the white dress, the disappearing and reappearing jewelry, the television turning off and on, the shades opening and closing.

She nodded, looking from me to Will and back again.

"Sounds like a haunting." I know that's why I called her here, the word still sent a chill up the back of my neck. "There's really no other explanation," Mira went on. "You know that, right?"

Will gave me a look. "Actually, Mira, there is another explanation," he began tentatively. I could see he wasn't sure of whether to go on or not, but I nodded, giving him the signal to continue. "I had the idea that perhaps Hallie's mind is delivering bits and pieces of memories back to her," Will said. "You know, she was so traumatized by the death of her playmate that she didn't speak until after she and her father built a new life away from here."

"I do remember that." Mira nodded. "You stopped speaking altogether. Your parents were frantic."

"Considering that, I was thinking the very fact of being back in this house was triggering memories in Hallie's mind," Will continued.

"I'd go along with that theory if it wasn't for the other things happening," Mira said finally. "How can you explain the jewelry disappearing and reappearing? The shades? The television?"

"That's why you're here," he admitted. "I *can't* explain those things. If it was just Hallie seeing a girl in white around the house, I'd recommend a psychiatrist."

I continued Will's line of thinking. "The thing is, Mira, all these little happenings—a necklace gone here, a television turned on there—wouldn't bother me too much if it wasn't for some rather distressing information I've learned about my family in recent days."

Mira squinted at me. "What sort of information?"

"I've learned that over the years there have been a number of—well, what I would call *suspicious falls* on this property and in this house, including—not incidentally—Julie Sutton's fall out of a third-floor window thirty years ago."

"Tell me more about these falls."

I leaned in toward Mira and told her what I had learned from Iris.

Mira grimaced. "That doesn't sound good," she murmured.

"No." My account was picking up steam, heading to its conclusion. "But the last straw came the other night when Will fell down the front stairs."

Aghast, Mira looked at Will for an explanation. He told her how he thought he heard someone calling his name in the middle of the night and how he felt hands on his back, pushing him down.

"That's the reason we called you," I concluded. "It's become dangerous. If there's a malevolent spirit here, I want it out. I want to be able to live in my new house in peace."

That was the full story. Now that Mira knew, she opened her bag, spread a deep-purple velvet cloth out on the table, and placed five votive candles on it.

"Do you have any idea who this ghost might be?" Mira asked, as she lit the candles one by one.

I exchanged a sidelong glance with Will. "I think it might be one or all of the little girls who died here in the 1913 storm: Penelope, Patience, and Persephone."

She looked at me in the flickering candlelight. "I'm not familiar with that event. What storm?"

And so I told her all about it—how nearly a century earlier a freak November snowstorm had caught Penelope, Patience, and Persephone unawares outside and how they died in one another's arms at the bottom of the cliff.

"So you don't think it's the spirit of the girl who was killed here thirty years ago?" Mira asked.

Will and I exchanged glances. I hadn't even considered this. "The reason I thought our spirit is one or all of the girls from 1913 is because of the family lore I've recently learned. My relatives have all assumed the girls were still around. Their mother especially was tormented by the thought that her daughters didn't make it to heaven. She believed it until the day she died, and even tried to contact them once. And all the falls—"

Mira nodded. "I just wanted to be sure. If you think you know who the ghosts are, it helps. Whenever possible, it's best to try to contact specific people on the other side."

She explained what was going to happen tonight. She would spend a few quiet moments meditating—going into a trance?—and then we'd join hands while she called the girls, inviting them to join our circle.

Mira took a deep breath and closed her eyes. *Here we go,* I thought. But then she opened them again. Something had occurred to her. "Do you have anything that belonged to the girls? It's really helpful to have something from the person I'm trying to contact."

I shook my head. "It was nearly a hundred years ago, Mira. Their stuff might still be around here packed in a box somewhere, but I wouldn't have the first idea where to look."

As Mira collected herself, taking one deep breath after another, grasping our hands, squeezing them tightly, all I could think of was that perhaps it was a good thing we didn't have those ribbons.

"Penelope, Patience, Persephone," Mira chanted, in a voice that was not quite her own. "Penelope, Patience, Persephone. Girls, we are calling to you. We are asking you to join our circle. Come to us, girls. Join us here at the table. "Penelope, Patience, Persephone. Penelope, Patience, Persephone."

Mira sounded just like Iris when she had said those same words, chanting, calling to the girls. Her voice was scratchy and oddly pitched, as though it wasn't she who was speaking but someone else. I was beginning to feel something, an electricity in the room prickling at the back of my neck and running down my arms.

"Penelope, Patience, Persephone."

I heard it first in a distant corner of the house, the rumbling of something awakening and coming to life. A century-old wind snaked its way into the room from where it had been lying dormant on the third floor, swirling around the three of us at the table, wrapping us like a python and constricting us. All the candles, those on the table and those in the chandelier, were extinguished in one collective *whoosh*. We were in total darkness. And then I heard it.

Say, say, oh, playmate, come out and play with me.

I tried to scream but my voice had no sound. I tried to open my eyes, but it was as though they were glued shut. I tried to let go of Mira's and Will's hands, but I could not unclench my grip. Their hands had gone cold, stonelike, completely without feeling. It was as though I were holding the hands of the dead.

Somewhere in the distance, Mira was murmuring. "You're cold as ice. You're freezing. You're frozen. You're dead."

I smelled it, then. Suddenly and immediately the room was filled with it. The scent of roses, overpowering and thick.

"Hey!" It was Will, his voice high and awkward. "Stop it!"

From Mira, in a whisper: "You're cold as ice. You're freezing. You're frozen. You're dead."

"Ouch!" Will was on his feet, trying to wrench his hands free of ours. I opened my eyes but it was no use, I could see nothing but blackness.

The dogs burst into the room from the kitchen, snarling and barking. I could feel them circling the table and hear them panting. Finally—it must have been only a few moments but it felt like forever—Mira loosened her grip, pushed back her chair, and ran toward the wall. She flipped on the light switch, and the three of us uttered a collective gasp at what we saw.

The table was covered with white ribbons.

They were piled high between us, covering the velvet cloth, the unlit candles, and the tabletop itself. They spilled onto the floor. One lazily danced its way across the room as the dogs growled, soft and low.

Mira was standing at the light switch, her eyes wide, panting. Only then did I see Will's face. It was covered in scratches. Little rivers of blood trickled down his cheeks from what looked to be razor-thin cuts. He just stood there, open-mouthed, unable to comprehend what had just occurred.

I tried to hide my terror and slid up to Will, resting my hand gently on his arm. "Let's get you into the kitchen and clean you up." I led him into the other room and sat him down at the kitchen table, Mira following close behind us. I grabbed a clean dish towel out of a drawer and wet it down before gently and softly dabbing the blood from Will's face. He was looking at me with the eyes of a frightened little boy.

"There's a first-aid kit under the sink in there." I pointed Mira in the direction of the bathroom off the kitchen. She returned with the kit and I opened it to find an antibacterial cream for cuts and scratches, which I rubbed on Will's face. Luckily, none of the cuts were very deep. Scratches from tiny claws. Or a child's fingernails. I wondered if they'd leave scars.

Meanwhile, Mira's hands shook as she opened another bottle of red wine. *Good thinking.* She poured three glasses of it and downed one immediately, pouring another in its place. Then, we all started to talk.

"I've experienced a lot of things in my life, but nothing like that," Mira said.

"I couldn't let go of either of your hands," I reported.

"Something was in that room with us," Will murmured, touching the scratches on his face.

"Tell me exactly what happened to you," Mira said to Will. "When did you start feeling the scratches?"

Will thought for a moment. "It was right after I started to smell the rose petals. You smelled them, too, right?"

Mira and I nodded.

"So the scratching began as soon as they came into the room," Mira murmured. "Does either of you know the significance of the ribbons?"

"Family lore has it that, a long time ago, another medium called the girls with ribbons. They used to wear them in their hair every day."

Will's eyes were wide, but Mira did not seem at all surprised by this news. "Sometimes that's how the spirits of the dead come to us," she murmured. "They'll place something significant to them around us, so we'll notice they've been there. It's quite common, actually. Sometimes it's a butterfly hovering close by for an unusually long period of time. One woman I know sees an eagle perched on a tree outside her window and knows it's her dead son sending a message of protection. Another family finds pennies in strange places—in their shoes, in the bottom of a bowl of pasta, frozen into a compartment in an ice tray. It's how the dead tell the living they're still around, still watching."

Neither Will nor I said anything. We both just sat there, holding hands, shaking our heads in disbelief at what had just occurred. If only all we had to be concerned about was pennies or hovering butterflies.

Finally, Mira said, "Well, at least we accomplished one thing tonight."

"What's that?" I wanted to know.

"It's absolutely clear that you've got a ghost. Three of them, actually. Penelope, Patience, and Persephone."

"So now what?" I asked her. I was truly at a loss. I had no idea what came next. And I was suddenly very, very tired. All I wanted to do was to fall asleep in Will's arms without any worry about mischievous, murderous ghosts.

"We go on to Phase Two tomorrow." Mira smiled.

"Which is?"

"Getting them out of here," she said. "I'm assuming you still want to stay in this house, right?"

"Right."

"And I'm assuming you want the girls gone?"

"Definitely."

"Well, there are ways to take care of that," she promised, pushing her chair back from the table. "But I think we've all had about enough for one night."

I didn't want her to go, I'll admit it. I was afraid to stay in the house. Suddenly, I had an idea. "May Will and I come with you and stay in a room at the inn tonight? I'm really not excited about spending the night here."

"You can have your old room." Mira smiled, patting my hand.

"We could go to my house, you know," Will offered, as he dabbed at this face.

I shook my head. "You live clear on the other side of the island and Mira's just down the road. Plus, Tundra and Tika won't fit in your buggy and I'm not leaving them here alone." I turned to Mira. "We *can* take them to your place, right?"

She nodded quickly. "I don't usually allow pets, but I can make an exception tonight for these girls."

And that's how the three of us came to leave my house together that night. In retrospect, I see it was a mistake. Hindsight can be particularly cruel when one goes down a wrong road. Perhaps if Will and I had braved the night in that place—faced the girls head on—we would have been spared what happened the next day. On the other hand, I don't have any way of knowing what might have befallen us if we had decided to spend the night in the house after those spirits had been called, awakened, and stirred up. Who knows what manner of horror we might have experienced?

PART THREE

· 30

You're not going back there alone," Will said to me, over breakfast at Mira's the next day.

When we arrived at the inn after a damp, rainy ride in Mira's carriage, we simply fell into bed and into a deep sleep, dogs curled up at our feet, not awakening until midday. I didn't even have a change of clothes with me, so I thought I'd head back to Hill House in the light of day and pack a few things.

"It's daytime," I said stupidly. "Nothing's going to happen to me. And anyway, I've been living there for two weeks now. If they wanted to do anything beyond tease me, they've had plenty of opportunities. I'm not afraid now. I was last night but I'm not afraid now. I'm really not."

How afraid did that sound?

Mira had run into town for some groceries, so she couldn't dissuade me, and Will wasn't convinced by my bravado. He was shaking his head, and only then did it occur to me: The scratches on his face were all but gone. I could barely make out their faint trails on his cheeks. It was as though they, too, were phantoms or figments conjured up by Mira's call to the dead, dissolving with the light of day.

"I just wish you'd come into town with me," he muttered, knowing he wasn't going to win this battle.

"It's a beautiful day," I told him, as though that meant anything whatsoever in the context of what we were discussing.

But it was true. It was one of those rare late-fall days, just as you're preparing for the onslaught of snow and chill and cold, that surprises you with a burst of summer, a day of respite and reprieve from the harsh weather that will certainly be descending in very short order.

"Here's what I'll do," I began, by way of compromise. "I'll pack some things for us, just in case we decide to stay here at Mira's again tonight. I'll clean up all the debris from the séance, and then I'll take a picnic lunch outside and wait for you. And I'll keep the dogs by my side the whole time. How's that?"

The sky was a deep cloudless blue and the temperature must've been climbing into the sixties—not a heat wave but, in late November on this island, quite an unusual occurrence. I leaned against Will as we walked toward my house, the dogs running in long circles around us.

"You know what didn't occur to me until just now?" I said. "Iris. She'll be there. I won't be alone."

Will smiled. "Small comfort. Like she can do anything if the ghosts try to push you down the stairs. But it's something, anyway." He kissed me as he veered into the barn to hitch up Belle, who had spent the night in a stall vacated by one of my mother's horses.

I ran up the steps, took a deep breath, and opened the back door. Iris was already here: the glasses were washed and put away, chairs pushed neatly under the table. I opened the door to the dining room and found her, broom and dustpan in hand, sweeping up the ribbons. The scent of roses was still overpowering.

She gave me a sharp look. "What happened here?"

Suddenly, I felt like a small child caught in the act of doing something wrong, something forbidden. Had we? I was almost afraid of saying the words, but I managed to squeak out, "We tried to contact the girls."

"Tried? I'd say you succeeded." She sniffed as she picked up the dustpan full of ribbons and made her way to the kitchen door to dump them. "That was a mistake, Halcyon. The last time someone contacted those girls, somebody died."

I remembered the story of Hannah's séance and shivered at the thought of poor Jane going over the cliff.

"I think it's time you heard the tale of Halcyon Crane," Iris said, and walked out the back door, leaving me alone with my fears and my questions.

It took a moment before I followed. Iris had gone down the drive and into the garden, where she was sitting on one of the stone benches. As the dogs curled up on their beds in the kitchen, I trotted down the drive and joined her.

"You need to fully realize your gift," she said to me there in the garden. "You need to own it and use it, now that you've called the girls to you in this very real way. You are more powerful than they, and much more powerful than any supposed medium you had here. Now is the time, Halcyon, to realize who you are."

I sighed. "I have no idea how to do what you're suggesting. I've tried, but I—"

"That's why I'm here, child: to teach you, to unlock your sight with my stories. And now I'm convinced that this last one, *your* tale, you need to see on your own. It's the only way." She fished a few black-and-white photographs out of her apron pocket and handed them to me. "Look deeply, Halcyon, and then empty your mind of all thought. Let your spirit drift in the ether. When you're hovering there between worlds, call the spirits to you, your mother and father, and they will show you what you need to see." She fell silent, leaving me to ponder the photographs in my open palms without benefit of her explanation.

I saw me, as a baby, my mother and father smiling broadly. A birthday party with just one candle. My father lying in the grass with me sleeping on his chest. I let myself become absorbed in the photographs until I could almost sense the moment in time they contained—the smell of the grass that day, the taste of sugary frosting . . . I closed my eyes and tried to clear my mind of other thoughts, listening to the sound within my own ears, feeling the soft breeze on my face, until another scent swirled about me: a familiar cologne. *My father's cologne.*

I opened my eyes but was unable to see what had been in front of me. There was no stone bench, no garden, no cliff beyond, no Iris. Only my dad, younger than I, sitting in a room in Hill House that I took to be his study. He was staring out the window absently, running a hand through his hair. How full it looked, back then. My mother, obviously pregnant, swept into the study wearing a long purple dress and dangly earrings and kissed him on the forehead.

"Money's not the issue, Madlyn, you know that." My father sighed. "I'm just worried about what kind of father I'm going to make. Am I ready for this? Are we?"

Madlyn laughed, a musical trill that sounded familiar and sweet. "Nobody's ever ready to have a child, silly. They come into our lives when *they're* ready."

Noah looked into his wife's eyes and collapsed in the face of her optimism. "I guess you're right. This baby's coming, whether we feel ready or not."

That scene dissolved into thin wisps of smoke taken aloft on the breeze, to be instantly replaced with the image of me, wriggling in my bassinette, my father leaning over me, beaming. "Let her sleep, Noah." My mother smiled at him and led him out of the room.

I saw another image then. My mother, her long auburn hair pulled back in a scarf, was sitting at the desk in her bedroom suite, squinting and scowling at a group of photographs she had laid out in long rows. I watched her gather them up in a hurry and shove them into a file when my father came into the room.

"I'm worried about Halcyon," he said to her.

"What else is new?" My mother rose from her desk and took him in her arms. "You've got to be the most doting father on this planet. What is it this time, my love?"

"Madlyn, I know we've talked about this before, but you really have to listen to me this time. I've been trying to tell you, honey, our little girl is blind." *Blind?* My father went on. "She never makes eye contact with anyone, not even you. She doesn't react to toys or faces or animals. You've got to face it, honey. We need to take her to a doctor."

His earnest, pleading words sent a familiar chill up my spine. I watched a curly-haired toddler, unsteady on her feet, turn and walk directly into a wall. But that image didn't jibe with the next one that floated in front of my eyes: me as a toddler, looking directly at a woman whom I recognized as Hannah and laughing as she covered her face with her hands and then dropped them, crying, "Peek-a-boo!" before she dissolved into the air as my mother swept into the room. Image after image flickered into view then, like a slide show, me talking and laughing and playing with Hannah and Simeon and Amelia. I wasn't seeing what was in front of me—but I *was* seeing beyond the veil into the world of the dead.

Noah tried again one afternoon. "Madlyn, I think we might have another problem with Hallie. I know it sounds crazy, but I heard her talking to your mother today. And it's not the first time."

Madlyn laughed. "That's ridiculous. She has an imaginary friend, that's all there is to it." But I could hear what my mother was thinking. She herself had spent her childhood talking to a dead twin, so to her this was normal behavior.

"How can she talk about pretty white ribbons and that brown furry teddy bear and the red leaves in the garden when she's blind?" Noah wanted to know.

"Honey, don't question it," Madlyn told him, turning him

around and rubbing his shoulders. "This house has a way of doing strange things to people. Don't worry about it. My dad didn't *talk* until he was five years old, and look at him now."

Another image materialized: Will, as a boy! With me in the garden, right where I was now sitting. He was chasing me around one of the benches and suddenly I stopped, turned, looked directly at him, and leaped on him. I knew I was seeing the first moment of my own sight. Will's was the first face—other than a ghost's—I had ever seen. A warmth overtook me and I laughed, watching my young self lying on top of Will, tickling him mercilessly. I grinned, thinking of the night before. Not much had changed.

"I can't believe it," Noah murmured tearfully to Madlyn as he held me tightly in his arms.

"It's just like my father and his speech," Madlyn whispered over my shoulder. "I don't care why it happened or how, only that she can see now. That's all that matters."

As I learned from the next vision, I had not lost my ability to see beyond the veil, and I saw how frazzled my dad was becoming with my mother's constant denials that nothing out of the ordinary was happening. "Hallie! Halcyon Crane!" he would call as he pounded through the trees in front of the house, looking for me yet again. I would disappear during the afternoons, exploring the house and the grounds and especially the woods. More often than not, he'd find me lazing in the grass watching the sailboats come and go in the harbor, or brushing the horses with my grandfather, or playing in the shade of one of the great oak trees that stood near the cliff. But on this day I wasn't in any of those places, and it was getting dark.

Noah's breath started to catch in his throat as he ran through the grounds, calling my name, the exposed roots and gnarled branches clawing at his shirt and his hair. He was lumbering through the stand of trees in front of the house, nearly blind himself with the fear of never seeing me again. "Hallie!" His voice was shrill, frantic.

"Here, Papa," came my voice from within the trees. Noah stopped and looked around wildly, but he couldn't see me. "Not there! I'm over here!" Suddenly, a rustling in the bushes. "Boo!" I cried, leaping onto my father's legs and holding on tight. Beads of sweat had begun to dot my father's forehead. He bent down and scooped me up, holding me close to his heart. I saw that I had been perilously close, three or four steps, from the edge of the cliff.

He held me tight; I could smell the baby shampoo in my hair, mixed with wildflowers and lavender and water and night.

"What's the matter, Daddy?"

Noah put me down and knelt beside me, face-to-face. "You know the rule about the cliff."

I squirmed and shrugged. "I was just playing."

"I don't care, young lady. You've been told never to play by the cliff alone."

I looked at him with innocence in my eyes. "But I wasn't alone."

Noah shook his head and sighed, confusion and dread apparent on his face. "Who was with you?"

"My friends," I explained. "We were playing hide-and-seek."

A dark shadow crept over my father's face. A childhood game had become dangerous. It had led me to the cliff edge.

What I saw next made me suddenly cold: me on the bluff with three ghostly playmates—the girls. We were sitting across from one another, playing patty-cake and singing:

Say, say, oh, playmate!
Come out and play with me.
And bring your dollies three.
Climb up my apple tree!

The sound wrapped around my throat like an ice-cold hand. I saw my father scooping me up away from them into his arms. I saw them waving at me. I saw his terrified face before I put my hands over my own.

"But I play with them all the time, Daddy! And other people, too! Grandma and great-grandmother, especially. Grandma fell and lost a baby."

My stomach began to tighten and I was having trouble breathing. *This is it,* I thought to myself. *I'm about to learn everything now.* I had an overwhelming urge to get up and run from that bench, to shake the vision from my eyes, because I knew what I was going to see next—my repressed memories of the day Julie Sutton died.

The memories had stayed hidden in some dark recess of my brain for a reason, I thought, in a wild attempt to justify not hearing the rest of the story. Maybe I shouldn't know what happened. Up to now I had been just fine not knowing, after all. Why dredge up the past? But then again, what was the point of hearing all these family tales from Iris if I wasn't going to hear—or see—my own?

Somewhere, very far away, I heard Iris's voice. "Keep looking, Halcyon. It's right there before you."

But I didn't see Julie, not just yet. What I saw was my mother, entranced with her photography, her own gift, oblivious to everything going on around her. The capturing of souls was a heady thing; it intoxicated her, I could see it in her eyes. Every time she developed one of her photographs, she was like an addict, insatiably drawn to what she would find there. I saw it clearly: This gift, this obsession, left very little time for other things, like husbands and children. That's why she didn't see I was in danger. And I knew then this part of the tale was cautionary. I made a mental note to remember that I, too, risked addiction. I needed to keep my eyes on what was really important.

"So what if she's having visits from previous occupants of this house?" my mother said to Noah, waving off his fears. "They're my *relatives*, for heaven's sake."

"Maddie, I think we should leave the island," he pleaded. "Let's get away from here."

"Are you kidding?" she spat back at him. "Leave my father here alone? No, Noah. Absolutely not."

I saw more arguments, then. Doors slamming, tears from both of them. "This is a wonderful place to grow up," Madlyn told her husband. "Hallie has friends and a great school and a whole island to explore—without cars to run her over. You've got a fine job, and I can do my work from here. These are my roots and they're Hallie's roots. You can't seriously want to take her away from all of that because you think she sees ghosts."

She said that last bit with a kind of sarcastic venom that Noah had never before heard from his wife, and I saw the defeated look on his face. Nobody was leaving the island. Desperate, grieving, and frightened, he whispered into my ear that he'd protect me as best he could, promising to watch me with a hawk's keen eye.

Then the scene shifted, and I saw somebody new on the island shopping for groceries. She followed my father and me out of the store and touched him on the sleeve. He turned and saw a young woman. She looked into his eyes and said, conspiratorially, "I can see that your daughter has quite a gift."

I could almost hear Noah's heart beating. He took a deep breath and whispered, "What do you mean, a gift?"

"The sight. I have it, too."

He grabbed the young woman's arm and hustled her over to a quiet corner of the street. "Listen, I don't know who you are or how you know what you know, but I really need to talk to you," he said to her.

Now I saw the woman's face more clearly than I had before. Mira? *It couldn't be.* And yet there she was, her face younger and brighter than I knew it to be, but plain as day.

I watched my father meet Mira for a clandestine dinner on the mainland that evening. Of course they couldn't be seen together on the island—word would get back to my mother in a flash—so they picked an out-of-the-way restaurant not far from the ferry dock. He told Mira everything: how I didn't see until I was three years old but was constantly talking about visual things and people and animals, how I regained my sight in an instant one day, how I was immersed in stories of my ancestors' pasts, how I had always played with imaginary friends but now those games were turning dangerous.

"What does your wife say?" Mira asked him shyly.

"She discounts it, all of it. She is totally in denial and says I'm insane to be worried. I've tried everything to make her understand, but she won't listen, she won't . . ." His words trailed off into a sigh.

I watched as a coy grin appeared on Mira's face and knew she was very glad to hear this. I saw images of the two of them meeting again and again, intimate dinners and rendezvous at out-of-the-way hotels. They had had an affair? I felt sick. All those times she had been so friendly toward me, so helpful, she had never once said anything about this.

Then I saw Julie Sutton's parents drop her off at the house for the afternoon. My father found us playing in a third-floor room, sitting on the floor with a tea party spread out before us. I was pouring imaginary tea from a pot and chattering away to Julie and to the stuffed bears I had positioned as the other guests.

"You girls are playing so happily up here, honey." He smiled at me, relieved to find me immersed in a normal child's activity—a tea party with a real live friend—and went on his way down the stairs.

But then came the screaming: high-pitched, horrible screams. My father flew back into the room and found me, scratches bleeding all over my face, locked in a struggle with, to him, what was an unseen foe. But I could see exactly who it was.

I saw myself screaming, holding my arms in front of me to fend off a girl in a white dress: Patience—but her face was not the face I had come to know. It had morphed into a grotesque worm-eaten skull, its flesh paper-thin and flaking. Her eyes were gone—only empty black holes remained—and she was yelling, "We weren't invited to this party! You didn't invite *us* to this party!"

Julie was crying and cowering in the corner, and then Persephone was upon her, scratching and pushing her, tearing at her dress, and finally putting her tiny hands around Julie's throat.

Seeing all this, I was stunned into a stupor. I couldn't shake the images from my view and I couldn't move; the images held me captive even though I wanted to get up from that bench and run more than I had ever wanted anything in my life. This scene now before me was what my mind had locked away.

• • •

I kept screaming and fighting against this unseen enemy—unseen by my father, that is. I knocked over lamps and tore bedding off beds, I fell and tumbled and screamed. My father was just standing there—paralyzed with shock, I assumed—until one of them—Penelope—knocked into his legs and he felt, with certainty, her presence there.

He dove into the fray and tried to grab whatever it was that was torturing me. In doing so, he turned Penelope's wrath against him. She flew at him, scratching his face and biting and tearing his shirt—he could not see her, but I was seeing it all—until he was backed into the wall near the open window.

I couldn't catch my breath. There I was again, on top of a roller coaster, about to plunge toward the ground whether I wanted to or not.

In the confusion, with me fighting off Patience and my dad fighting off Penelope, Persephone saw her opportunity and took it, pushing Julie out of the open window. I ran to the window and watched her fall. She locked eyes with me as she tumbled all the way to the ground, mouthing my name. The last thing I saw was her terrified face before her skull hit a rock, making a sickening cracking sound.

My father didn't see exactly what happened, but he saw me leaning out of the window. When he looked out the window, he saw, to his horror, the body of Julie Sutton lying on the ground.

"Oh, my God," I murmured to myself. "He thought I did it!"

Noah flew through the house, down the stairs, and outside, stopping only when he reached Julie. I watched from the window as he attempted CPR, but it was useless; she was dead. He called the police and the Suttons.

"It was the girls," I whispered. "They killed Julie. But my father thought it was me. That's why we left the island."

The vision swirled into view again. My mother was away when it happened, so my dad asked Mira to come to the house that evening. She did, and he told her everything that had occurred during the day—by that time, of course, the whole island knew there had been a death at Hill House. And Mira hatched the plan for escape—leaving the island. Within Noah's panic, she saw a clear road leading to what she wanted, so she took it.

"I'm going to take the blame, Mira," I heard my father say. "Just so long as none of this touches Hallie."

Mira shook her head. "Your daughter is in grave danger," she told him slyly. "I can feel it. This is not the end of the matter. You need to get her out of here. With you in prison, who is going to watch over Hallie? Your wife?"

Noah sat down hard on one of the kitchen chairs, defeated.

"Listen," she said, in low conspiratorial tones. "I know a man on the mainland. He can come up with a whole new identity for you. For us. We can run away together and start a new life somewhere, pretending that this never happened."

I put my head in my hands, feeling the beginning throb of a migraine. Or was it my father's head I felt hurting? Somehow, I could see it in his eyes. He never intended to take Mira with us; she was merely his means of escape.

"I've given Madlyn several chances to see that something is very wrong here," he murmured, nodding. "Hallie's in danger, that's never been more clear. But Madlyn won't see it. All she keeps saying is that she herself was perfectly safe growing up in that house. But Hallie's life could very well be at stake."

Noah arranged everything with the man on the mainland: a new driver's license, birth certificate, college degree, everything. And he waited for the right time. Meanwhile, the police investigation was turning nasty, as was island opinion. Everyone was horrified by Julie Sutton's death and there was only one person who could be responsible: Noah Crane. He allowed the police to believe that he was the one who killed that poor girl. Never once did the harsh eye of blame come to rest on me.

I saw my father and Mira cooking up an escape plan. She would tow a fishing boat to the designated site; she would find our overturned kayak, thus making everyone think we had died. Noah would send for her later, when he reached our destination.

Still, he waited and wondered. Was leaving really the right thing to do? The last straw came the day Madlyn showed him the latest photo she had taken of me, swinging in the backyard. Noah saw it loud and clear, his mute daughter calling out: *Help me.* That was it for my father. He tried, one last time. "Can you not see she is in danger here? Can you not see that, Madlyn?" But she was as blind as I had been during my first years of life.

It was time to go. In the middle of the night, Mira towed a fishing boat to the enormous arched rock formation known as the Ring, where she left it moored securely, along with a change of clothes and some supplies. The next day, after kissing my mother goodbye, Noah Crane paddled the double kayak toward the north side of the island with me sitting still, as I knew to do, in the front seat. Young as I was, I knew that keeping one's center was the most important part of kayaking. If you lost it, you'd tip. My dad had taught me that.

Noah knew we were just minutes away from death, a death he had carefully planned. He was paddling toward a remote part of the island that could not be seen from shore, a spot that few people frequented. It was a tricky thing, dying. The calm weather that was perfect for kayaking on this great lake called many people to the water. It was difficult to find the solitude he needed. He scanned the horizon. If he saw any other people nearby—a kayak, a sailboat, even a swimmer—he would have to abort the plan and try another day.

My dad's face was stern and determined. He was so close. The plan seemed to be falling into place perfectly. Nobody was around, as far as the eye could see. Just a few more strokes. He poured on the steam, as though he were paddling for his life; in a way, he was. His arms began to ache, his muscles tiring. Still, he couldn't stop now. It was really happening. He was really doing it.

If Madlyn didn't believe we were dead, she would surely hunt us down and bring me back to the island; my father would go to jail. But Noah wasn't worried about failure on this day. He was a methodical man, and he had calculated every eventuality. His plan would work.

The image shifted slightly, and I saw my dad withdrawing money from his bank account again and again and again, sums not large enough to attract notice, but enough. It was easy for him to squirrel this money away for himself, and he had traveled to the mainland to open a bank account under his new name, Thomas James. He had managed to stockpile almost six figures. He had a few thousand more stuffed into his jacket pocket. Not a fortune, but enough to start us in a new life.

I could see it on his face; the enormity of this thing was overwhelming to him. What he was doing was illegal, never mind the cruel immorality of taking a child away from her mother. He still loved Madlyn and knew he always would. But love comes a distant second to the safety of your child. He told himself that, over and over, until it took root in his soul.

I saw my dad think of all these things that day, as he paddled his kayak under the Ring. Local legend had it that the Ring was the gateway to the spirit world. It would be our gateway, too.

"See that, Daddy?" I called to him, silently, from my mute world. (I was not to speak a word for two years because of the trauma.) I was staring back toward shore. Then I turned my head and looked back at him, the fear apparent in my eyes. Noah had no idea I was also seeing the girls, standing on the shoreline, angry. He tried to say something to me, but the words caught in his throat. If he had had any moments of doubt about what he was doing, they were put to rest. Thank God he was getting his daughter away from this accursed place.

He passed through the Ring and found what he knew would be there, a fishing boat tethered to a rock on the sandbar, all gassed up, ready to go. Mira had stuck to their agreement. *Now,* Noah prayed. *Please let us get away.* He slowed his paddling and floated onto the bar.

"Hallie, we're going to do something fun today," he said, in a voice that was not quite his own. "Are you ready?"

I nodded and smiled, always up for a fun adventure with my dad.

"Okay," he began. "I want you to climb out of this kayak very carefully and stand on the sandbar. Can you do that?"

Of course. I was delighted that my father trusted me enough to do this important thing. He had never let me get out of the kayak before until we were on shore. But I wasn't afraid. I knew I could do it. I slithered out of my seat and stood on the sandbar, wiggling my toes inside my sandals.

Then my dad did the most curious thing. He got out of the kayak, too, and turned it belly up, shoving it out into the water. Then he threw his wallet and hat into the water. I watched it all float away.

"This is our boat now," he said, motioning toward the fishing boat. "Look. I've got some things in there for you."

What could those be? I waded to the boat and looked in. Two backpacks, a hat, an old jacket, and a blanket sat on the bottom of the hull.

"Climb in," Noah said. "This is the surprise I was telling you about. We're going on an adventure, just you and me. Now, I want you to crawl into the boat and get under the blanket, and stay there until I tell you to come out. You're hiding. It's a game. Can you do that for me?"

Sure! It was simple. I hid under blankets all the time. I did as I was told, shivering with anticipation, wondering what would come next.

Noah untied the boat and started the engine. As we puttered slowly away, he put on a fishing hat with a wide brim and an old jacket he had stuffed in the boat. He took out a fishing rod and laid it over the side. Anyone watching from shore would see a lone man out fishing, not a father and daughter in a kayak.

It was done. We were dead, or would be, hours from now, when Madlyn began wondering why we hadn't come home. Noah imagined the frantic search, the cries of anguish when the kayak was found, the funeral of father and daughter. He pushed those thoughts out of his head and focused instead on the next tasks he would have to accomplish: finding an isolated spot to ditch the boat, hailing a taxi, getting to the airport. I saw all this swirling around my father's head like an ethereal to-do list.

Thomas James was glad his daughter was obediently huddling under the blanket so she couldn't see the tears in his eyes as he steered the boat toward the opposite shore.

This vision blurred, and I heard crying, a baby's cry, and knew the tale wasn't over. I saw Mira holding an infant. Was this my father's child? I sat there in stunned silence for a moment or two as the vision floated out of view. Was there anything else about Mira I didn't know? She had never told me she was a mother. I wondered if the baby had survived. Did I have a brother or a sister somewhere? Had my dad known?

I shook my head, sweeping the last wisps of the vision away, and suddenly became aware of my surroundings again. Iris was still sitting next to me on the bench. She now seemed impossibly tired, as though this tale had sucked the life out of her. I also saw that the bright November day had turned dark and foreboding, as it had on so many other days here. Clouds were swirling and turning above us; the wind was changing direction; the horizon looked dark and threatening. A storm was brewing. It was time to go inside.

"Iris," I said, taking her cold hand in mine, "let me help you into the house." But Iris shook her head.

"My work here is done for the day, miss." She started to stand up from the bench on what looked to be painful and creaky legs, but then I remembered what I wanted to ask her.

"May I ask one more thing before you go?" I spoke gently, holding her steady.

"What is it, child?" She was dead tired; I could see that clearly.

I began hurriedly. "Iris, my father took me away from here because of the girls. They're still here, and they have harmed Will—pushed him down the stairs and scratched him. I want to live in this house for the rest of my life. It's my legacy, my family history. I don't know how to thank you for telling it all to me. But right now, I need to know one more thing: How do I get rid of the girls?"

Iris's smile was weary. "They're just children, Halcyon, and spirit children at that. You are a living adult. As such you are much more powerful than they are. You now know how to use your gift. You must simply tell them what to do."

"And what is that, exactly?"

"To go, of course," she said. "They have been earthbound for too long now, doomed to stay in a house where they have committed murder and mayhem for generations. They are confused and lost without their mother and father. They view new people coming to the house as intruders, strangers to be feared—especially other children—Jane, Charles, Amelia, all the poor babies, Julie Sutton. And now your Will intrudes. You must tell them their family is waiting, Halcyon, or he will continue to be in danger. They're not aware that they are dead, you see. It's time for them to go where they belong."

"That seems too easy," I said, unconvinced.

Iris wrapped her arms around my shoulders and brushed her paper-thin cheek against mine, pressing her lips to my face. "I have done what I was to do, Halcyon. I have kept your family's lore safe and tucked away in my heart until you arrived. And I have shown you their faces and told you their stories and, in the doing, helped you unlock your gift. You're correct, child, in knowing that you belong in this house. Three little girls, even murderous ones, cannot take that away from you."

I got the strangest feeling, then, that Iris had somehow taken us outside of real time and space, as though *we* were shadowy figures floating somewhere in the ether as she told her stories.

When I finally pulled away from her, I was up to my calves in snow. How long had I been standing there in Iris's embrace? I whirled around, and all I could see was a wall of white. No house, no trees, no garden, no Iris. Only the blizzard that had suddenly descended upon me.

· 31

Why hadn't I noticed that it had started to snow? Had I simply lost all awareness of everything around me? I couldn't see the house, and I had no idea which way to turn. *It's just like the storm that killed the girls.* This idea gave me a very sick feeling in the pit of my stomach, but I knew I had to be strong in order to get Iris and me back to the house.

"Iris!" I called, reaching blindly into the snow for her. "Iris!" But there was no answer. I bent down to the bench—perhaps she had simply sat down?—but she wasn't there. She had wandered off into the storm.

The last thing I wanted to do was look for Iris in a raging blizzard. I wanted to get back to my warm house. But I knew I had to find her. And so I put one foot in front of the other, slowly and slower still, calling out her name. I rubbed my bare arms for warmth. That's all I'd need, to freeze to death out here. Then I'd be another of Iris's strange family tales. But whom would she tell? The last Hill—me—would be gone.

Then I heard it, soft and faint in the distance. "Hallie! Hallie! Where are you?"

Will! All of a sudden I remembered I had told him that

morning I'd meet him on the cliff for a picnic. Surely he didn't think, in this weather . . . But there it was again. "Hallie! Hallie!"

"I'm over here!" I screamed. "By the garden!"

"Hallie?" But his voice was getting fainter and fainter. He was going the wrong way.

I started running toward the sound of his voice, stopping only when I remembered that there was an actual cliff somewhere nearby.

"Will!" I called out, and then, remembering, "Iris!" I had two people to find in this storm.

But I heard no response from either of them. I could see nothing but whiteness swirling in the air before me. I had no idea where I was, and no idea how to get back to the house. I was lost.

"Will!" I tried again. "Will!"

The silent snow wrapped around me. Panic was setting in as the whiteness descended around me, piling up at a very rapid rate. Now it was nearly to my knees, and I was having great difficulty moving around. I thought how restful it would be simply to sink to the ground and let that blanket of snow cover me. I slumped to my knees, almost giving up.

But then I heard it: laughter. "You're ice cold!" I heard a voice say. "Hallie! You're ice cold!"

I heard the voices clearly. It was the girls, I was sure of it. "Come on! You can't stop now! You're ice cold. Come and find us!"

Were they trying to lure me off the cliff? No. I remembered how Hannah always believed they had saved her life in that storm. Their voices were getting louder and louder, as though the words were being shouted into my own ear. I put one foot in front of the other and began to move. "You're getting warmer! Warmer now, Hallie!" A few more steps and then: "Colder! Colder! Turn around before you freeze!" I turned and walked another couple of steps. "Warmer! You're getting hot!" A few more steps. "You're burning up! You're burning!"

My foot hit something hard and tall. I recognized it immediately as the stone wall adjacent to the stairs leading from the drive to the house. I was home. I was saved. I climbed the stairs blindly, feeling each one with my foot as I went.

"Hallie!" I heard, louder now. It was Will.

"Will! I'm at the stairs! Follow the sound of my voice!" I just kept shouting until he collided with me. *Thank God.* We stood there for a moment, holding each other.

"Iris is out there," I said to him. "We've got to look for her."

"Hallie, I'm getting you back up to the house. Right now. You're freezing."

He led me up the rest of the stairs, one by one. I nearly died of joy when we reached the back door. I opened it and fell into the kitchen, shivering. Will ran to the living room and got me an afghan, which he immediately wrapped around me.

"My God, how long have you been out there?"

"I have no idea," I said, though chattering teeth. It was then I noticed a pot of stew on the stove and smelled the bread in the oven. "Did you make that?" I asked him, knowing he hadn't. He shook his head. It must have been Iris. Who else would've done it?

Much later, after we had showered and eaten and thoroughly warmed up, I told Will the tale of Halcyon Crane. He kept shaking his head, muttering things like *Unbelievable* and *Wow.* I don't know whether he took what I said at face value—especially the part about the girls saving me—or if he believed Iris was embellishing my story the same way she embellished the others.

I wasn't sure either, but at that moment I didn't much care. I was back in my house with the man I loved, and we were both safe from the storm. Iris had made it, too, as evidenced by the fine dinner she had prepared. I took Will up to bed that night with the distinct feeling that everything was going to be all right.

· 32

I had it out with Mira after the storm passed. She had been planning to come to the house the night of the storm to help me exorcise the triplets—"Phase Two," she called it—but there was no way she could get through the snow. So she came by a couple of days later when the island had begun to dig out.

"Thanks for the offer, but I think I can get the girls to leave on my own," I told her.

"On your own? Are you sure?"

"No, I'm not," I admitted. "I still might need your help. But the way I'm seeing it now, the girls aren't the only demons of the past that my coming here has stirred up. Other things need to be exorcised, too."

Mira seemed worried. "I'm not sure what you mean."

So I confronted her with what I knew. She tried to deny it, sputtering and posturing and pretending that she was the wronged one—how could I possibly *think* such a thing?—but I stood firm and she basically collapsed under the weight of the truth.

"I'm sorry, Hallie," she said finally, after pulling out a

chair from the kitchen table and sitting down hard. "I looked for you and your father for years. The man who I put him in touch with for new identity papers disappeared around the same time, so I couldn't get your location or new name from him. It was impossible to find you, and then I realized Noah didn't want me to. It's true that I was furious when your father left me. I've been holding that grudge ever since. But I really felt as though I was helping him back then. He needed to get you out of here."

"Why didn't you tell me?"

She made a face. "I'm not exactly excited about anyone else finding out. I don't know the statute of limitations, but I might be charged as an accessory to murder. Or whatever they charge people with for helping murderers."

Oddly enough, I felt for her. I don't know if it was pity or empathy or something else, but seeing the way she was so resigned, I just couldn't hate Mira. She was right. She had helped my dad, her selfish motives notwithstanding, and in doing so she had probably saved my life. Right then and there, I forgave her.

"But what about the child, Mira? Did you have my father's child?"

At this, Mira's face went white. "Who told you that?"

"The source is not important," I said to her. "I just want to know if it's true. No more lies, Mira. I've lived half a lifetime based on lies. I want the truth now, once and for all."

She shook her head. "I've kept this secret for thirty years, Hallie. Nobody on this island knows who his father is."

"His? So you do have a child. A son, then?"

Mira looked at me and smiled. "I thought you knew I had

a son. Everyone here on the island knows him. He runs the coffee shop."

I sat there, open-mouthed. Finally, I managed to say, "Jonah? Are you kidding me? Jonah is your son? My dad's son?"

She nodded in confirmation. I could hardly believe what she was saying. My thoughts were racing. Jonah was my half brother? That would explain why he felt so familiar, so like my dad in so many ways.

"He has known who his father was for some time," Mira told me. "In fact, what he's been going through the past couple of weeks isn't so different from what you went through. He thought his father was dead all these years—that's what I had told him—and now he finds out that he was alive and living just north of Seattle until just before you arrived. When you think about it, it's exactly what you went through after learning about your mother."

"Not exactly," I said to her. "He had you to come to for answers."

"And when he did, I told him the truth. I looked for your—and his—father for years. I tried everything I knew to find him. But he had disappeared into thin air. Jonah was angry with me at first, sure. But I think he realizes I was just as much a victim as he was."

A painful thought occurred to me. "Mira," I said carefully, "did my dad know about the pregnancy before he left here with me? Did he leave you, knowing you were carrying his child?"

She shook her head. "Even I didn't know it then. If I had, you can be sure I would've told him. I loved your dad, Hallie. I wanted to spend the rest of my life with him."

My mind continued to swim. So this is what Jonah had wanted to tell me. I thought back to our evening at the wine bar, and now it made perfect sense that he had asked so many questions about my growing-up years. He was trying to learn about the life that might have been his and about the man who was his father.

I sighed and looked at Mira, feeling a mixture of confusion, defeat, and regret. "What a tangled web this is," I said to her.

She smiled a weak smile. "Do you have anything to drink? Stronger than tea, I mean?"

And so we opened up a bottle of wine and sat together drinking it, talking about what was and what might have been. We both saw that nobody, not my mother, not my father, not Mira, not me—and certainly not Jonah—was to blame for any of it. The affair notwithstanding, everyone had acted with the best of intentions, and this was simply how it had turned out. All our lives had been thrown into turmoil as a result of the epic tale of my family, and now, after thirty years, several deaths, and more than a few otherworldly occurrences, the circle was closed and we were back where it all began.

Much to Mira's relief, Jonah wasn't ready to tell the whole island who his father was. Neither was I. It would be between us for a while. But the fact that we were siblings was not lost on either of us. We saw more and more of each other, becoming good friends. We even decided that one day when I stopped reeling from the tales I had heard from Iris about my mother's family, we'd look together for our father's family on the mainland. Other stories about other ancestors were swirling out there in the wind, waiting to be learned.

One day not long after this, I ran into the Suttons downtown. I took a deep breath, walked over to them, and told them I had gone to the police to request the file on the case. "I wanted to find out for myself what the evidence against my father was, and I can see how it looked suspicious," I said to Julie's parents. "But all I can tell you is that I don't believe my father would have ever intentionally hurt your daughter. I'm sorry that I can't give you a better explanation of the accident that day. I know you want it as much as I do."

They accepted my apology—what else could they do?—and we went our separate ways. I assumed word got around that I tried to dig into the case and uncover the truth, because not long after my meeting with the Suttons, I noticed a great thawing in island opinion about me. People stopped staring and whispering, and I became a prodigal daughter of sorts, one of their own who had left and returned. Some of that goodwill, I believe, came from what I decided to do with my days during tourist season.

One snowy afternoon while Will was at work, I found myself at the front door of my mother's art gallery downtown. It hadn't been opened since her death. According to Will and Jonah, it was one of the more bustling and popular shops on the island during the summer months, selling not only my mother's photographs but other pieces crafted by local artisans: jewelry, pottery, watercolors, the occasional sculpture. The thought of it sitting there, unused, had begun to nag at me. The moment I turned the key and stepped inside the dusty building, I knew I had found what I would be doing with my summers.

"I'm going to open the Manitou Gallery in the spring," I announced to Will that night over dinner.

"That's fantastic!" He smiled and lifted his glass. "I know people have been wondering about the fate of the shop. To a new chapter!"

A few days later I was at the shop, taking care of the many details that needed to be completed before spring came—dusting and cleaning and calling the artists whose work was displayed there, many of whom lived elsewhere during the winter, to let them know the shop would be open before the first tourist ferry arrived.

In the back room where my mother had her studio, I noticed several boxes labeled MOSAIC MATERIALS. I found them filled with old cracked pottery, tiles, and pieces of what seemed to be foggy antique mirrors. I picked up one of the larger mirror bits, and it seemed to me I could see the hint of a face within it, as though it had captured the reflected image of the mirror's previous owner when he or she gazed into it long ago. Could that be true? Could they be reflecting an image of the past? I remembered what I had seen that first day in my mother's house—her image reflected in the mirror in her bedroom. A jolt of possibility traveled up my spine.

I began to work with the shards, arranging them on a small table, and before I knew it, day had passed into night and I was staring at a colorful mosaic I had created. In the coming weeks, I created many more, becoming immersed in crafting them, positioning the mirrors just so. Will commented how beautiful and haunting he thought the pieces were, although he didn't understand what I meant by reflected images of the past. Perhaps I was the only one who could see them. Was it my particular family gift? I wasn't sure. But I was beginning to think a new Crane woman would have artwork to sell in the shop when it opened in the spring.

I was turning off the lights before bed one evening in Hill House when I found the girls standing before me in their white dresses, white ribbons in their hair. They looked so pretty and sweet, not at all like the ghouls I had been seeing. They were just little children.

"Come play with us, Halcyon," Persephone said, extending her small hand to me. I noticed slight smiles creeping as one across their faces, their eyes hesitantly anxious.

I folded a stray afghan and set it on the chaise. "Playtime is over now, girls," I told them.

"You never play with us anymore." Penelope pouted; the others narrowed their eyes.

The force of their gaze gave me a chill. My voice wavering just a bit, I said, "That's because it's time for you to go."

"Who says so?" Patience wanted to know, her chin jutting defiantly forward.

I put my hands on my hips and faced them. "I say so. It's time for you to go home."

The girls smiled then, eerie ice-cold smiles. "But we *are*

home." Patience grinned, as the three of them dissipated into the air like wisps of smoke swirling around me.

And then I felt it, the poking and prodding and pinching of unseen fingers, on my face, my arms, my legs, my hair. Three pairs of hands on the small of my back, pushing me forward. I stumbled to my knees.

"Stop it!" I screamed into the empty room, covering my face with my hands. And just like that, their assault ended. The air in the room began to seem lighter and fresher, as it is after a spring rain. I stood up. Could they be gone, as easily as that? I took a deep breath and closed my eyes, thinking it was over.

It wasn't. They were there again, in the doorway leading to the living room. But instead of the innocent little girls in white dresses who had been with me moments before, I saw a macabre vision of the moment of their deaths, three children frozen together, silent screams of terror coming out of their gaping mouths. I quickly turned away, only to hear their giggles echoing throughout the room.

Now they were walking slowly toward me, the flesh hanging on their worm-eaten, eyeless faces, the skin on their arms rotting and falling away with every step, their white dresses now black and tattered with dirt and decay. It was as though they had risen from their graves.

"You don't frighten me!" I shouted at them with conviction, but my trembling legs told me otherwise. What would they do when they reached me? What would I do? I tried to run from the room but found I could not move. Was it fear or something else holding me firmly in place?

My mind was swimming. Iris had said I could get the

girls to leave, but how? I thought of the stories she had told me. I thought about Hannah and Simeon, about the old witch Martine, and about Iris's doomed cousin Jane, driven over the cliff by these demons. I thought of Charles, whose animals protected him, and of Amelia and the unborn children she lost when she was pushed and fell. I thought of my mother and my father, driven apart because she couldn't accept his fear of the girls, and finally I thought of poor Julie, who spent her last moments on earth in terror, battling these unseen enemies. I'm not sure where it came from, but I had an idea. I recited the names of my relatives out loud, over and over—"Hannah, Simeon, Charles, Amelia, Madlyn, Noah!"—as though the names themselves were incantations. Or prayers.

Then I whirled around to face the girls, their ghoulish faces dancing ever closer to my own. "This is going to end now," I growled at them, with every ounce of strength inside of me.

And then I saw them, my ancestors, hovering and shimmering near me as though I were seeing their reflections on a glassy lake or in one of the antique mirrors at the shop: Hannah and Simeon, Charles and Amelia, and—my breath caught in my throat—my own mother and father. The girls must've seen them, too, because they dropped their horrible façades and in an instant were the sweet-looking little girls they had once been.

"You're leaving now," I told them. "You have been very naughty for a very long time and caused this family untold grief."

"But Halcyon—" Penelope started.

"But nothing," I told her, pointing toward our ancestors. "Look. Your parents are waiting for you."

As I spoke, Hannah and Simeon had their arms outstretched. "Come, girls!" Hannah called to her daughters. "It's time to come inside! It's getting cold out there!"

"Mama!" Penelope cried, as the three girls ran to their parents. "Where have you been? We've been looking for you for so long!"

And then all of them were gone, dissipated into the air like fog when the sun shines. It was truly over.

· 33

When spring came, I found myself wandering with the dogs on the other side of the island, ending up at the old cemetery. I decided to tidy the graves of my relatives, pulling weeds, dusting off headstones, talking to all of them. Visiting. Telling them my news: Will and I were happily in love. Maybe there would soon be a new generation of the family whose stories would intertwine with theirs.

Later that night, I had the strangest dream. I was back in the cemetery, among the graves of my Hill ancestors. I noticed the gravestone of Iris's cousin, Jane Malone. As I bent down to pull some weeds near her grave, I felt a chill wind rush through me.

"Grave tending, miss?"

I wheeled around and my eyes couldn't quite take in what I saw.

"Iris? My God! Where have—"

I was going to ask her where she'd been; I hadn't seen her since the storm. But my words trailed off, because just then Iris's face began to change. Before I knew it, I was looking at a woman I didn't recognize.

"I thought you deserved to know the truth," she said, her speech now heavy with a French-Canadian accent.

I couldn't make sense of what I was seeing. "Iris, I—" I started, but she cut me off.

"Not Iris, *chérie*. It's time we dispensed with that ruse. My name is Martine." She smiled, and as she did the age seemed to evaporate from her face, her deep wrinkles replaced by rosy, smooth skin. She reached up and ran a delicate hand through her hair, shaking out the gray. It was now long and flowing and auburn. She moved at the waist, and her dress, now a vibrant green, swayed this way and that. "It feels wonderful to finally shed that skin."

Martine? I leaned against a tombstone, afraid my quaking legs wouldn't support me. I tried to speak but couldn't formulate any words. I wanted nothing more than to run away from this woman, as fast as my legs could carry me. But where would I go? I couldn't get away, not really.

"When Iris went over the cliff that day along with her poor cousin, I saw my opportunity." Martine smiled.

"Opportunity?" I croaked.

Martine smoothed the folds of her dress and sniffed. "Hannah had done a pitiful job raising my three children. That was my mistake, giving the spell to someone so weak."

My skin went cold. "*Your* children?"

"Oh, *chérie*, you are so naïve. Of course they were part of me. I gave them to her. They were as much my children as they were hers. But when I saw what she did to the girls—my three babies—I had to step in before she could hurt the others who would come later."

I shook my head. "What do you mean, step in?"

"I mean just that. I stepped in. I had been planning to leave the island. I had had enough of these wealthy people who would scorn me outwardly, only to come creeping to my back door when they needed something. But then I saw how incapable Hannah was of raising children—the girls died because of her!—and I knew the herbs I gave her would allow her to conceive again and again. Something had to be done. Someone had to protect future children. So when poor Iris went over the cliff—"

"Iris died?"

"No, Hallie." Martine shook her head. "She went over the cliff, just as her cousin did. But I saved her. I knew I could use her to live within the house and watch over my children and grandchildren, so I put her body around mine like a cloak. Just as I said: *I stepped in.*"

"How—" I started, my eyes growing wide.

Martine laughed and shook her head back and forth, her long hair blowing in the breeze. "I'm the Witch of Summer Glen. A little thing like that isn't so difficult."

I sat down, hard, on the cold ground next to the grave, not quite knowing how to formulate coherent thoughts out of the muddle that was my mind. Finally, I said, "So you were Iris, all those years?"

She nodded. "I had to look after them: Charles, Maddie, even the girls, such as they were. I had brought them all into the world, so to speak. I had a responsibility."

An undefined anger was bubbling up in my throat. "You certainly didn't do much to protect *me.*"

"You?" Martine laughed again. "You didn't need my protection. You were stronger than all of them combined. So like me. That's why you were able to rid the house of those naughty triplets. Soon after you left with your father, I left as well. Look at the gravestone, my dear."

I shuddered, thinking I was going to see my own name there. Instead, I noticed a small stone. IRIS MALONE. *Faithful daughter, servant, and friend. 1905–1976.*

"Wait. Iris died? But—"

Martine shrugged. "My work was done. And I was so tired of that horrible black dress."

"So—" I couldn't quite grasp what she was saying to me.

"When I learned you were coming back to the island, I decided to put on that dress once again. You didn't know anything about your family—my family. I had to tell you, *ma chère*, to make sure you kept their memories and mine alive. You needed to know the truth, about them and about yourself. And there was only one person who could tell you. Me."

With that, my eyes popped open and I was sitting up in bed, Will breathing low and shallow next to me. The room was dark except for a shaft of moonlight shining in through the window.

"What's the matter?" Will murmured groggily.

"It was just a dream," I whispered. "A crazy dream."

"Curl back in." He held out his hand to me. And so I did, slipping down under the covers, snuggling next to the man I loved.

Acknowledgments

I grew up in a family of storytellers. Some of my earliest memories involve sitting at the kitchen table, listening to my parents, grandparents, cousins, aunts, and uncles tell tales about the people and places in their pasts, so it's no wonder I should grow up to tell stories for a living. My first acknowledgment, then, goes to my family. To my mom and dad, Joan and Toby Webb; my brothers, Jack and Randy Webb; and Gram, Elma Maki. I know how proud you are to see me fulfill my lifelong dream. Your confidence in me is what got me here. And to everyone else who has ever sat around my parents' kitchen table and *raconteured*, thank you for a lifetime of inspiration.

To my wonderful, funny, fabulous agent, Jennifer Weltz. The gratitude I feel for your belief in me, your hard work on my behalf, and your friendship is boundless. I wouldn't be here without you. Writers—you may have written the next best seller, but without a great agent all you've got is a ream of paper. Thanks to everyone at the Jean Naggar Agency for your unwavering support.

To my talented editor, Helen Atsma. Thank you for

believing in a first-time novelist, for loving this story as much as I do, and for your wise, insightful, and careful editing. Your skill has made this book infinitely better, and working with you to hone this tale was an absolute joy.

To my long-suffering friends who have endured the process of me doing something so audacious as writing a novel and trying to get it published, Sarah Fister Gale, Kathi Wright, Mary Gallegos, Bobbi Voss, and Barb Smith Lobin. I fully expect you each to buy a case of these books and give them out as gifts. (Just kidding, though it's not a bad idea.) Really, what I want to say is, thank you for your encouragement and for making me laugh every day. And to my sounding board, plot untangler, and kindred literary spirit, Randy Johnson. Thank you for being so happy to see my dream come true. Next it will be your turn.

Finally, to my spouse, Steve Burmeister, and my son, Ben. I know living with a writer, especially this writer, isn't always easy. Your love means everything to me. I'm so happy to be walking through the world with you two, creating the tales we will tell others around our kitchen table.

One last word about the story itself. Although it was modeled after Mackinac Island, Grand Manitou Island is a figment of my imagination and, now, yours. This novel is a work of fiction, save one thing: the 1913 storm that killed the Hill triplets. That was very real and remains the worst storm in the history of the Great Lakes.

extras...

essays...

etcetera

more author
About Wendy Webb

more book
About *The Tale of Halcyon Crane*

... and more

Meet Wendy Webb

Steve Burmeister

Wendy Webb grew up in Minneapolis and has been a journalist there for nearly two decades, writing for most of the major publications in the region. Currently, she lives in the gorgeous Lake Superior port city of Duluth with her spouse, photographer Steve Burmeister; her son, Ben; and their enormous Alaskan malamute, Tundra. She is at work on her next novel. Please visit her website at www.wendykwebb.com. ■

Although you are making your fiction-writing debut with *The Tale of Halcyon Crane*, you've worked as a journalist for more than twenty years. Was it difficult to make the switch from nonfiction to fiction? What were some of the challenges?

It was difficult at first. I didn't realize how different the two styles of writing actually are. One of the cardinal rules of fiction writing is "Show, don't tell." But as a journalist, you "tell" a story, and as I'd been writing that way for so long, it was second nature to me. It took a while before I even understood the difference between showing and telling well enough to break that habit. Also, plotting and pacing a novel was a completely new experience for me because it's something you never have to do when writing a magazine article. The timing of when to let a bit more of the story unfold is an art unto itself. And consistency—you never even think about it as a journalist, but I found myself constantly going back to make sure Halcyon was wearing the same outfit she left the house in fifty pages earlier.

Loving, lively animals play a role in *The Tale of Halcyon Crane*—from the animals that Hallie's veterinarian grandfather cared for to the boisterous dogs Hallie inherits from her mother. Do you have pets?

We have a 130-pound giant Alaskan malamute named Tundra. Readers will notice Madlyn's dogs are also mals, Tundra and Tika. Tika was our husky-samoyed cross; she passed away about five years ago. I believe there's a special connection between people and their pets that fits very well with the magical realism I like to convey in my writing. Pets sense our fears and our sadness, and want only to help. There's something enormously comforting about that. I also love the unqualified joy my dog experiences in the moment—going for a walk, chewing on a bone, giving me a hero's welcome when I walk in the door after a long day.

I believe there's a special connection between people and their pets that fits very well with the magical realism I like to convey in my writing.

The Great Lakes clearly occupy a special place in your heart. Have you spent a lot of time on or around the lakes?

I grew up in Minnesota and have a great love for Lake Superior, where I now live. It's a spiritual, mystical place filled with ancient lore and legend. Many local residents actually do have a vague sense that the lake itself is a living thing, which is how the native peoples in this area viewed it. Here's an example: A few years back, a man set out to swim across all the Great Lakes. But he couldn't make it across Superior despite many attempts. In the press, he had been "trash talking" the lake, saying its reputation for being dangerous was a myth. People here thought the lake simply wasn't letting him pass because of it. I think all of the Great Lakes hold that kind of fascination for residents and visitors.

Any special hobbies?

I like to row and kayak on Lake Superior, and we've got a cabin in the Boundary Waters Canoe Area Wilderness that separates Minnesota from Canada, where we spend a lot of time. It's a gorgeous area that offers the best of both worlds—unspoiled wilderness and beautiful lodges with great restaurants.

My friends joke that my two major vices are expensive wine and lots of new books, and I love nothing better than a morning of kayaking or rowing followed by an afternoon sitting with a glass of wine on the deck of my cabin overlooking our lake, reading a great book with my dog at my side. And it doesn't hurt if my son and husband are there, either.

My friends joke that my two major vices are expensive wine and lots of new books.

Have you read any good spooky fiction lately?

I'm always reading. My favorite book in the genre that I read last year was *The Spiritualist,* by Megan Chance. I read it in one day, sitting on the aforementioned deck of my cabin. It's absolutely fabulous. This year, one of my favorite books is *The Little Stranger,* by Sarah Waters. It's deliciously creepy and I could not put it down. I highly recommend those two novels for people who want a little tingle up their spines.

The Tale of Halcyon Crane begins on the West Coast, north of Seattle. Do you have any personal connection with that area?

I lived in Bellingham, Washington, for a couple of years, and I absolutely love that area. It reminds me of Minnesota in a way. But of course, here on Lake Superior we don't have seals or whales. One of the things I loved best about living out there was that I could actually hear the barking of the seals from my house. It's a very relaxing sound. The San Juan Islands are hauntingly beautiful—maybe I'll set a novel there one day.

I think this world is filled with things we can't see and don't quite understand.

Your tale is filled with ghosts. Do you believe in them?

I must admit I do. I think this world is filled with things we can't see and don't quite understand. I dedicated the book to my brother, who died of a sudden heart attack a few years ago. Since he passed away, several of us in the family have had odd experiences we can't really explain. Here's just one: I was sweeping the wood floor in my bedroom shortly after my brother's funeral. After doing the entire room, I turned around and saw several pennies strewn on the floor . . . the floor I had just cleaned an instant earlier. It really happened, folks. I can't tell you how or why. ■

On Writing *The Tale of Halcyon Crane*

I come from a family of storytellers. Some of my earliest memories involve sitting at our kitchen table, listening to my parents and relatives tell stories—some of them hilarious, others tragic—about my family's past. These tales were filled with unforgettable characters and fantastic situations, and I know them all as well as I know my own name.

But as much as I loved hearing these stories, I've always wanted to spin tales of my own. In Halcyon, I found a woman whose background is the opposite of mine: I grew up hearing everything about my family; Halcyon knows nothing about her past. It isn't until she is in her thirties that Halcyon learns of her childhood abduction and sets out to find some answers. What happened all those years ago? Who was her mother? Who were her ancestors? And most important, who was *she*?

I wanted to include an element of magical realism in the story because I love the notion that something otherworldly can be right around the corner, waiting for you on any given Monday; that the world is filled with things we don't understand and many of us can't see, and that fairy tales, Grimm's especially, could really have happened. I love the goosebumps and tingles up my spine I get from shows like *Medium* and *The Ghost Whisperer* and books like *The Ghost Orchid*, by Carol Goodman, and I wanted to write a story that would give people that same type of deliciously haunting, eerie feeling.

I decided to set the story on Mackinac Island because the Great Lakes hold a magic and mystery unlike anyplace else. Many people think the lakes are actually living things, with moods ranging from benevolent to murderous.

I fictionalized Mackinac's name—calling it Grand Manitou Island instead—so I could be free when writing about the specific places, happenings, and people there, but readers who have been to Mackinac will recognize it right away. When you go there, you really feel like you've traveled back in time—I think it has to do with the fact that there is no motorized traffic and everyone gets around by horse-drawn carriage. It's a place filled with beautiful Victorian homes, grand hotels, great restaurants, fudge shops, wine bars . . . and a very creepy old cemetery. It seems to me that the whole island is teeming with spirits—if anyplace in the world is haunted, it's Mackinac Island.

What better place for a woman to go looking for the ghosts of her past?

There does happen to be a Grand Manitou Island in Lake Nipissing in Ontario, but it's not inhabited. I've since learned that this Grand Manitou Island also has a reputation for being haunted, interestingly enough.

What better place for a woman to go looking for the ghosts of her past?

Another reason I set the story on the Great Lakes was because I wanted to work in a real-life tragedy that occurred there: the worst storm in the history of the region, which happened in November of 1913. I came upon newspaper accounts of the storm when researching another story. They called it the Frozen Hurricane, and it destroyed harbors, piers, and shorelines, demolishing buildings, tearing up concrete streets, dumping feet of snow on land, and, most horrifyingly, sending nearly every ship on the Great Lakes that day to the bottom, all hands aboard. One of the newspaper accounts told of drowned sailors, frozen together, floating out of the fog and in to shore. When I read that, I knew I had to include it somehow in my story.

Halcyon does eventually find the answers she seeks, and in doing so gains a greater awareness about who she really is. We're all on journeys of one sort or another—some of us to the past, looking for answers; some of us tentatively moving forward, unsure of what the future holds, and I very much hope *The Tale of Halcyon Crane* speaks to that journey. ■

1. Hallie's father talks about seeing Madlyn at the nursing home the day before he died. Do you think he really saw her spirit, coming for him? Why or why not? Do you believe the veil between the living and the dead is lifted as a person passes from one life to the next?

2. Hallie has twice been sidelined by men she loved: her husband and her father both were different men than she believed them to be. How did their deception—non-malicious though it was—affect her? Did she do the right thing by ultimately trusting Will?

3. Each child born of the spell from the Witch of Summer Glen has a special otherworldly ability or gift. With Hallie, her gift develops as she stays on the island. Do you think Hallie simply grew more aware of her innate talent, or did being on the island somehow change and enhance her abilities?

4. What is the significance of mirrors with respect to Hallie's ability to "see"?

5. Why couldn't Madlyn understand the danger the island posed to her young daughter, Hallie? Was Madlyn a good mother?

6. Was Hallie's father justified in taking his child away from his wife and their home? Did you think he could have handled

that situation differently—perhaps more openly and truthfully?

7. Mira befriends Hallie, but she also harbors a great secret that isn't revealed until the end of the book. Did you understand Mira's decision to keep the truth to herself for so long, given that she barely knew Hallie, or should she have revealed it sooner? What secrets would you keep from a friend?

8. Did you enjoy the way Hallie's "tale" is slowly revealed to her? Are there storytellers in your family who have kept family lore alive?

9. Forgiveness is one of the themes in this novel. Who most needed to be able to forgive? Who most needed to be forgiven?

10. Have you ever seen a ghost? Do you know anyone who has? What are some of the best ghost stories you know?